About the Author

CeCe began writing in earnest in elementary school, when asked to pencil one paragraph using that week's spelling words, but kept going and produced twelve pages instead. Since then, CeCe has served in the United States armed forces, analyzed bonds for investment management firms, and lived in or visited all the United States, the United Kingdom and dozens of countries, but never stopped writing. Today, CeCe runs every morning, and works a respectable job during the day, but reserves the late afternoon, when possible, for writing.

Tara, Princess of Brythrony

The Complete Adventures

CeCe Loop

Tara, Princess of Brythrony

The Complete Adventures

Olympia Publishers
London

www.olympiapublishers.com
OLYMPIA PAPERBACK EDITION

Copyright © CeCe Loop 2024

The right of CeCe Loop to be identified as author of
this work has been asserted in accordance with sections 77 and 78 of the
Copyright, Designs and Patents Act 1988.

All Rights Reserved

No reproduction, copy or transmission of this publication
may be made without written permission.
No paragraph of this publication may be reproduced,
copied or transmitted save with the written permission of the publisher, or in
accordance with the provisions
of the Copyright Act 1956 (as amended).

Any person who commits any unauthorized act in relation to
this publication may be liable to criminal
prosecution and civil claims for damage.

A CIP catalogue record for this title is
available from the British Library.

ISBN: 978-1-80074-977-1

This is a work of fiction.
Names, characters, places and incidents originate from the writer's imagination.
Any resemblance to actual persons, living or dead, is purely coincidental.

First Published in 2024

Olympia Publishers
Tallis House
2 Tallis Street
London
EC4Y 0AB

Printed in Great Britain

Dedication

For Katherine, to whom I originally told these stories.

Book I: The Prithrath Ocean

I'm Princess Tara

Princess of the Realm Tara of the House of Hession of the Kingdom of Brythrony sat on her bed and, by turns, glared, then stared, then pondered her situation. How boring it was in the castle! What lay out there, beyond not just the castle grounds but in the kingdom, even beyond? Idly, she let her toes brush the floor as her feet kicked back and forth over the side of the bed. The floor needed sweeping, she noted, and not for the first time. But it was almost never swept. This was because Princess Tara refused to allow any of the maids to enter her room, and Princess Tara rarely, if ever, and certainly not of her own volition, swept the floor herself.

Why was it so boring? Princess Tara slumped backwards onto her bed and frowned up at the bedroom ceiling, one of the several rooms of a suite in Castle Stonedell's North Tower. Of course, there was always something for her to do. She could be making herself busy improving the palace's topiary gardens, or in the stables combing her horse, Daystar, or even engaged in something civically useful around the kingdom. Her mother and father had urged her more than once to become more familiar with the proceedings of the law courts or check into the progress of the construction of some important building. Her mother certainly wanted her to do that. But Tara scorned those distractions as tedious and stultifying.

Tara was her parents' only child. They told her—regularly—that she was spoiled. She disagreed. She had lots of responsibilities to fulfil, she would retort, that other children didn't. Like having to go to the law courts to try to understand the happenings there, and suggest changes to the palace topiary garden, and open important buildings around the kingdom, and things like that. Sometimes she had to stand in the throne room for what seemed like hours during official court functions. These were deadly dull events, and Tara sought to evade them whenever she could. How many other children had to do similar service? During these times, she would seek some pretext—any pretext—to go down to the stables to see Daystar. Or she might go out into the field, either on foot or astride Daystar, to practice her archery. She thought she was becoming pretty good at it.

This afternoon, even these couldn't seem to hold her attention.

Tara groaned and rolled her slightly-tall frame for her age over such that her face was buried in the mattress. So boring! Strands of her just-below-the-shoulder-length brown hair were caught in her mouth again; she yanked them out angrily. Why was she so bored? Deep down, she knew that part of the problem was that she didn't have any real friends, and that was why she was bored. At least, she feared that. Her parents had told her that once. She pushed that thought away also. She had Daystar. But a horse couldn't be a friend. Not really. A horse was just an animal, a mount, no matter how special.

This led Tara to silently formulate another tart rejoinder to her parents regarding her supposedly spoiled nature. She wasn't spoiled, because her life in the palace practically precluded her having friends. Who could be friends with the kingdom's only princess, the heir apparent, after all? And it wasn't like there were any proper neighbors near the palace. There could only be one king and queen in a kingdom at any one time, and this particular set had only one child, her, named Tara. True, some of the courtiers always in attendance at the court had daughters, and some were her age. But, just as true, they stuck to each other and none really wanted to include her in any of their games or activities. Yes, they would—if she were to ask them to include her. But how much fun was it to have to ask to be included? Either it was natural and spontaneous or they were including you because they had to, because your parents ran the kingdom.

Frustrated, Tara pulled herself upright on her bed and began groping beneath it for her shoes, as that was where they generally were found and at various distances underneath when she kicked them off. She'd go downstairs and find something to occupy herself. Somehow.

Just as she was starting to descend the spiral staircase leading to the ground floor, a voice floated up toward her. "Tara?" it called. "Tara?" It was her mother, Queen Armorica.

"Yes, Mom?"

"Are you almost ready? Are you coming down?"

Tara stopped in mid-stride. Ready? For what?

It was if her mother had sensed her confusion. "For the opening ceremonies! For the new docks! We have to get going!"

Only then did Tara remember, and with a thunderclap. The opening ceremonies for the new docks at the port on the River Vahaval! Tara gasped.

She had completely forgotten. Her mother would be furious! "Uh, almost! Almost! Another few minutes, that's all!"

There was another moment of silence, which Tara knew indicated mounting impatience. "Well, hurry UP! We have to leave very shortly if we are to arrive on time!"

Tara dashed back into her bedroom and wrenched off her shoes; they skittered to rest underneath the bed next to the several pairs already there. The dress! The dress she had been instructed to wear! Where was it? Tara tore it out of the closet and flung it onto the bed. Just time enough to get it on; no time at all to fix her hair. Maybe her mother could do that. On the carriage ride to the docks.

This was miserable, Tara said to herself. Why had she forgotten about this event? It was the third time this week that some sort of appointment or event had slipped her mind. But, like with her loneliness, she also knew why she kept forgetting. It was because she didn't want to go. She disliked these duties. She referred to them, privately and disparagingly, as "princessing." "Princessing" meant going out and about the kingdom and being a silly, simple, simpering princess, and nothing more. Vacuous and smiling, laughing at everyone's jokes and banter and making the same empty bantering conversation back. "Badinage," her parents called it, and encouraged her at its practice. Incredibly dreary, Tara thought it.

"Tara! Tara! Where are you?" The voice floated up, rising in pitch with each word.

She'd better get down now, or her mother would really be angry. "Coming!" she bawled through the open door as she made for the staircase. Then she darted back to grab a brush, which she suddenly realized might be useful on the carriage ride. "Coming!" Once more she returned, now furious with herself, for a ring she often hung by a chain to her mirror. It had been bequeathed to her by her grandmother, Queen Ysolde, who had died when she had been very young. It was all she had of her aside from some stories her mother had told her. She frequently wore the chain around her neck, as a sort of connection, she felt, to someone who, if alive, would surely take her side in all her disputes with her parents, be mindful of her likes and dislikes, and be terrifically interested in all she was doing.

"Coming, Mom!"

A moment later, Tara practically tumbled to the base of the stairs, breathless and flushed. Her dress of royal blue silk was wildly askew, the accompanying white royal sash fluttered like a banner from one shoulder, and her tawny brown shoes with an elaborate embroidery of flowers across the toe and vamp in a cream-yellow thread were still grasped in one hand rather than on her feet. Like her other formal dresses, it incorporated the House of Hession's colors of blue and brown, with the white in the sash.

Tara leaned on the banister as she struggled, as discreetly as she could, to slip her right foot into a shoe.

Armorica frowned in obvious disapproval. Tara knew what was coming: how could she arrive in such a state? Why was she always so late? How could she be so cavalier with respect to her duties as Princess of the Realm? Still, Tara thought to do her best. "Here I am! Ready to go!" she called gamely, affecting a cheery voice.

"You are not ready to go! Look at you; look at your hair!"

Tara couldn't look at her hair, it being atop her head. Still, she knew full well what her mother meant. "But, look: I brought along this brush. For my hair. I thought that maybe you could help me with it as we rode to the event!"

Her mother opened her mouth in outrage with a ready riposte, then closed it to consider this unexpected concession. Tara rarely suggested mother–daughter sorts of activities. Mostly it seemed as if she preferred to be by herself. This caused no end of unhappiness on Armorica's part, recollecting fondly as she did her own close relationship with her now-deceased mother. "Your hair?"

"Sure! You could fix my hair on the way there—whichever way you thought best. And, we could talk!" Tara held out her hand holding the whale bone brush, inlaid with silver and her mother's initials, whose brush indeed it had been.

Armorica eyed the brush sceptically, then slowly reached to accept it. She considered Tara's unkempt, disheveled mop. It would be a challenge. A severe challenge. But maybe it could be fixed in time. The ride would take an hour. Maybe, with concerted effort… "It may pull some!"

"That's all right. I understand." Tara straightened where she stood, her foot at last in its shoe. Sullijee, one of her mother's ladies-in-waiting, had noticed that most of the buttons down the back of Tara's dress were unbuttoned and those that were had been jammed into the wrong buttonhole, and had begun to work intently to rectify this. Tara just smiled still more broadly at her mother and said nothing, even as she worked to manoeuvre her left foot into its shoe while balancing unsteadily on her right.

Armorica grimaced and weighed the brush. "We had better get going, as soon as you're properly buttoned. I'll do what I can with your hair. But don't blame me if it's not perfect!"

Tara had no intention of blaming her mother for her hair, however imperfect it might turn out. She sighed with relief at having avoided another argument and dutifully followed her mother, who had already turned on her heel.

A courtier led them through the reception hall and out the great double doors to a courtyard in which stood a traveling state coach. Its sides were of a dark, varnished wood, with gold trim and the arms of the royal House of Hession emblazoned on the door. A small honor guard, consisting of four brilliantly attired soldiers astride pawing and snorting horses, waited patiently behind. The coachman reined in the four horses in the traces, which had been stamping impatiently; a groomsman before them soothed the lead with one hand and held its harness with the other. "We must start off at once if we are to arrive on time," the courtier reproached no one in particular as he helped the queen and then her daughter into the coach. He gestured to the coachman to start, then mounted his own horse and took his position in the cavalcade immediately behind.

With a confused clatter of horseshoes on pavement, the company started forward.

"Come here. Sit over here, right next to me. No; face away from me, so I can work on your hair! That's it, like that." Queen Armorica wasted no time in getting her daughter into position. "He's right, you know: we're late, and so we'll ride faster, and that means less time to work with this, this wreck on top of your head!"

Tara winced as her mother immediately began wielding the brush. "Ow, Mom! Ow!"

"You said you wouldn't cry out!"

"Ow! No, I said I'd understand if it pulled!"

"Tara!" remonstrated her mother, shaking her head. "You'll have to learn that you need to brush and comb your hair more often. Or it will become hopelessly tangled. Like it is now. Do you ever brush it? At all?"

"Of course, I do, Mom." From time to time.

"It is why I gave you this brush. MY brush."

"Yes, Mom."

"Honestly, maybe we should cut it off. Cut it down sharply, so it's easier to deal with." Armorica stopped for a moment to gauge her daughter's reaction to this most dire of punishments.

But, to her dismay, Tara came to terms all too readily with the proposition. "Maybe it might make sense," she agreed, and far too cheerily for her mother's liking. "I do have trouble keeping up with it. Besides, it'd grow back anyway over time."

"Absolutely not! You're a princess, and you must have the hair to match! Honestly, what would everyone else in the kingdom say? What about all the other princesses in the neighboring kingdoms?"

Tara wasn't sure what they'd say. It wasn't even apparent to her they'd care. But she didn't say anything.

"How would you show your face at events such as these?"

This was almost more than Tara could bear. As if she wanted to attend such events in the first place! But Tara knew that she had little choice. "Mom—ow!—Mom, you know I'm not so excited to go to them anyway!"

Her mother was too busy fussing with Tara's hair, applying the brush in a series of rapid, short strokes to work out some of the more obstinate tangles, to consider that remark. "Really, Tara: this is simply dreadful! Maybe we should just cut it all off after all!

"No, we mustn't. Because you must go to these events. Absolutely must. You are a princess, the only princess of Brythrony. You must look the part. That means gorgeous, shining, flowing locks of hair. Why, when I was your age, I brushed my hair constantly! It shone like the sun! I must have been the envy of every other girl for miles and miles around!"

Tara grit her teeth as much against the pain as the recitation of a story she had heard countless times. Her mother had suggested in the past that Tara had inherited her hair from her, and then indicated extreme disappointment that Tara was not caring for her inheritance as she should. It was almost like, Tara thought at times, it wasn't Tara's hair, but her mother's hair, and Tara was only growing it for her.

"Then, what about the Season coming up very shortly? This year's will be very grand, I am told!"

Tara very quietly heaved a sigh. The "Season." She dreaded this as well. It consisted of an interminable series of society balls and parties at the various mansions and palaces and stately country homes of the nobility of Brythrony. She was invited to all of them as a matter of course—she was, after all, Princess of the Realm. Every now and then her mother and father threw a ball; this, thankfully, occurred only rarely. She thought it had something to do with the attendant expense, which was great. But she never enquired further, for fear of leaving the impression that she wished for another to take place at Castle Stonedell. Which she didn't. While her mother would have been delighted to host one, as Armorica thoroughly enjoyed all the associated preparations, her father, King Childeric, was less enthusiastic and generally demurred, citing Tara's own lack of interest.

"Yes, Mom. The Season. We'll see, I guess. And, I guess, also, we'll have to keep my hair, if only for that." Our hair, thought Tara, disconsolately.

Her mother suddenly paused in her work. "There! I think I have it! And, with only this hairbrush to work with! Absolutely amazing what I've done! Here, take this mirror—"

Armorica produced from within the folds of her dress a small pocket mirror which she offered to Tara, and which Tara dutifully unfolded and gazed into. It was so small, all she could see clearly was a single brown eye looking despondently back at her. She tilted the mirror up to try to catch sight of her hair, but the reflecting glass was so small and the carriage's ride so uneven, it was hard to focus it. She spied in quick succession the tip of her smallish, slightly upturned nose, then the roof of the carriage; there was a fleeting glimpse of the top of her head, and of the carriage window behind her. "Mom, it looks great. You have done wonders."

Her mother puffed herself in pride. "It is truly wonderful, what I've managed to do. And, look, we are just arriving at the docks! Just in time! I am amazing!"

The courtier riding immediately behind them pulled even with the carriage's window and addressed Armorica. "Your Majesty, we arrive! May I ride before you and lead your carriage to the opening ceremonies?"

Armorica granted permission with an expansive gesture and the coach started forward again with a jerk and began to rattle over cobblestone streets.

Armorica turned back to Tara and began to speak earnestly. "Now listen: you are to speak to everyone. Everyone. This is an important event for these people, and so it should be important for us, too."

Tara nodded. She received these instructions from her parents before each event of this nature.

"I do believe the mayor of the town will be present. Make a special effort to say something to him. Something kind!"

"Yes, Mom."

"Just do as I do. Keep your conversation light and airy. What's that word for it? I know it…"

"Badinage."

"That's it! Right. Remember that. Badinage." Armorica glanced out of the window. The rumbling and rattling cobblestones under the wheels had given way to the regular thudding and bumping of flagstones. "Oh! Look! We are indeed arriving! Get ready! Here we are!"

The coach drew to a halt and, clearly on cue, a cheer erupted from the gathered crowd. Armorica stretched out her hand to wave, then retracted it as her door was opened. A footman appeared at the running board to assist Armorica to alight; Tara took the proffered hand of the same footman and stepped down herself, as it happened into a passing sunbeam filtering through the massy clouds overhead. The white royal sash glittered briefly as Tara waved, too, as she hastened to join her mother.

A band began to play. Local dignitaries approached to make their obeisance, the mayor first. Tara murmured her thanks and made sure to say how delighted she was to be present to officiate at the ceremonies. She idly adjusted a pleat of her dress, composed herself, and smiled a practiced smile. "It's such a pleasure," she repeated several times, now in the "court" accent reserved for official occasions and in which she had been trained from childhood. "These new facilities are important, not only to your lovely town, of which some small part we had the pleasure to see as we drove in, but to the entire kingdom!"

A man who had introduced himself as the foremost alderman of the town bobbed his head enthusiastically. "You are ever so correct, Your Highness! Ever so! These are very important facilities! We expect to expand considerably our ability to handle cargo, both in terms of volumes and in types!"

Her mother was in apparent earnest conversation with the mayor and moving toward a temporary stand erected, doubtless, for the event. Tara fell in behind her mother. "Is that so? What sort of cargos do you expect? And how much more?"

The alderman was ready to supply all manner of facts and statistics to substantiate his expectations. Tara listened as attentively as she could and occasionally even injected a relevant question or observation, even as her mind began to drift. It was not that she disliked doing everything her parents wanted her to do. It was that she just preferred doing other things. Other than princessing. For example, she loved to ride Daystar. This her parents tolerated but wished she loved less. She also liked to get out and about the kingdom, though on her own rather than in large companies of people whose sole interest was picnicking. She liked doing active things, like horse archery and exploring, rather than dressy, showy things, like parties and evening gowns.

She had been reasonably good at her studies but had mainly shown interest in those with a practical application. She had played for hours with water and inclined planes and materials, to the delight of her instructor, but had shown little aptitude for literature and poetry. Her tutors had also attempted to school her in dance, a musical instrument, and singing, because it was well understood that every princess should have a background in fine arts, but she had proved an indifferent and even unwilling pupil. Her mother had assumed responsibility for these lessons at last, greatly fearing for these aspects of her daughter's education but had no more success in engaging Tara's interest than the music master. Armorica had despaired as what Tara would do during the "Season" when attendees would frequently exhibit their abilities in these arts to great acclaim. Tara had attempted to console her mother. "Don't worry, Mom. I can just hum along when they sing. And, I'll always have your hair!"

The speeches spoken, the docks opened, and the badinage exhausted, Queen Armorica and Princess of the Realm Tara regained the traveling state coach and sank back into the inviting softness of its upholstery. The same courtier as before materialized outside Armorica's window. "With your permission, Your Highness?" he enquired, and this time Armorica granted it with a much more languorous wave of her hand. The coach wheeled and commenced the return journey to Stonedell, the queen and her daughter grateful for the opportunity to be silent and alone after an intensively social afternoon.

Tara stopped and dismounted in the shade of a sprawling and ancient apple tree. It was the day after the opening of the docks, and Tara had gone to the stables early in the morning to exercise Daystar before she was due at the law courts to listen to and understand better the turning of the wheels of justice. She walked Daystar over to a patch of especially green grass, thought to tie him to a nearby tree and then shrugged and simply let the reins drop. Why did Daystar need to be tied up, after all? Like she, Tara, was most every day. Tara dwelt morosely for a moment on this sad simile. Yes, let Daystar move freely for a little, and according to his own whims. Just for a little. No, there weren't other horses around for you to play with, unfortunately, but at least you can run free for a bit.

Tara walked over to the mighty trunk of the apple tree and leaned against it, her back to its broad bulk. She groped for a moment for the necklace she wore and, at last finding it, dragged it from beneath her blouse. At the end of the chain, hanging like a charm, was the ring her grandmother had owned. Tara examined it minutely. It was just a ring, nothing more than that. It was set with a ruby, but hardly the largest ruby and certainly not the most perfect, as a number of inclusions deep within it were plainly visible. Still, to Tara, it was of the very greatest value.

She had never really known her grandmother and had only heard stories of her from her mother. These her mother had willingly recounted, but it was clear from her mother's tone that she hadn't approved of her own mother's adventurism. "Now, don't you go doing the same," she had chided a raptly attentive Tara on each occasion. This was because, according to her mother, her grandmother had been on all sorts of expeditions, such as the time she had hunted for dragons, explored deep caves at the seaside, and even, most dramatically, defended Castle Stonedell itself from its very ramparts, shoulder-to-shoulder with the palace guard, when it had been besieged by a neighboring kingdom.

Tara sighed. She had never known her grandmother in that way; the dim memories Tara retained were of her as a frail and nearly helpless invalid. Hard to reconcile that with the Adventurous Princess, as she had once been known, but that is what her mother and father had insisted. If that were true, Tara thought, she would surely have approved of Tara's spirit, sympathized with the impossibilities of learning to play a musical instrument, and encouraged her interest in the wide outdoors over the claustrophobic chambers of the law courts. Tara surveyed the forest about her gloomily. Her grandmother would have understood. She would have been someone she could have trusted and spoken to about how, on occasion, her mother could be so overbearing. Always wanting more of this, more of that, wanting more of Tara. Mom! Enough, huh?

Tara returned the ring back to within her blouse. She wished she had friends. Even a sibling. Even though she had heard that siblings always fought with each other. Geez. She would welcome having a sibling, even if it came with the occasional quarrel. So long as it also came with companionship.

Queen Armorica trailed King Childeric through the rooms of the royal suite. "Won't you listen to me? Why won't you listen to me?" she complained. "I'm worried!"

"Dear, worried about what?"

"About Tara! She's alone out there!"

Childeric shrugged. "I think she can defend herself pretty well with her bow and arrows; she's an excellent aim. She also has Daystar, so she should be able to outrun most any other horse. Besides, she's only in the pastures nearby."

"No! Not that. Though I also mean that!" Armorica became exasperated. "What I really mean is that she's all alone! And I'm troubled by how it's starting to look like she prefers being alone!"

"We can't make her be with people if she doesn't want to."

"You know what I mean. Don't you see? The Season is starting again soon. She'll seem… strange… if she just wants to be alone all the time. It's called the "social season" for a reason. For socializing. Because it's about getting out and being with people, other people!"

Childeric replied evenly that he knew what it was called and why. "I don't think Tara really likes the Season. She's never expressed much interest in it."

"But she should! It's important!"

Childeric held up his hands as if to suggest there was nothing he could do. "I suppose we could make her go, but we could never make her like it."

Armorica ignored that point to focus on her broader meaning. "She needs to start meeting people. She can't become a recluse, or some sort of hermit! Not when she has to be queen someday!"

Childeric acknowledged that his wife had a point. As far as he could tell, Tara's only interests seemed to be archery and Daystar. She should have a broader set of interests and expanded outlook. Childeric recollected. She had shown little aptitude in her studies beyond certain select subjects, shown minimal interest in the arts, and demonstrated absolutely no patience with governance. Yet, obviously, one day Tara would be ruling Brythrony. If it was to be governed well and properly, Tara's disinterest in such matters as law, protocol, diplomacy, even good leadership had to be remedied. Maybe Armorica was right that Tara needed to get out more. "Maybe you're right," sighed Childeric to his queen.

Armorica drew herself to her full height, visibly savoring her triumph. "I'm very glad that you agree!"

"She needs to get out more and become better acquainted with the serious responsibilities of ruling."

Armorica frowned and considered. This wasn't exactly what she had in mind, but at least it was moving in the right direction.

"Let me ask: how did she do at the opening ceremonies for the docks?"

Armorica pursed her lips. Tara had done well, all things considered. Better than Armorica had expected. Especially given the disastrous start. But she hesitated to compliment too much, for fear of undermining her recently successful argument that Tara's social skills needed remediation. "She did... all right. I suppose. Though it could have been better. And her hair needed lots and lots of work."

"Did she speak with the local officials? Did she make—whatever it's called—that small talk?"

"Badinage. The badinage."

"Yes, that's it. That sort of thing."

"In a very basic way. And, well, I guess I'd say she was polite and attentive."

Childeric smiled and was about to add something, but Armorica rushed forward to interrupt him. "But it was only after I addressed her most sternly on proper protocol before we left! And, also, I warned her again about it on the way over. She doesn't like it."

That seemed understandable, thought Childeric. Who did? "She did it though, right? And the badinage as well?"

"Not as well as she could have."

"So there's hope! Maybe she'll get better at it with practice."

Armorica said nothing, and her mouth twitched as she formulated a response. They both knew that this point took them right back to the start: that the problem was that Tara was not socializing enough, and, when she was, it was only because she had to be practically dragged into it by her all-too-frequently unruly hair.

Childeric sighed. "I have an idea," he continued, daring to broach a thought he had pondered from time to time over the past weeks. "Maybe what Tara needs is to get out and around the kingdom. It will be hers someday, right? So far, she really hasn't seen that much of it, save for the occasional excursion to open a dock or to go to a party. Other than that, all she really knows are the fields and forests near the castle, where she's been on Daystar."

Armorica waited sceptically, her arms folded.

"Well, I'm thinking, let's ask her to take a tour of the kingdom. We could find a reason for her to go, or even make one up. Anyway, in the course of that tour, she'll get to know the land, meet a lot of the nobility, and surely attend a great number of functions. This will expose her both to our kingdom and its good subjects. Then, with that understanding, she should be much more amenable to our instruction on the importance of good and wise governance."

Armorica mulled over this suggestion for a moment. It was startling, and radical, but it would get Tara out and in the company of more people. Rather than holed up in the North Tower or on that horse, riding around. But—

"Also," added Childeric, recollecting his wife's very recently expressed worries, "She'll get plenty of practice at being social—"

"Hmph!"

"Social, because I expect she'll have to meet many people wherever she goes—even as she gets more practice at that badinage technique!" Childeric paused. "What do you think?"

Armorica considered. It wasn't exactly a promise that Tara would be required to embrace the social season, but surely she'd be back in time for that anyway. Armorica liked how a tour would thrust Tara into greater visibility. Even if a tour would be a bit more unsupervised than Armorica would like. Still, it would force Tara to interact with people on her own, rather than become even more retiring and forcing her parents manage her entire social life for her.

"Possibly," she replied, cautiously. "But she can't go out alone on a tour. That's just impossible. It's also not safe."

"That's true; it's not safe. She must be properly escorted."

Maybe it was too dangerous after all. "Why shouldn't we just insist she attend all the events of the Season? Like every other princess? Wouldn't that accomplish what is necessary anyway? Without all the dangers of a tour?"

Childeric shook his head. "She's going to be queen someday. She needs more than just parties. She needs to see the kingdom and meet her future subjects. I think a tour is just what she needs."

Armorica's eyes narrowed in calculation. It would have to be more than a tour. There would have to be social events too. That was part of being a queen as well, and an important part of her education. Armorica could, would, look to that aspect herself. "What about a reason for her to go? We would need that."

"Let me think on that a day or so more."

"If she goes anywhere in an official capacity, she'll simply have to dress better. She can't seem to dress herself properly. Maybe I'll send someone with her to look after that. I know the person: Sullijee. I can count on her. She can arrange the wardrobe, and maybe even her hair." She might even help provide Tara with some guidance, thought Armorica. That might not be so bad at all. And maybe Tara could come to trust Sullijee too, and be a good influence on her. Maybe a tour was sounding better the more she reflected on it! "Yes. Think on it a day or so. Yes, please."

Childeric and Armorica sat patiently through the monologue of the spokesman of the delegation from Sea Sprit. Tara sat nearby, draped listlessly across a chair.

"Your Majesties, Your Highness," bowed the spokesman to the sovereigns and to Tara, "This is a topic of great importance to the people of Sea Sprit. If it please Your Majesties, Your Highness, may we lay before you our humble petition for assistance?"

Childeric and Armorica, from their thrones, gave their royal assent with the slightest inclination of their heads. Tara, just at that moment, appeared to be fiddling with a loose decorative element on her gown, flicking it back and forth with her pinkie finger. Otherwise, she had passed the duration of the audience thus far staring dejectedly at the floor.

Armorica noted this with displeasure out of the corner of her eye and cleared her throat. "Yes, please: it is Our will that you set before us this petition. In detail."

The spokesman bowed again, three times, once to each. He turned to an aide just behind him, who proffered him a scroll and what appeared to be a small pamphlet. Holding both before him, he approached the thrones, bowed again, and placed them on a small table placed there. He bowed yet again and stepped back, still facing the king and queen, until he resumed the place where he had stood before.

A servant stepped forward to retrieve the items. He inspected them closely and suspiciously.

What's he looking for, wondered Tara irritably. Does he think they have something in them? Like, snakes or something?

The servant, apparently satisfied that they contained nothing untoward, proceeded to the sovereigns and delivered the papers with a deep, ceremonious bow.

So ridiculous, thought Tara. Just take the silly things already! It's just a list of things these people want. Or something very much like that.

King Childeric cleared his throat and unrolled the scroll. "It appears to be a map," he stated, his right eye just visible above the upper edge and fixed on the spokesman.

"Yes, Your Majesty. You are very perceptive!"

Tara rolled her eyes. This, she had been told, was protocol and that she had to learn it. Endure it, more like, she thought.

A counsellor stepped forward to assist the king. Childeric thanked him wordlessly and pointed to a large dot prominently placed on it and next to a hatched area ornately labelled "Prithrath Ocean."

"And this is… ahem… Sea Spit?"

Tara convulsed but had the presence of mind to stifle the outburst of laughter that had arisen within her. But it would not be quelled, and Tara hastily bent her head to bury her mouth in her sleeve.

Her mother glanced sharply down at her. "Tara!" she hissed, venomously.

The more Tara tried to control her hilarity, the more impossible it became. In desperation, she took an enormous mouthful of the sleeve of her dress, which helped only because its taste made her gag. The gagging gradually overwhelmed the impulse to laugh, until at last Tara's spasms subsided, though her eyes still watered. Childeric smothered his own smile, then eyed Tara reproachfully. Tara bowed her head low, affecting mortification.

"Sea *Sprit*! This is *Sea Sprit*!" continued Childeric after all had settled.

"Yes! Yes, Sire!"

"Very good! Now, please: may the worthy delegation from Sea Sprit summarize its petition for Our ears?"

"Sire, with great pleasure. But first we thank Your Highnesses most kindly for your royal indulgence for granting us this audience!"

Tara stifled a yawn. It had been funny there—for a moment. Now it had gone back to being deathly dull. Still: Sprit. Spit. It had been funny. Tara suppressed a last giggle at the memory.

Armorica waved languorously for him to continue.

The spokesman bowed elaborately again. Tara grimaced. Finally! At last they would get to what this tiresome delegation from Sea Spit wanted! "Sire: the humble townsfolk of Sea Sprit beg to intimate to Your Highnesses that it may be Your royal pleasure to consider reinforcing the maritime approaches of Sea Sprit, for reasons both of national protection and of natural protection!"

Childeric listened intently but said nothing.

The spokesman waited a moment, but not seeing the expected dawning of understanding on the face of his monarch, continued. "Sire! If it be Your royal pleasure! The loyal and worthy people of sea sprit beg you to supplement the town's defenses so that they may provide protection from both the sea and from maritime marauders who seek to prey upon Your Majesties' commerce!"

Armorica leaned over to her husband and whispered. Childeric nodded after a moment. "I see! A sea wall! Is that it? Sea Sprit desires a sea wall?"

The spokesman, relieved, bowed deeply again in acknowledgement that this was, indeed, the object of the delegation's mission. "Yes, Sire! With a fortress, also, built integral to it. So as to defend most completely your loyal city."

"Hm! Ha!" Not just a sea wall but a fortress too? Childeric hesitated. "And, worthy delegation of Sea Sprit, tell me, do the townspeople of Sea Sprit have an estimate of what the cost of these desired fortifications might total?"

The spokesman bowed deeply again and indicated with an open hand the pamphlet that now lay upon the small table between the king and queen. "Your Highnesses: with tremendous effort and with an exceptionally stern eye on economy, the people of Sea Sprit have arrived at a figure that is believed to be the most economical that could be obtained!"

Tara's eyes strayed back to the floor. First petitions. Now cost estimates. How much longer could this audience continue?

The spokesman concluded. "This project would be of tremendous value to not only the town but to the kingdom for the protection it would afford all the land! It is for this reason that this delegation importunes Your Majesties with these entreaties! Because the protection would be to the benefit of all, we beg to put before Your Majesty the thought that all might assist in its financing, through general taxation of the kingdom."

Rather than through raising the funds locally, thought Childeric sourly. But then a thought occurred to him. "This wall and fortress, you say, would offer protection against the sea and from lawless elements who range the same?"

"Oh, Sire! Yes! Absolutely! Sea Sprit is wracked almost continuously by the most ferocious of gales!—"

Childeric raised a hand to call for the spokesman to cease. He turned to Armorica to look at her significantly. "It may be Our royal pleasure to undertake an on-site investigation and inspection of this project before We make a determination."

The spokesman rocked back in astonishment. "Sire?"

"Yes! Yes. It may well so be. Since you request funding from our kingdom...?"

"Yes, if it please you, Sire."

"Then it behoves us to conduct an assessment of this project first-hand. In person. That is to say, We or a trusted emissary."

"Of course, Your Majesty! If and when it may be your pleasure!"

Childeric thanked him with a gesture and dismissed him. He then turned to Tara, leaning forward in his throne so he could see her beyond his queen. "Princess Tara," he called. "You are excused also, if you like. The audience continues, but I see no need for you to stay further. That is, unless, you would like to."

Tara shook her head quickly and leapt up. What luck! The afternoon was not so far gone that she couldn't get out to Daystar for a short ride. She slipped around her chair and, with a goodbye wave to her parents, dashed up to her room to change to her riding clothes.

Tara sat on her bed late the next morning. It had not gone well at dinner the night before. It was true that Tara had arrived just a little late for the first course and a little flustered, as she had ridden Daystar a little further than she had intended. But the weather had been so perfect! And Daystar had been so happy to see her! They had ridden out to an old stand of apple trees and she had let Daystar browse amongst the lowest branches for fruit. He had absolutely been the happiest of horses. Tara sighed. She loved Daystar.

But then she had been late getting back to Stonedell, and she had had to change, which she had done poorly, and then she had had to rush down to dinner. She had tried to gain her chair as unobtrusively as possible but had been noticed anyway. Her mother had been irritated with her and told her so promptly.

"Mom!" she had complained. "I'm not really late! Not really!"

"You are. Because you're spoiled. Why can't you arrive on time? Were you out on that horse again?"

"His name is Daystar!"

"Daystar! Were you out on him?"

"Mom!"

"No, sit closer to me; right next to me here. So that I may observe your table manners more closely! Do you think to escape notice by sitting so far away? We are not so numerous here!"

"Mom!" Tara had wailed. She had looked to her father pleadingly.

"Now, Armorica. We don't need to be too rough with Tara, do we? Can't we just have a nice, friendly, family meal this evening?"

Armorica had glowered and resumed her seat. Dinner was served, and the servants retired to the rear of the room. Presently, Armorica had turned to her daughter again, and, after correcting, in mid-bite, the manner in which she held her fork, announced she had not been pleased with Tara's outburst during the audience with Sea Sprit. "It was the most impolite thing I could imagine," she sniffed. "That unfortunate spokesman: he was just trying to find the money for a construction project for his town and you had to laugh at him! Embarrassing, really, for your father and me!"

Tara hadn't said anything and stared into her plate. She had long ago learnt that it was better to say nothing when her mother was in a mood such as she was. Replies and rejoinders only escalated the criticisms, which, invariably, turned acrimonious. Tara shrugged, almost to herself. All right, Tara had been terrible. Again. Nothing she could do was good enough.

Tara had put down her fork. She had been hungry before, but she wasn't any longer. Too bad she had not taken one of those apples she had let Daystar munch on earlier in the day. Then she would have had something to eat. She had mumbled an excuse of being tired and unwell, stood and fled the table before her mother had hardly the chance to react.

"Wha?— Did you?— Tara! Come back here this instant!" her mother had loudly demanded, but Tara had imagined that, by that point, she had been far enough away so as to be able to argue plausibly that she had not heard.

Safely back in the North Tower, Tara had tossed her shoes angrily under the bed and then thrown herself on top of it in near despair. So unhappy. So unhappy! She had rolled over to gaze through the window at the stars, a few visible between the clouds that had rolled in over the course of the day. What was it like, she had wondered for a long time, far, far away from this room, this tower, this kingdom? What other lands and waters had those clouds passed over? She wished she could leave that instant to one of them—any of them.

At length she had grown tired, thrown herself back on her bed and gone to sleep.

Now, come the morning, she still wasn't inclined to go downstairs. She couldn't deal with her parents. But she hadn't had anything to eat except for an old crust of bread, sequestered at the back of the drawer of her night stand and which she had been saving for just such an emergency. Hunger was forcing her out. She located her left shoe, tugged it on, then bent back down to grope around some more to find the right. Just as she was jamming that one on, there was a knock at the door.

"Tara? Tara? Are you in there?"

It was her mother. She rarely came up to the tower, as she didn't like climbing all the stairs. This was one of the reasons why Tara so liked living in the tower: hardly anyone bothered to come up. Tara dropped her head into her hands.

"Tara! Are you in there?"

"Yes, Mom." What could it be, she wondered wearily. "I'm here—but I'm coming right out!"

Armorica waited outside the door, her attention momentarily occupied by the generally untidy state of the landing and the steps leading up to it. She guessed that the last time they had been mopped or swept in any way was never. Cobwebs were in the corner near the ceiling too.

Just then, there was the sound of scuffling on the other side of the door. A moment later, Tara cracked it open and, contorting herself artfully, contrived to slip around it such that only barely did she open it further at all. She immediately closed it behind her. Her mother, despite craning her neck, was unable to see what lay on the other side beyond the very briefest of glimpses of the grey wall opposite.

Best to put the bravest of faces on things, thought Tara as she presented herself. "Yes, Mom?"

Queen Armorica eyed her suspiciously. "What were you doing in there? But it doesn't matter," she interrupted herself. "Come down with me. Your father and I wish to speak with you."

Oh no, lamented Tara, as she followed her mother down the tower stairs and across a reception hall. What now? Were they going to pick up this morning where they had left off last night? Childeric was already waiting for them at the family's private dining area.

The queen stopped and motioned for Tara to proceed her. Tara demurely took a seat at the table and waited in trepidation. Had she done something else wrong? But she had been upstairs in her room last night!

The king cleared his throat preparatorily. "Thank you for coming down, Tara."

Tara glanced back and forth between her mother and father. "Well, Mom made me come down."

"Thank you all the same. Now, you may be wondering why we've asked you to come down."

Tara feared much but said nothing, thinking that her silence would best answer that question.

Childeric thought back quickly to the conversation he had had with Armorica last night after Tara, clearly upset, had run from the table.

He had put down his utensils to address his wife directly. But, before he could speak, she had whirled on him.

"She's being very difficult! Did you see that? There's nothing I can do! And I didn't even mention her hair! How awful it was, how she hadn't brushed it!"

Childeric was glad she hadn't. It would've only made things worse. "I think this shows how clearly she needs to get out and about. You saw her at the audience. She showed no interest at all in the affairs of the kingdom."

"She doesn't show any interest in anything!"

"We were talking about this just the other day. I've got an idea on how we might address this."

Armorica had thrown up her hands in resignation. "It's impossible! Maybe she can just marry someone who will do it for her!"

"Marry? I don't see that any time soon. She much prefers archery and horses and exploring."

"She's turned out to be a tomboy," Armorica had concluded, morosely.

"That's not entirely true. She doesn't mind balls and dressing up. It's just that she doesn't have tremendous patience for it."

"Like her studies," had sniffed Armorica. "She wouldn't focus on those either for any length of time!"

Childeric reflected. It wasn't that Tara had been intractable. Rather, it was that her responses had often hinged on some loophole in the problem's phrasing instead of a more conventional approach to its solution. Childeric had at first been amused at her cleverness but had come to conclude that it was probably more indicative of boredom. He also knew through hard experience that managing affairs of state was not about over-clever solutions and implausible premises.

Childeric had held up his hand in a gesture of abeyance. "We spoke of her taking a tour of the kingdom. In which she would be exposed both to our subjects and their concerns and have certain social duties. Do we agree that she needs that?"

Armorica, lips compressed tightly, had assented.

"I've got an idea on this. Just listen for a moment."

Childeric returned to the present. "Thank you for coming down to speak to us," he repeated. "This is because your mother and I need your help on something."

Help? Her help?

"Do you remember the audience with the representatives from Sea Sprit? Yes? Then you remember also that they have asked for assistance from the kingdom in financing the construction of a sea wall and an associated fortress."

Tara seemed to recollect all this, if vaguely.

"This could be a very important project. Not just for the city of Sea Sprit but for the kingdom."

Tara nodded.

"Because it is so important, we think that, before we do anything, someone we trust—someone we completely trust—ought to first take a look at Sea Sprit's plans and make sure they make sense. Someone smart and clever and who knows how to make this assessment."

Tara nodded again. All of this made sense, but what did it have to do with her?

"Well, your mother and I have been thinking that, at some point in the future, you shall become the ruler of this land." Her father paused, perhaps waiting for a reaction. Seeing none from his daughter, he continued. "We don't expect that day to come soon! But, and somewhat in preparation for this, your mother and I—" he gestured to Armorica, who smiled, "—think it would be a good idea for you to be that person. To go to Sea Sprit and inspect their proposal. And then tell us afterwards what you saw and what you think." Childeric paused again.

Tara studied her parents intently by turns, unsure of how to react. Sea Sprit? To look at a wall? Why? She had no experience in building walls.

Her mother continued. "That's right. We also think it's time that you get to know some of the kingdom. See it. Meet some people in it. If you're going to be the ruler one day, you should know Brythrony better."

"But I've been around Brythrony. Are you saying I never get out?"

"Of course not. We're not saying that. What we're saying is that you need to see more of the kingdom than you have so far."

Childeric broke in. "And we need someone to go to Sea Sprit. To see this important project!"

Tara didn't seem to hear her father's point. "Like, what parts of Brythrony do I need to know more about?"

"Like those parts beyond the fields you ride around and the places you go to shoot archery," replied her mother, evenly.

Puzzled, Tara let her eyes wander the room. "Like, like… the Sea Sprit parts?"

"Among others," inserted Childeric quickly. "And this is an important project! We need someone to make sure that it is real and necessary!"

"You should be more familiar with this part of the kingdom. And see the ocean," added Armorica, allowing a measure of enthusiasm to creep into her voice. "And some of the towns on the coast—they're quite lovely! And there'll be balls thrown for you on your arrival. In many places! It will be so fun!"

Tara winced privately. She had a hard time enduring balls. The first hour was manageable, but after that it was tedious.

"It wouldn't be all social engagements. Not at all. Because the defensive fortifications are an important project!" reminded Childeric, anxious to wrench the conversation back to Sea Sprit and its request.

Tara considered. Maybe it wouldn't be so bad after all. Maybe she could find a reasonable balance between the two. Neither sort of activity—viewing defensive fortifications nor attending afternoon teas—appealed all that much, but seeing another part of Brythrony might be interesting, and she could put up with a little bit of badinage and fortifications. Hadn't she been complaining recently about being bored? Maybe it might be a good idea.

"Can I take Daystar with me?"

Her parents nodded. "Of course. You can either ride or take the carriage. If you would prefer to ride, that's fine."

"Though the carriage is very nice!" enthused her mother. "Shady too, on a hot day!"

Not a chance, thought Tara. Her horse was her best friend. Maybe, sadly, her only friend. Tara shook her head. "I'll ride Daystar."

Childeric and Armorica looked at each other with the relieved expression of, well, then, it was settled! Childeric turned back to his daughter. "Good! Why don't you pack some clothes—"

"—Probably won't need much more than I'm wearing—"

"—You'll need to take some ball gowns!—" insisted her mother.

"—I suppose I'll need some money too—"

"—And anything else small you might like to take with you—" her father interjected.

"—Like, hey, my quiver and bow!—"

"—So you can get started in a few days. What do you think?"

Tara was already thinking ahead about the journey. No, she didn't know where Sea Sprit was, except that it was on the sea or the ocean, but the more she thought about the idea, the more she liked it. Not so much about getting out to see the kingdom because she might be its ruler one day. After all, that wasn't going to happen, probably ever, because she couldn't imagine her mother and father not being there. Instead, it was about getting out and around to places she had never been to before. The balls and fancy receptions and such that her mother seemed to think she'd have to attend she'd find a way to skip. Yes. It could be fun.

Tara nodded her head with increasing vigor as she thought the proposal over. "It sounds good. I like it. All right! I think I can be ready pretty quickly. Just throw together a couple pairs of shoes and some clothes and I'll be ready!"

Her father demurred. "What about Daystar?"

"Daystar? That's easy. He's ready to go anywhere most any time!" Tara laughed. "He doesn't ask for too much advance notice!"

Her mother stepped in. "Tara: we also need to prepare some other people to go. With you."

Tara's easy, relaxed expression changed to one of suspicion. "What do you mean?"

Queen Armorica chose her words carefully. "You won't be riding out alone. It's not safe. There will be some people with you."

"For safety's sake," added her father, quickly.

"What do you mean? How many? For how long?" This didn't sound good. Was she to be escorted the entire way? To be supervised all the time?

"It would not be safe for you to ride out alone around and about the kingdom. Remember that you are a princess. You can't just ride around like, just, a normal person."

Tara's shoulders sagged. Of course, she knew she was a princess. Being a princess was really grand and all, some of the time. But too often it seemed a complete pain: like in this instance. Couldn't she just be herself and on her own for a while? Have a little adventure on her own? Without all these courtiers and stifling advisers all the time, like at the palace court?

"You can't just go alone," repeated her father. "No. You will travel with a retinue of perhaps… maybe ten. Heralds, guards, footmen. And so forth."

"But!—"

"No 'buts'. You will not travel alone. It would be dangerous!"

"Plus, you'll need someone to handle all the trunks you'll have with you. Such as the ones holding the ball gowns and shoes!"

"And which you will take!"

Tara opened her mouth to speak again, but her parents both cut her off, and so vociferously, that she immediately gave up. So much for adventure! Now she would have to travel at a crawl amongst an enormous parade of people. She might even have to talk with them. She groaned inwardly. This would turn out to be awful and not at all fun!

Tara turned and sulked back to her room to begin packing.

Her parents turned to one another after she had disappeared. "I thought it was going be more difficult than it was. I mean, at first," began Childeric, trying to remain upbeat. "It did get a little more difficult at the last. I guess."

"I don't know," replied Armorica doubtfully. "Are you sure—really sure—this is a good idea?"

Childeric hesitated to answer. Partially because, on some level, he was as uncertain as she was. On another, while he was sure getting Tara out was for the better and necessary, he was no longer positive that a review of Sea Sprit's desired defenses was the best vehicle to accomplish this objective. So, he answered her question simply. "Yes, I still think it's a good idea."

"Maybe she'll meet someone out there. Someone handsome and dependable."

"Maybe she'll meet some other noble ladies out there with whom she might become friends."

"Maybe," thought both silently. But only "maybe." Not "surely."

"At least, she'll get out and about. And be social."

"I hope she remembers her manners!"

Childeric expelled a sigh. "I'll give the orders to the palace guard to ready a detachment to accompany her. I'll ask for someone dependable and intelligent to lead it. Someone discreet. You'll see," he added, turning back to Armorica and forcing some confidence into his voice. "It'll be fine. She'll have a nice little wander around the kingdom and meet some people. She'll grow up a little!"

Tara on Tour

It was a week later. Princess Tara was at last on her way to her first stop, a small town called Jiswith at the edge of the Prithrath Ocean on the west coast of the kingdom. It had taken what had seemed like ages to get away from the palace, what with all the boxes and trunks and bags her mother had insisted she take. All of those trundled along behind them in a cart pulled by a team of horses. Tara rode near the front of the procession, astride Daystar and with her bow and quiver of arrows slung over her shoulder. The soldiers of the palace guard had been uneasy, at first, with her riding in the van of the procession—and not even in a carriage—rather than toward the rear, protected. But, once beyond sight of the palace, Tara had made it clear, in no uncertain terms, that she would have it no other way. The captain of the guard, Rohanic, after initially protesting, had bowed to her royal insistence and Daystar had fallen in step just behind him.

The hours had passed thus, and at last it was drawing on to mid-afternoon. It would not be long until the procession would arrive at Jiswith, where it intended to pass the night. Jiswith had very little to offer, Tara had come to understand, other than being about one third of the way between Stonedell and Sea Sprit. There was an inn there, also, of suitable size and quality that might host Her Highness. Tara wasn't optimistic about what she would find but, then again, she didn't really care so much. She hadn't really spent too many nights outside Castle Stonedell anyways; anything would be new. Besides, she told herself, wasn't she used to riding all day on Daystar? She didn't need a feather bed wherever she went!

An advance messenger rode up to confer with Rohanic, who promptly dropped back to inform Tara that, shortly ahead, there would be a delegation from Jiswith waiting to greet them. Rohanic asked Tara if that would suit her. Tara bit her lower lip and signaled her consent with a single nod. She hardly had much choice since they were to stay in Jiswith and she couldn't very well arrive without meeting the delegation. Time to haul out those despised badinage skills and put them to work. Well, it would be her first opportunity to see how it went without her mother supervising her.

Suddenly remembering her mother's voice, Tara's left hand flew to her head. She should make some effort to order the many stray hairs not hidden under her hat, she thought guiltily.

The delegation was small, in that it numbered only ten. There was the mayor, his wife, a few of the local constabulary, and a couple of curious onlookers. Tara was grateful it wasn't larger.

The entire delegation bowed low as soon as the procession came into view around the bend and remained in an attitude of submission until they had stopped in front of the mayor. An expectant wait developed, and Rohanic glanced significantly at Tara. With a start, Tara realized that she was supposed to be doing something. But what? Her mother had always handled these initial moments. Tara racked her brain for a moment and realized that her mother always said something, something to put the others at ease. Something protocol-ish. Words like that.

"Ahem! Dear Esteemed Mayor… of Jiswith! And delegation!" she began, awkwardly. "So, um, greetings to you! And to the lovely Village of Jiswith!"

Maybe it had been enough. Put on a smile, Tara, she told herself. Everyone likes that. The mayor straightened and, seeing Tara wreathed in a broad smile, did so likewise. "Your Highness!" he began. "Greetings! We welcome you and your entourage to the humble Village of Jiswith!"

"A great pleasure!" returned Tara. Pretty soon, this would be over, and she could have something to eat and go to bed, she figured. Wow, this was tiring already! Except—oh, wait—wasn't she supposed to dedicate something or another or give some money to some local and worthy cause as she passed through? Her father had instructed her as much and given her some money for that express purpose.

"Your Highness, you do us a tremendous honor by your visit!"

"It is my very great pleasure!" Tara repeated. How in the world were they supposed to get going and get this over with? "I look forward greatly to viewing the lovely Jiswith and dedicating…" Tara's voice trailed off. Uh-oh. They hadn't said anything about dedicating anything. And, come to think of it, her father had said they MIGHT ask her to dedicate something. But the word "dedicating" still seemed to hang awkwardly in the air, unfinished and echoing, and all the delegation was looking at her in confusion. "Dedicating a lovely night to the enjoyment of Jiswith and its… its loveliness!"

The mayor bowed again. Tara hoped he was pleased and honored, rather than mystified and convinced Tara had lost her mind. "Yes, let us go there, to Jiswith, right away!" she added, to paper over the silent perplexity that had settled over the group.

The delegation promptly mounted their horses, the mayor riding alongside Tara. He began to tell her of the prosperity of Jiswith, how good the harvest had been lately, and that the townsfolk were very happy and peaceable people with little to complain of.

"This is wonderful news," acknowledged Tara, trying to focus on managing her horse—maybe this was why her mother had suggested a carriage—amongst all the other horses of the delegation while trying to listen attentively to the mayor. "I shall be certain to convey this to my mother and father." In addition to managing Daystar, she was also trying to think of something for badinage. Something to chat about idly with him. Something other than the harvest, about which she knew absolutely nothing, except insofar as it meant apples for Daystar.

"Yes," the mayor continued, and proceeded to recount, in detail, the bounty of their fields and orchards and the great promise that the coming season must surely hold for them. "We are extremely loyal to the throne and happily share our prosperity through our tithes to Brythrony!"

Tithes! recollected Tara. She had heard about those quite a bit during her too numerous visits to the law courts. No one seemed to like taxation. It must be onerous. Couldn't that be a useful topic for badinage? It seemed like most everyone coming to the law courts had an opinion on them; surely the mayor would as well. At the mayor's next pause, and eager at the chance to show she was engaged in the conversation, "Taxes! I have heard talk of them. What do you think, Esteemed Mayor: they are high, are they not?"

The mayor nearly fell from his horse. "Your Highness?"

"Taxes. Taxes. I understand they are high. What would you say?"

The mayor looked furtively to the other nearby members of his delegation, all of whom were wide-eyed in amazement. His wife shook her head covertly, mouthing discreetly the word "no." Was this some sort of trap? The mayor's mind raced. Had Princess Tara been sent to Jiswith and maybe points further away to assess local attitudes toward taxation?

Or, rather, had she been sent to investigate discrepancies? Come to think of it, wasn't the village behind by two months on the excess owed from a better-than-expected crop, which they had deliberately under-reported?

Meaning, this visit was not the bolt from the blue that he had initially thought it. How foolish of him. Of course, there was purpose behind it, royal purpose. And that innocent affectation of awkwardness at first: a feint, to throw him off guard.

The mayor gulped. "Uh, Your Highness, no… no, not at all!"

Tara looked at him sharply. "No? Not too high?"

"Your Highness: I would never suggest dissatisfaction with our taxation! We are proud—Jiswith is proud—to make its loyal contribution to the throne for the common defense of the kingdom."

"That's not what others say," replied Tara darkly, thinking of the general tone of the complaints she had heard in the law courts. "Some say they think they pay too much and would like to pay less. Less than they do," she added meaningfully.

The mayor fidgeted with the reins on his horse. How did Stonedell know? How could it? Yet, obviously, it did. "Your Highness, if I may be so bold…"

"Yes, Esteemed Mayor?"

"Your Highness, if there might be any dissatisfaction—any at all with Jiswith, at court… you would be so kind as to tell us, would you? If it be your royal pleasure?" The voice was almost pleading.

Tara eyed him glumly. So much for an innocent badinage topic. It was supposed to have been something that the mayor could have spoken on for the rest of the journey to Jiswith. Instead, it had prompted him to question her about court life and how her parents perceived Jiswith, something about which she had not the faintest idea.

"Some people like to pay less than they do, that's all I mean to say, Esteemed Mayor. Nothing more."

They are furious with us, panicked the mayor. And they know all. Everything. He rued the dark day that he had first thought to hide from the court what was its due. It had been a vain and stupid effort to increase his popularity. His council had warned him that her visit might be more than a mere stopover.

They were nearing Jiswith; the houses on its outskirts lay ahead. "What a pleasant town," stated Tara tonelessly, making a last, vain effort at badinage.

And now she threatens us for failing to pay our taxes in full, wailed the mayor silently. Childeric's troops will ride in and take everything! So discomfited was the mayor he could say nothing in reply.

Another attempt fallen flat, concluded Tara. Best to end this quickly and say she was tired. When Rohanic fell back to ask her what was her pleasure, she replied in a faint voice that she wished to be taken to the inn immediately, as the demands of travel had over-wearied her.

Rohanic saluted her and directed the procession toward the inn that had been identified for their stay.

The mayor's heart sank. This could well be the end of him. Maybe even of Jiswith. He must surrender the owed taxes immediately. Childeric must be enraged, to have sent his daughter, the princess, to collect them personally.

The delegation and the procession parted at the inn, with the mayor professing everlasting loyalty and fealty, Princess Tara dispiritedly accepting same but resigned to being a failed conversationalist on her first real independent effort. Bleakly, she expected that, the ride having gone so poorly, they would not ask her to dedicate anything or appear before any local cause.

She mounted the stairs to her quarters, Rohanic having promised to ensure Daystar was well cared for. She was so tired, come to think of it, it was just as well that there would be no official duties that evening. "Send something up for me for dinner," she requested of Rohanic. "Anything. Nothing special on my account; just whatever they're serving you and the others."

"Yes, Your Highness," he replied, and, an hour later, a tray of simple stewed meats and vegetables arrived at her door. Tara ate with relish and fell asleep immediately.

She awoke the next morning to a soft tapping at the door from a maidservant. "Your Highness! Something for your breakfast?"

Whatever the rest were having, replied Tara, sleepily, and accepted shortly afterwards the tray left at the door as she had the night before. She dressed and went downstairs to find Rohanic and the rest of the guard ready to continue their journey. "Something very strange occurred, Your Highness," remarked Rohanic after they had departed Jiswith and, unexpectedly, been seen off by a very large, boisterous crowd, which must have comprised the entire town's population. "Late last night. Just before I was intending to retire. The mayor visited me."

Tara regarded him questioningly.

"Your Highness: the mayor asked me to accept the unpaid taxes of the town and presented them to me, right then and there!"

"Indeed?"

"Yes, Your Highness. In a small chest. Which is behind us, in the luggage wagon." Rohanic inclined his head in the direction behind them and toward the rear of the train. "Hidden amongst the baggage, Your Highness, as I suspect it is a certain quantity of gold."

How very strange, thought Tara. That Jiswith should choose to pay its taxes now, and to her, rather than at the annual assessment! "But, I suppose that means we'll have to carry it with us, doesn't it? All the way to Sea Sprit?" she observed, peevish at the expectation that the procession would move even more slowly than before.

"Yes, Your Highness. It is an additional burden, I suppose. Though, usefully, and if necessary, we might 'borrow' from it for expenses as need be."

True, admitted Tara. So, they needn't run out of money. Not that that had been a concern to begin with. In the meantime, they had the extra bother and security to consider for the taxes.

"Your Highness: a thought occurs to me. The next town, called Sylvan, is very little and has only a small inn. Rather than overwhelm this inn, why not have the majority of the guard camp in the woods outside the town, while you, under an assumed name and accompanied by me and one other trusted person, stay at the inn. In this wise there will be no knavish temptations to pilfer from the chest, as we can most easily set a guard on the baggage cart."

Tara agreed to this and, as the day drew on toward evening, she, Rohanic, and his lieutenant approached the inn. It was just as well, as there were only two rooms available: one for Tara and the other for her two escorts.

Though Tara received the best room Sylvan had to offer, still it was rudely furnished with but a bed, chair, and wash basin. Tara was a bit surprised at first, but quickly warmed to its simple, honest welcome. The bed was hardly the most comfortable either, being stuffed with straw, but it was sufficiently fresh straw as to still be fragrant, and it reminded her of being out in the fields with Daystar.

In private, Rohanic apologized deeply and repeatedly for the rustic accommodations, but Tara, charmed by their simplicity, laughingly brushed him off. "Really, Rohanic! Stop this at once; I'm quite beginning to like it. And only one utensil with which to eat! I can surely use that one properly; my mother the queen would at last be proud of me!"

Tara joined the others at supper downstairs, with her escorts to either side of her. The meal was eye-opening. Rather than servants bringing them their dishes on fine plate, they ate out of rough wooden bowls which had been scraped smooth on the inside by hundreds of hungry, questing wooden spoons. A weak beer was poured out into brown glazed crockery and each allowed only one refill. Tara caught the eye of Rohanic at one point during the meal, and he appeared to be in agony at the contrast with her usual palace fare, but Tara smiled back, laughed, and plied her spoon zestfully. "Wonderful!" she cried softly. How she welcomed being totally anonymous for an evening! No functions, no dedications, no badinage, and no one cared about her any more than anyone else there.

Tara climbed the stairs to her room, absolutely blissful. Though the day's travel had been long, this day had been the best so far. Being away from the castle wasn't bad at all. True, the bed was shorter, harder, and the sheets rougher. The room was smaller too, and the furnishings spare, to say the least. But no one questioned her table manners, the extent to which she had or had not brushed her hair, and if she was properly wearing whatever gown that Sullijee, her assigned Mistress of the Robes, had chosen for her. Because no one cared. No one! She could really come to like this, she caught herself thinking. But, turning sorrowful, that could not be, as they were to arrive in Sea Sprit on the morrow, and surely there would be a reception for the visiting princess. In fact, she recalled that Rohanic had told her that they would arrive midday so that she could properly prepare herself for the long-planned gala reception. She frowned. This evening and the next morning were all the time she had left to herself before "princessing" began in earnest.

Mid-morning the next day, Lieutenant Rohanic reined his horse in slightly so as to fall back and ride abreast of Princess Tara. Unlike the days before, and in order to cut a more martial figure on arrival in Sea Sprit, he wore his dress helmet, burnished to a brilliant reflection of the blue sky overhead. After saluting her with a touch to his helmet of his gloved right hand, he spoke.

"Good day again, Your Highness. I hope you breakfasted well?"

Princess Tara indicated disinterestedly that she had and to repletion.

He touched his helmet again to signify he understood and that this was well and continued. "We are fast approaching Sea Sprit, the objective of our journey. I have sent ahead two of our entourage to announce your arrival so that a suitable welcome may be prepared."

Tara shook herself free reluctantly from the lovely languor into which she had settled over the course of the morning of just her plodding horse and the dappling sunlight and focused her attention on Rohanic. Yes, Sea Sprit was their objective. All too soon she would have to start princessing again, engage in that hateful badinage, and dedicate something or another. Then, also, the brushing of her hair. She tried to console herself. Perhaps, and despite what her parents and several others had told her, Sea Sprit was little more than a port and not overly grand. If so, she just might be able to avoid any further receptions and balls. Then, the next morning, perhaps she would and without too much fanfare, take a quick look at the site for the proposed works and depart quietly. Her hopes rose fractionally.

Lieutenant Rohanic was speaking again. "We should be arriving in an hour or so."

Tara repositioned herself restlessly in her saddle. "A welcome, suitable or otherwise, is probably not necessary, Lieutenant. Why not let the good people of Sea Sprit go about their normal affairs without that distraction?"

Rohanic stared back uncomprehendingly. "But, Your Highness, how can this be? When a member of the royal family arrives for an official visit, the townspeople must be made aware so that they may pay their proper respects."

Tara frowned. This was much how her father and mother had told her she had to do it. With a lot of drama and excitement. "I suppose," she replied carefully, "those two you sent ahead are already away and cannot be recalled?"

"Yes, Your Highness: they have already departed."

Tara sighed. "Very well, then; we shall have whatever reception Sea Sprit sees fit to render us."

The people of Sea Sprit had indeed been turned out to greet their princess. There was a band to receive her and cheers that, on command, resounded up and down the road. Goodness gracious, thought Tara, they can't possibly be that glad to see me! They must have been threatened with dire harm to shout so! Tara did her best to wave to either side of her in equal amounts but feared that she might be favoring the right since she was right-handed.

The royal procession drew up to a small, elevated stand, where the gentry of the town had been assembled. In the stand, calmly, even smugly gauging her, and with expressions ranging from faintly amused to that of scandal barely concealed, were the so very local upper crust of a seaside port town. Tara surveyed them from below for a lengthy moment, conflicting currents coursing through her. Her heart beat faster, her breath quickened. Acutely, she realized how stained and untidy she must appear, how disheveled and unkempt her clothes must look, how mussed and tousled her hair surely was, and how appallingly dirty and travelworn her features must be. Yet, was she not Princess of the Realm? How dare they inspect her with such clinical detachment as they might some specimen fished from the depths just beyond the quay?

A flash of pride prompted her to straighten in her saddle. Her face reddening brightly, she composed her features into their haughtiest expression. If they could only know how little she wanted to be there! A wave of irritation, anger, and humiliation swept over her, and she wanted to ride far away from Sea Sprit that instant. Before she could flick the reins though, the pride within her overcame the humiliation and irritation. No. She would stay, she resolved, and attend their absurd little ball so as to demonstrate publicly the caliber of the House of Hession.

The mayor, a round, ruddy fellow, doffed his tall green hat, bowed low, and welcomed her to Sea Sprit. Tara eyed him up regally, and, in a single, fluid motion that would have done her father's horse guards proud, dismounted from Daystar and swept up her traveling skirts to approach the stand. The mayor fell back in astonishment and even alarm to make way for her.

She was dimly aware that, behind her, her procession had come to a halt and that Rohanic was frantically manoeuvring his horse so as to be as near as he could to his charge. Tara stepped lightly onto the platform and advanced on the mayor until he could back away from her no further. She gazed down directly into his face as if to bore a hole through him with her eyes. Then she turned to the assemblage to her right. "Greetings, Esteemed Leadership of Sea Sprit! We thank you for your hospitable welcome!" she called, and the whispering and gesturing amongst them stilled as her voice rang out, for she had enunciated her words in the distinct "court" accent reserved exclusively for official occasions.

The mayor bowed again and, bobbing and babbling, repeatedly welcomed her in what sounded like the same words, only uttered in varying combinations.

She listened but for a few moments. "Loyal Subjects!" she cried, abruptly turning to the crowd at her feet and to either side. "It is with great pleasure—" she continued, now switching to the everyday accent of Brythrony, "—tremendous pleasure!—that I visit you! Too long have you and your very genuine needs been neglected. But today, I arrive to perhaps remedy both, and I thank you all, in advance, for your kind hospitality!

"Thank you, and good day!"

The crowd erupted in a wild cheer which seemed, this time to Tara's ears, absolutely genuine, though conceivably solely so because of the brevity of her speech. Tara, more measuredly, turned back to the mayor and, shifting back into the court accent, thanked him again. Then, setting her jaw, she proceeded amongst the rows of the local dignitaries to meet and greet each and every one of them. This accomplished, she tripped lightly back down the stairs and sprang to her mount. "Rohanic!" she commanded.

"Your Highness!" he answered immediately.

"Let us proceed!"

"Your Highness!" he acknowledged and barked the order for the procession to continue. Tara set her face in a fixed smile and nudged Daystar forward.

"Your Highness," murmured Rohanic, dropping back to ride even with her, "We are scheduled next to be present for the unveiling of a central administrative building for Sea Sprit."

Tara gritted her teeth. "Very well!"

"Shall we then proceed there?"

"Yes, and directly. If you please!"

Rohanic saluted in acknowledgement. "Forthwith, Your Highness!"

Tara called him back after a moment. "And, if I may, where to from there?"

"To the inn, Your Highness. To prepare for the gala ball this evening."

There really would be no surcease from this accursed princessing, concluded Tara with bitter finality, and her gaze hardened as she stared out into the road ahead. "Very well; so be it. Let us go and dedicate this facility."

"Yes, Your Highness."

Tara had a sudden idea. "Rohanic, a last time, please!"

"Your Highness?"

She lowered her voice and breathed, "Is it not traditional, when visiting, to show a measure of largesse to the population, and conspicuously so?"

"Your Highness?"

"A gift!"

"But—Your Highness—we have no such monies to bestow!"

"The taxes from Jiswith. SOME of them. Some. Have them to hand. At the dedication."

"By your command, Your Highness."

Tara sensed reluctance in Rohanic's tone, but she was unperturbed. Sea Sprit would not forget the visit of a member of the immediate royal family, however she might have arrived. Yes, on some level, she knew she was being childish, but Tara could be stubborn and willful at times. Just at that moment she was supremely exasperated with every aspect of princessing, from her parents' idea that she come out here, to the superior reactions of the local dignitaries, and, yes, by her own daft decision to come by horse rather than by carriage. In spite of all these things, or maybe because of them, she refused to be cowed by the people of Sea Sprit or by the demands of princessing or by anything else associated with what she was, might, or could be confronted with on that trip. A very resolute and coldly furious sort of bloody-minded determination had come to her, and she fiercely vowed to see it all through, no matter how many hands she had to press or how many versions of thanks she would have to mouth in an official capacity.

The procession wound its way through the gaily decorated streets of Sea Sprit toward the administrative building which, to Tara's eye, resembled a small, mean, low affair and hardly worthy of the attention being bestowed on it. But it was what it was. Tara summoned her court accent again and dismounted to do her best.

Queen Armorica proceeded to read aloud the message to King Childeric once they had gained the privacy of their royal apartments.

"'Your Majesties,'" she began, then groaned loudly and stopped.

Childeric became impatient, as it was clear that Armorica was reading ahead silently rather than to him, as she had told him she would. "Well? What? What after 'Your Majesties'? Surely it says more than that!"

Armorica groaned again, and her hand dropped to her side. "Will she leave a trail of destruction in her wake? Oh, Tara! This has got to mean the end of our House!"

"What does it say?"

"Yes, yes. Just wait a moment!" Armorica massaged her temples as she ran her eyes back to the top of the page. "Yes, here. Yes! I begin:

Your Majesties! My humblest and most earnest greetings to you and—

"Oh, do skip all that!"

In accordance with your royal direction, I report to you on our progress and adventures to date in making our way to Sea Sprit.

As planned, we overnighted in Jiswith, having made that journey in good time by taking the Royal Route as we had discussed extensively—

"I'll skip some of these extraneous details too—

—to meet the mayor and a delegation at the town gates. Our interaction with this mayor was most strange, as it was not long before the mayor began to evidence the most extreme signs of discomfort and agitation in speaking with Her Highness, Princess of the Realm.

"What on earth did she say to him?"

"Just wait!"

It became perhaps a bit more clear—or maybe much less so—later that evening, when that mayor, accompanied by several alderman, came to my door and, with a great show of contrition, offered us, in a small locked chest, the taxes he said to be due and owed, and entreated me to take these and for Your Majesties to be merciful toward Jiswith, said town having now discharged its debts, or at least so he maintained.

"Tara wrangled more taxes out of them? Well done, Tara! Who would have ever thought she could have that sort of impact!"

Armorica looked up from the paper, glowering. "She is not some common tax collector! She is supposed to be representing the crown! This is beneath her!"

Childeric waved his hand in dismissal, as if it were all the same to him.

Armorica continued:

We made good time the next day and overnighted, again as planned, in Sylvan. I accompanied Her Highness into Sylvan, though most of the escort remained outside the town and camped, in order to guard the monies we had unexpectedly obtained in Jiswith. Her Highness and I, and one lieutenant, stayed incognito in Sylvan and, I must say, to no discredit to Her

Highness at all, she took to her role quite readily as a traveling noblewoman and blended in quite well; no one suspecting of anything else.

Armorica stopped and looked up again. "I wonder what THAT really means. That she 'blended in' so very well!"

Childeric waved his hand again casually. "Only that, I'm sure, and no more. That she understood this necessity and undertook it to the best of her not inconsiderable ability!"

"Humph," grumbled Armorica, but resumed:

We again made good progress the following day to approach Sea Sprit as anticipated. Her Highness, as you know, decided in her superior judgement to ride her own mount rather than travel by carriage. It was because of this, perhaps, that the assembled dignitaries of Sea Sprit, I am most sorry to say, were not the most welcoming to the Princess of the Realm upon her initial approach to the reception platform.

Armorica broke off. "She must have been a mess by the time she arrived! An absolute mess! They probably didn't even recognize her!"

Childeric's mouth twitched, but he said nothing.

However, I hasten to add that Her Highness, with superb dignity and poise, recovered herself remarkably well and greeted the population, which had turned out to a man, woman, and child to greet us, with a very brief speech, which was clearly well received by everyone.

"Well done again, Tara!"

We proceeded from there immediately to the dedication of the administrative building. There, the Princess of the Realm surprised all, and earned great admiration and approbation, by distributing a portion of the taxes obtained from Jiswith to the people of Sea Sprit.

"No! No, Tara, no!" moaned the king.

"Not at all!" expostulated his wife. "Yes, this was quite the right thing for her to do. Perhaps the ONLY thing she's done right the entire tour so far!"

"Is there anything more to this extended recitation?" demanded Childeric, fast becoming annoyed.

"Very little. Only that… let's see… they attend a gala reception at some local worthy's mansion that evening… they are to tour the town's defenses to inspect them as they currently stand the next day… and, hm… signed, Lieutenant Rohanic." Armorica put the message down on a nearby demi-lune table and regarded Childeric. "Are we SURE it was a good idea to put her on tour?"

Childeric drummed his fingers for a moment. There was nothing to be done for it now. She wasn't doing that bad, surely, anyway. "She's certainly learning a great deal. I'm sure she'll be fine. And Rohanic will look after the rest, I expect."

It had actually been somewhat charming, reflected Tara later that evening, as she sank gratefully into the finest bed at the finest hostelry in Sea Sprit. Yes, there had been a reception for her to attend, but it hadn't been too demanding, as it had not been as "gala" as she had expected, more a kind of extended receiving line in the house of the wealthiest sea captain locally.

Tara thought back as she lay on her bed, awaiting sleep.

First had come the preparations. The largest room in the inn had been set aside for these. Her Mistress of the Robes, Sullijee, had had a bank of cheval mirrors positioned in a square open at one side and a box placed in the center and upon which she was to stand. Sea Sprit's finest seamstresses had been placed at her disposal to ensure her dress was perfect. For the most part it had been, though a button was in need of tightening, and there was a general need for fussing, which Tara bore with as good a grace as she could. Of course, there had been the hair brushing. Tara had not been allowed to do this herself; a loaned servant had performed this function but at least much more gently than her mother was wont. Tara was only to watch and ensure that her hair was just as she might like it, the ribbons placed just so and affixed in just such a particular way, and so forth and so on.

Over all of this Sullijee had presided. Sullijee was older than Tara, perhaps by a few years, and Tara didn't know her that well as she was more closely associated with her mother's retinue. Her mother had thought it best that Tara have someone to assist her in preparations for social occasions, she had explained, and thought Sullijee might do this best. To a certain extent, Tara was grateful, as she had no interest in fretting over dresses and shoes herself. On the other hand, she wasn't sure just how far she could trust Sullijee. She was from her mother's household, after all. What would she report back to her mother? Thus, while she was careful to remain cordial with Sullijee, she was careful not to confide in her.

A cobbler had worked with her shoes. He had been perplexed at the condition he had found them, which was badly worn, rather scuffed, and overall in an advanced state of disrepair. Several times he had glanced up questioningly at Tara, but she had kept her gaze firmly focused on her hair in the mirror. Of course, the shoes were in poor condition, Tara admitted silently. She had only just dragged them out from under her bed before departing and only on repeated prompting from her mother. Only just had she noticed that she had not hauled out a pair; she had had to reach back twice again for the other. Idly, she wondered how Sea Sprit would have taken it if she had worn mismatched shoes to the gala. Would they think it deliberate and the newest style at Stonedell? She smiled to herself. They would never guess it was because she had simply been too rushed and uncaring to have made sure of a match.

A suitable coach had been sent by the host, a retired sea captain. It had clattered to a stop outside, the horses snorting and frisking. She had shooed away the attendants, slipped on the shoes of burnt umber silk with a smile as thanks to the cobbler, and turned for the door. Momentarily, she had stopped and closed her eyes. It was time at last for some serious princessing. Ready or not. She had opened her eyes, nodded graciously to the doormen, and wide open they had thrown the double doors to the porte-cochère.

The effect had been dramatic. To the breath-taking amazement of the small knot of onlookers gathered, Princess Tara had emerged, resplendent in her favorite ball gown of lapis blue with carob-brown stripes diagonal up and to the left across it, a checked stomacher panel in darker tones of indigo and chocolate completing it. As on all such formal occasions, the royal sash of purest white silk was pinned from her right shoulder to her left hip, such that it contrasted in direction with the diagonal stripes in her gown.

The door to the carriage was flung open and, though she had hardly needed it, she had accepted the footman's hand. Rohanic, in parade dress, had appeared alongside as escort as soon as they were on the horseshoe drive leading to the street.

The sea captain's mansion had been situated atop a bluff overlooking the town. The reception had been held in the ballroom, which had, at its very end, a commanding view of the harbor. Though Tara had not had the opportunity for a tour of the residence, having been immediately engaged in the business of the reception, that which she saw surprised her pleasantly with its easy elegance and self-confident refinement. How much lovelier and lighter as a room it was than anything at Stonedell! Mirrors alternating with polished brasses reflected in prismatic hues the multitudinous lights of the crystal chandeliers hung at regular intervals overhead. Underfoot, and in involved parquetry, a depiction of Sea Sprit in a storm had been figured in the floor.

Surrounded by such opulence, it had been easier for Tara to maintain a regal demeanor and her court accent. She had tried to mind her mother's voice, always in her ear and reminding her to stand up straight, look in the eye the person speaking to her, be kind, and smile—a lot.

Tara had been introduced first to her host. "Captain Jarvis," she had murmured and offered her hand as she was introduced. "How very kind of you."

"A very great pleasure, Your Highness!"

Captain Jarvis was a tall, slightly stooping man in, Tara had guessed, his seventies. He wore the retirement uniform of the Brythron Navy, which largely consisted of a blue cutaway with all medals displayed, paired with grey trousers and grey shoes. Tara had eyed the medals discreetly. There seemed to be a lot. She didn't recognize any, but then she had never had much interest in such things anyway.

"Captain, you served in our navy with great distinction," she had remarked as an opening gambit at badinage and with a gesture toward the impressive rows of ribbons and medals at his chest.

"Ahem! Your Highness! It was my honor to serve our great kingdom in that capacity. Mostly during the reign of Your Highness's grandmother, Queen Ysolde, I should say. Later, for a time, I sailed a commercial vessel, trading up and down the coast."

"My grandmother, did you say?" Tara had asked, seizing this element of his remark and recalling to mind the ruby ring from her grandmother, which lay in her desk in her room in the tower at Stonedell.

"Yes, Your Highness. A fine queen, who maintained a fine navy and who oversaw a fine era for Brythrony!"

"Did you ever meet her, Captain?"

"Indeed, yes, I did, Your Highness. Once only, though."

"Oh! Tell me about that instance, if you would, please."

Jarvis had paused a moment and looked up at the ceiling as if in thought. "Your Highness, it was a very long time ago, as you might imagine, but I still remember it quite clearly."

Tara had stopped with the captain and waited for him to continue.

"Yes, yes: I was the second in command of the *Gyrfalcon*, a warship of some two hundred men, if memory serves me correctly.

"Ahem! Yes, we were moored, and the Queen was passing through and thought to pay us a visit. We received notification of this intended visit early in the day, and we had all ship's personnel 'turn-to' to get *Gyrfalcon* ready for a state visit."

"Indeed, Captain."

"Indeed, Your Highness. But I do believe that we needn't have, as Her Majesty, when she appeared at the foot of the brow, was hardly dressed for a state occasion! She had clearly been traveling and was not in state dress at all."

Tara had smiled to herself. Wouldn't that be so like her grandmother. Probably just coming back from the ends of the world, or similar. "She was known to travel, wasn't she?"

"Yes, yes. Quite right, Your Highness. And so, your grandmother the Queen stepped aboard our vessel, but not so much to pay us a visit, I suspect, but rather out of curiosity and perhaps even as a means of conveyance somewhere in the future."

"Is that so! What do you mean, if you please?"

"Ahem! Well, Your Highness, I mean to say that she showed a great deal of interest in the quarters and the eating facilities but no interest in the honor guard or ship's armory or any of her other capabilities. To be very honest with Your Highness, I believe to this day that she was thinking of some sort of mission for *Gyrfalcon* and with her on board!"

Tara had nodded in understanding. "She was one for excitement."

"Yes, Your Highness."

"But, if I understand you, it sounds as if no such mission ever materialized?"

"No, Your Highness. We never heard of such. And, sadly, I never had another opportunity to encounter your grandmother the Queen." He had turned to regard Tara with his keen eyes, then offset them with a benign smile. "Your Highness, you are not at all like her in that respect. Your Highness is magnificent in her ball gown!"

Tara had returned his smile, but it had been forced, although Captain Jarvis could not have known. How irksome, thought Tara, though she had broadened her smile just a trifle to offset this contrary thought. Her grandmother had been able to board ships whenever she liked and undertaken exciting missions, whereas she, Tara, had to go princessing.

So much for that avenue of conversation, to Tara's dissatisfaction. But another had come to her just as quickly that she was certain would be even more fruitful. "Captain, I've learnt that I am to board a vessel tomorrow morning for a day's sail in the general area."

"Indeed, Your Highness?"

"Yes. Indeed. And you mustn't tell anyone! State secret, I imagine, but I'm sure I can trust you, depending as I am upon your past service to the Crown."

Jarvis had harrumphed something to the affirmative.

"I expect I am to be shown the coast and some of its more prominent features from the sea. Fortifications and so forth, I believe."

Captain Jarvis clasped his hands behind his back and commenced to walk alongside Tara, though maintaining a respectful distance and always a step behind.

"Tell me, Captain: what sort of weather, wind, and wave might I expect? For what sort of conditions should I prepare myself?"

"Your Highness, this is momentous news that you will inspect Sea Sprit from the sea! You will bear witness to the truth that, though she is stoutly defended, she could yet put further reinforcement to good use."

"Indeed, Captain; tell me more," Tara had continued, selecting as she passed a lightly sugared sweetmeat from a proffered silver salver.

Captain Jarvis had then begun an explanation of the purpose of the sea walls, the various elements of defensive architecture that Sea Sprit already had, when they had been built, and what more the city could use, in addition to his expectations as to the weather the next day.

Tara had listened and attempted to concentrate as best she could, but the activity all about her had been a tremendous distraction. She had felt obliged to acknowledge the curtsies and bows made to her, and the prismatic play of colors from the chandeliers had seemed to wander errantly across her dress and up her white silk sash to linger mischievously in her eyes. The half-heard strains of a string quartet moving through vaguely recalled musical phrases had also hampered her comprehension.

The captain had eyed her as they had approached the French doors at the far end of the ballroom, and which opened onto a large balcony overlooking the ocean. "When do you sail tomorrow morning, Your Highness, if I may be so bold as to ask?"

"Not at all, Captain. I believe with the tides; at least, that is what I recollect being told. I'm not sure when that would be, exactly, though I suppose I will be informed."

"And your ship, may I also ask?"

"The *Dolphin*, as I remember."

The sea captain had nodded. "A fine ship," he observed. "Well captained and well crewed. I recall now being consulted as to which ship might be best to take Your Highness out. *Dolphin*: she's highly manoeuvrable, even in the lightest of breezes!

"Indeed, *Dolphin* represents an investment on the part of Sea Sprit in her own defenses."

"Really, Captain? How so?"

"Yes, Your Highness, in that her conversion into her present form was paid for by the people of Sea Sprit, as is her manning complement and supplies."

"So, then, Captain, she is the embodiment of Sea Sprit's self-reliance and efforts to date in her own self-defense."

Jarvis had bowed wordlessly.

Tara had then thanked her host for assisting in the selection of *Dolphin* and had had to take her leave, as she had been asked to meet others at the ball. This had continued until she had feared that she might collapse on her feet she became so exhausted.

At length, she had begged leave of her host and his guests to depart, as she had had a full day and expected to have another on the following. Then the same coach, again escorted by Rohanic, had conveyed her back to her rooms.

Now she lay in her bed, fatigued beyond description. Yes, it had been so very tiring. But at least it was done. Tara yawned and thought about the morrow. She was sure it would be pleasant. Out there, on the sea, with the sun and the waves. Not much to do but be shown the seawalls and fortified towers and so forth.

The next day, Tara bade good morning to Lieutenant Rohanic. He had been somewhat uneasy with her presence on board without the full complement of their escort, but not all of them would be able to join, as *Dolphin* was a smallish vessel, only a cutter, and could not accommodate them all. "No danger here," had replied the vessel's captain, Captain Sisti. "We'll hardly be out of sight of land. Besides, this is a hardy crew here," and he gestured broadly to the sailors preparing the vessel for getting underway. "There'll be no trouble!" Lieutenant Rohanic had had no choice but to accept this reassurance. He insisted, though, that the royal ensign of the Princess of the Realm, quartered, with a canton of her coat of arms and solid blocks of the colors of House Hession in the other quarters, not be flown from the rigging so that they might sail, insofar as possible, unknown. This concession obtained, he, with two other trusted soldiers, came aboard and the rest stayed behind with the horses, the wagons, and the remaining tax monies from Jiswith.

Dolphin got underway with a roll of drums and to the cheers of the assembled crowd. Princess Tara stood on the quarterdeck and, with one from her retinue to either side, Rohanic remaining with Sisti, waved as gaily as she could. "Bye-bye!" she murmured. "See you soon! Later on today!"

The cutter pulled out of the harbor, a freshening breeze filling her sails. The ship began to rise and fall gently as it met the swells from the open sea. Tara felt just the tiniest bit queasy at first but then told herself sternly that it had to be much like it had been riding Daystar at first: some jolting up and down but then, as soon as one had the rhythm of it, everything would be all right. She smiled more steadily, kept a grasp on the lifelines to maintain her balance and gazed steadily back at the sailors eyeing her out of the corner of their eyes. After a few minutes, they ceased to watch her for signs of seasickness and went about their assigned duties. Tara straightened triumphantly, delighted that she had passed that "test."

They rounded a cape, and Captain Sisti began to point out various notable aspects of the coast, including lighthouses, forts, and other prominent features. A chart in one hand and shading her eyes with the other, Tara did her best to follow him.

She asked in particular about the seaward defenses of Sea Sprit. "Captain, how often does Sea Sprit experience storms of sufficient violence so as to overwhelm the walls now in place?"

Sisti hesitated. "Your Highness, of course that depends on the year and the season, with some years seeing several, and some seeing none at all. This past year, I believe we suffered just two, but the last was of such violence that none in living memory could remember its equal."

Thus prompting the petition for aid, surmised Tara. "Doubtless they are seasonal, too? Maybe mostly in the spring and summer?" For such were the thunderstorms that she seemed to remember having had to take shelter from when out riding Daystar.

"No, indeed not, Your Highness. Mostly during the autumn. Mid- to late-autumn, I should say."

"And do they quite overwhelm Sea Sprit?"

Sisti smiled. "No, Your Highness; not yet. Though we did have to resort to sandbags to weather the last one!"

"What about other threats from the sea, Captain? Does Sea Sprit suffer from attack? And, if so, does not our navy offer all the defense she might require?"

"Your Highness, this is somewhat of a new phenomenon. Only within the past few years has Sea Sprit been the victim of what we might call piracy."

Tara pulled back and regarded Sisti with surprise. "'Piracy?' In Sea Sprit? Sea Sprit been attacked then?"

"Not exactly, Your Highness. Sea Sprit, the city, has not been attacked. Not yet." Sisti thought for a moment, then continued. "Your Highness, if I may explain myself: Sea Sprit itself has not yet suffered a seaborne attack. But some of the commerce leaving from and arriving to Sea Sprit has been attacked and there have been losses. It is unclear if it is a single ship or several, but it is always the same type of ship—a brigantine. Sea Sprit has thought it of sufficient concern so as to man and equip *Dolphin* for her defense."

"Really, Captain! Where is our navy?"

"Well, Your Highness, we have petitioned Your Majesty's Navy for assistance in this regard. And—" he hastened to add, seeing a building sense of outrage in Her Highness's expression "—that help has been forthcoming in the form of occasional patrols! But, it has been difficult to locate the source of this piracy, to find this brigantine, no doubt due to the existence of so many hidden coves and inlets along the coast, which the pirates must use to their advantage."

"They must hide their craft there."

"Exactly, Your Highness."

"But why, then, does not the navy come across these pirates during their patrols?"

Sisti shrugged. "Maybe the ships sent have been of too deep a draft to get close enough into shore to locate the pirates. Be that as it may, the piracy has continued. Not every ship entering or leaving Sea Sprit has been attacked, of course. The pirates strike only from time to time and at random intervals; no one has been able to understand when or where to expect them."

Tara gazed out over the sparkling water and its endlessly restless surface. On such a sparkling, sunlit day, it was hard to imagine such skulduggery.

Sisti continued. "The people of Sea Sprit are beginning to fear that, with the growing frequency of attacks, perhaps the pirates might become emboldened sufficiently to overrun Sea Sprit itself."

Tara nodded in understanding. Thus also the interest in the fortifications. But such works would be very expensive and more than the citizens of Sea Sprit alone could bear. Thus also the delegation to Stonedell.

Eight bells struck, and Captain Sisti begged Princess Tara to accompany him to a table to enjoy a light repast prepared by the ship's galley. Tara accepted happily. "But, please, Captain, may I also sample what the crew has for their meals on an everyday basis? Out of curiosity?"

Captain Sisti very reluctantly obliged after repeated warnings that she should sample this fare only in moderation, as it surely would not be the same as to which she was accustomed. But Tara insisted. Why not, and what was it like, she wondered, to eat as the sailors did, to have what they had every day? Surely it couldn't be inedible. And, hadn't her grandmother done something similar, according to Jarvis?

Both meals sampled, with Tara readily admitting that the one reserved for her had indeed been much tastier than that granted to the sailors—"But they are used to it, Your Highness!" reassured Sisti—Tara returned to the weather decks to view more of the coastline. Borrowing Sisti's spyglass, she confirmed for herself that, indeed, the coastline was dotted with inlets and rocks and small harbors that, who knew, could contain any number of craft. "Interesting," she murmured. "Perfect for smuggling, too, I would imagine."

Not long after midday, Rohanic mentioned to Tara that they should consider returning to Sea Sprit. To this Tara gave her assent, and *Dolphin* swung back out to sea. They soon lost sight of land, Sisti and his first mate explaining that *Dolphin* sought a current to help offset a land breeze that had sprung up and was delaying their return. The current, explained the first mate, should more than offset the winds and they should be back in port on time, she should have no fear.

Very shortly thereafter, though, a lookout, stationed in the very bow of the ship, hailed the first mate to inform him of the sighting of another vessel on the horizon. Captain Sisti whipped out a spyglass and focused on the distant dim, dark shape. He mumbled to himself some words Tara couldn't make out. Curious, Rohanic asked the first mate what the significance of the sighting might be.

"He tells me it's unusual," Rohanic explained to Tara in a low, guarded voice, after beckoning her to the lifelines so that they might stand apart from the others. "He tells me the other ship is matching our course changes and appears to be closing.

"And, it doesn't show any colors. Not to alarm Your Highness, that is."

Tara murmured her thanks at that act of kindness. But it was somewhat alarming all the same.

The captain shortly ordered all hands to their stations and for the ship to undertake evasive manoeuvring. "How strange," thought Princess Tara, but before she could give it much further thought, Rohanic hustled her below decks to Sisti's cabin. The other ship was closing fast, she overheard one of the sailor's exclaim, and *Dolphin* seemed unable to shake its pursuer, even as fast and as responsive as she was.

Tara watched through the porthole as the other ship paralleled the course of *Dolphin*. It neared and she saw it run up a signal flag which, to her, had no meaning. However, on the decks above her, there was sudden agitation. Unable to stay below decks, Tara dashed back up the ladder to the main deck and stopped one of the sailors to demand what the signal meant. "It's pirate ship, m' lady! An' it's a-tellin' us to heave to!" By which, Tara inferred quickly, he must mean that *Dolphin* was to cease evasive action and allow herself to be boarded.

"Never!" stated the captain flatly, and, raising his voice, called to his crew to order them to assume battle stations. "Stand by to repel boarders!" he roared.

Tara turned to Rohanic, who had appeared beside her. "Procure for me a sword," she ordered. "I have some practice with it, and I'll do my part!" But on this one occasion, and of all that she could ever remember, Rohanic failed to answer her. Instead, and in concert with his lieutenant, he instantly seized Tara and quick-marched her back down the ladder into the captain's cabin and dogged down the door from the outside.

Tara hammered on the hatch from the other side in protest. How dare they! "Let me out! This instant!" she raged. If only she had brought along her quiver and bow!

But Rohanic refused. "Your Highness must remain out of sight," he stated in a tone so firm that it brooked no argument from the other side of the hatch. "I have no doubt the pirates seek you, most probably to ransom you. How they knew you would be at sea today and where is anyone's guess, but that must be their intent!"

Tara's heart pounded. The pirates! They wanted her? Hadn't she and Captain Sisti just been discussing them? And now they were right outside the porthole! But, maybe Rohanic and Sisti were wrong that the pirates knew she was on board. Maybe the pirates were just looking for a ship to prey on. After all, their plans had only been solidified the day before, around noon. Impossible that the pirates should know she was on board. Perhaps, if she hid well enough, she might be able to escape detection.

Tara returned to the porthole and peeked through its very edge. On the pirate ship's transom she could just make out what must be her name, *Storm Wrack*. What a nasty name, she thought. Then, when the occasional swell allowed, she noticed something not on board *Dolphin*. It looked like a long cylinder affixed to the pirate ship's deck and lashed down such that it was aligned fore and aft. It must be some piece of piratical equipment, gathered Tara.

But even as she watched, a few of the pirates approached the tube, and, working with a laboriousness suggestive of moving a great weight, they swung it about to point it menacingly at *Dolphin*. As *Storm Wrack* fell back to draw more abreast of *Dolphin*, she saw that the cylinder was nothing more than a hollow tube. But why would they point a hollow tube at *Dolphin*? What could it mean?

The crew of *Dolphin* clearly knew what it meant, though, and there was a sudden spate of activity in response. The pirates behind the tube tilted it upwards to aim at *Dolphin*'s rigging and then, to her horror and shock, a moment later, with a guttural roar, the tube belched a lengthy tongue of green and yellow fire.

The flames licked the sails and rigging, instantly setting much of it alight. A wail of dismay arose from *Dolphin's* crew and she almost immediately ceased to make way; the breeze that was present served only to fan the flames from sail to adjoining spar. Voices cried for "Water!" but others—and here she heard Sisti's—countermanded those. "Water's of no use!" she heard him cried repeatedly. "It's sea fire! Cut the sails and rigging!"

Sisti knew the situation was hopeless as soon as he had seen the great iron tube made ready. He had heard of sea fire projectors, but had not imagined the pirates had had one. With sea fire, the pirate ship could burn *Dolphin* to the waterline with no effort at all. Yet the pirate ship had aimed the weapon at her rigging and only used a little. That could only mean that the pirates wanted to take *Dolphin* intact. But, as a naval cutter, she could have no treasure. This meant that the pirates could not be after coin. Rather, concluded Sisti grimly, the pirates surely wanted Tara.

As for the rest of them, they would probably be put to the sword.

In which case, decided Sisti, they might as well resist. "Prepare to repel!" he called, but it was very difficult to marshal his crew as, whenever he thought he had them ready to repel the pirates, a still-burning spar or part of the mast would come crashing down, and it would be necessary to break ranks to either smother it and the cinders raining down with it or roll it overboard.

The pirates opposite guffawed at the crew's desperate efforts. At last, having judged that enough damage had been done, *Storm Wrack* nosed toward *Dolphin*, and dozens of grappling hooks were thrown across to lock the two ships together.

Though resistance was valiant, after a very brief struggle, *Dolphin* was taken. A broad gangplank was flung down to bridge the gap between the two vessels and a loud, filthy, bilious man, shabbily dressed in patched clothing, strutted across, his breath redolent of alcohol. He steadied himself aboard his prize, eyed the luckless crew now at sword point and commenced to swagger up and down the deck of the stricken cutter.

"Ha! Ha!" were his initial words of greeting as he paraded back and forth. "Where's the captain of this 'ere vessil?" he demanded at last. Sisti motioned that it was him. "Ha! Wrong!" the man bellowed back, whirling on him. "See's here!" He thumped his chest. "I'M the Captain! Cap'm Braunzin, tha's me! Aye!

"Ha! Ha!" he roistered again, and the rest of the pirates joined him in his horrible fit of hilarity. Watching from below decks, having slipped out of Sisti's cabin, Tara recoiled from the very little she could see through the small gap between the hatch and the deck.

"Ha!" The pirate captain whipped out a cutlass that shone incongruously bright against his filthy vest and placed its very tip beneath Sisti's nose. He toyed with it a moment, as if threatening to carve up the face of *Dolphin*'s master, then pushed the captain's nose up with the flat of the sword. "Ha! Didja think ya cud outrun us? Ha!"

Sisti, a model of resolve, did not deign to respond. He stared coldly back, his mouth tightening into a thin, white line.

But this meant nothing to Captain Braunzin, who a moment later withdrew his sword to place it under the nose of another crew member and affect the same set of manoeuvres that he had with his captain. "Ha! I shud cu'chur nose off, jus' like that! I cud, ya know! I oughtta too, aye. But, well, lessee… mebbe I won'. I say—ha!—mebbe I won'. If, IF ya tells me what I wants!"

There was dead silence from *Dolphin*'s crew.

"What's I wan'!" continued the pirate captain, lifting his voice so that anyone within some distance could have heard, "Is to know where that princess is!"

He paused, perhaps waiting for a response.

"Aye, 'cause I know she's here! On board! Ha!"

Still no answer from anyone.

"Tara's 'er name!"

Still silence.

"Ha!" responded Braunzin, echoing himself. "Ha! I mightta 'spected 'z'much. No surprise!" He paced up and down, eying the crew with a lordly look crossed with a wolfish smile. "Ha." He thought for a moment, then abruptly wheeled to face his crew and thundered, "Search the ship, boys! Fin' tha' princess!" Gesturing to the captured ship upon which they all stood, he concluded, "Then's we give 'er to the sea fire!"

There was a lunge by some members of the cutter's crew, which was easily contained. The pirate captain grimaced a vile, evil smile and stepped forward. "E'r'ywhere!" he cried, flourishing his sword dramatically. "Search e'r'ywhere!"

Tara heard everything down below; how could she have not? She instantly retreated to her cabin and barred the door, even as she knew that she would be found anyway. Desperately, she tested the porthole: no, it was far too small for her to fit through. The hatch above had to be the only way out, and this hatch opened at the very feet of the pirate captain.

The door was tried a moment later. Finding it locked, a sustained pounding commenced on it from outside. Tara looked frantically around for anything she might think to take with her. Her eyes lit on a small knife, not much more than a jack-knife, which she pounced on and secreted in her blouse just as the door crashed open. The ruffian pirate crew instantly seized her and dragged her up to the main deck, where she was rudely thrust forward for the pirate captain's inspection.

He ran his eyes over her lingeringly, brazenly. "Aye. That's her! Ha!" He turned away, sheathing his cutlass, it evidently having served its purpose. "See that no 'arm comes to 'er," he chortled to both crews, gesticulating now with his free hand. "She'll fetch us a better price that way!"

There was a moment of silence. Then the pirates broke into a wild, uproarious gale of laughter and slapped each other on the back in anticipation of the riches awaiting them. They paused a moment to rub their hands together in anticipatory greed then hauled her across the gangplank to *Storm Wrack*. Down a ladder they rudely pushed her, though the process took longer than expected and required five of the crew, since she resisted at every forced step. Tara had just the opportunity to catch the anguished expressions of Rohanic and his lieutenant before she was swallowed by the pirate ship's hold.

The lines between the two ships were cut and the currents and seas caused them to drift apart. After enough distance had opened between them, the great iron tube that had already wreaked havoc on the sails and rigging was swiveled again to point at *Dolphin*. This time, to the morbid glee of the pirate crew, the wallowing *Dolphin* instantly erupted in flames.

Tara imagined the crew leaping overboard or into the ship's boats to row to shore. It would take them hours to make land, then hours more to find someone to whom they might report their story. Maybe days. Tara sank into despondency. She was trapped. And in the cabin, from its shabby and threadbare appearance, which all too closely resembled the garb of Braunzin, of that of none other than *Storm Wrack*'s noxious captain.

The one exception, an ornate cabinet constructed of a very dark wood that had been elaborately carved and many of its decorative motifs gilded, stood in one corner of the cabin. Struck as she was by its opulence, Tara approached it to examine it further. Then the cabin's hatch suddenly banged opened, startling her. The pirate captain staggered in and Tara leapt back, consciously resisting the temptation to seize the knife from her blouse to attempt a desperate self-defense. But he only leered at her, leaning heavily against the bulkhead. Then he snarled. "Wha' chu doin' over there at tha' there cab-y-net? Don' tuch-it, I tellz ya! Yu'll 'gret it!"

Tara backed away to the bulkhead behind her. The words "Horrible, loathsome man" kept running through her head, and the rank reek of alcohol rolled forth from his exhalations. "Aye; yu'd 'gret it, sure 'nuff!" he affirmed, then, with a last look back at her as if to satisfy himself that she might be well and thoroughly cowed, he worked some latch on the cabinet and, opening it, thrust inside something resembling a white cylinder. Braunzin leered again, slammed shut the cabinet door and locked it, then staggered out, securing the cabin hatch behind him with a great fumbling and clattering of dogs and keys.

The afternoon wore on with agonizing slowness. Occasional hoots and yells from the decks above came with increasing frequency and volume, accompanied sometimes by scuffles, snatches of songs, and cheers. Tara couldn't imagine what was going on. The door was locked tightly; this she knew from testing it several times. The porthole, though open, was far too small for her to wriggle through. She gazed down cheerlessly into the deep blue-green depths just beyond her. Fathoms and fathoms of water must be beneath the keel, she realized dully. And leagues and leagues of it between her and land.

Slowly and sadly, the sun sank toward a darkening sapphire ocean, and the shouts and shrieks of gaiety above deck merged cacophonously into what Tara presumed was the commencement of a celebration. Celebrating the occasion of her capture, she surmised, morbidly. What would they do with her? Ransom her, was what Rohanic had predicted. At this point, that might be the best she could hope for. Her parents would pay for her release. She was hopeful for that but disgusted at the same time. That she would have to be ransomed free. That she required rescue. She didn't blame Rohanic or the rest of her escort. She didn't blame herself. She was just furious with her current state of helplessness, her inability to do anything, locked as she was inside a filthy, fetid cabin and obliged to wait for whatever mischief her captors might have in mind for her.

Tara sank into the only chair in the cabin she felt confident was not infested. Alone she sat, staring through the sole porthole into the fading light dimly illuminating a glassy sea only intermittently visible. At length she fell asleep.

All at once, she was violently tossed to the deck by a tremendous explosion. *Storm Wrack* jumped, shuddered, and went dead in the water.

Tara picked herself up, instantly awake. The silence was total, with not even the accustomed rhythmic creak of timbers and flexing of the deck with the waves. She felt her way through the dark to the porthole. It must be just before dawn. A grey light was appearing in the east, and the quiet sea was a vast expanse of rippling blue-black velvet extending into a dark infinity. Directly below her, a faint wash was breaking against the hull; the foam from it stained the sea's velvety surface like spilt salt.

Another explosion, more tremendous than before, knocked Tara to her knees. *Storm Wrack* shuddered again. There was the clatter of hurried activity above her mixed with shouting and cries; it sounded as though the crew were racing up and down the deck. What could it be now, demanded Tara silently, but she began to fear the very worst: such blasts must have severely damaged the ship; how many more could it sustain without being blown apart?

The shouts and cries continued for a while, until Tara heard a new and terrible sound: that of snapping and crackling, such as Tara had heard before from large bonfires. It was fire, and it smelt like the sea fire that had destroyed *Dolphin*. But now it was on board *Storm Wrack*. A whiff of smoke drifted through the open porthole that was filling with the glow of the rising sun. Tara's mind raced. When she had fallen asleep, the ship had been filled with the shouts and excitement of the pirates celebrating her capture. Could one of the pirates tampered with the sea fire and set it off?

There was another explosion, from what sounded like amidships, and flaming debris rained down past the porthole. To her astonishment, just beyond, she saw some of the pirates rowing frantically away in one of the dinghies. "They're abandoning ship!" Tara breathed in amazement. The night before, they had been celebrating her capture; this morning, the ship aflame and sinking, they were fleeing. Before Tara could consider further this ironic twist, the rising volume of the crackling flames brought her back to the moment.

Back to the cabin door she raced. No good: still locked fast. Now back to the porthole, but, try as she might, it was simply too small for her to fit through. From the increasing slant to the deck below her, *Storm Wrack* was listing further and further to starboard, her cabin's porthole declining by degrees closer and closer toward the water. After checking the door one last, frantic time, Tara darted back to the porthole and howled through it at the pirates in the receding boat for help. Even rescue by them was better than sure death by drowning! But they didn't pause; they didn't even look back.

Then, to her absolute astonishment, a face appeared in the water below her. Tara squinted in disbelief. A girl was swimming alongside the ship. Strangely, her eyes were the same sparkling blue-green as the swells amongst which she floated. Behind and around her head streamed flowing locks of blonde hair and in which Tara thought to discern flecks of pink, as if from some sort of ornament or hair pins. But, wondered Tara, how could anyone other than the pirates be nearby? No matter, thought Tara. "Help me!" she cried, and thrust her hands through the porthole and waved them frantically. "I'm locked in this cabin and can't get through the porthole! I'll drown!"

"Who are you?" asked the girl, lolling easily in the gentle waves alongside and in a tone far more casual than Tara might have expected from someone eying the trapped prisoner of a burning, sinking ship.

"I'm Princess Tara, of the Kingdom of Brythrony! Can you help me?"

"Oh!" responded the girl after a moment's thought. "I don't know that place. It must be far from here." But then, seeing the mounting anxiety in Tara's face, she added quickly, "Let me see what I can do!

"By the way," the girl called back to her, "I'm Princess Marina of the Coral Kingdom. Hold on, just for a minute, while I get help!"

Tara racked her brain for any memory of a Coral Kingdom. She couldn't recollect a place of that name from her geography lessons. Tara shrugged. It had to be that this Princess Marina was from some far-off isle and had been kidnapped just like Tara. Maybe Marina had been held prisoner in the forward compartments, whereas Tara had been held aft.

With a flick of her arms and her blonde hair trailing behind her, Princess Marina dove beneath the waves. To Tara's complete amazement, rather than showing kicking legs as she vanished, Tara saw a flash of green and the shimmer of a powerful fish fin. Impossible, thought Tara. But there it was, right before her: Marina was no kidnapped princess. She was a mermaid. No wonder Tara had never heard of the Coral Kingdom. It must be far out to sea and underwater.

"Hurry, please!" shouted Tara to the eddying surface Marina left behind. Mermaid or human, the pirate ship was sinking, and Tara was going down with it. Just now, she'd be grateful for any help, even that from a mermaid.

A mermaid. Tara shook her head in disbelief. But she was, had been, just there in the water in front of her. Tara had seen her tail when she dove:

it had been a kind of scaly, sparkly green, and streaked with a shimmery blue. Her nearly diaphanous tail fin, flecked with gold, had flashed briefly in the brightening sun before she had gone too deep to be seen.

Tara had heard stories of mermaids in her youth. Mostly they had ended with "…But, well, no one believes they exist any more. Even if, occasionally, there are reports of sightings." Tara wondered if her grandmother had ever seen a mermaid. Her mother had never mentioned Ysolde encountering one, but then maybe she had omitted it. Her grandmother had gone hunting for dragons; maybe she had also gone searching for mermaids? Maybe that was what she had intended to do on the *Gyrfalcon*? Though the deck creaked beneath her ominously, Tara stood just a bit taller in the cabin of the broken ship. Could she be doing something that her grandmother never had? Like, talk to a mermaid? Her grandmother would surely have envied that! And now, she, Tara, had met a real, live mermaid—and hopefully was about to be saved by one!

Tara glanced behind her. The ship was listing ever more sharply. The ornate cabinet behind her suddenly slid across the deck to crash into the bulkhead to the other side of the porthole, the shock opening a gaping split in the cabinet. The flames she had heard crackling before were growing louder. Looking up through the porthole, she could see a plume of smoke rising into the early morning sky. *Storm Wrack* was doomed.

Agonizing minutes later, Marina's face reappeared above the water. All around her squirmed the restless and churning tentacles of what, to Tara, resembled a giant squid. "Stand back from the porthole," Marina warned and gave an indistinct command. A dozen tentacles stretched out from beside her and felt their way by degrees up the side of the ship. The sight horrified Tara, and she backed away in terror but said nothing, because she quickly grasped what the squid and Marina intended. The tentacles first probed then entered the cabin through the porthole, the suckers curling and writhing along the bulkheads to either side. Then they suddenly went rigid and began to pull and strain until the wood around the porthole fractured and splintered outwards with a tremendous crash. Before Tara's eyes, the porthole was gone, and in its place gaped a jagged, yawning hole.

The ship was now sinking fast. "Hurry!" shouted Marina. "You can fit through now! Jump!"

Tara gazed down through the shattered bulkhead and into the heaving, sparkling ocean below her. Every few seconds, it was washed by a curling breaker, which would leave behind a stretch of foam, that to be taken up a moment later by the next swell. True, Tara was nearing the water by the second, but it still looked a long way down. "I—I…" she stumbled, hesitating, "I can't! I don't know how to swim!"

"Can't swim?" echoed Marina incredulously. As a mermaid, that was simply unimaginable! Couldn't most land people—landlings, her father called them—swim? "Can't swim? All right; let me get help for that, too. But you'd better hurry and jump now! Before the suction from the sinking ship pulls you down with it!" Marina vanished for only a moment then appeared again in the company of a pod of dolphins, all of them nodding, screeching, and clicking about her.

Where and how does she find all these ocean creatures, wondered Tara for a moment. But no time for that. Taking a last look around the cabin, she readied herself to jump.

Then, to Marina's astonishment, Tara seemed to think twice and rushed back inside and out of view.

"Where are you going?" demanded Marina. "You can't wait any longer; you have to jump—NOW!"

Tara had suddenly remembered something she had seen the night before. She darted back into the cabin, picked up the chair in which she had passed the night and swung it against the broken cabinet to smash it completely open. Out of it she grabbed the white cylinder she had seen Braunzin place inside and jammed it up her sleeve. She raced back to the gaping hole. "All right, I'm ready!"

Tara began to compose herself to make the jump, but felt the deck slide more quickly beneath her feet and a solemn quiver run through the ship, as if it were breaking apart. No time to think any further about it. "Here I come!" she cried, and, closing her eyes, leapt out and away into the air.

Princess Marina

Tara jumped just in time. As Tara fell toward the ocean's surface, the ship seemed to give a final groan and rumble as the main mast collapsed backwards into the aft-most cabins, where Tara had been standing only a moment before. She landed in the water, went under and came up, gagging and sputtering. "Help! Help!" she yelled, taking in a mouthful of salt water and flailing with both arms.

Marina struggled to position the dolphins to buoy up Tara; it was surprising how hard it was to help this land princess, even though she so obviously needed it. It was almost as if she were trying to prevent Marina from rescuing her, the way she kept whacking Marina with her arms all about the head and shoulders whenever Marina got close. But she had to help the land princess; she'd drown otherwise. That was the thing about these landlings, her father, King Aenon, had told her. They breathed only the atmosphere above the sea and could not live underwater. Mermaids and all merfolk, of course, could breathe both above and below the water.

At last, Marina had one dolphin placed under Tara and one to either side to steady her. The dolphin under her rose gently so that Tara found herself seated astride the dolphin like she would have sat upon Daystar. The dolphin was far more slippery than Tara would have imagined but bore her up reasonably well, even if Tara remained half-submerged in the water. The two dolphins to either side were a big help in allowing her to maintain her balance.

"That's right; that's the way to stay on. Try to use those legs you have on you to grip its body to either side," encouraged Marina, gliding alongside her and offering an occasional hand of assistance.

"I can't thank you enough for saving me!" Tara announced as soon as she had achieved some stability on her dolphin mount. Marina smiled back and ran her hand along the flanks of the dolphin. Covertly, Tara looked across at Marina. Yes, she was a real, live mermaid. The pink flecks in the great, golden mass of Marina's blonde hair she had seen from the cabin of the pirate ship were actually a tiara fashioned out of red coral spicules. So maybe she really was a princess too, if she was wearing such an ornament in her hair. Though, at the same time, nothing prevented women on land from weaving flowers and leaves into their hair, and they weren't princesses.

Marina seemed friendly and helpful too. This starkly contrasted with the stories she had heard at Stonedell which had suggested, darkly, that mermaids sought to lure unwary ships onto rocks and sailors to their doom. Marina seemed far from malevolent and hostile. Marina's blue-green eyes seem to twinkle with merriment and good nature as she assisted Tara, just as the sunlight flashed and sparkled in a thousand coruscant glints off the wavelets surrounding the two of them and the three dolphins.

They swam on, Tara gradually growing more confident until at last she said she was really getting skilled at riding a dolphin. In response, Marina tutted gently that Tara should know how to swim. "True," admitted Tara readily, "I should, especially with so much of the world covered in water." Still, glancing again sideways, though clearly at home in the ocean, Marina was hardly learning to walk, although a decent part of the globe was covered in land. Still, she rebuked herself for not having learned to swim long ago when it would have been easier. That very visit to Sea Sprit, in fact, had been her first visit to the Prithrath Ocean, and *Dolphin* had been her first experience in sailing it!

The bulk of the cylinder still secreted within her sleeve reminded her of her impulse to grab it before jumping from the ship. Marina had been right that it had been very risky to have hesitated. But she had done it anyway, because she surmised it must have been valuable. Everything pointed to that: hadn't the pirate captain made a great show of locking it in the cabinet and warning her about trying to get to it? It was the only thing that she had thought in the cabin to be worth anything, aside from the cabinet itself, which had obviously been too heavy and awkward for her to take. Even when it had been in one piece.

As soon as she got the chance, she resolved to take a closer look at the cylinder.

"We need to get you to a place where you can stand up," decided Marina aloud at last. "I know just the place. The Secret Island."

"'The Secret Island'?" asked Tara. "It's really secret?"

"No, not really," admitted Marina shyly. "But I don't think anyone knows or cares about it. I mean, nobody ever goes there, since it's way out in the middle of the ocean. So it's about the same as being secret."

By this time, Tara thought that she would be very glad to walk on dry land again, so she replied that it was a tremendous idea. That was good, explained Marina, as they had been making for it all this time. Indeed, it wasn't long before Tara was seated as comfortably as she could be on one of the larger rocks of a small island's beach, her toes wriggling in the sand. Marina relaxed nearby in a tidal pool, her tail flipping lazily back and forth in the brackish water.

"How do you like it? The Secret Island?" began Marina, flipping her tail up so that droplets of water spattered across her to keep her cool.

Tara looked around. It didn't appear to be large. A length of sand stretched away from her to what looked like a small forest of palms and grasses. She didn't hear any signs of life—no birds, no insects—just the sad, sighing sough of the waves relentlessly washing the sand. "It's beautiful," she stated. "It's wonderful to be back on land! Thank you so much, again, for saving me from the cabin and then helping me swim here!"

Marina giggled and flipped her tail back and forth. "I'm glad to rescue you! I heard the explosions underwater. They were very loud. I happened to be in the area, so I swam over to see what it was. It turned out to be a landling ship, burning and sinking. I'd never seen such a thing before first-hand, though I've seen plenty of wrecks. Then, all of a sudden, I saw you at the porthole, looking down at me and calling for help! I've heard stories of landling people—that's you, that's what we call people who walk on land—who hunt and kill merfolk, so I was a little afraid at first. But you didn't look like you meant me harm; you looked like you were in trouble! So I helped you. I'm glad I did!"

Tara nodded. "I am so glad you did also. You saved me." She thought for a moment, watching Marina flick her tail up and down and from side to side. "Tell me your story," she begged, suddenly consumed by curiosity as to what it was like to be a mermaid.

Marina proved to be very chatty and promptly began to tell her in considerable detail of her life in the Coral Kingdom and her home, Coral Castle. There she lived, she explained to Tara, far beneath the surface of the ocean with her father, King Aenon, who had a wonderfully powerful trident, and her mother, Queen Seafoam, who was universally acknowledged to be the most beautiful and wisest of all mermaids. And a brother and two sisters. "She holds court most every day," explained Marina casually, "in the Great

Hall, which is flanked all the way down on either side by tremendously tall living ferns with all sorts of seaweed around them! All the fish folk come to the Great Hall to talk with her and keep her updated with what's happening around the ocean.

"Dad's out and about the kingdom doing important things, I suppose."

Tara had to allow how impressed she was by all Marina had described. "Are there lots of mermaids and mermen? Beyond those in Coral Castle?"

"Oh sure! Lots and lots, and they live in all the different depths of the ocean, some in the shallower parts but most in the deeper. And they all have their own accents and traditions and on and on!" Marina laughed merrily at the recollection. "Sometimes it's hard to keep track of the different places they come from and their histories and so on." She sighed. "But, I'm supposed to make an effort and all. Because I'm a princess."

Tara could sympathize wholeheartedly with that feeling.

Marina paused to flick some more saltwater onto herself from the pool in which she reposed and turned to Tara. "So, hey, tell me about yourself! Like, where do you live, and what's it like walking around on the land all the time?"

Tara hesitated. Nothing she had to say could be nearly so interesting or grand as Marina's Coral Castle. Tara's life seemed so hum-drum, mostly consisting of badinage at tedious events. Still, Marina had been forthcoming with her; she should be just as open in return. Maybe she was as curious about Tara as Tara had been about her. "Well, I also live in a castle. Only it's made of stone and not coral. It's called Castle Stonedell. Like you, I live with my father and mother. They're the king and queen of Brythrony."

"Does your mother hold court each day in a Great Hall? Like mine?"

"No, she doesn't. I mean, I don't think so. That is, I've never seen her hold one.

"But my father often has important meetings in our reception hall. Maybe that's like your Great Hall? That's where he arbitrates disputes and receives legations from other kingdoms."

"Wow, a legation!" Marina could hardly imagine what that must be, but it sounded grand and special. No legations, to her knowledge, ever came to the Coral Kingdom.

Tara was pretty proud that she had remembered the legation aspect of her father's business, even though she only dimly understood what a legation was or what its importance might be. "Legations. All sorts of important legations," she emphasized, pleased with the impact of the term on Marina. "And frequently!" In fact, it occurred to her, the group from Sea Sprit might have been a sort of legation sent to see her parents.

"So, anyway, I have a horse named Daystar, and we often go riding around the woods and fields around the castle."

"What's a horse?"

Tara glanced over at Marina quickly, thinking that she may be teasing her. But no, Marina's face was as innocent as could be. Because, Tara reminded herself sharply, there are no such things as horses in the Coral Kingdom! Not like Daystar, at least. Tara described Daystar and how fast he could run and how much she enjoyed riding him out to the apple orchards, all to Marina's delight and amazement. She could ride dolphins and other creatures, but she could never imagine going that fast, because the water impeded such movement.

"And I have a bow and quiver of arrows, which I can shoot very accurately," proclaimed Tara proudly, because she was pleased with her marksmanship.

Marina quickly asked about bows and arrows.

Tara considered briefly how to answer her new friend. "A bow shoots arrows," she stated at last. "A quiver holds the arrows for you before you shoot them. And you hold the bow thusly," pantomiming the act of holding the bow with her right hand, "in your right or left hand, depending on handedness, and then reach back behind you into the quiver to grab an arrow out of it, then fit it to the bow, and then shoot it! If you're accurate, you can hit a target from a long way away!"

Marina nodded in growing understanding. She had never seen a bow or arrow before. There were no such things under the sea, as the water wouldn't allow anything thrown to travel very far. Most merfolk used handheld spears and thrust them when they hunted or had to do battle.

"Why did you run back into the ship at the last minute?" asked Marina, changing the subject again. "You were very nearly killed by that falling mast. You only jumped just in time!"

What a funny world, thought Tara and, for the first time, with strong conviction for a spur-of-the-moment thought. She had lamented the tedium of the world, the silliness of the world, the unfairness of the world, and the meanness of the world many times before, but now, for the first time, she reflected on how strange and unusual it could be. In this instance, in a good way. She looked about her. Days before she would never have guessed that here she would be, days later, on an unknown island in the Prithrath Ocean conversing with a mermaid.

Tara turned to Marina and smiled mysteriously. "I'll tell you," she replied, lowering her voice, thinking, in a moment of whimsy, to adopt an overtone of drama. And why not? What was commonplace about the last twenty-four hours she had lived, what with pirates and mermaids and a sinking slip and now this cylinder? "I ran back to get this," Tara continued, letting the cylinder slide forward out of her sleeve to catch it in her hand such that it appeared as though she had produced the cylinder from the very air. With a flourish, she presented it to a gawping Marina. "The day before, I saw the captain of the pirate ship take efforts to lock it securely in what looked like an intricately carved cabinet. So I guessed it was valuable. That's why I ran back to get it. I figured it had to be worth taking!"

Childeric stood in the royal chambers, facing Armorica, having earnestly entreated her to sit or even lie down on the nearby couch.

Why, she had demanded of him, immediately alarmed. For what reason?

But he had refused to say, and had only repeated himself.

"Is it about Tara? It's Tara, isn't it?"

Childeric waited, expressionless until, having no other choice, she seated herself. Only then did he begin reading aloud from a scroll he produced from behind his back. "It's a message from Rohanic," he explained to her softly. "I read it, thus."

Your Majesties! My humblest and most earnest greetings to you and—
"Yes, yes; we know all that!"

Per your royal direction, I report to You on the most recent and very unfortunate developments in our mission to Sea Sprit.

Armorica nearly jumped to her feet.

"No, no; you must remain seated. I will not continue unless you are!"

Anxiety and frustration playing across her face in equal measures, she gesticulated angrily to him to read, irrespective of whether she were standing or seated. Childeric saw she would not be moved, shook his head, found his place on the scroll, and continued:

Your Majesties! I very much hesitate, but nevertheless it is my bound duty, to report to You a terrible and tragic series of events that have occurred since I last wrote.

Armorica made to rise again, aghast, but only arose halfway, and that unsteadily.

Your Majesties may recollect that I last wrote upon our having gained the town of Sea Sprit per Your Majesties' direction. That night, there was a gala reception held for us at the mansion of one Captain Jarvis, late of Your Majesties' Navy but more recently a captain of a commercial vessel.

This gala passed without incident, though I would point out that Her Highness the Princess comported herself with the greatest dignity and altogether in a manner befitting a Princess of the House of Hession and of a long line of noble and gentle rulers.

A wan smile passed across Armorica's face as she heard these words. Childeric's voice swelled in noticeable pride.

The next day, we boarded the cutter "Dolphin," which Sea Sprit, for its own protection, had outfitted for maritime patrol. The vessel was small though, and there was little room for others beyond the ship's natural complement. I and a few of my most trusted joined Her Highness on board as her escort.

The sea cruise began well with fair seas and light breezes, and Captain Sisti, master of the vessel, showed Her Highness much of the coast and seaward defenses as You had requested she view. But on the way back, we were beset by a pirate craft named "Storm Wrack," which, immediately and with great effect, used sea fire to destroy Dolphin's sails and rigging and so prevented our escape.

Dolphin was boarded, despite a most valiant resistance.

"Pirates!" choked Armorica. Childeric nodded soberly.

The pirates then searched Dolphin with the object of finding Princess Tara, who the pirate captain—who identified himself as Braunzin—knew was on board. It was impossible for Her Highness to hide, the Dolphin being too small to conceal much, and she was discovered and taken aboard the pirate ship. Dolphin was then burnt to the waterline.

"No!" cried Armorica and clutched at the arm of the sofa. "Taken by pirates! We'll never see her again! Oh, I knew it was a horrible idea to send her unescorted and alone into the world! Why we didn't see, why we didn't understand that, I'll never know!"

Armorica cast herself down on the couch and commenced to wail. "Tara! If only you come back to us in one piece, I'll never make you go out again to a social event!"

"It's terrible news," agreed Childeric, "but we never could have expected this."

The entirety of the crew escaped, as did I and the escort, by leaping overboard or by boarding the ship's small boat, which, by good fortune, had been secured to the side opposite that which was set alight. Most of us either clung to wreckage to stay afloat or to the sides of the small boat. At length, another vessel, sighting the pall of smoke from the burning Dolphin, sailed to our rescue, and saved us from the wind and waves.

As I mentioned, the lawless pirate Braunzin knew Her Highness was on board, as he demanded her surrender as soon as he boarded Dolphin (and which the crew rejected, to a man). This behavior leads me to conclude that these pirates sought Dolphin with this sole objective in mind, to take Her Highness, and undoubtedly with the intent to ransom her from Your Majesties.

It was impossible to pursue the pirate vessel at the time of our rescue, the rescuing ship being an unarmed merchant incapable of pursuit. But, now that I have made land, I have contacted Your Majesties' Navy and made representations of who I am and the rank of my charge, and I am informed that a corvette will shortly be made available with which we shall at once commence an exhaustive search of the coastline immediate to Sea Sprit, and whence these pirates most surely have set forth. Upon apprehending these sea-borne brigands, and I have no doubt we will, we will rescue Her Highness, and, depending on the degree of resistance they should choose to offer, either extirpate them or bring them justice in Your Majesties' courts.

Childeric lowered the paper slowly until his arm hung slack at his side. "It ends there," he mumbled.

Armorica groaned and flung herself back upon the couch in despondency. "Poor Tara! What have we done? How could we have done this to you?"

Childeric sat down on the couch and attempted to comfort his wife. Though he didn't admit it, he was shaken as well. How could there be pirates, he wondered, off Sea Sprit? The delegation from Sea Sprit had complained that they suffered from "maritime marauders" as he recollected, which was why they had asked for support in reinforcing their defenses. But, come to think more of it, how could pirates operate so boldly that close to the shores of Brythrony? How could such impudence have escaped the notice of the navy?

"Dear, dear," he attempted, stroking first her arm and her hair, even as Armorica dissolved into tears, "I'm sure she'll be all right."

"How can you say such a thing? You can't know that!" moaned Armorica from the depths of the couch's cushions.

"You're right. I don't know. But they took Tara with them. Pirates—and those types—generally just want money. Riches. I'm sure they intend to—pretty sure—ransom her. Rohanic said as much himself. Because she's a princess."

"Our princess!"

"Our princess," soothed Childeric. "Our princess. I'm sure they won't harm her, as they will want us to ransom her."

"Oh, Tara: I'm so sorry! I'll never make you go out again!"

"I'm confident we'll hear shortly from the pirates with their demands. In the meantime, Rohanic and the navy are searching for her."

"I know they are. I'm sure they'll find her."

Armorica sobbed again. Childeric heaved a sigh and simply held his wife's hand. His mind went back to the delegation from Sea Sprit. They had spoken the truth when they had complained of pirates, even though Childeric had had his reservations at the time. But, Childeric began to ask himself, how had these pirates known that Tara would be on board *Dolphin*? And how had they known where *Dolphin* would be and when that day? Surely Tara's survey of the coast had not been arranged until a day or so before; how had word gotten out so quickly, and even to seafaring pirates, about who she was, that she would be on board, and when and where *Dolphin* would sail that day?

Childeric's hand gradually loosened as his mind raced. Somehow, the word had gotten out. Somehow, someone who knew when and where Tara was going had conveyed this information to the pirates. That was the only way Tara could have been betrayed so quickly. Only a few people could have known this information, realized Childeric. A few in the escort party—including Rohanic—and a few in the town of Sea Sprit.

That person would undoubtedly be looking to share in the ransom for Tara.

Childeric's heart grew cold to think that Rohanic could be behind this. The same Rohanic he had long trusted—a traitor? He had entrusted his only daughter to a traitor? But then he caught himself. Impossible. Not because

Rohanic had remained behind on board *Dolphin*, which had been set alight and left for lost, but because the pirates had operated for some time before Rohanic had ever arrived in Sea Sprit. Impossible to believe that Rohanic had been in league with these bandits, then allowed the delegation to appeal for help, then arranged for Tara to be kidnapped and ransomed, when it would have been impossible for him to know she would be sent.

No, far easier to believe that someone in Sea Sprit was working with the pirates; this would also explain how they could prey with such impunity on commerce but avoided the navy for so long.

Childeric took a deep breath, quivering with fury. Someone in Sea Sprit, who regularly informed the pirates about valuable incoming and outgoing cargos, had also tipped them that Princess Tara would be at sea and that she would make a rich prize. That person or persons, Childeric vowed, would be found and punished very harshly. Indeed, with extreme severity if any harm were to come to Tara.

Childeric strode to his writing desk and began to compose a missive to send back to Rohanic. He would seal it with his personal signet and brittle sealing wax, such that it would have to be broken to be read, and such breakage would be obvious. It was important to convey this realization to Rohanic as soon as possible and confidentially. It could be of assistance in locating Tara.

Rohanic was thinking along the same lines as his sovereign as he waited impatiently for the naval corvette to begin the search for Her Highness. How, he was wondering, could pirates be so well informed as to the quality of the person who had been on board and where she would be in her survey of the coastline? Sisti? One of the crew? One of his escort? Rohanic dismissed this last thought instantly: he knew them through and through and had hand-picked them for this enterprise. Not a one of them was disloyal, not in the slightest.

No, the traitor had to be in Sea Sprit.

But who? His suspicions centered on the mayor or someone from the mayor's council. Someone who would have been privy to their plans and with sufficient advance notice to communicate them to the pirates.

That would exclude any of *Dolphin*'s crew, though not her captain.

Rohanic clenched his fists with impatience. Not for the first time did he accuse himself of cowardice in failing to prevent Her Highness's capture.

But he also knew any resistance by him or his men would have been vainglorious and pointless. Not that his life mattered so much, but the pirates would have taken her anyway and there would have been no one to take charge promptly of a rescue effort. True, they were sworn to defend her, but how were they to rescue her if they were dead? No, it had been the more prudent and wiser course to bridle his impulses and escape. If only to avenge the House of Hession on the pirates and exact a dire punishment on the traitorous wretch in Sea Sprit.

Marina clapped her hands in excitement. "Let's see it," she begged and, taking the cylinder from Tara, began to examine it. "It looks like it's made of whale bone. And, look! It's been carved with all sorts of geometric designs!" She turned it over in her hands several times then returned it to Tara. "It's scrimshaw, and very impressive, even a work of art. Someone very skilled carved this; it's clearly something special."

"I think it's more than that," whispered Tara. She held the cylinder up to Marina's ear and shook it. There came a rustling noise from within. "I think there's something inside it!"

"Oh! So exciting!"

"Yes, we just have to open it."

"Well, okay then: let's open it!"

"The problem is… I don't know how. It doesn't look like it has a cap. It looks like a single piece of bone!"

"Let me see," requested Marina, and she inspected it again but likewise couldn't find a crack or hinge or any evidence that it opened. Yet, without question, a noise did come from within when it was shaken or rolled.

"There must be something important inside it! Like, a map, or some kind of document. And there must be a secret spring to open it," enthused Marina. She had heard a great deal about maps and treasures being buried on land. The many wrecks that littered the ocean floor were generally without much in the way of treasure in them, she recalled. This was because, all the stories went, the treasure had been buried on land before sailing.

Tara agreed that something important must be inside it, and the size and shape of the container suggested a rolled paper. They both studied the cylinder, running their hands over the design. Tara thought to start pushing or depressing the carved bas-relief decorations and discovered quickly that a triangle depressed. Both girls cried with delight at this discovery and they became more excited. By turns, they pressed all the decorations and found that, in total, the shapes of a circle, a triangle, a square, a diamond, and a hexagon all depressed or moved in some way.

"Maybe in some order? But what order?" wondered Marina. "And what if some more than once and others not at all?" Tara had to admit that, were that the case, they might never guess the correct sequence for depressing the shapes.

"Let's see," spoke Tara thoughtfully. "These shapes, in order, have no angles, three angles, four angles, four angles, and six angles. I'm wondering if the sequence was set so it would be easy to remember by the person who set it but difficult to guess otherwise."

"Like how?"

"Like, say, pushing the symbols in order of the count of angles: circle, triangle, square, diamond, and hexagon." Which she tried, but nothing happened.

"Great idea though!" exclaimed Marina. "Try the reverse order."

That didn't cause anything to happen either. "It didn't work," admitted Tara.

"It was another good idea! But the square and the diamond have the same number of angles, don't they? How about if you swap their positions but otherwise keep the order the same?"

Tara did this, in reverse order. Nothing. So she tried it from fewest angles to most, pressing the circle, triangle, diamond, square, and then, finally, the hexagon. To their delight, something within the cylinder clicked. They looked at each other in triumph and inspected the cylinder minutely. Looking very closely, Tara saw that a small aperture had opened in the cylinder, into which she squinted, holding the cylinder up to the sunlight. She groaned and lowered it.

"What is it?" enquired Marina anxiously.

"It's a keyhole! And we still need the key!" explained Tara. "So whatever's inside is protected both by a secret catch hiding a keyhole and the need for the key that fits it!"

Marina was silent. "Whatever's inside must be real important," she said at last.

They both gazed dejectedly at the cylinder for a while. Tara suddenly remembered that when she had groped for the cylinder deep inside the cabinet onboard the ship, she had seen a key ring next to it, but had not taken it in her rush to escape. She groaned a second time. "The key! Maybe now I think I know where it could be!"

"Where? Where?"

"Where we'll never be able to get it: at the bottom of the ocean! In the wreck! In the pirate captain's cabin!"

"There? Then it shouldn't be too difficult to find."

"But it's at the bottom of the ocean!"

"But look at me! I'm a mermaid! It's easy for me to go to the bottom of the ocean! I do it all the time!"

Tara laughed. Of course: she had forgotten that she was talking with a mermaid princess, who could as easily swim through a wreck on the ocean floor as Tara could stroll through the ruins of a castle on land! "Why, I had forgotten! How silly of me! But... how will you find the wreck, and then search it, all by yourself?"

"Oh, I won't do it by myself. I'll ask the dolphins to take me back to where you started riding them. They have a good sense of direction; they'll know where that is. That'll be about where the ship went down. If not, it can't be too far away."

"Sure, that makes sense. And that's a great start. But what about the wreck? How do you search it when the debris field may be scattered over a large area?"

Marina shrugged casually. "That's easy too. I'll call up a whole bunch of squids, or octopuses, and ask them to sift through it for me. They have a lot more tentacles than I have hands."

"Brilliant!" exclaimed Tara, impressed. "I would never have thought of that!"

"That's because you're not a mermaid!"

The two girls laughed and hugged. Tara didn't even mind getting wet again. "But I'll have to stay up here until you come back. What will I do on this deserted island?"

Marina considered. "You'll have to look for some water. What with all the trees and plants inland, there's probably a spring toward the center.

"I wish I could take you with me. But you can't breathe underwater." She thought a little longer. "But I could ask my father if there's some way to bring a land dweller down to the Coral Kingdom and still be able to breathe. He'd know.

"But let me first go look for the key. I'll be as quick as I can!" With that, and into a swell that was just rolling up, Marina slipped off the rock and into the water. She waved to Tara once then vanished beneath the surface. Tara caught a glimpse of her gliding away to the ocean, and she was gone.

Tara was left alone. After watching the surf roll in and out for a few minutes, she stood and looked behind her inland. Marina has said she thought there was water on the island; could there be anything edible also? Like, maybe some tree fruit that Tara might recognize?

Over fallen tree trunks and through vines Tara moved, hearing nothing but the distant and intermittent hum of the surf on the beach, which grew ever fainter with each step forward. She guessed that made sense. After all, the island was distant from the mainland and maybe no animal life could get to it. Tara paused to gaze into the blue sky through the palm fronds. How alike this sky was to the sky over Brythrony: the same cerulean blue and wispy clouds, but seen through the waxy leaves of palms rather than through maple, oak and apple trees. They swayed gently overhead in a light, sustained rustle that Tara found wonderfully soothing. It still seemed so unreal.

She wondered about her parents. Probably they didn't realize yet their daughter had been kidnapped. When they found out they would be terribly worried. Tara chuckled at the irony. They had wanted her to get out and around the kingdom, and now here she was—even if, probably, this tiny island wasn't a part of Brythrony.

They would want her to return as soon as possible. Tara started forward again, slowly, thinking carefully. The cylinder was a mystery she wanted to solve. What was the paper it contained? Could it be something very special? If she returned to Brythrony immediately, she might never find out! What would her grandmother do? Tara thought of the queen she had never met and had only heard stories about. Her grandmother would surely want her to unravel the mystery of the cylinder. Surely. Not to make her parents worry, but she would be back very soon, as soon as she figured out what it contained.

Poor Mom. And Dad. And Daystar! But they would all get along just a few more days all right without her. And, what if the cylinder contained something wonderful that would help them all so much they'd be very glad she had pursued its understanding? Besides, Marina was already looking into the recovery of the keys. How could she toss it all to Marina now, having come this far?

Tara's mind became set. She wasn't hard-hearted, but the secret of the cylinder was simply too much to resist. She felt pangs of guilt, but told herself it would only take another day or so. Not too long at all.

A few steps further, and pausing again, she heard a distant gurgling. Pausing intermittently to gauge its direction, she found the source in the center of the island just where Marina had guessed it might be, bubbling up through rocks in a hollow.

Tara bent and drank gratefully then gazed deeply into the spring's depths. The little hollow from which the spring flowed looked sheltered from the elements and of sufficient size to hide the cylinder so she would not have to carry it with her all the time. There weren't any animals around either, to find it and toy with it. Why not hide it here?

Tara turned to head back to the beach, thinking Marina might be back with an update. As she made her way through the undergrowth, her mind went back to the turbulent hours when the pirates had overtaken *Dolphin* and its crew. She hoped they had been able to escape the fiery ruin of *Dolphin* without mishap. Odd, it suddenly occurred to her, that the pirates had boarded *Dolphin* and immediately demanded her. They hadn't asked for anything else. Just for her, and right away. How had they known she was on board? Who she was, where *Dolphin* was, and that her escort would be minimal?

Dolphin had been a fast and manoeuvrable ship. Captain Jarvis had told her so. Meaning, the pirates would have needed to have positioned themselves at just the right point such that *Dolphin* could not yet gain the current that would have sped her back to Sea Sprit. The pirates would have needed to know just where to wait so as to catch *Dolphin* when she was most vulnerable.

Who could have had all that information? All three components: the details of Tara's excursion, a comprehensive understanding of her craft, and intimate knowledge of the seas in that area?

Jarvis. Captain Jarvis. It had to be. The realization struck her quite suddenly, but it was obvious after a moment. Only Jarvis had all that knowledge. And she, Tara, had confirmed the night before that she would be on board *Dolphin*, a ship he had helped to choose for her, and sailing the next day with the tide.

Tara shook her head. She had been betrayed by a sea captain who had served in her grandmother's navy and who had hosted her the night before. Such perfidy. Jarvis clearly had expensive tastes; the ballroom had been exquisite. Was this how he had paid for it? By informing the pirates of the movements of the most valuable shipments in and out of Sea Sprit and then sharing in the spoils? There was nothing she could do now, not on a deserted island. But she would return to Brythrony, most definitely, and then there would be a reckoning.

Still shaking her head in disgust, Tara regained the beach to find Marina waiting for her.

"Great news!" cried Marina as Tara re-joined her. "We found the shipwreck! I have a team of squids sifting through it now for the key!"

That was good news, and Tara was thrilled. "You found it so quickly! I wish I could help, as I would remember roughly where it is in the pirate captain's cabin."

Marina's eyes twinkled. "I checked into that as well. Like I said, my father has told me that he has brought land dwellers down to our kingdom from time to time over the years. When I let him know what we were doing and asked, he sent me this." Marina pulled a wad of dark green-and-black seaweed from a pouch that Tara noticed was belted to her waist. She handed it to Tara happily, who received it cautiously. "Eat it! It will allow you to breath underwater and withstand the pressure!"

Tara turned it over in her hands, weighing it. "This? All of it? It's not poisonous either?" she added, anxiously.

"Yes, all of it. No, it's not poisonous!"

Tara held it up close to her left eye to scrutinize it distastefully. "All of it? I mean… it looks like a lot. I can't cook it, or something?"

"No time for that!"

Tara gingerly nibbled one of the leaves and gagged. No time to cook it or boil it or anything. Not even any seasoning, except for its very strong taste of salt, to help get it down!

"Go ahead; it's the only way," remonstrated Marina. "And you must be hungry anyway!"

Tara grimaced and squeezed her eyes shut. She'd have to eat it. But, if it would let her swim underwater, it would be worth it. Wincing, she forced it into her mouth and chewed. The seaweed had a vile, bitter taste, as if she were chewing on a section of old tapestry back at her palace. "It's awful!" choked Tara.

Marina stifled a laugh at the looks of disgust and repugnance crossing Tara's face. "Really? Sorry about that; I guess I've never had to try it."

Tara could imagine why as she swallowed the last of it. An anxious minute passed. "I don't feel anything," she said, her heart sinking.

"Give it some time!"

Another minute passed anxiously, Tara staring first out to the ocean, then reproachfully at Marina. "I still don't feel anything!"

Marina smiled knowingly. "I think it should be working by now. Come on; dive in, and let's see!"

Warily, Tara slipped into the water and dunked her head beneath the surface. She didn't feel any change. "Dive deeper," urged Marina. "You shouldn't feel any pressure either. That's when you'll know for sure it's working."

Tara dove deeper and to her surprise felt no discomfort. Very tentatively, she opened her mouth and noticed how the water no longer tasted salty but like the water she might find in a stream. Her eyes opened wide: it was working! How easy it would be to learn how to swim when she couldn't drown!

"You'll learn how to swim quickly!" confirmed Marina, and, after letting Tara experiment for another minute or two with her arms and legs, took her by the arm and pulled her further away from the shore. Once well clear of the rocks, Marina summoned two dolphins and, grasping their dorsal fins, they caught a ride out into the ocean.

Tara and Marina arrived at the wreck site to find a team of squids and octopuses combing the debris meticulously. Tara directed them to what looked to her like the remains of the pirate captain's cabin. At last a tentacle curled out of the wreck with a small metal item in its grip. It looked like a key. Marina rejoiced and was ready to leave but Tara caught her arm. "Have them pull out everything from that cabin and lay it to the side here," she counselled. "There might have been other keys in the cabin, and we wouldn't want to have to come back to this wreck a second time if the one we have here didn't fit."

"Great thinking, Tara!" exclaimed Marina. Very sensible, too, Marina thought, since it had not been the easiest thing in the world to assemble all this sea-help, even if she had been casual about it back at Secret Island.

The squids found a variety of other items of varying degrees of interest but none like the key ring Tara had remembered. With that in hand, they returned to Secret Island and Tara raced back to the freshwater spring to retrieve the cylinder from where she had hidden it.

The two examined it together. "Okay, let's try the keys," said Tara at last. One after another, with mounting excitement and trepidation, they inserted the keys into the hole in the cylinder. Of course, it was the last key that fit. To their delight, the cylinder unlocked with a barely audible click and a panel on a hidden hinge folded out. So cleverly had it been fit to the rest of the cylinder that it had been impossible to see that there had been a seam there all along.

Breathlessly, Tara probed the interior of the cylinder with her smallest finger, the only one that would fit into the tiny space. Yes, there was a piece of paper inside! Working her finger deliberately and pressing the paper against the inside of the cylinder, Tara wriggled it toward the opening. Then, with a triumphant grin, she extracted it with thumb and forefinger to display a rolled piece of parchment. The two of them unrolled it ever so slowly and carefully to find—Marina gasped—a map! The princesses cheered their success. But, to their dismay, they found that what looked to be an explanatory text had been written in indecipherable symbols and characters.

"Oh no!" wailed Marina. "All that for nothing!"

"Wait!" said Tara. "Look closely! We've seen some of these symbols before. They're the same as on the exterior of the cylinder!"

Marina looked more closely at the cylinder and compared the symbols incised there to the writing on the map. "Why, that's so! You're right! But how does that get us any closer to understanding them?"

Tara frowned down at the cylinder, tracing a symbol with her forefinger. "I guess you're right. That doesn't get us any closer."

The two princesses looked at each other, crestfallen. So much effort, but they were no better off and no further along than they had been hours before: seated on an island holding a cylinder they couldn't understand. At last Marina spoke. "Let's take it to my father. It's a long shot, but he might be able to help. It's possible he'll recognize the language. If not, well, maybe he might have an idea of how we could figure it out." Would Tara be willing, she asked, to come down to the Coral Castle and meet her father?

Tara certainly didn't have any better ideas on how to proceed further, and Coral Castle sounded like a far more hospitable place to spend the night than exposed to the elements on Secret Island. Tara readily agreed. With that, they closed the cylinder and placed it carefully in a case that Marina said would surely keep it protected from the water and pressure and dove back into the ocean to make their way to Marina's home.

Further out to sea, they were met by an enormous manta ray. They clung to its wings to take them to the depth at which the castle stood, a princess trailing to either side. Tara asked if it was heavy work for the ray to tow them. Marina giggled. "They've never complained to me! I don't think so anyway; they're very strong." Tara mulled over this for a moment. Come to think of it, none of her horses had ever complained to her either.

The Coral Castle hove into view, behind and beyond an intricately woven canopy of seaweed. "Down and around," Marina urged the enormous ray with a squeeze of its pectoral fin with both her hands, and they banked off a chilly ocean current and downward toward the castle, its wings rising and falling majestically. Tara could make it out better as they approached. Unlike an above-ground stone castle, it was an elaborate and fantastic construction of living creatures, wondrously brilliant in color and variety.

How amazing, Tara thought. It was living and growing all the time, a structure in constant change, even if slowly. Could it be that Coral Castle didn't require repairs and maintenance, like Stonedell did, and just needed tending and pruning to keep it growing in the right direction? And to keep the windows and other apertures open? They descended in tightening circles, gliding toward an opening that, to Tara, looked as though it was in the fourth or fifth level of the structure. It made sense, she realized with a smile. She had to enter her castle on the first level, because gravity forced her to enter through the ground floor. But in an underwater castle it could be far easier to enter on a higher level.

Marina motioned to Tara to slip from the ray, and they swam on their own through a grand entrance that Tara later came to understand as the Main Gate. A stout phalanx of squids, their tentacles interlocked, guarded the entrance but relaxed their posture as Marina identified herself and indicated that Tara was under her sponsorship.

"We'll head for the Great Hall. I expect my father, King Aenon, will be there," Marina explained. Noticing that Tara was tiring, she offered Tara a nearby attendant fish to pull her. Tara gratefully accepted and Marina led the way as soon as Tara had taken hold of it by hugging its dorsal fin. "I know you're not as used to swimming as I am. But you're really learning quickly!" Tara smiled back. She did feel like she was making progress.

Very shortly, they were in the castle's Great Hall. Up, up, it soared, and indeed no roof to it was discernible; maybe it had none. It was as Marina had described it, only incomparably grander. An ordered row of ferns and seaweed fronds to either side of a wide aisle rose seemingly up to the surface, swaying ceaselessly in the shifting currents. Coruscating shafts of sunlight from the world above dimly lit the vast space and picked out the hall's innumerable coral planes in an ever-shifting panoply of tones and hues. A million motes hung suspended, each by turns illuminated in the gem-like light such that the entire space of the room glistened and sparkled. Speechless in wonder, Tara glided through what for all the world looked to her like a night sky swarming with stars in twinkling, shifting constellations far, far beneath the dome of the sky above.

King Aenon, surrounded by floating knots of courtiers, half-reclined on a throne consisting of a giant half-open clamshell, the open half behind him intricately worked with jewels and mother-of-pearl to form a shimmering mosaic of sea life. Marina and Tara approached and waited; at length the king caught sight of them. Where was his trident, Tara wondered, as he was not holding it, nor did it appear to be nearby.

The king, an older but still clearly hale man, greeted his daughter warmly. Marina curtseyed by lifting the right flipper of her tail back with her right hand and inclining her upper body, then introduced Tara as her new friend and the person on whose behalf she had asked permission to come to Coral Castle. The king turned to Tara and eyed her closely with, clearly, a practiced eye. Tara, blushing, attempted a curtsey like Marina's but, unpracticed, instead completed a half-flip. The surrounding courtiers tittered and Tara blushed; even the King chuckled.

"Come! What can I do for you?" he asked when introductions had been formalized all around. Marina asked if they might have a moment with him in his library, nearby. There, producing the case containing the cylinder, she explained what they had done so far and what they had found, concluding with the request that he examine the symbols himself, as perhaps he might recognize them.

The king placed the case in a large evacuated translucent bottle on a nearby coral shape serving as a table. Through the bottle's clear walls he first studied the cylinder itself. Then, he unrolled the map and stared long moments at the writing on it, slowly fluttering his fingers atop the bottle in thought.

Turning to the two princesses, he said, "These symbols do remind me of others I have seen before. Let me find one of my reference books and we shall see." With a single stately flick of his tail, he shot to an upper shelf and, picking through what looked like tablets from below, drifted back down again to them to show them what he had retrieved.

"This may confirm my thinking," he said, with a wink, and turned over several mother-of-pearl plates collated together in a kind of book. Each pearlescent plate had been densely incised with characters and figures, none of which Tara could ever recollect seeing. The language of these sea folk, she guessed, noting how so many of the figures seem to consist of wavy rather than straight and angular lines, as the characters in her language did.

After flipping through to nearly the last plate, he tapped his finger on the bottom of the plate. "Yes. This one. I believe so." He turned to his daughter and her friend. "The figures on your map are in the language of landling people who lived long ago atop a promontory not far from here. While they themselves did not venture too far in their surface vessels, their principal city was so advantageously located it became a great trading hub."

"A trading hub!" exclaimed Tara. She certainly knew what that was and explained it to Marina, who was unfamiliar with the concept.

"Just so," affirmed the king. "As I said, they did not venture too far from their city, even if many came from far away to trade in their city. Thus, I would suggest that, in choosing a place to start in following this map, you choose that promontory."

He continued. "This plate has at least some of the same symbols on it with another language I understand next to it, and so helps us to— partially—understand your map. Not all the symbols, I'm afraid though."

"I'm sure it's a big help!" ventured Tara.

"Only you will know if such is the case," he replied. "I cannot join you on your adventure. I have other matters to attend to here. But, what I can do is provide you with a translation of those symbols I recognize on this map and point you toward what remains of the promontory where the city stood. I can also offer you the use of my chariot—" and here he frowned slightly at Marina "—but you must promise not to abuse that privilege, as it is a very special boon to grant."

Marina's eyes grew wide at the prospect of taking her father's chariot.

"So you must not wreck it!" concluded the king, fixing Marina with a sharp gaze. Marina sighed and rolled her eyes. The king then suggested they spend the night in Coral Castle and depart the next day for the promontory.

Tara was more than happy for the rest, particularly since she had spent the previous night sunk in dejection in a pirate captain's chair. She did have to choke down more of the nasty seaweed, but there was no other way, she knew, as she'd be drowned and crushed in an instant if she didn't.

Dinner was a satisfying meal, the main course of which looked to be a sort of soup composed of four types of seaweed into which had been mixed clams, scallops, and various other molluscs Tara could not identify. Upon enquiry, she was told that they were harvested from depths which "landlings" could not dive or reach, like they could those dwelling in shallower waters. The soup had been cooked atop a vent at a nearby fumarole complex, the same which provided heated water by pipe to the entire castle.

Marina and her siblings, Aenon, Queen Seafoam, and Tara were served at a large shelf rock table in a dining area off the Great Hall. The soup arrived at the table in enclosed vessels. Fancifully, and because Tara had come from the world "above," the palace cook staff had chosen to serve dinner in amphorae of varying sizes, salvaged from wrecked ships over many years.

Tara passed the meal in lively conversation with the rest of Marina's family. It had been a long time since anyone from above the surface had been to Coral Castle, and they were fascinated by what it might be like to live in a world lit so brightly by the sun, and in which water fell from the sky, in drops—rather than it being all around—and through which it was possible to move very rapidly, as Tara could on Daystar.

Afterwards, Marina led her to a chamber for rest several levels above where they had dined. By this time of the evening, and particularly at that depth, there was no sunlight at all, and all illumination was provided by alabaster lanterns in which anglerfish had been pent. Marina gestured toward the bed—a real "seabed," Tara smilingly termed it—and gratefully sank into it. It was deliciously soft and yielding, the underlay being woven of bands of seagrass. The bed's posts were of spiral whelks, stacked tip-to-tip. Overhead a canopy of sea silk undulated imperceptibly, silently, in the ever-present sea currents.

Marina collected all save one of the anglerfish lanterns to leave a single pool of wan light beside the bed. "Just in case," she explained, "you wake in the middle of the night wondering where you are."

"How will I know when I should get up?" Tara asked groggily, almost asleep already.

"I'll come for you. We've got to make an early start tomorrow if we are to reach the site of the ruins before night falls. Get some sleep now! See you in the morning!"

Marina, not hearing a response, bent closer to check on Tara. She needn't have: Tara was already fast asleep. "See you in the morning!" whispered Marina, and departed for her own sea bed.

The dawning day found the two girls in King Aenon's gold-and-green chariot, drawn by a team of leaping orcas, *en route* for the site of the ruined city. With enough provisions on board for several days, Tara and Marina relaxed in the rear, chatting away like the firmest of friends. The golden sun, the occasional splash of the salt spray, and the light, caressing breeze lifted Tara's spirits, and she felt a kind of carefree joy that she could never recollect having felt at Castle Stonedell. Of course, she missed her parents, who must be increasingly anxious about her, and she missed taking Daystar out for rides, but when was the last time she had ever hunted for treasure using a genuine pirate map? Never! When might be the next? Well, possibly never again. As soon as she found the treasure, certainly she would get back to Brythrony and all that badinage and court events and so on and so forth and reassure everyone that she was still alive and well.

Tara glanced down at her new dress—well, one she had been encouraged to borrow. It was fabricated from a selection of wide-leaf seagrasses of a palette ranging from a deep evergreen to a faint mint, its "cloth" a twill weave, and its multitude of shades forming an intricately repeated pattern. Tara delighted that, whenever droplets of spray fell upon the dress, rather than stain it, the salt water restored the grasses' rich, natural colors. As a decorative touch, colorful cowrie shells had been threaded intricately in bands across a basket-woven bodice panel which Tara fingered idly as she rode through the waves.

At Tara's feet, in a compact bundle, lay her "landling" clothes, tidily folded but stiff and rough from extended immersion in salt water. She would rinse them out in a freshwater pool once they reached land, but she was in no hurry as the sea dress she wore suited her just fine. On impulse, she positioned the skirt such that it covered her legs and imagined she was a mermaid, even positioning her trunk and hips like she saw Marina, out of the corner of her eyes, lounging against the side of the chariot.

At length, unable to resist speculating, Tara turned to her mermaid companion and asked, "What do you suppose is the treasure?"

Marina attempted a frown but unconvincingly, being naturally light-hearted and playful. She shrugged her petite shoulders, and her blonde hair was momentarily caught in the ocean breeze to fan out behind her. "Gosh," she exclaimed. "I have no idea! Maybe jewels! And all sorts of gold and riches!"

Tara couldn't guess herself. "It has to be something pretty important, don't you think? Or whoever made the map would not have gone to so much trouble to keep it secure, using the scrimshaw cylinder."

Marina agreed, now seeking to restore some order to her hair by running her fingers through it like a kind of comb. "I think it's gold. Silver too, maybe. We don't have that in the Coral Kingdom, only that which comes to us from the sunlit world, from a ship that sinks, like in storms."

She turned to Tara with suddenly very bright eyes. "So that would be really amazing to find that!"

Tara could imagine. It would be impossible to operate a smelter so far beneath the surface of the ocean. "But you must have pearls?"

"Oh! Pearls! Sure, we have lots of those. There's nothing special about those—unless they're super big; if the regular kind, that would be really boring."

Tara smiled and explained that most any pearl would be special on land, even as gold and silver were special at the bottom of the ocean.

"Hey," mused Marina. "Maybe we can trade? Like, some of our pearls for some of your gold? What do you think?"

Why not, answered Tara, since the Coral Kingdom had loads of pearls and the dry land comparatively more gold and jewels. But soon she returned to studying the map. "I wonder where and how people from the ships ascended to the high promontory on which your father says these ancient people's city was located?"

"We'd just swim up, but you can't do that on land, I know."

"Good point! So maybe there was a staircase? But how would they haul all those goods up stairs, that must have arrived most every day?"

By mid-morning, they had neared the shore, sufficiently so that Marina changed the team pulling the chariot for one composed of sea turtles. The closer they got though, the less and less the features of the shoreline resembled those that Tara expected from her close study of the map.

"Some of it must have fallen into the ocean over time," she eventually decided, tracing the shoreline shown on the map and pointing to that in front of them. "If we're in the right place."

"No worries. I'll dive in and check underwater. Something should be down there if it fell from the cliff." Marina was gone only a short time before her head broke the surface again. Placing her cheek on the chariot's gunwale, her shining blonde hair spilling inside, she confirmed she had spotted what looked like the jumbled remains of stone docks and roads some ways off the coast.

"I'm afraid you'll have to take it from here. On land. I can't go there," she ended, smiling shyly.

This would require her to swim to shore, Tara realized. By that point, the wad of seaweed which had allowed her to breathe underwater had worn off. Tara would have to swim on her own for the first time since leaping from *Storm Wrack*. Still, with all her recent practice, how difficult could it be? Tara closed her eyes tightly and jumped overboard. Bobbing up promptly, she began kicking her feet and paddling with her arms toward the shore. Marina was soon sculling alongside her. "Oh, I had forgotten about you and the swimming! But you seem to be getting along okay." Marina inspected her with a more practiced eye and came in closer. "But you really should be a little smoother in your strokes. Kick your feet together, like I do with my tail. Or, no, don't you landlings flutter kick? Well, kick a little harder! Pull—harder! That's it! Now your arms! Harder!"

Tara at last arose, coughing and spluttering, when her feet touched the sandy bottom sloping up to the shore. Clearly her swimming still needed work. Marina was a harsh taskmaster too. She meant well, of course, but unsolicited lessons had maybe been a little much.

Tara staggered from the surf, and commenced to search for the easiest way up to the promontory. Shortly, she spied a slightly flatter expanse that ran uphill in a kind of zig-zag around hillocks in the general direction of the higher ground above her. Maybe it was some sort of ancient road, she thought, and began to pick her way uphill. The higher she climbed, the more flagstones, though cracked and broken, she found. It was a road and it had to have been the route along which goods had moved many years ago.

Arriving at the top, she pulled the map from the cylinder and unrolled it on a weathered chunk of marble. Based on what she could discern and from what Marina's father had told them, she gathered that she should start her steps at what appeared to be a large temple. Tara looked up. She now stood on a kind of plateau overlooking the ocean, littered with marble blocks and column segments, as well as portions of still standing columns.

Tara took a closer look at one nearby. It was of marble, if crumbling, and fluted. Maybe, she thought, such a temple might have large, grand columns composed of many segments such as this one? Much further down the promontory she spotted a jumbled mass of columns and bleaching marble blocks. Amongst them she also thought she noted a chunk of entablature from what had to have been a roof and which, by its thickness and sheer size, suggested that the building to which it had belonged had been substantial. Tara walked over to it to examine it more closely. It still retained a series of elaborate, if worn, carvings. Maybe this was her temple? It was, at least, a reasonable start.

Tara opened the map again. It looked like she was to proceed forward, toward the ocean. She couldn't read for exactly how many steps, but King Aenon had thought it was for about four hundred, until she spotted a "sign" of some sort. He couldn't be clear as to what she should expect by way of a "sign," since the writing had been indistinct, or untranslatable. All right: four hundred steps. Tara started pacing from what she judged would have been the front of the temple. But, impossible: taking the full four hundred steps would take her off the edge of the promontory! Tara's spirits sank. That part of the city must have long ago slid into the ocean!

Tara retraced her steps to the beach and then, after wading out into the surf, swam out to the chariot, which was drifting in the swells. Marina was on board, sunning herself.

"Hey," Tara greeted her, rocking the chariot some.

Marina roused herself from her torpor. "Mmph? Wha'd'ja find?"

"A city! I found a city!"

Marina rose on one arm in real interest. "Really? That is something! Tell me what you saw!"

Tara told her what she had seen, concluding with "The rest of the city must be underwater; it must have collapsed into the ocean as the waves eroded the cliffside below."

Marina nodded with understanding. "My turn again. I'll dive down to see what more I can see. This time searching closer to the cliff's face underwater."

Marina returned presently with the report that there was clearly something down there, but that so many rocks and boulders were in the way that it was hard to make out what was there. She had tried to shift some of the smaller ones, but there were just too many of them and most of them were very large. Marina floated beside the chariot for a moment in thought. At last she spoke. "My father's trident can direct water into a jet. I think that should be enough to move the boulders. Maybe I should ask for his help on this?"

Tara couldn't think of another way, so Marina asked her father, imparting the message to a passing skate, if he could help them, and could he bring his trident with him. He showed shortly, carrying his trident, which was a great green-and-silver staff topped by three golden prongs. Marina told him what she had seen below and how they needed his help in moving aside the rubble.

"For this? You summoned me from Coral Castle for this? To move debris? I thought you were in trouble, or that you had been injured!"

Marina's face took on a pleading expression. "But we do need your help! Honestly, we can't move it ourselves!"

Aenon scowled. "Now that I'm here, I might as well help you! But do not call on me again for so trivial a task. This is supposed to be your adventure. I have many responsibilities and duties to attend to in Coral Kingdom, and not just shift rocks!"

Abashed, the girls promised not to call him again and down he dove. Marina joined him below and directed him to ply his trident back and forth and focus a jet of seawater on the tons of boulders and debris toward the base of the cliff. He lessened the jet's force as he progressed though, so as to disturb as little as possible any ruins or structures that might lie beyond. When Marina judged that the remainder she and Tara could manage on their own, Marina thanked him extravagantly and, with a last admonishment, he departed. Marina returned to the surface.

"I didn't mean to upset your father!"

Marina shrugged. "Sometimes he's like that. He wasn't as upset when he left as he was when he first arrived; I know because he wasn't so frowny. I mean, I wish we could have moved those big rocks on our own, but they were just too heavy."

Tara agreed with that. She would not have been able to help at all. "What's down there now?"

"It's kind of a wreck, but clearly there are more ruins. You were right:

a huge section of the city must have slid into the water all at once. I think some of it is kind of intact too."

This was an exciting development, thought Tara, and she pulled her map from the cylinder. Too bad she couldn't go down herself to see! But there was nothing to do for it, as they hadn't brought along the necessary seaweed. She did her best to control her excitement. "That's great news," she replied. "Can you tell me what it's like down there? I mean, I got about a hundred paces from the temple and was very close to the edge. I still had another several hundred more to go."

Marina dove back down to find an answer to Tara's question. Shortly, she reported that what looked like the pavement below was relatively intact, if littered with rubble, and that it had come to rest at a slant, and she pointed her arms in the direction she thought it sloped.

Tara considered. How might the ruins, now at the bottom of the cliff and underwater, have looked when they had been intact up on the promontory? How to re-orient these mentally such that it would be possible to reconstruct where Marina—who had no feet to pace—should look now? Tara sighed. This was impossible. How were they ever going to figure this out? She looked at her friend though, and the round cornflower eyes gazing expectantly up from the gunwales, great masses of tangled blonde hair floating all around, and determined that she could not give up now. Not after coming this far. She'd have to keep trying, if only for Marina's sake.

"All right! I think that much of the land that was once above water has shifted slightly and rotated. Based on how you've described it to me. I'm thinking that what was once 'north' is now more, really, say, to the northeast. So, I'm thinking we have to pace in that direction for three hundred steps."

She thought a little further. "But, with the collapse, the pavement was probably compressed or piled up, one flagstone on top of the other. So, instead of three hundred paces, let's just say two hundred. Or so."

One more thing, she recollected! "Finally, this is about a pace—" and she held out her hands to show what such a distance might look like for Marina. "So, swim that distance, times two hundred, to the northeast. What do you think of that?"

"Sounds great! I'll do it!" Down Marina dove eagerly to carry out Tara's instructions.

Back again at the base of the cliff, Marina swam to the northeast the equivalent of the distance Tara had shown her. She floated to a stop and looked around. Well, here must be the place, she decided. But all around there were still piles of rubble, along with various shattered pieces of column segments and mounds of masonry overgrown with seaweeds. They would need some real strength to move these items, as Marina couldn't do it alone, and they had promised not to call on her father, King Aenon, again. They would have to think of a solution themselves.

Marina swam back up to the surface, and the two princesses conferred in the chariot. "How about a blue whale?" volunteered Marina.

"A blue whale?"

"Yeah, that could move most anything! But maybe we'd be too close to shore for a blue whale to swim in safely."

"That's true. They are awfully big, aren't they? But, also, maybe it would be so big that it might actually destroy or damage things in moving the rubble. While trying to move things around."

The two lapsed into silence again. They needed something really strong but of more moderate size. Tara felt helpless. She hardly knew any sea animals. Dolphin and whale—plus a few seafood delicacies—were about all she knew.

"Hey, how about an orca? Or several?" asked Marina, on impulse.

"What's an orca?" responded Tara, and when Marina explained that those had been the animals which had drawn their chariot, Tara thought it a wonderful idea.

"They're really smart too!" enthused Marina. "That could be a big help."

Marina returned to the water and called for three orcas. Soon enough they showed, swimming together as a pod. "Just wait up here," she urged Tara, who, not able to do much else, readily complied. She leaned out of the chariot to stare into the depths but was unable to make out anything beyond a deep, silent, endlessly restless blue-green.

The orcas were most happy to help and with only a bit of direction nudged aside the sections of columns that lay scattered across the base of the cliff to expose large flagstones set in a decaying limestone cement. This had to be the pavement that Tara had seen up above, realized Marina. But there was still a lot of mud, rock, and silt covering everything. "Could you, like, fan your tails back and forth to move away the sand and mud?" asked Marina of them.

This they did willingly, but it stirred up such a cloud that Marina was left choking. After it settled or drifted away with the current, what lay clearly exposed was a long, oblong marble slab, cracked in two, but otherwise intact. How unusual, compared to what otherwise was down here, thought Marina, with rising excitement. It also looked as though it had been originally hidden in some way, but that its collapse into the sea had more fully revealed it. She swam back up to the chariot to tell an anxiously waiting Tara.

"You've found it! It must be it! I mean, under it!" gasped Tara, almost leaping with excitement. She must have been correct in her estimations! "Can you lift it in any way?"

Marina thought hard, recollecting how large even half the slab was. "Uh, no. I mean, I really can't. It's way too heavy." She thought some more and then frowned. "And I don't think our orca friends could push it out of the way either. Or lift it."

"But we've got to find out what's under it!" pleaded Tara. She tried to imagine what the marble slab might look like. How frustrating that she could not go down herself to see how it lay on the bottom! "Let me ask," she turned back to Marina, an idea forming in her mind. "Just how does it lie on the bottom? Flat? Or at some kind of angle?"

"I guess… well, at an angle. A little bit."

"With, perhaps, some part of it jutting up, such that the entirety of it is no longer flush with the pavement around it?"

Marina guessed so, though she had not inspected it all that closely and wasn't sure.

"So, here's what I'm thinking: can you check all around the edges of the slab, to see if some of the sand has been swept or eroded away to expose gaps through which something could slip? Not our hands, because we couldn't reach very far underneath. But, maybe something very small, like a little sea creature?"

Marina at once understood what Tara was thinking. Perhaps the lobsters and crabs could help. With a giggle, she noted that they had had to call for help that day from not just the larger creatures of the sea but the smaller ones. "I'll have to keep it simple for them," she explained to Tara. "They aren't as quick—in that sense—as the killer whales." She chuckled at her own joke. "They can be quick to scurry around, though!"

Diving down again to the slab, she summoned a swarm of crustaceans, which she asked to explore beneath the slab and report back to her what they might see or sense. It wasn't long before several came back to tell her that there was a single object, comparatively large to them, well wedged underneath. And that it was not something which they might eat or which would want to eat them. Marina understood their preoccupation with those details, even if they were not of immediate relevance. She enquired as to the shape of the object and was told that, as best they could tell, it had multiple sheer sides, which would be difficult to surmount, leading Marina to understand it was a box or case. That had to be it, nodded Marina, and asked them to push it toward her. While they did, she set to work with her hands to scoop out enough sand underneath one corner of the slab to make room for it to pass. It was slow work, but at last it came close enough for Marina to grasp it and pull it out.

As she had guessed, it was indeed a sealed cube. Marina dismissed her crustacean helpers and considered the long-sought trophy she now held so lightly in her hand. Surely it would be best to open it above the water, she concluded, since it was originally from the sunlit world. Around she spun and, with a quick flick of her luminous, fluked tale, up she rose in a swirl of settling sand to the shimmering surface.

Princess Ariel

With Tara's help, Marina landed the box in the chariot. The two hugged each other with excitement and, with shining eyes, pried open the lid. To their astonishment, they found only a tablet of white marble engraved with the same signs and symbols that the map had been.

"Oh no!" exclaimed Marina, crestfallen. "Still no treasure! Still no gold or jewels! Just more marble!"

Tara was deeply disappointed as well. She really had expected this to be the end of the treasure hunt. It was getting late in the day too. She took a closer look at the symbols in the marble all the same.

"Oh, this is awful," complained Marina, swishing her tail overboard disconsolately. "Is this really all there is? Just another chunk of marble? Throw it overboard!"

But Tara was taking a real interest in the marble tablet. "Hold on, Marina. Take a look: see how many of the symbols on the marble are like those on the map?"

Marina let her eyes flicker over the marble in a cursory glance.

"See? Well, we know that the symbols on the map were directions—step a certain number of paces this way, for example. This one must be similar!"

"Step out more paces? To find more marble tablets?"

"Marina! Of course not! No, it's just another stage in finding the treasure! We'll use the symbols we know from the map and fit them in here to see if we can't figure out where the treasure ultimately lies!" Tara straightened proudly. "I know we can do it! Just stick with me a little ways more!"

Marina glumly acknowledged that she had little choice, and the two decided to spend the night in the vicinity. Tara would stay on land with half of the provisions they had put on board the chariot, and Marina would stay below the surface of the water where it was more comfortable for her.

The two met back together again the next morning. Tara had already been studying the tablet. "From what I can make of it," she related to

Marina, "It directs us to return two hundred and fifty paces, descend a staircase, and open a door."

Marina was impressed that her friend had figured out that much and her hopes rose ever so slightly.

Tara continued, pausing to look up at the ruined city far above them. "But how far back is two hundred and fifty feet? Is it still on the promontory, did it slide into the ocean, or is it somewhere in between, maybe in the side of the cliff?"

"Back to you, sister!" laughed Marina. "I can't go up there today any more than I could yesterday! But," she added, "I'll go back down to see if I can't find anything beyond that big marble slab."

Just so, thought Tara, and climbed to the top to look out over the promontory again. She walked back and forth along the windswept perimeter but couldn't find anything that might look like a staircase or a trapdoor into the ground.

She sat down, dejected, along the column sections and thought about the map. Hadn't it told her to take four hundred paces forward? Of which she had only been able to achieve about a hundred? Meaning that there had been a further three hundred to take, which they had completed underwater?

Tara gazed up into the bright blue sky. One hundred paces plus three hundred paces made four hundred paces of which the marble tablet had directed them to take two hundred and fifty back. Meaning, obviously, that the trapdoor or door or whatever it was for which they were searching could not be up on the promontory. Tara felt chagrined. If only could she have done her addition and subtraction before searching underwater at the base of the cliff. Very possibly the staircase they sought was still within the cliffside, and only the initial steps of it had slid into the sea.

Back down she trudged to wait by the shore for Marina to return. She sat on the rocks, wondering how she might get her friend's attention. She dared not throw rocks into the sea for fear that one might fall on Marina's head.

At length, Tara, out of sheer boredom, began to scan the face of the cliff. Tedious it was, moving her eyes back and forth in as straight a line as she could, left to right, until she came to the edge of one side, whereupon she lowered her eyes just a tad and began scanning back, right to left. Just like reading, she realized. She was reading the face of the cliff, she told herself, as her eyes began to hurt from the sustained concentration.

A third of the way down, she thought she spied something unusual, though it was hard to be certain at this distance. There, far up above: a white dot, like of marble, set into the hillside. Hadn't the slab under the ocean been of white marble? And the tablet that had lain in the box beneath it? Could those be a set of white marble steps in the side of the cliff?

As Tara shaded her eyes to try to make out the dot better, Marina appeared behind her. "There you are! I've come up, repeatedly, but you haven't been here! Guess what I've found!"

Tara grinned and asked her to tell her.

"Down there, not far beyond the broken slab I saw yesterday, I found some steps jumbled amongst the debris! I had to call in more sea creatures to help clear the debris! But I'm thinking, could these be the steps from up above, at least some of them?"

Tara nodded. It made perfect sense. It matched what she had been thinking. With that, she explained to Marina what she had been thinking.

Marina's eyes grew wide. "Ooh! You were right! It was the next step in finding the treasure! We're almost there!" But then her eyes narrowed. "But how will we get up there? It's so far up there!"

They both turned and shaded their eyes to scan the face of the cliff. Could that white dot up on the cliff really be the remainder of the stairway? It was hard to tell, it was so far away. The two exchanged glances. That high up was too high for Tara to climb up to and too perilous to reach climbing down from the top.

"No!" Marina began to wail. "It's not fair! If only we had a way to get there! But it's so far away and so high up! But we deserve it!"

Tara had to admit that they had done all they could to gain the treasure, and it seemed horribly unfair not to be able to claim it when they were so close, and it seemed so certain. "But we need help, Marina. You can't get up there, and I don't see how I can either. It's like we would need to fly!" If only they had a trained bird that could go up there and take a look for them, thought Tara. But, what would that accomplish? They wouldn't be able to speak with it afterwards anyway, and it could hardly pick up whatever was inside and fly it back down.

Tara looked back to Marina. "I don't know what to do. I guess we could try to think of something..."

An albatross alighted nearby with a squawk and tumultuous flapping of wings. "See how it mocks us!" accused Marina. "Go away! Shoo!"

As if in obedience, and after a sidelong, quizzical look, the albatross spread its wings and lifted off with the breezes.

The next minutes were spent throwing out ideas on how they might somehow reach that spot in the cliff face. "Come on: any idea is a good one," urged Tara, but Marina seemed to have lost her spirit and only stared angrily and silently out over the foaming surf.

At length, Marina turned and pointed wordlessly down the beach. A figure was walking toward them. Tara and Marina stopped all conversation to watch. As the figure drew closer, they saw it was another girl, like themselves, only perhaps a little older than they, and a little taller, maybe by half a foot. Her hair was a shade darker than honey and her light skin contrasted with her light brown eyes. She wore a dress composed of countless layers and overlapping, narrow pieces of fabric, the colors of it blending such that it was near white at the throat but verged to blue through the bodice and the waist until it was dark grey at the hem. Her feet were shod in white slippers that made only the slightest indentations on the sand, she seemed to step so lightly.

The figure approached them and stopped four feet away. The three of them surveyed each other silently for a long moment.

"Good morning," at last she greeted them in a tone that, to Tara, sounded rather grand and even contained a trace of hauteur. "I have heard that you are in trouble. Are you in need?"

Marina and Tara glanced at each other. "Who are you?" they responded in unison.

She straightened proudly to her full height. "I am Princess Ariel, and I like to help others in need."

Tara and Marina look at each other, again puzzled. Tara turned back to their visitor. "I'm Princess Tara."

"And I'm Princess Marina! And where did you come from?"

Ariel stretched an arm overhead and described an arc with it. "I came from… above," she murmured, loftily. "Yes. That's it. From above."

"But are you in need of help? Or," she added, suddenly down-to-earth, "would you like some help anyway?"

Tara sceptically eyed the girl who called herself Princess Ariel and who claimed to come "from above," and then glanced up at the face of the cliff. "Well, we do need help. But I don't know that you can really assist us. That's because we need to get up that cliff."

"What do you mean?"

Tara pointed. "I'm not sure you can make it out, but that white dot up there—"

"Of course, I can make that out."

"—Right, that's good then! Anyway, that white dot: it's actually—"

"—It's actually a staircase. More accurately, the remainder of a staircase. Into the side of the cliff."

All right, so she really could make it out, thought Tara. She had super-sharp eyes, that was for sure.

Marina spoke up. "We need to get to it. But we can't. It's too far up for us to climb to and too dangerous to descend to from the top. So there we are."

"Why is it so important that you get to those stairs?"

Marina hesitated and looked to Tara. Tara looked to Marina. Should they tell this person who called herself Princess Ariel? Could she be trusted? Tara was tempted to demand what a princess, such as she called herself, was doing walking along the beach as she was, except that then she and Marina both would have to explain themselves as well.

"Well," said Tara slowly, at last, "we just saw it and thought it might be interesting. That's all."

It was Ariel's turn to eye them both sceptically, but she said nothing. Instead, she craned her head around to peer more closely at Marina. "Aren't you a mermaid?"

"Why, yes, I am! I live in the Coral Kingdom. My father is the King of the Coral Kingdom!"

"I've never met a mermaid before. How interesting that you are a mermaid!"

Marina's face glowed happily. "Now you have!"

Ariel turned to Tara. "And you're Princess Tara. Of...?"

"Of the House of Hession. Of the Kingdom of Brythrony."

"You aren't a mermaid."

"Uh, no, not a mermaid," admitted Tara. Just a regular human. Just me, that's all. "And you're Princess Ariel. Of...?"

Ariel drew herself up again and seemed to preen. "Of Cloud Kingdom!"

Tara had never heard of Cloud Kingdom. Yet it must be very nearby, as it appeared as though Princess Ariel had simply walked to meet them on the beach. "Oh," was all Tara could muster in response.

But Marina couldn't contain herself and burst out with a question right away. "Where is that? I've never heard of Cloud Kingdom!"

Ariel drew herself up even taller, if possible, and lifted one hand as if to encompass the heavens. "Up above. Overhead." She seemed to circle one of the larger cumulus clouds hanging directly over the bluff, and across which the remains of the ancient city were strewn. "Up there is Cloud Kingdom, and up there is where I live. In Cloud Castle." Then, to the astonishment of Tara and Marina, dramatically behind Ariel in a complicated sequence unfurled two pair of sweeping wings, golden and gossamer, like those of an enormous dragonfly, shimmering with a slight iridescence in the morning sun.

Tara and Marina gasped. "You have wings! So, you can fly?"

Ariel smiled knowingly. The wings beat the air in a brief flutter, and ever so lightly Ariel lifted from the ground. Just as easily, she set back down again, noiselessly.

"Are you, like, some kind of fairy?" blurted Tara.

Ariel frowned and furled her wings. "I am not a fairy. I'm far too big for that."

Tara wondered, if she wasn't a fairy, but she had wings, what was she? But Tara didn't ask any further questions, as it sounded, from Ariel's reaction, that further enquiry could offend. "Sorry! Of course, you're not a fairy. Sorry about that."

Ariel relaxed. "No problem at all." Her eyes drifted over Marina's green tail. "Is it… fun to be a mermaid?"

"Sure is; I like it a lot! I can swim everywhere there's water and down to most any depth."

"Wow. That far down, huh? But just like I can fly to most every height!"

Princesses Ariel and Marina looked at each other with sudden smiles. "How fun! To be able to go all over and see everything from so high up!" stated Marina, with an excited flip of her tail.

"I can ride a horse!" piped up Tara anxiously, who had neither flipper nor wings and could only walk.

But Ariel only favored Tara with a quick and cursory nod before returning to Marina. "I can also talk with all the birds, and they are my friends."

"I can also…" began Tara, interrupting, but stopped as she had to rack her brain for something else that would differentiate her. She had never been good at playing a musical instrument or singing, for example.

"That's neat! And I can communicate with sea creatures!" re-joined Marina.

I can't talk with any animals, and sometimes I can't even seem to talk to my own parents, Tara admitted silently, sighing. I can't even talk with Daystar. Why can't I talk with Daystar? "Hey! I can shoot a bow and arrow!" she volunteered, hopefully.

"That's really something," acknowledged Ariel, who at least seemed to know what a bow and arrow meant.

Marina suddenly remembered the scrimshaw cylinder in her hand. "Oh, but, hey! Princess Tara figured out this cylinder! She's really smart!"

Ariel looked more closely at the cylinder Marina held in her hand. "What is it? What did she—you—figure out?"

"She's really smart. I would have never understood what to do with it, but she figured out how to open it, all on her own, and then how to find the last clue to the treasure! Even though she didn't know the language at all!"

" 'Treasure?' What treasure? You figured out how to find a treasure?"

Marina bit her lip and looked to Tara. Sorry, she mouthed.

"That is, if you don't mind telling me."

"Well, we think it's treasure. We just can't get to it. That's all."

"Hm," considered Princess Ariel and glanced up at the cliff face. "I wonder: is this the help you need?"

Tara looked to Marina, who was looking at Tara. Tara thought of the marble steps high up in the cliff wall. How were they to get to them without the help of someone with wings? Clearly Ariel had already figured out that the stairs were connected to the treasure; they might as well tell Ariel everything, since she could fly up on her own at any time to investigate with or without any further information from them.

Tara nodded. "Yes. This is the help we need. This is how you might be able to help us. If you can, we are happy to share the treasure with you. Evenly. One third apiece." Why not? It was either one third apiece or none for anyone. Or maybe all for Ariel! Tara began to explain how they had got to this point, with Marina joining in at points, until at last they arrived at the moment, pointing to the cliff's face, when Ariel had come walking toward them on the beach.

Ariel eyed it critically. "Yes. I could fly up there. Even though the winds around the cliff face are a little gusty. I think I could do it."

Tara and Marina looked again at each other. Marina seemed a bit disappointed at having to share but there really wasn't any choice.

"All right. Yes, please. Would you go take a look? Please?"

Princess Ariel nodded confidently, then to the surprise of Tara and Marina, reached out and shook each of their hands in turn. "We'll share! I'll be right back. Watch me!" Then she unfurled her wings and commenced to beat them rapidly, as fast as those of a hummingbird. In a moment, Ariel had lifted from the ground in a hover, and then, moving swiftly, shot upwards toward the cliff. Within a minute, she could no longer be made out distinctly.

She returned about ten minutes later, breathless. "Yes! We were right! There're the remains of a stairway going into the cliff. And yes, the upper portion has fallen away into the sea. But there are still some eight or nine steps left, and at the bottom of the steps is a door."

Marina shouted for joy. "We're almost there! The treasure!" Even Tara was thrilled.

"So? Did you open the door?" they asked together.

"No. I think it's a door, because I can see what look like hinges at one side. But there's no handle, and the door wouldn't budge when I pushed on it. No keyhole, yet there is a slot, like, for putting a message through. Even though that makes no sense! So," Ariel shrugged helplessly, "I flew back!"

Tara fell silent into thought for a long moment, and Ariel and Marina did likewise, watching her. The only sound for what seemed like an entire minute was the ceaseless wash of the waves behind them. At last Tara looked up. "Did the slot have dimensions like so—" she gestured with her hands "—and so?"

Ariel studied Tara's hands closely. "Why, yes, much like that! How did you guess?"

Smiling knowingly, Tara picked up the marble tablet she and Marina had studied so intently. "I think the door does have a keyhole. And this is the key. It's both the map and the key. Let's insert this tablet into the slot and see what happens!"

Ariel's eyes widened in astonishment at this bit of deductive reasoning. She turned to Marina, who tapped her forehead with her forefinger. "I told you she could figure it out! She can figure out anything!"

Ariel nodded, took the tablet from Tara, and flew up again.

She returned a few minutes later, now without the tablet. "It worked! It worked! The door opened!"

"Well? Did you go in? What did you see?" demanded both Tara and Marina, who had been waiting with steadily mounting impatience.

Ariel shook her head, suddenly a little embarrassed. "It was dark. And," she added, "a little scary."

Tara immediately spoke up. "I'll go with you. If you can carry me." If Ariel needed support, Marina could hardly go—not when walking down steps was required. Tara had come this far; she couldn't turn back now.

Ariel evaluated her critically and decided that she could, though she wasn't confident about a very long distance. But, after looking back and forth between Tara, the beach, the cliff face, and back to Tara, assured the latter that she was "reasonably" confident she could get her to the stairway. "Hold on," she said stoutly and grabbed Tara tightly from behind about the waist.

Gee, thought Tara, I won't ask what she means by "reasonably confident"; I just hope it's enough to get me there and back. But what she said was, "I'm ready!"

"All right; hold on!" Ariel said again and, holding on tightly, Tara heard the wings beat behind her, and then slowly, gradually, the sandy beach began to fall away and she could see below her the receding face of Marina, waving her hand anxiously up to her as she and Ariel began their ascent to the cliff face.

The wind blew in sudden and sharp gusts at points as they made their approach to the cliff, and Ariel seemed to stagger in mid-air, but she held firmly to Tara, and then suddenly there was the edge of the stairway before them. There was one short, heart-stopping moment as Ariel found her footing on the narrow ledge which had to suffice as a landing, and then they were there.

Ariel pulled her down two steps quickly. "We can't be sure if the outermost steps might crumble away if we stand on them too long," she explained quickly.

"Very good point," acknowledged Tara. "Great thinking!"

Ariel beamed.

Just as Ariel had described it, at the bottom of the steps was a door, now open. With the sun lower in the sky behind them, the room had begun to catch its afternoon rays. They entered, cautiously, to find a smallish room that was almost totally bare except for what looked to be a pile of items in each of the four corners. Each of the items in each corner were the same, but different from those in the other corners.

In the first corner were small brown leather bags that Tara thought to be a size that could be worn at one's waist.

In the second was a pile of vials containing a clear liquid.

In the third was a stack of what looked like bronze sticks or short rods.

In the fourth were small sachets of what proved on closer inspection to be multi-colored particles resembling flakes of mica.

Tara and Ariel inspected one of each of the four items intently and wondered aloud to the other what they could possibly be. "Let's take them back to the beach, where we can look at them better in the sunlight," suggested Ariel, and that made sense to Tara, so they grabbed a few of each of the items. Tara held them fast in her hands so that Ariel would have both of hers to hold onto Tara, and back they flew to Marina.

They gathered on the sandy shore at a spot where all three could rest comfortably in their own element, and Tara distributed to each one of the four items found in the room.

"That's it? This is the treasure?" asked Marina, listlessly turning over the items in her hands. "Just some bags and sticks? And some dust? Not a single piece of gold? Or even one jewel?" She looked from Tara to Ariel in confusion. "All that work… and this is it?"

Tara didn't say anything, but she was also downcast. They had worked non-stop for days to figure out this puzzle! Why so much effort to hide packets of dust, glass vials, rods and a few bags? Yet, that was all that there had been as she and Ariel had made sure there had not been anything further in the room. Aloud, she put on the bravest face she could. "Look: we owe it to ourselves to take a closer look at what we found. Maybe it's more special than we think!"

To Ariel, they didn't look any different in the light than they had in the room in the cliffside. Disdainfully, she picked up one of the bags next to her to more closely examine it. It looked as though it could be belted about the waist of the wearer, or worn over the shoulder. She looked at it from all directions then tried to turn it inside out. Nothing in it. Nothing special about it from what she could see.

Tara picked up the short rod nearby. It was very dull and plain.

Marina inspected a sachet. Just as Ariel and Tara had determined in the cliffside room, it was filled with powder. She sniffed it. It didn't smell like anything. She hesitated a moment then stuck a finger in cautiously and stirred. "Maybe it used to be something, but it's turned to dust over the years?" She pulled out her finger and examined it. Her fingernail was now very shiny, and there were colorful bits under her fingernail as well. She reached inside to bring out a pinch and eyed it closely. It looked like it was composed of tiny specks of something very sparkly. But beyond that, she couldn't tell. She held it up into the sunlight, and seeing nothing different, let it drop, glittering, into the air after calling to the others to show them.

Immediately Tara and Ariel turned away with sharp exclamations of pain. "Ow! Stop! It's so bright!" they both cried out immediately.

"What?" asked Marina. "I didn't see anything!"

"Well, we were practically blinded! Whatever that was."

"Wow," exclaimed Marina, looking more closely into the bag. "It IS really sparkly. But I didn't see anything like it sounds you did when I dropped it."

Hm, thought Tara. That was surprising: we were practically blinded by all sorts of sparkling and flashing light, but Marina didn't see anything. "Let me drop a little bit," she requested. "Watch, but only out of the corner of your eye." With that, Tara dropped a smidge in front of her, and Marina and Ariel confirmed that they saw intense brightness as soon as Tara let fall the dust.

Tara replied that she hadn't been affected at all.

The three princesses gathered to look at Tara and Marina's outstretched fingers. "I think the dust gathers up and reflects the light," said Ariel, slowly.

"So, wow, it's like a special kind of dust," exclaimed Marina. "It's super bright for anyone looking at it, dazzling even, but the person throwing it isn't affected."

Tara nodded. "Dust that dazzles." She looked to the others. "It's dazzle dust," she dubbed it, and the others agreed: dazzle dust. Maybe there was something of use in that room after all.

Tara next took a closer look at the small rod she held. The others stopped their investigations to watch her. After the discovery of dazzle dust, maybe this rod also had potential to surprise. Squinting at it closely, she noticed that the rod actually appeared to be ringed by a series of bands at set intervals. More closely still, she saw that the rod was ever so slightly narrower after each band. She turned it over carefully. It looked to be made of some very light, strong metal. Could it be that the rod was actually a joined set of rods that nested somehow within each other? She shook it, pointed it, twirled it, and tossed it from one hand to the other, but nothing happened.

At last she shrugged and turned to her friends. "It's supposed to do something, I think, but I can't figure out what that might be." She tapped it on the rock on which she sat. It rang slightly, as if it were very hard and strong. How strong?

"Let's see if it can withstand bending when we insert it between these two rocks next to you," suggested Ariel, pointing to a large rock resting at a slant atop another next to Tara.

Tara stood up and jammed it as best she could beneath the large, black slab of the rock and tried to pry one from the other. The rock didn't move and the rod didn't bend, but then it was short, maybe too short to be able to obtain sufficient leverage. Tara shook her head. "Not a good test," she said. "I'd need it to be longer," she added, half to herself, "like, by about three or four more feet." To her astonishment, the rod immediately telescoped out that length. "Amazing," breathed Tara, and the others clapped.

"It extends!" cried Marina.

"Great idea! Let's see how far!" Tara pulled the rod out from underneath the rock and asked it to extend to its full length. It promptly extended to about fifteen feet or so. "Look!" Tara shouted, motioning to the others. "It extends, on command, and to an ordered length!"

"Is it strong?" asked Ariel, now picking up the rod before her.

Tara returned to the rock that was half atop the other. She inserted one end of the extended rod under the rock and put another under the tip of the rod as a fulcrum. She tested the rod: it flexed but did not break. Tara put more and more weight on it, then jumped up and, catching it, hung from it. With a creaking, grinding sound, the stone at the tip of the fulcrum flipped over and Tara landed lightly on her feet. She grinned at her friends. "It's strong AND flexible!"

The others nodded, eyeing the rod appreciatively. After a moment, Marina took exception, though hesitantly. "All right, so it can extend—and, I guess, contract. But, what do we do with that?"

Ariel didn't say anything. Tara guessed it was because, at the back of her mind, she was thinking along the same lines. First, Tara thought to have it contract to test what Marina had thought might be the case. Quickly and smoothly, the rod retracted as Tara requested. She looked up triumphantly at her friends. "Why, of course, it is of tremendous use!"

Ariel and Marina waited, expectantly.

"Sure! For example," Tara looked down at the rod, "it could be used for, well, for, like, for moving things. Like heavy stones, as I just did. If we needed that!"

"Oh," said Marina, not obviously impressed.

"Right! Or, well, we could maybe hold onto it really tightly and have it lift us up to the full extent of the rod. When it extended!"

"I have wings that can do that for me," responded Ariel.

"Or, what if we needed to prop something open for a long time, something really big and heavy? We could have this rod extend and hold it open for us."

Marina took another look at the rod, somewhat less doubtful. Maybe it might be of some use, sometime, somewhere, she thought.

"Or," continued Tara, warming to the topic, "maybe it might be used as a kind of bridge, like to stretch over a chasm, if we had to go across it, and we could either balance on it or cross, hand-over-hand!"

"I have wings that can—" began Ariel, but Tara interrupted her.

"Sure, and yes you do! But for me, and because I don't, it still might be useful." Tara could see her new friends were not yet convinced of the telescoping rod's utility, but Tara was. No, it wasn't as amazing as the dazzle dust, but it could be of use nonetheless.

Marina and Tara now turned to Ariel. It was her turn to explore the last item they each had: the little vial. Ariel held it up to the light. It had some sort of liquid in it, and she could feel it slosh in its vial as she shook it. She held the vial and shifted it from hand to hand and peered closely at it, but it was just a featureless vial, stoppered by a tight cap. Looking at Marina and Tara, she put her hand on the cap. "Might as well see what's inside," she muttered and pulled and twisted it until it came off.

Nothing happened. After a moment, Ariel stared directly into it as the others watched closely. Then, the others still watching, she poured a drop into her hand. It was smooth and oily, she told them, rubbing it between her thumb and index finger. Very smooth. She put her other hand to her palm and rubbed the two together. Nothing. But when she drew her hands apart, a film stretched between them briefly then collapsed to form a clear, glistening bubble on her left palm.

Marina and Tara were fascinated and gathered to look more closely. "What is it?" they asked. "What does it feel like?"

"Like, nothing; it's as light as air!"

Ariel turned to the others. "I have no idea what this is, but maybe Princess Tara can figure it out. Right, Princess Tara?" Then she blew on it softly, just to see if it would move. To her surprise, the bubble suddenly leapt from her hand to float into the air, where it moved and drifted for a few moments and then returned to earth but hovered above Tara. Tara extended her hand to let it drift into her palm, whereupon she looked up at the others and smiled. "How fun! It came to me!"

She brought the bubble right up close to her eye to look into it. It was empty, of course, but the world through it was just slightly hazy and streaked with colors, as she had remembered looking through soap bubbles. Soap bubbles had been somewhat resilient when breathed on, she remembered, too. She blew on it ever so softly, on impulse. The bubble in her hand popped, noiselessly, and immediately they heard distinctly Ariel's voice again. "I have no idea what this is, but maybe Princess Tara can figure it out. Right?" as if from the bubble itself.

The three were silent for a moment. "Did you see how it came right to me?" said Tara softly, when they had thought about what they had just seen and heard. "It came right to me, because Ariel said my name. Just as if she had addressed it to me. Like a letter. And then it repeated what Ariel had said."

"It's like a message bubble," observed Ariel, and so they thought it must be. These would be wonderful, they agreed, to use to stay in touch with each other. How many times in these last few days, Marina and Tara recollected, they had wished they had some means to talk to each other when they had been outside of earshot.

"And bubbles can pass through the water, drift through the air, and float over the land! So a bubble sent by any one of us should surely reach any other!" Marina added excitedly.

There were no items left to examine from the room in the cliff. "All right, well, no gold or jewels, but there was this dazzle dust, some telescoping rods, then the message bubbles.

"I guess I like the message bubbles most of all."

"As for me, I think I like the dazzle dust," declared Ariel.

Tara hesitated. "And, as for me, I guess I like…" she surveyed the three items before her. "I guess I like the message bubbles too."

"But what about the brownish bags that were in the fourth corner?" asked Ariel.

It was true, remembered Tara, thinking back to the room from which these had come. The bags had not been piled in the middle or with one of the other three items but had been placed in their own corner. Placed, as if to suggest that they merited as close an examination as did the other items, and possibly as useful.

"Take a look, Tara!" urged Ariel, handing her one.

"Let's all of us take a look!" replied Tara, passing another bag to Ariel and then turning to hand one to Marina. Each rummaged around inside her bag and reported it empty. They appeared to be just plain, fawn-colored bags, edged in black, that could be fastened around the waist or worn over the shoulder.

Tara examined the exterior of the bag closely and turned it inside out as best she could but saw nothing noteworthy. It was in good condition, which was remarkable for being locked away for what must have been many, many years. So it had to be more than any ordinary handbag. Plus, since all the other items in the room in the cliff had been extraordinary, mustn't this one be as well?

"It must be meant to carry the other three items," announced Tara at last. "Because it was in the same room as the other three. But, funny, I don't see any clips or loops to hold a vial, a rod, or packet of dazzle dust."

Tara frowned. No, the bag did not look specially constructed to hold the other three items, but Tara was confident it had been intended for just that purpose. Tara placed the telescoping rod into the bag and it wasn't apparent at all that the rod was within. What about the vial? Tara put that in as well: no sign of it being within either, nor did the bag feel any heavier, and the same with the dazzle dust. Interestingly also, the bag didn't feel any heavier for containing these items.

The other two princesses were now watching Tara, who held up the bag to them. "Hey," she called to them. "Show me your bags. Put them side by side." They put all three next to each other, and Tara shifted them around so as to mix the three up. "Now, tell me which bag contains the rod, the message bubbles vial, and the dazzle dust?"

"It doesn't look as if any have anything in them. They all look the same," observed Ariel.

Marina looked up. "If I hadn't seen you put them in one of those bags, I'd say all of the bags are empty."

Tara picked up the one she had put down. "This is the bag in which I put the three items. It looks just like the others, even though—see?" and she opened it and brought forth all three items, one by one. "Isn't that amazing?"

Tara put her bag down. "Let's get some rocks to put inside, like, about ten. To see what it looks like then."

Not only did the bag readily accommodate the stones, but there still seemed to be room for more. Moreover, the bag wasn't any heavier or bulkier.

"It's a really special bag!" concluded Ariel for all of them. "It's a super-capacity bag that, no matter what's inside, doesn't show it's holding anything. And it's not any heavier either from what's inside."

"Wow; it's the ultimate traveling bag," whispered Marina, in awe.

"It's a special purse," agreed Ariel.

"A princess purse!" added Tara.

"I don't think we want to leave any of these items in the cliff-face room, to crumble away eventually into the ocean," said Ariel. "I'll fly back up and get the rest and carry it all back in one of the bags!"

Marina and Tara were left alone on the beach. "Now what do you think of our treasure?" Tara asked Marina.

"It's nice, even if it there aren't any gold or jewels!" replied Marina, brightly.

"I've been thinking," remarked Tara, scanning the skies to see if Ariel might be back in flight yet to re-join them, "that, although Ariel joined us on this treasure hunt a little late, we could not have found everything we did without her."

"I agree!"

"I think it's right that we shared equally with her. What do you think?"

"Yes, it is the right thing to have done."

"And, also, what do you think of this idea: we each take a bag, and into it we place one of the three items. Then we each have one each of our found treasure items."

Marina looked down at the ground before her where the rods, vials, sachets, and purses lay, then up to the cliff face. "What will we do with the rest? We have more than three of each."

Tara shrugged. "Keep the rest for spares, I guess?"

Ariel was landing just then, her arms full of purses, each identical to the next. Tara and Marina told her of what they had decided, and Ariel accepted with delight.

"I'd love to use the message bubbles to stay in touch with both of you!"

"Yes, of course! How fun!"

"I just know we're going to be fast friends!" exclaimed Tara, then frowned and fell silent.

The others immediately asked why her demeanor had so suddenly changed.

"No one, not my mother and father, not anyone in the entire court, know what's happened to me," she explained. "Marina found me in the cabin of the sinking pirate ship and, for all anyone in this whole world knows, aside from the two of you, I drowned! They may not even know that the pirate ship sank; they may think I'm somewhere over the ocean, still kidnapped."

Ariel laughed and grabbed Tara's hand. "Why didn't you say something before? I can take you back home. Easily!"

"How? I'm too heavy for you to carry very far. And," picking up a princess purse, "I won't fit into one of these."

"I won't carry you! I'll send for my sky chariot instead. It's pulled by swans. I'll take you up to Cloud Castle, then when we're over where you live, I'll send you back down the same way. By sky chariot. Easy!"

Tara smiled and relaxed. "Sky chariot? Cloud Castle? Well, if you'd take me, yes, please! My parents will never believe any of this!"

Tara turned to Marina. "It's time for me to go. Thank you ever so much for saving my life!"

Marina smiled happily, then reached behind her with her right hand to grasp the right flipper of her tail and pull it up ever so slightly while inclining her upper body. The merfolk curtsy, thought Tara, remembering suddenly; what she had witnessed Marina perform in the Coral Castle to her father. Tara smiled in recollection, then impulsively rushed forward and wrapped Marina in her arms.

"Mmph!" Tara heard as she squeezed Marina tightly.

"Thank you, Marina! For rescuing me, for taking me to Coral Castle, and even for giving me clothes to wear!" Tara said, gesturing to her woven seagrass dress. "For everything!"

"Oh, I'm so happy to have done all that; I'm happy to have met you! And it's been such an adventure; I had such fun!" Marina's eyes seemed to moisten. "Let's be friends?"

"Absolutely! Friends forever!"

"I'll see you again? You promise?"

Tara nodded. "Yes! In the meantime, we have the message bubbles."

Marina nodded too, as if remembering. "It's nice to have you as a friend," she added, shyly. "Because all my siblings are much older than I am. They sort of, well, do their own thing."

"I'm an only child, so I don't even have siblings." Tara had thought that a sibling would be fun to have, to have something in common with, but maybe not always did it work out like that. She looked down at her seagrass dress, which was now damp across the front from hugging Marina. She could have a mermaid friend instead.

Marina giggled, just as Tara had so often heard her giggle over the last few days. "That always happens when you hug a mermaid! But the seagrass likes the saltwater. In fact, if it's away from saltwater too long, it'll disintegrate."

"I understand. But I'll keep it forever as a souvenir from my night at Coral Castle."

"Goodbye, Princess Tara! Please don't forget me!"

"Never, Princess Marina! I know we'll see each other again. And please tell your parents 'hello' for me and thank them again!"

Marina waved again as Tara climbed into the sky chariot, which Ariel had summoned and which had just set down on the sand. Ariel climbed in after her and took the guidance reins to hand. With a surge, the wings of the swans fluttered, the traces went taut, and the sled began to glide forward. Tara turned and waved a last time at the receding Marina, who was waving frantically with her right hand even as she wiped her eyes with her left. Then she was indistinct against the black rock upon which she had been sitting.

Tara leaned back in the seat to contemplate a ride in the skies, at considerably greater comfort than her trip to the cliff-side face had been earlier. But on the way up to Cloud Castle, Tara had a second thought. "Um, Ariel, I wonder if I might ask you to take me back to Sea Sprit instead of

Castle Stonedell?"

"Sea Sprit? Why? Don't you want to go home?"

"Yes. Absolutely. But, there's a, well, a little problem that I should address first, I think." Tara then proceeded to relate her suspicions that the same Captain Jarvis who had hosted her the night before she had sailed was, in fact, in league with the pirates who had captured her and sunk *Dolphin*. "And so I want to look into that a little further. I'm sure that Lieutenant Rohanic and the rest of my escort are still in Sea Sprit. Once I find them, we'll be able to arrest Jarvis. If I'm right."

Ariel was aghast. "What a horrible man! Of course, I can take you back to Sea Sprit: it's a very short ride. We don't even need to go up to Cloud Castle. I'll land my chariot outside Sea Sprit and we'll both go the rest of the way on foot."

Ariel was insistent, and Tara was happy to have the company. Ariel reversed course and the chariot banked steeply, came about, and followed the coast line until Sea Sprit came into view in the distance. Ariel brought the chariot down and they alighted on the sand. Moments later, the chariot had departed to return to Cloud Castle and the two were alone on the sand together.

Tara pointed. "Up there, on the bluff: do you see the house up there? That's the manse of Captain Jarvis. I really do believe he's behind all this!"

Ariel nodded. "Why don't I flit right up there to see if anyone is there? I'll peek through the windows to see if I can find him. He'll never imagine anyone looking for him through the upper windows!"

Tara smiled. No, he certainly wouldn't! "Great! Thank you. I'll start walking toward Sea Sprit along this strand. If you see something, you'll know where to find me."

Up Ariel flew, a shrinking dot against the bright blue, cloudless sky. Tara had not walked far through the soft sand before Ariel had returned and set down before her. "I saw the person you described as Jarvis," she related. "He's in that big ballroom you mentioned. Also, it looks like a bunch of men are arriving. They're dressed in rags and carrying cutlasses and led by an especially large and ugly man who shouts a lot!"

Tara considered. Could these be the pirates, led by Braunzin, who had manned *Sea Wrack*? But why would they be meeting with Jarvis now? "Were they trying to hide at all? What were they doing?"

Ariel mused for a moment. "They didn't seem to be all that concerned about being seen. In fact, yes, some even were singing!" She wrinkled her nose at the memory. "Terrible singers too!"

Tara nodded. They had to be Braunzin and his crew. Those who had escaped from the wreck of the *Storm Wrack*. They must have just found their way back to Sea Sprit. Maybe they were seeking refuge at Jarvis's place. It was looking more and more like Tara was right about the connection between him and them.

"Listen, I know this is really difficult, but could you carry me one more time? Up to the bluff where the Jarvis house is located? One way only! I'd like to see what happens!"

"Tara, that's way too dangerous! What if you're discovered?"

"I'll be careful! Besides, after dropping me off, you'll flit down to Sea Sprit, find Lieutenant Rohanic and tell him where to find the pirates and me. That's when they'll be arrested and we'll see justice done." If there were problems, she added as an afterthought, why, she'd immediately send Ariel a message bubble!

Ariel hesitated. This was turning out to be a lot more work and danger than she had expected. But she had promised Tara her help. Furthermore, it was Tara really doing all the dangerous parts; all she was asking of Ariel was to fly her up there to the house and then leave and find Rohanic. Surely she could do that. She nodded in agreement, if with hesitation. "All right; I'll do it. Come on, let's go!"

Ariel tightly encircled Tara again with her arms, as she had done before, and, with a mighty effort, beat her wings hard. Slowly, sluggishly, she lifted off and up they began a laborious and even erratic ascent to the mansion. Now more aware of the strain on her new friend, Tara caught herself biting her lip in worry. Several times, she thought she might slip from her Ariel's grasp but, at last, and with a final lurch, Ariel landed to that side of the mansion with the fewest windows.

Tara turned to thank her friend who saw she was bright red from the exertion. "Rest here a while," she encouraged Ariel. "I'll wait a bit. I won't start until I know you've recovered."

This seemed to give Ariel heart and she straightened and proclaimed herself ready to fly down to Sea Sprit. Tara gave her last instructions. "Ask for Lieutenant Rohanic. They were last quartered at the finest hostelry in the town, which looks out over a secondary square. You'll see it easily from the air. Go there straight away! State that you know where the pirates and I are, and that he must come at once!"

Tara stopped for a moment. "Here: take this. It's my signet ring. Show it to him. He'll know it's from me. That's your proof that you know me."

Ariel turned to leave, but Tara stopped her again. "One more thing! When you land in Sea Sprit, could you fold your wings right away, so no one sees them? So that you don't... uh... attract undue attention!"

Ariel smiled. Of course she could, and, before Tara's eyes, they folded up in a complicated process that occurred in a blink. Then she unfolded them and took flight for Sea Sprit.

Now for Jarvis's mansion, thought Tara. Up she climbed the remainder of the hill and approached a window. It was closed and shuttered. It was small also, though, prompting Tara to think that it might not let into a larger room but to a small one and hence was more likely to be empty.

The shutters were locked fast and would not yield to either tugs and pushes. She cast about for something with which to smash the lock on the shutters and so open it. No, that would make too much noise. Then she recollected her new-found princess purse. The telescoping rod, extended and used as a lever, could surely pry open any shutter, no matter how tightly locked.

Indeed, at sufficient length, it took only the smallest push on it to spring the shutter open. Handy, that, she thought, as she returned it to her purse. It was enormously strong and yet flexible and compact. She had originally thought it the least of the three items in the purse, but it had been the first she had called on for help.

Tara climbed through the window and into the darkness beyond. It turned out to be a sort of storeroom. Fortunately, the door leading out of it was unlocked. Out she slipped and into a hallway. Around a corner, she recognized the route through which she had entered the mansion for the reception days before. Good. She would start there, in the ballroom, where Ariel had reported Jarvis was—maybe already with the pirates?

Up to the ballroom stairs she crept, staying to the shadows. She didn't hear anyone around, which was good. Though, come to think of it, where were the servants?

Tara began to discern faint, indistinct voices coming from the ballroom. Up the stairs she crawled, then behind a large ornamental cabinet just beyond the threshold. Now she could hear them better, and even see them, far down at the other end of the room near the large doors leading to the balcony she recollected from the night of the gala function. She pressed herself flat against the cabinet and strained to listen.

First she recognized the voice of Jarvis; he was speaking. Then, when he paused, and without difficulty, she heard unmistakably a voice that she thought she would never forget: that of that horrible pirate captain Braunzin. She hardly breathed for straining to listen and didn't dare look around the cabinet for fear of being spotted.

"—'s a purty nice place as ye gots here, Jarvis!" Braunzin was saying.

"What are you driving at, you old sea dog?"

"Jes' sayin', purty nice… all this here, wit' mirrers and all, and lights, and sich. Aye. Ha. Nice, huh, lads?"

There was murmured assent. So, there were a number of them present, and not just the captain, realized Tara, her blood running cold. How many, she wondered.

"And you'd'a had something about the same yourself, if you had kept some of what you'd been given—rather than drink it away!"

There was a moment of shocked silence, and Tara, despite her anger at him, feared for Jarvis's life. But instead of a furious eruption, there came a roar of coarse laughter. "'Drink'? Drink, he sez! Well, never did I! Ha! Ha! An' I cud use a drink now, methinks! Huh. Aye, lads, wha' 'ya thinks a' that?"

There was an answering roar of approval from what Tara now gauged to be at least five or six voices.

"Nothing of the sort; absolutely not at all!" Jarvis admonished them, having to raise his voice to be heard above the din.

"Oh? Butcha wants us to leave, eh? Ha! Well, ha! I thinks we needs us some money to leave, eh, boys? Somethin' so's ta buys us passage outta here. Eh, boys?"

There was another growl of assent.

The voices then sank lower, and Tara guessed some sort of negotiation must be in progress. Just as well, she thought, as she had enough to have them all apprehended and punished for the traitors they had so clearly revealed themselves to be. She stood cautiously and began to back her way to the stairs down to the ground floor. But in backing, she stumbled against a display table set against the wall and fell sprawling to the floor. Worse, the porcelain vase atop it teetered from the impact and, before she could dive to catch it, it tumbled to the floor with a tremendous crash.

Jarvis whirled and, seeing Tara picking herself up off the floor, turned as white as sea foam. "By the Great Kraken! It's Queen Ysolde!" he choaked.

"I can explain everything…!" he began to babble, but Braunzin cut him off.

"Ya' ol' fool! It's that Tara princess! Git her, boys! She's our ticket agin!"

Tara had just enough time to regain her feet, reach into her princess purse and throw up into the air before her a pinch of the dazzle dust. Though only a pinch, Tara threw it high, and it spread out and descended before her as a curtain would. The beams from the myriad lamps and mirrors lining the ballroom were caught up and reflected in the drifting, settling motes, and the wall before her sparkled and flashed as if of a thousand tiny mirrors.

The four pirates rushing toward her howled in pain and staggered but charged on, drawing their cutlasses as they stumbled forward. Tara reached back into her princess purse and this time grasped the marvelous telescoping rod. "Extend four feet," she commanded softly, and it promptly stretched to the length of a staff, featherweight and unbreakably sturdy.

At that very moment, galloping madly up the road to Jarvis's mansion rode Rohanic, followed distantly by his corporals and the rest of his contingent. A strange woman had appeared before him not long before and, producing a signet ring, had identified herself as a friend of Her Highness the Princess.

Rohanic had been astonished. "A friend? Of Princess Tara? How do you know her?"

The woman had thrust the ring toward him and, her face betraying great anxiety, had replied, "Unimportant! See her ring, here, as proof of our friendship; I come to tell you she is in danger!"

"What sort of danger? Where is she?"

The woman had half-turned and pointed up the hill. "In the Jarvis house on the bluff. Quickly! The pirates are there also!"

A multitude of other questions had raced through Rohanic's mind, such as how this woman knew Tara, and how Tara had come to be at Jarvis's mansion, and how the pirates were there also, unbeknownst to anyone else in Sea Sprit, but the woman had thrust the ring forward a second time, insisting that Rohanic confirm its authenticity. Yes, it was the Princess's. He returned it. "How come you by this ring?"

"I am her friend. She gave it to me! You must go immediately!" With that, the woman had turned and fled the room. Rohanic had jumped from his seat and run after her, but she was nowhere to be found. Impossibly strange, he had thought, but he was duty bound to investigate and had called to his men to ready their mounts. But as he had begun to ride, he had quickened his pace, thinking that, if the stranger were right, and Her Highness were in danger, it would behoove him to ride as fast as he could. Very shortly, he was galloping up the road, the nostrils of his horse flaring, and he himself panting from the exertion.

Tara sized up the four pirates rushing her. Taking the rod by one end, she stooped and swung it wide and fast, connecting with the knees of the one furthest to the right. With a yelp, he collapsed heavily.

Tara was by no means an expert with a staff. Her specialty had always been bow and arrow. Still, she had managed to cadge an occasional lesson from the guards' instructor, and she felt confident enough to parry the wild and clumsy thrusts of the pirates at least for a time, particularly since their eyes were still half-dazzled. She just had to hold them off until Rohanic or anyone showed to relieve her, which she fervently hoped would be soon.

Braunzin and the other two pirates watched in high amusement as the three remaining pirates grimly pressed their advantage of greater numbers. Occasionally, Braunzin would hoot when Tara would catch one of the pirates on the side of the face with the rod and leave a stinging welt. "Ha! Spirit! I likes it!" he guffawed in approval once.

Even so, Tara was being forced steadily backwards. Throwing a quick glance over her shoulder, she saw she was too far from the stairs to break and run. Unless help came quickly, she would be overpowered shortly.

To his complete amazement, as Rohanic rounded the last bend around which lay the mansion, he saw again the same woman who had spoken to him in the city below at the steps up to the front door. Impossible, he muttered to himself. He had ridden at full speed; how could she have arrived before him?

"The ballroom! Quickly! There is fighting!" she urged him.

Up the stairs dashed Rohanic, drawing his sword as he ran. He burst through the door with his shoulder, turned to look back for the mysterious woman, but she was gone again. A witch of some sort, he thought. Was it a trap? But he could hear for himself, upstairs, what sounded like a sustained scuffle and occasional grunts, oaths, and shouts from what was clearly some sort of struggle.

Rohanic leapt the stairs to the ballroom three at a time to find an exhausted Tara backed against a wall by three ruffians, though their inexpert swordsmanship hindered their efforts as much as advanced them. "Unhand Her Highness!" he roared and charged, his broadsword raised.

The pirates whirled to confront the more proximate threat. Braunzin immediately sent in the other two who had heretofore held back to exchange sneering observations on their fumbling junior colleagues. For a wild moment, it looked to be an even match: Rohanic, animated as if by the fury of ten, against six pirates. But their greater numbers were too much, and even Rohanic was forced, step by step, back to the wall to join Tara.

It was then that the rest of Rohanic's contingent came clattering up the stairs. The ragged and ill-trained pirates were no match for the professional guardsmen. There was the briefest of scuffles, and the pirates were disarmed or surrendered.

Tara spotted Braunzin at the far end of the room sidling toward the double doors leading to the balcony. "Stop him! He's going to get away!" But Braunzin was too far away to be intercepted. In a moment he had reached the doors' handles to fling them wide and escape.

Indistinct through the windows was a figure who, to Rohanic, appeared to be the same strange woman he had encountered in Sea Sprit and again at the foot of the stairs. Now, somehow, she was on the balcony. The doors rattled and flexed with the desperate strength of Braunzin but held.

"It's her again!" gasped Rohanic, pointing. "She's holding the doors!"

Sprinting, Rohanic covered the length of the ballroom in short seconds. Braunzin spun and, with surprising dexterity, slashed with his cutlass in a sharp chopping motion that, had Rohanic not deftly parried, would surely have cloven him in two. Before Braunzin could reply with a thrust, Rohanic had dashed the cutlass from Braunzin's grip, and he was staring in horror down the length of the broadsword's blade, a tiny drop of blood welling at his throat from the prick of its point. Tara, arriving a few seconds behind Rohanic, just caught sight of Ariel pulling her telescoping rod through from the two outside door handles, wave quickly, and flit away.

Tara kicked the cutlass so that it skittered far down the ballroom's intricate parquetry. Once Braunzin had been frisked for hidden weapons, of which they found several, Rohanic sheathed his sword and, turning to the double doors, opened one wide. "Now I find out!—"

But, to Rohanic's stunned surprise, the balcony was deserted. "Where did she go…?" he demanded of no one in particular. "Wasn't she just here?"

"Nobody's here," Tara observed, joining him at the threshold to the balcony and electing to state the obvious. "Maybe the door was just stuck, and that was why he couldn't get out? Bad luck for him, right?"

"But I saw…!"

Tara made a show of inspecting the empty balcony. "I don't see anyone here, Lieutenant. I don't know where anyone could have gone either, yes?"

Rohanic shook his head in disbelief. "It's impossible! She showed me your signet ring in Sea Sprit, she was at the base of the steps to this house when I arrived—despite galloping as fast as my horse could carry me—and she was on the balcony to prevent the pirate's escape! How?"

Tara grinned and shrugged. "I'm lucky to have such a guardian—wherever she might be! You arrived just in time to prevent my recapture!"

Rohanic glanced over at her sharply, but Tara had already turned to go back inside.

Two days later, in Sea Sprit's central square, Tara approached again an elevated stand erected in the very center, constructed around the plinth of a statue to some forgotten municipal leader. Again, the gentry of the town had been assembled for the occasion. They stood to the rear and at a respectful distance from a podium placed equidistant between the edges. Before the stand milled the citizens of Sea Sprit and even some from the surrounding farmland. The atmosphere was expectant and hushed.

There was a tumult of horseshoes on cobblestones. An ornate carriage rolled up to the stand, none other than the carriage of the disgraced sea captain, Jarvis. The door opened and Princess Tara of Brythrony, in a sky-blue dress trimmed at the cuffs and the hem in cedar brown, emerged into the bright sunlight. Her white sash of royalty, pinned at shoulder and waist, fluttered gently in the salt sea breeze.

Tara mounted the steps at a dignified pace. "Greetings, Esteemed Nobility of Sea Sprit!" she addressed those on the stand using her "court" accent. They bowed or curtsied deeply and very nearly as one in response. Tara favored them throughout with a reserved, regal smile.

The round, ruddy mayor approached and swept off his great hat in a deep bow to complete the formalities. Tara maintained the same regal smile for him but added some murmured words of thanks she imagined to be suitable. Then she turned briskly to the raised dais and faced the citizenry of Sea Sprit.

"Loyal Subjects!" she cried, switching to the everyday accent and gesturing toward the crowd with one arm outstretched for emphasis. They fell silent to a man, woman and child. Another half-second Tara waited, then continued. "It is my great pleasure to speak to you again! And I come before you with good news!"

Tara paused again.

"In weeks past, your fair city was besieged by pirates, who preyed upon your commerce and threatened your livelihoods. But now it is my very great pleasure to inform you that this threat has been eliminated. Their ship is a wreck on the seabed floor. Its cannon, which spat fire and death, is no more. Finally, not two days ago, the last members of its crew and captain were apprehended by none other than Lieutenant Rohanic and his men of your kingdom's guards!"

The crowd cheered lustily. Tara motioned for Rohanic, also seated on the platform, to rise.

"The arrest of these pirates is an act of heroism and deserves recognition. Thus, it is my great pleasure to brevet Lieutenant Rohanic for his courage and service." Tara requested Rohanic to stand next to her. "Lieutenant Rohanic, you are henceforth to be addressed as Guards Captain Rohanic!"

The crowd cheered again, and Rohanic saluted Her Highness and the crowd and resumed his seat.

Tara continued after the cheers had largely died away. "Now to the unfortunate part of what I have to relate to you." Tara paused, as if to draw her breath. "There was a traitor amongst you. One you trusted and who occupied a position of respect in your community."

Many promptly cast their eyes downward in the traditional Brythrony expression of disapprobation toward those convicted of the most heinous crimes, but from others came a storm of catcalls, hisses, and shouted imprecations against Jarvis. She motioned for the crowd to be still so that she might continue, but in vain. At length she looked to the mayor for assistance, who promptly stood and roared out, in a most impressive voice for a man of his stature, for silence, and at last the tumult stilled.

"Thank you! To continue: this malefactor has been apprehended and will face justice."

There were renewed cheers but with darker cries for vengeance as well.

Tara held up her hand for silence. "For his crimes, his accounts, his housing, and all his possessions are at once forfeit to the crown.

"However, Sea Sprit and its citizens have suffered much from him and his accomplices, and it would not be just for you to go uncompensated. Therefore, representing the Royal House of Hession, of the Kingdom of Brythrony, I today deed to Sea Sprit and its population, from now until forever, all of his property and effects, which I understand to primarily consist of his mansion, its contents, and the grounds immediately surrounding it. These I give to you for your municipal use and enjoyment! And," she quickly added, the thought suddenly occurring to her, "which you might well consider adopting henceforth as your center of municipal governance and administration!"

The crowd leapt to its feet as one, and the clamor rang from one side of the square to the other, repeatedly and ever more loudly. Tara responded with her reserved smile. Good idea, she told herself, silently, to suggest its use as their municipal administrative center. They should surely prefer it to the hideous, squat building she had dedicated on first arriving. Without question, the view from it would be much better.

"I thank you all, again, for the very kind hospitality you have shown me during my visit!" And with this, Tara stepped back from the podium. The mayor approached, and in a babble of thanks, expressed his and the city's gratitude for her magnanimous gifts.

Tara encored as her response her reserved, regal smile.

After another flourish of the great hat, the mayor stepped to the podium and the din of the crowd abated ever so slightly. "People of Sea Sprit! We are grateful indeed to the Royal House of Hession—most grateful!—for ending the pirate menace. We entreated Your Highness for assistance, and we received it, in fullest and promptest form!"

The mayor paused, now quite out of breath. After a moment's panting, he resumed. "And, and! And we are most grateful—most grateful indeed!— for the generous gift of the mansion. Most grateful! In our thanks, and speaking for Sea Sprit, I hereby decree before you all that this mansion is to henceforth be known as 'Princess House'!"

The uproar from the crowd was immediate and tremendous, and the commotion echoed and re-echoed throughout the square. Tara took a half-step forward in acknowledgement, and began to form her features to resume the now-familiar regal smile but, her eyes filled with the cheering, frenetic crowds, she found herself swept up in its emotion. Before she could stifle it, before she could bow even fractionally to cover it, an elated smile had begun to steal across her face, and tears had started from her eyes. Only through a supreme effort did she regain control of herself, yet, transported as she was by the host of joyous, upturned faces, all cheering as one for their town, their princess and their kingdom, she could not help half-raising both arms in a kind of open-armed embrace of the multitude and mouthing, speechless, her gratitude.

Then she recovered herself. "GC Rohanic!" she called.

"Your Highness!" he responded, jumping to his feet.

"We can be ready to leave?"

"Your escort awaits Your Highness at the rear."

"Then let us depart."

"Your Highness!" responded GC Rohanic, and Tara stepped quickly down the stairs at the rear of the platform, Rohanic at her heels, to the surprise and confusion of the gentry of Sea Sprit, who hastily arose in a series of waves to acknowledge her departure.

A few moments later, Tara was seated side-saddle atop Daystar. "Daystar, oh Daystar, how are you?" cooed Tara, stroking his mane gently.

"For Stonedell, GC Rohanic! If you please!"

"By Your command, Your Highness. Guards, forward!" called Rohanic from the head of the procession, and the train set off.

That evening, again in Sylvan, and at the same inn as before, Tara retired for the evening after another simple meal. She heaved a sigh of contentment, delighted to be back in a comfortable, if simple, bed.

They would overnight the following night at some town other than Jiswith, Tara had decided, so that for just a bit longer she could travel incognito. Enough princessing, surely, for this trip! She paused at the open shutters in her room to gaze into the night sky and smiled in satisfaction. For the rest of the journey back, she would be nothing more than a local noblewoman, not Princess Tara, and would silently celebrate her wonderful, glorious anonymity.

Tara was seated at the private dining table of the royal family at Castle Stonedell. Her father was questioning her with great interest.

"So, how in the world did you escape those pirates?"

"Well, like I was saying, the ship caught fire and all the pirates jumped overboard. So, it wasn't really that I escaped, but that the ship broke apart. That's how I got free."

"That's an amazing story! What did you do when you were in the water? I didn't know you could swim."

"Well, I can't really. Not so well. And that's something I really intend to fix, believe me! So I just, well, floated. On some debris. Flotsam… kind of, sort of thing."

"You clung to flotsam?"

"Exactly!"

"And you floated all the way to shore?"

"Um, no, just to an island. I washed ashore on an island."

"Poor dear!" interrupted her mother. "You must have nearly starved!"

"I really was hungry. For sure. But there was a spring there. So there was water to drink."

"What about food? What did you eat?"

"There was, you know, fruit. Berries. Bark."

"Bark! You had to peel bark off trees? Like some sort of animal? Poor darling!"

"Now, Armorica, she had to eat whatever she could to survive!"

"Of course, but… bark! How horrible…"

Maybe that had been bit far, with the bark. She had only thrown that in to be what she imagined was convincing. Wasn't bark edible though? Because some deer eat bark in the winter, she recollected.

"And then I made a raft and floated to shore and then got back to Sea Sprit." Best not to mention Marina and her role; her parents would hardly believe her anyway. They might think she was crazy and in need of "rest" or, worse still, more princessing.

"Indeed. And what's this about capturing the pirate captain? And Jarvis?"

"Oh, that. That was all Rohanic. He did all that." Best not to mention Ariel either. If they wouldn't go for a mermaid, what would they think of a winged woman with a magically extending pole?

"Rohanic swore that he encountered a woman who kept urging him to rescue you. Swore it. He said she seemed to be everywhere!"

Tara smiled deprecatorily. "I think he's just being modest. It was his conscience motivating him, I'm sure. That's why I brevet-promoted him.

"Quite right, too."

"Besides, how can anyone be everywhere anyway? Rohanic can't expect us to believe that!"

Neither one of her parents had anything to say to that.

Tara thought to ask a question. "What about the pirates and Jarvis? What will become of them?"

Childeric was grim. "There is a justice for traitors. They will be tried—though there is little doubt of their guilt—and be punished appropriately. I don't expect they will trouble Sea Sprit or the high seas ever again."

Tara asked no more on that, thinking it best to leave it there.

Later, Tara returned to her bedroom in the North Tower. It had been fun to have an adventure or two, but it would be nice to sleep in her own bed again.

Tara looked around her room. The walls were a dull, drab grey. Maybe it might be nice to have them painted blue. Wouldn't that remind her of the Coral Castle, where it was always such a lovely deep blue? Or the sky, where Ariel lived in her floating castle?

On impulse, Tara stood up and walked to a chest of drawers opposite her bed. She pulled open the top drawer, which yielded with resistance. That was good; Tara liked that. This was because in the drawer, toward the very back, Tara kept some of her most precious mementoes. To this small collection she would add her princess purse. Secreting it in the very rearmost depths, Tara came across something she knew well. Her fingers closed around it and she withdrew the ring of her grandmother. She smiled. Her grandmother, Ysolde. What would she have thought of Ariel and Marina? Tara squeezed it in her fist tightly and then replaced it in the drawer, next to her princess purse.

Evening was drawing on. Tara moved to the window and threw open the shutters. The stars were starting to show far overhead and the leafy tops of the trees were receding into the gathering darkness. Tara looked up into the velvety black and thought for a moment. Then she retraced her steps to the chest, pulled open the drawer and reached again for her princess purse. Out of it she pulled the vial of the substance which created message bubbles.

She wet her hands at the wash basin, then dripped a drop from the vial into one hand. She clapped the other to it and slowly pulled them apart to form a bubble; into it she whispered, "Hey, Marina, just to let you know everything is fine with me and I'm back home again! I hope you and your family are good too!" She wished Marina well and that she hoped to see her again soon, then whispered Marina's name and blew the bubble into the night with a puff. The bubble drifted off in the direction of the road along which Tara and her procession had so lately come from Sea Sprit.

Tara watched the bubble vanish into the darkness.

She reached for the vial again and let fall another drop into her still-wet palm. This time she addressed her other new friend. "Hi, Ariel! I'm back home again! Thank you so much for all your help in getting back to Sea Sprit, and especially for hastening to my rescue. And," she giggled, "for preventing that terrible pirate from escaping! Rohanic still can't figure out what happened!" Then she murmured "Princess Ariel, of Cloud Castle," and blew the bubble softly into the night. It headed straight up into the darkening sky. Up to Cloud Castle, mused Tara wistfully, and followed it with her eyes until it was out of sight, merging with the darkness and the twinkling stars.

Several flights downstairs and in another wing of the castle, Childeric and Armorica relaxed in the royal suite. Queen Armorica sighed. "I can't believe she was stranded on an island and had to build a raft to float off it!"

"Yes, that's very exciting, isn't it?"

"Thank goodness she's safe! After all those adventures with pirates and then in Sea Sprit and on and on!"

Indeed, though Childeric. The raft story was especially interesting. He wondered how she had been able to do that, without a hammer or nails or anything of that nature to hold the logs together. To his knowledge, his daughter didn't know any of the knots that would be needed to bind such a platform together. "And having to eat bark," he added, trying to keep his voice from becoming wry.

"So awful! I can't imagine."

"Neither can I." No, and what about what Rohanic had said? That there had also been some woman who had been helping Tara? No, she couldn't have been everywhere, as Rohanic had claimed. But Rohanic was absolutely trustworthy and not given to exaggeration. There was something more here, thought Childeric, but Rohanic didn't know any more. Only Tara would know, and she had stuck to her story.

"Anyway," he offered, "as I recall, you had sworn that, should Tara return safe and sound, you would not ask her to go out any more on any of these 'Season' events."

"I said that? I don't think so! Why, it's even more important than before, I should think."

Childeric let his facial expression convey his disbelief at what his wife had said.

"Why, yes! More than ever we have to make sure she doesn't become some sort of half-wild tomboy! Eating bark, indeed! No man will ever want to marry her!"

"Someone married your mother. She was somewhat of a tomboy."

Armorica sniffed. "That was a different day and age. This is today. You must understand that.

"No, absolutely not. Tara must attend the Season, participating fully, because she lives in today's world and must find a husband in today's world.

"And that is how it is done."

Then, with finality, "No one today has time or interest in a tomboy."

Childeric turned away, not wanting his wife to see the half-smile spreading across his face. Impossible to convince his wife otherwise when it came to the Season, he knew. But, at the same time, he knew it would be just as difficult to convince Tara that The Season should be important to her. For the moment, though, it hardly mattered. He heaved a contented sigh of relief. Tara was back, the pirate problem had been solved and the taxes collected from Jiswith! Tara, all told, had done well! Tomboy or not.

The Library of Syssalin

"Aa-choo!" Princess of the Realm Tara sneezed. Princess of the Realm Tara had a cold, and a nasty one.

"Ugh! It's, oh, it's, it's all over my face! So disgusting!" Tara reached for her handkerchief and wiped her nose, then, absentmindedly, wiped her eyes and face from the detritus of the previous sneeze. Then she remembered—with a start—that she had wiped her face *after* wiping away the nasal mucus draining from her nostrils in what seemed like a never-ending flow.

So, she had just wiped her own snot all over her face.

"UGH! That. Has. Got to be. The most DISGUSTING thing! Ever!" she whispered fiercely to no one and flung the handkerchief toward a hamper at the side of the bed, moved there expressly for the purpose of catching used handkerchiefs.

Princess of the Realm Tara lay sprawled across her bed, writhing in misery. How could this be so awful? She was tired without having done anything, was hungry every ten minutes and then not, and her face was swollen and puffy. Her nose had turned a bright red from wiping and blowing it so much.

Speaking of which… she reached for another handkerchief from the now badly askew stack on the table next to the bed.

What an awful cold she had. Exceptionally awful. From somewhere, someone; she didn't know. The only person she knew who could not have given it to her was her horse, Daystar. Daystar would never give her something like that, she consoled herself. Even if he could.

Also, her new friends Marina and Ariel never would. Of that she was sure. They were far too considerate and kind. Why, Marina probably couldn't even get a cold! Probably the same for Ariel. Speaking of which, it had now been a few weeks since she had come back from her adventures in Sea Sprit. She wondered what they were doing, Ariel in her castle in the clouds, and Marina far below in her castle amongst the coral. And she, Tara, in her castle midway between the two.

Tara rolled over and stared at the ceiling. They had to be doing something a lot more fun than she. When would she see them next? It didn't seem possible, ever, at least without an extended and complicated explanation to her parents, who never believe her anyway. Tara rolled to her side. How could she see them again, she began to ponder, when suddenly her diaphragm began to convulse as she felt another sneeze coming on, and she was wrenched back to the present moment. This absolutely had to be one of the most terrible things to have happened to her in a long while.

"Aa-aa-AA-CHOO!"

It was so nasty, she muttered, reaching for yet another handkerchief.

Just as she was tossing that in the general direction of the hamper, there was a hesitant knock on the door. "Dear? Are you in there? Tara?"

Who else would be in her room, sneezing like this? "Yes, Mom. I'm here. Sneezing."

"Tara, I brought you some more handkerchiefs. I thought to check on you."

That was nice, Tara allowed. She sat up on the bed, stood and shuffled to the door to open it.

Princess Tara kept to herself in a small suite of rooms in the North Tower. Despite her parents' numerous suggestions at numerous times in numerous veiled and not-so-veiled ways, she steadfastly refused to move to the ground floor and into what they insisted were more princess-like quarters. There were several reasons for this. First, Princess Tara had everything she needed in the rooms in the North Tower. These consisted mostly of her bed; a window that looked out on the fields in which she often rode Daystar; a semi-secret exit to the rooftop and the other towers, and a chest of drawers in which were hidden, in the top drawer, toward the very back, her most precious mementos.

A second reason were the stairs themselves. Her parents argued that the steep and dark flights were dangerous to ascend each night going to bed but Tara thought them one of the most important features of the North Tower suite because they were a strong deterrent to too many or too regular visits from her parents. On those rare occasions when they did climb the stairs to her suite, Tara met them on the landing outside. But Tara thought to make an exception today, partly because it was thoughtful of her mother to bring up more handkerchiefs, and also because Tara was too achy and miserable to resist anyway.

Tara opened the door with a sudden jerk. Her mother was standing just beyond, her hand partially extended and holding a short stack of handkerchiefs. She was clearly surprised by her daughter's sudden appearance. "Oh, Tara! I just, well, didn't expect—"

Didn't expect me to actually open the door, finished Tara silently, but smiled and said aloud "Hi, Mom; thank you so much for bringing those up for me. Come on in!"

Her mother took a tentative step across the threshold, as if she were stepping into a strange and foreign land. Her eyes wandered to the left, the right, up to the ceiling, and then around, unable to disguise her interest. How long had it been since she had been in this part of Castle Stonedell? "Thanks, dear."

"Come on in, Mom," repeated Tara and slouched onto the bed. "Thanks again for the handkerchiefs, I could really use them." She motioned to the diminishing pile at the table by her bed. "I kind of need a few more."

Her mother nodded. "How are you feeling, dear?" she asked, stepping to a chair opposite Tara, gingerly shifting to one side with her thumb and forefinger a white sash tossed over its back. It was the white sash of her royalty, her mother noted, the one Tara was supposed to wear to all formal events. She was about to admonish her daughter that she should take better care of it and hang it up properly so that it would always look presentable, but stopped herself. Tara was clearly feeling poorly; best to just let it go on this one occasion.

Queen Armorica lowered herself delicately into the chair. "Feeling any better, hm?"

Tara sniffed, then darted out her right hand to the table for another handkerchief. She felt a sneeze coming on. "Oh, wai-!—" but none came. "Um, maybe better, Mom. Maybe a little."

"Poor dear." Armorica looked around. It didn't appear as if anyone had been in this room for a long time, and by which she meant anyone to clean it. There was dust everywhere, except along the most trafficked corridors, such as the one leading from the bed to the door and from the bed to the chest of drawers. And to the window. And then there was a spiderweb up high in the corner at the ceiling. And there were crumbs and, things—who knew what those were—over there.

And the handkerchiefs fallen from the bedside table, though those must be recent—

"Hello, Mom? Are you listening to me?"

"Of course, dear."

"So, what do you think?"

"Um, I guess, well," Armorica inspected her daughter's face carefully. It looked innocent enough. "I guess, yes, I guess that's fine. Yes."

"Thanks, Mom. I think that would help a lot!"

"Really?"

"Yes. Really."

Armorica suddenly became unsure of herself and what she had agreed to and began to reconsider her most recent answer. "But I think I should check with your father first to make sure." That still left her wondering what she should be checking with him about.

Tara watched her mother carefully and noted that one side of her mouth had pulled down in just the slightest hint of a frown. From many years of observation, she knew that often betrayed uncertainty. "Sure, Mom. Go ahead."

Armorica looked down at her feet and the dust prints she had made in the floor, then back to her daughter. "Uh, tell me again…"

"Mom! Were you not listening to me?"

"Of course, I was!"

"Then why…?"

"No, no, it's all right, don't worry!—"

"Because, you always ask if I'm listening to you, and it just looked like—"

"Yes, yes; you're right. It's fine. Don't worry."

"Thank you, Mom. I think it will be very good. I do believe a few days in Sea Sprit, in the ocean air, will help me recover from this illness more quickly. I think, also, that the people of Sea Sprit won't mind at all that I'm there."

Armorica considered. Sea Sprit wasn't all that far away, something like a day or two, and Tara would surely be welcomed there. The fresh air might indeed help her recover more quickly. Why not? She smiled at her daughter. "Sounds like a good idea, dear. For a few days. Then hurry back!"

Armorica had a sudden idea. "Oh, and please take something nice to wear! There might be a ball or reception in your honor!"

Tara frowned, and reached for another handkerchief. "Mom! I'm not well, remember? It's hardly a good idea for me to be getting together with people feeling as I am, right?"

Armorica's disappointment showed. "I suppose you're right. Not as you are."

"Yes. Thank you, Mo—aaa-CHOO!"

Armorica hastily stood to leave. "Will you need help getting ready?"

In between successive sneezes, her daughter waved her off to indicate she would not.

"Very good then. We'll send word to Sea Sprit that you will be arriving in a few days for a stay of, oh, maybe a week. But, that your visit will be low key."

Tara expressed her gratitude with a smile and a wave, while blowing her nose loudly. Her mother backed out of the room, closing the door behind her.

Tara waited a decent interval, listening for the steady tread of her mother's footsteps down the stairs to die away, then went straight to the chest opposite her bed. She pulled open eagerly the top drawer and reached all the way into the back for the princess purse stuffed there. After a moment's groping, she pulled it out and withdrew from it a small vial. She uncapped it but, before pouring out a drop, reconsidered. Didn't she need a bit of moisture for her hands—and certainly not the nasal mucus? Wetting her hands with a small splash of water from the cup at her bed, she let fall a drop from the vial into one hand, clapped the other to it softly, and then pulled them apart to produce a glistening bubble, slightly smaller than the palm of her hand.

"Hello, Marina! I'll be back in Sea Sprit soon! Can you believe it? Maybe we get could get together again? It would be so great to see you again!" She explained why she would be there and gave a rough estimate as to when and puffed on the bubble to send it on its way. Ariel was sent a similar message immediately afterwards.

What fun, thought Tara. And the idea of combining an escape from dampish Castle Stonedell with a visit to the seaside, where she could see her friends had occurred to her only on the spur of the moment, even as she had been speaking with her mother. Importantly, her mother had agreed. This meant her father would as well, because that was the way things always worked in these matters. Tara smiled. It would be good to see Marina and Ariel again. Now to kick this cold, and quick!

In conversation with his wife later that day, King Childeric was supportive of Tara passing a restorative week in Sea Sprit. "It sounds like a good idea. The fresh ocean air will be healthful." He mused for a moment. "Maybe we'll visit Sea Sprit as well as she finishes her convalescence. I've become rather interested in the little city that the pirates were so lately terrorizing!"

Armorica agreed. "Yes, and this will get her out some too. Which she sorely needs more of. Even if Sea Sprit isn't exactly a new place and certainly not the grandest. Tara wants her visit to be low key, but there will simply have to be some kind of reception! There simply must! Which is why I have told her to pack something in which she can be presentable." Armorica made a mental note to follow up with Tara on this. Tara must be sure to take something creditable to wear, and she mustn't forget her white sash. The same sash which had probably been hanging casually off a chair for days.

Which sash would surely need a stern pressing beforehand thought Armorica, fiercely.

"Yes," she said aloud, composing herself again. "It might be quite nice to visit little Sea Sprit. Perhaps just for a few days. We could see this newly named Princess House too. By then, Tara will have recovered and there could surely be a reception for all of us. And, why not? Yes! It could even take place in Princess House!"

Childeric considered his wife. She was growing more enthusiastic about Tara's second trip to Sea Sprit by the minute. What a pleasant contrast to her feelings about the first trip.

The next day, as Tara was gathering up a few of the personal effects she wanted to take with her to Sea Sprit, in through the open window floated a bubble. It hovered just over and beside her, patiently, until she stood upright and noticed it. She smiled. From one of her friends! She stretched out her left hand and down it settled to nestle just inside her palm. Tara blew on it with the softest of breaths, and it burst. She heard Marina's voice.

"How wonderful, Tara! It would be GREAT to see you again! But I hope you're feeling okay? Anyway—"

Tara smiled. Marina was irrepressible.

"—I can swim over and see you, no problem! And, guess what? I showed the purse to my father, and he decided to do some further research on that city. It's really interesting! I'll tell you more when you're here! See you soon!"

Tara let fall her hand as Marina's voice died away. The city. The ruined city, the rubble of which she had wandered through a few times looking for what had turned out to be the princess purses. Marina's father, King Aenon, had inspected the purse and its contents and been intrigued enough to look into this city further.

She wondered what that could mean. Maybe something exciting? It had to be. If it was nothing, Marina would not have bothered to mention it. Tara shivered with anticipation. This cold she had contracted was turning out to be one of the best things that had happened to her in weeks!

Several days later, her parents gathered at the carriage window as Tara prepared to set off. She had learned from the first trip to Sea Sprit that it was better to ride by carriage. Daystar could trot alongside, rider-less.

Besides, it was better in keeping with the image she wanted to maintain of still being ill.

Tara waved with her right hand, in her left a fistful of handkerchiefs. "Good-bye! Don't worry about me!"

Her mother was speaking. "Take care, dear! Get plenty of rest! Do not—do not—exert yourself!"

"I'll try not to!"

Now her father addressed her. "Tara, please take care of yourself and get well. We'll come ourselves in a week to join you. It will be a nice holiday for all of us. So we shall see you shortly!"

"Yes! How wonderful!" cried Tara, the carriage starting to pull away. Inwardly, she found their promise disconcerting. Her parents coming out to collect her? In a week? Not that she was so anxious to stay longer, but it could be problematic if they were to have any contact with people who might report that she had been far more active than a recuperating princess might be expected to be. Tara bit her lip, becoming anxious. No, a week should be long enough. That was plenty of time to see Marina and Ariel. Plenty of time to go on long—unescorted—walks. And rides, alone, on Daystar. All of which would restore her spirits and health. There'd be enough time for all this and to dispel any rumors before her parents arrived.

Tara settled back in her seat, coughing and then wiping her nose again with a handkerchief. Come to think of it, maybe her parents wouldn't come at all. Maybe they were just talking and had no real intention. Or maybe they'd change their minds. Tara's spirits began to lift. The sooner they got to Sea Sprit, the better.

"Rohanic! Guards Captain Rohanic!" she called, peering out of the carriage window ever so slightly.

"Your Highness!" came the prompt answer from the head of the column.

"You needn't have concerns on either the road or the ride as we make for Sea Sprit! I am anxious to breathe the fresh ocean air and recover!"

"Of course, Your Highness," he replied, and the column increased its pace appreciably. What a contrast, thought Brevetted Guards Captain Rohanic, pricking again the flanks of his mount. How great her interest was on this occasion to reach Sea Sprit, compared with her previous disinterest.

They arrived two days later in Sea Sprit, making reasonable time, even though the carriageway was in poor condition at stretches. We simply must improve these roads, thought Tara with annoyance, as she was sometimes violently jounced about the interior. Handkerchiefs scattered everywhere with each bump. Tara soon learnt to segregate those which had been used appreciably from those which had not.

They also detoured, at Tara's request, to avoid Jiswith. Tara was worried that her re-appearance might prompt the townsfolk to rebel at what they might perceive to be a further effort to squeeze more taxes from them.

They were met by a single gendarme at the city's limits, Stonedell having emphasized that this visit was meant to be entirely private and not one of state. After conferring with Rohanic, Tara learned that Sea Sprit intended to host them at Princess House, which had not yet been converted to the municipality's administrative center.

"Princess House?" she asked. "But won't that be conspicuous?"

Rohanic acknowledged that Princess House would be more visible. However, it was perhaps the only location in the city at which her entire retinue could be comfortably housed all at once. "Moreover," Rohanic pointed out, "the house has a fine garden, in which Your Majesty might take her repose, if she should be of such a mind."

Tara considered. At first she had been inclined to balk at staying at such a high-profile location, but, as she thought about it, it might actually be perfect. Situated as it was high up on a bluff, no one would see her comings and goings. "Very good," she replied. "Excellent idea. My parents intend to join in a week or thereabouts; it should be commodious enough to host us all, I expect." And, Tara reminded herself, and recollecting the lovely ballroom from her own reception upon her first visit, do so in lovely style.

"What a thoughtful idea," she concluded, and with that, the procession at once turned onto a side road leading to the former mansion of Captain Jarvis.

Tara was received in the ballroom she admired so much and offered refreshments, which she received with a gracious smile, and then was shown to the former sea captain's rooms. These consisted of a suite off the main hallway of the second floor of the mansion and largely situated at one corner of the house, somewhat remote from the other rooms. The suite consisted of an antechamber, which was a sort of private parlor, a dressing-room, a bedroom, two closets, and a bath.

Tara and her Mistress of the Robes Sullijee, who had arrived in a separate carriage, were conducted on a tour of the rooms. The décor was comfortable but hardly opulent. This made sense to Tara, since Jarvis had surely spent much of his life in tiny sea cabins. Tara liked that they were apart from the other rooms; that could be important, should she want to go out alone to be with Marina. And Ariel, who had yet to contact her but who hopefully would soon. Tara pronounced herself quite satisfied with the accommodations and in particular admired the impressive marble and tilework in the bath.

Sullijee thought the stonework was fine too, and very much liked the full length, gilt-framed mirror affixed to the bedroom wall, which Tara, having seen much grander, gave only a cursory review. Sullijee objected to the suite's distance from her own room though, arguing that it made serving Her Highness much more difficult, as how was she to respond promptly to Her Highness's every need? Her protests were silenced only by Tara maintaining that she was satisfied—quite satisfied—with the rooms. As for Sullijee, in that she anticipated Tara's every need, would she always be at hand at the instant required anyway?

The tour complete, Tara dismissed Sullijee to unpack herself the relatively few items she had brought, again overruling Sullijee's objections. Sullijee departed, tight-lipped and reluctantly. Tara smiled. Yes, odd that her Mistress of the Robes was not unpacking her clothing, but Sullijee must not come across the princess purse: doubtless she would communicate that to her mother at once. Best, thought Tara, picking it up, to hide it somewhere Sullijee was unlikely to go.

Tara checked the back of the closet, thinking to hide it there, maybe behind anything that might have been left behind? But the closet had been cleaned out, and all that she found, on a shelf above some dusty racks, was an old brass button.

She turned it over in her hand, eying it closely. It looked to have an anchor stamped on it. Probably it had belonged to a uniform Jarvis had worn, and maybe from his commercial service. Tara placed it back on the shelf. She didn't want it, even as a memento. She shook her head slowly. A discrete enquiry had revealed that the usual punishment for traitors was death by hanging, and, for those who had been seafarers, from a yardarm. Tara shuddered. Jarvis had been a traitor, to be sure, preying on his fellow citizens to fill his coffers. Tara's work had revealed that, and so she had had a hand in his undoing. Still, it had been his own treachery which had brought him to that pass.

Tara glanced around the bedroom a second time, still looking for somewhere to hide her princess purse. No, there was not much of note beyond some furnishings of reasonable quality and a painting or two of modest artistic ability. Out of place was the full-length, gilt-framed mirror Sullijee had expressed approval of earlier. Tara took a few steps closer to inspect it. Odd, a mirror like that, wasn't it? Jarvis had not been married, and wouldn't it be the lady of the house who would want such a thing? Jarvis had been a man of the sea, and full-length mirrors and the associated vanity was not what she would have expected from that type.

Tara stepped still closer to the mirror to stand directly in front of it. The glass looked to be of high quality and all one piece. That made it unexpectedly valuable, as most mirrors were smaller, those being easier and cheaper to fabricate. Tara glanced around the room again, her eyes flitting from one article of furniture to the other in turn. The mirror was clearly of greater value than the other furnishings present—far greater. Tara ran her hand along the gilt frame: plaster, of decent quality and with good attention to detail in the gilding. On impulse, she pushed on the mirror itself and was surprised to find that the left side gave ever so slightly. Was it not firmly set in its frame? She tried the top and found it to be solid. But the right side gave like the left had, whereas the bottom did not.

How could this be, puzzled Tara, stepping back to contemplate intently a mirror she had given no thought whatsoever to five minutes before. She pushed again. Yes, both sides rocked back and forth ever so slightly. But the very center of the top and bottom did not. It couldn't be, unless... unless—

it occurred to her in a flash—the mirror rotated about a central axis. It wasn't rotating freely though, so there must be a catch to release it. But the catch would be close by, she reasoned with mounting excitement, because it would not be feasible to run such a mechanism for any distance.

She looked around the room: no sconces or shelves nearby on which to push or pull. But the gilt frame itself consisted of a series of ornamental bosses; maybe one of those might release a catch? Tara began to push on them, one by one. At last, at the top rightmost corner, the boss depressed ever so slightly with a barely audible "click" and the mirror quivered. Holding her breath, Tara pushed first on one side of the mirror, then the other: she had been correct. It did rotate, and about the center! With a sly smile, Tara pushed the mirror to reveal a thin, dark slit, through which she slipped without a second thought for her cold, a handkerchief, or anything else.

Almost immediately, she returned. It would not do, she reminded herself sharply, to explore without her princess purse! Also, it would not do to explore blind; she needed light. Tara cast about for anything she might be able to light and carry with her, until she at last remembered having seen a candle in a hallway sconce outside.

Finally, before she went far, and before the mirror should close behind her, she should identify the release from the other side so that she would not be trapped behind the mirror.

Quickly, she grabbed her princess purse, purloined the candle and stepped back behind the mirror. Tracing the outline of the mirror with the lit candle, she easily spotted the lever that released the mirror from the interior side; there had been no effort to hide it. She tested it twice to satisfy herself, then, heart pounding, closed the mirror so it latched and, holding the candle aloft, turned to face the corridor onto which the mirror entrance had opened.

It was very, very dark in the corridor beyond the mirror. The wan circle of light from the candle seemed to illuminate so little of the way ahead. Tara held the candle up to the wall nearby, to her right. The wall was hewn, it seemed, from the solid rock of the bluff on which the mansion stood. She reached out to touch the wall. It had been roughly cut, and still had sharp edges. She bent to inspect the surface on which she stood. It seemed a little smoother, as if there had been some effort to chisel away some of the larger trip hazards, doubtless to minimize stumbles in the dark.

Tara held the candle up so that she could just glimpse a bit of the grey rock overhead. The tunnel seemed ancient, she thought, though she was no judge of the construction of passages. Maybe it even predated the mansion? Maybe the structure now known as Princess House had been built on the ruins or foundation of some other, much older structure.

Tara turned back to regard the other side of the mirror, behind her. A very faint light, almost a glow, emanated from it and was slightly brighter around the edges, such that the actual mirror seemed silhouetted. She retraced her steps to look more closely at it. Just at the edges, near where the glass met the frame, she could see into the bedroom beyond. She placed her eye to the gap; even as she did, Sullijee entered and glanced around, evidently looking for her. Tara smiled. Of course she couldn't be seen behind the very mirror her Mistress of the Robes had so recently admired. Sullijee criss-crossed Tara's field of vision, obviously puzzled by Tara's absence when no one had seen her leave. Tara could just barely make out her name being called—and then, shrugging, Sullijee left.

Useful hiding place, thought Tara, if it ever came to that.

She turned back to look down the passage stretching out into the darkness. It was then that she spotted next to her, on a kind of ledge, what looked like a bullseye lantern. Tara nodded. That made sense. Jarvis must have left the lantern on the ledge and lit it as he passed through the mirror, then blew it out when he came back, leaving it for the next time. She picked it up. It still had quite a bit of oil in it. Tara lit it with her own candle, which she blew out, and proceeded, now with the much better light from the lantern illuminating the dusty, uneven passage.

The path was generally straight, but it had occasional turns to it. It was also generally one path, though Tara counted one branch at one point and what also looked like what could be a larger room off to one side. She would explore those later, she resolved.

She stopped at a juncture with another passage. Which one to take? The one down to the open air, she decided, and lit the candle again. The flame guttered ever so slightly along the way she was originally moving and did not when held aloft in the side passageway. She would keep moving along her original course, she decided, as that way seemed to lie fresh air, as evidenced by the very slight breeze coming from that direction.

The path generally sloped downhill and must lead to the base of the bluff, she decided. This suggested that it was not just a bolt hole in which to hide, or a hidey-hole in which to secrete contraband but a secret exit from the mansion! A little further and down a rough and long flight of steps, Tara came to a wall. She shone the light all along it. Impossible that such a tunnel had been cut into the rock only to end. And there was the breeze too. No, it must be a door, she reasoned, and she only had to open it. She shone the light on the floor, and this confirmed her conclusion: there were marks along a smooth surface in a quarter turn, suggesting that part of the wall swung inwards. She shone the light a little further around the wall and soon found a handle, which she pulled on with all her weight, and slowly, silently, in swung the door, letting the sunlight gush into the passageway and, so brightly, it temporarily blinded her.

Tara found herself looking into brush and scrub but clearly able to hear the surf beating against the base of the cliff not far away. It was as Tara had expected: a secret exit from the mansion down to the water's edge. Perhaps Jarvis had used it to effect his rendezvouses with the pirates and not be seen to be leaving the mansion.

Just then, a small bubble floated down from overhead. Tara stretched out her hand to receive it and blew softly upon it to hear its message. It was Ariel. "Hey, I'm overhead Sea Sprit; when will you be around? I'll come down to see you!" Perfect, thought Tara, noting that the sun was starting to descend toward the horizon. What about tomorrow morning? After replying to Ariel and updating Marina, she headed back toward the open entrance to the tunnel.

As she had expected, it closed from the inside the same way it had opened, using the handle. Then, carefully holding the lantern in front of her, Tara began retracing her steps back to the mirror door to the bedroom. Much as she would like to explore the tunnel further, she feared that if she didn't return soon, the household staff or Rohanic might become alarmed at her disappearance. Best to get back in plenty of time for the evening meal so as not to arouse suspicion.

Tara checked the room beyond before unlatching the mirror. No one was there. She unlatched the mirror and stepped through, then quickly closed it behind her. It swung noiselessly on its axis. She was left gazing at herself in the mirror. She saw a figure with bits of grey dust in her hair and in streaks across her dress and bodice. This would never do, she determined, dusting herself off as she appraised herself in the mirror. She rang for Sullijee.

Sullijee appeared almost at once. "Your Highness!"

Tara smiled and nodded. "Dear Sullijee, might I ask for my bath before dinner, please?"

"Of course, Your Highness! I came earlier to enquire if you might wish for one, because it can be refreshing when one is ill, but I couldn't find you!"

Tara nodded. That was why Sullijee had been in her bedroom. "I must have missed you somehow! Well, it's no matter. May I have the bath now, please?"

Sullijee curtsied and rushed to fulfil the request.

Tara smiled to herself. She'd have to be careful with Sullijee. She was attentive and intelligent but very curious, even to the point of prying. Tara had no idea of the company Sullijee might keep, but she could not have her Mistress of the Robes speaking with Rohanic of any suspicions, or, worse still, to her mother.

After breakfast the next morning and a very public walk about the gardens of Princess House, during which all the various flora were identified and their deliberate arrangement within the parterre garden explained, Tara retired to her room, pleading fatigue. As soon as she had closed the outer door to her suite and thanked Sullijee for her services, Tara retreated to her bedroom and sent a message bubble to Ariel, explaining to her where to meet her. Then she changed into sturdier clothing, belted her princess purse to her waist and stepped through the mirror. She lit the bullseye lantern from a tinderbox she had brought along for that purpose, and which she had purloined from the kitchen that morning and started down the tunnel to its outlet at the beach.

She found Ariel wandering aimlessly in the scrub as she emerged from the tunnel. "Ariel! Over here!" she shouted, causing her friend to jump in surprise.

"Tara! How did you get there without me seeing you…? But it's so good to see you!" The two friends embraced warmly, then Tara stepped back.

"I'm staying up there," she pointed up to the mansion on the bluff, "but look at this!" she continued and walked her friend back to the mouth of the tunnel. "See? It's a secret passage I discovered from my bedroom down to the base of the cliff!"

Ariel whistled in a low tone. "Wow, that's a surprise! So you can come and go whenever you like, right?"

Tara nodded. "I'm also thinking this is how Jarvis—remember how he used to own the place—got down to the water's edge unsuspected to see his pirate friends."

Ariel nodded. "It makes sense. But come with me: we want to get down to the water. Marina's waiting there for us!"

Marina was lounging on the rocks, flipping her tail back and forth and playing with a small crab in a rock pool. As they approached, Tara saw Marina using the tip of one fin to hollow out a cavity under a rock so that the crab might have a place to hide from predators when the pool, intermittently filled and drained by the waves, was empty. She looked up to see Tara approaching and gaily waved to her.

There was another set of warm greetings, after which Tara was obliged to brush the water off her clothes, and then Marina, with shining eyes, pulled both Ariel and Tara closer by an arm. "Listen! I've got the most interesting news to tell you!"

Ariel and Tara looked to each other as if to ask, what could this be?

Marina pulled them still closer and lowered her voice to a low tone. "Listen! Do you remember how we parted at the beach beneath that cliff where we found the princess purses?"

Both Tara and Ariel remembered.

"Right! So I swam back to Coral Castle. That evening, I told my father, King Aenon," turning to Ariel, "that's my father, King Aenon."

Turning back to both Ariel and Tara, she continued. "Anyway, I told him what happened! What we found in the cliffside!"

The others nodded again.

"He took a look at my purse and listened to what I had to say about what was inside, and became super interested! So, after dinner, we went back to his library to learn some more about this city!

"Yes! Well, what we found was that the city was named "Syssalin" and that it was a great trading center long, long ago. Well, we knew that already! But, while we knew that, we did not know that, in addition to acquiring considerable wealth from its trading activities, it also acquired great knowledge. This was because people from all over the world passed through Syssalin on their way to some other place to buy and sell things, and they passed their knowledge on to people in Syssalin. Well, this knowledge was said—" she lowered her voice still further and the others drew closer "—to have been written down over the years—in books and manuscripts and plates and so on, you know what I mean—and stored in a fabulous library!"

"A library!" breathed Tara, nodding. It wasn't the sort of place she tended to want to visit, though she understood Stonedell had one, but still, libraries were supposed to have all sorts of knowledge useful for finding all sorts of wonderful things. Such as the city where they had found the princess purses, as revealed in the library of King Aenon.

"A library," concluded Marina, emphatically. "And it's supposed to have been hidden inside the city someplace."

Tara spoke up. "But I've been to the top of that bluff. There's nothing there but ruins. That's all that's left of—what did you call it? Syssalin. Just fragments of columns. The city was razed to the ground!"

"Yes! And that's just what happened, when Syssalin was attacked. It was looted and destroyed. By barbarians. But they never found the library. The barbarians searched for days and tore down every structure. At last they gave up and left. But the library just has to exist, because there are simply too many references to it that are too specific and detailed.

"So it's still there! It's got to be!"

"A hidden library," said Ariel slowly. "How interesting." She paused for a second and looked thoughtful. "Did your father say what might have been in that library to make it so important that the barbarians would want to tear down everything to find it?"

That was a good question, agreed Tara. Because, while books and knowledge were valuable, it was hard to believe that barbarians would want these so badly that they would go to such lengths to find them. Or had there been something else in that library to prompt its invaders to search so thoroughly for it?

Marina nodded, a smile spreading on her face. "Yes! Yes! That's it! The records mentioned something of great value, of power, but it wasn't quite clear what it was. That was because we could only find it mentioned in a fragment, and it wasn't well preserved. Plus, it came from the barbarians, and not the people of Syssalin."

Tara spoke. "Could that mean that there wasn't anything powerful there after all? Maybe it was just a rumor?"

Marina shook her head. "No, it sounds like there was *something* there. It's just not apparent what."

The three princesses looked at each other. "Well, what do we do next?" asked Ariel at length.

Marina looked brightly at Ariel, then at Tara, then off into the distance up the beach where they knew the ruined city lay, then back to focus steadily on Tara with her blue-green eyes, now shading to an innocent sky blue. "Why... we have to go look for it! Obviously! I mean, right?"

Tara's mouth twitched ever so slightly. "I guess..." she said at last. "All right. But we have to do it in a week. That's all we have."

"A week? Why?"

"Because that's when my parents will be coming to Sea Sprit, I expect, to take me back to Stonedell. It will be impossible for me to get away then. So we'd only have a week."

Ariel shook her head and gazed out to sea. In endless, tireless succession, the foaming breakers rushed toward them to break on the rocks and sand, then slowly retreated back out to sea as if always for another offensive. She heaved a big sigh. "All right. If that's all we have, then that's all we have!"

"But, but... how are we supposed to find that library when a host of barbarian invaders couldn't? And nobody since?"

Tara shrugged. "That part's easy. Because they weren't us, that's why!"

Ariel laughed. "But thousands must have searched those ruins over the years! Maybe more! What else could there be to find?"

"That's true. But—and this is important!—they didn't have someone who could go underwater and look at things from that angle. Nor," and Tara nodded to Ariel, "did they have someone who could fly up and see everything from above!"

"And they didn't have Princess Tara either!" chorused Marina and Ariel, and all three of them laughed together.

"Good, then. We have another six days to find this library. Let's do this..." Tara thought hard for a moment while the others waited expectantly. "Marina, can you reconnoiter the base of the cliff again to see if there is anything left that we should look into? I know you took a pretty hard look at it when we were looking for the purses, but could you look again?"

Marina nodded, her face now flushed with excitement.

"And, Ariel, could you fly up and?—"

"And take a look from the air for any sort of marks or anything obvious that might suggest something we should look further into!"

Tara nodded, a big smile now on her face too, in anticipation of the adventure that may lay ahead for all of them. "And I'll look in that sea captain Jarvis's library to see if he has anything. Remember that pirate captain Braunzin, with whom he consorted, had that cylinder from Syssalin. Maybe they both were interested in Syssalin and had other information on it. It's worth a look, I think!"

Marina clapped her hands in delight. "Great idea, Tara! I love it! Let's get going!"

With that, the three took their leave and Tara returned to the tunnel to ascend back to the mansion. First stop on passing through the mirror back into the bedroom, she told herself as she closed the tunnel door behind her, was the library of Captain Jarvis. Was there anything there that could be useful?

Princess Tara looked away from the book she had been skimming and, after a moment, put her hand up to her eyes and rubbed them. This was very tiring. Her head hurt from trying to make out so many different sorts of scrawls in so many sizes and hands. Then there were the maps and marginalia scribbled in every which direction. She rubbed her eyes again. Research was tedious, even if done sitting down.

"Are you well, Your Highness?" It was Sullijee, doubtless being solicitous of her mistress's health.

"Yes, Sullijee; I'm well, thank you. Just a little weary."

"Your Highness must not wear herself out with these books!"

No, she shouldn't. But she had to do her part in looking for anything on the ruined city. "Maybe, Sullijee... might I ask for a cup of tea? That would be so lovely!"

Sullijee dropped a quick curtsy and promised to return promptly.

Tara stood after Sullijee had rounded the corner. Just as well: she felt as though Sullijee had been watching her the entire afternoon from various corners of the room under the pretext of being present to fulfil any of Tara's wishes. Tara didn't feel she was being over-suspicious, either.

Tara stood to return to the bookshelf. At least this room had not been touched by the workmen preparing the mansion for conversion to municipal purposes. Probably because removing the books would have required many trips down Sea Sprit for their storage. This meant Tara had all the books to herself. Unfortunately, there was no apparent organizational sense to the collection, meaning Tara had to go through them, volume after volume, in the dwindling hopes of finding something that could be of use. All of which had attracted Sullijee's curiosity. What, Tara could imagine Sullijee wondering, could have attracted such an ardent interest just one day after arriving?

In her peripheral vision as she glumly contemplated the shelves loaded with all manner of volumes, ranging in size from personal diary to unbound folio, Tara saw Sullijee return with the tea, which Tara heard placed on the table next to the reading desk with the slightest clink of porcelain cup on porcelain saucer. Then, after just a second's pause, came the soft rustle of layered skirts approaching. Sullijee. Surely coming to enquire as to what Her Highness was doing.

After a momentary silence, "Is Your Highness searching for something? Could I help in any way?"

"Oh, hello, Sullijee! I was just looking through the former owner's library—"

Sullijee cast her eyes downward in the traditional manner at the reference to the traitor.

"—just looking to see if there might be any suggestions here on… something to do in the area, around Sea Sprit, while I'm convalescing."

Sullijee looked back up again. "Indeed, your Highness? I do believe I can help you! This is because I am originally from this region of your kingdom!"

"Really, Sullijee? I had no idea."

Sullijee performed a half-curtsy. "Yes, Your Highness! So I am familiar with Sea Sprit. Very much so."

This could be a stroke of luck, thought Tara. But she'd have to make her enquiries without betraying any special interest to this very inquisitive young lady. "Please, Sullijee," continued Tara, returning to her reading table. "Tell me more about Sea Sprit and its environs. What might be, uh, enjoyable to see and do?"

Sullijee composed herself before her mistress. Tara noted how her eyes wandered across Tara's damask dress and settled for just a fraction of a second on her grandmother's ring, which today she wore on her right hand, then reverted to address her. "Yes, Your Highness," she replied, and absent-mindedly began to curtsy again but stopped herself.

"Yes, Your Highness. Well, I suppose it might depend on how Your

Highness is feeling and how adventurous She might feel… but one might venture to the morning markets in Sea Sprit, just to take in the atmosphere. All sorts of things are sold and bought there. Such as foodstuffs. And all manner of crafted items."

Tara strove to affect interest in this suggestion.

"Yes. And, one could visit some of the cultural aspects of Sea Sprit. For example, I believe that one of the important Sea Holidays is this week—there are six over the course of the year—and you could attend. The dancing is quite intricate and meant to reflect the movement of the waves at that particular time of the year."

Tara replied that this was a good suggestion too, and well worth consideration. "I am also thinking that it might be pleasant to go out into the country around Sea Sprit. To take in the fresh air. Are there any especially picturesque spots that you might recommend?"

Sullijee considered. "Your Highness might consider the woods further inland, which are very pleasant and shady and cool. Though I would recommend you maintain an escort for this, as there have been reports of banditry."

Tara signified curiosity and indicated for Sullijee to continue.

"Also, there is the high bluff overlooking the sea, which we call Point Syastic. That has a very nice view out over the sea, though it is somewhat of a steep climb."

"Really? A view? Tell me more."

"Yes, Your Highness. It has a fine view out to sea and indeed was the site of a city once. All that remains, though, of that are ruins."

"How romantic! Is it worth exploring?"

Sullijee shook her head. "Hardly, Your Highness. The ruins consist now mainly of tumbled stones and some sections of columns. Little more."

Tara could attest to that herself, she recalled, half-smiling. "I can imagine. But you say there was a city there, at one time?"

"Yes, Your Highness. Long ago." Sullijee looked wistfully into the distance for a moment, then back to Tara with a somewhat sly expression overlain with craftiness. "But, Your Highness, some say…"

Tara motioned for her to proceed.

"Legend has it that there's still treasure there!" Interpreting Tara's impassive face as an invitation to explain, Sullijee continued, her eyes momentarily aglow with the telling. "It was a long, long time ago. Hundreds of years! The city had a great treasure—a weapon!—which it could use against its enemies. This couldn't be kept a secret, of course, and a great barbarian warrior learnt about it and decided to take it for himself to become the most powerful king of the known world. He amassed an army to attack the city and, using spies to open the gates, stormed the city and captured it in a great battle!"

Tara nodded. At last. Finally, the discussion was moving in the right direction. Somewhere beneath the many layers of legend there was the truth; she just had to sort it out. "How interesting! Did the barbarians ever find the treasure-weapon?"

Sullijee shook her head. "No, Your Highness. They searched and searched, and even razed the city looking for it, but couldn't find it. Well, some say it never existed. After all, if there were such a mighty weapon, why wasn't it used to defeat the barbarian warrior king?"

Tara acknowledged the same with a slight smile.

"But, others say it was just too well hidden, and the city wasn't able to get it out in time to use in its defense. Because it was taken by storm in the middle of the night. They say that the weapon was hidden, along with all their other treasures, in the caves and caverns deep beneath the city."

"Beneath the city?"

"Yes! Because it is also rumored that a network of caves is beneath the city. Maybe from tunneling, maybe from the ocean waves, but that's where people say the weapon and all the other treasures of the city were kept."

Tara nodded again, mindful to remain interested and be perceived as such, but not so interested as to arouse suspicion. "Oh! So, maybe the barbarian king thought to find the treasure in a building, when, in fact, it was below ground."

Sullijee nodded. "And no one in the city would say where the caves were. I guess many didn't know, but those who would, wouldn't say."

"Any caves must have long ago fallen in, or been blocked up," surmised Tara aloud, as if in summary.

Sullijee drew closer and leaned in toward Tara. "No! They're still there! But no one can get into them!"

"Really? Why?"

"Because. Because some of the caves are said to be flooded and too long to swim holding your breath. And others have pits, or parts of the floor that have caved in. And, of course, it's totally dark down there." Sullijee straightened. "People have tried to explore the caves but never with any success. Some have never returned!"

"Some have never returned." Understandable, considering the insuperable obstacles in the way of the lost treasures of Syssalin. But such barriers would be insurmountable only to those without friends who had wings and fins. With rising excitement, and so slowly as to be imperceptible, Tara slid her hand from the arm rest where it had rested throughout the entirety of Sullijee's tale to beneath the table, down to the seat cushion, which she gripped with such tightness that her hand went a bloodless white. For Tara did have friends with wings and fins. Maybe the caves could be accessible after all.

"Where," asked Tara casually, "are the entrances to these caves? Does anyone know? Because it might be interesting to see them. Of course I could never go in them: far too dangerous! I couldn't possibly hold my breath for any length of time anyway!"

Sullijee laughed with Tara.

"But it might be interesting just to see them. Just the entrances."

Sullijee nodded. "Yes, Your Highness, you could. But by boat. I understand some can still be found in the face of the cliff around the waterline. Above or below, depending on the tide. I've never been myself." She shrugged. "I think the wind and the waves have caused some caves to fall into the sea over the years. Who knows? Maybe the treasure rooms themselves have fallen in. If they ever existed!"

"Maybe so. Maybe so. Well, if it would require me to go by boat, I think I have no interest in seeing the mouths of these caves. The seas must be very treacherous next to the cliff, and the boat would have to venture very close in."

"Just so, Your Highness."

Tara made a show of sniffing at this in disinterest. "Little sense in risking one's life just to see a hole in the rocks, is there? I'll be content with the view; that will be sufficient. That's probably all the 'treasure' there's to be had anyway."

"Quite right, Your Highness," said Sullijee, in clear approval.

Tara thought to drive home her disinterest. "Besides, I had plenty of excitement out on the water with the pirates during my last visit to Sea Sprit!"

Sullijee laughed again merrily, and Tara joined her wholeheartedly, delighted that she had found out as much as she had about the ruined city, and from someone she would have imagined to be the unlikeliest of sources. Tara was certain that, if Sullijee had been monitoring her movements for her mother, she was now surely totally thrown off by Tara's voiced disinterest in the treasure. But Tara fully intended to pursue it via the secret passage down to the ocean from her bedroom. She just had to communicate what she had learnt to Ariel and Marina. All they had were six days!

That evening, after a simple—at Tara's specific request—repast, and after Tara could finally get away, she retired to her bedroom suite, feigning fatigue and assuring Sullijee she would not need assistance. The others will be happier with me gone, thought Tara as she closed the outer door of her suite. Now they can get about playing cards or exchanging gossip or any of those other things they like to do when the royal family isn't around.

And it was just as well anyway, continued Tara, in the same vein. She had two messages to send and wanted to get some rest. "Marina!" she whispered into her first, "Swim in, when you can, to the base of the cliff beneath the city! I understand there are some tunnels there, maybe at the waterline or just above, depending on the tide!" Next she created a bubble and briefed Ariel. "Check the face of the cliff," she concluded, "particularly near the base, at the water's edge! I understand there might be tunnel mouths which are worth exploration. Tell me tomorrow what you find!" Those words wafted into the late evening sky, Tara slipped between the covers of her bed.

By the time Tara could get away the next day from such princessing responsibilities as a reception for a ladies' gardening club in the potager, it was nearly noon. She pleaded fatigue again and requested that her lunch be sent up to her room. She ate as she changed into exploring clothes, grabbed her princess purse and, depressing the boss, stepped through the mirror to the other side. Just as she was reaching for the bullseye lantern, she heard approaching footsteps in the rooms beyond and she immediately swung the mirror shut to be left in total darkness.

Tara pressed her eye to the crack at the edge of the mirror to see who was entering her room. It was Sullijee again. "How curious she is," breathed Tara. And despite Tara's request that she not be disturbed! Why was she checking on my whereabouts, Tara wondered. Sullijee looked this way and that around the chamber but found nothing except Tara's lunch tray. Thoroughly puzzled, Sullijee at last picked up the tray and passed outside

Tara's field of vision, the door to Tara's suite opening and then closing shortly thereafter.

Tara smiled triumphantly. The nosy Sullijee had been defeated! But it also meant that Tara would have to concoct a story to explain why she had been missing when she had told everyone she had been retiring to her room. Or Sullijee might well have something to report to her mother after all. Tara lit the lantern and started down the passageway. All of that would have to wait until she returned. Just now she wanted to get down to the base of the cliff and meet with Marina and Ariel.

But Tara had taken only three steps down the rock passageway before she halted. Hold on, she caught herself. Was this the smartest way of getting to the ruins? Maybe not. Slowly, Tara turned and headed back to the mirror. Reaching it, she blew out the bullseye lantern and, checking again for any sign of Sullijee, re-entered her bedroom. Quietly, she changed into her riding clothes, then nonchalantly stepped into the outer chamber of her suite.

There, as she had expected, she found Sullijee fiddling with the draperies, as if waiting for something. She jumped at Tara's appearance. "Your Highness! I didn't expect!—"

Tara smiled sweetly. "Didn't expect what, Sullijee? Me to be in my own bedroom?"

"Of course, Your Highness!" she replied, curtsying quickly.

"I think," Tara continued, switching to a contemplative tone, "I think I will take Daystar and ride to the ruins of Syssalin this afternoon. That was a good idea you had earlier today." Now there would be no need for an explanation for her absence from her room.

"Beg your pardon, Your Highness? To where?"

Tara recollected that Sullijee didn't know the actual name of the city in ruins. "That ruined city! I believe one of those books from Jarvis's library mentioned its name as Syssalin. Or something like that."

Sullijee curtsied again. "Of course, Your Highness. It won't be too demanding for you to ride out there, in your current condition?"

Tara shook her head gently. "I'll ride very slowly."

Another curtsy. "Of course, Your Highness! I will communicate your wishes to the stables. Daystar will be made ready at once."

Less than an hour later, Tara was on her way to the ruins astride Daystar, at her belt the princess purse. She consented to an escort but only to the outskirts of the ruins. So that she may better commune with the atmosphere of the place, she explained.

"Hello, rocks and columns," called Tara softly as she arrived at the crest of the bluff, leaving her escort behind. "How nice to see all of you again!" Tara glanced behind to make sure the escort was out of sight, then sent Ariel a message bubble to tell her she had arrived.

"Hi there!" exclaimed Ariel shortly, rising some distance from the edge of the bluff, then settling down gently next to Tara. "How have you been?"

"Super, thanks! How has the hunt gone?"

Ariel sat down next to Tara on the stump of a column. "Wow; sure feels good to sit down and take a load off my wings!" She eyed Tara. "Must be nice to always be on the ground and not to have to keep yourself up in the air!"

Tara smiled. What she wouldn't have given to be able to fly like Ariel. Surely Ariel knew this by her knowing smile in return. "Hey, I'm sorry to come out so late. But I had some official work to do. And I had to get away from a nosy Mistress of the Robes. At least I got some useful information from her."

Ariel agreed. "It's been a big help, honestly! Marina and I immediately switched to searching the waterline of the bluff. She took below the water, I took above."

Tara nodded.

"Listen to this: I think I found something, just above the shore line. Right where the sea washes in and out at low tide. It's hard to see, unless you are really close in, because it looks a lot like jumbled rocks. But I think it's the mouth of a cave."

"Could you look in?"

Ariel shook her head. "Too dangerous just then. But Marina said she would swim in and take a look at high tide, when the water should be deep enough."

Tara looked out to the water. "When should that be?"

"'Round about now. I'm hoping we'll hear from her shortly. You're here just in time!"

The two turned to the vista in front of them, that of the sun slowly heading to the horizon in front of them. How wonderful this was, it suddenly occurred to Tara. Out of the palace, away from badinage, away from princessing, and out in the world with friends and intent on some meaningful purpose! Just her, Daystar, friends, and an objective. She breathed deeply in satisfaction.

Ariel turned to her questioningly, almost as if she could hear Tara's excited thoughts.

"Just taking in the view and the sea air," replied Tara, innocently.

Shortly, a bubble floated up over the edge of the cliff and hovered, wavering between the two. "It's for me," said Ariel confidently, and Tara knew this had to be true but put out her hand anyway.

Of course, it settled in Ariel's outstretched palm. She breathed on it gently, and they heard Marina's excited voice. "Hey, Ariel, I think I found something! It's a cave all right, and it goes deeper! Much deeper, I think! Tell Tara to come out and take a look! I think this is it!"

Ariel turned to Tara. "You heard for yourself: better come out and take a look!"

Tara gauged the sun's height above the horizon reluctantly. "I want to. But I'll have to wait for tomorrow. It's too late in the day now. Let's plan on tomorrow morning, if the tide is right. Meet me up here!"

Ariel nodded. "I guess I'll have to carry you down, huh?"

"Yes. Sorry about that!"

"No problem; I can manage. It's easier going down than coming back up!" They both laughed.

Shortly afterwards, Tara returned to her escort and rode in silence back to the mansion. She stated, upon returning Daystar to the stables, that she expected to go out again in the morning and to the same place. "I quite like the atmosphere," she told the groomsmen. "It's very tranquil."

With that, she returned to her rooms. On the morrow, it would be only four days until her parents were due to join her. Would that be enough time to find the lost treasure of Syssalin and bring it back to Princess House?

The next morning, early, Tara was standing again at the edge of the bluff. Daystar she had left behind with the escort she had again allowed to accompany her, but they were again ordered to remain far removed and not to disturb her the entire day. She had also told them to steer any curious sightseers to other parts of the bluffs, though she doubted any would come. Finally, she had brought along a picnic lunch—big enough for three, she thought, which had earned her some enquiring looks from the kitchen and some observations, thought to be outside of earshot, of what a fine appetite she had. Now she stood again at the edge, one foot atop a chunk of pillar and her hands on her hips, waiting.

Ariel showed shortly. "Ready to go? Ready to hold on tight? Oh, lunch! How nice! Leave that behind and I'll come back for it; I'm not sure if I can take both it and you at the same time.

"All right; are you holding on tight? Then, let's go!"

Tara was slowly lifted off the ground and into the air. She hugged Ariel all the tighter but this time kept her eyes wide open, peeking as they were above Ariel's right shoulder. The sea seemed to fall away from her vision, and she rose up into the sky. There was a bit of hesitant and unsteady movement laterally, then she fell herself gently sinking downwards, with the sea and its endless march of whitecaps coming back into view as she descended.

"Just a little bit further, and in," she heard Ariel mutter, and felt the strain pulling at Ariel's back from her wings bearing the extra weight. Her feet were sprayed wet with seawater, and there was a crash of surf, and then all of a sudden she was touching ground. "There! Made it!" Ariel said. "You can let go of me now!"

Tara let go and stood back. She was standing on a rocky surface and, upon stepping away and looking around, she saw she was facing out the cave's opening and could see, just beyond, the foam-flecked surf washing across the rocks ringing the mouth and, occasionally, creeping inward to where they stood. Everywhere were small, irregular pools of standing seawater, intermittently refreshed by the surging waves. Dotting the cave walls and rock floor were lichens, barnacles, and other intertidal life. "It's low tide?" she asked Ariel.

"Yes, but the tide is coming in. Marina looked around some yesterday, at high tide. She said it went back pretty far. Now's our opportunity to explore it."

Tara surveyed the roof above her. No wonder not many had come here to look for the fabled treasure of Syssalin. Just getting to the cave itself was hard enough, and that had been with wings. "Let's get going then, and see what's inside!"

The two princesses turned and ventured into the cave. Tara and Ariel had to pick their way forward with great caution, as it was very slippery with the standing water underfoot and all the slimy seaweed.

Before long, the daylight from the mouth of the cave was just a dim circle behind them. They stopped, unsure of how far to keep going. With a sigh, Tara realized she should have brought the bullseye lantern from beyond the mirror with her.

Ariel spoke. "Uh, Tara... Are we sure this is the right cave to be exploring?"

"Funny: I was thinking the same thing. I'm not sure at all myself."

"We need some light. We could be in the right cave, but we wouldn't know, because we might be missing something."

Tara had to agree. "Let's go back. Back to the mouth. Let's talk with Marina and see if she has found anything else underwater that looks more promising. Besides," she added, peering ahead into the darkness, "this cave doesn't seem to go much further than as far as we've come."

Back at the cave mouth they found Marina, sunning herself on the rocks. So like a mermaid, thought Tara. "Hey, how are you?"

"Hi!" Marina returned brightly. "Good to see you again! Did you find anything back there?"

Tara and Ariel looked to each other. "Nothing, really. Basically just seaweed and barnacles and lots of slime."

"It's not 'slime'. It's seagrasses and sea carpet, and it's important for sea life and very useful besides."

"Of course! Still, we didn't find anything. And it looked like it ended about where the sunlight from the mouth faded out."

Marina ran her fingers idly through her hair. "Okay, that makes sense. When I explored it at low tide, it seemed to end about there for me also. I just thought you might be able to find something more, having legs and all. I thought you might be able to climb up the walls and find something."

"We didn't see anything."

Marina sat up. "Well, no worries. Because I think I may have found something much better!"

The two others immediately wanted to know.

"Yes! It's another opening in the cliff. Almost directly below this cave, but underwater. It's kind of deep down for a landling. And," looking to Ariel, "a flying person. But not for a mermaid, of course."

"Of course."

"Right. So I went in to investigate, and the tunnel sort of thing went up pretty quickly, and it wasn't long before it opened into a larger room filled with air!"

"An undersea entrance!"

"Right! Maybe! I couldn't explore any further than that, because, while I can breathe air, I can't go ashore. Only up to the water's edge."

"Did you see anything else?"

"Yes! Something more! I took a closer look at the walls, and those of the underwater entrance were natural. But the opening into the air-filled room was of finished stone and had clearly been laid by people. So the entrance to the room was man-made!"

Tara was thrilled. "Marina! You did it! That must be the entrance to the complex! It has to be!"

Marina preened herself in obvious pleasure.

Though Ariel wanted to go immediately down to see the entrance, and Tara didn't want to waste any time either, she held herself back. "Let's plan our next move instead of going down right away. Ariel, maybe could you fly back up to the edge of the bluff and grab our lunch? Then, while we eat, we could decide what to do next?"

This was done, and over the next hour, the princesses agreed that, for the remainder of the day, Ariel and Tara would attempt the dive down to the cave mouth to test their ability. In the absence of light, Marina would have to lead them. They would return the next with the bullseye lantern for the light they would need to negotiate what Sullijee had warned might be pits and other obstacles that would be in the tunnels.

"Can you swim?" Marina asked Ariel on impulse. "I mean, how is it with wings? Underwater? Can you use them to help you swim?"

Ariel drew herself up and her voice assumed some of the same hauteur they had heard when they had first met her. "Of course, I can swim! And my wings fold! They fold very neatly behind me, and then I swim just fine. Just like Tara!"

"Just checking," replied Marina hastily. "You can swim, just like Tara," she echoing, recollecting that Tara herself was still new to the exertion.

By the time afternoon was drawing on and after a number of attempts, Tara and Ariel decided they could not reach the mouth on their own because it was simply too deep. "Don't worry, you'll just hold onto my waist and I'll pull you! It's no trouble at all," Marina reassured them.

"Are you sure?" asked Tara. "It won't be too much for you?"

Marina shook her head. "I'm naturally a strong swimmer. Just keep your head down and your body in line and we'll make it without a problem!"

There was no other way, so the three agreed to meet the next morning, Tara as before waiting for Ariel at the top of the bluff. All of it sounded very good, thought Tara, as she rode back to her room, her escort following a discreet ten paces behind. Only three days left until her parents came, though.

"Ready?" asked Ariel the next day, when she drifted up from below the edge of the bluff to alight next to Tara. Tara nodded, wordlessly. "Good." Ariel glanced at the bag Tara had brought with her. "The lantern?"

"Yes. And, well, a little something to eat too."

"That's good too! I'll make a second trip for that, just like yesterday. All right. Here we go again; hold on!"

Tara grasped her friend tightly around the waist and put her chin on her left shoulder. The ground fell away beneath her, and she again rose just slightly to clear, then drifted slowly out over the booming surf, then descended quickly to alight just inside the cave mouth. This time the floor of the cave had about a foot of water in it. Tara grimaced to be set down in the chill, sloshing water.

"I guess the tide's coming in," she said, picking up her foot and shaking it.

"I guess so. It's wet, but we'll be a lot wetter soon, so I didn't think we'd mind."

That was true, allowed Tara mentally and composed herself for the full immersion in the saltwater that she would soon experience. She peered out of the cave over Ariel's shoulder. The seas looked rougher than they had the day before.

Marina showed up a few minutes later. "Hey, you two! Are you ready?"

Both nodded that they were.

"Good! Wrap up what you have tightly so it stays dry, and we'll go."

Tara answered that she had taken especial precautions for the lantern and lunch to remain dry, and so, with a last look between them, they pronounced themselves ready.

"Good." Marina paused for a moment, then her hand dove into her princess purse. "Hang on! I think I still have a little of the seaweed on hand from when I took you, Tara, down to the Coral Castle! Let me see…" Marina looked thoughtfully up into the ceiling as she rummaged through her princess purse, then her eyes lit up. "Here it is! It isn't much—" she said, pulling out a small wad not much bigger than the ends of three fingers,

"But it ought to help." Marina distributed half each to the other two. "Take that. It's not enough to let you breathe underwater, but it should help a little with the pressure. You'll want that; we have to go pretty far down."

Tara and Ariel swallowed the bits given to them without hesitation. Tara didn't even mind the sour taste so much, knowing how much it would help.

Marina continued after a moment. "Let me warn you: the waves and currents are stronger today than yesterday. So you have to hold on extra tight and take an extra deep breath. On account of the water being colder."

"Are you sure you can take the two of us? At the same time?"

"Pretty sure. Each of you could take an arm, and I would be fine kicking with my tail. We could make it."

"But, in one breath? Tara and me?" asked Ariel, nervously.

Marina hesitated just a fraction, allowing Tara the opportunity to cut in. "I'm sure she could. But the water is colder, and maybe we wouldn't be able to hold our breath as long as we could yesterday. So, just to be safe, and so Marina can swim as quickly as she can, maybe, Marina, you could take us one at a time? What do you think?"

Marina thought this over for a second. "All right; that's a good point. We'll do it that way. One at a time." Marina took a deep breath. "Who goes first?"

Tara frowned in reflection. She was dying with curiosity as to what to was down there, but would going first be risky? Then she caught herself. How could she ask Ariel to face a danger she wasn't willing to first face herself? Tara was ashamed of herself. "I'll go first!" she said immediately.

Just as she spoke, Ariel raised her hand. "I'll go," she said shyly. Then, hearing Tara speak so forcefully, she added, "But, you go first, Tara, if you like. We've come this far mostly on your ideas, after all."

Tara chuckled in spite of herself. "Ariel! I only volunteered to go first because I was worried there might be danger. No: if you want to go first, you go!"

Ariel laughed too. "No, you go first! It's your treasure hunt!"

"Ladies!" interjected Marina, smiling and motioning for silence. "One of you has to go first. Just one. But one must!"

"You go," said Tara. "Take the lantern with you too. See if you can light it as soon as you arrive where there's air.

"Now, go; get going!" She made shooing motions with her hands.

"Go!"

Ariel turned with a smile. "All right then, Marina! I'm ready!" With that, she splashed into the deeper water just beyond the cave's mouth and took hold of Marina about the waist. She made a face. "Gosh, you're right: it is colder!"

"Kick a little yourself too, just to help me out, if you would," Tara heard Marina request of Ariel, then she saw Ariel take the deepest breath she could, and with a last *1-2-3 Go!* the two vanished beneath the surface.

The wait seemed interminable. Tara tried to time it, holding her breath for as long as she could imagine, and then some, to gauge how far it was and when Marina would be back. It was longer than she expected. When Marina's head finally popped up above the surface, her face was grave.

"What happened?"

Marina was sober. "It was longer than we thought. With the stronger currents and all. And you were right to have me take you one at a time: the colder water means you can't hold your breath as long."

Marina's voice began to trail off, and her downcast expression turned to deep dismay. Tears began to well from her eyes. "Honestly… Ariel, well, almost didn't make it. She nearly blacked out. I think she was about to drown, even. I got her up into the air only just in time. I had to—sort of—revive her. Even. It was awful." Marina swallowed hard and looked directly into Tara's eyes, as if she were pleading for understanding. "It was really close."

Tara rushed to her friend and hugged her. "It's not your fault, Marina! No, it's not!" Far, far in the back of Tara's mind, she felt the wetness spreading across her that always came from clasping Marina close, but she welcomed it this time, as if absorbing it would be, in some way, like wicking away Marina's distress and pain. "Marina! Don't blame yourself! How is Ariel now?"

"She's all right, I'm pretty sure. But I was really worried. I mean, I had to, sort of, well, pump her chest a little. To get her breathing again!"

Tara was stunned. That was serious. The dive was far more demanding than she had imagined it would be. In retrospect, Tara really should have gone first, and she felt a terrific wave of guilt sweep over her. Poor Ariel! No wonder no one from what Marina called the "sunlit world" had discovered the entrance—it was simply too deep and the currents too treacherous to reach unassisted.

She took Marina by the arm. "Look: you did the most wonderful thing when it had to be done. You saved Ariel's life! I'm sure she's all right now; that's all that counts. And I'm ready too. Any time. I'll take an extra deep breath, that's all. I'm ready when you are."

Marina nodded and wiped away her tears. "Are you sure…?"

"Yes, I'm sure! And I won't leave Ariel there alone!"

"All right; if you're sure. Hold on tight, though. And I'll swim extra hard, as fast as I can!"

Tara waded into the water, hobbling across the rocky floor of the cave, and then, more slipping than stepping, into the deeper water where Marina was waiting. Ugh! It was cold and the waves were rough, even in that sheltered location! Marina turned her back and Tara grasped her around the waist, her hands overlapping each other so that each hand gripped the wrist of the other, as if to lock them. "Hold on tight!" Marina cautioned once more, and then she submerged, Tara trailing after her, with only an instant to take one last, extra-deep breath.

Tara held tight, her eyes firmly shut. She willed herself to be absolutely motionless, conserving all her energy and her breath. She must, she repeated, shut out everything and concentrate on only those two imperatives: holding tight and holding her breath. But her heart raced wildly, and her thoughts flew to Ariel and how she had nearly drowned. Would she, Tara, drown? She mustn't, and she wouldn't, she felt, if she held fast and firm and kept faith in Marina.

Down, down they swam, the water becoming icy and biting her skin. The little light that had impinged on her eyelids vanished completely. They must be getting closer, thought Tara. They had to be. Her teeth began to chatter, and she bit her lip to stop them. But it didn't help, and she found herself gnawing on her lips instead.

Tara shivered—a great, deep shudder that convulsed her entire body in a single, involuntary spasm. Both hands began to lose feeling, and she told herself fiercely she must not let go, but still she sensed her grip loosening involuntarily. Marina must have noticed too, as Tara then felt the warmth of Marina's hands grasping hers in assurance. Dimly, she felt Marina's tail thrash beneath her as they dove ever deeper to inhospitable depths to which Tara, with her two frail legs, was impossibly ill suited. The sounds of wind and wave had long ago faded; now the numbing cold supplanted even the endless swirling of water around her. And the pressure was relentless, even with the seaweed Marina had given her. No light, no sound, no feeling, no taste except salt, nothing at all except the merciless cold and the pounding in her head from the mounting pressure.

With a faint start, Tara realized that it was now too late to return to the surface, even if she let go of Marina that instant. A sense of panic began to claw at her, starting in her stomach and mounting into her throat. She could never reach the surface now; she was too far away. It was too far to go back. They had to be close to the underwater entrance; they simply had to be. They had to reach it, because it was too late to go back.

Then the pressure was all that was left, and it ached fiercely. It had started in her ears, but now it surrounded her, crushed her. She began to see tiny stars, and the memory of the sunlit world became incomprehensively distant. Nothing existed except the thudding in her skull, harsher and stronger, and the limitless stars, of every possible color, whirling all about her, around her, inside her. The stars seemed to coalesce and get larger and larger, and Tara felt her consciousness ebbing, her breath beginning to give out, and it *was* giving out, and she knew this, more and more faintly, and she was trying to hang on, but it was so difficult and so cold and—

And then suddenly she was up into air, and the relentless pounding began to subside. Tara gasped and choked and didn't dare breathe for fear she was still underwater, but she had to and couldn't stop. Distantly, she was aware of Marina guiding her to the edge of the pool into which she had emerged, and it was all Tara could do to cling to its edge and heave great gulps of air. She coughed, once, twice, and then threw her head back for more air. Two hands grasped her by the arms, and she felt herself being hoisted up. It was only then that she thought to open her eyes and saw the shadowy form of Ariel pulling at her with both hands. Of course, she realized, infinitely tired. Ariel. Ariel had lit the bullseye lantern. Ariel was trying to help her from the pool. Tara, with a tremendous effort, half-hauled herself out and Ariel dragged her the rest. Tara retched again, rolled over on the cold stone floor beneath her and stared blankly into the darkness.

At last she sat up to find Ariel staring anxiously into her face.

"Are you all right?" asked Ariel.

"I think so. That was quite a trip."

"Sure was. Do you think you can move at all?"

"Yes. I think so. What about you?"

"I'm all right." Ariel smiled hesitantly, which came across particularly feeble in the dim light, and marked more by shadows than by actual sight. "It was rough all right. I think I only made it because of my lungs—I've got extra capacity, just because I fly pretty high, where the air is thinner."

Tara nodded.

"Good thing I went first after all, I think. I only just made it; had you been first, and without any warning, you might have… well, not made it."

Tara nodded again. Maybe it had been best for Ariel to have gone first. She heaved a great sigh and glanced around. "I think I can stand now. Let's see." With only a little assistance from Ariel, Tara stood. Ariel picked up the lantern and played it around the room, resting the beam on an opening in one wall. It had to be the passage out.

Just then, Marina's head reappeared above the rim of the pool. She heaved a bag out and onto the floor. It was the food Tara had brought for the three of them. "Here we go!" Marina called cheerfully, as she almost always seemed to be. "Lunch is served!"

Tara sat down near Marina and let her legs dangle over the water. "There is no way either of us could have made it without you pulling us here," she began, speaking down to her friend in the water.

Marina nodded solemnly. "I'm happy to do my part. If only because this is as much as I can do. I can't go any further."

Tara agreed. "That's for sure. Ariel and I will take it from here, but we'll ask you to wait for us here, if you would. We'll send you a message bubble to let you know where we stand or if we have problems—or need some ideas." Tara thought further. "As I was told, there are pits and gaps in the passages. Those are the legends, at least. Ariel, how quick are your reactions? Could you fly quickly if you had to? Like, if you were falling?"

"Like, if I suddenly walked off the edge of a pit?"

Tara nodded that that was just what she was thinking.

"Pretty quick. I mean, very quickly. If I had my wings spread."

"That's really good. So, why don't I hold the lantern, and you could walk just a pace or two ahead of me, with your wings at the ready? I'd shine the light, and we could look for openings ahead of us together. But if we should miss one, you wouldn't fall much. Whereas," and Tara smiled ruefully, "I'd go all the way down."

"Sure; makes sense. No problem!"

"Aw! I want to go too!" cried Marina, slapping her tail twice on the surface of the pool to make a sound like clapping.

"You've done plenty all ready," soothed Tara. "You found the entrance and got us here. Now it's our turn!" Waving goodbye, Marina promised to stay near the edge of the pool. Down the passageway Tara and Ariel started out, the latter in the lead by a few steps, the former holding the lantern and swinging it slowly back and forth to light the path ahead.

The passageway ran straight for a way then turned upwards and continued at an increasingly steep slant. At one point, the two stopped to catch their breath, the incline was so steep. "We must be heading for the top of the cliff," said Tara, thinking that was a good thing, since it suggested that Sullijee's musings that the library was underground and thus had not been found were correct. An underground library in the cliff would have had to have had an entrance at the top accessible to the city's leaders.

They started forward again. A few minutes later, the wisdom of Tara's suggestion that Ariel precede her was proven. Very suddenly and unexpectedly, and just as the two were rounding a slight turn, Ariel dropped out of sight with a gasp and a slight "Oh!" Tara stopped instantly.

"Hello?" she called. "Ariel?"

A few seconds later, to her relief, Ariel rose up from the darkness to hover in front of her. "Hi! I'm back! Good thing you stopped yourself; it looks like a long way down!"

Ariel re-joined Tara at the edge of the pit, which gaped in front of her. "I have to admit, it took me by surprise. But fortunately, I was ready, with my wings out." Tara guessed that beating her wings in a fall, for Ariel, was about the equivalent of the human reflex of putting out one's hands when tripping.

"It's pretty deep," continued Ariel. "Deep enough to really hurt. I'd need the light to see if there is anything down there; it's too dark without it to see."

Tara acknowledged that she had been lucky to avoid so narrowly a possibly deadly fall. "Could you flit over to the other side of the pit to see if there is anything there? Like, if the passageway continues."

Ariel became indistinct and then returned. "There's nothing on the other side; the passageway doesn't go any further."

Funny, that, observed Tara, and shone the lantern's light on the walls to either side of the pit. The pit seemed to go to the very edge of the walls to either side, and the walls themselves were extremely smooth, almost as if of melted glass. There were no cracks or crevices to permit someone to make one's way around the pit by clinging to the wall. "Very curious," said Tara aloud. "The people who made this pit wanted to be extra sure that the only way across was the one they had in mind. Which seems to be long gone," she added, examining the lip at her feet.

"But there isn't anything on the other side anyway. It just ends," Ariel pointed out. "And I felt around some too. I didn't feel any cracks, like there were doors or anything."

"What about at the bottom of the pit? Could you fly down there? I'll give you the lantern."

Ariel took it and flew down, the beam of light from it rapidly growing smaller as Ariel descended. Tara saw it move about at what she guessed was the pit's floor, then it began to grow larger as Ariel returned. "There's nothing there! Just solid stone: no door, no nothing! But, it can't just end like this! There has to be something more!"

Tara agreed. No, it couldn't just end. She supposed she could ask Ariel to carry her across the pit so she could see herself but Ariel had already checked the other side. What could Tara's inspection add?

Tara thought hard to try to recollect everything she knew about Syssalin and its ways. Not much, honestly. The only direct contact she had had was in opening the cylinder to obtain the map inside and then finding the marble tablet. She mentally retraced the steps they had taken to find the princess purses. First, there had been the cylinder. That had been opened by depressing the shapes in the required order. That had revealed a keyhole, which had required a key retrieved from the wreck of the pirate ship.

The opened cylinder had then revealed a map, the directions on which had eventually led to a once-hidden marble tablet. Inscribed on the tablet had been further directions, which had taken them to the stairway in the cliff, at the bottom of which had been a locked door. Opening the door had required the insertion of the tablet. Then and only then had they been able to enter the room to find the princess purses. There was a pattern, Tara realized. Every step in finding the room with the princess purses had come in two parts: two steps to extract the map from the cylinder, two steps to obtain the marble tablet from where it had been hidden, and two steps to find and open the door.

Tara took a deep breath and shook her head slowly. Always two steps. Always two. Never just one.

Ariel watched in fascination. Her friend was clearly thinking very hard;

even in the dim light of the lantern she could almost see the thoughts flitting across her face. Tara had to be figuring it out, even as she was watching! Ariel hardly dared breathe for disturbing her.

So, there must be two steps to get to the lost library, concluded Tara. It wasn't that they were on a wrong track, or had come to a dead end. The first step must have been locating the opening under the water. What and where was the second? A door in the wall on the other side of the pit? But Ariel had checked that. No, that wasn't it. It must be... Tara looked into the blackness to the other side of the pit. It must be in the pit itself. At the bottom. But, no: Ariel had checked there too! Or, could it be, somewhere in the wall of the pit and not at the very bottom? Tara shivered. How clever it would have been to do that. Anyone who had fallen into the pit would have been too injured to have investigated further; anyone avoiding the fall would not have been able to see a door midway down. Hadn't Sullijee mentioned that the treasure was hidden deep beneath the city and that pits were an obstacle?

"I think," began Tara slowly, "I think..."

Ariel waited expectantly.

"I think we need to go down into the pit. I think we need to look in the pit."

"Both of us?"

Tara shook her head. No need for that unless necessary. Even though she very much wanted to investigate herself! "No. Not yet, at least. Here: you take the lantern and descend very slowly and shine it all the way around as you go. See if you see anything in the walls of the pit, above the bottom."

Wordlessly, Ariel took the lantern. Her wings beat in a blur and, with a wave of her free hand, she sank out of sight into the pit. The light from the lantern gradually dimmed as it revolved about the pit, deeper and deeper.

There was a sharp cry of excitement from about halfway down. "Tara! Look at this!"

Tara bit her lip. If only she could! "What do you see?" she called instead.

The lantern light grew brighter as Ariel ascended. "Stairs! Stairs! There are stairs cut into the side! Grab on to me and I'll take you to them!"

Tara immediately seized her friend about the waist. Without another word, Ariel lifted off and began the descent, until she placed Tara on a narrow ledge halfway down the pit. "I'll carry the lantern and stay alongside you as you descend, in case you should lose your footing," she whispered.

Tara was grateful for this offer, as the stairs, though cut from the solid stone itself, were crumbling at the edge with age. How they had been carved there in the first place, and how anyone got to that point without them was a mystery to Tara, but she didn't stop to think about this. She was too excited that her suppositions had been correct. They had to be close to the library now! Finding the stairs had to be the second step in locating the library!

Tara stepped cautiously down the crumbling stairs, clinging to the wall to her right and keeping her hand on the shoulder of a hovering Ariel to her left. As she walked, she remained alert to changes in the rock under her fingertips, hoping to feel something that might suggest a door or passageway as they made their way down to the bottom.

Nearly to the bottom, Tara stopped short. "Wait! There's some sort of recess here in the rock. Like…" she felt the shape "…a door!"

Ariel shone the light and illuminated what indeed resembled a doorway in the wall. As with the door to the room containing the princess purses, there was no handle. This time, though, there wasn't even a slot through which to insert a tablet. Just bare rock. Nothing else.

That could only mean that the way to open the door was there itself. Tara felt all around inside the recess, pushing, probing, prying, and poking. At last, pushing on a rock projection which resembled a lintel, a low grinding noise came from the stone, and one side began to swing outwards. Tara stepped back to make way for it and would have surely fallen off the stairs had Ariel not caught her.

The grinding began, then slowed, then, all too suddenly, stopped. Ariel shone the light. An opening was apparent, but it was too narrow even for the slim Tara to slip through. "I need it to be just a little wider! Just a little!" She grabbed at the rock door and tugged. No use! It was too heavy!

"What do we do now?" wailed Ariel. "It's so unfair!"

Tara stared hard at the gap between the wall and the door. The ancient machinery had failed too soon. But the gap it had provided was more than wide enough to insert the telescoping rods they both had. She whipped out hers. They were strong too, she knew.

She passed hers to Ariel. "Let's see if we can pry it open, just a little further."

"With just this rod?"

"Well, we'll extend it. To its full length!"

"That's far longer than the ledge on which we're standing!"

Tara smiled. "But not for you, who can hover! We'll extend it fully, then you'll push on the very end. It's the way leverage works, right? The longer the lever, the greater the applied force! It might be enough!"

Ariel eyed the rod dubiously.

"We've got to try!"

Wordlessly, Ariel handed the lantern to Tara, then floated out until she was about in the center of the pit. She extended the rod toward Tara, who inserted it deep into the opening. Tara then stepped up the stairs to be well clear of any debris that might be dislodged. "Start pushing!" she called.

Ariel took the end of the rod in both hands and, straining, pushed against it. The rod bent and creaked, and Ariel pushed even harder, feeling just the slightest bit of give in it. "Push, Ariel, push!" cried Tara from the darkness.

Ariel pushed as hard as she could. There was further creaking and the sound of cracking, then the rod jumped forward and Ariel nearly went tumbling over the rod's end. "Something just happened! Check it now!" she cried.

Tara shone the lantern into the recess and whooped with excitement. "You did it! You did it, Ariel! We can fit through now!"

A moment later, she was joined by her friend and, after congratulating each other on their success, they slipped breathlessly through the narrow aperture that had been opened.

They emerged into a much larger room, and one that appeared to go back some way into the cliff. Tara looked around in wonder. How had this room been carved out of the rock as it had? She lifted the lantern and shone it high, up and around. Set into the wall and running its entire width was a single shelf, which ran continuously around the semi-circular room. In some spots, the shelf was bare. But in others, tantalizingly, there were items resting on it.

"We have to go take a look!" she said excitedly to Ariel. But in so doing, she saw that the lantern was almost out of oil. They didn't have much time left to look. Tara groaned. "We'll have to move quickly! We don't have much time!" She groaned again. "And I didn't bring along an extra flask!"

Ariel nodded. "We'll have to do the best we can. I suppose we could always come back," though neither she nor Tara were enthusiastic about the dive down to the entrance to the complex through the cold seawater. "Let me send a message bubble to Marina, telling her we found the library. You start to look at the shelves and I'll join you!"

Tara was already at the shelf, scanning the lantern's beam back and forth to discover whatever might be on it. The first items she found appeared to be a kind of stack of tablets, bound at the top by a kind of wire. There was a number of them, scattered across the shelf and at various intervals. Over each stack, whether it be of several or only one, was a symbol of some sort that Tara couldn't read. Doubtless they had meaning and maybe explained how the tablets were organized but there simply was no time to try to figure them out.

Over everything lay a thick layer of coarse dust. Fallen from the rock itself overhead, she guessed. Tara picked up one of the tablets in her hand and glanced at it to assess what it might be made of. It looked like some sort of shell, or horn, as if from an animal. It did look like it would fit in her princess purse though, which she knew to be capacious. She stuffed the stack she was holding in and moved on.

Ariel soon joined her excitedly. "These are the books! The books of Syssalin! We really did find the library!"

Yes, nodded Tara. It was unlike any library she had ever seen, even if she had only seen a few. Instead of stacks of books up to the ceiling, and row upon row of shelves, there was only this single shelf, which wrapped around the room. And, instead of books, there were these tablets piled at intervals.

The lamp sputtered and flickered.

"We've got to go quickly," muttered Tara. "We can't be trapped here in the dark! Grab as many tablets as you can. Let's see what else there is, if anything!"

They completed the circuit of the room but only saw in the time they had and with the lantern's waning light two items that were not tablets. One was a collection of glass-stoppered flasks that had been bound together so that they could be picked up as one. The second was a box which, when opened, was found to contain a ring and more tablets.

Quickly, the two princesses stuffed as many more of the tablets into their princess purses as they could readily seize, then they backed toward the way they had entered. "Bye, library! Maybe we'll be back!" called Ariel softly into the darkness, now lit only feebly by the dimming glow of the lantern.

And with that, they backed out of the chamber to emerge back onto the ledge. "Quick, grab me about the waist! We've got to fly; we don't have the oil in the lantern to walk up the stairs! You hold the box and I'll hold the flasks!"

"But how am I to hold both the box and you about the waist?"

"No time for that! Just do it!"

Tara promptly threw her arms around her friend, gripping the box in her right and then holding the wrist of her right with her left hand. Ariel immediately lifted off, holding the lantern and flasks in her two hands. The flight up was unsteady, and they weaved back and forth and swayed while ascending. Tara tightened the hold of her hand around her wrist as close as she could but even so could feel it slipping. But she couldn't drop the box either, she knew she just couldn't, as she was sure it must contain something valuable. Just as she thought her fingers must fall off from holding so tightly to Ariel, her feet touched ground on the upper side of the pit.

Ariel took a deep breath. It had been difficult for her too.

"No time to rest. We've got to run. Quick! We didn't see any branches," urged Tara, already starting. "But it's possible we missed them! If we take a wrong turn, we'd never find our way in this darkness!"

That was enough to motivate Ariel. Wordlessly, she chased after Tara, who was already ahead of her, the lantern light from the bullseye Ariel held seemingly getting fainter with each passing second. "Run! Run!"

Tara pounded forward, inwardly reminding herself to pick up her feet as high as she could so as not to stumble over uneven surfaces. Ariel could catch herself with her wings, after all; Tara had no such back up. In between sharp reminders, Tara demanded silently of herself why she had not moved more quickly down the passageway to reach the pit, why she hadn't found the secret door in the pit more quickly, or why she had not brought along another flask of oil. It was no good now, of course, to reproach herself, but she couldn't help it. If only! If only!

On and on they ran, Ariel not daring to fly for the stones jutting down irregularly from the overhead. How could the passageway be so long, wondered Tara. Faster, faster, she goaded herself: if the light goes out, they would be lost forever in impenetrable darkness. And now Tara was realizing how hungry she was. She had eaten a little back at the pool, but now she was finding herself almost faint from hunger. What a time for this!

The lamp grew fainter and fainter, and then, right in mid-stride, it flickered and cut abruptly. The darkness was total and instant. Tara stopped, and Ariel promptly crashed into her, so close behind had she been following. Tara heard the sudden, urgent beating of Ariel's wings behind her though, and rather than tumble to the floor, she felt herself caught and held and then brought back gently to a standing position. Wow, she realized. Ariel caught me just in time!

All each could hear for the first moments was the panting of the other's breath. "Tara?" came the quavering voice of her friend from just beside her.

"Hi, Ariel," answered Tara, for a moment forgetting the darkness and their plight and smiling. Who else would be right beside her?

"It really is dark now."

"We must be hundreds and hundreds of feet inside the cliff," answered Tara, simply. She reached out her hand. The wall next to her was intermittently rocky, as if chiseled, and other parts a glassy smoothness, just as at the pit. "I don't know how much further it is to get to Marina."

"Me neither." Then a long pause before she said, "I guess we could just start walking. In the dark. Carefully? What do you think?"

Tara thought for a moment. She guessed they could. She didn't like the idea of walking completely blind, but it would take them forward. Hopefully, there was nothing else out there lurking in the darkness and waiting for them. Horrible thought, she told herself, and refused to take it further.

Then Tara had another thought. A terrible thought. "But I can't remember which way we came. I mean, I got turned around some when I almost fell and in talking to you. I don't know any more in the dark which way is toward or away from how we got in!"

There was absolute silence. Then she heard Ariel's voice, miserable in the dark. "Me neither. I got turned around too. Oh, Tara; what are we going to do?"

Tara concentrated. They had to think of something. Funny, it flashed across her mind. In the absolute darkness, it was like she was beginning to see little lights before her eyes. They weren't there, of course; they were just tricks of her mind. But it seemed like they were really there, flashing and dancing and fading in and out and changing colors. Tara stared, fascinated, and the more she stared, the more they swam before her, and chased each other, and hid around the corners of her eyes, and grew and shrank, as if in mockery.

It was like when she had clung to Marina and swum to the hole to gain entrance to this complex.

Marina. Marina! Tara felt for her princess purse and located the vial of message bubble liquid by touch. "We'll send Marina a message bubble and ask her to call our names! We'll follow her voice! Maybe she's nearby; maybe the cavern will echo her name and we'll be able to hear her!"

"Oh, great idea, Tara! You always think of something!"

Tara whispered into the bubble, using a drop of water from a canteen she always carried to wet her palm to create it, and pleaded with Marina to start calling their names, or to sing to them, or anything that would make a noise they could hear and so follow it back to her. "Hurry, Marina!" she whispered, and then blew it off with a puff.

They waited, for what seemed like long, anxious hours.

At last, very faintly, Tara thought she heard a faint, silvery voice. Was it Marina? It didn't sound like her. Was it the auditory equivalent of what had been swimming before her eyes only minutes before? She closed her eyes, only for concentration, since there was no light to shut out. Was it Marina?

"Do you hear that?"

"I'm not sure!"

"It's singing! It's Marina!"

Tara breathed a sigh of relief. "I wasn't sure if my ears were playing tricks on me!"

"No, no; they aren't! Come on, Marina's calling us! This way!" Tara felt a hand grasp her shoulder and start to tug her.

"You're sure? That seems like the wrong way, like the way we came!"

"Absolutely I'm sure! Follow me!"

Tara followed. If the song grew fainter, they could always turn back. It was strange, thought Tara, stumbling forward. The tune was indefinable and the voice haunting, not even Marina's, she would have sworn. The notes wandered through otherworldly glissandos, as if chasing some forgotten, alluring tune up and down an unfamiliar scale, and to no particular endpoint.

Steadily, the notes grew stronger and clearer. "We're here!" cried out Ariel suddenly, surprising Tara.

The song stopped and the voice Tara recognized as Marina's returned. "At last! But don't fall in the water!"

Another minute of careful edging forward and Ariel and Tara were seated again at the edge of the pool. "I can't believe we made it," exclaimed Ariel, her words punctuated by the splash of Marina's tail in the pool.

"Good thing you used the message bubbles," said Marina. "I had gone back up to the surface, it was so dark!"

"Now to head back to the surface ourselves," said Tara, not without a little bit of trepidation in her voice. "I guess it will be like it was getting down here?"

They heard Marina's tail flip idly in the pool below them. "No, I don't think so. I think it will be a lot easier. Because we'll be swimming up; it should be faster.

Ariel spoke. "I came down first; let me go up first. We'll test it on me." Tara agreed, remembering what Ariel had said about her greater lung capacity. Once all three of them were at the surface, they would all take a look at what Ariel and Tara had found. Ariel lowered herself into the water with the softest of splashes, then Tara ceased to be able to hear her. Tara began practicing breathing deeply, but before she had gotten to twenty, Marina was back.

"Ready? It really is easier going back, since we will be swimming toward the surface. Take a deep breath anyway!"

Before long, they were at the mouth of the cave below the cliff where they had gathered before diving, only now the sun was setting. Tara felt she should return right away. She promised to meet them the next morning at the base of the cliff beneath Jarvis's mansion "—where I met you the other day," and asked Ariel to carry her back up to the edge of the bluff.

Though mad with curiosity to learn what they had recovered, the other princesses understood. Tara took back the lantern in exchange for the box, as she wanted to avoid questions back at the mansion.

Ariel held the box tightly. "I'll keep it safe for us in Cloud Castle until tomorrow! And I promise not to peek!"

Tara rode Daystar back to the mansion in good spirits, having evaded with vague answers of climbing and exploring the queries of her worried escort. It was wonderful to be back in the light of day again, even if it was drawing on to dusk. In fact, Tara was grateful for the dimming light; it helped to hide her very bedraggled appearance. Good thing she had worn clothes about which she cared little.

Sullijee, though, was most distressed by the state of Tara's garments.

"Your Highness! My goodness! And you've taken a tumble, I fear? Are you all right?"

She paused, recollecting in horror. "And your illness?"

"Over that, I expect, Sullijee, thank you. Yes, I'm doing much better. But, I suppose I ought to change for dinner?" Tara added, with an arch smile.

Sullijee hadn't heard her, perhaps fortunately. She had gone already to draw a bath for Tara and to lay out fresh clothes. The faintest undertone of disapproval crept into her voice as it floated out from the bath. "It may have slipped Your Highness's mind that we receive visitors this evening. Your Highness hasn't much time, I'm afraid, to prepare."

Tara groaned inwardly. Visitors! When had this been arranged? But she didn't dare ask. Probably she had been told days ago and it really had "slipped her mind." More princessing. And the awful badinage. At least it was following a day in which she—of all people—and her friends had penetrated the fastness of the cliff and walked inside the ancient library of Syssalin.

Sullijee stepped out of the bathing room into the suite to eye Tara's head critically. She sighed, just audibly. Tara shrank under the intensity of her gaze. "I will have to dress your hair for you also, Your Highness. While you are washing, I'm afraid. For lack of time to do it otherwise."

The visitors that evening turned out to be the mayor, his wife, plus several local dignitaries, whom Tara received in a formal drawing room. Tara concentrated on maintaining her court accent but had to be vigilant, as occasionally she caught herself slipping into the vernacular, from fatigue.

Her guests were kind and complimented Tara on all she had done for Sea Sprit on her first visit. Tara protested that she had done very little, if anything. The mayor, as round and ruddy as when she had first met him, was effusive. "Well, my goodness! Your Highness! We are so delighted to have you join us this time for a few days!"

His wife leaned forward in her chair to add, "Yes! Just staying with us brings us such great honor!"

Tara replied easily that it was her great pleasure to return to Sea Sprit.

"Yes, Your Highness, and it is our *very* great pleasure to host you, and even if in such, ahem, a low-key manner—when it would be our far greater pleasure to celebrate your sojourn!" He bobbed twice in his chair as if to accentuate his enthusiasm, and Tara smiled kindly. With a start, the mayor remembered himself and signaled, not over-discreetly, for an aide, fidgeting in the background, to approach. The aide stepped to the mayor's side and proffered His Eminence a box. "Your Highness!" he announced, puffing himself up greatly, just as he had at the reviewing stand when Tara had first appeared on her mission to inspect the proposed site for the sea walls and prefatory to all his speechifying, "The People of Sea Sprit are most anxious to thank Your Highness and demonstrate their gratitude to you!"

"That is hardly necessary, Your Eminence, as it is kind of you to let me stay as it is."

"No, no, Your Highness—" he caught himself. "I mean to say, if it please Your Highness, the people of Sea Sprit beg your permission that I offer you a token of their thanks. If I may, please?"

Tara surmised that the box in the mayor's hands was for her. Her normal impulse would be to simply accept it from him and open it. But this was an official function, of a sort. She shifted her eyes to Sullijee and then darted them over to the partially outstretched hands of the mayor. That was how it was done, wasn't it? How her father and mother received items, at audiences, intended for them?

Sullijee stepped forward and graciously accepted the box. She then turned to Tara and opened it toward her, bending slightly so that Tara might see inside. Nestled within a gathered white cloth was a miniature bejeweled device in the shape of a white cresting wave. How kind of them! Tara looked up and smiled with genuine happiness.

The mayor smiled as well, seeing she was pleased. As then did his wife, observing in turn his reaction. Then the aide, if in a more formalized way. Tara began to reach to take the box, then recollected herself and gestured with a short sweep for Sullijee to display it to everyone in the room, which she did to a low buzz of approval.

The mayor continued, but such were his pauses and hesitations that, to Tara, it sounded as if he were recalling words and phrases from a hastily rehearsed speech. "Your Highness! It is The White Wave of Sea Sprit; this is from our flag. It is only a small token from the people of Sea Sprit, and which, we hope—and long may I have the honor of representing them as such!—will recollect to you your stay in our city. And the tremendous esteem in which the population holds you. For Your Highness must know how extraordinarily popular she is in Sea Sprit! Having defeated the pirates and unmasked the traitor single-handedly!"

All immediately cast their eyes downward at the mention of Jarvis, recalling his criminality. "Though Your Eminence knows quite well that this was not the case at all," resumed Tara, breaking the silence as the ranking member of the party after an appropriate interval.

The mayor's wife piped up instantly. "Your Highness is very modest! Why, indeed I believe all the girls born in the past month have all been named 'Tara' after you! Your Highness is even the subject of songs! A new dance, the Tara-Tella, is all the rage! Oh, so many young ladies in Sea Sprit are most envious of you and near despair!"

That struck Tara as highly unlikely, but she voiced her gratitude to her and the people of Sea Sprit and promised that, henceforth, the device would surely remind her of the generosity of the people of that city. The mayor's wife pointed out that the device could be affixed to a garment by a pin on the reverse and was clearly ready to continue on how it might be worn, when they were interrupted by the announcement that, if it pleased Her Highness, dinner was ready to be served. Tara, hungry, arose, and everyone in the room immediately did as well.

"Your Highness, we had thought to make a presentation to you in the square, but did not, knowing your desire to remain secluded," said the mayor, accompanying Tara to the table.

"Quite right, Your Eminence, quite right. I am recovering, after all, from a slight illness—"

The mayor's wife broke in a with a short squeal of dismay. "Your Highness is unwell?"

"Recovering! Recovered, even! It must be the… lovely sea air and the fresh breezes that blow in. Off the sea."

"The sea breezes are wonderfully refreshing, aren't they?"

"Absolutely. Such a tonic."

"I understand," added the mayor's wife slyly, now at dinner, "that Your Highness has enjoyed an afternoon or two at the ruins on the nearby bluff?"

"Why, yes, I have. The view is tremendous. Sweeping, even. And it's so, well, romantic, to idle about the ruins, here and there, and look at… this and that."

"It is. Very much so." All the guests nodded. Tara wondered if any of them had even been up there. Isn't that how it is with sites near to home: we never bother to see the ones we could see every day, because they're so close at hand. So we wind up seeing the more distant sites, because they might never be seen again.

"Yes, it's been lovely. And I think it's been instrumental in my recuperation. Oh, very much so."

"That's wonderful news indeed," replied the mayor, his smile broadening. Then his voice took on a conspiratorial tone. "I have a secret to tell Your Highness, if I may!"

"A secret!" murmured the others around the table.

A secret, wondered Tara. What could this be?

"Yes! Your Highness knows that she will be joined shortly by her mother and father, the king and queen. But what Your Highness may NOT know is that, in fact, they are already on their way here! And may even arrive tomorrow afternoon!"

Tara started in amazement, which must have surely gratified the mayor and his wife, who stifled a titter at her reaction. "I see that Your Highness IS surprised!"

Incredible, thought Tara. Whereas she had thought she would have two more days to look for the lost library, as it turned out, there would have been only one. This also meant that she would only be able to see Marina and Ariel one last time, tomorrow morning!

The mayor was speaking again, his head bobbing, much as his entire body seemed to bob at moments of intense excitement. "Yes! And may I also reveal that Her Majesty, your mother, has proposed that Sea Sprit host a grand ball, which, in fact, will launch this year's Season. All of this tomorrow night! As a surprise for Your Highness!"

"How wonderful."

"Yes! Can you believe it? We are so honored!"

"Yes. Yes! It is a great honor. And I am… very… honored. To be so honored." Tara toyed with her fork and purposefully maintained her smile. So now there would be more princessing, and shortly. Ugh, and then the hair. What a way to end what had been a wonderful holiday. She swallowed, inwardly glum, if outwardly maintaining a cheery expression.

Mercifully, the mayor changed the subject. "Has Your Highness heard that there are supposed to be secret doors in the mansion?"

Tara looked up sharply. "Really?"

"Yes! It's rumored that there is a network of subterranean passages behind these supposed secret doors, leading everywhere!"

Tara smiled. "Surely that can't be the case. Leading to everywhere."

The mayor wagged his head. "That is what is said."

And so it continued, for another agonizing hour. At last, Tara was able to plead fatigue and retire for the evening. Fortunately, there were others there to take care of the obligatory pleasantries, and so Tara could be excused. She mustn't take sick again, the mayor's wife reminded her. Not with the first ball of the Season coming the next evening!

"And you please mustn't tell your mother that I've revealed it to you!" admonished the mayor in a mock serious voice.

"Ooo—and I understand the Queen is bringing a most fabulous dress for you too!" intoned his wife, excitement and jealously mixed in equal parts in her voice.

Her friends were waiting for her at the bottom of the cliff the next morning, which she only reached when the sun was already high in the sky.

"Where have you been?" asked Marina, clambering from the surf to the rocks. The three had gathered on the sand so they could be together comfortably.

"I came as quickly as I could," replied Tara, sheepishly. "I had to go to an event last night. Dinner. With the mayor and his wife. And some others."

Marina and Ariel nodded knowingly, mollified. "I know what you mean. It's difficult to get away."

"Really! And they stayed and stayed!"

"C'mon, let's get going!" interrupted Ariel. "Down here, at the rocks. I've got everything here!"

The three turned to the pile Ariel had assembled on the other side of one of the rocks. "Let's take a look at what we have. Remember what we found in the side of the cliff? Maybe it's like that!"

None of them could imagine what they might find. Though Tara remembered how unimpressed they had been at first by what they had discovered, and then how practical each had proven quickly. Ariel hoisted the first princess purse and opened it. She plunged her hand into it and dragged out stacks of tablets. She laid these on the rock before them.

The princesses studied these for a moment and then looked to each other. Tara reached out to take one in her hand and look more closely at it. "It's got writing on it. In some language. I don't know it though." She flipped through it. There were drawings incised in the material, along with diagrams and lots of the squiggly, scratchy writing. Staring at it intently, she could just make out what must be individual letters. She put the stack down and gestured to the others. "These must be the books of the library. They look like they would be." She picked up another, and it was similar to the first. "Yes, these must be some of the books of the long-lost library of Syssalin."

The three princesses considered the pile of "books" before them for a long moment. "So, this is what everyone sought for so long," concluded Marina, quietly. "No one else ever found them. But here they are, right in our hands." She looked up at them in turn. "You found it. The library."

"*WE* found it," corrected Tara. "The three of us. It would have been impossible otherwise."

"And everyone else—hundreds of people—looked for centuries. We, just the three of us, found it in only three days. Maybe four," added Ariel, in a soft, wondering tone.

Tara nodded. It was true, if a little incredible. But, then, none of the other seekers had had both a winged and a finned friend. "Let's see what else is here," she said.

Ariel hefted the cluster of bottles for the other two to examine. "They're empty," observed Marina.

"But stoppered. I guess they're meant to hold something? Or, do they already hold something?"

"Maybe they can hold a lot? More than they look like they would? Like our purses?"

Tara was doubtful of that. The purses were so effective at that; the bottles seemed too fragile to take out and around. And who would want to hold limitless liquids? She shook her head. "We'll have to figure that one out."

The last item was the box that Tara had held so tightly to in her flight out of the pit. Ariel held it before her and lifted the lid backwards toward her to present it. Tara and Marina peered in.

"It contains… a ring! And a book."

Tara looked at it closely. It was a ring made of a strange metal and set with a red stone and so looked, in some respect, like her grandmother's ring. But the metal in this ring was of a composition Tara didn't recognize, and the stone sparkled and flashed, even in the relative darkness of the box. The book looked very much like the others except that its cover was purple and silver.

"It's magic. The ring is magic; I can feel it," breathed Marina.

Ariel turned the box so she could look in. "Yes," she said after a moment assessing it. "The ring's magic. For sure!"

Ariel put down the box and the three of them looked at the items and then at each other. Now it was time to divide amongst them their discovery. Marina spoke first. "Tara doesn't have any magic. How about she takes the ring and the book? Because it looks like they go together."

"Marina! No, that's not—" expostulated Tara. That had to be the most valuable third of the treasure, and obviously so.

Ariel nodded in agreement, cutting Tara off. "That makes sense. And I'm thinking that you, Marina, should take the tablets. For your library. Which Tara has mentioned to me." She smiled. "That leaves me with the bottles. But that makes sense, too, because I don't think they'll survive at the depths of your Coral Castle!"

Marina agreed instantly. Tara, seeing that it had been sorted, just like that, felt she had no choice but to agree. So it was done that quickly. She picked up her box with both hands and held it close. "Thank you both so much. I'll figure out what the ring can do and what the book says. I'll be sure to let you know."

Marina said she would pass the books to her father, who would surely be delighted to add them to his already considerable collection.

Ariel promised to figure out what the bottles could do and relay that to them as well.

Tara looked up into the sky, then to the mansion where she was staying overlooking the bluff. She should head back up, she told them at last, reluctantly. How sad it was that she had to leave her friends again, and for silly princessing duties too! But she felt better this time in taking her leave, because she felt that they had become fast friends in trusting their lives to each other in finding the library.

Marina's cheery, ebullient spirits immediately sank. "I'll miss you two!" she said dejectedly, her tail fin suddenly limp in the tidal pool in which she rested. "You'll send me a message bubble?"

Both Ariel and Tara immediately promised they would. "I wish you could come up with me to the mansion. Not for the silly ball, of course; but to see things."

"Me, too!"

Some other time, though, they all thought, not saying anything. After another long moment, they exchanged a second, muted round of good-byes, and then Marina, covering what Tara thought for sure must be tears, suddenly turned and slid into the water. Only when she was far enough away so that they could not make out her features distinctly did she turn and give a final, slow wave. Then she clasped close a dolphin's dorsal fin, was towed out to sea and vanished amidst the ever-rolling waves.

Tara and Ariel waved until long after she was out of sight. Ariel sighed. "Guess it's time for me to fly back too."

Tara stepped forward and gave her a hug. "You saved me back there. At the pit. You got me down safely and back up again."

"And you saved us both with your quick thinking. Several times and, each time, you were right!"

"I guess we owe each other then, huh?"

Once more they said their good-byes, then Ariel unfolded her wings in the complicated and fascinating way that they always unfurled and, in a moment, they were a blur behind her. She lifted from the ground silently and gave a short, quick farewell wave, then darted up into the bright sky toward the single cloud hanging overhead. Cloud Castle, of course, realized Tara, following Ariel's trajectory with her eyes. Then she was gone too. Tara sighed, disheartened. Time to get back for sure. Her parents might even have already arrived. She turned away from the shimmering tidal pool in which Marina had lately rested and the footprints in the sand in which Ariel had just been standing to make her way back through the passage to the swinging mirror door and her room.

Her parents arrived toward the evening. Tara was dressed and ready to meet them at the top of the steps leading to the ballroom, the crystal chandeliers lit behind her so that she was silhouetted, she thought, to best advantage to impress her parents that her week's stay in Sea Sprit had been beneficial. She had even had Sullijee elaborately coif her hair in a coiled braid that took forever, in Tara's estimation, to complete.

"Oh, Your Highness," Sullijee had remarked on catching sight of Tara's right hand while arranging her hair. "That is such a lovely ring you're wearing! I've never seen it before!"

Tara had laughed and held it up to eye it, as if out of novelty. "Oh, that! I found it in the ruins of the city!"

Sullijee had caught her breath and nearly dropped her brush. "Your Highness! That's—that's just amazing! You have the sharpest eyes! People have wandered those ruins quite literally for centuries and never found anything!"

Tara had shrugged casually. "Well, I was up there for nearly two days straight, wasn't I? Just sort of enjoying the view. And poking around. So, one might have expected I would find something."

Sullijee had stared in disbelief. "It is most remarkable, Your Highness. It must be ancient, but it's in such marvelous condition. And the stone… it simply glows!"

Tara had glanced down at it again. "Just the light, I would imagine. I'm sure it's nothing more than a curiosity. But it is another nice souvenir of my time here, isn't it?"

Sullijee had gaped at Tara's "luck" in finding the ring; Tara had been secretly amused. There, she had thought: now Sullijee would have something to report to her mother. And they both would have a story as to what Tara had been doing up on the bluff for two days straight!

In fact, her mother remarked on the ring that night at dinner. Tara repeated the same story she had told Sullijee. Interesting, she observed privately, that her mother had noticed it so quickly. Even if it did gleam strangely, and seemingly more so by firelight and candlelight than sunlight.

"You're looking so much better!" her father observed proudly

Tara smiled. "From the wonderful ocean air! It's refreshed me. I think I've fully recovered from my illness."

"That's very good," her mother agreed, her hand fluttering. "Because of course we will have a reception. Here. In this very mansion." She sniffed. "Put it at last to some good use, I should think."

Ah yes, the ball the mayor had mentioned. So it was true. Tara's shoulders drooped fractionally. "When is it to take place?"

"Why, tomorrow night, in fact! In celebration of your time here! In Sea Sprit!"

Of my stay here? Tara wondered at that. Who would be celebrating that? Only her mother. And as a pretext for a social event. She was glad to have been forewarned by the mayor and his wife.

The entire mansion glittered the next evening, preparations having begun early that morning. Her mother sailed up and down the ballroom floor, back and forth, sternly directing the requisite last-minute preparations for the many arrivals due any minute. That glass polished again, those candles straightened minutely, that table arranged and re-arranged just so.

Tara followed in her wake. You must learn how to prepare for an event like this, her mother had insisted. Tara had dutifully obeyed, at her heels with every step, splendid in a voluminous ballgown patterned in deep blue, wider, horizontal stripes alternating with narrower, pecan-brown stripes, and which her mother had produced for the occasion. Her white sash of royalty was fixed at her shoulder with an enamel of her royal ensign and pinned at the waist by the newly given White Wave of Sea Sprit.

All this she wore for the reception, for the House of Hession, and for the Kingdom of Brythrony. But for herself, on a chain around her neck and far too far down the bodice for anyone to ever suspect, was her grandmother's ring. Additionally, on her right hand, on her index finger, was the fascinating ring she had recovered from the lost library. Occasionally she studied at it as she trailed her mother up and down the floor or caught sight of it reflected in the mirrors lit by so many shining candles, or distantly in the glass doors at the very end of the hall. Didn't it sparkle, as if with its own, inner light? Tara resolved to investigate if the book that had come with it offered any explanation.

"Princess Tara! Whatever are you doing? Are you listening to me? You understand this, yes? That the arrangements must be centered, like this, so that they balance those over there and reflect your appreciation of symmetry?"

"Yes, Mom."

"Were you at *all* listening to me?"

"Yes, Mom. Of course I was."

Just then, they heard from downstairs the rattle of the latch to the front door being thrown open. The stentorian voice of the butler echoed up the staircase. "His Eminence, the Mayor, and his wife!"

"Come, Tara! Quickly! They're arriving!"

"Yes, Mom, I'm right beside you."

"Oh, and your hair! If only we had a few more minutes. But, oh, no time for that now! Remember, say something to everyone—kind things!—and keep your conversation light and airy!"

Princess Florence

"I wonder what on earth Tara is doing?" wondered her father, King Childeric, aloud. "I mean, we have hardly seen her for days!"

His wife, Queen Armorica, looked up from the papers in which she had been thoroughly engrossed. She had been reviewing the proposals on themes and venues for the upcoming Season that had been arriving over the past week. Some of them seemed quite good too, she murmured thoughtfully. "Hm? What's that, dear?"

"Tara. Where has Tara been?"

"Up in her room, I suppose. Or with Daystar." Armorica seemed strangely unconcerned.

This was unusual. His wife was almost always exceptionally interested in what Tara was doing, even inadvisably so at times. Now she seemed indifferent. But—yes—he remembered: it was because of the Season. That time of year again. Childeric's mouth twitched. The season—no, it must be capitalized: The Season. It was of inordinate importance to Armorica and to certain others in particular social circles in the kingdom, even if much less so to Childeric and not at all to Tara.

On this Childeric really did sympathize with his daughter. No one minded that he had little interest in the Season; the males of the kingdom were not really expected to do much with it, really, except fund it. The married males, that is. As for the unmarried males, they were invited to attend, and it was desired that they attend. Their role was to dance with the ladies, comment on dress and supply some amount of gossip, depending on the event. Yes, Childeric had been to a few of these events in his time. That had been before—he seemed to recollect—they had assumed the importance they had today.

It was generally the more dandified males who regularly attended those events. Childeric was proud that he had not met his spouse through the Season. Rather, he had met her while he had been on campaign. Through her mother, he was proud to say—proud, because she had taken a liking to him because he had been very much an out-and-about sort of prince, and it had been on one such out-and-aboutings that he had encountered Queen Ysolde. Chasing bandits, or something like that. Childeric smiled to himself. Ysolde had never been a fan of the Season either, though she had tolerated it on account of her daughter's interest. Which interest, unfortunately for both daughter Tara and Queen Armorica, had not been inherited by the next generation.

Odd, though, that he hadn't seen his daughter very much in days. What *was* she up to? He resolved to enquire into it when an opportunity came up.

Tara was indeed very busy in her rooms in the North Tower. So busy that she had hardly come down, except for meals and to regularly currycomb Daystar. She took him out for rides too, lost in thought. Stablemaster Geoffrey noted her distraction. Something's on her mind, he decided, but knew it was not his place to ask as to what.

Just then, Tara was bent over a book, a book with a purple cover and silver—no, gold, depending on the light—writing on it. This was unusual for Tara, as she had never been studious. Ever. It had never come to a question of ability. Rather, it had always been lack of interest and a refusal to apply herself. She had shown some interest in applied physics, such as why things worked and functioned the way they did, but little in rhetoric, hardly at all in song or versifying, and had proven virtually impossible to instruct in any instrument.

Tara read well, but selectively. No patience for the history of Brythrony, to Armorica's mortification, though quite a bit about her maternal grandmother, Queen Ysolde. Armorica had been delighted, at first, but her happiness had waned when it had become clear that Tara's interest was mainly in her grandmother's most tomboyish adventures. For example, she had been asked repeatedly to tell the story of how Ysolde, in her youth, had personally strode the battlements of Stonedell, rallying its defenders, when it had been under assault by a neighboring kingdom. Not at all about her contributions to governance, diplomacy, or to relations with the nobility of Brythrony, which required attention and had to be managed just as much as those with external parties.

At this particular point, Tara was wishing she had put a little more effort into history, because the book from the library of Syssalin she was poring over was nigh unintelligible. Maybe, she was thinking, if she had absorbed more history, some of the words—not all of which she could make out— might be sensible and combine to make decipherable sentences. Too often, understanding was frustratingly just beyond her grasp!

Or a foreign language? Would a foreign language have helped her to understand these impossible sentences?

It was irritating! Tara replaced the book in its box and then back in the top drawer in which she kept her special mementos. She tossed herself on her bed, her legs dangling over the side at the knee, kicking slowly back and forth, her toes barely brushing the floor. Here she was, the same Tara who had figured out how to find the book and ring but unable to understand what they were all about. She lay back and looked up at the ring on her finger. What was it after all? It looked special. It had to *be* special, because it had been found in a hidden library.

For the first time since returning from Sea Sprit, Tara looked hard and long at it. Not just admiringly and from arm's length, but closely and searchingly. She brought it up to her eye and scrutinized it from every angle. She still didn't recognize the metal that formed the band; its color was not one she had seen before in jewelry. She blinked twice and screwed her eyes up tight to focus. Was that something inscribed on the band? Yes, characters of some sort and formed by a series of thin swirls and lines. Tara studied them intently. They looked much like the characters in the book that had been in the box alongside it. Tara let her hand fall to her side. They were. She had assumed that the book and the ring were linked, because they were in the same box, but had not explored the thought further. Tara lifted her hand to examine the ring again. Yes. The characters were the same as those in the book.

A thought occurred to her. Were the characters the same as those on the map that had led them to the princess purses? It would make sense, if those who had left the princess purses had also made the ring! And this was exciting, because Marina's father, King Aenon, had been able to decipher some of the writing, meaning perhaps he could help with the book and the ring.

Tara smiled and nodded eagerly. King Aenon could surely help her read it. Maybe the tablet-books Marina had taken back to Coral Castle from the library might be of further assistance in translating her book.

Marina had said the ring was magic. Ariel had agreed. It certainly looked magical to Tara. The book had been stored together with the ring and had similar and maybe the same characters inscribed in it. If the ring were magic then, perhaps, the book was as well? Suggesting that, if translated such that Tara could read it, Tara would have magical powers?

Tara sat fully upright. This was an amazing, incredible thought: a magical Tara! But why not? Ariel was a magical person because she could fly. Marina was too, as a mermaid, and her father had a trident with what could only be described as magical powers in the way it could control water. Tara had no magic, none whatsoever, but maybe this book could change that! Tara grinned broadly and began to kick her feet back and forth faster as she began to imagine herself doing the most phenomenal, magical things to the incredulity of her family, the entire court of Brythrony, all the world!

But what would she do with such powers? Make everyone immediately and totally forget the Season! Tara smiled. That was silly, of course. If she had magic, she wouldn't care about the Season, and the frowning disapprobation of all those who thought it so important wouldn't mean anything. No, she couldn't imagine what sort of magic the book contained, but it had to be powerful and special, as it had been secreted in the city's closely guarded library.

A thought occurred to her: perhaps the book had even been the secret weapon of Syssalin that the barbarian warrior king had sought! That would mean that the book must contain unbelievable powers, so much so that, had it been employed, it would have repelled a vast barbarian horde!

Tara jumped up to fumble through the top drawer of her chest for her princess purse. It was time to send a message to Marina, whose father's help she needed. But how to get the book in their hands? Tara stood motionless for a long minute, the vial of fluid for message bubbles in one hand and the other still on the drawer handle, until at last a slow smile crept across her face. Then she formed the message bubble, whispered into it and sent it into the sunlight with a puff of breath.

The next morning, Tara awoke to find a message bubble hovering over her head. It drifted down a little as she sat up, as if anxious for her to extend her hand and listen to its message. Tara rubbed her eyes, adjusted her position so that a few pillows were supporting her back, yawned, and only then stretched out her right hand. The bubble promptly settled into it.

Tara puffed on it gently, and she heard Marina speak. "Hey! How are you? What an interesting idea! I've never tried it, but I guess I could. I mean, freshwater shouldn't hurt me, although I've really never swum up a river before! Oh, and sure: how about later today, since I'll already be in the area? A little after noon? I can make that, with some help from my sea-creature (as you call them) friends!"

Perfect, thought Tara, yawning again. I'll ride Daystar out and pass her the book this afternoon. That decided, Tara dressed and trotted downstairs for breakfast. Her parents were already at the table.

"Hello, dear, how have you been?"

"Fine, Mom, thanks. How're you?"

"Very well, thank you. You look very pretty today!"

"Thank you, Mom! That's so nice of you!" But inwardly, Tara's suspicions were aroused. She had just thrown on what she called her "any ol' clothes," which she kept mainly for activities involving curry-combing Daystar and riding. She knew she was hardly looking grand; there had to be some other motive behind her mother's compliment.

Or was she being too suspicious? Because hadn't her mother just paid her a compliment? Tara reflected, smiled pleasantly and took a seat at the family table in front of her bowl of porridge.

"So, what have you been up to these last few days? So alone and withdrawn in your room?"

"Oh, not much, Mom. Just, you know, working. On things. That sort of thing."

"Hm," replied her mother, unconvinced. Tara, working? Like, being studious? That was hard to believe, based on experience. A sudden thought occurred to her. She looked over to her daughter, a sly expression coming over her. "Were you, maybe, thinking of someone? Was that it?"

Tara started, as much from the subtle shift in her mother's tone as the half-hidden smile that had stolen over her face. Her mother couldn't possibly know of Marina and Ariel, could she? Or could that Sullijee have somehow seen something and told her mother? Maybe when the three of them had been together on that last day in Sea Sprit, at the base of the cliff beneath Jarvis's mansion? "Uh, no, not really, Mom…"

A triumphant smile settled on her mother's face at watching her daughter's reaction. "Dear, it's all right. I'm thinking you met someone at the ball we held in Sea Sprit! It's perfectly natural! Won't you tell me who he is?"

So that was it. "Mom, no. I didn't meet anyone at the ball. That's not it."

Her mother's face fell momentarily, then that same crafty look slowly reappeared. "Then what is it? What were you doing? What's the matter then?"

"Mom! It's not that… it's… nothing." How could Tara tell them now about the magic ring and the box and the tablet-book she was going to pass to Marina in the hopes of learning magic? How?

Childeric looked up from the document he was studying. "Armorica, let her be. If she doesn't want to tell you who she's thinking about, that's all right. Isn't it?"

Armorica's face was a mix of perplexity and disappointment. "Well! I suppose you're right. But, I guess, well, I mean, I had no trouble talking to MY mother about the boys to whom I took a fancy!"

"I know, Armorica. But, if she doesn't want to… Maybe she shouldn't have to."

Her mother composed herself. "Of course not." She turned back to Tara. "Of course, you don't have to tell me just now. You can tell me later, as you're ready. That's fine."

Tara had to resist rolling her eyes. She hadn't met anyone at that silly ball in Sea Sprit. The entire evening had consisted almost entirely of following her mother around. Yes, and there had been heaps and heaps of badinage. And some dancing—which she had done her best to avoid—and receiving lines and complicated greetings in the court accent. Still, because she could hardly admit the truth to her parents, she sat there instead and stirred her porridge, perhaps a little too fiercely. "Thank you, Mom. When I'm ready. Yes."

This position appeared to please most of them, or at least displease the fewest, and the meal returned to the usual morning topics, punctuated by the regular click of spoons against bowls.

Armorica spoke again shortly, and striving to affect artlessness. "When you're ready to tell me who he is—whoever he is—I'm hoping you'll let me know in advance of the next ball we're planning. So he can attend. So you can see him again."

"The ball?"

"Yes. The ball. The Season is upon us, you know. We need to be planning for it."

Tara took a measured breath. The Season. Yes, because hadn't the Season been launched at the ball at Princess Hall in Sea Sprit. Tara hesitated. On the one hand, she would like to know when the next event she would be expected to attend might be, the better to steel herself for it. On the other, she dreaded conveying to her mother even the remotest flicker of interest in it. So she just nodded and said nothing.

"I have the plans for the next event. At my desk. Wouldn't you like to come and take a look at them with me?"

Tara was devoutly wishing she had stayed upstairs. Now she simply had to look at the plans. If she did not, her mother would be very upset with her for failing to show interest in events which were supposed to be, in some way which she would never be able to fathom, for her benefit.

Tara looked glumly down into her nearly empty bowl. Hardly anyone she knew would attend, and those who would be present would be either better connected, or more attractive, or wealthier, or somehow something more than her. About the only thing that Tara could be sure of being more than anyone there—at least from Brythrony—was of a higher station. But then again, princesses from other, larger kingdoms frequently attended and, as far as kingdoms went, Brythrony was, quite frankly, smaller and poorer. "Yes, Mom," she replied simply. "Right after breakfast?" Best to get it over with.

Her mother straightened involuntarily in her chair. This was exactly the answer she was longing to hear! "Very good, Tara! Good idea! You'll see: it will be so exciting! Why, I remember doing this with my mother each and every Season!"

It took Tara several hours to extricate herself and get away to ride Daystar. "He's been waiting for you," chided Geoffrey the Stablemaster. Daystar whinnied as Tara approached. She stroked his mane. "But you'd never be angry with me, would you? And you'd never insist I attend a ball, right?" Daystar whinnied again and nuzzled her, nosing for the treat that Tara almost always brought him. Tara interpreted the response in the negative and smiled. "I knew you wouldn't," Tara whispered affectionately back.

"Will you be gone long, Your Highness?"

"No, Geoffrey. Just down to the river, I think, and back again. Maybe I'll go via the fields."

"Very good, Your Highness."

Tara brought Daystar to a brisk canter and off they set for the River Vahaval. That was not the direction she usually roamed, because she generally preferred the opposite direction, toward the forests and meadows. Today, and perhaps out of simple caprice, she wanted to go to the river. That was what she was sure Geoffrey was thinking, at least.

Effecting the rendezvous required the exchange of several more message bubbles, but at last it was done. Tara left Daystar to graze on the banks and met her friend some way from the shore, removing her shoes and leggings to do so.

"Hey! How are you!" Marina fairly shrieked on catching sight of Tara, so delighted was she to see her friend.

Tara smiled. It was fun how demonstrative Marina was. She was so earnest and likable! Tara knew she wasn't really like that, but it struck her that maybe she might like to try it, if only because of the happiness it must surely spread.

"I'm—well! Great!" enthused Tara, deciding to try out this new persona immediately. "Yes! Really great!"

Marina waved her arms about wildly, as if transported by excitement. "That's great! I'm great too!"

Tara chuckled to herself. Didn't it work! Marina had become even happier. And making people happier was a good thing, right? It had to be. Tara thought to experiment more with this new attitude.

"Right! I'm great! And here, in my princess purse, is the book I told you about!" Tara withdrew the tablet-book from her purse and placed it in Marina's outstretched hand.

Marina examined it critically. "The pages are like the pages of the other books from the Syssalin library. The same hard material." She tapped a page with her forefinger. "It's not shell, but then it's not bone or ivory. Strange, huh?" She looked up at Tara with bright eyes and shrugged innocently.

Marina closed the book and studied its cover. "Your cover looks to be made of the same material as the ones I have, but the color is more purplish... and with a sort of gold writing. Mine looks more like a frost blue. With silver writing." She flipped through the pages. "Binding's the same, I guess." She stopped at a page and examined it thoughtfully, her voice softening and her caudal fin carving eddies meditatively in the river's current. "Funny, though: the symbols inside are a little different than the ones in my books. I mean, some of them are the same..."

Her voice trailed off and she looked up to Tara, her pupils contracting in the bright daylight to tiny pinpoints, which seemed to swim in the Bleu de France and pastel turmoil of her irises. "But not all of them. My father has been looking through the books. He loves trying to understand them. 'Cause he really likes his library." She mused over the tablet in her hand. "He'll like looking at this one too."

"I'm sure he will," agreed Tara. "Let me know what he finds. Please!" she added, forcing an eagerness into her voice upon remembering her decision to be more demonstrative.

Marina promised she would and that she would return it "because, after all, it goes with the ring."

They chatted about Tara's parents and Marina's siblings until Marina said she should get going if she was to make it out to sea with the receding tide— it made swimming a lot easier, she explained. The two princesses said goodbye, with, as always, numerous promises to stay in touch, and Tara remounted Daystar and began the slow jog back to Stonedell.

Tara rode away, very satisfied. The tablet was in good hands. If anyone could figure it out, that would be King Aenon. That left her with the ring. Maybe the tablet explained the ring, but maybe it didn't. She slowed Daystar still further and scrutinized the ring again. What could a ring like this do, she wondered? She had heard stories of rings that granted wishes, rings that transported their wearers to wherever they wished, rings that cast spells, rings that did all sorts of things. Brythrony didn't have any magic rings to her knowledge. Maybe this might be its first.

She took the reins in her left hand and held out her right. What could it do? Maybe something wonderful! Maybe, too, nothing at all, thought Tara with a sinking feeling, despite what her friends had told her. But as if in answer, a tendril of warmth crept up her finger and spread across her. What was this, she wondered, her heart quickening. Something from the ring? Then, she suddenly understood what the ring was and what it could do. The knowledge was as complete as it was sudden, as if the ring had told her itself. But that was impossible. The ring wasn't alive; it couldn't communicate.

Yet, as of that instant, Tara knew what the ring was. It was a Ring of Shooting Stars and would project flame and fire in the direction in which she pointed the finger wearing the ring. She had only to specify the form the fire should take and use the appropriate gesture. The ring's crystal would provide the power.

"Amazing," whispered Tara. A Ring of Shooting Stars. "Could it be true?" She immediately thought to try it and pointed her finger at the tree to her immediate right. Then, thinking again, she hastily elevated her hand into the bright sky and whispered "fireball," and instantly the ring pulsed, glowed for a fraction, and from it soared heavenwards an immense ball of flame. "Incredible!" Tara fairly shouted.

Just like that, thought Tara. It had been so easy. I just had to put my mind to it, to start thinking about the ring, and there it was: full understanding! From the ring itself. Was it alive, somehow, in some way? Tara stopped Daystar and stared down hard at the ring. "Am I supposed to talk to you?" she finally asked it, hesitantly. But the ring gave no answer. Let me think hard, she decided. Hello, Ring! Um, how are you!

No answer to that either.

Ring, thank you for accepting me!

No answer.

Do you speak at all?

Still no response. Absolutely nothing. Tara waited a little longer, but still nothing happened. Interesting, concluded Tara at last, and nudged Daystar back to a trot.

So, the ring didn't talk. But she still felt the ring on her finger and still understood that she could put her hands in front of her, spread apart, thumbs touching, and call for a "spark shower," and from the ring would emanate a brilliant cascade of sparks. A fireball was produced by pointing and flexing the ring-wearing finger. Splaying the fingers of her right hand and requesting a "meteor swarm" brought forth half a dozen lesser fireballs that, though less intense, covered a larger area when they exploded. And maybe some other applications she didn't know she knew yet.

But the ring never communicated further or imparted anything more, despite repeated attempts to elicit more. Never, for as long as Tara would have it, would it reveal anything about its previous owners, how it was made, or how it had arrived in the Syssalin library. It was a fabulous ring, with extraordinary powers, but ultimately just a ring.

This caused Tara to start thinking about the book that had accompanied the ring. Maybe the book was as accessible as the ring, if she just tried harder with it. Maybe then she'd understand it, just as she had with the ring, and she'd be able to cast spells and do incredible things! Only good things though, she reassured herself. My power must be used for good only. Like—here she laughed again—getting rid of the Season. But no, not for trivial things like the Season or even, she frowned, princessing. Only for really important, serious things, like protecting Stonedell from an attacker, or rescuing people, or stopping barbarian warrior kings from razing Stonedell in a search for magic weapons, as had befallen Syssalin.

That made Tara think. She should be careful about this amazing Shooting Stars ring and the potentially magical book. If others found out about them, they might try to steal them, or even force Tara to abuse them. That must not happen. Tara resolved that, should she figure out how to work magic, she would let only her friends know, so neither she nor any magic she learned could be abused.

Tara nodded. That made a lot of sense. Keep it a secret until she was in control of it. Only then tell select others. Maybe her parents—eventually. Though she wasn't sure how they would react to magic. Tara thought about that for a moment. But she already had magic. She had the magic of the Ring of Shooting Stars.

No, she thought again, steadily making her way back to Stonedell, they probably wouldn't like magic. They didn't believe in it. Maybe because there had not been magic in Brythrony for a long time. There were tales of it, sure, and every now and then people came from afar talking about it, but nothing in Brythrony. Maybe it would be better, just for a while, not to mention it to anyone except her friends.

Queen Armorica approached King Childeric in the royal suite the next day, late. "I'm telling you, she's thinking of someone!"

King Childeric was taken by surprise. "She?" "Someone?" He thought for a moment. His wife gazed at him expectantly, as if it should be obvious to whom she was referring.

She took his hesitation as disbelief. "Yes, I know it! Call it mother's intuition, but I'm certain!"

"Mother's intuition," thought Childeric. So it was about Tara. Oh! Of course: about Armorica's contention that Tara was pining over someone she had met at the ball in Sea Sprit.

Childeric recovered easily. From long practice, he was dismayed to realize. "Really? But Tara denied it!"

Armorica smiled, knowingly. "Oh, sure she did! But I've known her since birth, of course! I know her better than she knows herself!"

Childeric was pleased that he had unraveled the riddle as to whom

Armorica was referring but took some offense at the insinuation that he had not known Tara since birth likewise. "See here, I'm no different on that. On knowing her from birth!"

"Well, then, I've known her since before birth! But whatever: I know her. And, I'm telling you, she's thinking of someone. I'm sure of it. She's met someone."

"Why do you think that?"

"Have you not heard how excited she is now? She's fairly bursting with enthusiasm! It's 'yes!' this and 'yes!' that, and with all sorts of excitement!"

"But you said yesterday morning that she was hiding herself away, and that it had to be because she was unhappy from wanting to see someone."

Armorica halted, but only for a moment. "It's all the same. These mood swings. They just go to prove my point."

Childeric said nothing. He was baffled as to how to respond to his wife's expressed argument that, far from undermining her position, all of Tara's behaviors—however contradictory they might be—were actually proof of Armorica's deeper understanding. It seemed most unlikely to him that his daughter's opposite moods could somehow simultaneously be evidence of the same emotion.

But maybe he just didn't understand his daughter like her mother did. Maybe he didn't understand his wife like he thought he did.

"Yes. I'm certain," she concluded, with finality, after again interpreting Childeric's hesitation as scepticism.

Something else occurred to Childeric. "But she hasn't received anything from Sea Sprit. So why the mood swing? But maybe you're thinking her romantic interest is someone in this very castle?"

This caused Armorica to pause longer. She had been confident that the interest had come from Sea Sprit. But as Childeric had pointed out, there had been no communication from Sea Sprit. "Not officially," she agreed slowly. "So it must have come in secret! By a secret courier! No, I'm certain! It's a prince from a nearby kingdom. But who? I have to—I simply must—find out!"

Childeric nodded thoughtfully. A "secret courier." Well, maybe. But he had a hard time believing in an ongoing exchange of messages between Tara and her mysterious beau without her two parents catching on. It would be very difficult to keep such a secret, even with some of the palace guard assisting. Still, he reminded himself, now that she had switched to an unrelated topic, the search for such a courier could occupy Armorica for a while.

Upstairs in the North Tower, Tara lay sprawled across her bed, drained. Not physically so, though she had taken Daystar on a lengthy ride, but from being so relentlessly cheery all day long. Tara rolled over onto her stomach. She wasn't a dour, unhappy person, but being constantly enthusiastic required real effort. It was surprisingly hard being like Marina. How did she do it, every single day? So many exclamation points. She hardly ever seemed unhappy when they got together. The only times that she seemed sad were when it came time to leave her friends, and that—if anything—illustrated how happy she was to be with them. If only. If only Tara could be so bubbly and friendly and happy.

But it was a good and wonderful thing to be so happy, she reminded herself determinedly. Good, because it made other people cheerier and happier, as she had seen in the impact on Marina at the River Vahaval. Further, maybe, the more Tara practiced being cheery, the more she would become cheery herself. It just required a change in mindset.

Tara's thoughts began to wander. Her mother often told her she was grumpy. Could it be true? Tara felt very uncomfortable thinking of herself as a grumpy person.

But was she grumpy? Really? Tara grimaced. Maybe cheeriness would come with practice. Think like Marina, she told herself as she prepared to crawl into bed for the night. Just keep thinking like Marina.

It wasn't long before Tara received a message bubble from Marina, relating how she and her father had made impressive progress on translating the text from Tara's book. Well, really, her father, she conceded. Yes, just as they had expected, it contained spells. She could pass it back in a day or two; would that suit? Tara responded enthusiastically with her own bubble that that would be perfect. She intended to study the book as soon as she had it again and cast her first spell in front of her and Ariel shortly thereafter. Wouldn't that be something to look forward to?

Tara immediately sent a similar bubble to Ariel. The book contained spells, King Aenon was translating it, and as soon as Tara had it back, she would learn a spell and cast it—her first ever!—before them. How did that sound?

Ariel responded in ready agreement and confided as well—in a voice that came across as an especially mysterious whisper—that she now understood what the bottles were and could do. She'd explain when they met up for Tara's spell casting.

A day or so later, Tara had the tablet back in hand but with the translation too. Tara retreated to her tower to study it, this time with a lot more cause for hope. At least it was a rest from trying to be so happy all the time about—oftentimes—not very much. But then she regretted that thought as inherently downbeat. No, better to say that at least this was a real project with a real outcome. It was an opportunity to learn real, live magic!

Tara sat at her vanity, staring down at the book's listing of its spells. Time to buckle down and really start studying, she told herself. But, wow, look at all the spells: there were pages and pages of them. There were spells of summoning, evoking, dispelling, dispatching—what was the difference?—entrancement, postponement, and even others, on the last pages, that, just looking at them, made her skin crawl. The characters seemed to squirm about on the page as she gazed down at them, and she felt slightly nauseous in reading them now that she had the translation.

Those spells must be darker magic. She didn't want to get involved in that. She wanted only good, decent magic. She turned the page back again. She should start with a "lighter" magic spell, and one of the easier ones at that. From the top of the list. But one which did something that she and her friends could see happening. How about a spell of summoning? Some had to do with the weather, she saw. That seemed harmless enough. Marina had mentioned that the second one under "summoning" was supposed to summon rain. Examining it, it looked pretty simple: just a couple of lines. Not too tough, right? The others had, well, eight or nine lines each. So then she'd summon a little shower.

Tara looked out of the window. This choice sounded really smart to her. There was little to go wrong with bringing some rain. If she was a little "light" on the power of the spell—however that might happen—then it would be a very, very brief shower. But still detectable. On the other hand, if she went too "heavy" on the power, well, because she would cast it down by the river, any flooding would promptly roll out to sea.

Yes, it was perfect, she decided. Simple, in that the spell wasn't long or complicated and its results would be benign. Really, the only worry was if it was raining already the day it came time to cast her spell, because then no one would be able to discern that the spell had worked. Why, even the gestures accompanying the spell looked easy! She followed with her eyes the described movements and even rehearsed them slowly but without the words so as not to create a thunderstorm in the tower. Easy, but she'd still study it diligently, and in a way she never had with history, and sums, and court etiquette.

But all of that was for the future. Just then, Tara was delighted she had decided which spell she would learn. She was also hungry, as she hadn't had much for breakfast, being so preoccupied with spell selection. She looked out of the window at the morning sky; it wasn't too late in the morning to go down and get a bite from the kitchen.

First, though, she needed a pair of shoes. She peered beneath the bed where, inexplicably, all her shoes seemed to wind up. Yes, there were shoes back there. She reached into the darkness and grabbed, by turns, five or six and paired the two that looked to be the most closely matched. After wriggling her feet into them, she clattered down the stairs for the kitchen.

Besides the usual complement of cooks, scullery, and suppliers, she found her mother. "Hi, Mom," she greeted her gaily, then hastily corrected herself. "Good morning, Your Majesty!"

"Good morning, Princess Tara," her mother replied, then eyed her daughter up and down quickly. Her eyes seemed to rest for a fraction longer on the shoes but passed on quickly, which Tara took to be indicative that her choices were indeed matched close enough. "How are you this morning, Princess Tara?"

"Super, Your Majesty!"

Her mother's eyes widened. "Very good. I'm glad to hear that."

"I just came down to see if I could get something to eat. Anything, uh, left over that I could have?"

One of the kitchen staff approached and curtsied. "Beggin' Your pardon, Your Highnesses, but it would not be difficult at all to make—"

"No, no, just something left over! I don't want to be a bother!"

"Well, we have the bread left over from this morning, just toasted?"

"Perfect!" Tara took it eagerly and, with a piece of cloth she intended to use as a sort of napkin, vanished out through the scullery's rear door in the direction of the stables. Armorica followed her with her eyes as long as she was in sight, then returned to giving her instructions to the staff on preparations for that evening's banquet for a visiting diplomat, an event about which Tara had already learnt and fully intended to miss.

"She's happy again," confided Armorica to Childeric later that evening, after the banquet. "Really, I'm happy for her. It's so sweet!"

Childeric noted that his wife had said nothing about Tara being absent from that evening's meal, when usually she would have insisted on her presence.

Armorica sighed gently. "I mean," she continued, turning to her husband, "you should have seen her this morning! Her shoes weren't even matched! She's so in love she can't even put together a pair of shoes correctly!"

Childeric said nothing, choosing instead to nod sagely and narrow one eye, as if expertly adjudging this sentiment.

Armorica understood that expression favorably. "It *is* sweet. She must have received another letter. Directly to the North Tower. That's why she was up there all this morning. It's so romantic, don't you think?"

Childeric was less enthusiastic about the possibility of correspondence entering and leaving the castle relating to the royal family without their knowledge, but then he doubted its existence to begin with. He only nodded again.

"No, and I won't try to interfere with it either. Of course, I'm tempted to find out *who* it is, but I won't. But on the other hand, the next ball is coming up soon, and we simply have to make sure he's invited. I have to find out, somehow, who he is, or she'll be crushed! Absolutely crushed! Poor Tara!"

"But how will you find out, if not by intercepting one of the letters?"

"Well, of course that wouldn't help me anyway! Because, naturally, it wouldn't be signed properly by the actual author!"

Of course it wouldn't, thought Childeric. It would be signed, Your Sweetest Strawberry, or similar.

"And, further, it would all be in code. They'd have invented a code. Oh, Tara's very clever; she's devised something very complicated so she can correspond with her special friend and not be discovered if the message should fall into the wrong hands."

Childeric assumed an inquiring expression.

Armorica became resolute. "I'll just have to find out who he is by other means. I can. I know how. I'll ask the other ladies of the Realm. Mothers know, you know!"

Childeric nodded again. If she were right, at least he would find out more about this correspondence occurring without their knowledge. "Time for bed, right?"

Days later, Tara, Ariel, and Marina gathered by the river bank. Marina had swum up again from the ocean, making a special trip to watch. First, Ariel had her story to relate.

"They're stasis bottles. That's what they are. From the library," she explained, calmly and knowingly.

Marina and Tara looked to each other. "But what are stasis bottles?" asked Marina. Tara had been framing the exact same question.

"They're bottles in which time stands still." The others eyed her, bewildered. "It's like this: if you put something or someone in a stasis bottle, that someone or something doesn't get any older, or get hungry, or thirsty, or anything. Whatever's in the bottle experiences no change at all, because time doesn't move inside a stasis bottle."

Tara and Marina mulled this revelation over for a moment. "But the bottle's so small. How would you put a person into it?"

Ariel pretended that she was holding a bottle and gestured with it. "That part's magic too, just like the bottle. You just put the mouth of the bottle right on top of the person, and the bottle sort of sucks the person into it."

"Wow," murmured Marina. "Just like that. Like, all of sudden, you're inside a bottle. Looking out!"

"Yes. But you can't get out once you're inside; you have to be released. In that way, it's like a miniature prison for all eternity and in which you never get older or change in any way."

That had to be serious magic, thought Tara. Super powerful, and sort of scary. "Could you accidentally put yourself in a stasis bottle? Just by mishandling it?"

Ariel shook her head. "No. Because you're holding the bottle. The bottle would be trying to put itself in its own bottle. That's impossible. So the bottle is harmless to whoever's holding it."

That made sense to Tara, and she said so, and everyone agreed with her. Then Tara's voice brightened and, having already explained the Ring of Shooting Stars in message bubbles, she picked up what surely had to be on the other princesses' minds. "Are you ready for my first spell? Do you want to see?" Both nodded eagerly, but Tara thought to caution them again. "Look, this is my first time! So I chose a really small spell. I know you've seen a lot of magic before but, well, it's my first time. I just don't want you to expect too much."

"Don't worry! We're very excited to see!" enthused Marina immediately.

Ariel clapped her hands quietly a few times in support and, with that, Tara closed her eyes and concentrated. She put her hands out in front of her and, to calm herself, imagined herself back in her room in the North Tower. Gesture like this, and this, she told herself, and moved her hands thusly. Say these words and then these, she continued. Finish with a flourish like THAT! She opened her eyes and looked around quickly. Marina and Ariel were watching her, riveted.

"What happens next?" asked Marina eagerly, after a breathless moment.

Tara looked up into the sky. Not a cloud in sight. No rain, no hail, no snow, no precipitation at all. She waited without responding until it was obvious there wasn't going to be a rainstorm. She sighed. "Nothing. The spell was supposed to bring a rain shower. But nothing happened; not even a cloud. I must have gotten it all wrong. Somehow. I don't know what, but I didn't do it right." Her shoulders drooped. She had had Marina swim all the way from the ocean for nothing.

"Don't worry, it takes practice," consoled Ariel. "All the magic-wielding beings I know either do it naturally, because they're born with it, or after lots and lots of study. You just have to work on it a little more. You're new to it!"

Evidently, thought Tara, dejectedly. But she thought she had put a lot of work into learning the spell!

Just then, there was a blur above them, not far over their heads, accompanied by a susurrus as of a gust of wind through tall grass. Tara looked up and pointed. A blue-green mist hung above them for a long moment, churned for a bit, and then sped off downriver, following its course out to sea. "That was it; that was the cloud," Tara said, wonderingly. "It didn't look like the cloud I was expecting, but I guess that was the cloud!"

Ariel looked after it thoughtfully. "Yeah," was all she mumbled.

Marina watched it fly away too but said nothing. For once, she wasn't ebullient. Rather, her mood seemed to have become subdued, even fretful. "Yes, I guess so," she finally responded. "That was the cloud. I guess."

But Tara was excited. "Yes, it was! It had to be! I worked some magic!

I need a lot more practice at it, because it didn't rain, and it was supposed to be a rain shower. But that was the cloud that was supposed to produce the rain!"

"Then why," asked Ariel slowly, "did it, sort of, run off the way it did? Clouds don't do that."

Tara considered this objection. "I don't know. Wind, maybe?"

Both Marina and Ariel demurred, and their eyes wandered back to the course of the river and to where it flowed until out of sight around a bend.

"Well," volunteered Tara at last. "I guess I'd better get back to studying this tablet so I can perfect this spell. Marina, I'm so sorry you swam all the way here just to see a little cloud that flew off so quickly. Not very exciting at all, I'm sure."

Marina looked back from contemplating the course of the river. "That's okay," she answered, her voice starting to resume its normal perkiness. "It's all right. It's not that far, really. And Ariel can give me a lift back to the sea, right?"

Ariel smiled at Marina's half-in-jest suggestion and unfurled her wings. "A flying mermaid? Who would ever believe that? But I'll fly low for a little way with you on your way back out to sea. I'm ready to go when you are."

Tara waved good-bye to her friends, and they departed. She remounted Daystar and rode slowly back to Castle Stonedell, pondering all the way what could have gone wrong with her spell and how she might correct it.

Tara's mother motioned her over on catching sight of her passing through the reception hall. "Oh, hello, Princess Tara!" she called, using her formal title, since courtiers were in attendance.

"Yes, Mom—Your Majesty?"

"Yes, please. Do you remember those plans we were examining the other day? For that, for that function we had in mind?"

Tara's heart sank. The Season again. Still, remembering her decision to be more Marina-like in her attitude and enthusiasm, she strove to inject some pep into her voice. "Yes, Your Majesty."

"I have tremendous news! We've set a date for it: next week! Lady Alina will host! Isn't that wonderful?"

"Oh! That is tremendous. Yes!"

"I knew you'd be thrilled. And—guess what? Guess who I've asked to be invited?"

Tara bit her lip. She couldn't possibly imagine who, not knowing what path her mother's thinking might have wandered down in assembling the guest list. Tara shrugged and mustered a lopsided smile.

Her mother grinned slyly. "Prince Halliad. He was at the ball we hosted in Sea Sprit."

Tara's eyes darted around the room. The courtiers were pretending to be disinterested, and were ostentatiously either discussing some topic of great importance or studying papers they had for the queen to review. "Prince Halliad."

"Prince Halliad. Hm?"

"Sounds great, Mom—Your Majesty. Yes, I remember him. From the ball at Sea Sprit."

"Exactly! I knew you'd remember him. Hm?"

"It is great news, Your Majesty. I'll go up to my room—directly—and think about something to wear for it."

"Perfect! But not the same dress you wore in Sea Sprit!"

Tara slowly climbed the stairs of the North Tower, an overwhelming feeling of ennui rising within her. The spell had been a failure. The more Tara thought it over, the more suspect she thought the "cloud" had been she had conjured. Her friends had not been impressed in the least, either. So much effort wasted.

Now, Prince Halliad. She remembered him now, and yes, she had chatted with him for a few minutes in Sea Sprit. It had been mere badinage, of course, and only because his parents had been conversing with hers, but yes, she had met him. Well, fine, have him invited too. What did it matter to her? At last she arrived at her rooms. She locked the door behind her and dragged herself to her wardrobe to check its stock. Sure, she had some dresses to wear. Ones she hadn't worn in a while too. They'd do just great. Now, back to that spell book. But, suddenly unable to bear it longer, she threw herself on her bed in a fit of dejection.

Several floors below, King Childeric entered the reception hall. Armorica summoned him with one hand, even as with the other she motioned the courtiers to withdraw. "I knew it," she told him excitedly. "I just knew it! Prince Halliad. He's the one!"

"Who?"

"Prince Halliad. Prince Halliad! You remember: Tara had quite a nice conversation with him at the ball in Sea Sprit. Laughing and even flirting—

a little. She said she remembered him; of course she remembered him! And you should have seen her face when I told her he had been invited to the next event of the Season."

Over the next days, Tara recovered some of her enthusiasm for working magic. Upon re-reading her spell of summoning, she concluded that the reason why the rain shower had not materialized and in the form expected was because she had spoken too hesitantly. This was because timing was key, not only in how and when the incantation was spoken but in making the gestures just at the right time with the words. Exact pronunciation was important, too. Fortunately, Marina had been kind enough to rehearse the words with her several times and that had helped. All in all, it was a considerably more delicate than she had thought it would be, getting the spell right, and especially because the language was foreign.

One evening, as Tara was practicing the gestures, especially the important final flourish, there was a knock at the window. What could that be, wondered Tara. Her window was too high up for it to be a tree branch. Was it hail? Had she summoned a hailstorm?

The knock came again, deliberate and measured. Not a hailstorm, realized Tara, and stepped over to the window to peer through the shutters. It was Ariel, sitting outside on the sill and peering in for her.

Tara opened the other window and invited Ariel in. Ariel jumped off the sill, which nearly caused Tara's heart to stop, as she expected her to plummet, and then fluttered in through the open window and settled into a chair.

"What a surprise!" exclaimed Tara, recovering. "What brings you here now? Oh! What's wrong?"

Ariel's face was troubled. "Sorry, Tara. I'm afraid it's not good news. I mean, there's a problem."

"What is it?"

Ariel frowned more deeply. "Do you remember that summoning spell you showed us the other day? Down by the river?"

Tara nodded, dread rising within her at where Ariel might be taking this.

"Well, you did summon something. For real."

"You mean... that cloud that appeared over our heads? Which then went out to sea?"

"Yes. But it wasn't really a cloud. It was something else. I, well, wasn't really sure what it was. Because it didn't really look like a cloud to me, you see."

Tara remembered that Ariel had not looked persuaded that the cloud had been an abortive rainstorm. Neither had Marina. At least, not exactly. "Is that why you two were…? You and Marina…?"

Ariel nodded again. "We talked about it as I accompanied her back out to the ocean. She thought it was something else too."

"I think we were right."

"But… what… what was it then? And how come you didn't say anything at the time?" Oh no, thought Tara frantically. What had she done? What had she done?

Ariel fidgeted in her chair. "We weren't sure. And, well, you're always right. You know? You've always got the great ideas on what we should do next whenever we're in trouble. We thought you must be right again."

No, not this time! But Tara didn't say anything and just waited fearfully for Ariel to continue.

"I've been speaking with Marina. She's been investigating. She had a hunch, and she wanted to look into it."

"Please, Ariel! What is it?"

"It's a water sprite. You brought a water sprite into this world. By accident. Through the spell of summoning. Something went wrong—"

I must have mispronounced something, or gestured incorrectly, or mistimed something, thought Tara, miserably.

"—and the spell brought a water sprite instead of a rain shower."

"I did it. The spell didn't bring it. I did it."

"Oh, Tara! You didn't do it on purpose!"

No, it wasn't on purpose. It was incompetence. Tara put her forehead into her hands and closed her eyes in agony. "I've got to set this right. I have to. Oh no, what have I done?" She racked her mind for ideas, but she had no idea how to deal with a water sprite. She didn't even know what it was. She sighed dismally and looked up. "I have no idea what to do next. But, I guess, first things first: what is it? What is a water sprite?"

Far, far away, far out in the Prithrath Ocean, a small humanoid figure sat cross-legged in the swinging trough of the waves. He—for he looked boyish, though it was difficult to assign a gender, so androgynous he appeared—was, from his height and features, only of about the age of twelve. But the most curious thing about him was that he floated contentedly, just on top of the ocean's surface, as light as the flecks of foam on the waves themselves, no less so than as if it had been a restless seagreen-colored carpet and he quite entertained by its restlessness.

Another oddity about him was his dress, which was as restless as the waves and shimmered in the sunlight that glinted all around him. His garb was blue at times and then at moments green and looked altogether as if it had been fashioned of scales, like those of a fish. On his head and neatly covering a patch of his greenish-blonde hair was a small green cap that never moved, no matter how the boy swung in the waves and irrespective of the shifting breezes. Below the cap his eyes danced merrily, and he seemed to be having the greatest fun riding the waves up and down.

"Ha-ho!" he called to himself, or maybe to the curious fish below, "Isn't it so?" He trailed the fingers of his right hand through the water in a tight semi-circle from left knee to right, delighted by the small plash they made and fascinated by how the eddies they made in passing disappeared almost as quickly as he created them. He laughed to himself softly. "'Tis writ in water of Childeric's daughter, and how House Hession learnt a stern lesson!" He chuckled again, pleased with his poetastery. He stretched his arms out behind him and, gathering up a passing wavelet into a bundle, formed it into a pillow and stretched back into it to relax. There he lay, almost motionless, save for his dancing eyes, rocking between the waves just as easily as any "landling" would have stretched back and taken his ease in a hammock strung between two trees.

At length, in the distance a larger-than-usual wave appeared. It approached steadily, despite the necessity of having to pass through other waves and even moving counter to all currents and the wind itself. It built in size the closer it approached the blue-green boy until it loomed sharply over him as it came upon him. The boy watched all of this, from the wave's very origin until it was nearly on top of him, and took no heed except to wink once at it, a gesture too enigmatic to divine; otherwise, he lay perfectly still. The wave grew taller still until it towered directly over him, where it hung threateningly. Still the boy evidenced no concern.

"Well?" he spoke at last, looking up from the stray strand of seaweed he had been twining in and around the fingers of his right hand with his left. He sat up from his ocean pillow and shook his hand, casting the strand away.

"Sprite. At last."

The water sprite smiled archly and fingered his cap. "Ho-ha; you've been looking for me? Here I rest at your behest, an ocean billow for my pillow!"

The wave, topped by an enormous whitecap, hung over the sprite. Now it grew taller still, now it diminished in size until it was not much higher at all than the sprite. Ever it fluctuated, though never did it move from directly before the sprite. A long minute passed before the voice from the wave came again. "I have always known where to find you. I sensed you as soon as you came out to sea."

The water sprite fingered his hat, as if to tip it to the wave.

And so the two stared at each other, or communed silently with each other, for a full minute, until the voice from the wave spoke again. "How do you come here?"

The sprite batted his hat so that it spun quickly atop his head though it did not fall off. "Tara! Tara-Tara-Tara-Tara! Madera-caldera-chimera-fofera! Tara!"

The wave said nothing, but water swirled up and down its height, striated with foam and seaweed and such other flotsam found about the ocean.

"She brought me here. But she had nothing for me to do. Nothing. Why, then?" The water sprite commenced to sing in a high falsetto, not looking at all amused. "I suppose out of spite she summoned this sprite! I'll teach her a lesson for this sort of transgression."

The wave varied in size and height for a good time after the sprite had spoken. At last it responded but in a voice slightly quicker and deeper than before, as if sensing opportunity. "Why not bring me water? Water from her land. All of it. That will punish her and her house."

The water sprite doffed his cap and balanced it improbably by its very tip on the nail of his thumb. He breathed a puff of air on it, and it commenced to revolve slowly, as if a kind of vertical pinwheel. He said nothing for a space while he considered this invitation. At last, "What would you give me to do this? We must have equality."

The wave had a ready response, as if expecting this query. "You would have your revenge, and so you would be equal with Tara for the vexation she has caused you in summoning you to this world without purpose and then abandoning you here.

"You are right though, that I would gain, with you bringing me so much water. Thus, I would owe you equality on this count. I propose to offer you the crystalized parts of this world. To have. To take back with you. You would have these in satisfaction for the labor of bringing me the waters of this Tara's lands."

The water sprite allowed his cap to cease revolving on his thumb and then, with a flick, sent it spinning high into the air. It flipped many times, yet landed in the exact same place on his head where it had lain before the wave's arrival, and without displacing a single strand of his green-blonde hair. "Your Watery Wonder!" he exclaimed. "That is a fair offer and restores equality. I accept, and we shall exchange. I shall bring you all the waters of Brythrony, and you shall give me the icy reaches of this world—which I quite fancy—for my own."

Many and varied are the topics that badinage can encompass, Armorica had reminded Tara on multiple occasions. "They don't have to be especially deep or important or special," she was now emphasizing to her daughter, as Tara sat restlessly at her mother's vanity, Sullijee working diligently with Tara's recalcitrant hair. "Badinage can be about anything you want it to be! Sullijee, please—I think, I just think that lock there could…"

"This one, Your Majesty?"

"Oh, you are such a treasure! Yes, just so! Exactly!"

"Tara, will you look at the wonder Sullijee has worked?" To Sullijee she said, "Dear, show her the mirror, please, won't you?"

Tara accepted the proffered hand mirror but without enthusiasm.

"Isn't it just marvelous? Your hair—it really is magnificent, when expertly brushed with real care and consideration!"

Tara noted in the mirror that Sullijee had straightened with obvious pride at the compliment. Tara's mouth turned down at the corner. "I think it looks great, Mom. Thank you, Sullijee."

"Oh, Tara! You are impossible! Why aren't you more excited? It's *the Season*!"

Tara attempted to smile and really tried hard at it. Lately though, she had had trouble summoning her inner Marina. Try as she might, she couldn't find any reason to be mirthful or bubbly or anything but worried. Ariel had told her a water sprite was loose somewhere, and who knew what it was doing? She, Marina, and Ariel were trying to decide what to do, but

Tara felt she wasn't offering any help at all. She had caused the problem and was doing nothing to fix it.

"You'll see," offered Sullijee, in a tone Tara imagined was meant to be helpful. "Once you're there. It will be so exciting! So many beautiful dresses! Such a glittering ball!"

This time, and seeing that her mother had turned to refill her wine glass, Tara had no trouble summoning a smile for Sullijee, not one that was merry but one more akin to a grimace of repressed malice. Sullijee started with surprise, but Tara re-formed her lips into something more Marina-like just as her mother turned back around.

"So, and as I was saying: remember 'badinage'. Yes. Please do. With kind words for everyone. And especially to Prince Halliad. I know he'll be there. I know he's accepted the invitation."

Badinage, glumly ruminated Tara as she and Sullijee drove the short distance to Lady Alina's nearby mansion, Rohanic riding postillion. Topics could range the gamut from the current fashion in dress to all the many and various relationships between the aristocracy of Brythrony, both diplomatic and romantic, both public and concealed. Of course, Tara knew all this but felt woefully unskilled at the required wordplay and *double entendre* that seemed to come so naturally to everyone else. Further, she had no knowledge about anything going on outside Stonedell and so always sensed that she understood less than half of every conversation.

But as it turned out, and much to her surprise, Tara was startlingly aware and up-to-date on the topic that gripped the attendees that evening. This was because the topic on everyone's minds was the weather. Usually one of the more innocent and reliable topics for badinage, and invariably in the form of observations on how lovely the sun was, or how heavy the snowfall had been, this time it was about the lack of rain. Tara's heart sank as she increasingly comprehended just how widespread the discussion was and how concerned that evening's attendees were.

Baroness Crinum said, "I just can't understand! Normally it rains most every day this time of year. A shower or two. In the afternoon. But no. Nothing at all! My garden is quite dry! And brown!"

"I can't understand it either," fretted the Lady Alina, their hostess that evening. "And this is not just about filling my moat, or similar," she added, with a sidelong glance across the room, which prompted snickers from some but only bepuzzlement from Tara, as the reference was lost on her.

"No rain at all, not for days."

Tara glanced around the circle of faces into which she had ventured, employing what she thought was her best badinage. "But mightn't it rain again soon?" she offered. "Because it's only been a week or so?"

The others eyed her sadly, and Tara began to perceive that even those of considerably lesser social stature were coming to regard her as irredeemably pitiable. "Perhaps you are right," returned Baroness Crinum in her characteristic sharp, staccato manner but in a tone suggesting Tara was, if anything, very far from being right. "But—well—we should be having more rain! Especially this time of year!"

"Oh, and have you seen the River Vahaval? It does seem to be drying up!" piped up a younger girl, whose name Tara did not know and who was dressed, to Tara's eye, in a sort of lace confection, from her dainty shoes to the very top of her head. Surely her first Season, scoffed Tara mentally, before reminding herself to be a bit less disparaging and a bit bubblier. But the others nodded sagely, as if the debutante had propounded something tremendously erudite. "'Tis true," echoed the Lady Alina. "The water level has fallen. Which is very odd, as there seems no reason for this from only a few days' lack of rain. Why, I understand that stretches of the Vahaval are nigh close to unnavigable!"

Tara made a wan smile, swallowed hard and racked her brain to say something, but nothing came to mind. Nothing. No badinage, not anything. Had the water level of the River Vahaval really sunk that much and from just a few days of missed rain? How? But she knew how already: the water sprite. Ariel had told her that they were unpredictable, and they always worked mischief unless kept under tight control. What form the mischief might take was unknowable, and even depended on the sprite itself, but it was always something to do with water. It could be too much water, or too little water, or water in the wrong places or the wrong times. It was increasingly clear that Brythrony's problem was lack of water, and it could only be because of the water sprite Tara had summoned.

Tara thought to change the subject. Badinage. It could be anything one wanted it to be, right? "Um… maybe we are having a bit of a drought, but isn't it very colorful here this evening?"

The others fell silent, waiting. Tara suddenly felt exceedingly hot and red, to a degree she had not realized before and not altogether because she was wearing a fairly full silk Mikado dress, the skirt brown and the bodice blue, her white sash of royalty diagonally across her and pinned at her waist by The White Wave of Sea Sprit.

"I mean, I guess I should have worn more blue than brown this evening. For the lack of water. I mean, the drought…" Tara's voice died away in her throat. She had been trying to say something clever, combining her house colors with the lack of water giving way to the browning grass, but clearly this had been a mistake.

The silence began to lengthen.

What a dumb thing that was to have said, thought Tara. How simply, totally mindless. "Lace is a very nice addition to this Season," she attempted again, increasingly desperate for any conversational approval, even from The Young Confection she had dismissed but moments before as jejune.

But the eyes of The Young Confection, so moist and understanding earlier, had become as hard and obdurate as flint. Not a trace remained in their depths of their former kindness. Tara's propitiatory offering was, in effect, scorned. "The kingdom is drying up," she declared flatly.

Tara felt personally implicated.

At length, Tara cleared her throat guiltily. "I'll… I'll have to look into this," she stuttered. The circle around her waited expectantly for something more definitive than this empty-headed reply, but, miserably, Tara could think of nothing more. They—even The Young Confection—stared another long moment, just exquisitely long enough so that Tara was fully aware that she had said absolutely the wrong thing, or not enough of the right thing, and was unquestionably a complete nincompoop.

"Lace! Lace; very much so. Your Highness!" stated the Baroness authoritatively as The Young Confection studied the rim of her empty glass fixedly.

The Lady Alina cast her eyes downward and then away, a sequence which Tara, crushed, interpreted as indicating she should depart.

Tara muttered a few more choice words of badinage and extricated herself from the circle, the others stepping back all too willingly to allow her to go. Where to now, she sighed. How much longer was this excruciating ball to continue? Tara retreated to the nearby balcony, hoping to find some fresh air and a reprieve from the talk of the weather. Couples and small groups were there in quiet clusters, but the balcony was sufficiently large, and Tara felt sufficiently alone that she imagined she would be able to stare morosely into the darkness without being observed.

"Is that Princess Tara? Of the House of Hession? Of Brythrony?"

Tara heaved a quiet sigh. Who was this? She could not place the voice, but evidently he knew her. She composed herself for a moment and summoned a gay image of Marina to her mind, all shiny green scales and blonde hair with tiny points of red coral spicules peeking out. Marina's image waved to Tara, and a ghost of a smile crossed Tara's face. Then the image faded to reveal, standing before her, a young gentleman, maybe two or three years older than her. He was dressed somewhat foppishly, with quantities of lace at his wrists and throat. His surcoat was intricately embroidered in rich hues of crimson and silver, and at his belt dangled a small ceremonial sword that was little more than an elaborately bejeweled dagger.

"Hello, is that you, Princess Tara? It's me, Prince Halliad. Do you remember me? We met at the ball in Sea Sprit."

"Prince Halliad! Of course I remember you. From Sea Sprit. How have you been? Sunny weather we've been having lately, haven't we?"

Deep in the subterranean grottos of a small island, far out in the Prithrath Ocean, two voices were in conversation. One voice was high and lilting and spoke almost in musical notes. The other spoke in slightly deeper tones and much more sombrely and seriously. The first spoke more often than the second.

"Have you not seen? Where have you been?" asked the water sprite, dressed in the same shimmering scales as before. He sat perched atop a rock and was drawing, with his finger, a rivulet of water up from the inlet that lay just behind him until it had circled the rock on which he sat and then flowed back down again to the inlet lapping at his feet.

"I have seen, I have seen," came the murmured response, in the same voice as had emanated from the wave on the previous occasion the two had met. This time, the words were uttered by a figure in the form of a beautiful maiden. But only once beautiful as, days drowned, she now made a tragic spectacle. Her fine features had begun to bloat, and her pallid skin was cast over with a hundred ghastly green hues; her sunken eyes were rheumy and filmed over from long hours staring sightlessly into the depths.

Seawater streamed continuously from golden hair tangled with bits of kelp and dead man's fingers to a pool at her feet that neither expanded nor contracted. "You are making good progress. I sense that Brythrony is drying. You are achieving your revenge."

The water sprite inclined his head slightly in satisfaction at this acknowledgement of success. "'Tis true, 'tis true. There is progress."

"Where might you be holding the water as you accumulate it?" enquired the maiden, softly, and moving a step closer.

A gleam entered the water sprite's eyes. He turned his finger around in a circle, and the rivulet of water took to the air and proceeded to jump and dance and even describe shapes, as if it were a kind of liquid lasso under the control of his index finger. "Ah, Sea Witch! It is safe, as long as I am safe!" He began to chant in the same falsetto voice he used on all such occasions when moved to rhyming, now accompanying himself with the rivulet of water that he forced to dance in time with his words. "By the force of my will, I hold each rill, but should I disappear…" He paused dramatically, the diamantine droplets of the rivulet suspended in mid-air as if they themselves were also breathlessly awaiting the sprite's concluding words. "It reverts! To meadow and mere!" He eyed the drowned maiden keenly. His attention distracted, the rivulet splashed to the ground to find rest at last. "It shall be yours. But! Only when we have equality. Oh yes! All shall change when we have our exchange!"

"Very good," sighed the lugubrious maiden, turning to take tentative steps toward the whispering, dark inlet. The puddle of water at her feet, ever replenished, trailed her steps closely, just a half-step behind. She paused, directing her voice to the inlet. "You are making good progress. I am too. I have initiated the necessary magic to gather up the polar regions. For you."

"Wonderful, oh Witch! For it is right, to have equality throughout! As you gather snow, I induce drought!"

The Sea Witch made no answer but shuffled slowly into the water. When she was approximately knee deep, she collapsed with a rush and vanished entirely, only to rise again a moment later in the form of the suspended wave with the seething whitecap atop. "Let us keep this location as our rendezvous. In two days' time." Then, without another word, the wave subsided and all became quiet.

The next morning, Armorica, breathless with new intelligence, pulled Childeric aside after breakfast. "I knew it! I knew it! Admit it! Admit I was right!"

"Admit what about what?"

"About Prince Halliad! Tara was seen talking to him—extensively!—on the balcony at Lady Alina's! Ooh, I was so right!"

Childeric pondered his wife's revelation. Why not? He had never met this prince, but what did that mean? It could still be that Tara was smitten with him, even if unexpectedly.

Armorica tapped her head with her forefinger repeatedly. "Mother's intuition! Trust it!"

"How did you find out that she spoke with Prince Halliad?" Childeric partially knew the answer to this question but thought to ask it anyway, if only for the implied compliment to his wife.

She smiled broadly in receiving it. "Mothers know. Mothers know!"

At about that same time, Tara was at the banks of the River Vahaval, conferring with Marina and Ariel. The water level, she noticed immediately, was much lower than on that terrible day she had summoned the water sprite. In fact, the water was so low that the three had had to arrange to meet considerably closer to the sea, where the river was still deep enough for Marina to swim up unnoticed.

That terrible, awful day that she had fooled with something she hadn't understood, she repeated to herself and not for the first time. She compressed her lips to a thin line. Now she had to set things right.

They met at a bend in the Vahaval where Marina could remain unobserved. Ariel spoke first after they had greeted each other solemnly. "I've flown across Brythrony over the past two days. There is definitely a drought. I can see it from the air. Even though it's only been a week without rain."

"How?" asked Tara, in wonder. "How could we have a drought in so short a time?"

Ariel spoke slowly. "It must be because the water is being pulled out of the land, the lakes, the river, even the air. Not by evaporation. That means it really is being done by magic, or by some other magical agency." Which the three of them all knew could only be the water sprite.

"I'm worried for my Cloud Castle," continued Ariel, lowering her tone. "Look up. Do you see any clouds? Even the water is being pulled from the sky, from the clouds. If this continues, the cloud upon which my castle is built will disappear and my castle will come tumbling down!"

The other two acknowledged this truth with simple frowns. The water from the land, the river, the streams—even the water vapor in the air and clouds—all of it was going somewhere. "We've got to stop this sprite. Get rid of it, send it back to where it came from, something, anything. But the water has to come back," said Tara, with considerably more determination in her voice than she had voiced at Lady Alina's. "I have to take the lead on doing this."

Marina agreed. "All of us have to do something. Definitely. Because who's to say where it stops? Taking the water from the air is super serious! Not just Brythrony but everywhere! Because everything is connected through the air!"

That was true too. With no water on the ground and no vapor in the air, all the land would become a vast, endless desert. All life—except that in the oceans—would cease. Maybe also in the oceans, thought Tara with a start, because maybe they just couldn't tell yet if those were being depleted. She looked up into the endlessly, now ominously, blue sky. The house colors of Hession were blue, brown, and white. Blue was meant to symbolize the cobalt blue of the kingdom's skies and the water features dotting it. Brown represented the umber soil of its fertile tilled fields and the woodlands foresting so much of the land. White was for the snow-capped mountains to the west and the puffy, pearlescent cumulus clouds that so benignly provided shade during the summer. All of this was in jeopardy, as all of it depended on water, either directly or indirectly.

"The water sprite has to be stopped. I mean, *I* have to stop the water sprite," Tara announced with finality. No one else said a word, but Tara knew they agreed.

"Water sprites stay near large bodies of water, where they're most comfortable. They don't have to be in water, but they prefer it," Ariel mentioned quietly at last.

Tara considered this for a moment. "Marina, could you ask the sea life if they have seen or heard anything unusual recently? Like," she added helplessly, "a water sprite?"

"I can describe one for you," piped up Ariel. "I've read about them."

Marina nodded and listened closely to Ariel's description. "Great idea! Let me ask and see what I can come up with."

"I have another idea," said Ariel. "I know two sisters who live far, far to the north. They're the Ice and Snow Princesses. If the water sprite is pulling all the water from the air, eventually they'll feel the effects too. Let me see if I can contact them. Maybe they can help us somehow."

"And I have an idea as well," offered Tara, thinking now of the reception at the mansion of Lady Alina. She had spoken to Prince Halliad, and in speaking to him, she had gestured with her right hand, and the ring from Syssalin's library had caught the light of the myriad candles from within the hall and sparkled. "The sprite likes water. I guess that means it wouldn't like fire. Maybe this ring," holding up her right hand, "could help us if we had to confront it?"

Why not, thought the others. Anything was worth a try. Marina slid down from her rock seat into the river then turned back to face them. "But hey, one more thing. And I'm just thinking, that's all!"

"No, go ahead! What is it?"

"Well, I can double-check, of course. With my father. But maybe fire won't do anything against the water sprite after all. Because the sprite might be able to quench it. Instead, I'm thinking we may need a Spell of Dispatch."

"If that's the spell we need, I'll cast it," vowed Tara, despite her misgivings about magic. With those words, Marina swam back to sea, Ariel flew off to her castle, and Tara mounted Daystar to return to Stonedell. Well, who else would cast it? Having brought it to Brythrony, to their world, she must be the one to send it back. She shuddered. More magic. She and magic spells hadn't mixed so well so far.

Tara stabled Daystar, combed him just a little while still in thought, and then, after a moment's hesitation, walked up to reception hall. She heard voices; her father was receiving someone. Best to avoid that; it could be state business. She turned instead for the family's private rooms to the side, where they normally took their meals. Her mother was there, bustling about.

"Why, hello, Tara!" her mother greeted her gaily.

"Hi, Mom." Funny, thought Tara. Why was her mother so bright-eyed and joyful?

"How are you?"

"I'm all right, thanks." Probably just cheerful about something or another. Where is my Marina attitude? I should be trying to be more open-minded! "Fine, Mom! Thanks!"

"Lovely, dear! So, I heard you spoke with Prince Halliad at the ball at Lady Alina's." Armorica's voice trailed off ever so slightly, almost inviting Tara to answer some unspoken question.

Prince Halliad. So that was it. "Well, yes, a little. Some, sure."

"On the balcony!"

Sullijee. Had to be. She must have found out somehow and told her mother. "Yes, Mom. On the balcony. I thought to go and get some air and, well, you know, he was there. That was all."

Her mother's eyes twinkled, as if with a shared secret. "Now, I won't ask what you two talked about!—"

"It's all right, Mom. We didn't talk about anything special or important. I mean, you can ask; I don't mind."

Her mother looked disappointed but recovered her poise quickly. "No, no! That's not my business. What you and the prince discuss."

Tara waited a moment longer, just to see if her mother might want to ask further. But her mother began to bustle about again and make a great show of not being interested at all in Prince Halliad or the conversation on the balcony. How strange this was, thought Tara, contemplating her. Usually, I don't want my mother to ask questions, but now I'm fine with it, even as my mother, who usually wants to know everything about what I'm doing, obstinately refuses! But, surely on some level Mom really does want to ask about what Halliad and I talked about on the balcony, or else why bring it up in the first place? "I really don't mind," ventured Tara again, just to be sure. "I mean, it's all right if you want to know. Really."

But her mother showed no interest at all, and Tara departed in confusion.

Later, over dinner, Childeric related how he had seen a delegation from one corner of the kingdom that had pleaded for more time in paying their taxes on account of the sudden drought. "I told them I would think about it, but how can there be such a thing as 'sudden drought'? Drought happens slowly, and because there is no rain for a while, right? It sounds suspicious to me."

Armorica agreed, but Tara, and perhaps against her better judgement, spoke up. "Well, I've heard about this some. I mean, riding around with Daystar. Seeing it, too! It does look like a drought. Because we're supposed to have almost daily rains this time of year. And we haven't." Tara looked from her father to her mother, wondering what they might say. "So it is kind of like a sudden drought. Maybe they're facing real hardship."

Childeric scoffed. "'Sudden drought'! Tara, that's very kind of you to be so trusting and believe that story, but it can't be true! It just doesn't make sense!"

"Dear, it really doesn't make any sense. That's not how droughts occur. It's true that we haven't had rain for a little while, but that doesn't make it a drought."

Tara looked gloomily into her plate. Of course, it didn't make sense. Unless you knew about the water sprite. She looked up again. "Everyone at Lady Alina's party was talking about it too."

Armorica gazed at Tara sympathetically. "Dear, that's wonderful that you got to speak with so many at Lady Alina's ball. It sounds like you had a wonderful time, talking to everyone and Prince Halliad and, and, so many others!"

Tara looked back into her plate. That wasn't the direction she had hoped the conversation would turn. But that was evidently what her mother wanted. Tara sighed. She had better start learning that Spell of Dispatch as soon as King Aenon could supply it.

Almost as soon as she entered her room, a message bubble floated through the open window and toward her. Tara held out her hand to receive it. Marina's voice from within it told her, based on what King Aenon had read when he had had her tablet, to turn to a specific page in her tablet and begin memorizing the gestures and phrases there, as that was the Spell of Dispatch. Tara shuffled unhappily to her chest and pulled the tablet from the top drawer. It was something she could do, should do, to try to remedy this terrible situation. She had better get this spell right too. Brythrony—the entire world—couldn't afford her botching another.

Tara was awakened the next morning by a penetrating cold. The light was still grey, as if just before dawn. The window was open, as she had gotten in the habit of doing so to receive more promptly any incoming message bubbles. She wasn't sure, after all, just how long they would hover outside, waiting to be let in. She sat upright, shivering, and wrapped the bedspread around herself. How could it be so cold at this time of year? Her breath frosted before her in a white, wispy cloud. Then, over by her chest, she heard a sustained whispering, or sighing, as if of leaves scattering across flagstones before a stiff breeze. She drew back in alarm and suspicion. Was this some trick of the water sprite, her new nemesis?

A blurry cloud began to form at the opposite wall, roughly in the shape of a person of about Tara's height. In growing alarm, Tara stretched out her right hand, the one wearing the ring, as if to ward off the solidifying creature. If whatever this was made one false move, she told herself grimly, she'd flash-burn it with a fireball! Slowly, as if being constructed layer by layer, a greyish-white sleet occupied the blur, and it began to solidify, starting at the floor and rising gradually. It was human, Tara discerned, as the form took shape past knees, a waist, and then shoulders. From there it finished off quickly, and Tara saw what looked like a grey-white statue of a girl about her age and size. The cold momentarily became acute, then faded. Natural colors infused the form and the statue relaxed. She turned to Tara. "Hi!" she greeted Tara calmly, looking for all the world as if she had simply stepped through the door. "I'm Florence. Ice Princess Florence."

Tara got out of bed, conscious that she was still in her nightclothes and still keeping her right index finger cautiously trained on this person identifying herself as "Florence."

"Good morning. May I ask who you are and why you're here?" And at this terribly early hour, she added, mentally.

"Ariel sent me. Are you Tara? Princess Tara?"

"I'm Princess Tara."

"Sorry for the surprise entrance. I won't hurt you; you don't need to point your finger at me like that. Why are you doing that, by the way?"

"I don't know who you are. And this ring is my protection. And why did Ariel send you? And prove that Ariel sent you!"

Florence nodded understandingly. "Sure. This is all rather sudden. But I can explain. Ariel *did* send me. She and Marina think they've found this water sprite of yours," Tara flinched at the reminder, "and they've asked me to help. Which I'm happy to do.

"Oh, but maybe you want proof that Ariel sent me. Let's see: you, Marina, and her were down at the river when the water sprite first appeared."

"Thank you. But not something involving the water sprite. Because if you were the water sprite, or sent by it, you would—"

"—I would know that. Good point. All right, what about this? The three of you have princess purses, which you found at the ruins of a city, where you also found the book containing the spell which summoned the water sprite."

"What's in the purses?"

"Sure!" The girl who had identified herself as the Ice Princess concentrated intently for a moment, and her brows knit and her pleasant features creased in a sudden frown. "That would be—she told me that, didn't she?—that would be, let's see: a rod, a package of dust—something like that—and bubbles. Which you use to communicate with each other!"

That was close enough, if not exact. Tara lowered her hand, relieved. "Sorry about that. I was just unsure of who you might be. Would you like to take a chair and rest after your… journey?"

"Thanks," said Florence, relieved, and plopped down into the chair at Tara's vanity. "Look, don't mind me, if you need to get up and get dressed!"

Tara stood, yawned and stretched. This was exceedingly odd, to get dressed in front of a stranger, but it did sound as though she knew Ariel, and she guessed she wouldn't mind getting dressed in front of Ariel, which was much the same, wasn't it? As she hurriedly pulled on some clothes, she covertly studied her visitor, who seemed preoccupied in studying her very pale fingernails. Florence was garbed in a kind of silvery-white dress that fell to well below her knees. The dress was trimmed in a sort of sparkling tinsel at the cuffs and hem, and her shoes looked to be more like silver slippers better suited to marble floors than an ice-bound land. Atop her head was a silvery circlet, bridged across the top by a sort of lattice-work that shimmered in the light. Despite the austere colors of her dress, her face and demeanor seemed pleasant enough, and her smile engaging. She was very pale, though, her lips almost bloodless, and her eyes so light as be almost colorless.

"How did Ariel bring you into this?" Tara asked when she had pulled on a second shoe, found uncharacteristically immediately underneath the bed.

Florence nodded. "Great question. So, let me update you.

"Marina sent out her ocean friends to locate the water sprite. It wasn't long before she got the news back that the water sprite had met up with and joined the Sea Witch—"

"'Sea Witch?'"

"Right. More on that shortly. But they joined up with the same end in mind. Steal all the water from everywhere for the Sea Witch. The water sprite would do this. In return, the water sprite would receive all the ice and snow of the polar regions. THAT'S how I got involved. Because I'm Ice Princess—you can call me Flo, lots do—and that would mean the end of my home. It would leave my land with just cold, bare rocks!"

"That's terrible!"

"Yes. It would be. So these two have to be stopped. Fortunately, Marina believes she is very close to knowing where they are."

Tara spent all the next day at her studies of the Spell of Dispatch. It was difficult but not as difficult as the summoning spell had been. For that Tara was glad. Occasionally, she would stop and step over to her window to look up into the sky. It was a perfect, flawless, unchanging blue. No clouds to be seen anywhere, no matter how she craned her neck. These two definitely had to be stopped. This water sprite and Sea Witch, whatever she—it—was.

Almost as an afterthought, she wondered what her parents were thinking of her, again up in her room and not appearing downstairs. She shrugged. It couldn't be helped. She had to learn this spell. Probably they thought she was moping over something that silly Prince Halliad had or hadn't said to her.

Later that afternoon, Ariel stopped by to enquire about her studies. She also brought a fuller explanation as to what the Sea Witch was, straight from Marina.

Ariel sat herself down in the same chair in which Princess Flo had rested. "How's it going? I hope all right. That's because everything is getting dryer. Every second, it seems. I moved Cloud Castle offshore, where there is a little more water vapor, I was getting so worried about it." She turned to the side and unfurled her wings, buzzed them gently then re-furled them in the complicated way which always fascinated Tara. "There! That feels better; somehow they got all cramped up—must have folded them wrong. I don't guess that ever happens to you.

"Anyway, Marina sent out all her sea friends to find out where this water sprite and Sea Witch might be hiding. She found them all right. You'll never guess where!"

Tara couldn't imagine.

"At the Secret Island! Marina tells me you've been there—"

Tara nodded. The Secret Island! They were there?

"They're there. But, not *on* the island: inside it. There're in the island's subterranean grottos and passages, which were created over the years by the water and rain dripping through. That's where they meet."

"That's great news! So, once I have the spell mastered, I'll go there, wait for them and then send them back to wherever they came from."

Ariel hesitated. "Well, that'll only work on the water sprite. Because it was summoned. But the Sea Witch lives in the ocean and didn't come from anywhere else. So she can't be dispatched."

Tara hadn't thought of that. "Is that what Marina said? She knows?"

"She knows. The Sea Witch has been a real problem for the merfolk in the past. Just not recently. I mean, 'yes', she's a problem right now because of the water but not recently otherwise."

"What do we do about her?"

"Well! I've got an idea! Tell me what you think!" Ariel leaned forward eagerly. "Do you remember those bottles we found in the library? You and I?"

Of course, Tara remembered. She nodded. "Sure. You told me about them at the river. They're, like, a kind of magic prison?"

"That's right. They're 'stasis bottles'. Anything inside stays inside until someone lets it out. Forever. But never hungering or thirsting or aging in the meantime."

A magic prison with a life sentence for anyone inside. Only, even death didn't end the life sentence, since anyone imprisoned would be forever ageless. Tara reflected. Forever was a really long time, but maybe the Sea Witch deserved it, if she had caused all sorts of problems for the merfolk. "That sounds good: the water sprite goes back to where it came from, and the Sea Witch goes in a stasis bottle. Then she's no longer a problem for anyone. In which case, some good would come out of this terrible situation!"

Ariel nodded in agreement. "That's what Marina and I are thinking. Now," changing the subject, "I understand you've met Princess Florence? Yes? Good. Florence said she'll join us when we go to the grottos beneath Secret Island. I'm sure she's told you this, but the ice and snow where she lives are vanishing, just like the water is in Brythrony; I guess also because of this water sprite. So she's ready to help."

Tara glanced out of the window into the perfect blue sky. She was reluctant to ask for help when she had caused all the problems, but it could come in useful. Also, there would be no second opportunities so it had to go right this first time. "You're right. It's good to have her help. How do we get to the Secret Island? Last time I swam, but it took a while."

"No need to swim this time. We'll take my sky chariot. I've already been overhead it to check it out; there's enough room on the beach to land. The witch and sprite won't even know we've arrived, since they'll be deep within the island."

Tara stood. "You and Marina have thought of everything. I should be ready with the Spell of Dispatch tomorrow. Is that all right? Do you think they'll be there?"

"They seem to meet every third day, from what Marina—via her sea friends—tells me. Tomorrow is perfect. We'll leave early; be on the fields outside the castle and I'll come and get you!"

Tara went to bed late that night, coming downstairs only for dinner. She had to learn that spell, just had to. Her mother shot enquiring looks at her throughout the meal, which Tara did her best to ignore. She also saw her mother glance meaningfully at her father several times. Tara was too preoccupied with the difficulties of learning her spell to participate much in the conversation, though when she was addressed directly, she thought she did pretty well (if she did say so herself) in being upbeat and bubbly. After all, she reminded herself, if all went well, the drought would end and the rains would return. If not... well, better not to think of that. Maybe then she'd be the one stuck forever in the stasis bottle. She gazed out of her window before getting into bed: another clear, cloudless night. She'd never look at the sky the same way again, she vowed.

Early the next morning, she was aloft in Ariel's sky chariot. Looking over the rails as they climbed higher into the brightening sky, Tara saw that the land below was indeed looking very brown and dry. Ariel confirmed it, explaining that she had had to post Cloud Castle still further out to sea and at a lower altitude to keep the "foundations" of it secure. "Ready with the spell?" asked Ariel of Tara, by way of summarizing that conversation. Tara nodded. She had already practiced it mentally half a dozen times.

No further words passed between them until, well out to sea, the chariot banked sharply and Ariel pointed. "Secret Island," she announced. "I'll set us down on that strip of beach, there, between those rocks and the forest verge." Tara looked over at the island they were circling. If she had followed Ariel's finger correctly, they would be setting the chariot down about where she had first set foot on the island herself, long, long ago, when she had first met Marina after jumping from the pirate ship. How long ago and far away that seemed now.

Marina was waiting for them when they alighted from the chariot. "Ready with the spell?" she immediately asked Tara. Tara smiled tightly. "Good. They're down there. That's what some cavern fish have told me. Arguing about something or another, something about equality. That's good, because maybe they'll be distracted."

She held out both her hands, each one containing a small wad of seaweed. "Here: eat this. It's too far down to the entrance below for me to lead you without it. Come on, eat up! It's not that bad. And Tara, you don't need to make such a face!" Marina giggled despite the seriousness of the situation. Tara had to smile—maybe her first genuine smile in days—in imagining her sour expression as she choked down the noxious weed.

"Good. Are we ready now? Tara, I'll take you first, so you can get in position. Ariel, get ready; I'll be back shortly." With that, Tara walked into the water and then dove beneath the surface. Marina took her by the arm and down they went through layers of successively colder water, the light changing from a light, almost sky blue, to a deeper velvety blue and then to an imperial purple before it went nearly black altogether. Then, though the colors around her didn't change all that much, the cold lessened, and she felt Marina beginning to lead her upwards. They hadn't gone much further when Marina pulled her to the side, up against some rocks, and moved quite close to her, such that she was whispering directly into her ear. "The grotto is just ahead. I think they're still arguing. Let me tow you the rest of the way, so you don't make any splashes. I'll put you in what I think is a good position and then go for Ariel!"

Tara nodded in understanding, and they set off again.

A few moments later, Tara was crouched behind a rocky outcropping some distance from where the ocean water lapped gently at the pebbles and sand that constituted the tiny beach in the grotto of the Secret Island. There, in the faint, green glow of what had to be bioluminescent lichens, she witnessed what had to be one of the strangest sights she would ever see. Pacing back and forth, and speaking in what sounded like querulous tones, was a boy, maybe a young teenager, dressed in what looked to be a patchwork of blue and green that glistened in the wan light like fish scales. On top of what looked to be close-cut hair was a small cap that maybe was affixed to his head, as no matter how violently the boy—or was it a girl?—turned or gesticulated, it never moved. But what really caught Tara's eye was the other being with which the first was in such animated conversation. This was nothing less than what appeared to be an enormous lobster, sea-green in color, and speaking quite clearly, and gesturing with unusual facility a particularly large right claw.

The youth was speaking. "But what of all I have done for you? So much! Gathered for you, stored for you, kept safe for you! And what for me? For me?"

The lobster responded in soothing tones but in too low a voice for Tara to apprehend its words. The youth paced and spun, and the voice floating out to Tara through the cavern was hard to make out, what with the echo and the constant pacing and the rising and falling volume. Tara strained to understand but could make out very little. Ultimately, she realized, the nature of their dispute didn't matter. All she needed was to identify which was the Sea Witch and which the water sprite and then get close enough to the latter to get off her spell. But which was which? She hadn't expected this. Marina must know, she decided, as the merfolk had had many troubles from her. Mostly likely, the youth was the sprite, but she couldn't be wrong, as she would get only one chance to cast the spell.

Marina and Ariel surfaced next to her a short minute later. "All right, princesses, here we are!" whispered Marina when all three of them had caught their breath and their eyes had adjusted to the low lighting of the grotto. "What next?"

Ariel and Marina looked to Tara. Tara looked back. Time to get started. The moment they had all been waiting for. Tara darted a quick look around the rocks; the sprite and the witch were still conversing. Good. Tara took a deep breath. "Which one, Marina, is the Sea Witch?"

Marina pointed at the crustacean.

Tara snuck another look around the rocks. "So then the other is the sprite." She turned to Ariel. "You've got the stasis bottle with you?"

Ariel revealed it to them beneath the surface of the water, careful not to lift it above and make a noise.

"Great. So here is what, maybe, we ought to do." The others leaned in still more closely. "First, we call Flo to come join us. She wants to help; we need her help. But—" remembering her arrival in the North Tower— "when she shows, she'll cause a sudden chill, and they'll be aware of us. So that's why, right after we send out the call to her, Marina, you'll go out and distract them," with a nod toward the sprite and the witch, "as best you can. Say or do whatever you have to get their attention. While you're doing this, I'll sneak around from behind to the water sprite. As soon as I'm close enough and he can hear me—that's one of the requirements—I'll cast my spell. That will send him off. Then Florence, Marina, and I can deal with the Sea Witch, while Ariel rushes in with the stasis bottle to capture her.

"Got it?"

"Sounds like a lot going on all at once," mumbled Ariel. "Do you think it'll work?"

"That's the whole idea: a lot going on all at once. They should be confused, and we'll take advantage of that. Look, I just need to send that sprite back to where I brought it from, and then it will be the four of us against that witch. Those should be good odds, right?"

No one could argue with that arithmetic, so Ariel took from her princess purse what looked like a piece of glass and, shielding it, spoke urgently into it. They saw Florence's face appear in it. "Come on and join us," whispered Ariel. "As soon as you can make it!" She turned to her friends. "It's an ice shard, for communication. Like a message bubble but only with her and her sister. Whom you haven't met yet."

Tara nodded. "Why don't we give her a princess purse when all this is over?" she suggested. "She'll have earned it!" If we get out of this, she found herself remarking silently, but dismissing the pessimistic thought immediately. "All ready? Marina, out you go, as silently as you can until up you pop!"

Marina disappeared soundlessly. Ariel and Tara waited a few anxious moments until they heard a soft plash at the other end of the cavern, and the dim form of Marina appeared, silhouetted in the ghostly light of the cavern. Almost immediately came her voice from the darkness, challenging, but with a quaver to it, as if from an underlying nervousness. "What schemes are you working up now, Sea Witch? And with whom? Whatever they are, you'll never get away with them!"

"Time for me to get moving," whispered Tara, and, as quietly as she could, she clambered out of the water and on to the pebbly strand to commence a halting creep in and out of the shadows around the edge of the cavern. Focus, she reminded herself. Focus and preparation. One chance only to get this spell right!

Tara moved as quickly as she could, keeping one eye on picking the quickest and quietest path around the edge of the cavern and the other on Marina's efforts to maintain their attention. She seemed to be doing well. The sea witch, still in the form of a lobster, had scuttled about to address her and was now waving its enormous right chela at her, as if making admonitory counter-arguments, while the sprite had ceased pacing to watch the witch and Marina with an interest that waxed and waned, depending on what each was saying.

Marina didn't dare look over the carapace of the Sea Witch lobster to find Tara. She was too afraid of accidentally giving away the plan to sneak up on the water sprite. But she sure wished Tara would hurry! The Sea Witch seemed to be advancing bit by bit with every wave of its exceptionally large—and menacing—claw. Marina forced confidence into her voice, but out of caution and growing fear was slipping further and further back into the water.

The enormous sea-foam green crustacean was definitely creeping forward, decided Marina, and its chela was snapping with avidity. What if I should need help, she thought, and, submerging her head quickly, sent out a distress call. "Quickly! Help me! I may be in great danger!" she radiated urgently toward the sea.

Marina resurfaced to continue distracting the Sea Witch. "It's very difficult to be—ouch!" she cried as, before she could regain her bearings, the lobster's right claw stretched out and, in a single motion, plucked her by the waist out of the water. Marina was swept up to nearly brush the roof of the cavern. "Stop this immediately! Put me down! Gently!" she radiated to the lobster but, unlike normal lobsters, it didn't respond. Because it was the Sea Witch, she knew, despite its current form, though it had been worth a try. "Let me go! Put me down!" she cried aloud, struggling vainly.

"I could cut you in half so easily," snickered the Sea Witch, gently flexing her pincer, as if to give Marina a foretaste of such a fate.

Far to the back of the cavern, Tara's attention was entirely focused on the water sprite, now engrossed by the spectacle of Marina in the grip of the Sea Witch.

"Capital! Capital!" it laughed and leapt. "See the little mermaid, tight in your grip! Watch the little mermaid, cut with a snip! Oh, do give me the human half as a souvenir! The tail-ish portion is only good for chum!" The water sprite danced and jumped, spun and capered. It leered up at Marina, hooted again, and taunted her. "Poor little mermaid! Fishy friend nears her end!"

She wasn't quite as close as she would have liked to have been, but Tara could see that now was the time to step forward. Now or never. Suddenly, she felt a little dizzy, and the cavern swam slightly before her eyes. She shook her head, and the syllables of the spell she was to speak burned brightly in her mind, as if in anticipation of their imminent use. Tara hesitated as the cavern reeled before her. There was Marina, just above her, writhing in slow motion in the claw of a monstrous arthropod; the water sprite, below and rapt, had thrown its arms high in a grotesque parody of victory. Tara gasped and staggered: what had happened to her? Some counter-spell from the Sea Witch or water sprite? Marina was in grave danger, she told herself fiercely and pinched herself so hard on the arm she nearly cried out. But the sharp pain cleared the fog in her mind, and she stepped from the shadows, her right hand already outstretched and beginning the first gesture of the Spell of Dispatch. "Water sprite! Listen well!"

The sprite jerked around, perplexed. The lobster whirled, Marina still in its grip. In that strange and sudden instant, Tara saw directly through the sprite as if it were translucent, and it was not humanoid but an ebbing and flowing, oscillating and fluctuating green vapor. Then the syllables of her spell tumbled from her lips. In fleeting succession, the sprite evidenced supreme anger, outraged irritation, and last, resignation. "Tara!" it howled and dissolved into the same blue-green mist in which it had originally appeared on the banks of the River Vahaval. The lobster, its stalked eyes twitching, followed the water sprite's gradual dissipation into the upper recesses of the cavern.

Out of the corner of her eye, Tara saw Ariel appear on the other side of the cavern, dripping, stasis bottle ready in her hand. "Not yet, Ariel! Not until Marina's free! Or she'll be trapped too!"

The lobster instantly squatted into a defensive crouch. The antennae waved with mounting agitation and then, slowly, it backed toward the cavern wall. "No closer, or I chop the mermaid to pieces!" it threatened at last. "Aenon will have her back again… in chunks!"

"Let her go!" ordered Tara, stepping forward boldly to confront the gigantic crustacean and heedless of the claw hovering over her. "Do you see that bottle she has?" she continued, pointing to Ariel. "It's a stasis bottle! You'll be trapped forever!"

"You mean to do that anyway. That's no threat!"

This was true, Tara knew. Would they have to offer the Sea Witch her freedom in exchange for Marina's life? Could the Sea Witch be trusted?

Behind Ariel the water began to froth and churn. Hearing it, she scrambled up the short beach, eyes wide with horror. A moment later, a half dozen enormous, ropey giant squid's tentacles flung themselves out of the water at the Sea Witch. Before she could scuttle away, the tentacles had wrapped themselves around her thorax multiple times and begun to tug. Marina cried out in relief. "Pull! Pull!" she called excitedly. As she did, the water lapping in the inlet boiled as all sea life within a mile's radius, by all their innumerable means of locomotion, thronged to her aid, crowding and crawling, swimming and swarming, wriggling and writhing.

Ariel and Tara stared. A black tide of crabs and lobsters had surged from the water and were driving for the witch, and the beach became a roiling mass of squirming chelae, dully glinting in the faint green light. Behind them, the blood-orange tentacles of an octopus had coiled up out of the water, a boulder hoisted high in the air. The bulbous head showed for a brief moment, and the two keen eyes drew a bead, then, with a mighty jerk, the tentacles hurled the boulder at the lobster.

The lobster ducked, just in time, and the boulder sailed over its carapace to shatter against the wall behind it. The swarming crustaceans below, with a tremendous clatter of snipping and snapping, furiously attacked the Sea Witch's legs nearest the claw holding Marina.

The squid's tentacles strained for a moment, then they slipped directly through the lobster and fell flat to the rock and sand. Another boulder flung by the octopus, better aimed, passed through the thorax. The crustaceans, confused, found themselves snipping at nothing. "I am the sea; you cannot hurt water!" the Sea Witch mocked. The other, smaller claw now gestured threateningly, and the lobster lunged at Tara. "You next!"

Tara darted back, just before the chela snapped at the empty air where she had stood. "Ariel!" she screamed in terror. "Get her!"

The lobster wheeled back to face Ariel, who stopped in her tracks. It was a stand-off: the witch had Marina, but they had the bottle. Neither trusted the other.

Tara felt the tips of her hair stir, as if in a breeze. From where? How could there be a breeze in a subterranean cavern? Then she shivered violently. She opened her mouth in surprise but then shut it again promptly. Divert the Sea Witch's attention until the last possible moment. "You'll never get away with this! Put her down, and we'll let you go!"

"Ha! Let me go first. Then I'll set her free!"

"How do we trust you?" Just beyond the Sea Witch, just over its tail fan, Tara spotted what looked to be the figure of a human, a girl, about her size, starting to form from the ground up in striations of white and grey. Then a chill blast swept over the four in the cavern and Florence stood before them, whole and complete.

"Watch out!" shouted Tara as the Sea Witch, sensing a third threat, whirled to confront it. The smaller pincer claw rose high and fell toward Florence. Florence threw up her arm instinctively and a white flash burst from it to envelope the claw in mid-air.

It descended further a fraction, then seized up, frozen solid.

"Florence, save Marina!"

Florence understood immediately what Tara wanted. She panned her hand across the cavern until it swept across the overlarge crusher claw clutching Marina, but, so as not to freeze Marina, proximal to the carapace rather than across the claw itself. It too iced over in a moment. Marina beat on it ineffectually but needn't have, as turning about in fury, the Sea Witch's frozen claw inadvertently collided spectacularly with the wall of the cavern and shattered into pieces. Rocks, lichens, moss, ice, and Marina all rained down to the sand below.

Ariel saw her chance. Darting forward, the bottle unstopped, she thrust it against the witch. There was a brief *whoosh*, the air trembled, and the Sea Witch was no longer amongst them. Ariel popped the stopper back on the jar and held it aloft triumphantly.

The other three gathered around, Marina rolling over and groggily dragging herself across the sand to see. Inside, rising three quarters up to the rim, was a quantity of what looked for all the world like grey-green seawater. Only, occasionally, the water would resolve into a single wave with one tiny, unmoving whitecap atop it and race frenetically around the jar's minute perimeter.

Tara reflected the next day on the events beneath the Secret Island. The water sprite was back where it belonged. Marina had assured her that it could not return without being purposefully summoned, which Tara had many times vowed she would never do.

The Sea Witch was in stasis and, as long as she remained so, would not trouble the merfolk again. Already she was in safe "storage" in King Aenon's treasury room, where she would surely be secure for a very long time.

Princess Florence had a princess purse. She had deserved one after saving all of them, though she had been modest about that and even apologized for missing nearly all the excitement. "It took me longer than I thought it would to figure out in which cavern you were. I didn't want to appear in the wrong cavern, or worse, in the middle of the island. That wouldn't have been useful to anyone!"

Tara had determined she would never cast another spell again. The Spell of Summoning had gone disastrously wrong, and the Spell of Dispatch had made her woozy. "They can sometimes do that," Ariel had explained. "Magic can be like that. It depends on the spell, really. The person too." Enough, she had promised the others. She'd leave the magic henceforth to them. "And we'll leave the brainstorms to you that get us out of trouble!" they had replied, gaily.

Finally, Tara had decided to quit trying to be like the light-hearted and enthusiastic Marina and to go back simply to being Tara. She loved Marina, and adored how perky and effervescent she could be, but Tara couldn't be Marina any more than Tara could be magical like Marina. It was too much effort and wasn't her. Tara would have to be Tara, and she and everyone around her would have to be content with that. She could, and probably should, try to be happier rather than so introspective and pensive. But there was no way around it: 'happiness' for Tara would always be complicated and with reservations, not innocent and whole-hearted like with Marina.

As for her parents, they hadn't even noticed she had been gone. Well, it had taken less than a day. Her mother hadn't even asked where she had been all that morning, and Tara had been glad this time for the sympathetic eye and solicitous silence when she had come down from the North Tower for something to eat.

"Hi, everyone!" She had greeted them with the quiet happiness that had come to her from having resolved the water sprite problem. Her mother had been taken aback. She was happy again! When Tara had requested an extra fork from a servant, Armorica had leaned over to Childeric. "She must have received another message. From HIM!" she had whispered. Childeric had eyed them both in turn but concluded that on yet another occasion, saying nothing was the better answer.

Now she was upstairs in her rooms in the North Tower, reluctantly preparing for the next event of the Season. Sigh. But with the water sprite gone, the conversation could get back to the usual dreadful badinage and away from the awful drought. Sullijee bustled about, selecting a dress for her and assembling the necessary tools to manage Tara's hair. Tara sat at her vanity, doing her best to submit without complaining.

"Such fair weather we've been having," offered Sullijee cheerfully as she began the lengthy task of ordering Tara's locks.

"Yes. Lovely indeed. But I suppose the vegetation wants rain. So people say."

"Oh, I know people say that, but I shouldn't be surprised if we don't get plenty enough one of these days soon."

Just as she spoke, there came a tremendous, rolling boom that rattled the very foundations of the castle. Sullijee jumped, and Tara gave a short, sharp cry of surprise but, in sudden realization, laughed joyously. "That's thunder! It's going to rain!" Racing to the window and throwing open the shutters, Tara thrust out her hand. As she did, a sky purple with clouds opened and out poured a torrent so solid it appeared as if a curtain had come down about the castle. Tara watched a long, gleeful, triumphant second. The downpour was so heavy she couldn't see the forest across the field opposite—and it was mid-afternoon! She scanned the clouds overhead. It could continue for hours.

"It's rain! Rain!"

Sullijee was crestfallen. "Oh no; it's pouring! Simply pouring! And what a terrible time for this to happen too! The roads will be impassable; they'll have to cancel tonight's ball!"

Tara laughed aloud as she hadn't in days and spun about on the ball of one foot. "Rain! At last!" She turned to the despondent Sullijee and seized her by both shoulders, surely for the first and only time. "Don't worry; I'm sure it won't last too, too long! And haven't we wanted rain for days?"

Book II: The City Underground

Pentenok

A solitary figure, difficult to distinguish against her background, stood on a ledge projecting from a shadowy mountain. Behind her yawned the mouth of a cave; before her spread a panorama of rocky crags and lesser peaks. She stood there, silent, motionless, as if in contemplation, visible only as a slightly darker speck against the bulk of the rock wall.

Then the figure started. The far east had begun to glow with the dawn. A tiny, molten crescent was forming just at the hazy edge of the horizon. The figure reached to her neck and fumbled with a band that she lifted to strap with care around her head. As the sun lifted further into the sky, the flat twin disks over her eyes reflected its progress, and the distant, fiery glory of the rising orb showed twice in miniature upon her pallid face.

The whipping wind, numbing at that height, yanked fitfully at her black cloak. For the most part, she paid no heed but, occasionally, became sufficiently uncomfortable so as to impatiently rewrap it about herself. Though it was bitterly cold and she stood exposed on the ledge, so iron was her will that she remained there long minutes, oblivious and immobile. She might even have been supposed as part of the rock itself but for her frustrated efforts to keep her cloak from becoming a wind-caught banner, a fluttering black against the parti-colored grey, brown, and white of the mountain behind her.

It was a magnificent view from her perch, this final peak of the Grey Mountains. Immediately beyond, the range moderated to rocky ridges and then undulating hills. Beyond these were patches of green, merging in the distance to a rolling, verdant carpet. Here and again there were the blue dots of lakes, the glitter of their waters flashing back the light of the ascending sun.

The sky brightened steadily. Nearest the sun, it was a cornflower blue dusted with striated powder-white clouds. Across the arc of the sky, past and behind the figure, the sky deepened to a pure cobalt and still onwards to indigo, verging to wine as the night fled away.

The blazing sphere inched still higher. What the thin air, temperature, and wind could not do the light apparently could. The figure adjusted the strap which kept the dark disks over her eyes and, with a last glance out across the world—shaded by her right hand—she turned and strode into the cave behind to vanish into its depths.

Far, far below the Overlands—where there is bright sunshine, warm breezes, blue skies, lush vegetation, and snow-capped mountains—lies the Underworld. The Underworld is vastly unlike the Overlands. The Overlands are brightened by the cycles of the sun, but the Underworld is a place of perpetual dimness. The Overlands have seasons of hot and cold, while the Underworld enjoys moderate temperatures all year round. Overhead, the Overlands boast a sky of limitless height; the Underworld's caverns are limited by rocky ceilings, even if far above. Yet some of the Underworld's caverns are cut by abysses, unlike in the Overlands, where such features would be weathered away by wind and rain, and these chasms are of unknowable depth, as if to match and mimic the limitless height of the Overland skies.

The Overlands teem with life. There are creatures that flit through its restless airs, that prowl its chill seas, that roam its rolling hills, that scurry through the branches of its whispering forests, that twitch in its baking sands, or that worm through its loamy soils. Many live their waking hours under the sun; some fewer keep to the night and hunt through the darkness for food or water.

The Underworld also hosts life. Though dark, it is not an empty, lifeless place. There are no birds or flowering plants, but there are many darkness-loving, cave-dwelling creatures, and every ecological niche of the Underworld is as filled to fullness as its corresponding niche in the Overlands. There are fish and river creatures, if generally blind, in the underground rivers and pools. In the upper reaches lives the leathery lavalal, which glides from higher to lower rocks through the open spaces to escape its predators, while the fearsome mocurra, a kind of enormous carnivorous centipede, ranges the deeper levels. There are no green plants, but there is a tremendous range of lichens, molds, fungi, and other subterranean plant life thriving in the warm, dark, and less travelled strata.

Especially lichens: all sorts of lichens and all dependent on the natural radioactivity of their immediate environment for energy, rather than photosynthesis. Unique to certain depths and micro-climates of the

Underworld are certain lichens called "light lichens" and which, in their natural and uncultivated state, glow softly in tones of brown that range from a faint sepia to a soft caramel. Truly brilliant light lichens of the brightest hues are rare and prized. This has led some Underworlders to try crossing different species of light lichens to achieve ever brighter intensities and even to establish farms in an effort to develop particular shades and hues of luminescence. But the field of lichenology in the Underworld is more art than science; real success has eluded the farmers. The cultivation of a steady supply of low-quality illumination had been achieved, but the production of a high quality lichen was still as uncertain and inconsistent as the chance discovery of a "bright white" by one of the infrequent expeditions to the lesser explored regions of the Underworld.

At the top of the animal kingdom in the Underworld and analogous to the highest rung humans occupied in the Overlands were the Underworlders. They lived in communities of various sizes, just as humans did above ground, and preferred to be closer to the surface than deeper. Just as in the Overlands, many of these communities lay along waterways or the junctions of well-travelled trade routes.

One of the principal agglomerations of Underworlders was the sprawling city of Pentenok. Pentenok was widely assumed to be the oldest of the Underworld cities. Certainly it was the noblest and most prestigious of them, besides being the wealthiest and best organized. All things could be had in Pentenok, it was said. Certainly it had all things that Underworlders wanted.

Pentenok rose in tier upon faintly sparkling tier toward the roof of the great vaulted cavern in which, ages before, its foundations had been fixed. The city stood at the conflux of two mighty rivers, the Rivers Iilish and Liltenen, both of which were rumored to have their origin in the Overlands but which had never been traced. These waterways brought trade and a continuous supply of fresh water and represented a pair of riverine highways on which the many watercraft of the Underworlders plied their navigable reaches. Trade, as at the surface, varied and involved foodstuffs and wearables, mined elements—of which there was enormous range and of high quality—fashioned goods, and, perhaps, most important of all, light.

This light was furnished by light lichens. For, though the Underworld was a place of great and seemingly limitless darkness, and its inhabitants had lived there since beyond memory, its dwellers still prized light, and they sought it out and the colors it illuminated, howsoever it gleamed. For light was how they knew the reaches of their kingdom, and light was how they explored the caverns which honeycombed their world. And light was how they navigated the treacherous waters of their rivers, and light was how they even recognized each other. Light was precious and valuable, and the whiter it was, the more valuable it was, as whiter light brought forth greater color from all on which it shone, and color—in a world otherwise of darkness—was valued as exquisite.

Some ventured to the Overlands, thinking to glory in the brilliance of the unlimited light of the yellow sun high above in the "far ceiling" of the sky. But these were few, and they came back in just a few days. This was because most Underworlders found themselves agoraphobic in the Overlands, there being no solid roof overhead. Others returned because the light was too blazing, more than they could stand even equipped with the special dark quartz crystal goggles that had been developed to moderate the light. Even with these goggles, having lived their entire lives in dimness, the midday sun of the Overlands was profoundly disorienting, the landscape unnervingly dazzling, and its profuse colors overbold and riotous. The Underworlders envied the Overlanders their abundant light but had no desire to share in it above ground, overpowering as it was.

Pentenok functioned continuously. Its markets and work-places were open every day, with the exception of officially designated Rest Days. There was no day or night, or storm, or shine, so its citizens could wake at whatever hour they chose and sleep likewise. But, in practice, large portions of the population tended to rise and rest in the same twenty-hour cycles, if only for the sake of convenience or to facilitate the needs of some classes of citizens who tended to group and function in the same cycles. Over time, certain cycles had come to be associated with particular classes and metiers, with one the preference of the ruling classes and another, almost directly counter to the first, the favorite of artists and performers.

Arranged about these two primary and largely independent cycles were other partially overlapping cycles into and out of which the rest of the population moved as age, work, and fancy took them. Some never switched cycles and lived within the same cycle their entire lives, in which case, these Underworlders might never come across some sections of the population and would be ever ignorant of what they did, what they thought, and how they existed. Thus the great labyrinthine city of Pentenok stirred continuously, its markets nearly always populated, its merchants nearly always transacting and some portion of its citizenry nearly always meeting, conversing, dining, or working.

Besides being the home of a great many Underworlders, Pentenok was a city-kingdom ruled by a Sebastokrator, the title its ruler assumed. "Sebastokrator" being a word not the most amenable to everyday speech, the commonly spoken honorific was the reduced form "Sebastos." The Sebastos lived near the center of Pentenok, in a small though ornate palace, the principal feature of which was the Spire of Lothwell, the tallest, most prominent of the city's five spires. Sebastos Reynam, House Biss, occupied the throne, and while not particularly adventurous or innovative in his rulership, he was generally perceived as being predictable and inclined toward tolerance.

Sebastos Reynam's light touch to rulership greatly pleased many, especially the mercantile classes, as the relaxation of customs regulations had allowed trade to flourish. But others were unhappy with Reynam's easy going style. They worried about the city's defenses and, particularly, the readiness of the city's Guards. The guards themselves felt that their relevance had diminished and that counsellors, financiers, and trade representatives had displaced them. The guards still trained, still patrolled the main and secondary paths of the Underworld leading to Pentenok, and still maintained order in the city, but were acutely aware that their prestige had declined. Not that they wished for conflict to remind others of the necessity of their existence, but they often grumblingly wished for former days when they had been of greater importance.

The Sebasissa Sundra, sister to the Sebastos, was also displeased. She was older than her brother by slightly more than a year and perceived herself as much more capable and far-sighted. She chafed at his seeming indifference to the affairs of the kingdom. It seemed to her that he was happy to let his policies with respect to their trading partners—past allies, yes, but potentially future enemies—be determined by these merchants and their mercurial trading interests, rather than strategic objectives or the true long-term needs of Pentenok as she understood them.

The Sebasissa Sundra carefully closed a small folio she had been studying intently and placed it to one side. The folio was very old, and its leaves—which had been formed of pressed and dried fungi—were crumbling away at the edges, leaving behind a residue of fine grey dust on the mocurra scale-covered desktop. She placed the folio gently next to the stack of pamphlets of various sizes she had been reading over the past days and leaned back in her chair. Interesting, but nothing new in it. Nothing more specific about its location than what she had already gleaned from other readings, and only some vague hints about how to use it.

On the other hand, insofar as it repeated what other books had said, the folio would seem to confirm its existence and power and the Sebasissa's growing conviction that that which she already had learned had to be correct.

A corner of the portfolio she had just set down lay within the small pool of light cast by her desk lamp. Sundra gazed at the lamp. It was unique in that it was fashioned from a single elaborate spray of wire gold. Interspersed amongst the lamp's spreading branches were five light lichens glowing with a soft yellow light and, hence, a rarity, especially in that their light was matched in hue and tone. The lamp was very old, having been given many generations before to the then Sebastos. A gift of the Light Merchants, Sundra recollected. It had been discovered, so the Merchants had told its royal recipient, in an expedition for light lichens in deeper caverns. But Sundra had never found the story believable. The Light Merchants picked and plucked, whereas wire gold required digging and delving.

There was a knock on the door. "Yes?" Sundra replied, stepping from the desk and rising to her full, regal height. "Who knocks?"

"I, Sebasissa. Maribess. At your service, and by your command, am I here."

Very good, thought Sundra. It was Maribess, a trusted confidant. They had known each other since a very young age and had even been playmates. Maribess had stayed close and dependable ever since and had eventually become a member of Sundra's quasi-official personal guard.

"Enter, please."

The door opened, and a diminutive light-haired woman with great, round, light eyes noiselessly crossed the threshold but stopped just upon entering after the required three-quarters genuflection due the Sebasissa. She wore a black kirtle interwoven with a silvery thread, and the edges of it were finished with a deep brown fringe. Underneath was a light chainmail shirt, which she wore just as did all of the Sebasissa's personal guards. This was Maribess.

Maribess was petite, even for an Underworlder, and had never been especially strong. As an offset though, she was exceptionally dexterous and had developed an extraordinarily keen aim, becoming skilled in a wide variety of thrown weapons like knives, bolos, darts, the miniature bow and arrow, and still others. Sundra appreciated this, having herself a good eye, but had had only the opportunity and time to practice the full-sized bow and arrow, preferring it over the miniature, as she was taller and stronger than Maribess.

Sundra waived with a gesture the usual honorifics due her and motioned Maribess to a chair on the other side of the desk. Sundra moved around and joined Maribess at a chair opposite. This was a signal honor, as Sundra required most to stand before her, and at the requisite three swords' length that was the prerogative of the royal house. "Welcome, Maribess."

Maribess seated herself respectfully in the proffered chair. In the last month, she had received several summonses to the Sebasissa's chambers, the most recent in the week just past. What had struck Maribess was that no particular subject had been the purpose of the summonses. Once the Sebasissa had reminisced about their shared childhoods; on another occasion, the Sebasissa had asked her what she thought might be the future of Pentenok; the details of still other discussions Maribess couldn't recollect at all. It was strange and, try as she had, she couldn't understand. Yet Maribess brushed it from her mind. Such was the Sebasissa, while she was Maribess, only Maribess. She was a servant and sometimes companion to the Sebasissa, not someone who dared question royal prerogative.

This room, the room in which the Sebasissa had always received her, was strikingly beautiful. Maribess had glanced around furtively, almost guiltily, the first time she had entered, and it looked to be a study but also looked to function as a kind of antechamber, from the several doors in the wall opposite the one by which she had entered. The room was furnished sumptuously and in the colors of House Biss, in tones of grey, black, and brown, with silver borders or piping demarking each change in color. More than any fitting or furnishing though, Maribess was captivated by the room's light: rich, warm, and with a soft brilliance that made all the fixtures and furniture gleam darkly.

Most importantly, the lighting was surely the whitest Maribess had ever seen, and here it radiated not only from the lamp on the desk to her right but from clusters of shining elements in the four corners of the room.

Overhead, from a chandelier, were three placed at the end of spokes radiating from a silver axis. To Maribess's eyes, the shadows, normally omnipresent in the Underground Kingdom, were hardly present, as the bright glow had virtually chased them from the room, and she felt as if she were almost in a kind of spotlight, if such a thing could exist in the Underworld. So much light, so rich and bright, she had thought the first time she had taken the proffered chair. And just for the two of them! And for no special occasion; only to receive her! In the Underworld, it was an honor to show light to a guest. Maribess could hardly understand how she, who had no rank compared to the Sebasissa, could merit such magnificence.

The effect had taken away Maribess's breath the first time she had entered. That effect, she had remarked to herself later and only after retrospection, had pleased the Sebasissa inordinately.

"Sebasissa, how may I serve you?"

Though Sundra had shown Maribess to a chair, she did not take a seat herself. Rather, she stood behind one, eying Maribess closely, then abruptly turned and began to prowl the room behind it. There was a swish of fabric with each turn of the Sebasissa, but Maribess thought she heard more than just fabric. It sounded faintly like the chink of chain mail, though there was none of the gleam of it from what Maribess could see.

Sundra stopped before a guéridon at one wall and on which had been arranged a number of exceptionally large and fine crystal specimens. Her hand hovered over first one, then another, until she selected an intensely red chunk of carnelian and picked it up as if to examine it. "Maribess..." she began slowly, then hesitated.

"Yes, Sebasissa?"

Sundra looked up with a bright eye, that hand holding the sample of carnelian slowly falling to her side. "Maribess, do you prize light?"

"Yes, Sebasissa, as much as any other Pentenokian. We all know the expressions: 'Light is life' and 'By the light, we know our friends'."

"Yes. So. Those are our adages, aren't they? And properly so, because they have much truth in them." Sundra approached the empty chair opposite Maribess to grip its back with her empty hand. "Tell me, Maribess, and looking at me, and in the light, are you my friend?"

"Sebasissa! Since we were small children! And until my last breath!"

"Forgive me for asking! That was surely unnecessary! But let me explain. I too prize the light and believe that more of it would bring great wealth and honor to Pentenok. Yes, the merchants of our city offer for sale ever as many light lichens as we might wish and are always looking for newer and better varieties, but they can't, or won't, offer real light. REAL light. In the abundance and radiance we would like and deserve!"

Maribess said nothing, as she would have disagreed with none of what her Sebasissa had said. But what could she mean? What was this about "real light" and "abundance?"

Sundra released the chair to return the mass of carnelian still in her hand to the decorative table. Then she shifted back to the chair and grasped it by the ear of one of its stiles. "I have been reading, Maribess. Researching. We don't have a tremendous library here in Pentenok, so our knowledge is scanty. But I have read of something tremendous, something wonderful, something in the Overlands and which is simply astonishing!"

Maribess leaned forward in her chair with wonder. "What could this be, Sebasissa?"

Sundra let go the chair and stepped around to sit down and lean forward toward Maribess and to the same angle at which Maribess leaned forward herself. Maribess heard again the soft slither of chainmail from beneath the kirtle, except now it was unmistakable, distinctive.

"It is magic," the Sebasissa said softly and dramatically at last, when she had settled. "Magic. I have read about it. It is called different things—sometimes a Rod of Light, sometimes a Crown of the Rainbows, sometimes other names—but all must be referring to the same thing. The same thing!"

"A 'Crown of the Rainbows'? But—please, Sebasissa—what is that? And what does it mean, a 'rainbow'?"

"Yes. So. 'Rainbow'. I have researched this too. It is an Overlands thing, a rainbow. It is a great arch in the sky—up into the far ceiling and then back down—and it is composed of bands of certain colors. These colors are not colors that we see naturally in the Underworld."

"An arch into the far ceiling? Just, up and then back down again? For… why? Why so much light like that?"

"They have an abundance of light. So much! You have heard stories of the Overlands, surely. But this rod, or crown, or whatever this device is, would control it, control the colors."

"Control them!"

"Just so! And this device is in the Overlands. It produces light and color—all the colors of the Overlands! From what I have read, it was lost, far back in time. Doubtless because the people of the Overlands have so much light and color that they could not understand its worth. But if we were to find this device and bring it back to the Underworld, it would be of tremendous value! We would see all! We could place it atop the highest tower of Pentenok, at the very tip of the Lothwell Spire, and it would shine forth eternally for all the people of Pentenok! And should any other kingdom wish to take it from us, for its value, why, if the light were modulated properly, it could send forth blinding rays and turn back any attacker!"

Maribess gazed in awe at the Sebasissa. At last it was clear! All these summonses: this is what she had been leading her toward! She saw her childhood playmate transformed suddenly into someone she had not seen for a long time, into someone driven and intent, alert and decisive, focused and energetic. The figure before her was very different from the perennially dissatisfied and sometimes carping Sebasissa she had known over the last several years. No, she had reverted to be more like the girl Maribess had known as a youth and particularly during games when the score was close. Then, the Sebasissa's face would seem to shine with a fierce determination to win, and her mind was sharp and firmly fixed on nothing else.

Maribess gazed for a long moment in dawning understanding of her childhood friend. She seemed changed, yet, in a sense, she was more like she had ever been in a long time. Maribess nodded slowly, stopped, then nodded again. This was her old friend Sundra, from before she had become the Sebasissa.

Sundra studied Maribess closely, waiting attentively for her reaction. She wondered if Maribess fully understood just how revolutionary such a device could be if brought to Pentenok. Why, for all the Underworld! Sundra knew it would change everything, but would Maribess understand?

"Atop... the highest tower? The Spire of Lothwell? And... offering light to all? Rich, abundant, true white light... to all?"

Sundra nodded slowly but with determination, her hands now tightly gripping the arms of her chair. "For all. For Pentenok. Imagine: everlasting, pure, white light."

Maribess stared a long moment into the Sebasissa's pale eyes, swept up by the Sebasissa's excitement. Maribess did not have a library to consult and only had dim memories of the stories she had heard of the Overlands— mostly these had been told to her as a child, and principally to frighten her.

The stories always included a bright object in the far ceiling that provided all the light the Overlanders could want, and none had mentioned a magical device such as the Sebasissa had described. But maybe such a device did exist. It was of no matter anyway: the Sebasissa had researched it and believed it existed. Then, of course it could! Maribess swallowed. "Sebasissa, this would be… incredible! Amazing!"

The Sebasissa breathed again. "So. Yes. Would we not be heroes in Pentenok? Would not the poets recount this incredible deed forever?"

"But Sebasissa, where is this device, whatever it may be? How will it be located and retrieved?"

Sundra relaxed some from the tension which had gripped her. "This is where I need your help, old friend. I am thinking of venturing into the Overlands. But I cannot go alone. I must have help."

"But Sebasissa, where is this device? I beg your permission!—"

The Sebasissa granted permission with a gesture.

"But, but, has it been located? And what obstacles might lie between us and its final procurement?"

"Yes, Kobemy. Exactly. All those questions. It lies in the Overlands. And not far from one of the outlets from our world to that one. So the texts tell me. So! This is where I must go. But I cannot journey alone. I require two to accompany me, to help me, to offer me counsel along the way. You are one of the very few I can trust so completely as to approach like this!"

Kobemy straightened proudly in his chair. He had been placed directly opposite the Sebasissa and at considerably less than the three swords' length due by tradition to the royal household. This was significant, he knew. He also knew that the Sebasissa did not casually or lightly offer gestures of familiarity. "Sebasissa, you may depend on me. I am deeply honored to be considered worthy of your trust!"

"Yes, you are! And so I feel confident to tell you my plans, if you will listen and keep these confidences."

Kobemy bowed in his chair by way of assent.

"So. You and I and one other will embark on this adventure. You and the other are to be my personal guard, my assistance. My confidants. The three of us will go to the Overlands to scout. You will also meet some people to whom I have been introduced and who have told me they will help. Overlanders. But I wish to evaluate them more closely. You can help me in this too."

"When would it be your pleasure to leave, Sebasissa?"

"Good. So, you are with me?"

Kobemy bowed again.

"In eight cycles. We leave in eight. For there are still some preparations for me to make."

The very next cycle after her interview with the Sebasissa, Maribess walked purposefully into the markets of Pentenok. The markets—simply called, collectively, Market—were open air, but only in the sense that they were uncovered to the seemingly limitless darkness overhead. The markets occupied a significant fraction of the city's third tier. A well-placed ramp to one side with adjoining stairs offered direct access to the river docks; overhead, three magnificent arching spans cut from the very rock connected the markets with other, adjoining tiers of Pentenok. Market, with, at its center, Central Square, was one of the most accessible locations of the city. This made it easy for all the inhabitants of Pentenok to shop and socialize, and it was very common for groups and individuals to meet at Central Square before continuing onward.

Maribess entered Market through one of the lesser-used entrances. Knots of the idle curious as well as intent buyers were inspecting the many and varied goods and foodstuffs displayed across the rows of counters and tables. Most of the goods had wended their way to Market by the Iilish and Liltenen Rivers, but a significant fraction came overland via the many meandering paths of the underworld. Maribess paused occasionally to glance at a table when something caught her eye, but it was more out of habit than actual interest. Before long, she had arrived at her objective: that section of Market reserved for the light sellers.

The deeper one ventured into Market, the fancier and more sumptuous it became. That corner, for the Light Merchants, was at the very rearmost of Market and was the most luxurious. The very best light sellers, those offering the whitest, brightest light, were placed back from the main thoroughfares of Market, and even on somewhat elevated ground. Their wares were not placed on tables for the casual passer-by to examine but housed within permanent, fully enclosed storefronts, somewhat grandly termed "pavilions." Admission to the very finest, most reputable of these was by appointment only and, it was whispered, only on reference.

Maribess lingered amongst the milling crowds at the tables along the outermost edge of the Light Merchants' reserved area. These tables had the most garish displays and the most aggressive touts. Their lights were the least expensive, inevitably the dimmest and most yellowish, some even with a currently unstylish greenish tinge to their glow. These was the lights seen in the homes of the city's poorest residents. Maribess sniffed. Her family had always had better. Not so very much better, as they had not been wealthy by any means, but at least appreciably better, as her parents had set great store on the quality of light in the home. They had been fond of stating that better light made for better minds and better spirits.

Now Maribess shopped for her own light. At first, she had thought to save on this component of her everyday expenses. But it had not been long before she come to agree with her parents and soon sought out the finest light she could afford. It was so: by the light, we know our friends, and even ourselves. Maribess found herself visiting the tables further in, where the light might be somewhat dimmer but was purer and whiter. Sometimes, for a change, she would choose light lichens that were brighter but with green or yellow tones. It was a balance struck in every transaction, this one of radiance versus hue, but Maribess fancied herself reasonably good at it, having developed a keen eye for it over the years.

A light merchant attempted to interest her in one of the formations placed prominently on his table. It was large, surprisingly so for its location along the main thoroughfare, and it threw off a good quantity of light. Yet a closer investigation revealed sections of its surface to be mottled by small dark spots; this was indicative of poor growth, perhaps even disease. Maribess smiled politely and wordlessly declined. For someone else. Not for her.

She passed on. All her life she had shopped for light. She had shopped with her mother, and then with friends as a social event, and even with males in whom she had been romantically interested as a sort of casual entertainment. Light was fundamental to Underworlders. Maybe it was everything, surely because they had so little of it. Light was a traditional present at the birth of children. All wedding guests brought some small token of it as evidence of good wishes for the newly partnered couple. The extinction of a light was the final gesture in funeral ceremonies. But now the Sebasissa had conjured up a radical, impossible vision: everlasting light for everyone! Maribess still could not fully come to grips with the thought.

No more need for light lichens! No more need for Light Merchants! No more comparisons of one's own light to that of one's neighbors or rivals, as some did to indicate advantage or wealth. No limit on light at all!

Maribess shook her head and reviewed what she now had come to call the Sebasissa's Impossible Idea. It was a device of some sort from the Overlands which, upon retrieval and transport back to Pentenok, would be affixed to the tip of the Spire of Lothwell. And there, forever afterwards, it would continuously radiate light of the brightest and purest kind for all. But how? The Sebasissa had told her it was by magic. Well, Maribess supposed, magic could make all sorts of incredible things happen. But… light the entire city? Perpetually? It would have to be stupendous magic!

Maribess shook her head again, nearly oblivious to the crowds jostling her as they attempted to get around the compact, petite woman standing in the very middle of the thoroughfare, lost in thought. She'd have to see it to believe it. The Sebasissa said it was in the Overlands and that it only needed to be found. How to do that, when the Overlands were reputed to be immense?

Yet the Sebasissa seemed to have a plan. She had spoken of journeying to the Overlands and needing her, Maribess's, help. Yes. The Sebasissa had researched this matter and was convinced this device existed. Shouldn't this be enough for her, for Maribess?

Maribess turned away from the light tables and, re-joining the ceaseless foot traffic, directed her steps homeward as purposefully as she had directed them originally to Market. The Sebasissa was her old friend and childhood companion. She had grown up with the Sebasissa and, though there was without question an unbridgeable social gulf between them, felt close to her. She would accompany the Sebasissa and help her to the extent she could with whatever plans the Sebasissa had formed. "By the light we know our friends," Maribess repeated to herself. The Sebasissa had a plan to offer light to all Pentenokians. Maribess would prove herself to be the truest of friends.

There was a knock on the door. Sebastos Reynam recognized the rap by its characteristic rhythm and forcefulness. "Enter, please."

Sundra stepped into the room and closed the door behind her. Reynam eyed her for a long moment until Sundra, as if recollecting herself, genuflected deeply, as was required when entering the presence of the

Sebastos.

She arose and waited at the requisite three swords' length before approaching further. Reynam, a tall man with features similar to those of Sundra, though without her hardened eyes, motioned her to come forward as might please her after a pause in length exactly duplicating that which she had shown in genuflecting to him upon entering. "Sister, how are you? Welcome! What brings you to see me?"

"Brother, I wish for your continued health!" was Sundra's reply upon being invited to speak, a traditional and more formal salutation.

Reynam raised an eyebrow fractionally at his sister's slightly more distant tone. Then he turned toward a set of doors in one wall, sighing privately. Another one of these discussions, he determined dismally. Increasingly, it seemed, his sister came mainly to alert him to one evil or another. One cycle, it had been the poor training and equipping of the city's Guards; on another, it had been to warn him darkly about what she was convinced were efforts by other city-kingdoms to spy on their royal house. What would it be on this time? Of course, they had always had their disagreements on what the city needed and how the treasury should be used, but they now seemed at odds more often than not. "Thank you, sister, for your good wishes. I return them, of course, with my best wishes for your health."

Reynam opened the double doors and stepped onto the balcony beyond. "For what might I have the pleasure of your visit, please?" Reynam rested his hands on the carved stone railing and looked out over Pentenok, which stretched, in that direction, for what looked to be an infinity. Yet Reynam knew that it was not so very great, for it was not that the limits of the city could not be discerned for the distance, but because there was so little light, and what little was there was dimmest at the outer, poorest reaches. Closer in, in the houses of greater distinction and wealth, there were lights that could be seen even from the balcony as far up as they were, but further out, these dwindled to tiny pinpoints, or only the faintest of suggestions of light, rather than something actually visible.

Reynam considered the view thoughtfully. This was Pentenok, the largest, grandest, and most important city of the Underworld. Everything they had, any light they shone, was because it had been gathered by their own hand and theirs alone. The city's very existence was a triumph. Across the floor of the immense cavern sprawled the buildings housing the teeming commerce of the city, and overhead, always overhead, was the deep, velvety blackness, absolute, unchanging, a kind of warm, dark, enveloping comfort.

Sebastos Reynam pondered the dark panorama before him, intermittently lit with tiny sparkles of white and yellow. It had always been like this. He was the seventeenth of his house, House Biss, to have ruled Pentenok. The sixteen before him of his line had surely gazed similarly out over the very same view and come to the very same conclusions. Certainty and predictability had kept their line on the throne, not innovation. His father had impressed on him that innovation often brought change, which could all too rapidly turn uncontrollable and bring destruction. Reynam was pleased to have assumed the throne with little fanfare. His main concession to the passage of time had been an enhanced and increased permitting fee the merchants of Pentenok paid for the privilege of conducting their business, and that strictly to more fully fund the city's and the royal house's treasuries.

Sundra joined him on the balcony, but facing him, rather than contemplating with him the view so indistinctly spread below them. "Brother, you are Sebastos, to be sure, and I am Sebasissa, but I am obliged to bring a matter to your attention."

"Yes, sister? Is it spies again?"

Sundra flushed at the faint mockery in the Sebastos's voice. "No, brother. Not spies. Though I am quite certain they are present." She lowered her voice and inclined her head toward him. "They are everywhere! It is better that we are out on the balcony, where they cannot hear us."

Reynam said nothing. Of course there were spies, he was thinking. The other city-kingdoms wanted to know what Pentenok, the largest and wealthiest of them, was doing. Similarly, didn't Pentenok make strenuous efforts to place its own spies in their innermost circles? But Sundra had not been able to offer real evidence as to where and who the spies might be, so the warning had been too vague to be of any use.

"No, brother, it is something else. It is about the merchants. Especially the Light Merchants."

"What about the merchants, please, sister?"

Sundra lowered her voice still further and reflexively glanced about. "Have they not grown very rich off the trade that flows through this city?"

"Surely they are wealthier. But so is the city as a whole. As is the royal house. Everyone is wealthier on the trade that flows up and down the Iilish and Liltenen. Is this not a good thing?"

"So, it would be a good thing—wholly a good thing—if it did not come with a cost. At the expense of the rest of the people."

"How is this, Sundra? The merchants offer goods for sale. Our people buy what they like and as they like. Thus our people benefit from the trade and it is not at their expense. In fact, insofar as there are more and varied merchants offering goods, our people gain greater choice and selection in what they may choose to buy."

Sundra took a half-step closer. "The Light Merchants have purchased a license from the city and the royal house. With this license they extort higher prices from all Pentenok. Light is necessary, and their prices are like a tax."

"Really, Sundra! I mean, yes, the Light Merchants have purchased a license to sell. And the sale of the license added to the wealth of the royal house—our house—and the city. But this is fair, as it is a valuable privilege to offer their wares for sale at Market. And the Light Merchants have always sold light lichens to the people of Pentenok. This is long-established custom!"

"It is a great privilege to sell in Market," agreed Sundra readily. "But it is the people who actually pay for this privilege. The merchants only charge the people more to recoup the cost."

"You would have us raise the price of the license still higher? Would the merchants not just pass on the still higher price, and—if you are right—the people would be even worse off? Or should we charge less, in order to lessen the burden on the people? But then the city would have less to fund the upkeep of the guards and their equipment. And this is another concern of yours, yes?"

Sundra scowled and turned to the balcony rail. The merchants—the Light Merchants chief amongst them—had become over-mighty, she was certain, even if her brother did not seem to understand this. She was not the ruler of Pentenok, and that afforded her slightly more flexibility in her contacts than he. She knew people of strata other than the nobility, people of more modest means and backgrounds, like Maribess and Kobemy. And still others. Many in the Guards. They complained of the merchants' charges for everything they needed to live a decent life. In particular, they complained about the cost of light. This was a necessity, yet the cost of replacing spent light lichens seemed to be ever-rising, and the lichens of ever lower and lower quality. When confronted, some merchants said it was more difficult to find good lichens; others that the license fees to sell in Market were high. Others simply shrugged and replied that their own expenses were rising, and what else were they to do?

Light. Sundra surveyed the vast city that lay below them. Light. So little of it there in the darkness, only scattered flecks of it, to her mind, and those mostly close to the palace. The Light Merchants, the wealthiest of the guilds in the city, were hardly to be trusted. Doubtless they withheld from the people of Pentenok the best light for their own use, or for that of the royal house with which they sedulously curried favor. Wasn't that the measurement of the real wealth of Pentenok, it occurred to her? Light? More light, that is; not just light for the ever-richer merchant classes. But light for all, and light by which all of the city could see all of its surroundings, all of its detractors, all of its allies. Perceive, indeed, its future, just as the old maxims went. Just so. Sundra involuntarily glanced up to look up at the tip of the Spire of Lothwell, the highest point in the city and the landmark tower of the Sebastos's palace. Imagine never-ending light streaming from that spire for all! The grip of the Light Merchants would be broken and the people of Pentenok forever liberated from their oppressive taxes.

Sundra's gaze turned to the vast, silent, changeless blackness. This fabled device that controlled colors, if she could find it, would cast down the Light Merchants and solidify Pentenok's place as the wealthiest and most powerful city in the Underworld, all in one stroke.

"By the light, we shall see our future, brother," Sundra intoned, borrowing from the old phrase.

Sebastos Reynam half-turned toward his sister. Why the melodrama, he wondered, suddenly weary. The opaque adages, applied with such mysteriousness to everyday situations. He swallowed his frustration. "Yes, sister. And 'By the light, we know our friends'," he replied with a measured voice.

"Yes, that too. So, it should follow that, with more light, we should know our friends still better and see our future still more clearly."

Reynam nodded agreement, but inwardly he had lost interest. This was silly, purposeless talk that led them nowhere. He turned back to gaze out over the railing and sighed. "More light would be better, yes. If you should think of a way to bring us more, that would be a tremendous boon to

Pentenok."

Sundra peered more closely at her brother through the dim light that leaked onto the balcony from the room beyond the double doors. What was he saying? Could he have divined her thoughts? But no, she realized in an instant. He was just fobbing her off with another dismissive remark, couched now as an invitation. Sundra frowned. That was her brother. So content with how everything was currently arranged, with no eye toward the future or what could otherwise be. However things had been yesterday was how they should be today, and however they were today, why, why shouldn't they be that way tomorrow and the day after that?

"Brother, what if I were able to find another source of light? And bring it to Pentenok? What then?"

"I should think the Light Merchants have explored most every path within several cycles of travel and exploited every formation of any size. They have their farms too, of course, but these still have not yielded lichens of any value."

"But if?"

Reynam turned sharply toward her. "A new source? Of what kind? From where?"

She shrugged casually and relaxed. It wasn't apparent he had knowledge of what she had been discussing with Maribess or Kobemy. She should never have questioned that: those two were absolutely dependable. "Just thinking aloud, that's all. But what if I were to explore and find a source? One that House Biss would control, and not the Light Merchants?"

Reynam shook his head firmly. "No. I will not permit this. And we have discussed this. You are the Sebasissa and may not go off on some misadventure that may result in your death or capture. If anything should befall me—"

"May it be forestalled!" interjected Sundra, automatically.

"—then you would rule Pentenok. The succession of our House must not be endangered. We must have continuity. Without an obvious ruler, Pentenok could descend into strife, or even civil war."

"But I go to the shores of Dark Lake frequently!"

"That is different, and we both know this. Dark Lake is a known place, and safe, even if it is some distance from Pentenok. No," he concluded, shaking his head. "I am sorry, but the city's safety, and that of its people, cannot be compromised like that. It is our obligation as the ruling family."

Indeed, thought Sundra as she left the personal chambers of the Sebastos: rulership was an obligation. And one she intended to fulfil, if—increasingly—not in exactly the manner that the Sebastos had in mind.

"The Sebasissa!" rang out and, across the training field, all activity ceased immediately.

Sundra suppressed a smile. "Please. Please! Continue. Do not interrupt anything on my account."

"Continue! It is the Sebasissa's pleasure!"

"Thank you, Captain Ortiki. Please, arise."

Captain Ortiki stood from his three-quarters genuflection and waited for her further word.

"I wonder," she continued, after a short pause to check the immediate vicinity for any other than Kobemy, accompanying her, who might be within earshot, "how your training is going? By that I mean, that of the Guards."

Ortiki nodded. The Sebasissa had enquired about this on several recent occasions. "It is well, Sebasissa, thank you. But, I worry some about the Guards, as I have mentioned to you before. I sense that our importance is lesser these days, and to grow lesser still."

"Yes. So. You mentioned this concern of yours on a previous occasion. Because the allowance for the Guards, for recruitment, for upkeep, for pay, for weaponry, only shrinks."

Ortiki frowned and adjusted his helmet, which he had pushed back on his head to expose some of the typically nearly white, slightly curly hair that was so common of the Underworlders. Unlike with many others though, his was cut very short in the typical guardsman manner. "Yes, Sebasissa. But it is not in the sense that we receive less in our overall allowance. More that, it does not seem to keep pace with the expenses, which increase faster."

"These seem to be going up, always up. My guards can see this. I can see this."

Sebasissa Sundra nodded. "And the General of the guards? What does he say?"

Ortiki paused to remove his helmet altogether and to run his left hand through his hair, his helmet in his right. His face was craggy, and his pale eyes had an unusual intensity to them. A ragged moustache twitched beneath a slightly bent nose, and a faint, pale scar crossed down the left cheek to nearly his chin, a memento of a close-fought swordfight some years before. "Sebasissa, and only in response to your direct question, I have brought this concern to the General, but..." Ortiki paused meaningfully and lowered his eyes.

Sundra closed her eyes thoughtfully for a moment then opened them and looked out over the training field and into the blackness outside the walls. As before. No word on obtaining a greater allowance. Sundra closed her eyes again. This was how it would be? The merchants, the Light Merchants, garnered more and more wealth, while the Guards, who actually contributed to the safety of the city and its citizenry, got less and less? Because why? Because they had nothing to sell at a table at Market?

Sundra opened her eyes again and turned back to face Captain Ortiki. "This disappoints me greatly. I do not agree with my brother's policies on this matter. I will—"

"General! What a great pleasure!" announced Ortiki loudly, his eyes focused over Sundra's shoulder on a figure approaching her from behind. Kobemy whirled to meet the General of the Guards, who was striding toward them from a low structure set to one side of the field.

"A pleasure indeed," he replied, though the tone of his voice did not mirror his words. The General was a tall, elderly man, as thin as a wraith, his hair silvered like the Dark Lake might be near a clump of light lichens at its edge. "Sebasissa!" he cried, recognizing her as she turned, and he hastily genuflected the requisite three-quarters' depth.

"Arise, General," she murmured, accenting her words with a gesture of her right hand.

"What brings you here to our training ground, and to speak with Captain Ortiki?" asked the General, recovering his composure as he stood erect, a hint of suspicion creeping into his final words.

"Only some practice," replied the Sebasissa easily. "I thought to try my bow and arrow against Ortiki's best shots. And Kobemy, here," motioning, "thought to let us watch him in a trial with his short sword."

Here Kobemy saluted and, his hand on the hilt of his sword, shifted it slightly in his belt so that it became visible beneath the light cloak he wore.

The General eyed it. Though it was in its scabbard, it still looked like it would be somewhat longer and more supple than that generally used by Underworlders, fighting as they often did—when it came to it—in more confined spaces.

The General considered them both, one and then the other. "Very good, I should think. With your permission, Sebasissa, may I join the spectators in watching these trials of skill? I understand you have a very sharp eye with the bow."

The Sebasissa nodded. "Certainly. If Captain Ortiki can produce opponents for us...?"

Ortiki summoned two guardsmen who, after genuflecting, were introduced as Sarl, who would challenge Kobemy but using the characteristic Underworld short sword, and Bithorne, who would contest with the Sebasissa at archery.

Blunt sheaths were pulled down and over the blades of both Kobemy and Sarl's swords so that neither should be injured, and Sebasissa, Ortiki, Bithorne, and the General formed a rough circle around the pair to watch and officiate. Others joined as they understood the contest that was to take place. With a glance at Sundra for approval, Ortiki signaled for the two to begin.

There was a long moment of silence and stillness. Then Kobemy began to cut the air repeatedly with his longer, flexible blade in a figure-eight pattern as he eyed his opponent carefully. The latter weighed up the former for a moment, seemingly hesitant, then lunged forward, his blade outstretched, to take Kobemy by surprise. Kobemy darted to one side and parried deftly, then thrust as Sarl passed. Sarl just managed to avoid the blade with a lithe twist away. Sarl retreated, a cold smile now on his lips.

Kobemy swung his sword again, and the blade sang in the air. It was lighter and longer than the traditional short sword, the others noted. Not the standard sort of sword generally seen in the Underworld. Why Kobemy had chosen it was a guess; it wouldn't have the maneuverability and quickness of thrust that the short sword would. Perhaps Kobemy was gambling that its longer reach would be more effective in an open field?

Sarl advanced, step by calculated step. Kobemy held his ground, bringing his sword into guard position, but slightly higher and poised, as if ready to slash down and across if the opportunity presented. Sarl feinted with a thrust; Kobemy, unperturbed, stepped aside but kept his sword aloft and ready. Sarl feinted again with another thrust; Kobemy replied with a feint as if he would bring it down on Sarl's shoulder. Whether Sarl was fooled, or whether he was too focused on making his feint as realistic as possible, he appeared to have been taken in by Kobemy. He pulled back, losing his footing for a moment, and raised his short sword to parry. Kobemy's hand became a blur, and the sword whistled as it came around in a looping arc to swing up again and whack Sarl on the left side. In another instant it was up again, and Kobemy was back in guard position, the sword at the ready.

Ortiki clapped his hands several times in appreciation of Kobemy's manoeuvre, ignoring Sarl's sour expression. "Well done! Impressive, such swordsmanship!"

"Well done indeed," echoed the General, though with the faintest of tones of scepticism to his voice. "Perhaps a blade we should take a closer look at, though I wonder at its utility in the close quarters that we frequently confront on patrols. I see that it's flexible and quick, but I also wonder how sturdy it may be."

Kobemy saluted again and sheathed his sword, choosing to interpret the General's questions as rhetorical commentary rather than an actual question.

"Shall we have our archery contest now?" continued the General, motioning toward a row of targets Ortiki had had moved into position while Kobemy and Sarl had dueled.

The Sebasissa agreed and stepped to position—a spear hastily laid on the ground to denote the shooting line—one eye on her opponent and the other on the distant target. She reached around to grasp an arrow from the quiver over her shoulder and inspected it closely. These were the arrows she had had specially fabricated for her and to her exacting specifications. They had heads of fine steel, polished to a silvery bright; the black shafts were fletched in vanes of grey and brown bands; they were shorter, and overall smaller than the usual arrow, so she could carry more of them for the same weight. They would be finer than the guardsmen's standard issue, which were fletched in a dull brown with maybe twice the heft to them, especially the arrowhead, for greater penetrating power. Sundra took from Kobemy the bow he had brought and had been carrying for her and she tested it. Taut. Perfectly strung. Just as she always kept it. She pulled on it anyway, just to double-check. Yes, it was perfectly balanced and tensioned.

The General had requested the Sebasissa to shoot first, since she was challenger. The contest would be best two of three arrows. Sundra planted one foot forward and relaxed into her accustomed stance. Then she fit the arrow to the bow, pulled hard and, after a split second's hesitation as she aimed down the shaft, loosed it. The bow hummed for a moment, and the arrow was gone. There was a distant thud, and the arrow was in the target: a bullseye.

Heads nodded in appreciation, but no one said anything so as not to distract Bithorne. He frowned and studied the distant target disc, then, slowly, reached into his own quiver for an arrow and nocked it to his bow. His bow was not as well made and his arrows cruder standard issue, but he was far stronger and more experienced, and he had used these arrows and that sort of bow throughout his training. Sundra was clearly quick and fearsomely accurate, but he was a worthy adversary.

Bithorne nocked the arrow quickly and bent the bow far back. He stared hard downrange and a long moment ensued. Then his bow sprang back, and the arrow was gone. His was a bullseye too.

There was applause for both from the fifteen or so now gathered to watch. It was Sundra's turn again. She already had one of her arrows in her hand, as she had been inspecting it for perfection. As before, she advanced to the shooting line and assumed her preferred stance: slightly open and perpendicular to the distant disk. There was a short moment while Sundra pulled back on the bowstring, then the bow sang and the spectators looked downrange at the target. This time only nearly a bullseye, as it was just slightly outside the innermost ring.

If Bithorne saw an opening to pull ahead of the Sebasissa, he betrayed no emotion of the advantage. He too had an arrow in his hand, longer it was than the Sebasissa's and in the plain brown of the guardsmen rather than the colors of the royal house. He stepped confidently to the shooting line and nocked his arrow, then pulled back, held the string for a long instant, then fired.

This was two arrows apiece, and the contest was best two of three. Ortiki and the General went downrange to assess if there was a better archer, or if there would be the need for a third arrow. Sundra and Bithorne waited quietly and wordlessly for their return.

"Too close to tell," called the General as he approached the shooters.

"Too close," echoed Ortiki, allowing himself a small smile at how close the competition was proving. He knew the Sebasissa to be a keen competitor. What surprised him was just how good she was. Bithorne was one of his better aims; would he be able to win? "One more arrow apiece."

One more arrow, thought Sundra, narrowing her eyes as she took her stance at the shooting line. Last arrow. Now nock the arrow securely, now pull it back. Down the shaft at the disk. Focus, focus… loose! Only when the arrow was securely in the target did she relax, as if changing her stance while the arrow was in flight could somehow affect its accuracy.

It was a good shot. Not the bullseye that the first had been, nor as close as the second, but still close to the center and well within the dozen concentric rings that made up the Underworld target. It was hard to tell from where she stood, but it appeared to be in the third from the center.

Bithorne took his place opposite his disk. He pulled back hard on his bow, holding it, as before, for a long, long instant before letting go. There was a breathless pause as the spectators assessed. Ortiki signaled for the targets to be brought for closest inspection by all the spectators. Four runners fetched them forward.

They gathered around the two disks, the one with the three black shafts in it and the other with the three of brown. There was dutiful inspection of both, but the winner was obvious. Bithorne's last arrow was closer to the center by the smallest margin, but enough to put it just two rings away from the center rather than three, as Sundra's last arrow had landed.

All eyes turned—discreetly—to the Sebasissa. She bit her lip. Sundra did not like losing, but the location of the arrows was impossible to deny. She felt her eyes clouding with a rising anger and, had any of the others been close enough, they would have seen in those twin wells a sudden, seething turbulence. But she was before others, and her iron will was even stronger than her fierce temper.

The spectators she had welcomed to watch but minutes before were now witnesses to her humiliation. She could imagine her detractors laughing at her, particularly the General, who would surely recount every detail to her brother, and the thought flared and burned. But even as she prepared to admit her inadmissible defeat, it occurred to her how she might yet extricate victory, and in a manner credible both to her and House Biss. It caught Sundra short, so sudden and startling was this understanding, but this emotion too raced through her only for a moment, and then her strict self-control re-exerted itself. Yes. So.

Sundra bowed her head slightly to Bithorne. "Excellent shot, Guardsman!" she sang out loudly, so that all present could hear, and even those beyond the circle that had grown to more than twenty. "Excellent shot! All of Pentenok is fortunate to have such superb archers in its service!" She paused to reach with her right hand to the target to twist loose her three black-shafted arrows and offered them to Bithorne. "These I award you. You have won them. Further, I grant you permission to carry a device on your shield henceforth to commemorate this contest, that device to consist of these three earned arrows arranged in any way that may please you best. This," she intoned formally, raising her voice and with a gesture signifying a final royal pronouncement, "I so do: thus, and thus!"

Astonished and speechless, Bithorne genuflected deeply, even beyond the requisite three-quarters' depth, though not so low that the obeisance could be confused with that due the Sebastos. There was a moment as the audience strove to comprehend the Sebasissa's gesture, then all broke spontaneously into loud, sustained applause.

After the crowd had dispersed, Sundra walked down the field and back again with Ortiki. Kobemy trailed at a respectful distance, carrying the Sebasissa's bow and quiver. "Sebasissa, that was supremely deft of you! Not that I would ever have doubted you, but your handling of the competition was superb!"

The Sebasissa smiled a thin, self-confident smile. "Guardsmen are important to me, Ortiki. Were you surprised?"

Ortiki kicked a foot gently at the field's turf of lichens and molds which grew in such thickness atop a deep base of pebbles and powders as to perfectly mimic the grass carpets of like fields in the Overlands. "I will be honest with you, Sebasissa—"

"I would always ask you to be honest."

He genuflected quickly. "Your wishes, Sebasissa! But what I mean to say is that, well, I *was* surprised. Yes. I was surprised."

"Why is this, Captain?" replied Sundra, stopping and turning.

Ortiki shuffled his right foot, drawing a crease in the turf. Sundra watched him in his obvious indecision, waiting patiently for him to speak.

"Sebasissa... I know you take great pride in your archery skills. And that you are always looking to sharpen your aim. You practice as much as any Guardsman in the field!"

"I take that as a compliment, Captain."

Ortiki hastily affected another genuflection.

"But...? Your hesitancy betrays a reservation?"

Ortiki, with this prompting, at last looked up. "Sebasissa, I thought you might be upset, that was all."

"Because I lost to Bithorne?"

"Yes, Sebasissa."

Sundra resumed crossing the field, Ortiki falling into step beside and a half-stride behind, as decorum dictated. "Become upset with Bithorne? But he won fairly! We chose our own bow, our own arrows, and took aim from the same line at identical targets! No, that would have been unreasonable to have been angry for his superior aim."

The Sebasissa stopped again, and Ortiki drew up sharply beside her. "Besides, as I said to you, guardsmen are important to me. They are important to Pentenok and especially important to me. I could not punish—for no good reason—such a marksman for his excellence. And so my gesture, as a kind of investment. They can imagine how I might punish. But I would also like to demonstrate how I might reward and commend."

Ortiki nodded vigorously in agreement, though it was not apparent to The Sebasissa that he fully understood her meaning. She commenced walking again. "Tell me, does my brother ever come down to the fields?"

"Rarely, Sebasissa. And only for official events. Like for promotions. Or a review, on occasion."

"So. I am present more often?"

"Without question, Sebasissa! Your presence is well known. You come often to practice your archery, to review the guards; you are our generous patroness. All guardsmen know you as our most sympathetic voice in the Lothwell Spire!"

"That is good. I may have need of guardsmen loyalties one day."

"I wish for your continued health!"

Sundra stole a covert glance at Ortiki at his use of a phrase more closely associated with the Sebastos.

Ortiki grinned slyly as he dipped a knee, just slightly. "Because, may the fates ordain it, may you be our leader one day!" he explained.

Sundra nodded slowly, levelling her eyes at a point in the distance, far past the end of the field. "Perhaps it may be. One day. Perhaps, Ortiki."

The Overlands

Deep in darkness, three figures whispered amongst themselves. Kobemy, Maribess, and the Sebasissa had stolen furtively along the lesser-used paths of the Underworld to what the Sebasissa had confidently informed them was one of the closer exits to the Overlands. The Sebasissa had reassured them that she had been that way, scouting, on two other occasions. Then, as on this occasion, she had told her brother that she was holidaying at the Dark Lake. In actuality, she had gone adventuring in the world above. The other two had never been so far from Pentenok.

Now, having arrived, and after having labored up a lengthy if not so very steep climb, they waited far back in the cave in which they had arrived until the intolerably bright light flooding in from outside had dimmed. Only then had they ventured forth and only after carefully fitting to their eyes a pair of the goggles the Sebasissa had provided each. At last, cautiously edging around a last corner of the cave, and still squinting, they had come to the very mouth to survey the vista below.

These were the Overlands. They lay spread before them from where they stood, high, high up above them in these things called 'mountains'. The bright orb in the far ceiling was sinking, and a welcome darkness had begun to gather in the hollows and valleys of the lands below. Maribess shaded her goggled eyes with her left hand and surveyed the expanse below. "How bright it is! Will it get still darker? Ever?"

Sundra nodded. "So. Soon it will be darker. And remain that way for about half a cycle. Then, that fiery disk, which Overlanders call 'the sun', will appear on the opposite side—over there—and then it will be light again for as long as it was dark before. And so this repeats every cycle, and cycle after cycle, in the same manner. Indefinitely."

Kobemy murmured in amazement. He had heard whispers of this, and even read of it, but to see it was something else entirely. Imagine! Constantly changing like this! Dark and then light and then dark again! And then light! How had Overlanders ever gotten used to it? But his mind turned to another thought. "Sebasissa, you have provided us with these goggles so that we might better tolerate the light of the Overlands. Do the Overlanders in turn have eye fittings to help them see better in the dark?"

Sundra considered this question. At length she answered. "I have never seen one wear such as we have in the darkness. But also, I have not seen them wear anything during these periods of lightness. So. I believe that they do not wear eyepieces of any sort at all. I believe that they are only moderately adapted to both conditions, having to face them both regularly, such as I have described to you."

Both Maribess and Kobemy pondered this answer as they gazed out over the darkening landscape. Adapted to neither condition well, the Sebasissa had said. And she must know, having visited this place several times already. Then, Underworlders would see better than Overlanders in the dark but worse in the light. This suggested to Kobemy, and he voiced as much, that they should prefer the darkness as much as possible when interacting with the Overlanders. Sundra agreed, having come to that conclusion already. "So! It is well! Let us descend now that it is getting darker; it will be easier for us to pick our way down. It will also get colder up here, at this elevation. Yes. So," she added, glancing again at the rapidly sinking sun that was nearly hidden behind the far hills, "we had best start now."

Each of the three wore a backpack of essential clothing, as dictated by the Sebasissa. Kobemy also had his long—by Underworld standards—flexible rapier; Maribess had her miniature bow and a panoply of throwing weapons, including darts, daggers, and metal balls of various sizes. To their eyes, the Sebasissa carried no weapon; Kobemy and Maribess simply assumed that they were the Sebasissa's defense and she needed no other. To them, it made perfect sense and even filled them with pride. Yet, unbeknownst to them, she was armed, having secreted on her person two slender and cruelly pointed poignards and, to one side of her own backpack, an experimental folding bow that she had had the Guards' workshop contrive for her by special, secret assignment. Next to it nestled a slender bundle of her particular arrows, their vanes fletched in grey and brown, and their tips of the finest, hardest Underworld steel.

"We'll go as far as we can while it is dark. Then, we rest while it is light and harder to see," explained the Sebasissa as they carefully negotiated their way around boulders and away from what looked like loose debris that could slip and send them all sliding in an avalanche to their deaths. This would surely have been daunting to many Overlanders, but the Underworlders were accustomed to and adept at navigating treacherous fields of scree, having had great practice at it all their lives in the distant reaches of the Underworld along sometimes poorly travelled paths. "When we rest, I will explain to you who you will be meeting shortly. His name is Vedel, and he leads a band of mercenaries. So. He is hardly likable, but I understand he can draw others to our cause, and so he is useful."

Maribess and Kobemy saw Vedel for the first time a day later. Well hidden in a copse and as silent as the shadows in which they motionlessly stood, the Sebasissa identified him. "There," she pressed into their hands, holding in each of hers one of theirs and using the Underworld silent language of pressure on palm, fingers, wrist, and knuckles to communicate. While absolutely noiseless, it was limited mainly to directions to action and so afforded minimal communication, devised as it had been by and for the guards to facilitate military manoeuvres while concealed. "Ahead. Walking. Tall. At fire. Leader."

The two signed back that they understood. "Difficult," added Maribess as Vedel strode behind the fire and his face became fully illuminated. Given the circumstances and the limitations of the silent language, this comment could have been correctly interpreted as "entrenched," "tough," "intractable," or even "ugly." But because all of them seemed generally applicable, Sundra signed "Yes" in return, with additional pressure in Maribess's palm, which, in the silent language, indicated emphasis. "Very."

"How many?" questioned Kobemy after some further observation.

Sundra's fingers fluttered. "Fifteen. Twenty. Approximate. Unknown."

"Trustworthy?" asked Maribess, after digesting this rough count.

"Some. To our needs."

"When us?" asked Kobemy, which Sundra understood more fully as an interrogative as to when the three would break their concealment and reveal themselves.

"Soon. Kobemy. Me. Advance on my signal. Await."

Sundra paused and crossed each of the palms she held with her thumb to indicate she was beginning a new communication. "Maribess stay. Listen, very. Obey; follow." This was hardly clear, but it was the clearest the silent language could offer in the circumstances. Maribess understood though, that she was to stay behind in the shadows even as Kobemy and the

Sebasissa were to step forward. She, Maribess, would await further instructions on what to do which, she expected, the Sebasissa would issue from amongst Vedel and his men. Yes, and she would have her daggers and darts ready in case they were faithless. After all, had not the Sebasissa stated that they were not entirely trustworthy? Meantime, she would be sure to avoid any patrols, which they had already spotted and evaded, but might well come round again.

Maribess signed back understanding, adding pressure for "very." Unconsciously, her other hand felt for the miniature bow at her belt, the arrows to which were in a slipcase attached to her thigh. Her throwing daggers she kept in a holster behind her right shoulder, angled so that she could pull one out quickly when she drew her arm back to throw.

In front of the bonfire, in the middle of a clearing, Vedel peered into the darkness. He frowned with impatience. Where was this Sundra woman after all? "Princess," she styled herself, or something like that. This would be the third time meeting her, and she had seemed no more normal on the second meeting than on the first. From the Underworld, she maintained. She sure looked like she could have come from there: only wanted to meet at night, wore dark clothes, pale as a sheet, that sort of thing. Talked of the great riches she could offer him, if he would help her find something she wanted. Some sort of magical device that created light or something like that. He had said he had known of it. Well, he had lied, of course. He had only vaguely heard of such a thing, and it had been in stories as a child and told to him by his grandmother, but it was what the princess had wanted to hear, so it was what he had told her.

They had struck a deal. His job was to pull together the manpower to find it. Once he had it, he was to pass it to her and, in return, she would pay him off with some of the gold and jewels she said she had in profusion down in her Underworld. Huh. He'd like to see some of those. A suspicious man by nature, he was beginning to wonder. Riches some time in the future wouldn't mean anything to the rogues and ruffians he had been gathering around him and who wanted something today.

Meanwhile, she had proven more than a little irritating with her demands that he and his men do all sorts of work while she laid low.

She had also promised to set him up as a ruler, as a kind of satrap, of the land in which they were meeting. Vedel full well knew this to be the Kingdom of Brythrony. He was to be shored up by special troops from her

Underworld. He would have to have those to maintain control of the kingdom; there was no way he could rely on these brigands he had now! But like the gold and jewels, so far no sign of these troops.

Vedel toyed with the thought for a moment. Think of that! Him ruling Brythrony! But the current occupant of the throne would surely not be as willing to share his kingdom as this strange Underworld woman was. "Huh!" he said again, this time aloud. He would have to have her Underworld armies at his back to take Brythrony, and maybe these armies of hers didn't exist. He heaved a sigh. If none of any of this worked out, he figured that at least he could ransom her for some of those mineral riches she had. They had so much down there, they should easily be able to hand some over to get their precious princess back, right? That wouldn't make Vedel ruler of Brythrony, but it would make him rich. Assuming, of course, they even wanted her back. Given how irritating she was, maybe they didn't.

Vedel glanced up at the moon to gauge the time and stamped his feet in frustration. Where was she, after all?

A few minutes later, and without a further word or sign, Kobemy and Sundra strode directly toward the firelight from their concealment. Maribess stayed behind, a shadow within a shadow, her throwing weapons at the ready.

Sundra pulled out an arrow and her folding bow as she stepped fearlessly forward. Though fearless, she was not naïve. She knew this Vedel could turn on her. This was why she kept Maribess in the shadows, as a kind of insurance. She would dispose of him as soon as she could; he was far too untrustworthy to keep. But he was necessary just now, as he had been able to assemble very quickly a force that would look to a future reward rather than pay today, even if feeding it had required larger and larger raids of the surrounding lands with increasing frequency. This was not what she would have wanted, as it would prompt a response from the local ruler sooner and stronger than otherwise, but there was nothing to be done for that.

Kobemy and Sundra paused at the outer edges of the firelight, waiting to be noticed by some thirty men assembled around the fire. They were a ragged bunch, unshaven, some thin, some plump, some tall, some short, all dressed in varying degrees of now shabby finery—obviously stolen or filched over the years. So quietly though had the two Underworlders stolen up that it took nearly a full minute before one of them started and pointed.

"Looky! Two of 'em!" he gasped. There was an immediate ruction as all reached for weapons and staggered to their feet. As they stood, by varying degrees and from differing angles and with their own particular perspective, they came face-to-face with what must have been two of the most unusual humans they had ever come across in their lives.

Two humanoids stood before them, having taken several steps closer toward the leaping and flickering firelight on their recognition. One was male, one was female, but both were tall and thin, even willowy. In fact, so similar did they appear to the Overlanders that they could have been excused for thinking them to have been related. But whereas the man's hair was cropped close, that of the woman was much longer, though gathered in the back neatly. Neither looked particularly strong, at least not muscular, but both appeared lithe and limber, as if neither would be able to best the least of the group in hand-to-hand combat but either would easily outrace all.

Both had the widest, largest, and roundest eyes that any of them had ever seen before in a human, larger than that of any new-born baby. They were liquid, inscrutable pools that reflected to a great degree the dancing firelight, even as neither would look directly into it, even shied away from it, blinking and squinting as if, indeed, it hurt them.

Their skin was paler than death, unhealthily so, though both looked to be hale and well. Matching their pallid skin tone was their nearly-white hair, maybe platinum if any color, and slightly curly where it showed beneath their pulled-back helmets. Their fingers were long and sinewy, flexible they appeared, as if capable of tremendous dexterity. Their teeth were a uniform gleaming white, their gums so light as to be almost grey.

In sharp contrast with their skin and hair was their clothing. Both were clad in dark cloaks that blended in well with the darkness behind them. The woman additionally wore, subtly visible when the folds of the cloak parted, a silvery mesh of chainmail that glinted richly in the firelight and immediately excited the cupidity of those closest.

Over her shoulder was flung a black-and-grey cloak, which could be covering anything. At the belt of the male hung a long rapier-like weapon. His hand rested lightly upon the hilt, at the ready, though it was unsheathed not an inch.

A long moment passed as they sized each other up. Kobemy took all of them in a single, sweeping glance. These? These were associates, the tools by which the Sebasissa intended to search the Overlands for her magical device? He shook his head sadly, imperceptibly. What a sorry lot of bedraggled cutpurses they were, nothing more than petty thieves, with surely no discipline or focus amongst them.

Their leader, Vedel, barked at the others to be "on their feet" and, unable to counterfeit a pleasant smile, contented himself with a surly frown, cleared his throat, and demanded an explanation. "What is this, a' creepin' up on us like this? Hey?"

"We do not creep up on you," Sundra answered simply. "We stood here, awaiting your notice."

"You cud 'a announced yerse'f!"

"That would hardly seem necessary, I would expect. Did not your guards and patrols forewarn you of our approach?"

There was a growl of resentment and a muttered demand as to exactly where those guards were.

Vedel waved his hand in a curt expression of dismissal. There was nothing to be done about it now, though he would surely discuss this breach of security later with those responsible. "Sundra, huh? Nice t'see you 'gin."

Kobemy bridled at Vedel's omission of an honorific in his addressing the Sebasissa, but Sundra flexed her fingers discreetly toward him, as if to soothe his irritation. "Sundra. Yes, Sundra. And at my side is Kobemy."

"Who are they? What are they?" demanded one of band. "They're the ones we've been waiting for?"

"You know they are. Enough outta you for now!" called Vedel over his shoulder waspishly. Turning back to the two visitors he continued, modulating his voice to be more pleasant, however unaccustomed his throat was to the effort and his companions unfamiliar to the tone from him. "Welcome! Come, join us 'round the fire, and warm yerse'f!"

Sundra shook her head slowly and gently. "We are more comfortable at this distance."

This disappointed Vedel. He had hoped for a better look at Kobemy and that rapier he carried. Vedel shrugged. "Are there any more a' ya? Jus' tha two a' ya?"

Sundra sensed the possibility of treachery, not only in the apparent innocence of the question but in the half-hidden wolfish expressions of Vedel's unsavory companions. "So. Not just the two of us. We have a patrol too."

Vedel glanced suspiciously into the deeply shadowed woods just beyond the circle of firelight. "How many?"

"Your leader promised us our safety when we were with you." There was a murmur of disgruntlement at that. Sundra continued easily, "I promised the same to you, in return." One of the band guffawed, observing sneeringly that there were many of them and only two of the Underworlders. In direct response, Sundra snapped her fingers and pointed at the nearest tree at the edge of the firelight. Immediately there came a hiss and a thud as a darkly gleaming dagger buried itself nearly to the hilt in the designated tree trunk. Every man jumped and several half-drew weapons and began whirling about the circle in fear and fury, seeking the thrower.

Sundra's voice took on a brittle edge. "Of course you are watched; you must have expected this. But, brief me now," she continued quickly, making a deliberate effort to soften her voice and taking a half-step closer, "brief me as to what you have learned since our last meeting regarding this device that I seek."

"Jis' a momen'," demurred Vedel, who had recovered quickly. "I got ya sum'in' on that. But, before's we get to it, I'd like to know sum'in' a' you!"

Sundra stood motionless, waiting, the blinking of her eyes twice the only indication that she had registered these words as a preamble to a question, and that nearly impossible to have seen given her orientation away from the fire.

"Huh! There's s'posed to be some sort of additional manpower comin' a-here from your Unnerworld, an' I haven't a-seen it yet! When's it comin'?"

Now Sundra's voice was silken. "You are to provide the manpower at first, Vedel. Those were the terms of our agreement. First the device, then my Underworld army. Not the other way around."

Vedel scratched his side absentmindedly. "See here! How good is tha' army of your'n ennyways? For, ta be truthful, all I seen is two a' ya! And ya looks kin' a scrawny to me no-how!"

The rest of the band howled with amusement. Vedel half-turned to them and jutted his chin out in superiority at having executed this jibe.

"Are you sceptical of our swordsmanship? Kobemy, here," she gestured with her right hand, "would be happy to duel with your best swordsman as proof of our skills."

There was a murmur of approval. Kobemy, for his part, nodded vigorously and half-unsheathed his rapier.

"Please. Your best."

"Huh. I'd-a say with all conf-ee-dence tha' that'id be me! I'm the bes' swordsman here!" Vedel thumped his chest for emphasis.

Kobemy adjusted his goggles over his eyes and, from behind them, seemed to eye Vedel up and down carefully. Then he turned to the Sebasissa, letting his rapier fall back into its sheath and shaking his head sadly. "No, My Sebasissa. I am sorry; I cannot."

The band of brigands roared with laughter. Astonishment and black fury twisted the Sebasissa's features. "Kobemy! You are the best sword in Pentenok!"

"But the match is not fair, My Sebasissa. To him! Only if there are three of them will I accept the challenge!"

Sundra laughed. It was high and thin, like a single note struck from a crystal goblet, and she bestowed upon Kobemy a laudatory smile of supreme triumph. Vedel snarled and, with a sudden sharp move, whipped his sword out and lunged at Kobemy without giving fair warning.

Vedel would surely have skewered an opponent less prepared, but Kobemy had been watching and waiting for such or similar. He darted to one side and, in one smooth motion, tore out his own blade. It flashed up and down and cut the air in two—and surely Vedel himself had he still been standing there—but he had already leapt back and recovered.

"By what rules do these Overlanders cross swords, my Sebasissa?" enquired Kobemy, now cutting the air before him in a series of figure-eights as he eyed up Vedel anew.

"I'm not sure they—" the Sebasissa began, and Kobemy leapt forward, sword aloft, flashing in the firelight, "—have any," she concluded, as Kobemy brought his blade up and down in a series of lightning thrusts that forced Vedel backwards step by step, parrying frantically.

The burn of the bonfire at Vedel's back quickly became searing. Yet Kobemy pressed mercilessly forward, a wild, avid look on his face, the supple flex of his razor-sharp steel whistling closer and closer. Vedel began to realize he was overmatched and that he was more dodging the sword thrusts than parrying. So close was Vedel now to the fire that its leaping light behind him was fully reflected in the heretofore unreadable eyes of his opponent, and Vedel saw they were in fact circles of glass, or crystal. The scorch of the fire at this back, the relentless rapier before him, Vedel for a wild moment imagined he was battling a demon with eyes of flame, bent on forcing him to the very precipice of the infernal regions.

Vedel gasped. He would either be burned alive or cut to pieces. "Good 'nuff! All right! You'r'n the better!"

Kobemy pulled back on Sundra's command. Vedel hastened away from his over-close proximity to the bonfire. "All righ'! All righ'!" he heaved, breathless, fuming.

"Very well then," continued Sundra, after the briefest of pauses and successfully, for the most part, veiling her amusement. "Enough distractions and to business! So. Update me on what you have learned about that which I seek."

Vedel rubbed his singed backside tenderly, wincing. That had been incredibly uncomfortable. There was nothing he could do now, but he would settle with both of them later, somehow. "The 'thing'. Righ'. So's—say, could we jus' take a-step over here so's to keep this conf-ee-den-shal like?"

"Certainly," agreed Sundra, adjusting her goggles and motioning for Kobemy to join even though Vedel scowled at his inclusion.

The three conferred toward the edge of the firelight, the rest of the bandits now settling back down to sleep or games of chance, or, in pairs in rough conversation. "Huh. So's, here's whats we know's so far. S'far's I kin tell—I mean, from my inves-tee-gations so far—this dee-vice of your'n 's'not a rod or som'in' like that. No. 'T's a sort-a crown. Bes' es I can get. Mos' prob-bably." He paused there, to assess the impact of this intelligence on the two Underworlders.

Sundra considered. Some sort of headgear. This was a disappointment, as it meant she would not be able to bind it to the Spire of Lothwell for all to rejoice at and welcome, as she had from time to time envisioned. On the other hand, she realized cannily, it would mean that she could wear it, wield it, herself. Herself. Wouldn't this be even better, as all Pentenok would surely recognize her as Sundra the Light Bringer. Yes, Sundra, Bringer of Light. Unseen by Vedel, her eyes narrowed behind her dark goggles in appreciation of the image that swam before her. The power of this light would be hers alone, and she could be the conquering general of the armies that would unite all of underworld beneath her!

"Continue," she replied, striving to contain her excitement.

"Huh. Well, further—I mean, what my inves-tee-gations have uncovered—is that this dee-vice is in a place some say was named Sislin, what it once was. It's jis ruins now. Nuthin' lef' t'a' it."

"'Sislin?'"

"'Zactly. Somewhere in the ruins, but no one knows where. S's s'posed to be fearsome powerful, an' was s'posed to defend the city. But it was overrun enny-ways. Barbarians. Way back. Guess it didn't help after all when i' came ta it."

"It didn't exist?"

Vedel shook his head emphatically. This was not the conclusion he wanted them to draw. "No. They jus' didn't know how to use it! They forgot; they los' the knowledge as t' how ta use it. Some'in' like that. Enny-ways, when it came time a' las' ta use it, jis' when they needed it, they cud'n't. For whichever reason. No one knows why. It jis' wuddn't there. And the city was overrun!"

"So. You believe it must still be there?"

Vedel scratched his backside, which still throbbed from the singeing of the bonfire. He scowled again at Kobemy, then recollecting the latter's sword, quickly redirected his anger toward the ground. "Huh. Huh! Can' say. But, seems that's a-where's we ought's ta start."

Sundra considered this advice for a long moment. Vedel watched her closely. This whole story of the crown had been hastily assembled from half a dozen old children's stories and tales, as Vedel could hardly read, much less conduct research. Sure, he had asked around a bit, but who amongst his band was on any sort of terms with any who could read or research? No, it had been pieced together from fragments gathered from here and there, but all that mattered to Vedel was the question of whether it was patched together of sufficiently strong fabric as to hold up to this Underworlder's scrutiny. He watched her closely. Evidently it would, he noted with satisfaction, as, ever so slowly, she began to nod.

"Very well. Apply yourself in this direction. And where is this, this, "Sislin" ruin of which you speak?"

"In this very kingdom here. Name's Brythrony. Jus' at the coast."

"In this kingdom?" Sundra's eyes lit up behind her goggles. It was practically at hand! She ignored the mention of the word "coast," a word with which she was not familiar. "So. So. We shall apply ourselves in this direction. Gather your forces. Bring me more information on this crown!"

"Hey! Hey! Wha' 'bout the armies? The riches?"

Sundra returned to Vedel with a slight start. "The armies? They shall arrive in due course, when we are further along. Shortly I return myself to Pentenok to personally supervise their readying."

"An' the riches? How shall I feed my men?" Vedel made an expansive gesture, as if to suggest he felt personally responsible for the wellbeing of each of the disreputable souls behind him.

"You have yet to earn these riches."

"But how am I ta feed 'em?"

Sundra shrugged with a studied indifference. "This kingdom has riches enough to feed you in the meantime. I believe you and your men are well used to this sort of living."

The next night, the three Underworlders were on their way back to the cave by which they had exited the Underworld. For the most part, they journeyed in silence. Their Sebasissa had not asked them their opinion on Vedel or any of the others they had met, and neither had Maribess or Kobemy volunteered theirs. Lost in her own thoughts, the Sebasissa did not think of soliciting their reactions to the band they had encountered. For their part, being subordinate, it never occurred to them to importune her with theirs. As before, they rested during the day and travelled at night, pausing only on one occasion for Maribess and the Sebasissa to compete in an archery contest, the latter revealing her folding bow with the desire to test it.

"It is very good quality, Sebasissa," announced Maribess authoritatively, running her hands over it in admiration. "It is solid, strong, and fits together without hint of joinery."

Sebasissa inspected it closely likewise and for the first time at length. "So. It would appear. Shall we test it?"

Maribess was the superior shot at closer distances, but the strength of her miniature bow was insufficient to beat the folding bow further out. Sundra refolded the bow and stowed it, after removing her arrows from the impromptu target so as to leave no trace of their passage. "It is good. It is reasonably accurate and with good range, if not as good as the standard, fixed bow.

"It is somewhat between, in range and power, the miniature and the standard bow."

Both Maribess and Kobemy inclined their heads in full agreement with that assessment. With that, and wordlessly, they gathered up their packs and cloaks and recommenced their journey back to the Underworld.

Two hours later, something completely unexpected occurred. Maribess noticed it first. "My Sebasissa: the overhead—the far ceiling—it is dripping." She stretched out her hand and, catching a droplet in it, rubbed it between her fingers to test its lubricity. She held out her fingers as proof to the others.

The night was very dark. There was no hint of the so bright moonlight that had marred the other nights; none of the star-flecks in the far ceiling were visible. It was actually quite tolerable, this sort of darkness, Sundra had remarked to herself. Much like Pentenok. She examined Maribess's outstretched fingers, then felt it herself. A drop. Of water. Yes, it was. From out of the far ceiling called "sky" in this land.

Sundra searched the overhead through the leaves of the trees. All dark. She felt another drop on her face, then another. She frowned in concentration as she recollected. "These droplets: they are not condensation, like in Pentenok. Not the same, at least. We should seek cover under a tree, like the sort we use for hanging targets. Quickly too. These droplets: they could come in a rush." Sundra had heard of it, been told of it, this phenomena of falling water, but still it was surprising to feel it upon her skin.

The three sought shelter beneath the nearest tree having what looked to be the broadest, thickest branches. Gathered around the trunk, and at the Sebasissa's direction, they removed from their packs a light cloak to which had been sewn to the exterior a slightly oily surface, actually the treated leathery skin of the Underworld's flying lavalal. To prepare for the visit to the Overlands, Sundra had had sections of several skins sewn to three specially woven light cloaks. Her orders had caused great confusion among the seamstresses as, as far as they knew, such skins were only applied to the hulls of less well-assembled boats plying the Iilish and Liltenen, and as a kind of crude additional waterproofing.

Kobemy turned to Sundra after donning the cloak. "Am I wearing this garment correctly, My Sebasissa?"

Sundra inspected him critically. She then reached out to arrange the waterproofing better across his body, then did the same for Maribess. "Thus. So. These droplets. They can come down very fast, I am told. So much so that it is almost like standing in Dark Lake. But in the open."

Maribess gazed sceptically into the overhead far, far up. Like standing in Dark Lake? Very hard to believe! She looked out from under the branches though and saw the frequency of the droplets quickly gathering pace. She held out her hand to feel them. They plopped one after another, intermittently through the branches of the tree to fall on her outstretched palm. These drops, coming down, what was their purpose? They were cold, unlike the drops in the Underworld that fell from the cavern ceilings, which were warm. They fell irregularly, too, if at an intensifying rate, quite unlike the steady drip-drip in the Underworld. And finally, their pattern was quite clearly wide, as the entire area, as far as Maribess could see, was suffering from the falling water. In the Underworld, water from overhead was confined to that location directly underneath the point below which the condensation had gathered.

This must be the strange Overlands phenomena of "Weather," realized Maribess. The Sebasissa had explained it in a cursory way when they had paused once on the way to meet that scruffy and undignified Vedel. She had pointed to the far ceiling, toward one of the dark masses marring its complexion while the bright orb overhead had been descending. "It is called 'Weather'," she had explained. "It can cause the temperature to be hotter or colder, for it to be wet or dry, for there to be high winds or no winds. And so on." How strange, thought Maribess, to be so at the mercy of such an unpredictable force. So much better to be Underground, where there was nothing to make the air so harsh and cold, and it was always warm and calm.

Maribess watched the fall of the droplets intensify. "Weather" was puzzling. Some Underworlders maintained that all of them had originally come from the Overlands and that a principal reason for why the Underworlders had left the Overlands had been to escape "Weather." That made sense to Maribess. Life was unpredictable enough as it was; why also deal with the vagaries of extreme temperatures and winds?

Maribess eyed The Sebasissa covertly. She, Maribess, didn't like Weather. Kobemy did not appear to like it either. But it was not apparent that the Sebasissa minded. Maribess sighed. The Sebasissa was bold and adventurous and seemed to seek out the unusual. This was a positive quality in leaders, Maribess expected, and explained why Maribess knew she could never be a great leader like the Sebasissa. It was also why it was natural that Maribess should follow the orders of the Sebasissa, because the Sebasissa wouldn't quail at the unknown, as Maribess secretly feared she, herself, might. Maybe this willingness to challenge the unknown—up to and including the unforeseeable vicissitudes of "Weather"—was the same that compelled her to seek this Crown of Light. It was rumored in some quarters in Pentenok that it had been an excess of this quality that had caused her to be passed over by her parents as heir to the throne at Pentenok in favor of her brother, and even though he was a year or so younger.

The droplets descended thicker and faster, and the branches overhead afforded less and less shelter as, saturated, they began to yield that water which had accumulated across their leaves. Kobemy looked out sourly into the wet darkness, now accented by a rising mustiness. At first a novelty—to be as wet as if standing in Dark Lake, yet still on dry ground—the downpour had become thoroughly uncomfortable and unpleasant. Kobemy glanced at his companions. Maribess, though stoically silent, looked increasingly bedraggled; the Sebasissa's normally impassive face had become thin and pinched, and one corner of her mouth repeatedly twitched with distaste and displeasure. He could only imagine how he himself looked.

Still, to suggest that they leave their refuge under the tree was unthinkable. Such would be to suggest that the Sebasissa had need of his counsel, when only she could apprehend the greater import of each and every of their actions. Kobemy stared glumly into the soddening mold and the hollows into which the sky-water had begun to pool. Sometimes, when the bright orb in the sky went down, it was very pleasant in the Overland—very lovely, and very liveable. At others, such as now, it was frankly unbearable. It was this ungraspable "Weather" that caused it to be so. It was too often too unpredictable. Kobemy wondered miserably how the Overlanders could bear such uncertainty from day to day, not knowing whether it would be pleasant or not come the next minute, the next hour, even at any time in the future.

"How was your sojourn at Dark Lake, sister?" enquired the Sebastos Reynam.

Sundra smothered a smile, recollecting the weather of the Overlands she had only recently left. "Wet, brother. Very wet."

A corner of Reynam's mouth twitched. His sister must be in a jovial mood. It was unlike her to jest.

"I can imagine. Was it pleasant there? To get away from Pentenok for a few cycles?"

"Yes! Very. It was nice to have a little solitude. Away from Pentenok. I took only a few with me. Such as Maribess, a childhood friend. So. Maybe you remember her?"

"Of course. Maribess."

"Maribess," affirmed Sundra softly, and turned to the panoramic view over Pentenok from the balcony off the Sebastos's chambers. Flecks of light lichens, tiny in the dark, lay sprinkled across the black velvet of the city as if scattered by an over idle hand. It reminded Sundra of the star-flecks in the far ceiling of the Overlands. These pinpoints were spread below her though, and those others had been above her, and these were faint and constant, whereas those others had been quite bright, some of them, and had seemed to twinkle.

Sebastos Reynam contemplated his sister as she stood at the balcony rail. She was lying. Why, though, he did not know. She had never gone to Dark Lake, this he had been informed the day before. He had been given to understand, at the same time as his sister had been claiming to have been resting at Dark Lake, that Maribess had similarly gone missing. Also Kobemy, another familiar of his sister. Ortiki too, a prominent Guardsman of somewhat suspect allegiance and increasingly associated with his sister, had also vanished for the same period. Had they all gone some place together? Where, indeed, had his sister been?

He knew that she had not been at Dark Lake because of reports he had received. The Light Merchants had helpfully generated this information for him. They had explained, and it had made sense, that their business, by its very nature and necessity, took them to every part of the city and beyond. They saw a great deal in their travels and had found it useful initially to assemble this information to better understand their customers. Now they were honored to offer it the Sebastos. This information, coming now as it did regularly, had been useful on more than one instance in understanding unusual activities about Pentenok and even other city-kingdoms.

On this occasion, the Merchants had informed Reynam that there had been no need of any refreshment of the lights at Dark Lake, not before Sundra had said she would go, during, or after she said she had come back. This would have been required had Sundra or anyone been there. Meaning, Sister Sundra had not gone to Dark Lake.

Similarly, it had been the Light Merchants who had confirmed that neither Maribess nor Kobemy had been observed anywhere within Pentenok while Sundra had been away.

He sighed. So much intrigue and all so unnecessary. Wasn't there enough already in Pentenok without the two of them adding to it?

"Very good, Sister. Welcome back to Pentenok."

"Thank you, Brother. I wish for your continued health!" Sundra stepped back to the usual three swords' length, genuflected, and departed, having chosen to understand her brother's welcome as one of dismissal rather than an invitation to remain.

"And I, yours," called the Sebastos after her, although a long minute after her departure such that she could not have heard him. He sighed again. The Light Merchants had expressed guardedly the concern that Sundra was planning something. He feared they might be correct. Her coldness and aloofness strongly implied to Reynam that, whatever it was, it would not be to his liking.

He reached up and pulled on a cord that rang down to a room immediately below his and which communicated with his private quarters by a short flight of stairs. Within seconds, there was a soft knock on a panel of the room. "Enter," said Reynam, simply.

The panel swung inward noiselessly to reveal two guardsmen wearing tabards of the grey, black, and brown colors of the royal household. The chainmail beneath their tabards was light and supple but exceedingly strong, of the finest workmanship Pentenok could offer, and was recognizable even at a distance as being exceptional quality. The two guardsmen were Bakide and Lavinia and on "loan" from the guardsmen of the barracks. The Sebastos had determined that their loan would be permanent and had appointed them to be his personal bodyguards. Both were excellently skilled in the short, broad sword of the Underworld. Bakide was shorter, heavier, and more muscular; Lavinia taller, faster, and sharper. Both had been in the service of the city for many years, and their family for generations before that.

They genuflected silently before the Sebastos.

Reynam motioned for them to arise and addressed them quietly. "I believe it is more important than ever that you remain close to me. I worry that my sister has… plans… of an unknown nature that may be disruptive."

"Sebastos! A plot?"

"No, no; let's not say that. Not yet. I don't know what it is. If it is anything. But I think she has some sort of mischief in mind and I would like you to be aware."

The two genuflected again to represent their full understanding.

Reynam pondered them a moment longer then stepped over to a desk and scribbled a note on a memo-sized sheet of paper. He folded it, then placed it within a box to one side, sealing it with a length of thin wire which he tightened with a crimp. "Take this," he said, passing it to Bakide. Then, to the both of them, "One of you is to deliver it, the other is to remain watchful at all times.

"That is all."

Another genuflection, and the two wordlessly departed through the same panel by which they had entered. Reynam walked back out to the balcony by which he surveyed all Pentenok. Should he have more protection about him than Bakide and Lavinia? He toyed with the thought for a moment then dismissed it. That would attract attention and forewarn his sister he suspected something. No, better to be prepared for when whatever she was planning occurred and not to tip her that he suspected anything.

What she must also not be allowed to suspect—or clearly she would have had the light lichens refreshed at Dark Lake—was the ubiquity of the Light Merchants, and that they were now regularly funneling him intelligence. This fact was to be kept closely guarded and the secretive nature of the relationship maintained. That intelligence had proven valuable already; in the future it could prove critical.

"The archery targets have been taken down," Ortiki informed the Guardsman ahead of him, tarrying along the façade of the barracks but generally moving in the direction of the area reserved for that discipline.

The figure half-turned toward him and pulled back the hood, just sufficiently to reveal the platinum-combed and coiled coif of the Sebasissa, only wearing a slightly over-large Guard's robe.

Ortiki smiled and hastened to join her, she indicating with a gesture to omit the customary genuflection. "I was not sure it was you, so effective was your disguise!" he told her, with more than a trace of the unctuousness of which he was quite capable.

The Sebasissa smiled cautiously, all too aware of this aspect of his nature. She glanced around quickly. No one else was present, save for a

Light Merchant with several assistants engaged in the routine task of replacing the spent lichens spaced at intervals along the barracks to provide an adequate, if somewhat feeble, light. Good: they were alone.

Ortiki saw the work team as well. "We have seen them more often recently. Are we rising in the esteem of the Sebastos, maybe?" Then, adding hastily, "And I wish for his continued health!"

"It is not a sign of his esteem," Sundra replied but after a pause just long enough to suggest reservations with respect to Ortiki's sentiment. "I am certain that the lights are being changed more often because they are of lower quality than before. Meaning, in short, that the guards are being dishonored in yet another way by the Sebastos, my brother, and may I also wish for his continued health!"

Ortiki said nothing.

"The Merchants surely must find it lucrative to supply the guards their light: they charge much and deliver little." So typical of these Merchants, she continued silently. Grasping. Cheating. Abusing their privileges.

"The time is coming, I think."

Ortiki looked questioningly at the Sebasissa.

"We must be deliberate. Are you ready?"

Though the Sebasissa's remarks were cryptic, Ortiki knew to what she referred. "Yes, Sebasissa. I have confirmed the confidence of more than a third of the Guards. Another third are sympathetic. The final third can be neutralized."

Alizarin removed the last of his white robes and hung them on a peg. He turned to the mirror at the plain dressing table and ran his fingers through his thinning hair. Like nearly every other Underworlder, his hair was very light in color, and so it hardly showed any grey. But it did show his age, and the stress of his work, in that it was not nearly so lush and thick as it had been in prior years.

Alizarin gazed into the mirror and frowned. This was a difficult time. He was a bit worried. Would his leadership be enough to see them through? But it would have to be: there was no other leader. Alizarin shook his head, slowly, and his right hand drifted down to finger the outline of the key tucked into an interior pocket. It was a very special key, very special indeed. There was only one other like it. This was the key to the treasury.

Alizarin very much liked to visit the treasury, as it represented all that

that they had striven to achieve over many, many years. Wealth, sufficient wealth, to guarantee—inasmuch as wealth could—independence of action and a measure of indifference to the minor vicissitudes of fortune. Navigating larger setbacks and opportunities was the preserve of leadership. But wealth alone was sufficient to handle the smaller ones.

Alizarin didn't dare visit the treasury room that evening. There wasn't time. Still, by closing his eyes and concentrating, he could take himself on a quick mental tour of its contents, and this he liked too. Past the door unlocked by his key, of which the only other in existence was held by the Treasurer himself, there were several secret latches to unlock the vault door. Then, beyond, there were the chests of precious metals coaxed from the deepest depths of the Underworld. In shelves against the wall, there were the maps to the richest of the lichen farms. In upright cases lining the opposite wall there were the coffers of jewels and jewelery, painstakingly accumulated across countless cycles. All of this was not his but theirs. But the treasury was his in the sense that, when there were smaller setbacks and, yes, even opportunities, it was his from which to dispense and so manage.

It was "theirs" in the greater and more accurate sense in that it belonged not to him but to his organization. An organization of which he was but the current leader. That organization was the Light Merchants.

Alizarin was not his real name. His actual name was not known to anyone. Each leader adopted his or her own name but always a color, and a color such as that which could best be appreciated in white light, the purest, fairest, and most valuable of lights. This was to symbolize the ultimate striving of all Light Merchants, which was to develop and master white light underground. Alizarin was the twenty-third "First," the leader of the Light Merchants, and his program had been a focused effort to accumulate this wealth, which he saw as fundamental to the survival of the Light Merchants. The gathering and storing of this wealth, he had argued to the Light Merchants' council, was to be accomplished, and not contradictorily, by the spending of wealth. For lasting wealth, he had continued, could only be safeguarded over the long-term by spending. If wealth was not spent on enlarging it, inevitably it was dissipated slowly through a thousand different mistaken stratagems conserving it. He had been questioned closely on what he had meant by this. He had responded with the development of the network that was now present in virtually every corner of Pentenok. This network was called the Observers.

Alizarin exited the hall of the Light Merchants via a hidden passageway that let eventually into the basement of a lively tavern, its noise and the count of Underworlders at it affording him ample cover in leaving. He mingled with the others in the establishment only for long enough to pick up the odor of the place, then left to step into the street and become like so many others in Pentenok: just another person, just another Underworlder.

No one amongst the Light Merchants knew who Alizarin actually was. His council recognized him only by his white robes, the color reserved exclusively for him as "First." The others of his council wore other colors, in hues and degrees of brightness commensurate with their seniority. As with Alizarin, none knew the others' actual names and all knew better than to research actual identities. It was safer this way as, in the past, there had been plots to kidnap and hold hostage Merchants and force them to disclose the identities of their council.

Alizarin that evening had conferred with his Chief Observer, whom he knew by the name "Cinnabar," and who regularly collected and presented Alizarin with significant intelligence. Lately, they had been watching closely the movements of the Sebasissa. She was meeting more often with certain others and then vanishing with them for days at a time. Most recently, she had not been in Pentenok or at Dark Lake, where the family of the Sebastos holidayed. Where had she been? This had been the subject of speculation between the First and the Chief Observer. The latter was beginning to think it may not be meaningful. The First thought it meaningful that she had evaded their surveillance.

"Does she suspect she is being watched?"

"Yes. But not by us. She suspects spies from other city-kingdoms."

Alizarin was still thinking about this as he walked through the streets of Pentenok. She was suspicious but not of the Light Merchants. And she must not suspect them. Already the Sebasissa was not well disposed to them; she thought them over-powerful. It would never do for her to believe they were taking sides amongst the royal family.

Without conscious direction, his steps took him through Central Square and thence Market. With sudden realization, he saw that he was heading to the stalls of the Light Merchants. Well, why not check in—covertly—on what some of the lower orders might be doing? No one would know who he was anyway. He was dressed as any other Underworlder might be out and about shopping for the necessity of light.

He strolled the tables delimiting the section reserved for the Light Merchants. On display at these outer tables were the dimmest or those shedding the greenest or the most yellow light and thus of lowest quality. One particularly large lichen caught his attention. Its size indicated value. How odd it was out here, at the edge. He slowed to eye it more closely.

The Merchant noted his interest immediately. "Wonderful, isn't it? And at such a price! But this will be your gain. You will be the astonishment of all your family, your neighbors, when you walk through the door of your home with this!"

Alizarin sized the lichen up quickly, standing directly before it. It was diseased, to be sure, infested with a tiny mite that fed on the lichen. He had encountered specimens before with just such an affliction. Alizarin inspected it still more closely, his professional curiosity aroused. Sometimes, the lichen could be saved if the infestation was not too far advanced.

"Yes, yes! It is a beauty, yes? And what a wonderful price. How can I practically be giving it away, you are surely wondering?"

No, Alizarin saw: the mite infestation was very far advanced. Incurably so. Probably the lichen would shine another day, maybe a day and a half. At most.

"This is because I must sell all I have as quick as I can. I have more coming in and—as you can see—my stall is so small I have no room!"

Alizarin now turned his attention to the base in which the lichen was rooted for clues as to which segment of the Light Merchant's guild had prepared it, but the base was without signature or distinctive ornamentation. Probably if he picked it up and inspected it underneath he might be able to discern, but that would evidence too much craft on his part to keep safe his anonymity. Alizarin turned to the vendor. "How long have you had this specimen?"

The Merchant shrugged. "Some cycles. But it should go home with you. You see my price; make me an offer! We can discuss it!"

Alizarin pursed his lips. It had been a beautiful specimen—before it had been infested. Now though, this vendor was trying to pass it off as much more than it was. There would be trouble, stories, complaints, if someone bought this innocently and it failed within the cycle. He, Alizarin, didn't need that sort of trouble just now, not with rumors and plots swirling at the highest reaches of Pentenok. His voice hardened ever so slightly and he edged closer to the vendor. "How did you come by this lichen? From where?"

The Merchant's eyes narrowed. "From where? It only matters where it is going, home with you!" But uncertainty had entered his voice and his patter no longer had the playful lilt it had before.

Alizarin advanced another step and lowered his voice still further. "Remove this specimen from sale. Immediately. It is sub-standard— it is *sors*—and it is forbidden to offer such a one for sale. You know this."

The Merchant stepped around the table to interpose himself between Alizarin and the lichen. "Who are you to say this to me? The Light Lord himself?"

"Light Lord" was an antiquated term for the leader of the Light Merchants, and its use had been discouraged in favor of the humbler sounding "First" when, some time before, the Light Merchants had begun to amass significant wealth. "A member of the disciplinary council."

"Hah! The disciplinary council! I will pay your 'fine', if that is what you want!"

Alizarin nodded thoughtfully and turned away. He would ensure there would be more than a financial penalty for this vendor and enquire as well into the operations of the disciplinary council. He didn't like the emphasis that shifty hawker had placed on the word "fine."

Alizarin turned a corner to step deeper into the quarter even as the Merchant, still laughing mockingly at him, began anew his efforts to sucker a gull. A few steps further and the First stopped one of the guild's security personnel tasked with keeping order. With a sign indicating that he was a senior Light Merchant, Alizarin indicated the Merchant he had just left and instructed immediate remedial action. The guard signed back his understanding and, collecting three other security officers, moved decisively in the direction from which Alizarin had just come.

Alizarin continued his stroll through the quarter, ruminating on the business of light and how it meshed with the business of the city. Everyone needed light. Everyone came for light. The Light Merchants sold the light. Only the Light Merchants sold the light. This was by decree of the Sebastos, which decree had been promulgated to protect the quality and value of light. This was for the good of Pentenokians and was to guard against just the sort of chicanery that Alizarin had just encountered. Let anyone sell light, and these were the sort of hucksters who would come to dominate! No. It could not be allowed. Light was too precious to be sold like that.

Yes, Light Merchants paid for the privilege too, but there was no other way around it. The Sebastos had to run a city, and taxes and imposts were just a fact of urban living. At least, in the urban Underworld, it seemed.

It was all around him now. So much light, and in so many astonishing shades, shades across every hue that Pentenokians had ever seen. Grey-green, greenish, faint yellow, even ivory here and there, though in very small nubs. Some specialized in "fancies," small lichens with blue or even reddish-tinged formations; interest in these waxed and waned with fashion and Alizarin himself had seen a half dozen cycles. Shapes too. Even sizes. Sometimes smaller forms were more popular, sometimes peculiar shapes other than the most common cluster. It was no different in this respect than the cut of Underworld robes, only more prominently visible against the dark.

Alizarin circled back through the quarter and toward the main thoroughfare by which he had entered. The Merchant with whom he had exchanged words was no longer present, and his table had been emptied and draped with a heavy black cloth. Alizarin was satisfied: corrective action had been accomplished with speed and thoroughness. He expected the Merchant was even now being thrust before a member of the disciplinary council, a member of which was on duty every cycle throughout the cycle; what eventually became of him might be worth knowing.

Then too, it occurred to him suddenly, he should find out what had been the final disposition of the Merchant's wares. Where had they been removed to? Who had received those? And, as an after-afterthought, why had the mountebank not been reported earlier for selling *sors*? Why had no other merchant brought this to the attention of security?

This was unsettling. Alizarin acknowledged the temptation to sell sub-quality goods. Dues were high and had risen quickly in the last years, albeit after a period of no change at all. This had been necessary to finance the Observers and to pay the higher licensing fee The Sebastos had imposed. Many in the guild had questioned the need to pay a licensing fee at all. Did not they provide an essential service, the cultivation and sale of light? Was not bringing light to Pentenok service enough without the payment of a fee to the royal house? The question, and how to pay it, had convulsed the

Merchants' councils for several cycles. Some had been willing to pay immediately, reasoning it could ultimately be passed on to the customer through higher prices. Others had cautioned that there must be a limit to this and that they had to be careful.

Eventually they had found compromise by the guild itself funding some of the higher license fee through its treasury and for the total fee increase to be added to dues over three hundred cycles. Meanwhile, Alizarin had, in exchange for a temporary lessening of the fee, put the services of the Observers and a measure of the intelligence they gathered, at the disposal of Sebastos Reynam. It had been a tricky negotiation with so many parties involved, but it had at last been closed. That had been more than twenty-fold ago. It had help up reasonably well since then. Now there were further stirrings high up in Lothwell Spire. It would be tricky again, he feared. Soon. There may have to be more compromises.

The man known as Alizarin to the high councils of the Light Merchants at length arrived at his own home. It was an unremarkable dwelling in an unremarkable section of Pentenok. The building was small, only a few rooms. It had been a requirement to live thus to become First. There could be no ostentation, it had been impressed on him at his investiture. If he wanted to run his hands through riches, he could do so at the treasury. But he could have none of his own. The richer and mightier the Light Merchants became, the more unassuming and humbler they must appear.

Alizarin found two guardsmen in his front room waiting for him. As one kept his eyes on the door, the other saluted and offered him an object. "Sir, for you." Alizarin took it. It was a small, shiny box, exquisitely formed of interleaved sheets of brown-and-black mica, each corner and edge framed by a faint line of silver.

"Thank you."

The First broke the seal and opened the box as soon as the messenger had departed. As he had guessed by its container, the note was another summons to Lothwell.

He would have just enough time to summon a messenger of his own to request accompaniment. He could not see the Sebastos alone; guild rules prohibited it. Not only was it safer, it helped keep memories straight. He told his messenger to ask her to meet him at the gate and they would continue on from there to meet the Sebastos together.

The Guard at the Sebastos's door briefly inspected the proffered mica box, which represented their invitation, and waved the two through. "Proceed. The Sebastokrator expects you."

Reynam was standing in the middle of the antechamber, awaiting them, clearly forewarned of their arrival. His two visitors advanced to three swords' lengths and genuflected.

"Your servant Umber, Sebastos," said he.

"Your servant Mauve, Sebastos," said she.

"At your service," they said together, as if rehearsed, although it had not been. Then they fell silent and stood still, waiting for the Sebastos to address them.

Reynam eyed them keenly. "Thank you for coming."

"Sebastos, at your call and command," replied Mauve, bowing her head.

He eyed them closely a moment longer and then turned away. "I would like to thank you, thank the Light Merchants."

"Sebastos, there is no thanks due us. We and all we have is at your service," said Umber.

Reynam turned back to them. The two were highly placed members of the Light Merchants' guild, but he wasn't exactly sure which was more senior. Maybe her, maybe him. He had once asked them this question, but each had pointed to the other as the senior-most. He had not pressed the point; it had not seemed important. And it still wasn't, he supposed.

He had also asked, on another occasion, why there were two of them instead of the single individual he had expected in response to his summons. Both had explained that it was to obviate misremembering the commands of the Sebastos as well as to ensure that neither alone misrepresented the capabilities of the Light Merchants. Reynam suspected that there was more than this behind two emissaries rather than one but also did not press that point, it not seeming to be important at the time. This occasion also still wasn't one worth pressing for details or at least he supposed.

"Sebastos," continued Umber after a respectful pause, "may we beg of you how we assisted you, so that we might seek out further such opportunities in the future to serve you?"

Reynam considered. How much should he disclose about differences between him and the Sebasissa within the royal house? How much was wise? He focused again on the two emissaries. They stood waiting patiently, impassively.

Reynam weighed up the uncertainties. He hesitated, but if the Light Merchants and their Observers knew as much as they did about the Sebasissa and her doings, then they must certainly know about his differences with her. And, with a start, if they knew a great deal about her, they would also surely know a great deal about him!

"You can be of further assistance," he said at last. The two Light Merchants responded with another bow. "I worry—some—about the Sebasissa. You see, she does not bear the same burden as I do, being Sebastos."

The two Merchants bowed again, murmuring their natural understanding.

"Nor does she have access to the same information, the same reports, the same council. She has other interests," he added quickly, anxious to maintain the dignity of all members of the royal house, and the immediate royal family in particular.

Umber spoke after a pause gauged to permit the Sebastos any desire for further elaboration. "Your wisdom, your intelligence in this matter are beyond question and reproach, Sebastos. Your first interests are most naturally Pentenok and all Pentenokians."

Reynam nodded.

"This is your great responsibility," added Mauve sympathetically. "But if we could share in it, and so alleviate it in any way, it would be a signal honor for our guild."

Reynam turned away, as if lost in thought over the offer. Part of it was act, but part was that he truly did not know how much assistance he wanted. This was because, he realized sharply, he didn't know what his sister was doing—or plotting, as the case might be. If he knew more, he would know more about what he really wanted.

"Perhaps you can help me."

"We are ever at your service, Sebastos."

Reynam turned back to them and took a step closer so he could better gauge their eyes. "I worry about my sister. She seems increasingly disaffected. I think that, if you were able to assess better how she... might be manifesting this disaffection, I would be most grateful."

Mauve dipped a knee. "Sebastos, we will observe. Diligently. As soon as we have anything to convey to you, we will do so, through whatever channel you deem, in your wisdom, most expedient and convenient."

"Very good, then. I will let you know."

The Light Merchants were ushered from the Sebastos's chambers and exited the palace through an exit of which Reynam was confident his sister was unaware. Very good, thought Reynam again. The Light Merchants might bring him some understanding of his sister's doings. Then he would have a better idea what further actions to take.

Though there was no reason to suspect they would be followed, Umber and Mauve undertook a route away from the palace that involved multiple detours through abandoned structures and several instances of doubling back upon their track. By such a circuitous route they arrived at length in that section of Market reserved for the Light Merchants. Into one of the grander pavilions, against the very rock face on and about which Pentenok had been built, they slipped inside. Then and only then did Alizarin break his silence and speak with the one he knew only as Mauve. "We heard the Sebastos," he said simply.

She nodded. "We will focus the attentions of the Observers as he requested."

Alizarin nodded back and turned toward a panel that had slid to one side to reveal a stairway into the rock. "Right away. Something is happening. Or will soon. I expect that is what the Sebastos is wanting to know more about. This is what we want to know as well. His interest is our interest. In many ways."

"So. Yes. What is it?" asked the Sebasissa of the shut door and from beyond which a knock had emanated. She thought she recognized that touch. It sounded like Kobemy.

It was. He entered, accompanied by Ortiki, and the two made the obligatory three-quarters genuflection, then stood to full height, awaiting the Sebasissa's permission to speak.

"So?" Sundra stood from the small desk at which she had been writing and pushed the chair back but did not move from it. Across her desk streamed rays of the whitest, purest light that either Ortiki or Kobemy thought they had ever seen. The illumination was so fine, so pure, that they beheld it with awe. The brown-and-black desk seemed to almost glow, and the silver metalwork decorating the desk at either edge gleamed brilliantly.

Both hesitated until Kobemy at last spoke. "Sebasissa, Your health, always."

"Yes, yes, of course! But what is it? Why do you disturb me?"

"Because, Sebasissa, we believe… we believe there is… We believe we are being watched."

Surprisingly, Sundra said nothing. After a long moment, she stood and stepped away from the desk. "Tell me, why do you believe this?"

"A feeling, Sebasissa. I feel like, as I move through the city streets, that I am being followed."

Normally, Sundra would have dismissed this as ridiculous superstition. Maybe it still was. But she hesitated. "Tell me more. And tell me what you mean by 'we'."

Ortiki spoke. "I will tell you more, Sebasissa. This is what I hear from guardsmen. That some of us, those most closely associated with me, we feel like we are never alone. That someone is always nearby, around us. Someone maybe not of our interests and aims.

"Further, that your movements are also followed."

Sundra found herself next to the display table against the wall, upon which had been set a variety of mineral crystal specimens of different colors and shapes. Her left hand reached out to trace the facets of an inordinately large quartz crystal cluster, its prisms unusually clear and perfect in their pyramidal shape. "Interesting. And so?" She knew that the guardsmen were riven by factionalism, most particularly as to who they favored, be that the Sebastos or her. This factionalism she had done nothing to dampen and, indeed, perhaps had covertly encouraged over many cycles.

"And more, Sebasissa. More than a feeling." Ortiki glanced over at Kobemy, who nodded back. "Yes, more. My understanding, from certain favorably inclined persons, is that the Sebastos suspects you."

"'Suspects'? Suspects me of what?"

"Sebasissa, with your permission! Of Dark Lake. That you did not go to Dark Lake after all. On this most recent occasion."

Sebasissa's hand drifted from the rock crystal to a particularly fine specimen of geode, the amethyst crystals lining the vug an especially deep and vivid violet. Dark Lake. That last occasion. That would have been the occasion on which she had ventured to the Overlands with Kobemy and Maribess. She looked up sharply. Kobemy maintained an impassive, almost blank, expression.

Sundra's attention returned to the table and her hand moved further along the specimens to finger a citrine. "So. Does my brother say of what he suspects me? Or—that if I did not go to Dark Lake—to where I did go?"

Ortiki shook his head. "I do not know, Sebasissa, because my contact did not know. Perhaps the Sebastos himself does not know."

Sundra turned away from the table and swung toward her two lieutenants. To Kobemy, she said, "You came to me stating that you felt you were being watched." Now looking to Ortiki she continued, "You told me that the Sebastos suspected me, though of what is not clear. I believe you are both right. I believe that we are being watched, and this is because my brother suspects me of a plot." She took another step forward until she was well within the usual distance at which she kept visitors. "Now we must move. Now. The plans we have discussed: set them in motion. Within two cycles, we must be ready to act decisively."

Sundra, Sebastas

The Sebasissa Sundra, in a dark robe and with the hood pulled down so much that it accentuated her sharp features, summoned Ortiki, in a whisper. "Is he—?"

"Yes, My Sebasissa."

She eyed him closely and her lips drew back in a vulpine smile. Then she put out a hand to him and snapped her fingers faintly. Instantly he took it. "It is good," she signed to him, in the silent language of the Underworld. "I will see. Me, alone. One instance. Last instance."

Ortiki signed back that he understood, and she dropped his hand and advanced to peer around a rocky outcropping. Loitering around the corner, but still very much alert, were her brother's two bodyguards, Lavinia and Bakide, whom she had learnt accompanied him everywhere. Her brother was surely deeper in the cavern, as he was not with them. He would be out of sight, though surely not out of earshot.

This place was called Starmers, and its galleries were known for the unusual crystal formations that zig-zagged down its walls. Others stretched as columns from floor to a ceiling too high above to see. Starmers, it was thought, owed its singularity not to the steady drip of mineral-laden water over millennia but to the laborious work of a now-vanished underground river that had eroded softer rocks to leave the more durable ones behind as stalactites and stalagmites and which, when exposed to the dim bioluminescence of certain light lichens, veins deep within them glowed in weird and vibrantly fluorescent colors.

She snapped her fingers again for Ortiki to take her hand and signed rapidly, "Go, very! Quickly, very! Now my signal!"

Ortiki let go her hand and turned to the ten guardsmen behind him. With a curt gesture he brought them forward, and they obediently formed a semi-circle behind him. On receiving another command, they trooped out from behind the rocks, Ortiki in the lead, directly toward the two bodyguards.

Bakide noticed them immediately. "Captain! Hail to you! What brings you here?"

"Important business," responded Ortiki simply and continued to advance until he was no more than a sword's length from them.

"Well, what could it be, Captain? You know the Sebastos does not wish to be disturbed."

Ortiki's only response was another gesture, this time in a sweeping motion. The ten with him promptly sprang forward and seized Bakide and Lavinia, who were so shocked that they hardly uttered a word. Only when Ortiki produced two gags and passed them to one of his men did they realize with horror what was happening and called as loudly as they could. "Sebastos! Sebastos! A plot!—"

Sundra materialized from out of the darkness. "Are they bound? Not yet? Finish the job, and smartly, too! And the gags? A little tighter with this one! So, he struggles, does he?" She rapped Bakide's helmet sharply with the pommel of her dagger to stun him. "This may quiet him! Now, tighten it!"

A voice came out of the distant shadows. "What is this? Why am I being disturbed? This is my time, and Starmers is my place for meditation." A tall figure, little more than a greater depth of darkness, approached down the rocks toward the path where the others stood. He stopped short in disbelief. "How is this? Lavinia and Bakide bound? Outrage!"

Sundra stepped forward and made the required genuflection, though it came across as more a hesitant, shallow dip in her stride than a proper obeisance. "Brother, hold your anger! I have uncovered a plot against you—a plot to assassinate you! These two—these Bakide and Lavinia—were about to summon others to overwhelm you, thinking to take advantage of the fact that you had no other guards with you. But I have apprehended this plot and thwarted it!"

"Sundra! So you say! My own guards assassinate me?" In amazement, he approached the squirming duo closer and saw that they were frantically attempting to speak to him through their gags. "But these two—"

Even as he was speaking, Sundra clandestinely made again the signal she had made before the taking of the bodyguards. Ortiki, who had been watching for it, leapt for Reynam and pinioned his arms to his sides. The other guards joined him in a second, and Reynam was taken. "Sundra!" he sputtered with fury. "Traitress! Lies! The only plot is yours!"

Sundra falsified a chuckle. "My poor brother," she taunted. "So simple is he. It confirms how unfit he is to rule our noble city, doesn't it?"

Reynam struggled to voice a retort, but already a gag had been bound around his mouth as tightly as the others had had ones bound around theirs.

"Struggling will do you no good," crowed Sundra triumphantly. "It will only make it more difficult for all of us!" She turned to her lieutenant. "So. Let us return to Pentenok and thence directly to Central Square. I will immediately address the population and inform them that my brother's corruption has been unmasked and he taken into protective custody."

"Yes, Sebasissa. And what, may I be so bold as to ask, will you say to them?"

She shrugged, retaining her characteristic equanimity. "The truth. That Pentenok is in a state of disrepair, even though taxes are high, because my brother has defrauded the citizenry for many cycles. Solely to enrich himself!"

Ortiki paused for a moment but, catching the malicious glimmer in Sundra's eyes, gave vent through drawn lips to a rasping, harsh and horrible sound more akin to choking than the laughter shaking him. After a moment, Sundra joined in with her own, high and thin. To both prisoners and guards alike, their amusement sounded little different from the cold clatter of scrap metal tumbling to some smithy's floor in a jumbled heap.

There was a knock on the door and, after the briefest of pauses, it swung open. Sundra looked up from the desk at which she was studying a document. "Yes, Maribess?" she asked.

"Sebastas," she answered as she genuflected, using Sundra's title as ruler, her accession having been announced in Central Square only a few cycles before. "The Light Merchants have come at your request."

"Very well; show them in. Remain in the room afterwards to watch them."

"Yes, Sebastas."

Maribess departed to fetch the Light Merchants, and Sundra reflected on the sound of her new title to her ears. "Sebastas." How pleasant to assume rulership of Pentenok, and with her brother now in the dungeons far, far below the Lothwell Spire. So. Finally the moment had come for decisive action, the same for which her brother had always been so reluctant! Doubtless because he had been the prisoner already of forces far larger than he. But she, Sundra, was no such prisoner, and she was not afraid of pursuing those very courses to which her strongly held convictions prompted her.

The announcement of Reynam's perfidy in Central Square had astounded everyone. But she had used surprise to great advantage. She had hauled her brother up to the highest platform in the square and, expressing her own astonishment and sorrow at having to do what she had insisted she had had to, had explained to the population that the high and ever-rising cost of basic necessities, such as light and food, had come about through the granting of monopoly licenses, the proceeds of which had only flowed to Reynam and his cronies. There would be a trial, she promised, as soon as all the evidence had been gathered. That trial, she had assured, would be open to all, so that they would all be able to hear and see for themselves.

There would be no such trial, of course. She had long before determined this. Instead, her brother and his associates would be locked up until Sundra decided what to do with them. This would be in Sundra's own good time. Meantime, they would remain closely guarded. And silent.

That had been several cycles before. At this point in time, she had determined to receive delegations from the city's leading entities to ascertain where they stood on recent events and how far they could be trusted. She had summoned the Light Merchants first.

Maribess knocked again on the open door and led two figures in after a few seconds' delay.

"Two of you? Why two? I asked only for your leader."

The two genuflected as one and introduced themselves as Umber and Mauve in contrite tones. "Forgive us, Sebastas! We have always come as two, so that we may hear and understand your commands the better and so that no one of us mis-represents the guild!"

"So, do I understand that your guild does not have confidence in its self-selected leader? Why, then, don't the Light Merchants choose someone more trustworthy?"

Neither said a word, and only shifted uneasily from one foot to the other.

Sundra weighed them up. She distrusted—and disliked—the Light Merchants by nature. At least they had not hesitated to call her by her proper title, suggesting they held no overt allegiance to her brother. And she needed them, if only for now, to continue the supply of lichens until she could effectuate her other plans. She flourished her hand in an easy gesture of dismissal. "Be that as it may. The Light Merchants can select their own leadership as they like. I do not bring you here for that."

The two genuflected in acknowledgement, remaining silent.

That too was appropriate, thought Sundra, slightly more mollified. That they remain silent, awaiting patiently her next pronouncement. "Rather, I bring you here to tell you that Pentenok will not be run in the same way it was while my brother was Sebastos."

"Yes, Sebastas," replied Mauve. "We await your pleasure in this respect, and how we might serve you best."

Sundra continued after a moment spent trying to gauge their actual willingness to comply with this offer. "In particular, I will no longer grant the Light Merchants a monopoly over the supply of light to Pentenok. That monopoly is hereby rescinded!" She waited to see their reaction.

They evinced none, until, at long last, the male spoke. "Yes, Sebastas. If this be your pleasure."

"Further! The license fee you paid under the Sebastoship of my brother… for the monopoly!…"

The pause lengthened. "Yes, Sebastas?"

Sundra bit her lip. Would she tell them that the fee was no longer payable? In order to lessen the prices they charged Pentenokians? But crafty and conniving as they were, would they not simply retain the high prices and keep the difference for themselves? How greedy, how grasping they were! And Sundra would have helped enrich their loathsome guild still further!

"It is still payable!"

The silence that followed was clearly of a different sort, and the two were clearly stunned. Then the one named Umber genuflected, stuttering, "But Sebastas, we should pay a monopoly fee but have no monopoly?"

Sundra half-rose from her desk, mainly in irritation at how she had failed to think fully through how she might have intended this audience to go. "Enough! Do not presume to question my edicts!" Her pale eyes narrowed with suppressed fury.

She, Sundra, Sebastas, would not be, could not be outsmarted by these Light Merchants! But if these Merchants still paid the monopoly fee, would they still not just pass it on to the citizenry, and prices would simply remain high? How, then, would life for the average Pentenokian under Sebastas

Sundra have improved over that under Sebastos Reynam? "And! And! You are hereby ordered to reduce all prices for light lichens! By half! As of the end of this cycle!" There. That would solve the problem. The city would retain the income from the Light Merchants, and yet the people would still benefit. And immediately, as well. Sundra resumed her chair, pleased with herself for her quick thinking, though outwardly she maintained a fierce glower which she turned on first one, then the other.

The Light Merchants, she noted with a glow, were flabbergasted. "Sebastas!" gasped Mauve. "Pay the monopoly fee but receive no monopoly AND reduce prices by half?"

Sundra folded her arms. "Yes! So! As of the end of the current cycle. For too long the Light Merchants have preyed upon the people of Pentenok. No more. Not under Sebastakrator Sundra! So. This surprises you? Well! Prepare for more surprises! The Light Merchants are only the first; there shall be many others.

"Now, go! There are two of you present to hear my commands; you insisted upon it. So, let there be no mistake in my orders!" With a jerk of her hand, she dismissed them, and Maribess immediately marched them out.

Umber and Mauve exited the palace by the way they had come, through the front entrance rather than the little-used rear exit that Reynam had favored. The two walked in absolute silence while they were accompanied, and even beyond as they dodged around corners, passed through taverns, manoeuvred their way through occasional crowds, and stole through several abandoned houses. Only when they were in Market, within the Light Quarter, did Mauve turn anxiously to Alizarin. "Is this cause for concern?"

"Yes," answered Umber slowly, choosing his words carefully. "But in a general sense, and not so much because of the Sebastas's orders."

"But our license to sell?"

"No one else is in a position to sell as we are and so quickly and with as much variety as we can. Over time, yes, this could change. But it would take much time. Many, many cycles."

Mauve nodded with understanding. This was true. No one else knew where the lichen farms were hidden—she, the Sebastas, had not tried to expropriate those! Only the Light Merchants could supply Pentenok in the quantity and quality that it had long become accustomed to being supplied.

"The requirement that we reduce prices by half?"

Alizarin shook his head. "That is more problematic. This—I think—we will have to do. Certainly, at first. Then we will have to think up other ways to manage. For now, we can comply. But not forever."

Mauve nodded, and they separated. Alizarin, as Umber, was not willing to say more. Perhaps he had already said too much. Not that he mistrusted the woman he only knew as Mauve, disguised as he was certain she was, just as he was, but for the sake of the Guild's safety. What if she were taken prisoner?

"Not forever" had been his last words to Mauve. No, not forever. Not just because the treasury could not hold out long enough to fund the Observers and the needs of his guild on half the income, but because he was sure that however drastic this enforced price reduction clearly was, it would surely be followed by more restrictions. Ultimately, the Sebastas might wish to dispossess the Light Merchants of their entire livelihood. Alizarin frowned. The solidly stocked treasury was a bulwark against the fears and cares of uncertainty but, for greater problems, wealth was not enough: these required true leadership. Current events were shaping up to be one of these instances.

Later, the First met with his Chief Observer and related to him all that had transpired at Lothwell. Alizarin drummed his fingers on the table at which they sat but otherwise remained silent, until, finally, he asked gently, "The Sebastos? What happened to him?"

"The dungeons. Along with several of those most closely associated with him. Bodyguards, close councilors; most all his associates have been rounded up."

"Maybe a few still remain at large, in hiding."

"But he is alive? The Sebastos."

"Yes. In the deepest cell, but alive. And, I understand, receiving food and water."

Interesting, thought Alizarin. In the deepest cell. "The closest associates of the Sebastos: are they too in the deepest cells? Near the Sebastos?"

Cinnabar looked up at the First with a confident smile. "I don't know. Why don't we ask? I mean, ask of the Observers."

Alizarin clasped his hands together on the table in front of him. "It is impossible to escape the dungeons of Lothwell. They are very deep, and there is only one way out: back the same way one came in."

"Yes. Only one way."

The two gazed at each other, then down at the table for a long period. At last: "Only one?"

"No. There may be another." There was a pause. "But investigating this could be expensive."

Alizarin unclasped his hands and moved them to his lap, where he found himself clenching them into tight fists. Another way out of the dungeons of Lothwell. *Possibly* another way out. This could be tremendously important. For Light Merchants. For all Pentenok. It was too early to hope for more. First, it had to be ascertained if another route out really existed. But Alizarin was suddenly certain that this, THIS was the moment for which the Light Merchants had accumulated so much wealth. This was the vindication of those many years of saving.

Similarly, now was the time to test his other precept that true and great wealth could only be safeguarded by some measure of spending it. "Spend what you need to spend. These are important questions, and we must have answers."

The Chief Observer nodded silently. He had expected as much.

Alizarin stood to leave.

"First, there is one more item," Cinnabar added softly.

Alizarin turned back.

"One more item. I don't think it bears directly on the matter at hand, but it is something, nonetheless. And I thought you might be interested."

Alizarin waited.

"The Sebastas. Reportedly she has become fixated on an Overlands artefact. An artefact which creates light. Or emits it."

"An artefact?"

"Yes. An artefact. From the Overlands. It is a mostly a tale, but research suggests some substance to it."

Alizarin retook his chair and indicated that the Chief Observer should continue. An artefact of the Overlands which shed light? Alizarin's professional interest was piqued.

"Little is known about this artefact and only from a few Overland stories. It is some sort of device. Maybe a rod. Or headdress."

"Tell me more. What is this story? And what does the Sebastas know of it?"

Cinnabar sighed. "Impossible to say. The story concerns an Overlands city that grew prosperous from trade—much as Pentenok has—countless cycles ago. The city also had the device. At last, the city's wealth drew attention, and it was attacked and conquered. The story doesn't say anything about the people of the city using the device in its defense."

"So, maybe they city didn't have it after all? The device. Or it wasn't effective."

"No one can say. Perhaps it was lost. Or the knowledge of how to use it was forgotten. But the Sebastas seeks it. She has been researching it, reading everything which mentions it."

"Do we know why she seeks this device?"

"No. Only that she seeks it."

"Do you believe it exists?"

The Chief Observer shrugged. "Impossible to say. There are only stories. I doubt it, but who can know for sure?"

A thought occurred to the First. "Is it possible this device may actually be in the Underworld already, or even in Pentenok?"

"No. Not possible. We would know of it. If it exists, it is still in the Overlands."

The First drummed his fingers again briefly, ruminating. A curious interest of the Sebastas. But nothing more than that, as best he could understand. "Very well," he concluded, standing again. "Thank you for telling me this. I agree, it has no immediate bearing on what is happening now. But it is strange. And bears monitoring.

"More important, and more immediate, is a determination as to if there is an alternative way out of the dungeons of Lothwell."

Central Square was always the most active place in Pentenok, it being a common gathering and meeting point. It had ever been so, since the earliest days of the city. In the weeks following the shocking revelations of the corruption of the Sebastos—which still reverberated within certain circles—Sebastas Sundra had felt it desirable and even necessary to take urgent measures, and this had brought even more of the population into the square.

This was because the measures the Sebastas had decided to institute involved new and more laws. These, she was certain, would correct the excesses and laxness of her brother's reign.

By tradition, laws were not effective until their proclamation was affixed to an ancient stone pillar in Market and an announcement as such made from an equally ancient stone podium immediately to the right of the pillar. Such announcement was always accompanied by a herald's identification by gesture to the new law so that all the citizenry could examine it and understand it immediately. But there had been such a flurry of new laws and modifications to old ones that the heralds had run out of space on the ancient stone pillar and had been obliged to have brought in a kind of auxiliary ancient pillar. This pillar had been carted in by wagon from a ruined mansion on the outskirts of Pentenok. If not as old as the original column, it looked sufficiently old enough to deserve some respect and was thus promising in its ability to lend some of the same to the new laws of the Sebastas.

A small crowd gathered when the "new" ancient pillar made its first appearance in Central Square and its purpose made apparent. Factions formed and debate ensued. The first disagreement was on where to place the new pillar. Some wanted it to the right side of the stone podium, opposite the first, to offer balance and to frame the podium, as it were, between the two columns. This faction argued that the herald's identifying gesture to the new law would also be more obvious in that it would either be to the right or to the left, rather than ambiguous, as would be the case if both pillars were on the same side. Others argued that, because tradition placed the pillar to the left of the podium, so should be located the second, and next to the original, and slightly further from the podium, representing its status as an addition. This group pointed out that no one really identified the new law from the herald's gesture anyway, so disambiguation of the gesture was hardly necessary.

As if this controversy was not enough, another disagreement soon arose as to the appropriate height of the new pillar. Repeated measurement confirmed that it overtopped the original by more than two heads. Many believed that it should be slightly shortened, out of respect for the original ancient pillar. But others argued, and not without merit, that shortening the newer pillar would be imprudent from a practical standpoint as, with the slew of laws emanating from the Lothwell Spire, more space rather than less was required, and did anyone want to see—possibly—the necessity of a third pillar?

Ultimately, a compromise was struck that seemed to balance most concerns. Tradition would be observed by placing the second pillar next to the original, to the left of the podium, thus keeping the orientation of pillars and podium unchanged. But in a bow to the changing times, the new pillar would not be shortened and would be kept in its current size, possibly to signify the relative importance of the Sebastas's edicts and their impact on the city. Rather, and out of deference to the past, it would be placed a slight distance behind the original, ancient pillar. No one gainsaid these arguments, though silently, some acceded not so much out of respect to the Sebastas or even to provide more space for further proclamations, but because they were unwilling to undertake uncompensated the arduous work of reducing the newer column—of solid stone and very heavy—to a lesser height.

That outcome was surely for the better. For the Sebastas had many changes to make to the laws that had been in effect during and even before the misguided reign of her brother. She was very dissatisfied with the way the city had been run and was set on changing it. One of her first proclamations had been to reduce by half the prices charged by the Light Merchants. Pleased with the immediate and substantial impact of this edict, the Sebastas had ordered other prices reduced, such as those for wine, edible fluvial plant life (which were the vegetables of the Underworld diet), and then certain other edible fungi which were staples. It occurred to her also to cut the prices for those furnishings she imagined essential to a Pentenokian home, but she thought it best to wait and see how well these first edicts fared. Besides, she reasoned, these first decrees considered survival essentials: light and food. Furniture and furnishings could be addressed in the future.

The edicts drew mixed reactions. Those buying were enthusiastic. Those selling were distressed to find that they had to reduce their prices, immediately, and by considerable percentages, when the cost to procure their goods had not changed and indeed, they reasoned, would not change going forward. For the fluvial food merchants, for example, they still had to pay for divers, transport the food, and prepare it for market. They still had to display their merchandise. Where was the compensatory price cut for those costs?

These questions fell on deaf ears, if, even, they were asked. Few dared. No one knew what had become of the Sebastos Reynam and his closest advisers. They had simply vanished. This was enough to silence most. Of those who did speak out, most frequently from Central Square, and referring angrily to the offending proclamation, they were invariably visited later by Captain Ortiki, or a lieutenant, and a brace of grim guardsmen to inform the complainant sternly that adherence to the Sebastas's edicts was not voluntary but compulsory and that this warning would be the only one given. Alternatively, or if further explanation were needed, the captain or his lieutenant would continue, the complainant could accompany them back to Lothwell Spire to take the matter up with the Sebastas herself.

Never once did a complainant decide to accompany the guardsmen back to Lothwell Spire. The meaning of the warning was always clear.

On some occasions, there wasn't even a warning. Sometimes, the complainant disappeared. "Gone to join Reynam" was the assumption, wherever that was.

Thus, complaints ceased. And prices were reduced. Both of which suggested that the edicts of the Sebastas were effective. This should have earned the thanks of the consumers in the city, but they too had cause for unhappiness, because those foodstuffs which had been the object of the price reductions gradually began to disappear from the tables and shelves from which they were generally sold. Vendors apologized. Consumers complained. It was getting harder and harder to find what they needed, they said, lower prices or not. Inevitably, rumors began to run through the city, rumors of where to get this staple or that, and at what price, and through whom, and how. "Finding" clubs formed with the general aim of procuring goods at some price to accustomed levels of quality. No one at first dared form a "sellers" club, for fear of invoking the mandatory discount, but these too evolved, slowly and surreptitiously, for those who had desired items to sell at remunerative prices.

"An open door." That was how Cinnabar, his Chief Observer had explained it. Cryptic, as usual. No doubt to avoid compromise but cryptic all the same. He, Alizarin, had authorized Cinnabar all expenditure to look into it. Alizarin flexed his fingers. His hands were sore. He had been clenching and clasping them quite a bit these past two days.

"An open door." What could he have meant by this? How could there ever be an open door into the very dungeons of the Sebastokrator's Palace, the Lothwell Spire?

Deep, deep within the bowels of that very spire, the surface of a black pool rippled. A minute went by, and then it rippled again. A few more seconds, and the surface stirred. Some marine creature poked a strange appendage up from the water's edge. It was strange, because rather than some sort of grasping or grappling limb, it would have resembled more a dome, smooth and shiny, had there been light. But light there was, very shortly thereafter, right at the edge of the water, just above the surface. It shone a feeble beam this way and that and then round in a circle about the pool. The beam, and the associated dome, hesitated, then approached the pool's cut-stone edge, and the light was set down. Then, the dome heaved itself up, and it was now identifiable as a person, the dome having been a metallic and close-fitting helmet which, after another moment, the person removed and attached to his waist. Then, the figure turned and stuck a leg into the water, swirled it around, and withdrew it. Moments later, another figure emerged from the water and joined the first at the edge.

The first snapped a finger and stretched out a hand. The second took the hand of the first. With that, they stood still for a moment, then, letting go, they set off silently together toward an opening in the wall, the feeble lantern held in front of the first, a trail of wet footprints the only evidence of their passage.

These were the dungeons of the Lothwell Spire, and the pool of water, quiet and dark as it lapped the worked stone edges that hemmed it round, was an upwelling of the River Iilish. The jailors knew of this pool in the veriest basement of course, as they drew water from it intermittently for their prisoners, that being far easier than lugging it down from wells above. It was also used to dispose of unwanted items, quickly and quietly, rather than, again, lugging them up to the entrance far, far above. This, the pool, was the Chief Observer's "open door," as, properly suited to withstand the chill and guided to navigate its currents, it was a way out of the dungeons but by first diving deeper rather than climbing up many, many stairways.

The two figures prowled the corridors of the dungeons, remaining conscious of where the pool lay behind them so as not to lose their way back. They were searching and hiding. They were searching for someone cast into that lightless dungeon and hiding from anyone who might accidentally happen upon them in their search.

There was a rustle ahead of them. The two pressed themselves into a niche, melting into the deep shadows of a corridor lit dimly by very low-quality light lichens spaced at exceedingly long intervals. The rustle was a voice and, as it spoke, there was the scraping of a key in a lock.

"Heh. Heh-heh. There you go. How'z that?"

There was no reply audible to the two figures.

"Oh? So you sez? Well, that's not the way it is now, is it?"

Again, there was a short silence, as if a rejoinder were being uttered.

"Heh. Ha! We'll see about that. 'Bout that! Now, you don't go anywhere, you hear!—" and there was a pause, as if the voice, doubtless a jailor, were awaiting a response. But apparently none came, for the same voice picked up again. "—and take good care of yerse'f! But it'll have to be 'n the dark, as there's no light a-authorized for you, ya hear?"

There was another pause, and the two dark figures thought to hear now an answering voice, raised in a higher pitch, as if in anger or indignity.

"Sorry's that! Not authorized! It's too bad too, because, as they say, 'By the light we know's our friends'. Meanin', 'course, you'll never know me, this a-ways, as your friend!" There came a last "Heh!" and then there was the scrape of what sounded like more metal on metal, followed by the halting and shuffling footsteps of the departing jailor.

The darkness closed in almost completely as the jailor moved away with his feeble light source. But the two figures had crept in closer while he had been in conversation with his captive and, as soon as the jailor had disappeared around a corner and was judged some distance away, and then more for good measure, they stole forward to the door where he had been standing and held up their light to the barred window. Inside a bare stone cell sat a miserable man with only a cracked mug and a bare plate. He lifted his unshaven face upwards listlessly on perceiving the light, and the two figures were chilled by the empty, hopeless look in the eyes. But it was him they had come to see, as the code had been uttered outside his cell door.

"By the light, you know your friends," whispered one figure, reprising what the jailor had said, while the other turned away to keep watch on either side of the stone-flagged corridor.

The man inside convulsed in amazement and pulled himself erect. His bearing suddenly changed from one slumped in defeat to one of kingly self-possession. For, indeed, it was Reynam, lately the Sebastos, who had been thrust into that deep, dank, dark cell at the base of the palace from which he had so recently ruled.

Reynam straightened and took two steps toward the small, barred window through which the voice had whispered. "Who... who are you?"

"A friend. With light."

As the voice spoke, a tiny point of light commenced to hover in the window to prove the assertion. Reynam stared at it, transfixed. Yes, it was light, and he could see it, good and well. It was a very small glow but not like the very faint and diffuse sort incident from the jailor's barely visible lichen, but of much better quality; much brighter, and whiter in color; sharper and stronger and of real quality. Who could have such a light and be willing to venture down into these recesses to show it to him? "You are a friend, to show me light, and most welcome are you! Light is forbidden me, for no good reason, and it is like a torture!

"But," continued Reynam, taking another step closer to the barred window, "you did not come to me at considerable risk to show me light. You came with a greater purpose in mind."

The voice answered immediately. "Yes, there is a greater purpose. To communicate to you a possible way out. But it is not yet the time to disclose more."

"When will it be time?"

"That is not for me to say. Another decides."

Reynam was struck by misgivings. "Is this a trick?"

The figure at the door seemed to shrug, and the point of light bobbed. "Are you any the worse off for it yet, if so?"

Reynam paused and did not answer, acknowledging the implicit truth behind that question. "What should I be doing?"

"Be resilient. Be ready. Be strong. The way out, when it is time, will not be easy."

Reynam acknowledged this obvious truth with a curt nod.

"If you can confide with those who fell with you to this place so far beneath the Lothwell Spire, and can trust them, then do so. But breathe not a word to anyone else!"

Reynam nodded again. The dot of light at the barred window must have sensed his agreement, as it immediately vanished and the figure at the door retreated without another word. Reynam was again left in total darkness to ponder the meaning of this figure, and to wonder when it would "be time" as "another" might decide.

Maribess wandered through Market, half from habit, half from need, and—

why not?—another, third half out of interest in seeing the impact of the edicts of the Sebastas. In some places where she passed, she was greeted with deference and even with an honorific generally reserved for grander echelons of society than she understood herself to occupy. On the first occasion, it had caught her attention. She thought at first that maybe she was being mocked and had frowned in response. But as others did the same, she realized that it was because of the emerging perception of her as being an important figure in the household of the Sebastas. This had caused her to smile. Imagine: she, only a guard, a warrior, now being treated as upper society! Then she reminded herself sternly that she must not be flattered by such attentions. Yet, she liked it anyway, even if she were reluctant to admit it to herself.

As usual, she meandered past the stalls of the light sellers. Unlike on the previous occasion, she did not see the merchant with the large, diseased lichen. Maybe he was away gathering more. Another was now at what had been his booth. Maribess stopped to glance at her wares.

"Lady Guardsman! How are you today? My name is Sienna, and welcome to my table. How can I help you with your lighting needs?"

"Perhaps you can, thank you, though I may just be looking."

"Of course! Looking is good, and we look by light, and light is what I have to offer! By the light, we know our friends—and ourselves!"

Maribess made no reply and pretended to examine the display, when, in reality, she was trying to glimpse their prices. "This one, here," she said at last, unable to feign her inspection any longer and choosing one of the better specimens, "tell me about it."

"Of course! And may I compliment you on your discerning eye? This one is a lovely specimen; enjoy the golden glow emanating from it! It comes to us from the celebrated shelves that line the banks of the River Liltenen, far upstream, where there is sufficient moisture to encourage growth but not so much as to tend the light toward too greenish a tone."

Maribess eyed the lichen speculatively. It did have a warm, yellow glow to it, but she thought to detect undertones of an almost reptilian green, which were unfavorable. "The River Liltenen?" she echoed, idly.

Sienna nodded vigorously. "Just so! Isn't it lovely? Tell me, Lady Guardsman, what sort of space are you looking to illuminate? Do you look for restfulness? Because of your very significant responsibilities? Or, perhaps to focus? To better discharge these responsibilities? This lovely shade of gold can help with both."

Maribess had heard this sort of patter before. All that was new was that she was being referred to as "Lady Guardsman," when previously she had just been a sales prospect. She sniffed. "Tell me, what are you thinking would be the price on this one? Just out of curiosity."

Sienna replied, confiding that it was a special price because it was an honor to sell to the Lady Guardsman.

Maribess had heard that sort of line before too and did not find it any more persuasive than she had on the other occasions. "Have you heard," she asked casually, "that the Sebastas has ordered that all prices on light be reduced by half? And that was a cycle or so ago."

"Oh, yes, Lady Guardsman! And I have complied—all Light Merchants have complied. We hasten to obey our Sebastas. This lichen was, indeed, oh, just cycles ago, more than double the price I quoted just now. You are a very keen shopper to come after the edict came into force, you are!" Sienna gestured broadly to the other stalls around her. "See, everywhere: there are fewer lichens out for sale. But I must find a living somehow, so I am still here." Sienna's expression changed to one of dolor. "Your gain is surely my loss, Lady. But I am an obedient citizen of Pentenok and the Sebastas. May I wish for her continued health!" she concluded with a quick but appropriately deep genuflection.

Maribess looked around the space to which Sienna had gestured. It was true that the quarter was darker than usual, meaning fewer lights were out for display and—presumably—sale. Focusing, Maribess saw that far fewer tables than usual were occupied and that a fair quantity were empty or covered over by deep black shades. "Your gain is my loss, Lady" rang again in Maribess's ears, but she pushed the words away. They were probably hoarding their wares, hoping the Sebastas would reverse herself. Never! Or, they had retreated to some other, private venue and so were still keeping quality light beyond the reach of the common Pentenokian. Maribess eyed Sienna; she did not seem to be dissembling. But how could Maribess know who Sienna was? No, all Light Merchants worked ultimately for themselves. Themselves and their guild. That was how it had always been, The Sebastas had told her this several times.

Maribess's left cheek twitched in suspicion. "I wish for her continued health as well, the Sebastas! And I would suggest that the Light Merchants be as forthcoming with their wares today as they were before the edict, lest the Sebastas take further and greater interest in their doings!"

Sienna bobbed another quick genuflection at the mention of the Sebastas. "Of course, Lady Guardsman! I will communicate this to our guild immediately. And please! Spare a word for me, your poor servant Sienna, doing her very best to live a brighter, healthier life!"

Maribess, for the first time in her life, set her face in a supreme expression of hauteur by way of reply. Then, murmuring something she thought sufficiently vague as to leave uncertain just what she might say, turned and stalked back through Market to Lothwell Spire.

Sienna watched her prospective customer depart. When she had disappeared into the milling crowds of Market, Sienna signaled to a nearby Light Merchant lingering in the background that he could return to his table. Sienna must report this encounter to her supervisor, the Chief Observer. Indeed, hadn't the Lady Guardsman expressly directed her to do just that?

Sundra stood at one end of the palace's Receiving Hall, which occupied the larger part of the third level of the Lothwell Spire. A great ivory light lichen hung overhead, large enough to cast a soft, creamy pool of illumination across the throne of Pentenok and Sundra, who stood beside it. She watched dispassionately as Ortiki strode toward her down the length of the otherwise deeply-shadowed hall.

"Sebastas, I wish for your continued health!" he saluted her, and, as always, she glowed at hearing herself addressed as Pentenok's ruler. Her previous honorific of "Sebasissa" was used in address any female member of the immediate royal house, and which Sunda had considered little better than anonymity. Ortiki stopped and genuflected deeply when he had reached the requisite three sword's length. "Sebastas, you do not take the throne yet?"

She held up her hand. "If I thought it would mean anything, believe me that I would not hesitate to seat myself upon the throne. But I have little interest in that. In sitting and waiting."

She looked it over almost disapprovingly, which struck Ortiki as strange, as had she not very recently risked all to seize it?

"No, no time for waiting. I have much greater plans. So. They cannot and will not wait."

Ortiki stood silent, waiting for his orders and any explanation she might choose to give him.

"I am leaving, Ortiki. I designate you as ruler of Pentenok in my absence. But I shall not be gone long. Only a short time."

"Leaving, My Sebastas?"

"Yes. So. Back to the Overlands. For, yes, I have been there already. Soon I return. There is another world above ours, Ortiki, and I mean for some of it to be ours, to belong to Pentenok. And, because there must be many other underground worlds like ours—of course there must be!—I mean for those to be mine, and Pentenok's too. My brother lacked any sort of vision; he was content with what we already had and could imagine nothing more. But there is much more to be had, and I shall realize it.

"Now, you, Ortiki, come, come and sit on this throne! Sit and keep it for me." Ortiki reluctantly climbed the steps to the platform, turned and perched himself on the grand seat. "While I am in the Overlands, I want it well and safely kept. If I should find it less than this when I return!—"

"Certainly, My Sebastas! All shall be well!"

"I expect as much. And you know that you shall be under surveillance."

Ortiki grimaced in understanding.

"Keep it well, but do not grow over-comfortable on it." Sundra bared her teeth in a semblance of a smile. "As did my brother."

Ortiki straightened in the throne in a display of dignity, though inwardly he was shuddering. The Sebastas had promised him a reward for throwing in his lot with hers and, indeed, he had seen no other way toward immediate advancement. Ruling from Lothwell, even if only for a brief period and clearly in her stead, was surely what she had meant! But what was also becoming clear was that the Sebastas's rewards came with strict conditions, constant oversight, and no small amount of risk.

She swept her cloak around her in preparation to leave, the silvery suit of chainmail that he knew she always wore beneath her court garments flashing momentarily in the lichen light. A second longer she stared into Ortiki's eyes, her eyes pale and narrowing. The she turned and began to walk away down the Hall.

"My Sebastas! When do you depart for the Overlands?"

"Almost immediately," she called over her shoulder.

"But, but Sebastas! Wait, I beg you!" he called, starting from the throne after her. "When will you return?"

"When what I have to do there is complete. Why not always assume the very next cycle. And conduct yourself accordingly." With a last, short nod to her lieutenant, Sundra left, her soft trail boots making not the slightest sound on the great, dark flagstones of the silent Hall.

Not even a full cycle later, Sebastas Sundra, the usurper of Pentenok, was well on her way back to the Overlands. She had decided to use the same exit as on her previous visit. It was the closest and most accessible from Pentenok, although it opened high in the mountains of the Overlands, which came with its own dangers.

Sundra mentally reviewed the events of the past few days as she, Kobemy, and Maribess plodded along, seated on the back of a kind of large caterpillar, which served as a sort of pack beast. Sundra had chafed at her brother's lumbering ineptitude but had bided her time. It could only have been a matter of time until she had recruited the necessary allies to effect his ouster. Her vision, persuasive abilities, and the promise of favors had been sufficient. Ortiki had been useful in this respect and had only required the promise of being made captain of the guards to bring him around. So. Well, he had been furious at being passed over for this position some time before. Sundra could understand this anger, having been passed over herself for Sebastos. Now the former captain languished in a cell not far from her brother, the former ruler. Sundra smirked, entertained at the twist of fate for those two.

Sundra shook her head to clear it. Enough of thinking about the past. She had left Ortiki in charge, and he should serve well enough for the short time she expected to be away. Then she would return, in triumph. And she would return as the light bringer of Pentenok.

She savored the words in the darkness, swaying rhythmically to the rolling gait of her arthropod of burden. Sundra, The Light Bringer. She turned them over in her mind, and began to fancy them as a sort of cognomen. For though she had reminded herself many times that the future would not make itself, and that action in its construction would be far more decisive than dreams, yet she could not resist the seductiveness of the prospect that unrolled before her as they made their way upwards toward their objective. Yes, she would be Sundra, the Light Bringer, and also Sundra, Breaker of Monopolies. She would crush the monopoly of the Light Merchants, for perhaps still the crown could be set to shine from the Lothwell Spire every cycle, throughout the cycle. And Sundra, the Colorist, for the range of colors perceived in the Underworld consisted largely of silvers, greys, greens, and browns, but the crown Sundra would bear back would bring all the colors of the spectrum to the Underworld, and its people would grow accustomed to every hue and tint that Overlanders such as the unworthy Vedel took for granted. And why not Sundra the Conqueror, too? Because the device's brilliance would be the ultimate weapon in uniting under her rule all the other cities and peoples of the Underworld, as well as rendering Pentenok invulnerable.

Such a pleasing picture, Sundra determined, well satisfied with how events were developing. So. All she needed was this crown. Which was nearby, Vedel had said, in some ruined city on "coast," whatever that was. Not far away, though, as it was within the kingdom in which he had assembled his men. It wouldn't be long now, this was certain.

At length, Sundra indicated for the large caterpillar bearing them to stop. "No further," she called and signaled for the two Underworlders accompanying her to dismount. "We proceed from here on foot."

Without complaint, the three slung over their backs the heavy packs the caterpillar had carried for them thus far and set out on the path that stretched upwards toward the cave mouth. "These packs contain extra cloaks," she informed her companions as they staggered forward beneath the weight. "It may be extremely cold when we emerge in the Overlands, so we may need them."

But the Underworlders were fortunate. Though the air seemed thinner and colder—much colder—than on their last visit, it had turned toward summer in the Overlands and there were none of the freezing, snowy blasts that constantly buffeted the face of the Grey Mountains during the winter.

"In a short time, that glowing orb in the far ceiling will descend," explained Sundra. The other two nodded. As soon as it vanished, they knew it would become dark and they would more easily be able to descend.

"And what then, My Sebastas?" asked Kobemy.

"In the valley below, at a stream, a group awaits us. You have already met their leader, Vedel. No, he is no more trustworthy than before, in response to a question I know you must already be framing, but he—and they—can be trusted insofar as we need them."

"Shall I be prepared as I was on the first occasion we encountered them, My Sebastas?" asked Maribess.

Sundra nodded slowly. "So. You shall keep sheathed your sword, Kobemy. But yes, Maribess, you should have your darts and daggers at the ready. Secretly."

Then Sundra directed the others to unburden themselves of their packs but to pull out one cloak each to guard against the chill stealing up the mountain as they settled down to await nightfall.

They didn't have to wait long. Just as they had remembered from their previous visit, the orb in the far ceiling descended at last to disappear behind the rocky outcroppings behind them known locally as the Grey Mountains, and the three started down the slope.

Sundra motioned for them to stop as they neared a particularly dense copse of trees at the base of the mountain. Though it was pitch dark, with only a scattering of faint stars high above, Kobemy and Maribess easily detected Sundra's signal, so well adapted were their eyes to darkness.

A barely audible snap of Sundra's fingers from both hands brought her companions abreast of her. They each took one of her hands in theirs. "Ahead, soon, allies," she signed to them, by which they understood that this was the encampment of Vedel and his men, though it was unclear, given the limitations of the silent language, just how far ahead.

They each acknowledged understanding nevertheless.

"Now, more. Many, very."

Maribess and Kobemy understood this to mean that Vedel had successfully added more mercenaries to his ranks.

"We join. Together. Shortly. At my signal." With that, Sundra indicated that the conversation was over and they loosed hands.

The three slipped through the trees. Small brush, leaves, and twigs underfoot were new to them, but passing silently was not, and the challenge of moving noiselessly in the Overlands was similar to that of moving without a sound along the loose, rocky trails of the Underworld. Additionally, the three wore their thick, supple trail boots, which were especially absorbent of noises underfoot. They stole forward until they were just beyond the closest trees to the encampment, at which point Sundra motioned her companions to stop. Each took a position behind a tree while Sundra assessed when best to step forth.

The scene before them was much like the one that they had met the first time they had encountered Vedel and his ragged band. Still as disreputable, still of the same questionable loyalty, still as ill-disciplined as last time. Unexpected though was that their count seemed about the same. Hadn't the Sebastas said there would be more? The others must be patrolling? Kobemy guessed they were, rather than lying in ambush and positioned the hilt of his short, supple sword so as to draw readily and easily. Not that it would necessarily matter much if they were, he knew, grimly. Yet he would make sure—and he knew Maribess would as well—that they would feel some sting first.

There was a discreet signal from the Sebastas. They were to advance and disclose themselves.

The three stepped toward Vedel, the leader, who started unconsciously. Recovering quickly, he waved to them and called, if with a lack of conviction which belied his assurance, "There ya are! I was wondering where ya might have gotten on ta!"

Sundra stopped some distance from the fire Vedel always seem to keep burning. "We are here as agreed."

"Huh! Speakin' of promises, didja bring what you promised?"

Sundra reached into her tunic and produced a grey-and-black pouch, silver piping edging the seams. She held it out in her hand, as if inviting him to take it.

Vedel hesitated, as if he expected Sundra to step toward him to surrender it. But she remained motionless, her arm half-outstretched. He scowled and moved forward himself to take it. With a swift sweep of his hand, he snatched it from her palm then opened it and poured its contents into his hand. The pile glinted a dull yellow in the firelight. Vedel examined it carefully, flicking bits of it with an index finger. Then he looked up, suppressing a wolfish smile. "An' the rest?"

Sundra regarded him calmly, blankly.

"The rest!"

"That is the amount we agreed on. All of it."

Vedel readied a retort then thought better of it. "Huh! Hopes you got more of it where this came from! In that underground city of your'n."

Sundra nodded placidly. "And the rest of yours? As you promised?"

"Ya. Tomorrow morning. You'll see 'em."

"Very well. We start our search tomorrow then."

"By the Light, We Know Our Friends"

Vedel was speaking. "There," he grunted, as he motioned into the distance. "Got it?"

The semi-circle of men gathered around him muttered that they had.

"Good. So's, tonight. When the moon's up. So's we kin see. And ta really make 'em confused an' scared!"

There was a general mumble of assent and Vedel dismissed them, leaving only Sundra behind. She approached him and lowered her voice. "What is the purpose of this operation?" she demanded.

"Huh? 'Purpose'? Why's, what's the worry 'bout that?"

Sundra lowered her voice further but kept it level. "This operation. That you plan for this night."

Vedel stared into Sundra's face. Behind those glass disks she nearly always wore lurked the two pale eyes he had seen only a few times. He disliked the goggles, as they made it much more difficult to read what she might really be thinking.

On second thought, he realized as he stared into those impenetrable circles, maybe he preferred the goggles. Better to see the flat, blank disks than her near-white eyes. Gave him the creeps, their pallor, he had once confided to a lieutenant. As if they had been leached of all color, like she was some sort of walking corpse.

Besides, she being from the Underworld, it was about impossible to understand her anyway.

"'T'sa'n operation. 'S't's all it is."

Sundra regarded Vedel carefully. Vedel was a nuisance, and a worsening one at that. Their agreed objective was to locate the Crown of Light, and the operation planned for the upcoming dark cycle would seem to have nothing to do with that. How could a small village bordering a forest harbor such a crown of story and fable?

"With what purpose in mind?"

Vedel grunted and turned away. "Food. Mainly. Huh. Got's ta have that, right? Seein' as there hasn't been any munny comin' from your Unnerworld, and we got's ta eat somethin'."

Sundra considered this explanation. While Vedel was untrustworthy, she granted some minimal truth on this one occasion to what he was saying. About the requirement for food only, though. "So. Money comes for results. As you know. And regarding information or artefacts related to our objective."

Vedel resisted the temptation to expectorate. "Our objective!" Huh! More talk of art-i-fax and such. But where were the promised Underworld money and armies? "Men's got ta eat," he said at last. "An' if we don' have enny money ta buy no food, we hav' ta take it from wherever's we can fin' it." He hardly knew what the Underworlders ate. He had seen them once eating what—for all the world—looked like mushrooms and similar that you might find in decaying logs. It was very strange, he and his men thought: they never seemed to want a fire to cook a proper spit-roasted animal. It was almost as if, half the time, they lived on darkness itself!

Sundra frowned. Feeding Vedel's men was a secondary consideration; the crown came first. Still, she understood that the second was intended to be located by the first. Her concern was that brazen, large-scale operations within Brythrony, where the ruins of Sislin lay, must eventually provoke retaliation. Sundra did not want such a distraction. If Vedel wanted to wage a war later, when she had the crown in hand and was invincible, so be it. But not on her time.

Sundra had tried to explain to the simpleton Vedel the necessity of discretion, and that the rewards would be great for him when the crown was located but, while he would seem to indicate understanding, his behavior never changed. This had to be, she had concluded, because Vedel was too stupid to really grasp the import of the crown and its powers.

"When is Sislin to be explored? I ask this again. For I will go myself, as I have learnt how to ride these horses of your Overland."

Vedel suppressed a sneer. It was on the coast, and they were at the opposite border of Brythrony. Impossible for her to ride there on her own. "Got's several my bes' goin' there now. Through the forests an' fields. Should be there 'bout very soon."

Sundra reflected. She detested Vedel more with every passing cycle and probably would have had him executed many times over by now if she hadn't still had a use for him. Such an end could still come to him, she promised herself. But not yet. "Very well. I look forward to their report.

And," she added, pausing meaningfully, "with this operation you plan: do what you like, but do not attract too much attention. Do not run needless risks."

"I's jus' fer food!" Vedel called after the departing Sundra. "Don' chu min' at all! We'll be real quiet like!" She didn't turn back to acknowledge the mock reassurance. Vedel stared another moment after her then chuckled sarcastically to himself. Some day soon he would be rid of this weird Underworld princess. But not before he had received the full compensation he more than deserved for having had to deal with her.

King Childeric, King of Brythrony, was conferring with his counsellors and Captain of the Guards Valandal in the reception hall. They were gathered about the king on his throne yet retained a respectful distance. "But is there not always banditry, everywhere, at all times, as deplorable as that may be?" he asked.

His captain agreed. "Yes, Your Majesty. At all times. And in spite of our regular patrols. But these most recent instances have been something different entirely. They have been more organized, more daring, and far more destructive than others."

The king frowned. "In what way?"

"Your Majesty, just two days ago, a village near the Great Forest was razed. The raid was unusually coordinated and complete and clearly carried out by a sizable force. Bandits keep to the most remote fastnesses of the forests and prey on solitary travelers. Of course, occasionally, they will emerge to steal livestock and such, but then they come as pairs, or maybe several. No, this was much more than that, and it was calculated. And thorough."

"We could search the Great Forest for them?"

The captain shook his head. "Not possible, Sire. It's too deep and dark; there are too many places for them to hide. For us to be ambushed as well."

The king drummed his fingers. "So, they've attacked a village. What else?"

Captain Valandal nodded. "This is the third. This instance was particularly bold, as they put the village to the torch and even battled with the town's constabulary. Whereas, with the other two, they simply stole some livestock, most probably out of hunger."

"We must not allow this to happen again," insisted Donton, tottering up to the throne. He was one of the king's eldest advisors, and he spoke in a thin, reedy voice that was not much above a whisper. The others strained to listen. "This will not do! The people look to Your Majesty for protection, and if they feel they do not receive it, there will be vigilantism and organized resistance! Who knows where that could lead? No, we must deal with these bandits, and decisively!"

A younger counsellor, with a voice more suave but equally insistent agreed, adding, "Your Majesty certainly owes his loyal subjects his protection. But, in addition, the bolder, more organized nature of these attacks suggests another power may be behind them. Perhaps a neighboring entity, interested in assessing our reaction, is using these bandits as a kind of cat's paw. To test us, but to retain deniability as to their responsibility."

The king nodded at that. That thought too had crossed his mind. If true, it was a very unfortunate development. "Mortain? Could it be? Causing problems for us again, after all these years?"

"Perhaps, Your Majesty." The Kingdom of Mortain had been a headache in the past for Brythrony, and, meaningfully, it was on the other side of the Great Forest. It was Mortain, in fact, that had not so very long ago invaded Brythrony and even reached the walls of Stonedell before being turned back in a climactic battle. Mortain had been quiet of late, as it grappled with internal questions of succession, but perhaps those had been sorted out more completely than Childeric's intelligence had discovered. Or perhaps these bandits were prompted by that internal struggle.

"Yes, perhaps Mortain is behind this. Organizing and equipping the bandits. And then sending them toward us, perhaps to cause problems, perhaps to distract. But it doesn't matter. Whichever it is, or neither, we must deal with them decisively."

Childeric paused and frowned as he thought hard, his fingers very slowly drumming the arm of his throne. "Yet we cannot send our army to search for bandits who melt into the woods at the first show of force. That would render us vulnerable to attack from elsewhere.

"Captain, how about a small show of force in the area where they were last seen? To reassure the population and to prove we are alert?"

"Absolutely, Your Majesty! A small contingent, perhaps thirty men. That should be enough."

"Who will you choose to lead it? Someone intelligent, trustworthy, but brave!" urged Donton, his voice rising in pitch as if in insistence.

"I have just the person," replied the captain resolutely, and without a moment's further thought. "Brevet Guard's Captain Rohanic. He's trustworthy and brave and well liked. I know we can count on him."

Childeric nodded. Rohanic had performed with exceptional bravery in escorting his daughter in Sea Sprit and, later, rescuing her from the pirates. He could be trusted. "Very good. I think he's a sound choice. Are there any objections to this course of action?" There were none. "Any other thoughts?"

"Only this," piped up Donton. The others again found themselves leaning toward him to hear. "Rohanic and his contingent must be conspicuous and gallant with the villagers to show that Your Majesty cares. But, with the bandits, he must be ruthless and unyielding." This much seemed obvious, and there was no comment on this recommendation. "Still, he should try to bring one of them back, if he can. There may be much to learn if we can capture one alive."

Childeric agreed and, indicating as such to the Captain of the Guards, issued the formal orders to send Rohanic at once to that area the bandits had most recently depredated.

In the darkness, toward the very rear of the hall, Tara's mind was aflame. She had been passing through the reception hall on her way to visit Daystar when she had heard the conferring voices of her father and his counsellors. It had sounded important. Intrigued, she had paused to listen, then crept closer to catch every word (save that of Counsellor Donton, whose voice was difficult to hear even standing beside him), secreting herself behind one of the many columns marching down the length of the hall. The longer she had listened, the more amazed she had become. The more amazed she had become, the more her mind had whirled.

Bandits. Banditry. In Brythrony. And, very probably, the Kingdom of Mortain behind it! She knew well of the tremendous battle that had been fought against Mortain at the very walls of Stonedell, knew the story by heart. It was the story she had heard from her mother a dozen times, the one in which her grandmother, Queen Ysolde, had stridden the ramparts herself to fend off the invaders! Now, Mortain again threatened Brythrony and was using the bandits of the Great Forest to cause havoc in advance.

Tara stole out of the hall quickly and hid around a corner before Valandal made his way back down the hall to the barracks. She panted silently as he passed. Banditry. Mortain. It had to be stopped. But who would stop it? There was no Queen Ysolde to rally Stonedell's valiant defenders. She loved her mother, but she could hardly imagine Armorica handling this. She would be far too concerned about her hair, or badinage. Her father, Childeric, was of course a veteran of many campaigns, but maybe he was getting old for this sort of thing. Might it fall to her, Princess of the Realm Tara, to save the kingdom? It might. Her heart leapt to her mouth. The idea was crazy, madness. But who else? How else?

Tara exhaled a silent, dramatic sigh. It would have to be her. There simply was no one else. But she would need help. No, not from Rohanic or Valandal or any of the guardsmen, however brave and battle-trained they may be. From Ariel and Marina. Maybe Flo too. Only they, together, could save Brythrony. Tara dashed back up to her suite in the North Tower and immediately pulled the message vial from her princess purse. She had three messages to send.

"Tara? Tara?" The voice was firm and the knock insistent. "Tara?" It was her mother, Queen Armorica.

Tara jumped in surprise, then scuttled about the room collecting herself. The princess purse she was holding! Her mother couldn't see it! Where to hide it? Under the bed! No, what if she were to forget where she had put it? Some place obvious, but in plain sight, that would not attract overt attention. Like over the back of the chair. No, too obvious! But where? Of course: back where it belonged, in the top drawer of her chest of drawers!

Tara whipped open the door just as her mother was about to knock again even more loudly and insistently. "Oh! There you are!"

"Yes, please, Mom! Here I am." Tara clasped her hands behind her back and smiled innocently.

Her mother had seen that smile before. "Tara, what are you doing?"

Tara widened her eyes, as if in surprise.

"What's in your hands?"

"Nothing!"

"Tara!"

"But Mom!—"

"Show them to me!"

Reluctantly, Tara brought them around, clenched. Her mother looked down at them then gazed sternly into Tara's face. "What have you got in them? Don't play games with me!" she warned.

Tara opened them slowly and with almost painful unwillingness. There was nothing in them.

Armorica started and stared down intently. Why, her hands were indeed empty! Absolutely empty! Yet Tara had acted like she had been hiding something. Yet, she clearly wasn't. How very, incredibly strange…!

Tara hid a smile. Her mother had thought Tara had been trying to keep something secret. Well, she had been. Only, it was a thought, an image, rather than a physical object. Tara was still seized by the thought of being the savior of Brythrony, riding gloriously astride Daystar to its rescue, popular acclaim ringing in her ears, her three friends grandly accompanying her. Though how she saw Marina keeping up with her and the others, needing as she did water in which to swim, she kept vague in her imagination.

Armorica shook her head. Her daughter was impossible to understand at times. "Tara, your father and I have been talking." She paused, thinking Tara might have a response, but Tara said nothing. "We've been talking. We think it would be a good idea if you and I were to ride out to one of the nearby towns and pay a visit. A town like the one that recently experienced—" Armorica caught herself. Tara didn't know about the bandits and the disaster that had befallen one of the towns on the frontier near the Great Forest. Best not to alarm her unnecessarily or cause all sorts of needless consternation.

"Yes, Mom?"

"A town like the one that recently experienced a disaster. A disaster. A fire. Leaving many people homeless. Tomorrow morning."

Her mother was obviously referring to the town the bandits had attacked. But that town was at the edge of the Great Forest; were they really going to ride all the way out there? It was several days away, and her mother disliked travelling that far by carriage. Wait, though: hadn't she said LIKE a town that had suffered the disaster? "A town like the one that experienced a fire? But this town—itself—hasn't suffered a fire?"

"Yes. That's it. To show we care."

Tara hesitated in confusion. She and her mother were to visit a town that was perfectly whole and fine to show a town elsewhere that had suffered a disastrous fire that the kingdom cared? That didn't make any sense. Then Tara understood what her mother was really trying to say but perhaps couldn't because of niceties over the word "bandit": that they would visit a town like the one that had been raided to show they would defend it if it were attacked. To signal to all Brythrony, whether urban dwellers or rural folk, that no one would be abandoned to these highwaymen. Tara nodded her agreement. "Sure, Mom. I'm happy to join you. Let's go." Now it made sense. Queen Ysolde would have done this. Besides, it might be useful to see what a similar-sized town was like, in case it fell to Tara and her friends to defend it.

Another surprise. Armorica had expected resistance, as this was the sort of visit that Tara loathed as "princessing." "Why, that is lovely, dear! Thank you!"

"Sure, Mom. Tomorrow morning. Let's leave early too."

The next morning, early, Armorica and Tara were rolling toward the not-too-distant village of Memnal, escorted by a squad on horseback. The village was close enough to Castle Stonedell that no trouble was expected. Still, Queen Armorica was worried. "Be careful, Tara. Don't be too ostentatious and attract attention!"

"But Mom, we're going to Memnal to offer support and comfort. We have to be visible to the villagers to do that!"

This was true, Armorica knew, and she assented glumly. But she didn't like it. She knew it was her duty, as queen, to represent royal concern and protection, but it was her least favorite duty. She sighed. She recollected that her mother, Queen Ysolde, had relished it, but Armorica, now being privately frank, disliked it. It made her agitated. It could be dangerous. Why couldn't Childeric handle that sort of thing? But he was busy planning a military operation against the bandits, or making contingency plans, or something along those lines. She sighed again. Therefore, she had to—simply had to—do the consolation duties.

She glanced across the carriage at her daughter, who was raptly interested in the surrounding countryside rolling by. Tara didn't seem to mind at all. Even liked it, maybe. Probably because it wasn't the usual "princessing" sort of event. Rather than the usual elaborate coiffure, and to highlight the sombreness of the reason for the visit, they had simply gathered her hair back and left it at that. Tara had even brushed it, once or twice, Armorica had noted. Then, for perhaps the first time ever, Tara had even been waiting at the carriage at the appointed hour of departure. Well, it was for a good cause, Armorica reminded herself, turning back to her own window. It was duty. To console. She must bear up, she told herself yet another time. She must set the good example for Tara.

Tara hadn't minded at all. Armorica was right that Tara was glad to be able to dress simply for once. She hadn't even needed Sullijee's help to get ready, donning a brown Sussex round smock, plain except for some intricate embroidery in indigo and sky blue upon the collar, cuffs, and at the shoulders. Of course, she had had to wear the white sash of royalty, but that was kept narrow and devoid of ornamentation. No fancy shoes, no tiara, no required jewellery.

More significantly though, Tara believed this was an important journey. Tara knew enough about her grandmother to know that this was the sort of activity her grandmother would have embraced, reassuring the people and taking stock of the situation. Possibly preparing last-ditch defenses. This was why, unbeknownst to anyone, Tara had taken one piece of jewellery: her grandmother's ring. Tara fingered it in her lap, so discreetly even her mother didn't notice. What would Ysolde be thinking and doing? Reviewing with an expert eye the village, its fighting readiness, its strategic position, and so many other important considerations. Tara would do the same, even if it was unlikely Memnal would ever be attacked, since it lay so far from the Great Forest. On the other hand, who could say? Hadn't Mortain reached the very gates of Stonedell in its previous effort, not so many years before?

Yes, this was important. Saving the people of Brythrony, that was queenly, Ysolde-y stuff. Tara had faced challenges and problems before, but on those occasions only her own interests had been at stake. Maybe with the exception of the time she had inadvertently summoned the water sprite. But aside from that! No, this time all Brythrony was threatened. And again, as in her grandmother's time, by their archenemy Mortain.

The carriage and its escort rolled into Memnal before the sun was directly overhead. Tara was out of the carriage and surveying the small crowd that had gathered to meet them before the footman had been able to open the door. Most of them looked too old or young to fight. Heaven help them if Mortain penetrated this far into Brythrony! Still, and just in case, should they not be readying some form of resistance? Where were those of a fighting age, men and women alike? Could they really be still out in the fields when battle might be close at hand?

Armorica came around to join her daughter. "Stay close, Tara. Not too far away from the escort!" she murmured.

This advice Tara ignored. Who was the leader of this village, she wondered, boldly stepping toward the crowd, and what was the progress so far in erecting defensive earthworks?

Her eyes focused on the broader surroundings, she nearly stumbled into an elderly lady in a nearly threadbare, though carefully pressed, apron. "Your Highness!" she stuttered and affected a slightly lopsided curtsy, one hip being not as limber as the other.

Tara stepped back, startled, and refocused her eyes. "Your pardon, please!"

"Your Highness! Beggin' *Your* pardon, most surely!" The old woman grasped the hem of her dress and unsteadily attempted a better rendition of the curtsy, the second not much more successful than the first.

"What's this, Princess Tara?" demanded Armorica, addressing her daughter formally, as she always did in public. "Who is this?"

"Um! Mother! I mean, Your Majesty! Just, just speaking with… one of our subjects!"

Armorica joined her daughter and stared hard into the careworn face turned up toward her. "Yes? Who is this?"

Face-to-face with not just one member of the royal family, but two, and those being the queen and her daughter, the elderly lady began to quail. "Beg-beg-beg… beggin'!—"

"Princess Tara, what are you doing? We're here to see the village. To tour it and offer sympathy and hope!"

Tara's heart thawed. Maybe the village was far enough from the Great Forest to not need defensive earthworks, not yet. Maybe work in the field was the better use of their time, just now. Certainly, between readying defensive fortifications and comforting the subjects, this must be the moment for the latter. "Yes, Your Majesty, just so. May I have a moment, please?" Tara turned back to the peasant. "Madam, have no fear, but speak up, please. Tell me, where do you live?"

The crone babbled and gestured in the direction of one of the nearby thatched huts. Tara sized it up. It was small and mean, and in some disrepair, but it was home and kept out the wind and rain. She turned back. "And a lovely home it is too. You've lived there maybe all your life?"

The peasant bobbed her head in a series of affirmatives.

"Tara, shall we tour the village?" queried her mother impatiently and in a tone more of command than enquiry.

Instead of answering, Tara took a step closer to the trembling woman and looked deep into her grey eyes and lined face. She didn't live in a grand house, and she wasn't of aristocratic lineage, but she was a subject of Brythrony nonetheless. Just like everyone else, she deserved protection, rich and poor, powerful and powerless.

Tara clenched her grandmother's ring in her fist, tightly enough for her palm to feel each facet. Maybe it had been for someone similar that Ysolde had manned the battlements of Stonedell at that final, climactic battle. Not to inspire the archers at the merlons, not to encourage the halberdiers at the gates, and not even for the glory of her royal family, huddled below in the reception hall. But simply to defend the plain, common folk, such as this elderly lady, who were helpless before the sinister, grasping Mortain.

"Tara! At last? Can you be ready now?"

"Yes, Your Majesty. I'm ready." Tara bid farewell to the quivering old lady with a murmured thanks and stepped back to join her mother.

"Really! At last! Must you make every one of these outings so difficult? Now, come along," she continued. "We must go see the leaders of this village and explain that Brythrony is quite aware of the needs of all of its cities and villages and that We shall respond immediately if and when there should be a need!"

Tara agreed wordlessly with a nod and fingered again her grandmother's ring, now secreted once more in the folds of her smock. She was glad to have visited Memnal. She had been wondering what her grandmother would have been thinking and doing, and now she knew. The thoughts of Queen Ysolde would have been on the most vulnerable—and what steps she should be taking next to protect them.

Ariel returned Tara's message first, while Tara was out riding Daystar late that afternoon. The bubble caught up with her as she was at one of the many ancient apple trees in an abandoned orchard. The trees were still in fruit and Daystar before long found a branch low enough to contentedly munch an apple directly from a branch. That's fresh all right, commented Tara to herself, happy for her horse. She reached out her hand when she took note of the bubble hovering beside her. It settled silently in her palm and, blowing on it gently, she heard:

"Bandits! Now organized? How awful! Of course, I can help. Let me steer Cloud Castle over Brythrony and see if I can see anything from up above. I'll let you know what I find."

Perfect, thought Tara. No one else had aerial surveillance like Ariel. She might not be able to see into the depths of the Great Forest, but if they roamed abroad, outside it, in any force, Ariel would be sure to spot them. Or her birds would. Come to think, they couldn't even hide in the Great Forest, as no matter how deep they might venture, her birds would surely find them—why, they wouldn't even know they should be hiding from birds!

The second was from Flo later that evening, as Tara was getting ready for bed. "Let me know how I can help, Tara. The only thing is that I need it to be a little bit colder for me to be comfortable—you know how I am like that. But it's getting on toward autumn there and that makes it easier for me. Stay in touch!"

That was about all that she could expect from Flo, acknowledged Tara. It wasn't like Flo was magical or anything; she needed chillier temperatures to be at her best. Tara smiled. Well, Flo WAS magical, yes! But still she needed the cold. Otherwise, she came across as exhausted and unable to think straight. By the same token, the colder the temperature was, the quicker and the livelier she was.

Marina replied the next morning, also offering her help but reminding that she needed water of suitable depth to join.

Three days later, Tara stood with her mother and father at the top of the steps leading from the courtyard to the reception hall. Behind them were the great double doors of the castle, emblazoned with the arms of the royal House of Hession. Armorica and Childeric thought this location made a suitable location for viewing the courtyard where, traditionally, official arrivals and departures took place. A small formation of courtiers and palace officials stood respectfully to the side, listening as Childeric addressed a company of guards, Rohanic at their head, formed and equipped to address the bandits of the Great Forest. Others watched from windows and doorways.

"Brythrony looks to you for its protection," intoned King Childeric, in his best speaking voice and using the court accent expected on such occasions. "Our subjects look to you for their safety. This safety is threatened by the lawless brigands haunting our forests and glades and inflicting terror and fear on the innocent! Go now and bring back whatever information you may that will defend our kingdom, your families, and all the people of Brythrony from this threat to peace and security!"

A cheer rose. Rohanic bowed, raised his arm in a salute and, on cue from a motion from Valandal, set his prancing horse in motion. The thirty guardsmen behind him, plus the baggage cart, started forward and, minutes later, passed through the castle gates to further cheers from those waving them off.

"I expect Rohanic and his men will deal with those bandits," King Childeric said confidently to his queen and daughter as they watched the trailing baggage cart pass through the gates. "They may be fierce and they may overawe village constabularies, but Rohanic leads a well-trained and well-armed military force."

Tara nodded in agreement, not reminding him of the possibility that the bandits may be tools of Mortain and so may be reinforced. She knew she wasn't supposed to know this.

Another message came later that afternoon, as Tara was curry-combing Daystar. What she heard greatly agitated her. "Tara! I've found a huge encampment of bandits; I guess, maybe, several hundred! I've got them under surveillance by night by owls and by day by woodpeckers; I also have a couple of hawks circling overhead just in case. Anyway, it looks like they are preparing to do something. Something serious!"

Tara stood stock still as the voice of her friend died away. Several hundred! That sort of force had to have been organized by Mortain. Had to have been! And what about Rohanic and his company of thirty? They'd be crushed! Tara patted Daystar absentmindedly as her thoughts churned. How was she to warn Rohanic? How was she to tell her father and mother, when, in doing so, she would have to reveal who Ariel was? They'd never believe her, never.

Tara stood vacillating for the next several minutes. Finally, she took a step to the tack wall to hang up the comb, deciding that she absolutely had to warn her father about the far superior force Rohanic would be facing.

She stopped after one step. She couldn't do that. No one would believe her. Why, it would require her father to believe she had a flying friend who could communicate with birds. No, she'd be put to bed immediately and a doctor called!

But if she didn't, wouldn't Rohanic and his force be wiped out?

Oh, but it wasn't certain that Rohanic and his men would be

slaughtered, she reminded herself. This was because Rohanic might encounter just some of the bandits rather than all of them at the same time. Also, Rohanic and his force were trained, as her father had remarked, whereas the bandits were surely not.

Meanwhile, telling her mother and father about Ariel would have to mean explaining how she had met her. This would lead to telling them about Marina too. She sighed. They would be scandalized and frightened that their daughter had eaten seaweed from a strange mermaid and then swum to an underwater castle, flown up the side of a cliff held only in the arms of a winged woman, and so much more. Her parents would be so upset they would probably never let her out of their sight again. Then all her adventures would be over. Tara was suddenly sick with the thought of that, of never seeing her friends again. She would never see anyone her age again, outside of the hateful Season. No fun, ever again. Just badinage and having her hair dressed. By Sullijee. Tara's shoulders sagged.

Tara stroked Daystar's coat a few more times with the comb as she struggled a little longer with her conscience, then decided she would wait to say anything. At least for a little bit. And, maybe she might hear something more from Ariel. She smoothed Daystar's mane then hung the comb back in its place on the wall. "Sorry, boy. No ride today. My mind's just not on it. I've got to keep thinking about what to do next."

Daystar whinnied and tossed his head. How sweet, thought Tara as she closed the stable door behind her. He never complained and was always so understanding. She headed back to the castle for no particular reason and found herself just wandering from room to room.

That night, at dinner, her mother asked her if she was all right. "Yes, Mom," she replied, simply, and, before long, excused herself, even before dessert.

"I'm not sure she's all right," Armorica said to her husband when Tara was gone.

"I'm sure she's fine," he replied. "Just thinking of something or another.

"Meantime," he continued, frowning, "I've had other reports of still bolder raids on other villages near the Great Forest." He looked at Armorica but through her rather than at her. "I expect Rohanic to arrive in the area tomorrow and begin scouting. We need to put a stop to this!"

In her bedroom in the North Tower, Tara was whispering into a bubble in the palm of her left hand. "Hey, Ariel! Sorry to bother, but how many are there now out there? I mean, those bandits causing all sorts of problems. Are there more? Or, maybe, have some gone away? What are they doing? Can you tell me what's happening?" Tara thought for another moment but couldn't think of anything else, so she whispered Ariel's name to the bubble and puffed it away with a soft breath. Off it floated through the open window into the night. Tara turned back to her bedroom. She had hardly been coherent. She must have sounded like she couldn't think straight. Maybe she couldn't. Why couldn't she? Tara stared into the mirror on her vanity and into the face, her face, that looked back. Was she not able to think straight?

No, replied the face silently to her. You can't.

Why? she asked.

The eyes in the mirror stared directly back into her own. Because you are worried about the thirty-one men who might be going to their doom, and you, Tara, might be the only person who can avert this.

But my friends, she reminded herself, desperately. I'd have to explain all that, all about them!

The face in the mirror had no answer for her. Not, at least, one Tara wanted to hear.

Tara awakened the next morning after a fitful night. She had had dreams, but she couldn't remember any of them except to recollect that none had been particularly pleasant. She was hungry but reluctant to go down to breakfast. Instead, and to stall, she decided to brush her hair, which she did until it glossed a brilliant, shining, chestnut brown. The whole time, she studiously avoided looking at the face in the mirror. Only when she put the brush down did she catch sight, again, of her reflection. It seemed to glare back at her in silent accusation.

"I don't know how I'll explain," Tara pleaded with it.

The image's answer slowly formed in her mind. Your friends won't mind however you explain them. That's because they're your friends. It is more important that you tell your parents what you know than it is to keep the nature of your friends a secret.

"But they'll never believe me!" answered Tara, an image of her parents' outrage swimming before her. Yet, this time she didn't need an answer from her reflection. She knew already that she would have to make them believe her. She had to. And if they didn't, despite her best efforts? Well, they'd believe for sure when they got word that Rohanic and his men had been wiped out.

No, she had to say something right away. The lives of thirty-one faithful, unsuspecting guardsmen could depend on it.

Tara darted from the room and raced down the stairs. She encountered her mother still at the breakfast table. Her father wasn't there. "Hi, Mom. Where's Dad?"

"Well, good morning to you! You're up late! Say, hey! Your hair looks fabulous this morning; you brushed it!"

"Yes, Mom. Where's Dad?"

"Well! I suppose he went out to inspect the orchards. Or the gardens, or some place like that."

Tara thanked her and immediately left, without pausing to reply to her mother's voice demanding that she return to explain her inexplicably impolite behavior.

"Dad, I've got to talk to you," she said immediately on finding him at the castle's granary, as it turned out, and only after asking several palace servants and searching, in succession, the orchard, the vegetable garden, the reception hall, and even the scullery, where he never went.

"Of course, dear. As soon as I finish reviewing these accounts."

Tara waited a few minutes, fidgeting, then interrupted again. "Dad, today. Can I talk to you today? Now?"

"Tara, what is up with you? Can't you see I'm busy? Can you wait just a little? I'm almost done."

Tara heaved a great sigh and focused on what she was going to say to her father, to put the time to good use. Come to think of it, she hadn't decided what she was going to say to him, she had been in such a rush to find him. Tara considered. She'd have to mention Ariel. But maybe not Marina. Not yet. And not Flo, or her sister Crystal who, after all, she had only met by an ice shard Flo had shown her.

Her father broke into her thoughts by addressing her. "Yes, Tara, now. What is it? Please, I'm listening to you."

"Um, could we step outside, please?"

Her father obligingly stepped outside into the sunlight, though clearly perplexed at the request. "What is so sensitive that we have to confer in private?" he asked.

Tara bit her lip and shuffled her feet. "Uh, it's about, well, about…"

Her father said nothing, instead assuming an exaggerated look of enquiry.

Tara sighed again. "Rohanic. It's about Rohanic."

"What about Rohanic? Oh, are you worried about him?"

"No, not about that! I mean, yes, about that! I mean, all of them. Because they'll be ambushed!"

"What do you mean?"

"They'll be ambushed! They'll be far outmatched, because there are hundreds of bandits! They'll be wiped out!"

Childeric furrowed his brows and stared down at Tara. "Why on earth do you think this? How could you know? Tara, what has gotten into you?"

Tara took a deep breath. "I'm sorry, but I overhead you the other day in the reception hall. With Valandal. And the others. The bandits. Well, there are lots of them, many more than we—you—thought. Hundreds more!"

Childeric angrily seized his daughter by the shoulder and pulled her around the corner out of sight of the workers in the granary, who were pretending not to notice what was happening but very clearly were listening as closely as they dared. "Were you eavesdropping on my private councils? These are matters of state!"

"No! I wasn't eavesdropping! Not on purpose! I just happened to overhear. While I was passing by on my way to the stables to visit Daystar!"

"What did you hear? Exactly?"

Tara explained that she had heard about the bandits that had gathered, their raids on some of the villages, and that some suspected they were organized by the Kingdom of Mortain to cause chaos and upset in Brythrony. "And Dad, could you let go of my shoulder, please? You're hurting me!"

Childeric let go. He could see and hear that his daughter was telling the truth. Besides, they had all stood together on the steps to the reception hall to send Rohanic and his detachment off; how much more was there to reveal about this mission? Only the suspicion that Mortain was behind it all. And that was just that: a suspicion. "But why do you think Rohanic and his detachment will be ambushed?"

This was the hard part, Tara knew, and as she had always known. "Dad... I've got a friend. A friend who can, well, talk to birds. And they tell her that there are hundreds of bandits in an encampment in the Great Forest. With more coming. She has hawks—and other birds—conducting surveillance on them for me."

Childeric stared incredulously at his daughter and opened and closed his mouth several times in succession as Tara looked back at him pleadingly. Finally, he spoke and in a voice of genuine concern. "Tara, are you well?"

"Dad! I'm telling the truth! All right. Her name is Ariel. My friend's name is Ariel. I met her in Sea Sprit." Tara fumbled for words until she suddenly had an idea. "Do you remember what Rohanic said? That there was a girl who always seemed to be there, urging him on to rescue me? When Jarvis and the pirate captain had me? First in the town, then at the entrance to the house, and then that she had been on the balcony blocking the doors?"

Childeric thought for a moment then nodded slowly. "But you made light of that. You said that he couldn't be right, because no one could have appeared in all those places in such quick succession like he said she did."

"That's true. No ordinary person could have. But Ariel isn't ordinary. She could be everywhere seemingly at once, just like Rohanic said. In the town, at the steps, on the balcony, but then gone when Rohanic went out on the balcony to look for her."

"Because…?"

"Because Ariel has wings. She can fly. And she lives in Cloud Castle, up in the sky, where she talks with birds. She's even now over Brythrony, watching the bandits!"

There. It was done. Tara gasped out the last words, not daring to stop. Her father listened for a wild instant then, unable to resist the impulse, lifted his head and scanned the skies, as if he might find Cloud Castle overhead that very moment, watching them too.

"Tara, that's just… incredible! That's impossible!"

"No! It's true! Do you remember also that Rohanic said that she had showed him my signet ring as proof that I had sent her? I had! I had gone to confront the pirates and Jarvis and sent Ariel down to Rohanic in case I needed help. Which I did. Ariel flew down to Sea Sprit to get him then flew back up again to block their escape through the balcony doors. Rohanic thought she was everywhere at once but it was because she could fly whereas he had to take the road. And now she's over the Great Forest watching the bandits. She's just told me that there are hundreds of bandits there—Dad, you've got to believe me!"

"But how did she tell you all this? If she is up in some castle in the clouds? Did she send, maybe, a bird?"

Best not to go into the message bubbles just yet. Tara waved her hand as if to dismiss this question as unimportant detail. "Dad, you've just got to believe me. Rohanic and his guardsmen won't have a chance against hundreds of bandits, no matter how well trained they are. There are just too many! They'll be crushed!"

Childeric considered his daughter for a very long, astonished moment. This story about a flying friend who could talk to birds and floated around in the clouds was simply fantastical. Yet, it did offer an explanation, however incredible, for the amazing sequence of events of that day in Sea Spirit, which were otherwise inexplicable and had baffled the level-headed Rohanic. Well, maybe it was possible that some part of what his daughter had told him was true. But what was definitely possible was that there could be many more bandits than they had thought and that Rohanic was indeed walking into a terrible trap. Defeat was intolerable, Childeric knew; terrible for that detachment, terrible for his Guard's morale, terrible for Brythrony's prestige, and terrible in that it would embolden the bandits.

"Very well," responded Childeric slowly. "I don't know about your flying friend Ariel. But I will take your warning seriously. I'll send reinforcements. Immediately. Lives I don't want to lose could be in the balance."

Tara heaved a grateful sigh. "Thanks, Dad. For believing me. If only part of the way."

Childeric shook his head in bewilderment. "We'll see," was all he could say. How could he be upset with his daughter? She truly believed what she was saying. Either she was right, and Childeric should be tremendously grateful, or she had lost her mind and couldn't be blamed anyway. "We'll see. I will summon Valandal to determine who else he can send."

Another detachment, and one more akin to a rescue mission rather than reinforcements, departed the next morning. It was the soonest they could be mustered, equipped and instructed. Valandal had enquired in several ways how Childeric had come by his intelligence that Rohanic would encounter a far superior force than expected, but Childeric had declined to answer. But orders were orders, so Valandal had assembled another detachment, which took the same route as Rohanic, though there was scant hope of overtaking them, given their two-day head start.

Another two days later, the rescue detachment returned but with only a few of the original thirty-one. These were the ones who had managed to escape. The confrontation with the bandit invaders had been over in minutes, as, surrounded, they had had to surrender.

Tara had already known of this, of course. She had received a message bubble conveying a bare account of what had happened from Ariel. Ariel had assembled this as best she could from the sometimes-conflicting reports of her birds. "I can't really say how much of this really occurred, but it's clear that your guards were surrounded and taken prisoner!" was how she had summarized what she had been told.

Tara was despondent. It was just as she had feared. And, though she had warned her father, she had been too late. Rohanic and his men had still been taken prisoner. Now there absolutely was no choice. The guardsmen had to be rescued and the bandits and Mortain stopped. Before they stormed Stonedell and Mortain succeeded where it had failed two generations before.

Though Tara had wanted to depart immediately, she had resolved to stay long enough to get more on Rohanic's encounter with the bandits than Ariel's birds had been able to provide. This came from the most articulate of the escapees from the first detachment, who was brought before Childeric, escorted by Captain Valandal, almost as soon as he was back at Stonedell.

"Yur Mazhesty," began the Guardsman from the first detachment, a brawny swordsman named Saberht. "We wuz set 'pon, no question 'bout it! Most unexpectedly and most distressedly!"

"Go on, please. Tell me what happened."

"Well, like I wuz sayin', we wuz set 'pon. There we wuz, jus' a'ridin along, headin' for the Great Fores', jus' like our orders wuz tellin' us, and it wuz getting' a little darker, I giss, likewise, but GC Rohanic, he wuz wantin' to push on a jus' a li'l further. An' then we wuz a-goin' to stop."

Everyone in the reception hall unconsciously leaned forwards, or sidled a few steps closer, to better make out the words of the swordsman, who spoke in the thick accent of western Brythrony.

"An', an', like I said, that's when we wuz set 'pon!"

"Yes, yes, I understand. But could you give us just a little more detail? As in, how did this transpire? And how many were there? In your estimate!"

"Yes, Yur Mazhesty! 'Course! There we wuz, jus' a-drawin' to a halt, likewise, or mebbe jus' 'bout to, when, alluva sudden, Rohanic, he did, called a halt to us, the whole colum'. An', an', an' so we halted. Jus' like that.

"'Course!" Saberht continued, after a sharp word of prompting from Valandal. "Rohanic gives us the order to form up, form up, he sez, form up! As the way's blocked, an' we needs ta be ready! An', an' so's, Yur Mazhesty, we forms up, and readies our weapons, as that's what 'form up' means, ya seez, likewise."

Childeric urged Saberht to continue with a wave of his hand, maintaining his patience only with supreme effort.

"An' so's, we forms up. I'm on the right flank, as Yur Mazhesty knowz, an' I forms up, with my sword reddy, reddy ta go. An' likewise my fellow guardsmen do too, as ya know. An' Rohanic, he's at the head of th' column. An' I seez to what he's a-referrin' to, when I seez, there in the fallin' light, a large force of what looks like troops. Or like that. An' Rohanic, he forms us up, seez Yur Mazhesty, an' we falls into formation, likewise, but as we duz so, I kin see more of these troop-type-a-people off to me left, and I hears that there's others of 'em, now on the right. An' then I hears that there are still more of them, comin' up, why, jus' behinds us, jus' likewise."

"Could you see how many?" asked Valandal.

"Nossir, no. Nots too well. 'Cause of the fallin' light, ya seez. An' Yur Mazhesty."

"Were they mounted? Or on foot?"

Saberht shook his head. "Wuz hard ta tell. Buts, I think they wuz on foot. Fer the mos' part."

"Did you see their leader? Could you identify him again if you saw him?"

Saberht drew himself up proudly. "I cud seez! I's a-got sharp seein', that's what theys always a-sed 'bout me! So I cud seez. Not, jus', well, seez so well, on 'count a the fallin' light. Yur Mazhesty."

The reception hall fell silent, waiting for Saberht to continue. He coughed once and picked up again, apparently concluding that sufficient suspense had been achieved. "An' I a-heard the leader. We wuz ordered to surrender. Cuz—he sed—we wuz surroun'ned. An' I look'd ta-roun', and it looks as like we wuz a-surroun'ned, likewise. An' sum of us wanted ta fight our way out. Jus' like that. Like a-wise. But yuh cud see, Yur Mazhesty, and Cap'n Val'ndal too, likewise, that we wuz surroun'ned, an' it looked as if by lots a 'em.

"But the funnies' thing 'bout it, wuz—if ya wants to know it?"

"Of course, His Majesty wants to know!" hissed Valandal.

"Well, meanin' no disrispects ta ya, Yur Mazhesty—and Cap'n Val'ndal likewise—but, well, an', the leader of that force didn't look to be verry much of a leader!"

"What do you mean?"

"Yessir. Yessirs. Cuz, he sure was a-slight and willow-like, like he cudn't had much ar-mur on, an' likewise. An', further, the leader's voice: it wuz a-kinda high pitched. Like it wuz a boy a-leadin' 'em. That's it! Like that! Slight, like a boy, and with a-kinda high pitched voice, like a boy! An', an' likewise! Yur Mazhesty!"

Valandal took Swordsman Saberht back to the barracks, promising the king to quiz Saberht for further details on his escape. King Childeric assured Saberht repeatedly that he was a good swordsman, and that it was clear that the detachment of only thirty-one had been surrounded by a force far superior in numbers, and that the prudent thing had been to have done as Rohanic had, which had been to surrender, as nothing could have been gained from such a desperate battle, and, indeed, had there been such a battle, there may well have been no survivors to convey the news of their ambush back to Stonedell. Thus profusely and extravagantly promised that the encounter with the force led by a mere stripling would not detract from the Guards' otherwise unblemished fighting record, he was escorted out, leaving Childeric and his counsellors to confer as to how best to respond to these developments. All agreed though that a more substantial force would have to be mobilized as soon as possible.

As for Tara, she had slipped away as soon as she could into the shadows and thence up to the North Tower. After shutting the door, she pulled open the top drawer in her dresser. She was looking for a ring, a ring set with a sizable, if flawed, ruby and that had once belonged to her grandmother.

Rohanic stamped his foot with impatience behind the stockade within which he and his men had been confined. He was furious with himself, furious for having been caught and surrounded, furious at having no choice for the benefit of his men but to yield. Even if the force that had confronted them had been obviously superior in numbers.

For a wild instant, he had considered trying to fight his way out, but there had simply been too many. They'd have been massacred, he knew, and without taking very many with them. The surrender had been humiliating, but he had swallowed his pride and tried to think only of his men and their welfare, hoping that they might escape later.

His first real, independent command, and it had ended in ignominious surrender.

Rohanic had counted his men as soon as they had been left alone. They had started with thirty, plus Rohanic, but there were only twenty-eight, including him, now. Rohanic had not seen or sensed bloodshed, suggesting that three had escaped. He allowed himself a half-smile for that. If three had escaped, surely one would make it back to Stonedell to tell their story.

His thoughts were interrupted by the approach of several persons to the stockade. He could see their forms silhouetted by the flicker of a bonfire behind them and which half-lit the encampment in lurid, leaping shadows.

"Ho!" shouted one. "Who's the leader of ya lot?" It was the man whom Rohanic had overheard referred to as "Vedel" speaking.

Rohanic took a step toward the paling and peered through the narrow gaps between the posts. "I am. Guards' Captain Rohanic." He tried to keep his voice neutral but dignified. It would do no good to pretend defiance, now that they had already surrendered. At the same time, there was no need to truckle and especially not with the other twenty-seven of his men watching closely.

"Aye! Step forward here, to the paling. So's we c'n see ya better!"

Rohanic obligingly stepped up to the paling. Through the gaps he saw four persons standing a short distance away. All were bundled in cloaks for protection against the night chill. The one on Rohanic's left was Vedel, by his voice, though features were nigh indistinguishable in the dim light—probably purposefully so. One in the middle was of shorter stature and much slighter than the remaining two, while the figure on the far right looked to be only slightly less than the same height as Vedel, though, again, it was difficult to determine. "You can see me now?"

"Aye. We c'n see ya. But you c'n stop right there; ya needna' come enny closer!" Vedel guffawed extravagantly at his deprecating jest.

Rohanic didn't deign a reply. Striving to keep his voice even, instead he turned to the topic most on his mind. "The night is growing colder and there is no need for my men to be any more uncomfortable than they are. May I ask that we be allowed the blankets and cloaks from our baggage cart?"

Vedel and the two other figures turned to the fourth between them. There was a pause. Then that figure replied in a voice that, to Rohanic's surprise, was feminine. But the accent was very strange, one he had never heard before. It was even difficult to understand, it was so unusual. "Perhaps. If you will answer my questions."

The woman approached the paling to better examine Rohanic. The two studied each other for a time, and Rohanic saw that she was indeed slenderer than Vedel and the other one beside her. Though slighter and shorter than they, they appeared to defer to her as they would to a superior. With the light from the bonfire behind her, it was hard to make out her features, shadowed as they were. Yet her skin seemed very pale and her hair, where it was not covered by the hood she wore loosely over her head, almost white. About her neck was a strange necklace consisting of two large circular objects strung together by a cord.

Then she stepped back and Rohanic was not able to make out any other features clearly.

Sundra had stepped forward to gauge better this man's mettle. To her eye, he seemed unperturbed by his captivity, or at least wanted to appear that way. He stood tall and confident within the stockade and met her gaze evenly and without hesitation. His men behind him were quiet and watchful, so it was not apparent they were rebellious. Sundra's mouth twitched. This Rohanic may or may not be a problem, she thought to herself, and stepped back to re-join Vedel and Kobemy.

"I will answer completely and truthfully all questions customarily asked of prisoners," replied Rohanic simply to her question from a minute before, still careful to keep his voice neutral in tone and confident.

Kobemy, the figure to the right, took a step closer and tilted his head to one side to better inspect Rohanic through the gaps between the posts. "Where are you from? Who sent you?"

"I am Guards' Captain Rohanic. I command this detachment, and we are guardsmen of the Kingdom of Brythrony. King Childeric of Brythrony sent us."

Brythrony, mulled Sundra. Not a place she knew much of, to be sure. But then, why should she, since she knew so little of the geography and politics of the Overlands. "So. Why did your king send you?"

Rohanic paused, as it was important to be truthful here but also to be circumspect. "King Childeric has learnt of... activity in this area that is to the detriment of the kingdom. He sent us to investigate."

A likely enough story so far, agreed Sundra silently. They had been sent to understand the nature of the recent raids. Vedel's idiot raids. But she knew all this already; she wanted more. Considerably more. "Only twenty-eight of you? This king sent only twenty-eight of you to investigate?"

Good, thought Rohanic. So, their captors had counted his men and had not noticed that three had slipped away. "A detachment of this size was judged to be sufficient to determine the nature of the activity."

How many more could come, wondered Sundra. Stupid Vedel: he and his "operations" had prompted this too-predictable reaction. But there was very little to be done about it now except to try to assess this kingdom's resources. "And you, your men: this is an example of the fighting prowess of Brythrony?"

Rohanic ignored the implied taunt. She was baiting him, goading him, but for why he didn't know. "Why are you and your force disturbing the peace of Brythrony? What do you want?" he asked instead.

Sundra frowned. Why couldn't this simple guard captain, this Rohanic, be more forthcoming? She found torture distasteful, though Vedel would do it for her. But that could come later, if need be. In the meantime, there was another question on her mind. "What does Brythrony know of the Crown of Light? Have you heard of such a thing?"

What could this possibly be, wondered Rohanic. Were this strange woman and these bandits on a treasure hunt? "I know of no such thing; Brythrony has no crown of this nature. If you search for this in Brythrony, you search in vain."

Sundra narrowed her eyes in mounting irritation. He didn't know anything. Or wouldn't talk. Not yet. Fine. She could wait a cycle or two. "It will do you no good to evade my questions. You will talk. In time."

"May we have the cloaks? Please?"

"No. And you must blame yourself for this." She raised her voice so that all within the stockade could hear. "If you are cold, you may blame this Rohanic, this person you call your leader. All he need do is answer a few simple questions. But he will not, for he is contrary. So, for that and only that, you suffer the cold this evening!" With that, she turned back toward the larger group gathered about the bonfire, the other three trailing her. Facing the light from the bonfire, she pulled up around her eyes the pair of darkened glass lenses that had been hanging about her neck. Kobemy and Maribess did the same; the bright firelight, like the daylight, hurt their sensitive eyes, and the lenses ameliorated this greatly.

Sundra turned to Vedel as soon as she judged they were out of earshot of Rohanic. "It was easy to take them prisoner. This Brythrony: they are not to fear at all."

Vedel considered his response. "Well, aye, this 'un a-came easy to us, tha's true. There was less 'n thutty ov 'em. An' we were a lot more. But…" he hesitated, "some of 'em, they can be tough. They'll fight, aye, if it'd a-come to it. I think."

"So. Could there be more coming?"

"Aye. I'd 'magine."

"Are you ready to meet them?"

Vedel eyed Sundra speculatively. "We still have some tricks we kin use, I s'pose. But, what about tha' army a' your'n? Are you bringin' up enny reinforce-a-ments to help?"

Sundra looked away from the firelight. It was very bright, especially at the center. Why did Overlanders require such bright light each night? Didn't they realize that it defeated any ability to see past its circle? "My promise was to provide you with riches. Riches from our mines. Further, our agreement was that, once we had carved out a state from this weak and feeble Kingdom of Brythrony, you would rule it. All I asked for was this Crown of Light, when we found it, and which you assured me was here."

Vedel looked away into the darkness. All his stories about the crown had been only that, just stories, and recounted in the hopes of receiving military support from the Underworld to overthrow Childeric. But these troops didn't sound like they were ever going to show. Meanwhile, Sundra grew ever more irritating. "Huh. We won' never get to no crown or ennythin' if more guardsmen from Brythrony stan' in the way!"

Sundra adjusted her goggles. This fool Vedel could turn on her. This was why she kept Maribess watching at all times as a sort of insurance. "We have seen how they fight. Not at all. They should be easy to overwhelm. Then, this Brythrony can be yours."

Vedel grimaced. He knew Brythrony would not be overthrown so simply. Still, there was always the back-up plan of ransoming her for some of those Underworld mineral riches she was always dangling before him. They'd want their precious princess back, right? It wouldn't be the same as ruling Brythrony, but it would do nicely. He licked his lips in anticipation at the thought.

"Do it now! Just do it!" snarled Ortiki, leaning forward from the throne of Pentenok.

"Yes, Your Lordship!" gasped the Guardsman and dipped slightly with his knee, less than the three quarters required to the Sebasissa and certainly less than the full genuflection due the Sebastas. Ortiki watched him depart, not bothering to mask his irritation. Yes, his orders were being carried out, but he suspected it was only because he ruled by grace of and in the stead of the Sebastas. Not because of he, Ortiki.

He wished to be obeyed by his own authority, not because someone from House Biss had placed him on the throne. What House Biss could grant, it could take away. The Sebastas was out searching the Overlands for some artefact that was supposed to bring light. Ortiki snorted softly. He doubted such a thing existed. But even if she never came back, there were other members of House Biss that would argue their claim to the throne. Surely it was time Ortiki turned his attention to them.

Ortiki slouched back into the thin cushion of the throne. Honestly, it was abominably uncomfortable. He would change that too, and make it nicer to sit in for longer periods.

Oritiki twitched in hesitation, recalling the dark warnings of the Sebastas as she had departed that very Hall. There would be time for that later. When and as it became clearer if the Sebastas would return.

In the meantime, there was state business, of which the most pressing was settling scores that had rankled for years. Ortiki's long memory recalled many. Now was the time to even accounts. Some involved guardsmen with whom he had clashed over the years. Others had to do with Pentenokians who had treated him, he felt, with insolence.

Another aspect of state business was managing the various guilds within the city. To this, two Light Merchants had been by to see him the cycle before. They had come to plead to be left alone, largely. He had told them he would think about it, but that the price would probably be in the form of an increase in the privilege tax. He had said it very slowly and with emphasis. The two—they had called themselves Umber and Mauve—had done a decent act of hiding their surprise, largely by immediately effecting the knee dip. Ortiki took that to mean that they had understood. He liked that. As much as he liked being treated as ruler of Pentenok.

Ortiki wondered, and not for the first time, what the Sebastas had against the Light Merchants. They served a useful purpose, and they had a lot of wealth. Why couldn't some of that come to him? When they had dipped their knees again and begged to be allowed to present it to him personally, Ortiki had smiled. They weren't stupid. Good idea too, handing the extra tax directly to him rather than the treasury.

He still had to deal with certain members of Pentenok's nobility. According to reports Ortiki had received from sources he deemed trustworthy, some of these strata were objecting to the way his guardsmen had dealt with a crowd in Central Square. There had been some sort of demonstration around the ancient stone pillars and podium, where new laws were posted, involving how the new laws were being enforced. Ortiki admitted that the crowd, mostly artistic, counter-cycle types, had been treated roughly, but it had been necessary. Indeed, Ortiki thought they should count themselves lucky. Order had to be maintained, and the crowd had been ordered to disperse. Ortiki wouldn't tolerate his guardsmen being questioned any more than he would tolerate being questioned himself. Had they questioned the Sebastos? Or any of his predecessors? No.

The nobility should be on his side, Ortiki thought, the side of authority. If they weren't, then he should deal with these uppity aristocrats quickly to show that he, not that weak-willed Sebastos Reynam, ruled. Ortiki could settle scores with them too.

Deep underground, beneath the Lothwell Spire, a black pool of water rippled then splashed ever so softly. The time was somewhere near the middle of the third cycle, when the fewest jailors were walking the corridors of this, the lowest level of the dungeons of Lothwell Spire.

The water rippled again and was still.

One jailor was still present, his waist and little more illuminated by a faint light lichen held in one hand in a slotted metal cannister, which jiggled wildly in time with his peculiar halting and shuffling gait. He stopped with a grunt of recollection at one cell and lifted the battered metal can in his grasp to eye level.

"Ho! You there!" He peered within. "You!"

There was an answering remark from within the cell.

"Heh! Ha! So's ya think, eh?"

There was another brief pause for a response.

"Heh. Heh-heh. Well's, we'll all see 'bout that!" The lantern was lowered back to waist height, and the jailor took a few half-steps forward then stopped. The pool of light cast by the lantern revolved a half-circle, indicating that the jailor had turned. "So's ya think. Well's, you jus' won' know. You don' know who I am or where I am. 'Cause ya don' have no light, ya know."

The jailor paused, as if to listen for a reply, but none audible came. He turned back around, muttering, but paused long enough to throw back over his shoulder, "Ha. Tha's right. 'Cause, as ya know, by the light, we know's our friends."

These last words electrified the occupant of the cell. In the darkness, the absolute and utter darkness of his cell, he had had very little communication with anyone. As best he could remember, the only person with whom he had spoken was the same jailor who had just taunted him. He had heard a shout or two of cellmates elsewhere on the corridor and thought he recognized one or two of the voices but could not be sure. But in one of his previous "conversations" with the jailor, he remembered that those very words just uttered had been followed by a visitation from persons who had suggested they could offer liberty. Could that be the code again? "Be strong" they had told him. He steeled himself: he should be strong. Not just in case of release, but in case no one came, as he would be bitterly disappointed.

The captive was not kept waiting long. Soon, the tiniest of glows appeared at the barred window, and a voice whispered, so softly it could barely be heard, "By the light, we know our friends."

Reynam took the three steps to the window, all that was required to cross his cell, and grasped the bars. "Who are you?" he whispered fiercely, straining to see into the darkness beyond, the light lichen having been lowered again.

"Friends, Sebastos. With light. Are you ready?"

"I'm ready!"

There was a slight jingle of metal, and something scraped in the lock at the door. It swung open just enough to let Reynam pass through and to reveal two figures garbed in suits of leathery lavalal, dyed black: swimming gear. "Come, quickly; we have not much time!"

Reynam stepped beyond his cell, glorying in his sudden and unexpected freedom. Then a thought seized him. "Bakide. Lavinia. What of them? They must not suffer on my behalf!"

"Hasten, Sebastos! They are already free and await you!"

"Well done!" breathed Reynam then quickened his pace to a trot to keep up with his rescuers. "How—?" he began but fell silent on a quietening hand motion from one of the pair.

"Patience, Sebastos!" that one hissed. "You will see very shortly!"

Down the corridor they continued at a jog, round several corners, across an intersection, and down another corridor. Then they entered a larger room and abruptly stopped. Reynam saw what looked to be a pool of dark water in the center of the room.

The one who had spoken to him before turned and spoke again. "Sebastos, I am told you can swim. Is this so?"

Reynam nodded wordlessly.

"Very good. With your permission, we will tie this rope about your waist and then again to each of our waists. Then we, the three of us, will lower ourselves—silently—into the pool. We know the way to the surface and, because you will be bound to us, we will take you with us and away from this dungeon.

"Sebastos, is this clear?"

Reynam nodded again.

"Very good. You have only a moment to stretch your lungs, and then you must take the very deepest breath you can…"

Reynam gulped. How far would he have to swim? What if he drowned?

"…and then the two of us," pointing to the other black-garbed figure now hunched over the pool and staring into it, "will dive. And you will follow us."

Reynam nodded a third time. There was no other way. He could not go back to his cell. This was a chance at freedom. It was this or certain and eventual doom in this dungeon. And so it could not matter if this was a trap or not, as there was death behind him, even if moving forward could mean death. Reynam nodded a fourth time but now with the conviction of fatalism. "Yes. I will follow."

The other two exchanged glances, as if to make certain between themselves that he was being truthful. But there was no other way and, increasingly important, there was no time to lose. The other one, who heretofore had not spoken, answered gruffly. "We must dive. Now. And do not cry out as you immerse yourselves."

With that, the first turned back to the Sebastos and genuflected hastily and untidily. "Now is the time, Sebastos. You are ready?"

"Ready."

"For House Biss!" said the one who had spoken gruffly before but this time with an undertone of excitement. "For Sebastos Reynam! For Pentenok!"

With that, the two lowered themselves into the murky pool and Reynam, after hesitating a fraction, did likewise. The water was cold, and currents beneath the surface tugged strongly at him. It was deeply dark as well, and Reynam was suddenly very glad that he was tied about the waist to the two who had come to rescue him. Otherwise, in the murk, he could easily become disoriented and drown.

Reynam gasped sharply as the chill water closed over his chest and he began to kick his feet to keep his head up. The two beside him hugged the lip of the pool for a moment to grant the Sebastos a moment to adjust and take a last breath.

In the darkness and the silence, Reynam became conscious of the strange and intermittent voices drifting down the corridor from other inmates of the dungeon. Curious, he thought in a split second of extreme lucidity perhaps brought on by the frigid water, perhaps by the adrenalin coursing through him: he didn't remember so many in the dungeons before; they must have been confined very recently.

"Sebastos? Might you be ready? We must hurry!" said the first, anxiously.

Reynam grimaced. It was numbing, and he had not swum in a while. He must force strength into his limbs and breath into his lungs. "Yes," he croaked, awkwardly. "Now. For Biss. For Pentenok!"

The Crown of Light

The next evening, after the hour when she would have normally gone to bed, Tara was standing in the fields near Stonedell, anxiously scanning the darkening skies for Ariel's sky chariot. She had no real plan of what she should do next, but she knew that, in large part, it was her fault that Rohanic and his men had been captured. Had she warned her father sooner, maybe they could have been reinforced and saved.

Tara felt especially bad because it been Rohanic who had saved her from Jarvis and the pirates in Sea Sprit. It was he who had dashed up the road to the mansion to rescue her, heedless of his own safety. How had she repaid him? Not by racing to his rescue but by delaying. Not heedless of her safety but heedful only of keeping secret her friends and their activities.

Whenever she allowed herself the occasional moments to dwell on her behavior, Tara was ashamed of herself.

"I've got to do it," she repeated to Ariel as they ascended toward Cloud Castle in the chariot. "Just have to do it. I can't live with myself otherwise."

Ariel was silent until they were just about to land on the castle's Reception platform. "Tara, no. You can't. You'll only be captured as well. What good will that do? For the detachment or for yourself? For anyone?"

Tara silently gazed out into the darkness and the ground far below. Her thinking had been to stop at Cloud Castle only long enough to get a look at the encampment from above and hear the latest intelligence from Ariel's birds. Then, when darkness was complete, she had thought to return to earth to free Rohanic and his men.

"You want to do it anyway," resumed Ariel, as if there had never been a break in the conversation. They were seated on Cloud Castle's Vista Terrace, and every few minutes Tara would jump up to pace a few anxious steps before seating herself again.

"Yes. Within the hour. Could you set me down—carry me—as close as you can to their encampment? And I'll take it from there."

"No. Absolutely not. You will not 'take it from there', because I'm going with you."

"No way. It's far too dangerous."

"And it isn't dangerous—or less dangerous—for you, on your own?"

Tara sighed. "Yes, it is dangerous, but…" Tara knew it was dangerous and that she hardly had a plan. Ariel would be good to have along; she was very dependable. Tara couldn't, as well, force Ariel to fly off anyway after having set her down. "All right! Come with me. Thanks for the help. I mean that."

Ariel nodded. "I think you'll need help. Now, let's find out how many bandits there are, and exactly where this stockade is where Rohanic and his men are. As soon as it's dark, we'll descend to as close as we can to the stockade and free them.

"But, then what?"

"I've been thinking about that," said Tara. "Listen to this—and tell me what you think!" Good idea to relent on Ariel's involvement, Tara admitted to herself. It was good to have someone to talk to when it came to planning.

Ariel leaned forward, interested to learn just what sort of plan Tara had. Experience to date suggested that she should not expect much. She was beginning to conclude that Tara had a tendency to make plans up on the spur of the moment, with very little or even nothing thought through. Somehow, though, everything always seemed to work out right in the end. What was more, while success at the critical moment invariably seemed possible only through a miracle, it was always seemed equally inevitable and obvious afterwards. "Sure! Go ahead!"

"Right! Well, you've got the rest of the princess purses here, right? From Syssalin?"

"Yes, still. Well, except for the one we gave Flo."

"Of course! Well, let's grab all the telescoping rods from them and you'll take them. Here," Tara added, "take mine now! That's because you're going to use these to break the prisoners out of the stockade."

"How many do you think I'll need? Because, I mean, I only have two hands!"

"Take a bunch; they're not for you. Because," Tara added by way of explanation, "we don't know how strong the stockade is. The rods provide huge leverage, but we might need help from Rohanic and his men. That's why we'll take extra. You'll pass those through the stockade, already extended, and tell them to use them on the palings."

Ariel nodded. "What will you do?"

"Me? I'll provide the distraction. You'll need a distraction, because levering apart those palings could make a lot of noise, and there must be patrols or guards. Or something."

"True. What sort of distraction?"

Tara had already considered and discarded the idea of using her Ring of Shooting Stars; it would likely start a conflagration that could incinerate them all. "I've been thinking about that! Well, they're always around a campfire at night, right? Just as you'll take all the telescoping rods we have, I'll gather up all the dazzle dust, and I'll use that to create a distraction. Throw it in the fire, or something like that. They'll be totally disoriented!"

"And then?"

"And then, well, in all the confusion, we'll melt into the forest and evade them when they come after us. And, also, once Rohanic and his men retrieve their weapons, they'll have the advantage of surprise, if it comes to that!"

Ariel wasn't as confident in Tara's plan as its originator was, as she was worried about just how many bandits there were. Even with surprise, how were Rohanic and his men to overcome all of them? But she nodded anyway. "Look, if it doesn't look like things are going our way, we leave the extended rods with Rohanic, fly back up to Cloud Castle and try again later, all right? We can't take on all of them by ourselves, just the two of us, agreed?"

Tara did. She wasn't entirely convinced of her plan either, but it was something. There had to be some sort of distraction, as Rohanic and the thirty guardsmen could not possibly take on all the bandits head-on, especially without arms or armor. No, some sort of surprise was necessary. That would be the totally unexpected appearance of Tara and Ariel, literally from out of the sky, the dazzle dust, and then an unexpected attack by the suddenly-released Rohanic. "If it's not working, then we'll pull back. But you'll see! This plan is sure to work!"

After a quick snack to refresh themselves, Tara and Ariel stepped toward the edge of the Reception platform, the sky chariot now stowed in its hanger and the cygnets housed in their cote. Tara looked out into the gloom of the fallen night and then at the stars above. She wasn't very much closer to them, she thought, but she sure was a lot further from the ground. "You think you can do it?"

"I think so. I mean, I've carried you before—remember up to the cliff face at Syssalin? And then again up the bluff to Jarvis's mansion?"

"The ground is a lot further away from up here though!"

"That's true. But we're going down. The other two trips were hard because I had to fly up. I only have to break our descent going down."

There was no other way, knew Tara, to get to the middle of the forest; there was no place near enough to the encampment to land the sky chariot. "Let's go then," assented Tara. With that, Ariel unfolded her wings, wrapped her arms around Tara and, with a faint whir, they lifted from the platform.

It was a turbulent, terrifying ride down from such a far, far height. The wind cut and slashed at them, something Tara never felt when she was safe within the enclosure of the chariot. They then passed through a cloud, all wet and chill, and then out into the biting wind again, made all the more miserable for being damp. But gradually the darkness below resolved itself into patches of lighter and darker shadows, then trees, and finally Tara spotted the great campfire of the bandits. It did look enormous, even from that elevation. The tiny forms creeping about it must be men, rendered ant-like by the height. Tara shuddered, and not from the cold. Probably it had been just as well that she had not been able to see just how far up she had been when they had started from Cloud Castle.

Ariel set them down a short distance from the stockade, expertly manoeuvring through the tree branches. On releasing Tara, she gave a great exhalation of relief and swung her arms back and forth, as if to loosen them. "Wow! That was a little longer than I had expected! My arms were getting tired!" she whispered.

"So glad they didn't get *too* tired," replied Tara, with a feeble smile. They waited a moment longer to get their bearings and for their eyes to fully adjust to the darkness. "Ready?"

Ariel nodded quickly, held up the bundle of rods in her hand and began creeping toward the stockade. Tara watched her vanish into the darkness and started toward the great bonfire. There were patrols, they knew, but they both had guessed that they were much more distant from the encampment so as to better provide notice of anyone coming.

Tara edged forward and hid behind a tree. She was waiting, trying to give Ariel enough time to get to the stockade, pass out extended telescoping rods and position them to lever open the gate. She dug her hand into her princess purse to doublecheck that the quantity of dazzle dust she had poured into it was still there. Then she looked around the tree again to assess the campfire.

The bonfire was indeed enormous. A good eighty to one hundred men were gathered around it, at various distances, with what looked to be still more further back in the shadows. Those closest to the fire were brightest lit; they looked dirty and unkempt, and none wore any sort of uniform. Odd, thought Tara. If this was organized by Mortain, wouldn't there be some sort of leadership, and some sort of standard flying to signify their authority? But she couldn't see any sort of identifying banner or flag anywhere, much less any sort of tent that would suggest where the leadership was housed. In fact, she didn't see any evidence at all that Mortain was involved, not any symbols, house colors, or anything. "They must be trying to disguise their involvement," guessed Tara silently.

Just then, there was a commotion at the very edge of the circle of light flung by the crackling bonfire. Two figures approached out of the darkness, stopping just outside the brighter light. There was a brief tussle, and the two thrust forward a third from between them. Tara gasped. It was Ariel. Ariel had been detected and captured!

With all attention now on the captive, Tara dared move even closer to pick out the conversation.

"—by the stockade! In conversation with the one named Rohanic!"

A fourth figure appeared out of the darkness to stand opposite Ariel. Tara stared in astonishment: this figure was unlike any she had expected and appeared, by her form, to be a woman. She wore a dark cloak, though that part of her face turned toward the firelight was very pale, almost a ghastly white. Oddly though, she had the strangest eyes Tara had ever seen. They were over-large and flat and impossibly shiny. No, Tara corrected herself, peering more closely: she was wearing something over her eyes, as if for protection!

The other men around the campfire wandered over to gather around Ariel and her captors. The voice from the woman with the eye protection rang out authoritatively. "So! Who are you? What were you doing at the stockade? What did you say to that Rohanic?"

Ariel tossed her head slightly, drew herself erect and stared back defiantly into the expressionless, glossy eye disks of her interrogator. Tara noted that she had only one of the telescoping rods in her hand. Perhaps she had been able to pass the others to Rohanic?

One of Ariel's captors stepped forward and spoke. Also a woman, noted Tara, and she leaned in a little further to listen.

"I found her. At the stockade gate itself. I don't know how she was able to get so close to us." The voice lifted slightly in pride. "But she cannot get past me!"

The first questioner turned back to Ariel. "How is this? How did you get so near?" She turned to one of the men who had come from the campfire. "Why is it that your patrols are so ineffectual? Worthless! They detect nothing, while my companions guard everyone!"

Tara swallowed hard. Ariel was lost if she did nothing. But it was such a desperate gamble, what she was contemplating. But it just might work. And what choice did she have? Ariel was in danger! Tara reached into her princess purse and grabbed as large a handful of the dazzle dust as she could, essentially all of it, and moved stealthily until she was as close to Ariel as she could get but slightly behind her. Then, taking a last deep breath, as the first woman turned back to continue quizzing Ariel, Tara stepped from the shadows.

"You still missed me though!" she announced boldly and stepped over lightly to join Ariel, to the amazement of everyone gathered. "Touch me at your peril!" she snapped as imperiously and testily as she could to one of the bandits, who was approaching to seize her. He reeled away, astonished at her challenge.

"Tara!" gasped Ariel. "What are you doing?"

The woman with the goggles started with surprise but regained her composure instantly. "Another! So! One did get past us after all, Maribess?"

That one's pale face darkened but she said nothing.

"Who are you?" demanded the first. "And why are you here?"

"I," replied Tara calmly, gazing directly back into the flat black eyes of the woman opposite, featureless but for the way they weirdly reflected the firelight, "am Princess Tara—Princess of the Realm Tara. Of Brythrony."

Sundra listened attentively and became even more intrigued at the introduction. How interesting, she thought. "Terror?" Her name was "Princess Terror?" Maybe she could actually be an ally of some sort? "Princess? Of Brythrony?"

"Princess Tara. Of Brythrony. Who are you?"

"I am the Sebastas Sundra. What you might call 'Princess'. So, Princess Sundra. Of Pentenok and the Underground Kingdom. And my companions, Maribess," gesturing, "and Kobemy," gesturing again. Sundra did not bother to introduce any of the many bandits standing around her, not even Vedel, who was immediately beside her.

Tara's eyes widened ever so slightly. No wonder she had not seen any of Mortain's banners and standards. This Sundra princess was behind the marauding bandits, not Mortain. This was totally different than what everyone at Castle Stonedell had concluded.

Sundra continued. "So. Of Brythrony. From the same place as that Rohanic. Not a very impressive kingdom, from what I have seen of its fighting ability."

Tara's right hand again scoured the bottom of her princess purse to gather up any stray motes of dazzle dust from deep in every crevice and cranny. "We were certainly able to evade your guards and patrols," she replied easily. "Don't you wonder how we did that?"

Sundra glanced accusatorily over to Maribess, who scowled. "Yes, why not? Tell us how."

Tara lowered her voice to one suggestive of confident superiority. "It is because we can fly. We alighted behind your patrols."

A whisper of shock ran through the gathering crowd. "Fly? Fly? How, fly?"

"Oh, Tara! How could you?" cried Ariel in shock and dismay. "What will they do to me?"

Sundra's expression took on an avid, vulpine look in understanding that the one who had called herself "Terror" had betrayed the other. She took a half-step forward as her interest increased still further.

Tara gestured to Ariel discreetly for her to play along. Then she turned back to Sundra and the bandits. She really had their attention now; all eyes were riveted on her. She raised her voice dramatically so that all would be able to hear her clearly. "Yes! Fly! You want proof? Shall I show you?"

Who could resist? Not one word was said, which Tara understood to be encouragement. In her peripheral vision, Tara saw that the one Sundra had identified as Maribess had pulled out a throwing dart and was holding it at the ready.

"We can fly because... we have wings! See!" Tara gestured to Ariel to turn slowly and unfold her wings. She did so and, like gossamer, as they unfolded, they caught the dancing firelight and shimmered with a breathtaking sheen. A gasp of astonishment, a kind of collective catching of breath, went up. Even Sundra was amazed, Tara noted, both pleased and with mounting hope.

Tara lifted her left hand to gesture toward Ariel's glimmering wings. "You see? Wings!" Her right fist she had kept toward her side but slowly began to move it upwards, unclenching it ever so slowly as she did so. The more discerning in the crowd would have seen that that hand held something within it, something balled up tightly within the fist, that dribbled to the forest floor as she opened it.

The bandits' fascination with Ariel's wings was complete. But Sundra was the discerning type, having trained herself to be so, and she was near enough to see both of Tara's hands closely: the gesturing hand up high and open and the other down low, but rising, and with something within it. Sundra lowered both her hands and snapped the fingers of both softly. Kobemy and Maribess each instantly took a hand. Tiny streams of liquid fire had begun to trail through the fingers of this princess of Brythrony's right hand, just visible as long, wavering threads of gold in the flickering firelight. "Hand, see," she signed to each, hurriedly. Then, with rising horror, "Trick, very!"

How odd, Tara observed, that, just at this juncture, this Sundra princess had wished to hold hands with her companions. But there was no pausing. They had to act now or lose the moment. "Beat your wings," hissed Tara to her friend. "Hard! And close your eyes!"

The wings, facing them; the tiny rivulets of gold trailing from between the fingers, reflecting the firelight; the bonfire behind them—Sundra flung away the hands of her companions. "Shut your eyes! Turn!" she shouted to Maribess and Kobemy, clapping her hands across her goggles and whirling as she did so. A ruse! It had all been a ruse by this horrible, hateful Princess of Brythrony!

Ariel understood in a flash. Tara's unexpected and unnecessary appearance, the breathless revelation of Ariel's ability to fly, the theatrical unfurling of her wings; it all made sudden sense. "Tara, you're a genius!" she breathed as, with a mighty surge, she fanned her wings so violently they instantly became a blur. The great heap of dazzle dust in Tara's now open palm was caught up by the strong gust and billowed into the firelight as a vast, brilliant, blinding cloud that enveloped all the clearing with the bonfire at its center. There was a moment of stunned silence, then a terrific cacophony of agonized howls, moans, squeals, and groans from the men who had gathered over the course of the preceding minute to see the weird winged woman. For a long moment, in stark relief and as if lit by the flare of an impossibly bright sunburst, Tara saw the outline of every individual tree trunk around the clearing, the form of every bandit doubled over, or on his knees, and every detail of every item of equipment stacked or tossed idly about the ground.

Gradually, the dust settled, and the light flickered and died, leaving just the dimmer, ambient light of the bonfire.

Ariel turned around and surveyed the tableau before her. Many moaned that they were blind; some rolled on the ground in agony; others had staggered to their feet and were stumbling about the encampment, clutching at their eyes. Ariel strove to take it in. At last, she spoke. "Well done, Tara! That was incredible! But… where's Sundra?"

Tara scanned the crowd of unseeing men. None of them were Sundra and her two accomplices. "I don't know. They must have turned away in time. But we can't chase after them. We've got to liberate Rohanic and his men, then we'll be better able to manage these bandits. Their blindness is only temporary, after all."

It was true, thought Ariel. It wasn't possible to say for how long they would be dazzled, but it would surely only be for a short time. "This way; come on," urged Ariel, grabbing Tara by the arm and leading her back to the stockade.

Tara halted after only a few steps. "No, stop! I can't!"

"You can't? Don't you want to free them?"

"I mean, I can't free them; you have to! I can't be seen here, or there'll be too many questions about how I got here and why I was confronting the bandits alone, without the entire army of Brythrony behind me."

Ariel paused, confused. "So, what should we do? They already know we're here; I've given them the telescoping rods."

Tara smiled mischievously. "They already know *you're* here. But they don't know I'm here. You rescued them, Ariel! Now you're going to go back to check on them, after having single-handedly vanquished the bandits and Sundra!"

"Tara! That is simply outrageous!—"

"No, you have to. It has to be you. Or it will be impossible for me with my mother and father."

"I will *not* take all the credit, not when you were the one who devised the whole plan!"

Tara waved her hand in a gesture of dismissal. "No one cares about that. About taking credit. I have all I need anyway, from you. Now, quick: make sure they were able to get out of the stockade. Be sure to collect the telescoping rods; I'm certain we'll need those again. Then, Rohanic and his men can herd the bandits into the stockade, and all this will be over."

"Tara!"

"No more protests; just do it! Look, we don't have much time." Tara looked up into the sky. "It can't be that much longer until dawn. I have to get back to Stonedell by then or my parents will simply kill me!"

This left Ariel—briefly—to wonder about how someone who was so unafraid, even risking death, in her willingness to confront hundreds of bandits and a mysterious goggle-eyed princess with just a handful of dazzle dust, should yet be terrified of her unarmed mother and father, two people who, ostensibly, loved her. Ariel shrugged. If Tara had to get back, she had to get back.

"All right, fine. Let me call my sky chariot to the nearest clearing that can accommodate it. My birds have just informed me of one nearby. I'll take you back directly."

"But first to the stockade. To get the rods!"

"Yes, yes! Let's go! You hide on the other side of the stockade, where they won't see you!"

Ariel arrived just as Rohanic and his men had used the telescoping rods to pry two palings wide enough apart for a man to wriggle through. Rohanic was there at the paling, examining the gap made and assessing if it was big enough. "You!" he announced, startled to find Ariel again in front of him. "First in Sea Sprit and now here! Who are you, anyway?"

Ariel gestured to the paling. "Unfortunately, there's no time for introductions. I just stopped by to check on you; I'm glad you've made progress." Ariel half-turned away. "Oh, and don't be too rough on the stockade; you'll need it again for your prisoners."

Rohanic stared hard at her in incomprehension.

"The bandits are incapacitated but maybe only for a short time. You'll need the stockade so that, after you and your men have rounded them up, you'll have a secure place to hold them."

"'Incapacitated'? How? Who? You?"

Ariel smiled slyly and thought to borrow from Tara. "Why, you, of course, GC Rohanic! You and your men escaped and incapacitated them! Well done!"

"But!—"

"Go quickly, before they recover and you find yourself to have been captured twice!" Ariel waved a farewell then stepped aside around the stockade and fluttered up into a tree as soon as she judged Rohanic would be unable to see her.

Rohanic squeezed through the palings a moment later and darted around the side in search of her. Ariel giggled to watch him look frantically this way and that and mutter to himself. "Gone again! Who is she anyway, and how does she always know where I am?" But no one was there in the darkness, so back he ran round the other side again to urge his men to squeeze through themselves and join him.

Ariel re-joined Tara behind some trees further behind the stockade. "We should get going if we want you to make it back to Stonedell before dawn. My chariot is already on its way. We'll meet it in a clearing that's just a short walk away."

Tara listened intently for a moment. From what she could discern, it sounded as though Rohanic had the situation in hand. By now his entire detachment must be through the palings and have armed themselves with what weapons they would find about the bonfire. They'd corral the bandits shortly in the stockade. Some would attempt resistance but, still partially dazzled, this would surely be futile. Others might stagger into the forest and hide until regaining their eyesight. But this could not be a great number. The bandit gang had certainly been broken. This would be the end of the wave of brigandage Brythrony had been suffering.

"I don't know what to do about Sundra," Tara confessed to Ariel as they made their way through the trees toward the clearing.

"I don't think we can do anything. She and her two friends have got to be far away from here by now."

"I'm sure you're right. But, maybe, might you ask your birds if they can spot her? She couldn't have made it out of the forest yet."

Ariel pondered this request a moment. "Of course. Maybe she's on her way back to her own land, but my bird friends should catch sight of her along the way. I'll ask."

Tara stuck her hand in her princess purse and said sadly, "I'm afraid I used up all the dazzle dust. Every speck of it."

Ariel stared at Tara reproachfully. "Well, Tara, that's true, but isn't that what it's for? For using? And what better use could there be than saving your guardsmen and stopping these bandits from all their pillaging and burning?"

She was right, Tara had to admit. She turned her purse upside down, and the vial containing the liquid that created the message bubble dropped into her outstretched hand. It was empty, otherwise.

"At least I can give you back a telescoping rod," offered Ariel sympathetically, handing her one of the several she had retrieved from the stockade.

"Thanks." Tara slipped it into her Princess Purse, stopping to examine it for a moment and note that it bore no marks at all from having been used to pry open the palings. "And you're right. It was the best use of the dust. I'm just sorry there's none left for anyone else. But maybe I can find some more?" Tara threw a glance back over her shoulder in the direction where the stockade, now surely filled with bandits, must be. She imagined them still moaning, seated or leaning against the paling, stunned and in varying states of despondency and confusion. And only hours before, they had been so smugly self-confident and assured!

"I should instead be thinking about Sundra. I mean, what if she's just hiding nearby and looking to cause more trouble?"

"That's for another day," answered her friend firmly. "Let my birds find her. She can't hide from them. She won't even know she's being tracked and that we know where she is.

"Come on, let's get you back to Stonedell. I'll let you know of what they tell me when I have it."

Tara nodded. So sensible of Ariel. Didn't she have such good sense. Tara wished she had similarly good sense. But maybe their differing abilities was what made them such good companions and—even—so successful together.

They started forward again and soon the clearing was in sight. In the moonlight the sky chariot shone with a silvery sheen. The cygnets in their traces reared and beat their wings in greeting. "Hey, hi, my lovelies!" Ariel sang softly to them. "Are we ready? Yes?" She and Tara mounted the steps and seated themselves. Ariel took the reins and twitched them ever so gently. "Let's go then, my beauties! Up! To the sky!"

The chariot skidded across the clearing and lifted into the air. It cleared the treetops at the edge by the barest of fractions, and Ariel glanced round at Tara quickly to see if she might have been alarmed. But Tara wasn't looking down; she was gazing at the horizon, watching it redden in the far, far distance.

Alizarin was at the treasury before his Chief Observer arrived. He unlocked the door, worked the secret latches, and stepped through to take a quick visual inventory. This was the hoard of the Light Merchants, amassed and kept in this special, secure place. Alizarin reveled in its accumulation for a last, long moment for, very soon, a meaningful fraction would be gone.

The treasury would be depleted, but he felt no sense of loss. Instead, Alizarin felt exhilarated. The purpose of wealth, he had long maintained, was to create capabilities and options. The greater the wealth, the more significant the capabilities and the broader the option, and its highest and best use the preservation of the Light Merchants and the importance of their role in society. For, Alizarin affirmed silently, gazing at the treasure stacked and stored before him and glinting dimly in the lichen light, wealth could be gathered and scattered, but the guild of the Light Merchants could not be re-assembled once disassembled.

All previous Firsts had encountered and met tests of leadership in their time, and this moment's was his, Alizarin's. This very moment was a great moment, he sensed, and would require commensurate leadership, wealth, and competences from the Observers. He earnestly hoped all three would be adequate.

Just then, there came the knock on the door for which he had been waiting.

Alizarin opened the door. It was Cinnabar, his Chief Observer. "First," he named him simply, by way of greeting. Alizarin admitted him.

They regarded each other for a long moment. Alizarin spoke at last, his excitement rising. "Yes?"

"Yes. He is with us. As well as his closest associates who were nearby. Who could be extracted without notice."

"No alarm yet?"

"None. The jailors came to our side. And remain on our side."

Alizarin nodded. That had been critical to the initiative's success. "It was money well spent."

"Yes. Which brings me to…"

"It's ready. How far will that sum take us?"

"Most of the way. Perhaps all the way. Pentenokians are unhappy. The mood… it works in our favor. Because the uglier the mood, the cheaper it gets. To move minds."

Cinnabar was right. Alizarin had noticed it himself. The mood had shifted from shock and dismay to hostility and frustration. The random house-to-house searches for no one knew what, the arbitrary arrests on meaningless charges, the growing arrogance of the guardsmen, the filling dungeon: "Ever since Ortiki" were the words on more and more lips.

"That is good." Who knew how much more they might need, after all, or when? "How soon, do you think, would be wise?"

Cinnabar smiled. "You know the prohibitions! Soon. But I won't say more. Soon."

That would have to be good enough. Not just identities were kept unknown to protect the guild; planning was also compartmentalized. This absolute trust, even more than its monopoly and wealth, had to be the guild's greatest strength. "Then so be it. I will watch and wait like all other Pentenokians."

Even as Tara and Ariel rose into the sky in the chariot, Sundra, Maribess, and Kobemy were not all that far away. But they were on the move, slipping silently like shadows through the trees and moonlit glades to put as much distance as they could from the bonfire, the stockade, and the collapse of their designs.

At a brief stop for a drink at a stream and to catch their breath, Sundra looked up into the starry sky for a brief moment. How unlike it was from the calm, quiescent blackness always overhead in the Underworld Kingdom! The absolute darkness of the Underworld was a kind comfort, she realized, as opposed to the "stars," as Vedel had called them, of the Overlands. They were cold, silent, bright pinpricks of light that made her feel as if she were being watched from somewhere in the far ceiling. She turned back to the stream and her companions and put the thought out of her mind. What did it mean, anyway?

Maribess and Kobemy looked to her questioningly. The Sebastas clearly was preparing to tell them something, and they waited expectantly for her to speak. Gathering her thoughts, she explained shortly, her voice tight and under maximum control. "Those useless Overlanders—worse than useless! We have to do all the work for them! So! We regroup. Not here in the Overlands but back in Pentenok. There, we gather more to us. And we find out more about the Overlands and who would make better allies to achieve our objectives than those fools." She fairly spat the last sentence as she spoke, as if pronouncing it had been distasteful.

With that, Sundra set off again for the dark mass of the Grey Mountains bulking in the distance. Kobemy and Maribess, after adjusting their burdens, followed, one to either side of her, and half a step behind, as was due the Sebastas.

Half of Sundra's mind was on the route back to the Underworld Kingdom. The other half seethed, still furious at the reverse she had just endured at the hands of the princess from Brythrony and her winged companion. Her ambitions, thwarted! By a mere two Overlanders! When she, Sundra, the Sebastas, had had two of her own and all Vedel's men! Lost, at least for the moment, was the opportunity to find this place called "Sislin" and the Crown of Light. Lost also, most certainly, was the secret of her interest in the crown. This was because the cowardly Vedel would certainly bargain for his miserable life with any information he might have on her, the crown, or anything else. Sundra grit her teeth. If that Princess Terror had never heard of the crown before, she would take an interest in it now.

What if the hateful Princess Terror were to find it?

Sundra glowered into the dark. She had conducted intensive research to learn what she had about this crown. It was inconceivable that Princess Terror would know anything close to what Sundra knew. Even if she were to find it, she'd have no idea of how to use it.

Still, even if Terror might not find the crown, she would fortify her kingdom's defenses, set watches, and raise her guard. This meant that Sundra would have to be even stealthier on her next attempt.

Stupid, incompetent Vedel, to allow himself to be tricked as easily as he had been. He and his stupid, incompetent rag-tag army were all surely beneath the Sebastas for any sort of use. It had only been from expedience that she had employed them, ill-disciplined and untrustworthy vagabonds that they were. Like Vedel himself.

And so Sundra raged silently, forgetting conveniently that she had very nearly been fooled herself and had only realized the trick at the last second, and only because she had been standing the closest of them all and had seen

Tara's hand streaming the glittering dust it had held.

Yes, concluded Sundra bitterly. So. She was returning to Pentenok empty-handed. This time. But this time only. She would make another attempt to obtain the crown. The Crown of Light, with its fabled power, was worth the effort. But next time, rather than ally herself with those who were untrustworthy, unsubtle, and incapable, she would lead a select band herself composed of Underworlders only. No idiot Overlanders. And they would be secret and silent. Especially if this Princess Terror had located the crown and was learning how to use it.

"And," she added darkly, half to herself, and setting her jaw, "I will research this kingdom called Brythrony. And this 'Princess Terror' who rules it."

"Tara! Tara! Aren't you up yet? Tara! Are you all right?"

"Armorica, why not let her sleep? If she's tired?"

"I'm just worried that something's wrong with her! Look how late it is! What if she's up there, dead or something?"

"But if she's dead, it's too late to help her anyway, right?"

There was a moment of shocked silence. "How COULD you be so heartless!"

Tara rolled out of bed, groggy. Yes, it was late. She looked out the open window near her bed. The sun was high in the sky. Tara was still exhausted, of course. She had good reason to be, having spent the entire night dealing with bandits and a pallid princess and her associates, straight out of the Underworld. But none of this could she tell her parents. "I'm coming! Coming right down!"

That seemed to quiet her mother, whose voice lapsed to a mutter and whose steps Tara heard descending back down the spiral staircase of the North Tower. Time to get up, Tara, she told herself and sluggishly began to dress herself and head downstairs, maybe in time for lunch.

The next day, astonishing word came from the Great Forest. The bandits had been captured! Not only had the threat been eliminated but it would be possible to make some restitution from the booty seized. While pleased, Childeric wanted a detailed explanation.

Valandal did his best. "Your Majesty. Majesties," he added, with a bow to Queen Armorica, who was seated by her husband to receive the official word. Tara, the queen noted with acid irritation, was nowhere to be found at this important occasion and would have to be reminded of her duties and responsibilities. Probably riding Daystar through the fields. Really!

But Tara was present, only in the shadows of an aisle. She was very interested in the report, only didn't want to be seen for fear of prompting Valandal to say more than Tara thought prudent.

"Your Majesties," repeated Valandal. "Yes. The bandits have been captured. GC Rohanic effected this. With his detachment."

"But Captain! How is this possible? When he was held captive himself?"

Valandal cleared his throat. "Your Majesty, of course You are right. He escaped. He and his men. And, in the night, they captured the bandits and, very effectively turning the tables on them, are even now keeping them pent in the very stockade in which Rohanic and his detachment had been held!"

Childeric half-rose from his throne in amazement. "They escaped! And captured their captors? Well done! Or, maybe, their capture days ago was not actual? Did Rohanic allow himself and his men to be captured so as to be led to the encampment?"

Captain Valandal looked thoughtfully into the high ceiling of the reception hall. He couldn't say anything to His Majesty about the strange woman who Rohanic had sworn had provided him the tools by which he had been able to effect his escape. He would think them both mad! "Your Majesty, I don't have a complete report. Not yet. But as soon as I do, I will immediately provide it to you. Forthwith. What we know just now is that Rohanic and his men are safe and the bandits captured. The kingdom's borders to the west are secure, and the villages on the periphery of the Great Forest will no longer be troubled—no, not for a long time, since such an assemblage of such a force of bandits must mean there are now far fewer brigands and highwaymen at large."

This was good news indeed. Childeric was delighted and turned to his queen. "You see? GC Rohanic was exactly the man to send! What a cleverness, that stratagem!"

The queen nodded her approval, maintaining a regal demeanor. Where was Tara anyway, she wondered fiercely. Always shirking her responsibilities!

Childeric turned back to Valandal. "I look forward to the full report. In the meantime, you will ensure that Rohanic is appropriately rewarded. We shall also convert his brevet promotion to a full promotion. This is extraordinary; I am amazed. And very, very pleased!"

Valandal bowed. He was looking forward to the full report himself.

"But Mortain? Did we find evidence that Mortain was behind this?"

Valandal shook his head. "No, Your Majesty. In fact, Rohanic took great efforts to convey that Mortain was not behind this."

"Then… who?"

Tara stayed a moment longer as Valandal attempted a response then slipped back to her room. It sounded like Rohanic had indeed rounded up the bandit band after she and Ariel had left in the sky chariot. But what about Sundra, Maribess, and Kobemy; where were they? Most importantly, what was Sundra up to? She looked to have been the leader, despite her origin from a place she called Pentenok in an "underground kingdom." Sundra had not only been at fault for the chaos on the border, but she had nearly started a war between Brythrony and Mortain. She couldn't be allowed to escape and perhaps return to cause still more trouble.

Two days later, Tara found herself standing on a disk of solid ice, Ariel and Flo beside her. "Over there," Ariel was saying, pointing toward the forbidding face of one of the nearer peaks of the Grey Mountains. "That's what I was told. Can we get in a little closer to see?" One of Ariel's eagles had spotted the three figures making their way up the mountainside and had kept watch until it had seen them vanish into a refuge of sorts—a cave, Ariel had divined—that let out onto a ledge.

"Sure," replied Flo. "Let me take us there little by little. I need to be careful because of the air currents here: they can be a little violent and unpredictable."

Really, thought Tara, daring a peek over the side of the disk again, and adjusting the quiver slung around her back to do so. They were high up in the air, though not that far from the mountainside. Below lay a jumble of boulders and smaller rocks, interspersed with sparse grasses and krummholz. Further up the mountain was scattered patches of ice and snow, and further up still what looked like to be a cap of permanent ice. But at this level the snow had yielded to the summer thaw.

Flo was providing transport this time. The three of them were aloft on an ice disk she had caused to materialize and then kept solid underfoot. To keep her fellow riders proof against the winds and falling temperature, she had also formed about the disk a habitable sphere, and it was within this that the three clustered. Tara would have preferred Ariel's sky chariot, which would have been far roomier, but it would have been impossible for it to land on the mountainside. The cygnets would not have been able to tolerate the falling temperatures anyway.

But Flo's ice disk was perfect for the temperature and rough terrain. It could ascend and descend vertically, hover, and didn't need a flat surface on which to land. The colder it got, the more comfortable, happier and stronger Flo became. Tara was glad for this, as the colder it became, the more protection she and Ariel would need—and Flo have the wherewithal to provide—against the falling temperatures and rising winds.

Tara and Ariel scanned the mountainside keenly for evidence of the cave that Flo had described. "There it is!" called out Tara, excitedly, pointing. "I think that's it! Could you land us there? On that ledge?"

Flo made no response, but the disk began to edge in toward the spot Tara had identified. The cave mouth yawned as they approached. As they neared, they began to grasp how large it was. "Gosh, it looks immense," murmured Tara. "It *is* like an entrance. To someplace. Someplace maybe as big as an Underground Kingdom!"

Flo brought the disk just inside the cave mouth and they hovered for a moment as their eyes adapted to the dimmer light. While they waited, Tara asked, "Could you make this disk still larger if you wanted? To carry another person? Or even several?"

"Sure! I could make it really big, actually, and lift all sorts of people on it! It all depends on how cold it is. The colder it is, the bigger I can make it and the more I can lift. The warmer it is, well, you get the picture: the exact opposite."

Tara nodded. It was definitely getting colder outside, and the temperature would drop as night came on. She was thinking of Sundra. If they found her, Tara wanted to take her back to Stonedell to face justice. There was no reason, after all, why the bandits should be punished but not her and Maribess and Kobemy as well.

"How long ago did your eagle say they entered the cave?" she asked Ariel, turning to her friend.

Ariel recollected for a moment. "He said it had been 'the arc of the sun across the sky by half my wingspan'. Which, I'm thinking, means anywhere between four to six hours." She smiled at her translation.

Tara turned back to Flo. "How comfortable," she asked, "would you feel taking this disk into the cave?"

"Well…" she considered. "We could go some. We don't know how narrow it gets or what the overhead is like, but, just on the temperature alone, we could go a little way."

"Could you take us as far as you can, please? With their head-start, this may be the only way we can catch them."

Flo nodded, if unenthusiastically. The disk entered the cave mouth slowly and carefully, Flo concentrating on keeping them as high up in the cave as she dared but without getting too close to the overhead. Somewhere ahead was their quarry: three persons from the Underground Kingdom fleeing back to their city. They were on foot and growing more comfortable with their surroundings the deeper underground they moved. In close pursuit were another three, equally intent and surely gaining but becoming more wary and uneasy the further they ventured.

At length, Ariel tugged at Tara's arm. "Look! Down there! Do you see?"

Tara stared hard into the half-light of the cavern but didn't see anything. "N-no. Not yet. You must have better eyes than I do! Like your falcon friends!"

"Shh! Take a closer look. And don't look for three figures; look for motion!"

Tara followed Ariel's pointing hand and opened her eyes as wide as she could. The darkness was not complete, lit as the space was by a strange half-greenish glow that emanated from someplace that none of them could see and yet seemed to be everywhere, since the glow was mostly uniform. Far down below there seemed to be a kind of trail, or path, that wound its way in and out of various rock formations. Tara scanned the trail up and down below her and all the way until it wound out of sight into the darkness but still couldn't see anyone. How could Ariel possibly see anyone down there in the murk, she wondered. Was Ariel mistaken?

Then Tara thought she discerned a fleeting movement. It hadn't been on the path but just off it, as if something were moving alongside it, in and out of the rocks that lined it. Tara watched again, to see if it would reoccur. There it was again, just ahead of the previous instance! Tara uttered a low whistle. "I think I see them, Ariel. You have such sharp eyes! There, next to the path below us, right? Not on it, but next to it?"

Ariel nodded emphatically. "I think so." She turned to Flo and whispered, "I think we're just above them. Let's follow them a bit and see what they're up to."

"All right," granted Flo, "but not for long! It's getting warmer, and I don't want to drop any of us. It looks like it would be a long way down and a hard landing!"

Below them, Sundra stopped and turned to her companions. "A little further," she explained, in her lowest tones. "We'll stop and regroup at my brother's place of meditation. The place he calls Starmers. So. No one ever went there except by his command; I'm thinking no one does still. We will be safe there."

"How far?" asked Maribess. Moving too quickly in the over-bright world of the Overlands, she had caught her ankle between some fallen trees. Increasingly as they made their way down the path she was hobbling, though doing well in keeping up with the other two.

"A little further. Then we will rest. Come! Not much more!"

Kobemy bent to examine the ankle he had noticed Maribess was favoring. He frowned. "It is swollen. You have twisted it, though not too badly. But we should bind it. We can do this at Starmers; I have the materials with me. Give me your pack; that should make it a little easier for you."

Maribess gratefully bent to shrug off her pack and pass it to Kobemy. As he reached to take it from her, something caught his eye above them. He paused and narrowed his eyes.

"What is it? What?"

"Something… Sebastas, something very light in color, and high above. Following us."

"The Overlanders! They watch us from above!"

Maribess instantly sank to one knee. From her back she unslung the Underworld traveling miniature bow, which did not have the range of a true bow but which she hoped would have the advantage of surprise. From the small case strapped to her thigh she withdrew an arrow so short it appeared to be no more than an overlong dart. Then, deftly fitting arrow to string, she aimed into the darkness where Kobemy was pointing.

High up on the disk, Ariel gasped. "Up, Flo! Higher! They've seen us! And one's aiming something at us!"

Maribess caught sight quickly of what Kobemy had been pointing at. Humming to herself in satisfaction, she pulled back on the string and let fly the arrow. Up the arrow darted, but even as it flew, the ivory disk at which she had been aiming jumped, and the arrow passed harmlessly below.

"Overlanders!" hissed Sundra. "They fly! Like Overland insects! Again, Maribess, there is no sharper eye than yours!"

Maribess shook her head. "Sebastas, I thank you, but they are too high now. I would only waste the arrow. But perhaps they are also too high to see us and have lost us? Their eyes are poor in the dark. Shall we push on to Starmers?"

"Do you see them at all, Kobemy?"

"No, Sebastas. No."

"Perhaps Maribess's arrow frightened them away?"

Kobemy peered again into the velvety blackness surrounding them. "I don't know. I don't see them. But I have never seen such a flying disk before either, and it may have tricks to disguise itself."

Sundra hesitated. She had feared they would be pursued by that horrible princess from Brythrony. Having followed them this far, Sundra doubted they would be scared away so easily. In which case, they would follow them to Starmers. But there was nothing to be done about pursuers they couldn't see and who, being airborne, could not be ambushed by lying in wait. "So," she said at last. "Push on. We push on to Starmers." Besides, there would be help at Starmers. She had expected that Vedel and some of his men would return with her to the Underground Kingdom to claim some of the riches she had promised them as their reward. In anticipation of disgruntlement from either side, or perhaps both, she had instructed Ortiki to position a small detachment there to ensure she got her way if there was any conflict.

"Yes, on to Starmers," Sundra repeated softly. The detachment at Starmers could deal just as well with the airborne Overlanders as they would have with Vedel and his bandits.

High in the upper reaches of the cavern, the three princesses breathed a sigh of relief that no further arrows came flying out of the darkness at them. "That was close," murmured Ariel. Tara agreed, though she would have loved to have obtained one of the arrows that the Underworlder shot at her. Still, she would prefer to have it handed to her, or to find it, rather than to have to pull it out of a wound. "Too close."

Flo called over her shoulder, "I'll keep us up as long as I can, but, just to warn you, it won't be for much longer. It's just not cold enough!"

Where then should she set them down, wondered Tara. She knew the other two would be looking to her for the answer. Well, it *had* been her idea to chase this Princess Sundra, on account of it having been her kingdom that Sundra had been troubling! "They'll be watching behind them and above them, Flo. Take us ahead of them, and let's try to stay ahead of them based on the quality of the path they're on."

"What do you mean by 'the quality of the path'?" asked Flo.

"Yes. Let's assume they stay on what looks to be the broadest, most well-travelled path. As I bet they are going to some place where a lot of them reside. That city they mentioned, 'Pentenok', I think it was. So put us down ahead of them on that path. I think that's the best we can do."

Flo shrugged and took the disk forward, high up so as not be spotted by the three figures below them. Then she took the disk down and they hovered low, popping up every now and then to ensure they were still monitoring them. This worked fine, until, suddenly, their quarry vanished.

"Where'd they go? They were just here!"

"I need to set us down," cautioned Flo. "I can't be confident I can keep the disk solid."

That was too bad, thought Tara. Just when it would have been useful to see from above where their quarry had gone. But there was nothing to be done. Best to be set down safely than risk a long fall. "Yes, please!" replied Tara promptly.

Back on solid ground, Tara pointed and mouthed the words that they should hike up the path to where they had last seen Sundra and her companions. Back to where we last saw them, she tried to explain. The other two nodded with understanding and Flo and Tara moved forward on foot. Ariel spread her wings after a moment's hesitation and took flight, feeling more comfortable in the air but alert for the possible need to duck quickly should another arrow come whistling out of the darkness.

Tara and Flo crept forward anxiously. There were no shadows to keep to, because the dimness was so uniform. The scattered points of faint greenish light seeping from underneath rocks and from half-hidden crevices were all that relieved the gloom. This was not the time to study the source of this strange Underworld illumination, yet Tara found her attention caught, in odd moments, when her mind would wander for just the slightest instant, by the glow. From what she could tell, it emanated from some sort of lichen and grew directly on the rocks, the walls, and peeped out from beneath the largest boulders. Some sort of bio-phosphorescence, she marveled; how interesting and odd. Moreover, the light came from the plant itself, suggesting that, as long as it lived, the light would never cease or flicker. She had never seen anything like it in the world above ground, this unwavering, eternal half-light that never cast a shadow and yet offered neither cheer nor warmth.

Ariel alighted beside them and pulled both friends close enough to her to whisper to both simultaneously, "I hear something. Voices, I think. Though it could also be water, like a stream, flowing over rocks. But it sounds like talking." She pulled back and pointed off to the side.

Sundra and the others had turned down a side passage, realized Tara. Of course: that was how they had lost them. "Let's investigate. I'll peek around the corner. Ariel, you stay low: I don't want you to be a target!" Ariel agreed, gratefully.

Tara noiselessly pulled an arrow from her quiver and fit it to her bow. With utmost caution, she edged forward, looking for the spur from the main path which Sundra and the others must have taken. There it was, she saw in the dim, flat lichen-light. It was just a narrow path, off the main one. No wonder they had missed it from up above, on the disk.

Tara paused. Was she crazy, she asked herself. Yes, she was crazy, she had to be, to venture, however carefully, into a strange, dark, enclosed area in which at least several hostile Underworlders were lying in wait. But a moment later, she stepped forward, impelled by a memory. Had Queen Ysolde, of but two generations before, hesitated to stride the allures of Castle Stonedell when the fate of Brythrony had hung by a thread? The oft-told story raced through Tara's mind. Ysolde, almost alone and heedless of an unremitting hail of arrows, had dauntlessly rallied its defenders. A knighthood had been conferred on every archer who had manned a merlon that day and lived; a state funeral had been held for those who had fallen.

Now, again, the fate of the kingdom could be in the balance, even if the circumstances were very different. Then, the threat had been Mortain, whereas now it was this pale Princess Sundra of a strange underworld realm. The numbers were far smaller too, just three persons against three rather than one army against another. Yet, at bottom, the House of Hession had to defend Brythrony again, and was Princess of the Realm Tara to flinch when Queen Ysolde had stood fast? Tara tightened the arrow on the bow and, with renewed determination, stole forward into what she sensed to be a much broader and even darker space.

Yes, there were voices. Tara could hear them now. But they were few, not many. Yes, she thought she recognized Sundra's among them. It must mean that Sundra and her two companions were still alone, perhaps resting or deciding what to do next. Tara reached back with one arm and beckoned her friends to follow her. Now was the time to take her and her two accomplices captive, before they could escape again.

The voices suddenly fell silent. Tara guessed she had been heard, despite her utmost efforts to stay silent, and stepped out from the darker shade and toward what she was dimly aware of as the center of the space. "Sundra! Surrender!" she called, boldly. Spotting Sundra herself, she pulled back further on the arrow and aimed it directly at Sundra's chest.

The wrist of the woman named Maribess flickered, and a throwing dagger suddenly gleamed dimly in her hand.

"Lift that arm further, and this arrow goes through Sundra's heart!" cautioned Tara.

Sundra's voice was unperturbed, unruffled. "I wear the finest Underworld armor. Your Overland arrows cannot pierce it." Sundra peered more closely at Tara. "But you are alone! Are you alone? Where are your friends, your flying friends?"

Where, indeed, were they, wondered Tara. "Just behind me," she replied stoutly. "Give yourself up! You're well covered—all three of you!"

The man, Kobemy, stepped forward, his hand menacingly at the hilt of the sword at his side. "Overlanders have no will to fight. Like that Rohanic. They have only tricks. And you are alone. It was reckless to pursue us to our world, where we are the masters!"

"She is not alone," called Ariel's voice from above in the darkness. "And I am indeed covering you!"

Kobemy and Maribess instinctively looked up to search the upper reaches of the darkness for the speaker, though Sundra kept her eyes locked on Tara, remembering the devastating dust she had thrown into the bonfire. "So. The flying Overlander after all. Still watching from above. Even so, it is only two of you. Favorable odds, still, for us."

Tara couldn't be sure if Sundra really was wearing some sort of protective armor beneath her surcoat. Wouldn't she be the type who would, though? As for Ariel, she was unarmed, even if she was pretending to have some sort of weapon. The odds were definitely not in her favor; this was becoming more and more apparent with each passing minute. But had the odds been any better for Queen Ysolde when she had faced a much larger force and at the very gates of Stonedell?

"Kobemy, Maribess, a platoon, in the rear, only awaits our summons. Call them now. Then we shall throw this princess into the dungeons of Lothwell until we decide what to do with her. We shall return from the Overlands with something of value after all!"

The man named Kobemy directed back into the darkness a queer chittering, rattling sound that must have been that of some Underworld creature. A similar answering call promptly came from further back in the darkness.

Sundra smiled a superior smile. "Now you are our prisoner, 'Terror'! And never shall you return to your Overland world!"

Tara's spirits sank. A prisoner forever in a twilit world, leagues below the surface, never to see daylight again? She'd rather die now, nobly, in battle, than to waste away in some dank dungeon cell. She'd take Sundra with her, she vowed fiercely but silently.

A sudden chill breeze swept past Tara and whipped up the cloaks of the three Underworlders. They looked to each other. Wind? Down here?

The breeze strengthened and Tara's heart leapt in her breast. It was Flo, mustering some sort of defense, even though it was barely cool, much less cold. A thin sheen arching over and around the three Underworlders appeared, wavering at first but increasing by degrees in solidity. Wonderful Flo! Flo was encapsulating the three in a sort of ice shell, so that they could neither attack nor escape. The exterior of the shell reflected faintly the faint green lichen light scattered about the cavern, giving the three within a putrescent, chartreuse pallor. Tara saw Sundra mouth words to Kobemy, and it appeared as though he made the strange call again, but Tara could not make it out above the wind.

"Again!" she heard Sundra command, this time very loudly.

From the far back of the cavern came the distant sound of clashing steel, scuffling feet, and harsh voices. "Quick, Flo!" called Tara in rising worry. "Hurry! Before their reinforcements arrive!"

"I'm trying, I'm trying!" came Flo's voice from behind her. "But it's so warm! I can barely do anything; just a little, that's all!"

Tara's heart sank again. That was it? That would never be enough to hold them, nor the reinforcements which must be upon them any moment.

Maribess's arm flashed. Tara instinctively ducked, but the ice shell stopped the thrown dagger, though the impact brought it down in a thousand splintering pieces, so thin it had been. Sundra exulted. "So! This is all? This is your magic? It is ineffective in the Underground Kingdom!" She gestured to Kobemy and Maribess. "If this is their best, they are defeated already!"

Tara heard the movement of what sounded like many behind Sundra. And, indeed, multiple ranks of Underworlders, looking very much like Sundra and dressed similarly in black and silver, suddenly swarmed around her. This must be the end, thought Tara despondently. She would have time to loose just one arrow at Sundra, and then she would be taken or killed.

But the leader of the reinforcements, instead of advancing on Tara, turned and placed his hand roughly on Sundra's shoulder to spin her around. "Sister Sundra! We meet again, and again at Starmers!"

Sundra gasped and glanced to Maribess, who already had another dagger in her hand, even as she and Kobemy were seized from behind. There was the briefest of struggles as the dagger was struck from Maribess's hand, and her arms too were pinioned. Sundra writhed and twisted, as a serpent would in a hawk's talons, but to no avail. "Reynam!" she spat. "You! How?"

The leader, the man she had called Reynam, held up his right hand and answered loftily, "You, Sebasissa, will address me as 'Sebastos Reynam'." His voice took on a harder edge. "I place you under arrest for high treason!"

Sundra jerked a shoulder free and glared at her captor. Reynam, seeing her glance hopefully into the darkness behind him, smiled thinly. "No one is coming to rescue you, sister dear. My troops have already subdued the platoon you had waiting for you. That was the *very* brief scuffle you heard earlier."

Sundra sneered. "You'll be back in the dungeons of Lothwell as soon as we get to Central Square. I am the rightful ruler of Pentenok! The people know this!"

"Hardly. Your placeholder, Ortiki, overreached himself all too quickly. That little bit of power you gave him went straight to his head. I myself led the people of Pentenok against him and his myrmidons just a few short cycles ago. You really should choose better regents." Reynam's voice descended to a cold and menacing tone, which chilled even Tara. "It is he who is in the dungeons now. And, you," gesturing to Maribess and Kobemy, "who will be likewise, shortly. Bakide, Lavinia, take them away!"

"Sebastas!" called the futilely struggling Maribess as Lavinia commenced to drag her off, "I will never forsake you! Never!" But before she could say more, Lavinia gagged her with a strip of cloth she had kept ready for just that purpose.

In a final spasm of rage, Sundra wrenched herself half-free and whirled on Reynam. She had no weapon, but her glare was so fierce it was like an assault itself. Reynam, taken aback for a split second, shrank away, but the one he had called Bakide seized her again, roughly. "Reynam! Reyyyynaaaam!" she howled in an endless moment of unadulterated wrath, and then she was gagged as well. Bakide and three others wrestled her, still spitting and hissing, into the same fathomless darkness from which moments before she had expected salvation from her own reinforcements.

"Now," Reynam continued, turning to the awestruck Tara, Ariel, and Florence. "Who are you? But let me introduce myself. I am the Sebastos Reynam of House Biss, ruler of Pentenok, the Underground Kingdom."

Tara recovered first. "Of Pentenok? Like Sundra?"

"The very same city. We are siblings. But more unlike each other than you can imagine."

"She called herself Sebastas."

Reynam smiled the same thin smile he had to Sundra. "I am the Sebastos. She wrongfully took me prisoner and usurped the throne. As you have just witnessed, this has been undone, and she shall be punished.

"But forgive me: you? Why do you come to my kingdom to confront my sister?"

Tara recollected her manners with a start. "My friends," she gestured, and Ariel and Flo introduced themselves, Tara speaking last. "Princess Sundra came to the Overlands, to my kingdom of Brythrony, and assembled a considerable force of bandits and brigands. There she caused considerable destruction."

"She sought to extend her dominion to the Overlands?"

Tara shook her head. "I don't know what her objectives were. Perhaps she will tell you."

Reynam's face betrayed his scepticism that he didn't think she would. "And these bandits? Where are these malefactors now? Are they still at large?"

"No, they are captive. And they will each face justice, in time and in turns." Tara recollected her previous disinterest in her kingdom's law courts and reconsidered. Perhaps, on this occasion, she might look into just how they functioned. She continued, "Sundra was their leader, so we sought to bring her to justice also."

Reynam stared hard at them, each in turn, in mounting disbelief. "Just the three of you came to retake her? In her own land? Only three?"

Tara looked to Ariel and Flo, slightly sheepish at first but then with mounting pride. All right, maybe it had been extraordinarily foolhardy to have chased Sundra, Maribess, and Kobemy to the Underworld. Yet, hadn't they been successful? "We had reinforcements above ground. But we thought the three of us would be sufficient to bring her back."

Reynam shook his head in amazement. "I had no idea Overlanders were so bold. Were I not seeing it with my own eyes, I would never have believed it." Reynam shrugged. "Very well. I agree with you. You have a strong claim to try Sundra under your own laws, what with the wrongs you say she committed. But may I humbly request to try her first, since her first crimes were against me, Pentenok, and its people?"

"But Sebastos, how shall we of the Overlands obtain justice in our turn?"

Reynam bowed. "I admit your point. So, instead, may I beg you to trust me that I will seek the sternest punishment possible, given the gravity of her transgressions, and understanding the very real incentive I have to press these charges?"

Tara thought only for a moment. She would have liked to have returned with Sundra to try her in Brythrony's law courts. But how to do this speedily? Might it be simplest to give her over to Underworld justice? Reynam made a reasonable argument that he had very strong reasons to keep Sundra from ever getting free again.

Tara curtsied. "Very good then, Sebastos Reynam. I yield to Pentenok my claims and those of my kingdom. However, should she discharge her punishment in Pentenok, may I request that she be delivered to Brythrony to stand trial?"

Reynam nodded slowly. "Absolutely. Should she discharge whatever sentence she may receive, I will gladly render her to you and Brythrony.

"Now, I thank you, Princess Tara, for the tremendous service you have rendered the Underground Kingdom. You have thwarted her seizure of the Pentenok throne, her designs in the Overlands, and forced her back to the Underworld, where she has been captured. We are indebted to you."

Tara and her two friends curtsied again as their response. Reynam bowed again, deeply.

"And may I beg to offer you each my seal, as both a memento and expression of my appreciation? Should you ever find yourself in my realm again, show it, and the viewer will know that you have my gratitude and will be obliged to render any request for service you might make."

There was a knock on the door. Who could that be, she wondered. The knock had been more like a rap, firmer and more rapid than that she knew from her mother. "Who is it?"

"Just me," came a masculine voice in reply. It was her father. How strange. He never climbed the many steps of the North Tower to her bedroom.

Tara crossed the room from her vanity and opened the door a fraction. "Hi, Dad." There was a slight pause. "What brings you up here?"

"Could I speak with you for a moment?" Childeric squinted through the cracked door. Tara's room was virtually an undiscovered country; Childeric didn't think he had set foot within it for years. What he saw of the chamber beyond was a cyan-blue wall and a largely unmade bed, then Tara had slipped lithely through the gap to stand beside him on the landing and closed the door behind her to cut off even this momentary glimpse.

"So, um, Dad, what's the occasion?"

Childeric leaned back against the wall behind him. "Sorry to disturb you. Did I disturb you?"

Tara shrugged. "No. Just brushing my hair a little. That's all."

"Good. Well, I came up—I didn't realize there were so many stairs; it's as if this tower has gotten taller!—just to say thank you."

"Oh! Thanks, Dad! But what for?"

"For warning me that there were a lot more bandits than we had thought, and that Rohanic needed help. That prompted me to send out another detachment, which rescued those several guardsmen who had escaped. In the end, Rohanic and his men were able to capture the bandits on their own. Still, the intelligence we got from the rescued guardsmen, plus what you provided, made us send out a much larger force than we might otherwise have. Rohanic would not have been able to hold those bandits with just the men he had.

"The additional, upsized reinforcements we sent were crucial in keeping those bandits from escaping or maybe even overwhelming Rohanic and his men.

"So... I wanted to thank you. For your help. You and your friend—I can't remember her name now."

"Ariel."

"Ariel. You and your friend Ariel. Thank you for coming to me with that information."

"Thank you for believing me," replied Tara, simply.

Childeric made no move to leave though.

"Something else, Dad, on your mind?"

"Yes. Yes, there is. That Ariel friend of yours: did she play any part in helping Rohanic get free? In his escape?"

"Gosh, what do you mean?"

Childeric frowned slightly. "There are reports from some of the guardsmen that a woman appeared at the stockade door and handed them some very strong poles to use as levers to pry the stockade palings apart. Wide enough so that they could slip through. I'm thinking that was Ariel?"

"It had to be her. But I can ask her, if you like, and make sure?"

Childeric looked harder at Tara. "You weren't involved in that rescue in any way? Were you?"

Tara pulled back and assumed her best look of astonishment. "Me? But I don't have wings! How could I have gotten all the way out to the Great Forest and back again to rescue them so quickly?"

Childeric shook his head, puzzled. "Right. I know full well you don't have wings. But, well, I don't know. It just seemed that your friend Ariel knew exactly what to do and where to go and who to ask for and all that sort of thing."

Tara nodded as if she understood why her father might be mystified. "Her birds see everything. They must have told her. That's how she would know."

Childeric caught his daughter's eyes for just a moment and noted them bright with some enigmatic mischief, before the tell-tale twinkle vanished with a blink. He sighed. "Very well, Princess of the Realm Tara. Very well. We'll leave it there."

Now it was Tara's turn to hesitate. "But, uh, Dad, I've got something to ask of you."

Childeric nodded for her to continue by way of response.

"It's about Ariel. You haven't told Mom about her, have you?"

Childeric shook his head, no.

Tara bit her lower lip and shuffled one foot in the dust that had accumulated over many months of not being swept or scrubbed. "Um... I wonder, could we just keep that a little secret between us? For a little bit, at least, maybe?"

A thought occurred to Childeric as he considered. Maybe he could trade her desire to keep Ariel a secret for the story behind what had really happened at the stockade when Rohanic had been freed. Childeric gauged his daughter would yield.

But Childeric brushed the thought away. Why shouldn't she have secrets, if only for a little while longer? Both about the existence of Ariel and what, exactly, Tara's role had been in rescuing Rohanic. Something told Childeric that he should be trusting his daughter and that it would mean far, far more to her than his understanding would mean to him.

"Sure. Sure. This will be our little secret. I'll trust you—"

"Of course, Dad; thank you!"

"—to tell your mother and me everything when appropriate. Until then, our secret."

"Thank you, Dad! Yes, you can trust me!"

"All right." Father and daughter regarded each other for a long moment. Tara's hair shone in the sunlight slanting in through the lancet window above the landing. Her face, upturned, had a broad smile on it, one Childeric had not seen on her for many days. Her brown eyes glinted with just a trace of the mischievousness he had caught a minute before.

"By the way, your hair is looking lovely. Now that you've combed it. Your mother will be very pleased with what you've done with it."

Tara groaned loudly and turned away. "No, Dad, nothing about that either! Or Mom will want me to brush it like this every day!"

Book III: The Lost Quarter

Princess Atalanta

It was a shame about the dazzle dust, Princess Tara was thinking. Even if it had been put to very good use. She stood on the edge of a vast expanse of sandy scrublands, looking out into an endless distance of what she knew, come the morning, to be the heat and dust of the Lost Quarter.

The dawn was yet hours away, though there were reddish streaks in the far distance, just barely visible behind the morning stars.

Princess Tara gazed out silently, surveying the horizon, then yawned loudly. She couldn't believe how early it was.

She sat astride her horse, Daystar. Tara folded the reins in her hand and returned her gaze to the vast sandy wastes. Daystar whinnied. "Sure, boy, sure; it's all right," she reassured him, almost automatically. Probably thirsty. Or hungry. Or something like that, she thought.

All the dazzle dust was gone. Tara had used it to incapacitate the bandits that Princess Sundra had organized. There had been so many bandits that Tara and Ariel had even used the dust in the spare princess purses to create a cloud large enough to stun them all.

Of course, Tara had her ring, and that was very useful and powerful. The other princesses had their innate abilities too, and those could never be exhausted. But the dust served a very important function. Tara had thought about this one day while cantering through the forest on Daystar, her quiver over her back, as she liked to sling it, and her bow at her saddle. What was so useful about the dust was its defensive nature. Because it blinded temporarily those at which it was thrown, it was a kind of screen that allowed her and her friends to escape. It was quick, effective, and simple. Also, it didn't do permanent harm, like the arrows shot from her bow.

There was one thing else too, Tara had realized, the more she had thought about it. Something very important. As long as they were closely grouped together, the dust could affect more than one, without any further effort or using any more dust. This was also unlike her bow and arrows, which could only be aimed and fired one at a time, each arrow aimed at just one target. It was true that some of her friends, like Ice Princess Florence, had powers that could affect more than one person at a time, but that power was unique to that princess.

The more Tara had thought about it, the more certain she was that they needed more dazzle dust. They had to refill their princess purses. But from where, and how?

Tara had mulled this over for a few days before finally sending her friends message bubbles to ask them what they thought. All of them had thought it was a good idea to get more. But, characteristically, none of them had had any ideas on how to do so. At length, it had become obvious to Tara that if there was going to be more dazzle dust, it would have to be because Tara found it. She had sighed. Fine. She would go look for it. At least the others would help her, they had said. She would have to ask for that help, that was all.

She had thought hard about who she should ask for a suggestion on where to start. At last, she had pulled out a vial and dripped a drop into her palm, then rubbed her two hands together and drawn them apart to form a bubble, and spoken into it. "Hi, Marina, it's me, Tara! Listen, you know I'm thinking we need more dazzle dust. But I don't know where to get it! Any ideas on how we might figure out where? Could your father's library have any clues?"

Tara had puffed on the bubble and released it to the breeze. As with all the others she had sent, it had risen, quivered for a second and floated toward the open window to vanish into the evening. Tara watched with satisfaction. It would find Marina, and quickly. She was always surprised by how fast the bubbles travelled once they left a princess's hands. How useful they were!

It was natural to turn to Marina first on this. She could be a little dizzy at times, even if a fast friend. But that library of hers—of the Coral Castle—was simply incredible. They had nothing like it on land. Tara wondered how it had been gathered and kept; it must have taken centuries. It had proven hugely useful on several occasions already. Maybe it would this time, too.

But she shouldn't neglect the others, she realized, who might be able to help as well. Before turning in that evening, she also sent messages to Ariel and Florence. She was less confident of their ability to help but thought it wise at least to consult them.

Tara had made up her mind as the message bubbles came back from her friends. Marina had told her that their library had explained that a portion of the desert out to the west called the Lost Quarter (owing to the fact that no one ever ventured there) was understood to be the source of dazzle dust. One of the mother-of-pearl texts had indicated that they should look for a dry riverbed, and there, within it, they'd find the dust they sought. A crude map accompanying the text offered a reasonable indication as to where in the desert she should search.

Ariel herself had not had any clues as to how or where to get dazzle dust but had offered to help find it based on whatever Marina might unearth. As for Princesses Florence, she had replied—and in response to what Marina had discovered—that the desert was far too hot for her or her sister to comfortably handle, but that they might be able to offer assistance in dealing with the extreme desert heat.

Tara mulled this information over all the next evening through dinner and then that night as she sat on her bed, thinking. Her mother and father were away at a noble's mansion toward the other side of the kingdom. Tara had been invited but pleaded unwellness in order to avoid the long and tedious ball sure to last all afternoon and into the night that was to cap the visit. She decided that she would leave before they returned, the better to obviate the need for painful explanations and discussions.

Tara daubed her mouth with her linen napkin and then put it down. She'd send word to her parents that she was going to visit a friend and would be away for a few days. This was true, even if it was the case that this friend would be Princess Ariel and she expected to meet her somewhere in the Lost Quarter rather than at some dwelling in Brythrony. As for why she was well enough to visit a friend but not well enough to attend the noble's ball, well, she'd have to figure that out later.

She'd ride Daystar. Ariel would offer Tara a ride in the sky chariot to Cloud Castle, which was nice and beautiful and all, but the chariot couldn't carry Daystar, and how was Tara to find dazzle dust in the desert on foot and alone? No, she needed Daystar to get around, so she would have to ride out to the Lost Quarter, however boring that might be.

Up in her tower, getting ready for bed, a last message bubble came in from Ice Princess Florence. She repeated that she could not join her, on account of the heat. But, she continued, she'd meet Tara on the way and provide her with some items that she thought would be useful.

Florence appeared two nights later, while Tara was rooming, incognito of course, at a simple country inn. It had cost a bit more, but Tara had asked for her own private room rather than spend the night with various other guests lodging there for the night. She was glad she had, because, as Tara was washing her face, she looked up to find Florence appearing without any warning at all. Had anyone been in the room, there would have been a commotion that would never have been hushed up.

There Tara had been, at the wash basin and splashing cold water on her face, when suddenly the room had turned much colder. Odd, she had thought: no passing weather front would have changed the temperature as suddenly as that, and Tara had immediately looked up, dripping, alert to the possibility of some sort of mischief, perhaps from her old foes. But a slight sighing, or maybe whirring sound, behind her had caused her to turn and see the start of the process she knew Ice Princess Florence used to transit the world outside her frozen principality.

First there was a blur in the air in a space roughly like that which a person might occupy, then it solidified into the form, vaguely, of a human. Layer by layer, a greyish-white ice slanted into the area occupied by the blur and, ever so gradually, the form of a person accumulated such that it was distinguishable as a figure of about her age and size and pale to the point of pallid. A moment later for the dress to turn its usual silvery-white and the circlet to take shape atop her head, and presto! Ice Princess Flo was in the room.

Tara had not met Flo's sister Crystal yet. But she understood from Ariel that Crystal had always been more retiring and reticent. Flo, on the other hand, was far more outgoing and adventurous.

"So glad to see you!" sang Flo on fully materializing in the room and gaining her bearings.

"Same here!" replied Tara, then, looking around, quieted her friend with a motion of her hand. "But I'm not at Stonedell. We should keep it down here."

Florence had nodded. "Sure," she said, hardly lowering her tone. "Let's be quiet. But come over here and see what I have for you!"

Tara had seen that Florence's hands were full and that something was slung over her back. Tara motioned her over to the bed, the only spot where two could sit together in any kind of comfort, and spread her arms as if to ask, well, what do you have?

"Take a look!" had replied Florence and offered her a package from each hand. Then she had slung from her shoulder what looked to be a quiver of arrows.

Tara had received these with great excitement and unwrapped them as Florence had explained what they were. The first was a small bag full of hoar frost. If a pinch were sprinkled over the head of someone or something, Florence had told her, it would keep that person or thing cool for a while, no matter the heat. Staying cool for an extended time would require repeated sprinkling.

"How long would it keep a person cool?" Tara had asked. Florence hadn't known. It depended on how hot it was, she had replied, how much hoar frost was sprinkled, and over how many people or things it was sprinkled.

Tara had thanked her and placed the small bag into her princess purse, which could hold all sorts of things but still appear as if empty.

The next item, Florence had explained, was the contents to the quiver she had unslung from her shoulder. She had passed it to Tara, telling her she would surely know what to do with these. Tara examined them as she received them. They looked like arrows. Florence's face betrayed a certain amount of pride, and she explained that they were "ice arrows."

"When you shoot these from your bow, they'll freeze whatever they hit when they land. In a circle radiating from where the arrow strikes."

"How big a circle?"

Florence had thought for a moment. "I don't know. Maybe it depends on how hard they strike, so like, how high you shoot them? But I don't know. Great question; I guess I should have looked into that." Florence seemed disappointed in herself for a moment, until Tara told her it was a wonderful thing and didn't matter anyway, and that she would surely figure out how to use them after shooting the first one or two.

This had taken them to the final item. Flo was particularly enthusiastic about it. "It's like a message bubble but quicker! Crystal and I use them all the time to talk to each other!"

Tara had taken a closer look. It was an irregularly shaped shard of ice that fit neatly within her palm. She looked up. "How does it work?"

Florence had told her. "I'm so sorry I can't join you in person, but it's just so hot! You can understand, it being a desert. But you can use this shard to contact me whenever you like. Just breathe on the shard and rub it. Then call for me. I've got one myself, of course. I'll know it's you, because you will have breathed on the shard; that's what identifies you. So I'll answer.

Just hold up the shard and talk into it, and I'll hear and see you. You'll be able to hear and see me too!"

Tara had thanked her for that and asked to try it out right then and there to make sure she knew how to operate it. She had breathed on the shard, rubbed it, and called for Florence. Her friend, smiling, had whipped out her own shard and promptly called out Tara's name at it. Right at that moment, Tara had seen in her own shard her friend's face and heard her voice.

"There, now you have these three things. I'm hoping they will be useful to you. I know you'll like the ice arrows; you're such a good archer!"

"Thank you so much, but I'm guessing the hoar frost might be most important in the desert."

"Whichever it may be, stay in touch with me through the ice shard. Let me know how it's going. I'll help you however else I can, even though I'll be far away!" With that, Florence had waved good night and vanished the same way she had arrived.

Tara sighed. That had been the night before. Now it was morning, and she was here, looking out into the sandy distance. She had left a note for her parents explaining that she wouldn't be too long. She was sorry she hadn't been able to send her mother a message bubble instead, but then her mother was a queen and not a princess and so didn't get a princess purse. Tara smiled. Her poor mother! She would have trouble anyway understanding what to do with a bubble floating down to her from an open window! She would probably try to shoo it away rather than hold out her hand to catch it. It wasn't her fault, of course, it was just that this was something new that her mother had never seen before.

Tara took a last look behind her at the relative greenery she was leaving and then back toward the desert. She might as well get started. Ariel would find her when her Cloud Castle was overhead. Sometimes weather delayed its progress, Tara knew, so there was no use waiting. Tara repositioned her princess purse with the hoar frost in it and urged Daystar forward. Best to use the hoar frost sparingly, only when she really needed it. She didn't think she would get any more.

"C'mon, boy, time for us to get going," she coaxed, and with that they took their first steps into the Lost Quarter.

An hour later and Princess Tara was reaching for the hoar frost. The sun beat down pitilessly, and waves of heat seemed to radiate from the sand. Good golly, thought Tara. How awful this is! And the sun was yet far from its peak! She knew she had to bring out the hoar frost, no matter what, when she felt Daystar tremble slightly beneath her in the saddle. Poor boy, she thought and leapt off right away. It was fine for her to put herself through this but not her innocent mount as well. Pulling out a pinch of hoar frost, she leaned in close to Daystar. "Here we go," she whispered, holding her hand above both their heads. "Let's give this a try!"

Down fluttered a shower of crystalline, spinning, sparkling motes. They seemed to scintillate as they drifted down, somewhat like falling dazzle dust and, as they whirled past, Tara laughed in spite of herself. Daystar tossed his head and nickered.

"Hey, it's nice, huh?"

Daystar nickered again and nuzzled Tara.

"Poor boy! It was so hot! But now, with this hoar frost, it's quite tolerable, isn't it?" The heat had instantly abated, and Tara sensed it not as the nearly physical force that had beat down on her before but as a mild, soothing warmth, like sunshine on a chilly fall day.

Tara laughed aloud for sheer pleasure. "Flo! You are a wonder!" She turned to her horse. "How are you feeling now? Better?" The horse tossed his head again, with considerably more life. "Super. Then we'll get going again. And why not some water too." She offered him some from a substantial sack she had filled. With those words, she remounted, and they started off, keeping the bag of hoar frost close to hand.

Tara gazed up into the brilliant blue sky. It sure was awfully bright. No sign of any cloud either. This was of particular interest to her, not because she was expecting any rain, but because she was looking for Ariel's Cloud Castle. Ariel was supposed to bring more water and provisions for both Tara and Daystar. Further, Ariel was supposed to inform Tara if she was on the right track to the dry riverbed containing the dazzle dust.

Another hour and Tara dropped another pinch of hoar frost over their heads. It was easy to know when the last application was fading. The sun ceased to be a warm kiss and intensified into a rough, rude shove. Daystar snorted too, and Tara understood this to be a complaint over the heat. "Coming, boy, coming," she soothed and sprinkled the frost over them again. This stuff was superb, she told herself again, for the hundredth time. Absolutely brilliant.

She looked up with renewed vigor to check the horizon again and caught sight of a strange swirl in the distance. It was growing in size rapidly and seemed to be heading straight for her. What on earth could that be, she wondered. A breeze tickled the strands of hair at her ear, and she brushed them back unconsciously. Then, realizing how unusual that was after so many hours of absolutely no wind, understanding dawned on her. That strange disturbance coming toward her must be some sort of dust storm. Instantly, Tara dismounted and turned Daystar such that his back was to it. "Stay with me, boy! Close your eyes!" she muttered.

In less than a minute, the storm was upon them. How quickly it came, thought Tara in what seemed like a remote corner of her mind, for a little voice inside her observed everything even as she was frantically taking whatever steps she thought necessary to ensure they passed through the storm uninjured. All about their feet, the sand first stirred then suddenly and simply rose up and begin to churn about their legs. Tara staggered and Daystar shuddered. The sand rose in a whirling column and quickly enveloped them. Tara, choking and gagging, suddenly remembered that they should be breathing through a cloth to prevent being suffocated by the madly swirling sand. She quickly slipped her head covering down and around her mouth and grabbed a shirt from her bag to pull over Daystar's head to protect him. The horse straightened and shivered, but Tara held him tightly so he would not bolt and tried to whisper in his ear that it was all right, so as to reassure him.

The sky overhead became dim and lost. Red sand howled around them and even the shape of Daystar, next to her, became vague and indistinct. When she dared open her eyes, Tara could hardly see in front of her. Buffeted by the winds and stung by the tiny grains of sand driving at her, Tara crouched as low as she could while hanging on to Daystar's neck.

On and on the wind sang and the sand flew. The sun overhead flickered wanly and nothing was audible but the wind's scream. Then, just as quickly, it was past. The sun brightened, the restless sand fell to the dunes at their feet, and Tara looked up again. Fading away from her was the same swirl that she had seen coming toward her minutes before. The sandstorm had passed. She lifted her right foot. It was deep in sand. "Another drink of water, Daystar?" she asked her horse, and he accepted gratefully. They turned back in the direction they had been heading and continued.

Perhaps an hour later, and another pinch or two of hoar frost, Tara and Daystar arrived at a slight escarpment. Some distance away, maybe half a mile, and tracing an irregular line, Tara spotted a corresponding escarpment leading up and back to the regular undulating waves of sand that formed the monotonous terrain of the Lost Quarter. The surface of the bed was absolutely flat, without any rocks, declivities, or acclivities to mar its surface. Tara nodded. "A dry riverbed, Daystar! I wonder if this could be it, the place where we'll find dazzle dust!"

Tara glanced down at the edge of the slope leading down. It was sand, not rock, and crumbled beneath her feet as she tentatively tested it. She looked down at the surface of the dry bed. How strange, she thought. It was smooth, nearly featureless. Had it been running so recently that the wind and always restless sand had not yet had the opportunity to mark it? Tara looked about her and found a rock of some size. She tossed it out onto the riverbed on impulse. Nothing. Just a curiosity, she thought. Strange, but nothing else. She began to look for the best way to pick her way down the slope to investigate the dry bed. As she started down, she glanced up once more for the rock she had thrown. It wasn't there.

Tara stopped, puzzled. But she had thrown the rock just a few moments before. She shaded her eyes and scanned the surface more carefully. Nothing. Daystar stirred beside her and whinnied. "Hang on, boy, hang on," she muttered. No rock, no nothing. Yet it should be there.

Though her background as Princess at Stonedell Castle had been fairly sheltered, Tara had seen too much with her princess friends to dismiss as inconsequential anything even as seemingly innocuous as a missing rock. Where was the rock? Cautiously, she took a step forward and tested the surface of the riverbed. It seemed to hold up to her touch. She turned to her horse. "Stay here, Daystar. Stay!" Tara ventured out alone onto the sand, stepping as lightly as she could. She looked back. Daystar cocked his head at her from the edge of the bed, swishing his tail back and forth.

Tara took a few more steps and laughed. That had been silly of her. It was no more than a sandy riverbed, just sediment washed down from somewhere higher. She would go back and fetch Daystar and they would cross in confidence. She turned and nearly stumbled in the process. Her feet felt stuck. She looked down and saw that her feet were several inches mired in the riverbed. She pulled her left foot out and took a step back toward the bank. She freed it but only with some effort. It came loose with a sickening, sucking sound. The effort had caused her other foot to sink past her ankle.

Tara looked up at Daystar, and the horse whinnied again at her, as if in confusion. She looked down at her feet. She was sinking. With a start, she realized it was quicksand. She was standing not in a riverbed but what had to be dry quicksand.

Rising panic enveloped Tara. At least Daystar wasn't in it, she thought. With his narrow legs bearing his much heavier weight—and maybe hers too!—it would have been impossible to pull him out. And she could have never abandoned him to the unthinkable doom of dry asphyxiation by choking sand.

"Stay, boy! Stay!" she reassured Daystar and checked her feet again. Her legs now in up nearly to her calves, she felt as though she were sinking more quickly. Don't struggle, she reminded herself with effort; that only accelerates it.

The problem, she remembered, her mind racing, was that there was nothing stable beneath quicksand. Nothing. Not for yard after endless yard. Well, that was with wet quicksand. But it had to be the same with dry quicksand. She didn't think she could sink too far in it, she told herself: people vanishing forever beneath the surface of wet quicksand was just a tale, a scary story. But she could become so stuck in it, like up to her waist, that she might not be able to get out on her own, at which point she would eventually be overcome by the desert sun and heat, hoar frost notwithstanding.

Tara looked down at her legs. Now she was in definitely up to her calves. She tried to move a foot and found it virtually impossible, even with several attempts. But recollecting the hoar frost gave her an idea. Maybe there wasn't water beneath her, this being dry quicksand, but anything frozen would be solid and be a surface on which she could stand and stop sinking. It had to be worth a try.

Tara reached behind her in one smooth motion and pulled an ice arrow from her quiver. "Don't worry, Daystar! I'm going to get out of this real soon!" She didn't have her bow; that was still at Daystar's saddle. She dared not call him over for that. Instead, she looked at the arrow for a long second and then, holding it high up on its shaft, plunged it as hard and deep as she could into the sand in front of her, angling it toward her feet. The instant the shaft was in to the fletching, she let go.

The effect was near instant. Tara felt she was no longer sinking and was standing on something firm. She smiled weakly in relief. She must be standing on frozen sand. Funny that, she thought, standing on ice in the middle of the desert! But there was no time to waste. As soon as she had stabilized, she should get out.

Tara found she could creep forward a little with a solid surface beneath her feet. Not much, but it was progress. Tara pulled out another ice arrow from her quiver. She'd have to use several like this.

Using three successively to create a solid ramp beneath her feet, she was gradually able to make her way out and back to the escarpment. Just in time too. The hoar frost was beginning to wear off. Another pinch and some water for both of them and Tara, with a deep breath, was ready to try again. This time, she grabbed her bow and, aiming straight up, shot an ice arrow for the first time. It seemed to almost sizzle as it left her bow and trailed a faint trace of sparkles as it flew. It climbed high, high into the sky, then fell back to land only a little way from her, burying itself completely in the riverbed with a tiny swish. In a wide radius from where it landed, the riverbed flipped from a dusty tan to a dirty white that glinted dully in the brilliant sunlight. Tara smiled and picked up another rock. She threw it at the gleaming radius around where the arrow had fallen. The rock clattered on the now solid sand and skittered away.

"Come on, boy, I think we can build ourselves a path across!" Tara told her horse and, taking him by the bridle, led him onto the ice. When she had gotten about halfway from the center of the circle to the perimeter, Tara shot another arrow to take her most of the way across the quicksand. She looked back. Good, she noted with satisfaction: the sand still looked frozen solid where the first ice arrow had landed.

One more and she should easily be able to make it across, she figured. But this made her remember something that had occurred to her while she had been stuck fast in the quicksand. Marina had told her that the dazzle dust was within a riverbed. Hadn't the course of dry quicksand resembled a riverbed? She paused to check her princess purse for the traces of dazzle dust still in the purse. It was exceptionally fine, as fine as a powder. Was that what was underfoot, far, far down? Not yard after yard of sand but yard after yard of dazzle dust, underneath a layer of innocuous desert sand?

On impulse, she knelt down with the long knife in her hand she kept at her saddlebag. It was not a fighting weapon; it was too short for that. But it was useful for cutting ropes and branches and such things. Kneeling, she sliced into the frozen sand down to the hilt and around to cut out a square. Pulling the telescoping rod from her princess purse, she commanded it to extend a short way and, with a twist and some force, used it to lever out and flip over the block of frozen sand. She peered within. Nothing of interest that she could see. Just more frozen sand. Maybe she needed to go a little deeper to really see if there was anything. She cut out two more blocks of similar size to either side of the first then, deeper, cut out another square within the larger hole. Ordering the rod to extend a little further, she levered up a larger block within the hole. It was too heavy for her to lift out in one piece, so she cut it into chunks.

Tara paused and wiped her brow. Heavy work! And hot too—even with the hoar frost!

Tara glanced down again and thought she saw a grey powdery substance deep within the hole, something of a different shade of grey and a different granularity than the grey-white frozen sand around it. She looked up and wiped her brow then stuck her hand into the hole. It felt like powder. She shifted her position. There; now her shadow no longer fell across the hole. Instantly she had to avert her eyes. With the sunlight on it, the hole emitted a single coherent beam of light into the sky that seemed to outshine even the brilliant desert sun.

Dazzle dust. She had found it. At the bottom of a "riverbed." Just as Marina's library had promised.

Tara dove one hand into the powder and pulled it back up again, letting streams of the dust pour through her fingers back into the hole. Down it poured, thin, solid streams of liquid, scintillating fire that flickered as it flowed with all the colors of the spectrum. "Unbelievable," she whispered. "All the dazzle dust we could ever want. So this is where it comes from."

She looked up again. The sun was past its zenith. She couldn't stay in the desert much longer. It would be dark before long. She had to get going. She whistled and called to Daystar and, after first sprinkling another pinch of hoar frost over them both, grabbed the empty saddle-bags she had brought with her. She tossed them on the ground and proceeded to scoop out handful after handful of dazzle dust as quickly as she could. This should be enough, she thought, when she had at last filled them. If not, well, they could always come back for more, now that they knew where to find it and how to get it.

She pushed and heaved to move the blocks of still-frozen sand back in place, roughly fitting the chunks into the hole as best she could. The quicksand, as it thawed, would do the rest in filling in the gaps.

Making her way back across the dry riverbed was simply a matter of using a few more ice arrows. Once on the other side, Tara located her and Daystar's footprints leading to the escarpment. "C'mon, boy," she said to her horse. "We'll just follow them back to where we came from."

Not so tough after all, she mused, her back to the sun and their shadows beginning to lengthen before them. Maybe this would turn out all right. Funny, no sign of Ariel yet. Tara glanced up at the sky. Still cloudless. Must be some sort of weather system that was detaining her.

This made her think to check in with someone, and Tara reached into her princess purse to pull out the ice shard Florence had given her. Tara breathed on it, rubbed it and called for her friend.

A few moments later, Florence's face appeared, clear in the center but a little distorted toward the edges. "Hey! I was wondering when I would hear from you! How's the search going?"

Tara grinned back. "Hey yourself! It's going fine, thanks! I think I found our dazzle dust." Tara shifted the ice shard's field of view such that it included the saddlebags to either side of Daystar. "See this? They're full!"

Florence gasped. "Full? We'll never run out now!"

"Yes. Well, not for a long time. And there's more too. Lots more. If we should want it!"

"Tara, you're incredible! You did it! You found it!"

Tara smiled self-deprecatorily. "Well, I had plenty of help. From you, for example! The ice arrows and hoar frost you gave me were critical!

"And," patting her horse, "from this guy here, Daystar!" Florence laughed, but Tara's thoughts remained on something Florence had said, that they would never run out of dazzle dust now. This was true, now that they had so much. But what if someone else found it and used it against them, or in some way that none of them had yet imagined? Tara shrugged. They could hardly guard it, out here in the Lost Quarter, or take all of it back to Stonedell and keep it locked up! Besides, no one had taken it yet, so maybe no one ever would.

"Tara? Did you hear me?"

"Oh! Sorry! I missed that! Could you repeat, please?"

"Um, so I was asking you where you were and what was next."

"Sure! Sorry about that. Well, I'm still here in the desert, making my way back. I was supposed to be joined by Ariel. But she still hasn't shown. Fortunately, I found what we were after anyway, but I was wondering if you had heard from her at all?"

Florence shook her head. "No, nothing. Do you want me to check with my sister to see if she has anything?"

Tara considered for a moment. "No," she said at last, slowly. "No, no point in that. Probably not worth it. She'd be here if she could. Must be delayed for some good reason or another. I guess she's—"

"Tara? What? What is it?" Florence demanded. Tara had stopped talking, and the ice shard had shifted such that Florence could only see a small fraction of the sky overhead, as if Tara's hand had fallen to her side.

Tara's voice came distantly and without the image of her face, only the sky. "I don't know what that is… It's… enormous…"

"What is it? Show me! Hold up the shard and show me!"

Florence's view of Tara's world changed with dizzying speed. The deepening blue sky flashed upwards to be replaced with that of unrelieved sand in infinite variegated shades of brown and khaki. Then this blurred as Tara swung the shard up and levelled it at the horizon. Florence squinted into the shard, trying to make out the object in the distance. It looked like a red splotch, vaguely roiling and filling the horizon. Florence very nearly pressed her eye against the ice shard, so intent she was on trying to make out what was in the distance. It was something huge—and getting bigger. Florence knew little about deserts, but she remembered stories told to her as a youth, horror stories of deserts, the sort used to frighten her sister and her when they played games with friends. They had told each other of all sorts of desert monsters, including natural phenomena that they had never seen before and didn't know, really, the first thing about—

"Tara! It's a sandstorm! A giant sandstorm!"

"But I went through one of those on the way in. It was small and passed quickly! It wasn't at all like what's coming toward me."

"Well, I don't know what it was you met back then, but it wasn't a real live sandstorm like this one. Must have just been a dust devil or something like that."

"No; this is the real thing. This is a real sandstorm!"

"How do you know that? You're an ice princess! What do you know about the desert?"

"It's a long story. But trust me. Dismount Daystar, get some cloth—quick—and wet it and wrap it around your mouth so you'll be able to breathe. It'll be upon you in a minute!"

"And don't forget Daystar!"

Tara complied wordlessly. So she had only encountered a dust devil—was that what Florence had called it?—earlier that day. But she should prepare in the same way for the sandstorm now coming toward her.

Tara did as Florence recommended and wrapped her face and that of Daystar. "Here we go, boy; here we go again! Our backs to the storm, as best we can!" Tara glanced around quickly. No, there wasn't any shelter nearby. Nothing at all. The ground was very nearly flat, with hardly a hollow in which to hide herself. The wind intensified, and Daystar began to surge in his bridle, as if he might bolt. "Easy, boy," she urged and clung tighter to him.

Flying sand began to sting her calves and the back of her neck. Small eddies fled past her feet and into the dunes. Daystar's muzzle sought Tara's shoulder. Tara grasped his bridle and held it as close to her as she could to comfort him. The wind began to howl. She darted a glance over her shoulder and saw that the storm now towered over her and had turned a baleful, wine-dark red. Flashes of lightning flickered and traced through the blur, like luminescent veins, or like optical cracks of a whip, urging it onward.

Tara braced herself for the worst. She clung tighter to Daystar, as much as for him as for herself. Florence's image in the ice shard, still calling frantically to her, flickered and faded to a flat grey.

The edge of the storm swept over her and she staggered from the sheer force of the storm's edge. But even as she hunkered over to try to stay upright, she over-balanced and nearly fell backwards. The wind had ceased. She dared open her eyes and saw that she and Daystar stood within a small lacuna. Overhead and around her, lightning continued to spark menacingly through the claret-red, boiling storm, but she and her horse stood undisturbed within their tiny haven.

This wasn't just a sandstorm. Something else was going on. Tara straightened and shook the sand in a shower from her clothes. Whoever or whatever was behind this would show itself soon enough, she knew. She might as well meet that entity standing up rather than crawling.

A voice rasped out, as if out of the very air itself, startling both her and Daystar. "You."

Tara gathered her composure and lifted her head. In what direction should she face? The voice seemed to come from all around her. "Yes, me." Not knowing what to say next, she continued, trying to keep hers a statement rather than the accusation that had been levelled to her. "You."

"You!" came the voice again. It was feminine, vaguely, but with a hard, angry edge. It rasped too, and there was a faint susurrus, or slurring, in the way it trailed off at the end.

"Well, what about me?"

"You. Who are you?"

"I'm Princess Tara. And who are you?"

"I… I am the Desert."

"You perceive me as a storm."

That was true, allowed Tara silently. And what a storm she was! But Tara said nothing. So far, this desert "presence" had done nothing to molest her except use unconventional tones in addressing her. And that could just be a misunderstanding. So Tara hoped, at least.

Tara waited. What more could she do? She observed the flashing lightning all about her, brilliant white forking tongues that instantaneously licked the outer edges of the tiny sphere in which she was sheltered. The air reeked of ozone. The tiny space in which she and her horse stood seemed to throb and flux, as if from mighty forces pressing urgently from the outside. The sandstorm boiled around them, a blood-red blur of motion and horror laced with flickering, pure, liquid energy.

The moments lengthened. The voice came again. "You."

Tara waited longer. The tone of the voice edged from one of accusation to barely suppressed fury. Each time the voice came, the otherwise intermittent lightning around them lashed the sphere violently.

"What would you with me?" Tara asked at last, forcing a note of confidence into her voice. She worried as to where the tone might escalate next.

The lightning ceased to flash for a moment, and the storm paused such that for one tiny moment, all the grains froze in the air. Then it renewed with the same terrible ferocity. "I knew you earlier."

Tara hesitated, unsure of the meaning of this assertion.

The Desert continued. "Earlier, within this day. I passed through you. Like so." The voice hung in the air, expectantly, and the sphere in which Tara and Daystar stood expanded and divided across from her. The sphere pulled back to leave behind a tiny, human-sized sandstorm that whirled in sync with the larger one around them, then it grew and took shape. To Tara's astonishment, it divided and took the shape of a person and a horse, bent over, as if being buffeted by some invisible force. The figures were those of herself and Daystar, Tara recognized suddenly, formed of spinning sand, as they had been before the dust devil earlier in the day.

The voice spoke again, a note of triumph in it now. "It is you. The same."

Tara gasped. "That was you we encountered? Earlier?"

"One of my servitors. One. But all that they touch with any grain of sand, any breath of wind, they sense, and so I sense likewise. I do not have these 'eyes' that you and other creatures of my world have, yet I know even better every detail of you."

The lacuna shrank back to its original size, and the sand figures of Tara and Daystar were subsumed into the greater storm around them.

The voice continued, after a brief pause to savor Tara's amazement. "You, you have something. Something you did not before. The bags. They are full now, when before they were not."

The dazzle dust, Tara realized. The dust devil had conveyed every contour of her and Daystar to this desert thing, some kind of witch or something, including those of the empty bags. But when this storm had swept over them, the saddlebags had been filled to bulging.

The Desert Witch wanted to know with what Tara had filled them.

"What do you mean?" bluffed Tara. How much did the Desert Witch know? It didn't know what was in her saddlebags. Only that it had come from the desert and had to be valuable, because why else would Tara be in these wastelands and fill her saddlebags so fully?

Nor could the Witch know where the dust had been found, since the dazzle dust was deep below the sand and beyond the perception of the Witch's wind-borne grains.

The winds seemed to spin faster and the lightning flashed more proximate than before. The space in which Tara and Daystar stood contracted perceptibly. "You. You have something. Mine."

"Yours? Everything in the desert is yours?"

"Everything."

"And you too. When you are here."

Tara found the expansiveness of that claim profoundly disquieting. How could it be true that everything in the desert, even Tara, "belonged" to the Desert Witch? Not so! Tara didn't "belong" to anyone!

Now the Desert Witch wanted the saddlebags of dazzle dust. If Tara surrendered them, would she be released? Or would this monstrous thing compel Tara to reveal where she had found it?

Then what?

As if in answer, a roundish white object suddenly fell out of the cloud and bounced to the ground at the periphery of her vision. The irregularly shaped ball rolled to a stop at the very edge of the lacuna in which Tara stood. She peered more closely at it then recoiled. It was a human skull, its sightless sockets staring askew into the empty sky, its mirthless grin forever fixed. A moment later, the warning conveyed, it was swept back up again into the tumult and was gone.

That was enough. Tara knew that she could never give the Witch the dazzle dust. Just imagine the Desert Witch in possession of all the dazzle dust beneath the riverbed. Swept into her cloud and kept perpetually aloft by her fierce winds, she would become the most intense light in the whole world, second only to the sun. Tara was at a loss on how to deal with her now; she'd be invincible when no one could even look at her.

Tara snuck a peek at her ice shard. It was blank; somehow, the sandstorm must be interfering with it. She looked up into the maelstrom surrounding her; impossible to get a message bubble through that. And Tara dared not show the dazzle dust.

This made Tara think of the last thing she had in her princess purse: the marvelous telescoping rod. It was hollow and made of a strange metal. It extended quite far too, though Tara had never really tested its limits.

Tara gazed into the fantastically turbulent cloud around her, with its now almost constant lightning flashes. It was darkening steadily, from the color of blood to, increasingly, an ominous mahogany black. Wasn't it like a thunderstorm, in a sense, replete with lightning? Thunderstorms came every so often to Stonedell. For protection against them, metal batons had been attached to the roof of Castle Stonedell. Once, she had climbed out on the roof of the North Tower from her bedroom window to look at them. Her parents had punished her for that, and probably they had been right to do so, afraid as they had been that she could have died falling from such a height. Still, she had asked for the reason behind the small rods and the metal strips attached to them snaking down the walls to the ground below. She had been told that they were there to pull lightning away from the castle and send it to the ground, where it would do no harm.

"You have what is mine! Give it!" howled the voice, the threat in it now unmistakable. "Or…" and the voice trailed off. Just as it died, one of the forks of lighting leapt through the sphere surrounding them and touched the sand at the very edge with a sizzling crack. Daystar leapt in his bridle, nearly pulling Tara's arm out of its socket.

"Steady, boy!" she cried, hastening to soothe him. She turned back to the curved walls surrounding her. "I understand! I'll give you what you want! Just wait while I get it!"

It would be a terrible risk, but Tara felt she had no choice. Rather than reach for the saddlebags, Tara reached into her princess purse and stealthily pulled out the telescoping rod. She stepped cautiously to the edge of the sphere, rod in hand.

Impossible that the Desert Witch could know of the existence of the rod: the princess purse held whatever was placed within without any indication of the object's bulk or weight. Impossible also that the Desert Witch could see what Tara was holding in her hand at that moment, since no sand grains were touching her, and this was the Witch's main sensory organ.

So far, so good then. Now for the risky part.

Tara whispered for the rod to extend a bit and pushed it deep into the sand. Then she stepped back to Daystar.

"Give it to me! Now!"

Just like you want, agreed Tara, silently. "All right, I'll give it to you," she said aloud, obligingly. "Rod," she called softly, "maximum length, now!" Immediately the rod shot up from the sand to its fullest length and pierced the wall of the sphere.

The lightning strokes within the cloud instantly gathered to terminate at the tip of the rod, which began to shiver and glow with the continuous arcing. A high-pitched keening erupted from all around Tara, and the sphere pulsed fitfully. At first only at the far tip, but steadily creeping downward, the rod turned a brilliant incandescent blue-white, and the sand in which the rod was embedded began to glow.

The sphere began to shrink and the tornado around them slowed. The lightning flashed less frequently, even as the keening rose to a sustained wail. The rod began to writhe from the energy coursing through it and the sand at its base bubbled in a molten, smoking pool.

Tara stepped to the stirrups and into Daystar's saddle. "Just a few moments more, boy, and we'll be able to run for it!" If the rod could hold up. Cross our fingers for that though and hope for the best. She reached into her pouch and pulled out another several pinches of hoar frost in readiness.

Another few seconds and the sphere had retreated enough so that they were again standing in the desert, the sandstorm behind them slowly collapsing about the fiery, bowing rod. Tara looked around. From which direction had they entered the sandstorm, and in which should they continue? The sandstorm had effaced all their tracks. Most any direction away from the Desert Witch was the right direction in which to ride, Tara quickly decided.

"Now, boy! Let's run; run while we can!"

Daystar needed no further goading. He bolted forward with such a jerk that Tara was thrown back in her saddle. When she thought they had put some distance between them and the Witch, Tara dared glance behind her. She couldn't determine if the sandstorm was still deflating. Surely the rod would fail shortly, or already had, and the Desert Witch would regain her strength. Tara just hoped it would take a long time.

Far up ahead, Tara spotted what might be shrubs or trees. It wasn't where they had entered the desert, but it would be fine for where they would exit. The desert sand soon yielded to rocky, barren ground, and Tara found herself in what looked to be a barren field. Checking and seeing no sign of a regenerated Desert Witch, Tara dismounted and gave Daystar the last of their water, even though she was parched with thirst herself.

Daystar browsed disinterestedly at the sparse brown grass. It hardly looked appetizing, not compared to the green fields of Brythrony. There were stands of ragged trees in scattered clumps in the distance, none of them apple trees for poor Daystar. Tara looked up and searched the sky. This was when Ariel was supposed to resupply them. But there were still no clouds and so still no Ariel. Now, the sun was starting to sink. Tara sighed. Evening would be on them in an hour or two, and they should seek any sort of shelter and something for them both to eat.

Twilight found Tara wandering across the broken pavement of what appeared to have been meant as a courtyard but had to have been abandoned for years. It was within a large, rambling structure, once rather grand but now vacant and some parts of it tumbledown. It was a little creepy, to be sure, silent and dark like it was, but there was not much else for shelter that was more solid. Overhead, the stars were coming out.

Then, through an archway, Tara spotted what she least expected. A girl, of somewhat indeterminate age in the half-light, was playing alone in an adjoining courtyard. Tara squinted. She appeared to be playing a game with three metallic balls, each about the size of her two fists together, that rolled around and about her in an intricate choreography.

Tara's immediate reaction was to pull back and watch cautiously. Who could be living here in this abandoned place? Was she even real? Tara shrank deeper into the shadows. Perhaps she was another witch!

The girl suddenly looked up, took a single step in Tara's direction and halted. One of the balls commenced rolling directly toward her hiding place.

Strange to bowl a metal sphere toward me, thought Tara. What could it mean? But reasoning that there was no further point in concealment, Tara stirred up her courage and, trying to look as dignified as possible despite all the desert dust, stepped forward such that she was framed by the archway between the two courtyards. "Hello! Who are you, may I ask?"

The girl did not seem startled at all to see Tara appear. It was almost as if she had expected her. In the darkening twilight, Tara couldn't be sure whether the girl had retrieved her balls or if they had rolled to her on their own. She took another two steps toward Tara. "Who are you?" she replied, sharply.

Tara took a cautious step closer herself to better see the girl. Actually, she looked—roughly—to be Tara's age, just not as tall and with a more compact frame. Her hair was a deep black, her complexion a light olive, as many in lands lying close to the desert could be. "I'm Tara. I've come from far away. I'm a traveler now, and," she glanced around her at the gathering twilight, "I'm seeking shelter for the night."

The girl regarded her with an open, critical gaze that made Tara uncomfortable as it stretched into long seconds.

"Who are you?" Tara asked again, trying to keep her voice moderate and friendly since, after all, she was a guest in that land and that courtyard.

"We never have travelers here. Never. Where do you come from?"

"I'm from the Kingdom of Brythrony. It's a long way from here. Several days' ride." Tara did not feel it prudent yet to reveal she was from the royal house, recollecting her adventures with the pirates who had sought to ransom her.

"I don't know that place. But," she added, almost wistfully, "I haven't been anywhere. Not hardly."

The girl's change in tone brought out Tara's sympathetic side. How could someone like her be dangerous anyway? "What's your name? Please."

"Atalanta," the girl replied after a few moments' hesitation. "I'm Atalanta. Of the House of Orla. I'm the true princess of this realm, of Maurienne." She gestured broadly, ruefully. "And this is Orlaith Palace."

The girl's demeanor had unexpectedly changed from one of suspicion and reticence to innocence and forthcomingness and the last of Tara's concerns were allayed. "Are you really? Well, I'm a princess too! I'm Princess Tara of the House of Hession. Of Brythrony. My father is King Childeric and my mother is Queen Armorica."

The girl nodded soberly. "I think you're telling me the truth."

"I am."

Atalanta looked down at the three balls she was cradling in her arms, then into Tara's face as openly as she had before, though this time with incipient trust. With a slow, solemn movement, she began to open her arms. Rather than fall, the balls stayed balanced on her arms. Odd trick, that, thought Tara. As odd as bowling one of them toward me when she sensed my presence.

Atalanta opened her arms further, and the balls rolled off. Still they didn't fall but bobbed once and then floated next to her, then rose to the height of her head. Another moment and they had commenced circling her head in an interlocking series of slow and stately orbits.

Atalanta had kept her eyes locked on Tara the whole time. "These are magic balls," she said simply.

Tara nodded wordlessly. Clearly they were.

"They obey only me."

Tara nodded again.

"They obey me because I am the true princess of this land. They will obey only the true princess of this land, and only the true princess of this land can command them."

What a strange place this was! If she had not seen the balls orbiting Atalanta herself, she would have never believed it. "That makes sense," was all Tara could think to say.

"Let's go inside," said Atalanta after another lengthy pause. "And I'll tell you the story."

Clearly no one had been by in a long time, thought Tara. Atalanta was now anxious to talk to anyone. They walked into a hall lit only by several scattered torches. Though the light was very dim, Tara could tell that the hall had seen better days.

Atalanta commenced telling Tara her story, even as they were walking.

"It all happened a long time ago. Generations, for sure. Maurienne was beautiful and green, and rich from its crops and dairy farming. We were a peaceable kingdom, and didn't like war, so we allied with some of the neighboring kingdoms for defense. We said that, if any of the kingdoms had need of aid, the others would come to the needful one's assistance.

"We hoped that would mean there would never be a need for warfare.

"This was fine, for a long time. No one needed any help. But one day, one did. There was an invasion. I don't know what it was about. All the other allies sent help, like troops, or something else. All except ours. The king and queen at the time said that neither the ally nor the invader was right, and that it was complex.

"Then, they also said that maybe the other kingdoms with whom we were allies might not win against the invaders. Then what? And our troops and treasure will have been wasted on a lost cause."

"So Maurienne didn't send any help."

Atalanta paused to check that Tara was still listening. Atalanta resumed, shaking her head as if still unable to comprehend the story even though she knew it very well.

"But the other kingdoms won anyway against the invaders. It took longer and there was more bloodshed than there should have been, but they still won.

"One day the armies of the allies came back. A great queen was at their head. They surrounded Orlaith Palace. Everyone was afraid the palace would be stormed and burned down. The great queen called for the king and queen to show themselves when she had the palace totally cut off and at her mercy. The king and queen were afraid but had no choice. And so they went outside the palace gates, expecting to be killed.

"But the great queen and her armies didn't want to kill them. Or burn down Orlaith. Instead, they had come to pronounce a terrible curse."

Atalanta's voice had become distant and faltering as she had finished those last words. Then she picked up again, but not in the short, clipped sentences in which she had previously used. Rather, she began again in a far grander, more eloquent style, as if reading from a book describing the events. And perhaps she was, surely having read this passage of a chronicler many, many times.

"And a great queen was at their head. Her armies surrounded Orlaith Palace and stamped their feet and clashed their swords one against the other, demanding as one that the king and queen appear. And at last they did appear, trembling, and very frightened, for they were very afraid of what was to become of them and their house.

"From a platform just outside the walls, hastily erected from the shields of her troops piled one atop the other, the great queen stood and pointed her finger at them. She commanded the king and queen to their knees and spoke these words: 'Just as you failed your allies when they needed you, so shall your lands fail you and become desolate. Inasmuch as you would not risk what was precious to you on behalf of another, so shall your lands remain barren until you place in jeopardy for another's sake that which you hold most precious.'"

Atalanta looked up to Tara again, checking again that Tara was still listening. Reassured she was, Atalanta resumed but again in uneven, short sentences and a halting voice.

"The queen and her armies departed. Maurienne celebrated, because everyone had feared far worse. But within weeks, it was obvious that something was wrong. It was the curse. The sun never stopped shining, and rains didn't come. The land dried out, and the crops withered. No matter what we tried, we couldn't bring rain or water. And so all the crops failed and Maurienne became poor. None of the former allies would help or forgive us."

"Are you hungry?" Atalanta asked abruptly, and Tara gathered that the story had concluded.

"Well, yes, I am, thank you. But may I look after my horse first, please?"

Atalanta nodded and led Tara to the palace stables, which looked hardly used. Tara noted that Atalanta had seemed a little unsure at points as to how to get there. What a contrast, for Tara knew all the paths to the stables of Castle Stonedell.

Daystar fed and watered, the two girls returned to the palace's central hall. "Not to pry," ventured Tara, "but I hardly see anyone else in the palace. But you aren't alone, right?"

Atalanta shook her head. "No. I'm not alone. There are some others here. Most everyone left, though."

"Oh," was all Tara could think by way of reply. They left? But for where? Another kingdom? To try to farm the dusty fields? Tara couldn't imagine Stonedell without the gardeners, the groomsmen, the cooks, the guards, and so many more. In fact—a thought occurred to Tara. "Where are your parents?"

"They died," replied Atalanta, shortly, bluntly. Tara waited, but Atalanta offered no elaboration. "Nobody cares for me. Or about me." The golden balls around her head slowed imperceptibly in their ceaseless orbit, dropping fractionally so that they revolved just above the crown of her head. "I don't know that I deserve any better either. I am the true princess of Maurienne, but I have done nothing to save it."

Tara placed her spoon beside the bowl in which the simple soup on which she had supped had been served. Its pattern didn't match that of the plate beside it or that of the bowl containing Atalanta's meal. This was a dreadful situation, thought Tara. Simply dreadful. No parents, no one to look after her, no one who even cared whether she was happy or sad or lived or died. Tara eyed Atalanta sympathetically. Atalanta didn't meet her gaze but stared into her lap, her hands folded, her face set in an expression of resignation, hurt, and apathy. Her eyelashes trembled, but her jaw was set and there were no tears.

"Can I help in any way?" offered Tara impulsively. She was moved to pity for the poor girl, but even as she spoke she wondered how she could possibly assist. She was being foolish and silly: how could Tara possibly help Atalanta lift a curse that had been set many years before under circumstances she hardly understood?

But Atalanta's face brightened at Tara's offer and she looked up again hopefully. "Maybe you could? No one has ever offered to help before!"

Tara hardly knew where to start. Maybe, she suggested, could Atalanta think of anything more that might help her understand the curse and its origins? "And," she added tentatively, "you could also tell me about those golden balls of yours, which are always circling your head? I've never seen anything like it."

Atalanta nodded. "Yes. I can explain. The three golden balls. They're mine. They'll do anything I tell them to do, like roll or float or hover or fly. They can tell me what lies all around them, so it is like I can sense by them also.

"They're about all I have left of Maurienne's treasure. It wasn't huge to begin with, and all of it was spent trying to bring water to irrigate the land. But none of the projects ever worked that well. Maybe they failed because of the curse.

"The balls weren't sold, because my mother and father were sure they had special powers. Though they could never do anything with them themselves.

"Then, one day, when I was still a baby, my mother brought me into the treasury. The balls rolled over to me, all on their own, and clustered around my head. My mother and father were amazed. That was when my father remembered an old story that the balls would only obey the true ruler of the kingdom, that no one else could command them, and they would obey no other person.

"They've stayed with me ever since. Always. Ever since I was a baby." Atalanta chuckled, but sadness tinged her voice. "My mother used to tell me that whenever she looked in on me at night, she knew right away that everything was all right, because she could spot the balls circling over me. Silently, in and out of the moonlight. Like they were watching over me." Atalanta fell silent. Tara looked over at her quickly. The light was dim; it would have been hard to have seen her new friend's face, even if it had not been bowed ever so slightly.

"So, that's all I have," Atalanta concluded. "Everything."

Tara swallowed. What painful memories she must have of this place. She's lost everything; there's nothing left but an immense ruin.

"Let me see if I can help," volunteered Tara again. "Princesses need to stick together, right? I have friends, other princesses, and they are awfully capable and helpful. I'm sure they'd help too."

Atalanta looked up, and Tara saw in the flickering torchlight a single tear running down each cheek of her upturned face.

"Sure! I'm sure we can help!" Tara thought of Ariel and Cloud Castle. Ariel knew a lot about clouds, and clouds brought rain. Maybe she might have some ideas on what they could do to restore rainfall. "Tell me more about this curse. What we need to do is to lift it. That's it! Can you tell me more about it? More than the story you already told me earlier."

Atalanta nodded and, wordlessly, led Tara back down the echoing main hall nearly to its entrance. "See. See here." A length of what looked to be torn drapery lay on the floor. Atalanta yanked it aside with a single jerk and Tara saw, glowing by its own dim but steady light, an imprecation incised on the flag stones.

>Sear, scorch, sun, sand:
>I call a curse upon your land;
>Wind, waste, wither, wilt:
>See this now and recall your guilt;
>Burn, bake, blaze, blight:
>Such words henceforth shall speak your plight;
>Drought, dust, dry, dune:
>Make amends, or face your ruin.

"How did this get here?" gasped Tara.

"The curse. It appeared right after the queen spoke. It's been here ever since. At first, they tried to wash it away, but it wouldn't, no matter how hard they tried. Then they tried to paint over it, but it always showed through."

"At last," she concluded, and her voice softened, "they gave up, and accepted it as truth."

Tara shook her head. This looked like a serious curse. "You clearly need help. Do you see this?" she asked, showing Atalanta the princess purse at her side. "It contains some things you, as a fellow princess, need to have. I'm missing one," and Tara paused ruefully, thinking of the telescoping rod she had had to sacrifice to escape the Desert Witch, "but the rest is still here."

Tara opened her purse and reached within. "This little bag contains dust which is very useful, because it blinds temporarily everyone around except the person who throws it. And this," she said, pulling out the vial containing the fluid for the message bubbles, "is how we communicate with each other." Tara wet her palm from the mug of water she had carried with her then poured a drop from the vial into her palm. She clapped her hands together then drew them apart to create a small, glossy bubble. Almost kissing it, and to Atalanta's fascination, she whispered, "Ariel, when you come, please bring an extra princess purse with everything it should have in it! And also," adding as an afterthought, "please bring me an extra telescoping rod. Mine's gone, but it's a long story."

Tara lifted the bubble, blew on it, whispered "Ariel," and the bubble floated up, hesitated for a moment and drifted into the darkness of the hall's rafters.

Atalanta watched the bubble vanish, as if spellbound.

Tara turned back to her. "Now we'll get some help. Let me meet with them and we'll be sure to help you. Don't worry! I have to leave tomorrow to return to my own kingdom, but we won't forget you."

"Do you promise?"

"Absolutely." To seal it, Tara embraced her new friend, whose spirits seemed to lift before Tara's eyes.

The next morning the two set off, Atalanta desiring to accompany Tara as far as she reasonably could without a horse of her own. As they walked, Tara spoke of her own, very different childhood, and the two contrasted it with Atalanta's. Remembering the pain that the memory of her deceased parents brought her, Tara kept the discussion focused on happier moments, especially ones in which Atalanta had succeeded or coped well with adversity.

Inevitably, they spoke of Atalanta's golden balls. Tara was enthralled by the complicated, intricate pattern they wove, always moving and spinning, rising and falling, tightening or widening their orbit as they circled Atalanta's head and never once touching each other. It was as if they were aware of their own and the others' movements, for they moved too fast and too high for Atalanta to be controlling them herself.

Atalanta explained. "I've had them for so long that I don't know how it happens. That I control them. Or rather, maybe I should say that they have had me for so long!" She smiled for perhaps the first time Tara had seen. "I don't know how I communicate with them. I just think what I would like them to do, and they do it. Sometimes I whisper instructions; sometimes it's like they do what I want even before I think of it. It's like they're a part of me, we're so close."

"You mentioned last night that, when you were a child, they would hover over your head while you slept, protecting you."

"Yes. If I were threatened, I think they would fly at my attacker." She became pensive. "They can move quite fast, and they're heavy, so it would really hurt if they hit someone at full speed.

"But I've never had to do that. I guess," she admitted, looking up at Tara, "I've lived a sheltered life, even though I've mostly been on my own."

Tara told her she was lucky at least for that and recounted her encounter with the Desert Witch. Atalanta was amazed. "You thought of using your rod like that? On the spot?"

Tara nodded, a little proud, in spite of herself. "I did. I guess I've gotten myself into all sorts of situations, and I've had to get good at getting myself out of them! So far, at least!"

Shortly, Atalanta gauged by how far the sun had traversed the sky that she should make her way back to Orlaith Palace. They parted emotionally, even though they had only met the day before. "You promise you won't forget me, will you? You promise you'll help me?" asked Atalanta, and Tara heard her voice waver with emotion.

"Yes. I'll be back. We'll get you a princess purse first and then my friends and I will set about figuring out how to lift that curse."

Atalanta embraced Tara then drew herself erect and addressed Tara with a new solemnity. "I promise to help you also, Princess Tara. If you ever need help, I promise to come to your aid with whatever I have."

With a sudden gesture, Atalanta sent one of her golden balls to float beside Tara. "Let me help you right now. Let this ball lead you to the edge of Maurienne, so that you won't be wandering alone. Don't worry; I'll still have the other two."

"But how will you get it back?"

Atalanta shrugged. "We still won't be too far apart. I think that only if we got *really* far apart would we lose touch."

The spinning, floating ball led Tara for another hour or two, until she felt a sudden and unexpected breeze spring up. Daystar stopped also and required coaxing to continue. This was strange, thought Tara, looking around with concern. Then, behind her and from the direction of the desert, she saw a blurry shape that she had seen the day before, out in the desert. It looked to be quickly overtaking them.

"It's a dust devil," she thought and heaved a sigh. "Coming for me. Or could it be the Desert Witch herself?" Tara reined in her horse and dismounted. From within her princess purse, she whipped out the ice shard to contact Florence before she was overtaken entirely.

Florence came up quickly. Tara interrupted her immediately, before she could even open her mouth in a greeting. "Flo!" she called, worriedly. "I need help! That huge sandstorm is coming back for me, and I think it wants to get even! Can you help?"

The dust cloud looming over Tara grew taller and expanded, even though the velocity of the wind didn't change, nor was there more sand around to be swept up by the wind. Florence shook her head, horrified. "It's too hot for me! I won't have any power there! Can you shoot it with one of the ice arrows?"

Tara shook her head. "It's just whirling sand; there's nothing for the arrowhead to strike."

"What's that above your head?" asked Florence, pointing in the shard to somewhere over Tara.

"A golden ball," answered Tara. "A long story. It belongs to someone named Atalanta, whom I just met. She's a princess, like us."

"Can she help at all?"

Tara took a deep breath. It couldn't hurt. She looked back at the ice shard to answer, but it was beginning to dim. Florence was calling to her, her face increasingly desperate, but no sound was coming through. A moment later, the shard turned a dull grey, just like out in the desert when Tara had encountered the Desert Witch on the first occasion.

Tara looked up at the ball hovering before her. There was no time to feel silly about talking to a floating inanimate orb. "I need help! Can Atalanta help me at all? Maybe the other two balls, could they help?"

Tara had just time after uttering these words to turn to confront the now towering column of wind and sand. It spoke as it neared, in the same vaguely feminine tones of before, with again the same rasping edge and trailing slur.

"You," came the voice, and its wrath was unmistakable. "You. Princess Tara. I find you. Again."

Tara said nothing in response, only clutching Daystar's bridle more tightly.

"I have sought you. You. I owe you. A reckoning.

"See me now. I am diminished. Not so great as last we met. Away. In the desert."

The voice paused but not, Tara sensed, for lack of words. Rather, she guessed, to formulate the next threat. This came shortly in that all sorts of objects that might lie upon the ground in the wilderness or near the edges of habitation and which had been swept in the Witch's whirlwind were being spun to the edges. Surely, grimaced Tara, to intimidate her. Flashing by, just a short distance away, whirling but frozen before her each in turn for a brief moment so that she could see and recognize them, passed a tree trunk and branches, an assortment of brickbats, a section of roofing, a rusted farm implement, the broken wheel of a wagon, and sundry other items that Tara could not make out but which all looked heavy and dangerous.

"Even diminished, though, I am yet powerful…" The voice trailed off. So that was it, thought Tara. Though she had not yet fully reconstituted herself, she still had the strength to pick up all sorts of items to hurl at Tara and Daystar. Or, realized Tara with a sickening wrench, use to pulp them or to flay them alive.

"What do you want from me?" demanded Tara. Frantically, her mind ran through all the items she had with her. She no longer had a telescoping rod. The message bubbles were not a weapon. The dazzle dust she didn't want to reveal. What about the Ring of Shooting Stars? Tara eyed the swirling cloud and doubted its utility. But it might be all she had.

"What is mine."

Tara pressed her lips together tightly.

"You. You have it. Yield it. Mine."

In answer, Tara brought up her right hand, pointed her index finger, and called for a meteor swarm. The ring pulsed in response and a blur of fiery balls flashed up toward the whirlwind. But the cloud spun faster and each ball was caught and whirled out and away to explode harmlessly away from the Witch.

A horrible gurgling noise rasped from the tornado, and its top leaned over Tara, as if to taunt her. "You! You thought to harm me! With heat and flame!"

The tornado straightened and spun more tightly, and its color darkened. "I. I am the desert. I know well heat and flame."

At that moment, perhaps as never before, Tara had a sinking feeling that, this time, she had no last card to play, no last trick in her purse. She was at the mercy of this desert thing, and she knew it.

Still, even as Tara realized how desperate her situation had become, she could not bring herself to concede that she was truly doomed. Never, she gritted her teeth and told herself. The Desert Witch, who seemed to detest her for some unknowable reason, certainly had the upper hand, but Tara didn't have to surrender.

"What do you want?" she demanded, suddenly defiant. The Witch would have to name and ask for the dust. Tara refused to volunteer it. Not when volunteering it wouldn't make any difference anyway.

"You! Give! Mine!" screamed the Desert Witch.

As if in response, the golden ball over Tara's head advanced and dropped to hover a short way in front of her. A streak of yellow flashed to either side of Tara, and the first was joined by Atalanta's two other balls to form an equilateral triangle before her. Atalanta had sent her what help she could. Tara flushed, momentarily touched: it was a noble gesture, but it could only be symbolic. Three yellow spheres, by themselves, could not fend off the Desert Witch's whirling cyclone of debris, nor could they deflect large objects such as a tree trunk or a wagon wheel.

But Tara quickly apprehended that the balls did not intend to intercept missiles the witch intended to hurl at her. Rather, a thin golden disk, the balls at the perimeter, wavered and flickered into existence between them and seemed to undulate irregularly across its surface. The balls and their disk slowly commenced to spin then, together, the disk between them, they darted forward to vanish into the base of cyclone.

Tara waited an anxious moment. What could the balls be doing? But the Desert Witch, so vocal before, was silent. More importantly, she wasn't following up on her threats against her and Daystar. Tara put one foot in a stirrup; any reprieve was welcome. "C'mon, boy; this may be our only chance!"

Far away, Atalanta stopped in mid-stride on her way back to Orlaith Palace. She lifted one hand and held it aloft, spread, palm up. "Yes," she said, in reply to no one. "Spin. Opposite. As fast as you can." Inside the cyclone, the balls and their golden disk obediently spun faster and faster in the direction counter to that of the Desert Witch.

Tara jumped to the saddle. Still nothing from the Desert Witch. But the upper section had begun to sway, and the whirlwind as a whole was lurching erratically. Something was happening, and it had to be because of Atalanta's golden balls.

"Ride, boy, ride!" she called and spurred him to a gallop. Behind her, the cyclone careened as if it would topple, returned nearly to upright, overbalanced to lean far over the other direction, then bolted at high speed back to the desert from where it had come.

The wind died away and Tara slowed Daystar to a canter. Thinking of Atalanta, Tara turned Daystar back to Orlaith Palace, picking a path amongst the branches, leaves, and rocks that the Witch had left behind. There was no sign of the three golden balls.

Tara found Atalanta slumped in a chair in the palace's reception hall, disconsolate. Seizing the girl's listless hand, she called to her. "Atalanta! You saved me!"

Atalanta looked up with a wan smile.

"You saved me! You saved me!"

"I'm so glad. I promised you I'd help you, and I did."

Tara remembered with a sudden pang the promise she had made to Atalanta not to forget her, and how the other girl had so quickly, and perhaps lightly, made the reciprocal promise. How bitterly ironic that she would be the first to have to redeem that promise, and at such cost.

Tara knelt beside the chair to gaze earnestly into Atalanta's face. "You did help me. You saved my life! I can't express how grateful I am.

"But the balls—"

"I know. They're gone."

The words were uttered with a crushing finality that left no doubt. She started to speak some words of hope but realized that, if anyone could know the whereabouts of the balls, it would have to be Atalanta. "Are they really gone?" she finally asked, softly.

Atalanta shrugged. "I can't reach them. They don't respond. They must be gone."

Tara recollected her last glimpse of the Desert Witch. She had been racing back to the desert, maybe to try to regain strength.

"I don't know," continued Atalanta, her eyes unfocused, looking into the distance. "The Witch-cyclone was coming apart. I think she collapsed, out over the desert." She closed her eyes. "The desert," she repeated. "Out in the desert. The last I knew from them was that the Witch was disintegrating. Then, nothing. That's never happened to me before. To receive nothing at all from them. Absolutely... nothing."

Tara nodded, thinking. "Could it be they're out in the desert, just beyond your ability to reach them?"

Atalanta nodded sadly. "Maybe. But that's about the same, isn't it? Destroyed versus lost forever?"

No, there really wasn't much difference between the two, Tara agreed silently, standing. She looked out across the hall's flagged floor. In the distance glowed the couplets of the curse the queen had placed on Maurienne so long ago. Yet, to her eyes, the first couplet had vanished and only the second, third, and fourth were still visible. She stared harder as, before her eyes, the second disappeared. She grabbed Atalanta's arm and pointed.

Atalanta resisted at first, then looked up and started. "The words.

They're fading!" Pulling Tara with her, she rushed to stand before the glowing script. Only the final couplet was legible and even the first line of this was vanishing, leaving only the last line to linger a little longer. Then it too faded, and the flagstones were dark and bare, just like those paving the rest of the hall.

Atalanta turned to Tara. "What could it mean?" she asked, her voice fearful. Tara stared down at where the words had been, totally mystified. She moved her lips, but no sound came. I don't know, she was meaning to say, but she was interrupted by a loud crash that came from all around them. Atalanta jumped in surprise, but Tara recognized it at once: it was thunder. Thunder like she remembered hearing, and with the same sense of surprise, amazement, and welcome, as after she had banished the water sprite from Brythrony. It was thunder and coming rain.

A long, rolling boom sounded from all around them before it died away, echoing into the distance. It came a third time, this time rattling and reverberating through the bones of dusty Orlaith Palace. Before it had entirely died away came a sudden, sharp flash that momentarily lit up the hall from floor to rafter. Atalanta suppressed a shriek, but Tara grinned broadly with delight.

"It's rain, Atalanta! Rain! The curse is lifted!"

There came another boom, a flash nearly simultaneous with it, and a terrific downpour in waves. A moment later, more than a dozen rivulets of water were plashing upon the flagstones about them from high overhead. "The roof. No one's touched the roof for years because there was no need! But now—" said Atalanta in a tone of incredulity, turning and surveying the water streaming down all around them. She held a hand out wonderingly to interrupt the fall of one, as if to catch and examine it.

Tara held out her hand into a nearby stream too and let it run through her fingers. It was cool and—something she had not felt in days in that land—deliciously wet. She cupped her two hands to catch a small pool and poured it into Atalanta's. "You lifted the curse," she said, looking up into her astonished eyes. "You did what the queen required in that story you told me."

Atalanta's face became one of incomprehension.

Tara continued. "The king and queen refused the alliance their armies and wealth because they thought them too precious to risk losing. So the queen cursed Maurienne with drought until Maurienne was willing to risk losing what was most precious to it for someone else. You are the true princess of Maurienne and you just did this for me with your three golden balls."

Tara looked up to the roof, back wide-eyed to Tara, up to the roof again through the hundreds of rivulets pouring down, then, hesitantly, smiled tremulously. "You think… it's gone? The curse?"

Tara gestured to the rain pouring down around them as evidence.

Atalanta looked at Tara for a long moment and, with a lunge, embraced her. "I couldn't have done it without you."

"I didn't do anything! You saved me!"

"But you offered me your friendship. You promised me you wouldn't forget me. So I promised you the same, and I must keep my promises as a true princess."

Tara scanned the ceiling high above. They would need a lot of buckets to catch all that water. "Well, I sure am grateful to you for rescuing me from the Desert Witch. And I'm so glad that rain has come again to Maurienne. I'm hoping it will prosper again."

A thought struck Tara. "You told me the golden balls rolled to you because you were the true princess of the realm, right?"

Atalanta nodded.

"Weren't they right? That you are the true princess of this realm? Because you lifted the curse and restored the rains! Maybe the golden balls knew this, even from when you were a baby?"

Atalanta nodded thoughtfully again but said nothing.

Something else occurred to Tara. "How long, exactly, did the queen's curse lay upon Maurienne? You said it happened many generations ago, but how long?"

Atalanta bowed her head and Tara waited. The moment lengthened, until at last Atalanta stood straight again and looked Tara in the eye. "I… I lied to you about that," she said at last. "I was ashamed. It wasn't many generations ago. My father and mother were the ones who failed to honor the alliance. They brought the curse upon Maurienne."

Now Tara understood. So that was why the balls had turned to Atalanta. They had judged her father and mother and found them unworthy.

Atalanta continued, a note of steely resolve entering her voice. "I have learned from all this. I will be faithful to my friends and commitments. I will honor my word as I have spoken it. I will uphold the dignity of

Maurienne."

Tara straightened also. Just a day or two had passed since Tara had met her, but she seemed so much older than that. She seemed much more deliberate and resolute than when Tara had met her in the courtyard that first evening.

The next morning, Tara prepared to leave Maurienne a second time. Princess Ariel had flown in that morning and Tara had immediately introduced her to Atalanta.

"I have no golden ball to guide you this time," mourned Atalanta.

"Not to worry," replied Tara quickly. "Ariel will be able to scout ahead for us and keep us on the right path."

Ariel agreed, fluttering briefly her wings. "I would have arrived much sooner but, no matter how hard I tried, I simply couldn't steer Cloud Castle here. Something was preventing all the clouds from even getting close. Then, late yesterday evening, no problem any more!" Ariel shook her head, unable to figure it out. "I can't understand it."

Tara and Atalanta smiled at each other. Tara would explain it to Ariel later.

"Like I promised you: we won't forget you. We're going to find your golden balls. It was on my account they were lost; I won't let them stay that way!"

"Thank you, Princess Tara! Thank you, Princess Ariel! Thank you so much!

"And," she added, "Thank you again for the princess purse! I feel like I'm one of you already!"

Tara remounted Daystar, and Ariel's wings blurred, and she lifted off to hover alongside. "You're a princess, just like us!" She turned to wave as Daystar began to canter away. "Welcome to the group!"

Three Golden Balls

"I have to help her," Princess Tara told her friend, Princess Ariel, as they rode away from Princess Atalanta, still waving to them from the forecourt of Orlaith Palace. "I just have to. Those balls were her constant companions—maybe the only ones she had—during her childhood. I have to find a way to return them to her."

Princess Ariel frowned in perplexity. "But how is anyone to find them? When no one has the slightest idea of where they are?"

Well, really, thought Tara. How are we to find them, now that they've been swept out and away to who knows where? She patted Daystar's mane, then turned to eye her friend hovering beside her. "I think we've got a little bit of time for a story. Let me catch you up on everything that's happened over the past few days."

Tara told her the full story, concluding with the rainstorm that had swept through the previous night. Tara gestured. "Sure, she's glad. Maurienne is no longer under a curse, and her people can again hope for a life that they probably have all but forgotten. But she's also sad—"

"Of course!"

"Yes! Because she's lost her three gold balls. And they aren't just your everyday golden balls. Not that you run across golden balls lying on the ground every day," she added.

Ariel nodded in agreement. "No, they're not everyday balls. They're special."

"Very special. What's more, they saved me. That's why I owe it to her to find them and return them."

The two lapsed into silence.

Ariel spoke. "Why not send out a message to the rest of the princesses and ask if they have any ideas?"

Tara mused for a moment. Why not? "Do I need to send one to you?" she asked, jocularly.

"No," replied Ariel evenly, well used as she was to Tara's periodic purposeful silliness. "But you might send one to Atalanta. Just to let her know what you're thinking."

That was a good idea, thought Tara. Ariel frequently had good ideas like that, about asking for help from others and staying in touch with everyone. Tara tended to look only to herself and her immediate surroundings for solutions. Was this, she wondered, because, as an only child, she had always been forced to rely on herself? "I think you're right. I'll do it now," Tara said.

Ariel chuckled. That was so like Tara! Once she decided on something, she wanted to do it right away! "All right, you send bubbles to Atalanta and Marina; I'll send one to Florence." Within a few minutes, it was done. The two watched the three translucent bubbles float up and, after wobbling a moment, glide off in different directions. "There they go!" laughed Ariel again. "Bye! Send our love!"

Tara reflected. Ariel was right to include Atalanta. Tara knew what it was like to be on one's own; a message bubble would reinforce their assurances that she was one of "them" in full.

"Say, Ariel, I didn't send you a bubble, of course, but what about your birds?"

"My birds? Are you having ideas already?"

"You told me to ask the princesses for help. You're one of the princesses."

"All right, well, what about my birds?"

"You speak with your birds all the time. Could you ask them if they've seen anything? Particularly out over the desert?"

Ariel looked thoughtful. "Sure. Of course, I could. As soon as I get back to the Cloud Castle, I'll summon them and ask."

"Thank you. They fly everywhere; maybe they've seen something."

"Say," asked Ariel, "sorry to change the subject, but back to Atalanta: do you think she'd want to be involved?"

Tara sighed. "I know she would. But I think she has a kingdom to set back to rights." Ariel frowned, remembering that Atalanta's parents had died. "Maurienne needs her for leadership. Plus, she has to re-establish her court, fix her palace… all sorts of things. I'm sure she'd love to come along, but I think she needs to be with her kingdom just now."

Ariel murmured her agreement. Maurienne surely did need Atalanta's presence at this important moment.

"So I'll work on this problem for her. I don't mind at all." Tara smiled brightly. "She did save my life, after all."

The two parted ways after Tara was well on her way back home and in more familiar lands. Ariel flew back to Cloud Castle and Tara, only a day or so later, was back at Stonedell.

She had just seen to Daystar's bedding and fodder, which she always did personally, and bathed and dressed, when her parents returned. They found her in the reception hall, at one of the banquet tables, examining her quiver and its contents of arrows.

King Childeric eyed his spouse. "Looks like she's gotten a little sun while we've been gone," he said with a small smile.

His queen sniffed. "Probably out in the fields with that horse and those arrows. Rather than reviewing her lessons. Like on manners and protocol!"

The king stepped forward into the hall and cleared his throat. "Tara! We're back!"

Tara jumped up and ran to them to give them both hugs. "It's great to see you again! How was your trip?"

"Just lovely," replied her mother. "We had a lovely time. How have you been?"

"Fine, thanks. Just fine."

"What have you been doing while we've been gone?"

"Oh, not much. You know, just the sort of things I usually do. Same old stuff."

Armorica nodded knowingly. Probably out galloping through the fields and firing off arrows. That sort of thing.

"Have you been to see your friends?"

"What do you mean?" asked Tara, puzzled. She couldn't possibly be asking about Marina and Ariel. Tara had never mentioned them to her, as she would never have believed she knew a mermaid and someone with wings. She had revealed Ariel to her father but had sworn him to secrecy, and she didn't think he would have told her mother. She also had mentioned, in passing, that she had made the acquaintance of Florence. That, she thought, would be safe, as Florence looked normal, even if she had extra-normal powers.

She darted a quick look at her father; no change in expression there. It didn't look as though he had said anything about Ariel. "Um, like, such as which friends?"

"Tara! Are you being thick on purpose? Such as Lady Alina and Lady

Dominique!"

Oh. Those two. Tara worked to prevent her nose from wrinkling in distaste. They were hardly her friends. They thought themselves far more sophisticated and worldlier than Tara. Tara didn't care. It used to bother her, a lot, but since meeting her new friends, she had come to see how silly and vain Alina and Dominique were. Still, her mother insisted they were a "good influence" on Tara and liked to encourage her to get together with them.

"No… no, I didn't. Not them. I did see Florence though." This was true, strictly speaking, even if it was only through an ice shard. "But you weren't gone all that long anyway."

"No, not that long. I'm glad you saw some living creature other than Daystar. Honestly, I wish you would get out more—and, no, I don't mean into the fields and forests! Why won't you see those two nice young ladies? What is so wrong with them?"

That evening, back in the North Tower, Tara received a message bubble from Ariel. Her friend informed her that she had asked her birds to look for the balls, as Tara had described them. Nothing had come back yet, but she would continue to make enquiries. Tara nodded and went to bed. Ariel was very dependable with this sort of thing. If the birds saw anything, they would tell her, and Ariel would promptly let her know in turn.

A few days later, while at breakfast with her parents and toying listlessly with her spoon, a tiny round spot suddenly appeared on the linen tablecloth. Puzzled, Tara watched as it grew steadily in circumference from that of a pea to that of a chestnut.

"Tara, dear, stop playing with your cutlery, please. It's poor table manners. Really."

Tara nodded, half-hearing her mother. She gazed more intently at the tablecloth, then decided that some liquid below was staining it and that the stain was broadening. She reached out to pluck the tablecloth, but the stain didn't come with it. How extraordinary, thought Tara, letting the cloth drop again.

This action attracted another admonishment from her mother. "Don't play with the tablecloth either; you're supposed to be royalty!" The queen turned to her husband and gestured at Tara with her right hand. Do you see this, she mouthed silently. Childeric glanced up from a mapped proposal for the next season's planting and frowned but said nothing.

The dark spot reappeared as soon as the cloth settled. Oblivious to the silent conversation taking place between her parents, Tara stared. Whatever it was, it wasn't below the tablecloth. If it was a shadow… she glanced up toward the window to see what might be interposing itself between her and the sunlight streaming through it. Of course: it was a message bubble, floating steadily toward her, its intended recipient.

Tara jumped up. It simply wouldn't do for the bubble to land and burst and for the voice of the sender to begin to tell her excitedly of some new development. Her parents would go absolutely crazy.

"Excuse me, young lady? Just where are you going?"

"Just—uh—to get a drink of water!"

"Haven't you a glass at the table? Have you no sense of decorum? If you wish to get up, please *politely* request to be excused. Until you are, you shall remain seated!"

Her father looked up again. "Tara, do as your mother says."

Tara compressed her lips. This was going to be incredibly embarrassing. Yet she could think of nothing else that would get her quickly away from the table for sure. "But… but, well, actually, I have to relieve myself."

Her mother rolled her eyes in annoyance. "Well, if that's what it is, why didn't you say so? I don't suppose you could wait at all, no?"

Tara, out of the corner of her eye, saw that the bubble had descended to only ten feet above her parents' heads. She shook her head quickly.

Her mother sighed and closed her eyes, despairing. She waved her hand in dismissal, and Tara immediately made for the privy, the bubble following ever closer after her. As she left, she heard her mother whirl on her father to insist Tara improve her manners to those befitting a princess. "Simply awful! And she's not a child any more…!"

Tara had just made it around the corner when the bubble caught up to her. She put out a hand and the bubble settled into it. Blowing gently on it, it burst and, as clearly as if standing next to her, she heard Ariel say, "Hey! Guess what! One of my birds tells me it may have seen the gold balls! But guess where: way out in the Lost Quarter. I mean, way, way out there!

"Let me know what you want to do next."

Tara returned to the table, deep in thought. What to do next to recover Atalanta's golden balls, when they were far out in the Lost Quarter?

Her mother was waiting for her, wearing that stern expression which meant that Tara would be soon receiving important "information." No doubt about her lack of decorum, Tara gathered, with a sinking feeling, and prompted by her hasty departure from the table.

Armorica very deliberately folded her hands in her lap and fixed her eyes on Tara, whose own eyes had wandered down to the tablecloth. "Tara. We must review your manners. They are atrocious. Not acceptable at all."

"But!—"

"No! No. I will hear no disagreement. They are very poor. Very. They reflect poorly on you, on us and, yes, even on the kingdom. You *will* receive prompt and intensive instruction on this matter."

Tara sighed over-loudly and let her head fall to one side, as if her neck were partially broken.

"Don't push me, Tara!" Her mother's tone rose slightly and with a distinctive, harsh edge. Tara knew, from hard experience, that her mother was only moments away from being really, really furious.

"Hey, hey!" interrupted Childeric, evidently sensing this also. He put down the diagram he had been studying and frowned at the both of them. "Really, Tara, I know that you know better! Couldn't you just show it? Please?"

Tara nodded glumly.

"Thank you. I know you can." Turning to his wife, he expostulated, "I'm sure she will. Won't you, Tara?"

Tara nodded again, glumly.

"There. Yes?" this last word directed at Armorica.

"No. No. She needs additional instruction in propriety. Right away. From you-know-who."

Tara caught her breath. What could this mean?

Queen Armorica laid one hand flat on the table, as if enunciating an ultimatum and spoke to Childeric in her no-nonsense voice. "You promised me. That's what you said: if this happened again, we'd get help."

Childeric looked puzzled, as if he were trying to recollect that conversation.

"Yes. You agreed. That we'd send her to Duchess Eunice for a week."

Childeric opened his mouth to object when Tara broke in. "I'll go! If you think it would help, I'll go!"

Armorica whirled around, astonished.

"Yes. If you think it would be good for me, I'll go."

Childeric shut his mouth and stared hard at Tara, but she only responded with a bright, innocent smile and eyes she kept purposefully flat and unreadable. He narrowed his. He'd seen that face before, many times. Each time, that face, that mind, had harbored some ulterior motive, but, well, Armorica wanted her to go. And, apparently, so did Tara. Who was he to object? He shrugged.

"I'll leave... tomorrow! Or the day after! If," she added quickly, "you think it will help."

Armorica beamed. Tara's acquiescence had come impossibly more readily and easily than she could ever have expected. "You'll see! You'll learn a lot. The Duchess is really very nice. You'll have a fun week away with her!"

Thus, it was settled. And, two days later, early in the morning, Tara alighted from Ariel's sky chariot onto the reception deck of Cloud Castle. After warm greetings, Tara followed Ariel into her large receiving area where they seated themselves on the comfortable couches lining the sunlit room. It was always pleasantly disconcerting to find the windows of the castle in the floor rather than the walls, but, then, it would always make perfect sense to her a moment later.

Princess Ariel explained in greater detail how she had learnt what she had. "I put out the call to all my birds: if they saw anything like these three golden balls, they should let me know. I promised them a treat if they found anything," she added, proud of her cleverness in offering a reward.

Tara nodded. Very sensible, and very Ariel.

"None came back with anything. 'Course, I gave each one of them a little something anyway, because they are my birds and I want to encourage them."

This also made sense, because Ariel had a very soft spot in her heart for all her feathered friends.

"But then, just a few days ago, a pair of sand kestrels came twittering, very excitedly, that they had seen something like what I had asked them to look for."

"A sand kestrel?"

"Yes. They nest near the desert, though not in the desert proper."

"Interesting!"

"Right! Out near the desert. Like, toward the edge of Maurienne, now that the rains are back again. Anyway, the kestrels told me that they saw them in a part of the desert we call 'the Lost Quarter'."

"'The Lost Quarter'. That's it, exactly. That's where I went to find the dazzle dust!"

"Right! And also where you first encountered the Desert Witch, if I remember correctly, and where the Desert Witch was blown out or swept out, or whatever out in that direction."

"So I think we've found them."

"Could you call them back somehow, so I could ask them myself about what they saw? Through you, of course."

Ariel smiled knowingly. "I knew you'd want that! So I asked them to stay until you could come up." Ariel gave a quick "kee-kee-kee!" call and, very shortly afterwards, two diminutive birds of prey, much like small falcons flitted in and came to rest on Ariel's outstretched hand. She cooed to them, smoothed their wings and then set them down on an ornate golden perch to hand at the table next to her. "Here they are!"

Tara studied them. They were of an overall tan coloration with bars on their wings and spotted breasts. Pretty birds, they were, even if their plumage wasn't brilliant. They regarded Tara back keenly with tiny bright eyes, and Tara thought that, somehow, they seemed far more intelligent than they would if she had encountered them in the wild. "Ask them," she requested of Ariel, "to describe what they saw."

Ariel chittered to them briefly, and they replied, flapping their wings once. "'Three balls. Of the color of the sun. Much more brilliant than the sand'," she translated. "This is how they speak," she added to Tara, confidentially. "They don't know what gold is; the colors they know best are those of the desert and the land nearby."

Tara nodded in understanding. "Can you ask them how big the balls were?"

Ariel asked and then held up her hands to make a circle. "Of four eggs together, about, in size."

Tara smiled. "Perfect. And, how were they situated? Just lying on the sand?"

Ariel turned again and enquired. She turned back. "Yes, lying on the sand. Not hidden or in camouflage."

"But, they tell me also, there were tracks around them."

"Tracks?"

"They don't know what animal made them. Something large but not winged. So, some sort of land animal."

"They could show us where they saw them?"

"Yes. In fact, I'm taking us there now."

Wonderful, thought Tara. "We'll have them in hand shortly! Then we can pass them back to Atalanta and she'll be whole again!"

Ariel shook her head. "I think it'll be little more complicated than that. The kestrels checked on them again yesterday. They weren't there any more, just more tracks around where they had been the day before. There are some rocky outcroppings nearby though, and they think the balls might be hidden amongst them. At least, if they were pursuing them as prey, that's where they would look first."

It would have been too easy that way, wouldn't it, thought Tara. She sighed. "This means we'll need more help. Crystal and Flo won't be able to handle the heat—I've already spoken with them about that."

"So who then? Marina? But she's a mermaid! She'd be even worse off in a desert!"

"Funnily enough, that's exactly who I was thinking of asking for help!"

Ariel looked at her like she had gone crazy.

"No, listen: Marina may be just the person for us to turn to, because if there is something out there than can hold and hide the balls, then it wouldn't have much experience with water. It would be a kind of secret weapon to have Marina with us!"

"But how does she get to the desert? And stay there?"

"There's got to be water down there, a water table of some sort, even if it is far down below the sand. Let's just ask her if she can do anything with that."

Ariel whispered her thanks to the kestrels and sent them back. "If you say so," she said doubtfully, reaching into her princess purse for the vial which held the bubble fluid. "Let's send her a message and see what she can do."

To their surprise, a return message floated a few hours later. It settled into Ariel's hand and, when burst, immediately began in the chatty voice they knew and loved so well. "Wow! Sounds like fun! No mermaid has EVER been to a desert before! But how could I last even a second there? Although, if there were an oasis, maybe it wouldn't be so much a problem. And hey, my father's trident might be able to do just that. Anyway, meet me at the Secret Island and we can talk about it!"

Tara looked to her friend. "The Secret Island? But that's in the Prithrath Ocean, in the opposite direction of the Lost Quarter."

Ariel nodded thoughtfully, then arose to consult a complicated-looking device at the far end of the room. "Yes. It is. But we may be in luck. That's because the winds in that direction are blowing pretty swiftly, just at a higher altitude than where we are now." Ariel thought for a moment. "I think we could get to the Secret Island by early tomorrow morning, even late tonight, if we ascended now and rode those air currents back." She turned back to Tara. "Shall we do it?"

The next morning, the three of them were swimming from the Secret Island, having already met Marina and ingested some of the special seaweed which allowed them to breathe and withstand the pressure underwater.

Tara was explaining to Marina why she thought she could be so helpful. Marina was listening, intrigued but still dubious. "I mean, really, it's a DESERT! And take a look at me: it's like I'm part fish!" Ariel and Tara knew that she was not part fish at all and would have bridled at being referred to as such, and that this was purely for effect. Tara acknowledged that a mermaid in the desert must be unexpected but insisted she hear them out before making up her mind.

Marina led them through a skylight in Coral Castle and then down to the Great Hall, where she settled herself on a couch placed in the center of a circle of brilliant white sand near her father's elaborately decorated clam-shell throne. "Now, explain to me how a mermaid in the desert is going to do your friend Atalanta any good?"

Ariel looked to Tara. "Go ahead. What you said to me."

Tara still remembered the first time she had seen the Great Hall, trailing Marina and towed by a large ray. It looked as magical now as it did back then. Taking a deep breath of seawater, Tara explained to Marina the situation, including what the sand kestrels had told Ariel.

"What made the tracks?" asked Marina.

"We don't know. We haven't seen anything out there. They sound like pretty big tracks, at least from the perspective of a sand kestrel. And maybe that isn't very large at all. But it's hard to tell how big, because we don't know what made them."

"Oh." Marina fell silent and flipped her tail fin in one smooth flick up on to the opposite end of the couch.

"Here's the plan," interjected Tara, not wanting Marina to start thinking too deeply about the sort of adventure on which they were asking her to join them. "Ariel and I will go by Cloud Castle to the spot the sand kestrels identified. You'll join us through the water table underground. Then, you'll cause an oasis to spring up and we'll meet you. We'll find the golden balls quickly and head home. All done!"

"What if we meet up with whatever it was that made the tracks?"

"That's where your help will be so important. You'll bring up all sorts of water, like, using your father's trident, and nothing out there in the desert will have any idea of how to deal with that. We shouldn't have any problems after that; probably whatever it is out there is so unfamiliar with water it will be totally frightened away!"

The girls laughed together at the thought, particularly since they were at the bottom of the ocean.

"That's a fun thought," mused Marina. "Imagine: I could be the first mermaid to visit the desert. And imagine scaring things away with water! With water!"

But then she paused. "I really would have to have my father's trident to create a spring. I'm sure it could do it, because it commands all water. I'm just not sure he'd let me borrow it."

"Could you ask him?"

"Well, he's away. At some kind of mollusc convention. I think."

Ariel and Tara looked at each other. "Could you, well, borrow it? It'd just be for a day. Or two." Or maybe three, added Tara, silently.

Marina grimaced. "You don't think any longer than that? 'Cause he'd be awfully upset if he found it missing!"

"I think if we got moving right away, we could be back very quickly."

Marina mused for a moment, then looked up. "All right; wait here. I'll get it. I know where he keeps it and how to unlock its case."

Marina flitted off into the green darkness then came back a short time later with an enormous trident in her hands. "It's heavy," she told them, breathing heavily from the exertion. "Could you hold it for me a moment while I get something to carry it in? Like a backpack or something!" Marina passed the trident to Tara and swam away again.

Tara nearly dropped it, it was so unexpectedly heavy. Using both hands, she hefted it back up to waist level. Best just to hold it, exactly as Marina had given it to her, she decided. She dared not try holding it any other way;

what if that unleashed some catastrophic sea power?

"Need a hand with that?" asked Ariel, worriedly.

"No, I think I've got it. But take a look: it really does look powerful!"

The trident was a finely wrought weapon. Its handle was a narwhale's tusk, the base of the tusk bearing the three spear points, while its tapering length was the shaft. The tusk naturally spiraled; in the groove running clockwise up the entire shaft had been delicately laid a filigree of gold and silver. At the tip of the tusk was a knob of mother-of-pearl; the three spikes opposite looked to Tara liked carved coral but flecked with bits of gold throughout.

Ariel inspected the spear points from a safe distance. "They look really sharp."

Marina reappeared with a sack floating across her back and spread it open for them to push the trident inside. "It's really nice, isn't it? For that reason alone, my dad would be really, really angry if anything happened to it. Aside from the fact that it's also powerful.

"Quick, jam it in," she continued, flapping the bag at them, "before anyone sees us! We don't have much time!"

"Sure, but it sticks out a lot," Ariel said at last, having done the best she could with it.

"No problem," Marina reassured them. "We're leaving right away anyway. Back up through the same skylight!"

As they ascended, a voice came from behind. "Stop! In the name of King Aenon, I command you to stop!"

Tara's heart froze within her.

"It's just a guard!" whispered Marina.

"What is that you carry? Stop and be recognized!"

Marina turned and assumed the most regal demeanor that a sack across her back with a large trident sticking from it would permit. "It is I, Princess Marina. Who are you?"

"Your Highness! Forgive me! But I just saw…!"

"You were just maintaining an alert watch. That was good of you, and commendable."

"Your Highness is kind." But the guard's eyes strayed to the points of the trident projecting over Marina's head.

"You may be wondering about this trident?"

The guard nodded. "Your Highness reads my thoughts!"

"I commend your perceptiveness in this regard as well as the alertness of your watch."

The guard executed an underwater bow.

"As you know, my father is away. He has asked me to bring him his trident. For that is what I carry, as you see," and Marina half-turned to display it.

Of course, the guard recognized it. Everyone in the Coral Kingdom knew her father's trident.

"So, I only bring it to him. But what is your name, so that I may mention your thoroughness and alertness to your captain?"

This the guard gave, and Marina made a show of remembering it. "Very good. Now, I continue to my father. Remain as alert in all your duties!"

The guard retired and Marina and her friends resumed their ascent. "Let's hope he's happy with that explanation," muttered Marina, "and doesn't make a big deal out of seeing me!"

They parted when Ariel and Tara were back ashore Secret Island. Ariel and Tara promised to send a message bubble when they were back at Cloud Castle on exactly where to rendezvous in the Lost Quarter. Then, Ariel and Tara were back in Ariel's sky chariot, heading to Cloud Castle while Marina, pulled by a team of dolphins, set off for the shore nearest the Lost Quarter.

Tara and Ariel stood together on Cloud Castle's Vista Terrace a few hours later, watching the earth pass by far beneath them. Few features were visible from so high up, and patches of clouds obscured the view intermittently. Still, Tara could distinguish occasionally the silvery thread of a river, or the patchwork green of tilled fields; a more variegated green suggested forests, while a flash of light indicated a mirror-like lake, reflecting sunlight.

Ariel turned to Tara. "That's great that Marina's going to help us with her father's trident!"

Tara nodded, but doubts had started to creep into her mind the closer they got to the Lost Quarter. The most important of which was the question of just how prepared they were. It was true that Tara had ventured into the desert alone and with little more than hoar frost and ice arrows, but that was before she had ever guessed there were such horrors as the Desert Witch. What other creatures might be lurking out there in the most inhospitable section of the desert? The trident was surely powerful and water would be an innovative weapon. But did Marina really know how to use the trident? Was the trident enough for whatever might be out there? Tara grimaced. It was too late to turn back now.

She suppressed her concerns and turned to Ariel. "You're right. Marina will be a big help. The trident too. We'll be fine."

Early the next afternoon, the sand kestrels tweeted from their perches that they were nearly over the location where they had seen the golden balls. In a tight, descending spiral, the cygnet swans landed the sky chariot as close as they could to the rocks the kestrels had identified. Ariel sent the swans and the chariot back up to Cloud Castle immediately after they disembarked. They shouldn't be in the heat, she explained, any longer than absolutely necessary.

Tara watched as up, up they flew into the bright skies, leaving the two princesses alone on the barren, hot sand. Tara sprinkled some of the hoar frost she still had from Princess Florence over herself and Ariel and glanced around. "All right, let's start looking. Maybe we can find them quickly and get out of this place."

"The sand kestrels said they first saw them near the rocks. The next time they flew by, they were gone, but they thought they could be hidden in and amongst them."

In the rocks, murmured Tara to herself. Which ones? There were a couple of rocky outcroppings projecting from the sand nearby. She shaded her eyes and scanned the surrounding area. But this had to be the place. Everywhere else, the desert was just long, undulating waves of dunes. "Sounds good. Let's look in the rocks then."

A message bubble came to Ariel as she and Tara walked toward the rocks. It was Marina, telling them she expected to be joining them shortly and asking them to stay until she arrived. Tara checked her pouch of hoar frost again. Yes, there was enough for a few more applications for all three of them. Marina would definitely need a pinch as soon as she showed, or she would very quickly become a baked fish.

"Did the kestrels tell you which rock they saw the balls near?" Tara asked, scrambling across an especially large, hot boulder.

"No, nothing like that. Just near some rocks." She made a wry face. "They are only birds."

Tara frowned and, shading her eyes again, wished she had brought a hat with her. There sure were a lot of rocks, many of very odd shapes and sizes. She wondered why they were here. Why here, when everywhere else was plain, flat sand? "Well, let's keep looking. This could take longer than I thought."

The two princesses searched up and down the rocks, within each crevice, and in every cranny they came across, but found nothing. Nothing but sand and a few small, scuttling desert creatures, hiding in the shadows to escape the intense heat. Tara had had to sprinkle more hoar frost on the two of them twice over the course of the afternoon to ward it off.

Later still, Tara noted their shadows were starting to lengthen. At last she found Ariel leaning against a rock. One wing, stretched and bent forward, was a blur of motion like an impromptu, private fan. "Nice breeze!" commented Tara, standing next to her. "I didn't know your wings could do that."

"I didn't either until I tried. It's so hot! Even with the hoar frost."

"Well, here's good news for you. It's going to get cooler real soon."

Ariel's wing slowed. "Really? How's that?"

Tara inclined her head toward the horizon. "The sun will be setting before too long. It can get surprisingly cold at night. Even though it's really hot in the daytime."

"Really?"

"You'd be surprised."

"Pleasantly, I expect!"

Tara didn't respond. She wasn't sure how cold it could get. She imagined it could get very cold. Maybe they should be looking for shelter. Tara didn't feel they should fly back to Cloud Castle, having promised to stay until Marina arrived.

"Say, you haven't heard anything further from Marina, have you?"

"Nope, nothing."

Tara tried to think of all the nooks and crannies they had investigated that day. None had been large enough to shelter her and Ariel for the night.

"Um, Ariel, I'm thinking that maybe we ought to look for shelter. Just in case it gets really cold."

Ariel cocked her head and gazed at the descending sun. "Hm. I don't think we saw any sort of cave that we could crawl into."

Tara wiped her brow with her forearm. This wouldn't be the first time that she had been forced to fall back on her wits and, seemingly, at the last moment. She glanced anxiously at the sky. Probably only about an hour or so until sunset. They had best start figuring this problem out.

"Nothing at all?"

Ariel shook her head.

"Then I'm thinking we'll have to make one."

"But how? By digging under the rocks?"

That was impossible. They would never be able to dig enough sand with only their hands to hollow out enough room for the both of them. They had to think of something better.

Tara touched her princess purse. "Well, I've got an idea. Maybe we can use our telescoping rods. I'm thinking that we can use them as levers to lift up a rock and thereby create a kind of shelter. What do you think?"

"Sounds good. But what shall we brace them against? There's just sand here."

Tara had to concede that Ariel's point was a good one. She took out the replacement rod she had received from Ariel on leaving Orlaith Palace and considered first it, then the sand. No, the sand wasn't packed hard enough to use as a fulcrum. But if they could locate two adjacent rocks, they might be able to use one to lever up the rock opposite.

The two roamed amongst the rocks until they found two medium-sized rocks not too far apart. Tara seated her rod at the base of one rock and commanded it to extend until it touched the rock opposite. Ariel seated that end securely under the rock.

"Ready?" called Tara.

Ariel nodded.

Tara now commanded the rod to extend to its maximum length, and the two girls jumped up to grasp the far end over their heads. They hung from it for a long moment, and Tara feared that their combined weight still might not be enough to move the rock, but the rock opposite stirred and began to tilt upwards. "Hurry," she told Ariel. "Get your rod out and place it underneath the rock against something firm and make it extend also. We'll use your rod to prop up the rock. We can then add mine to yours."

With a worried glance up at the rock hanging over her and balanced only on Tara's extended rod, Ariel darted beneath it and seated hers in a depression in another rock beneath it, as near to the middle of the lifted portion as she could. Then she caused her rod to extend and lift the rock up from below.

"Great, Ariel, thanks! Now, hold the rock balanced from outside while

I put my rod next to yours to help keep it in place!"

"You want me to hold this rock up by myself?"

"No, just keep it balanced, that's all!"

Ariel rolled her eyes. How was she supposed to balance this gigantic rock? Tara would be squashed when Ariel proved unable to keep it balanced on such a thin rod! But she grasped the rock to either side of the rod and, as quick as a lizard, Tara was under the rock with her rod, had set it against a hard surface and stabilized the rock by extending it.

"Great! We did it!" announced Tara, dusting her hands off.

Ariel marveled at the trick. She would have never dared to attempt that on her own, or with anyone else. "But," she asked, after thinking a moment more, "how do we get our rods back without getting mashed beneath the rock when we remove them?"

Tara looked at her confusion. "Why, the same way we put them where they are now, of course! Except in reverse!"

Of course, nodded Ariel. Wasn't that typical of Tara to make it seem so obvious and easy.

But it was good to have the shelter, as the sun was nearly at the horizon, and a palpable cold was stealing across the desert. Fortunately, the rock was still quite hot from having been in the sun all day. Beneath it, it was nicely warm against the chilling air. "Great idea," sighed Ariel, as both princesses removed from their backs the small packs of food and water they had brought from Cloud Castle. "I just hope it holds through the night."

Tara did too. Though they would never know the difference, as they would be crushed in an instant. More immediately, and now that their need for shelter had been satisfied, she wondered what sort of creatures might emerge in this bleak place when the sun went down. "That's not exactly my greatest worry just now," she replied, a little louder than she intended.

"What do you mean?" demanded Ariel.

"Uh, well, when the sun goes down, it's not as hot, and different… things… might come out and look around."

"Look around for what?"

"You know, for, like, food."

"What sort of food? As long as they leave us alone, no problem, right?"

"They might not. That's the thing. Because they might be looking for food."

"'For food'? You mean, like to eat us? To eat us for food?"

"Just thinking aloud on this!" Tara hastily reassured her friend. "But, out of curiosity, tell me what else you have with you?"

"Just in case we need it?" asked Ariel, a trace of sarcasm in her voice. She heaved a sigh and rummaged through the contents of her belt pack. Like Tara, she had the message bubbles and the dazzle dust. But, observed Ariel, the dazzle dust required light to function against foes, and in the pitch black of the desert night, there was no light.

Tara agreed, as it was something she had realized herself. Again, looking out into the gathering dusk, she wished she had prepared better for this adventure. She had prepared quite a bit in advance of her search for the dazzle dust, what with the ice arrows, the hoar frost, and the ice shard communications device. Had she grown complacent?

"Anything else?" Tara asked, firmly working to keep worry out of her voice.

Ariel rummaged about and finally pulled out a crescent-shaped object. "Oh! I have this horn too. It's the Horn of the Winds. I put it in the purse a few days ago and never took it out."

The horn shone dimly pearlescent in the moonlight. "What can it do?"

Ariel turned the horn over in her hands. "When I blow on it, I can summon one of the four winds."

Tara thought that could be very useful indeed against anything advancing toward them out of the dark. That made her remember her Ring of Shooting Stars, which she kept on a chain about her neck when she was with her mother and father. She removed it from the chain and slipped it on her right index finger. "This ring: it also might be useful in the desert night."

With that, they nibbled at what they had brought as provisions. Both wondered what was keeping Marina. "I know it's the desert and all, but it sounded like she was almost here," observed Ariel.

Tara agreed. "I guess she ran into problems. Maybe the water table is so much deeper here than we thought and she's having trouble, even with the trident, in creating an oasis."

They finished and decided to get some sleep. "Why don't we take turns," suggested Tara. "You sleep first. I'll stay up. If I hear anything, I'll wake you." Ariel agreed, and Tara settled down to wait for her turn.

But the day had been long and the heat draining, and though Tara tried as hard as she could to stay awake, drowsiness overwhelmed her. She found herself back in her bed in the North Tower, though it was not nearly as comfortable as it usually was. Inexplicably, it was filled with sand and her pillow was lumpy. Then she was at the window in her room, and there was a sensation as of scraping, as if a tree branch from outside her room had come through the window and, moved by the wind, was brushing against her. Odd, she thought in her dream, that a tree could be so tall as to touch her through the window!

The movement faded, then recommenced, only this time much stronger and more steadily and insistently. Tara groggily half-opened her eyes, wondering what this could be, then awoke with a start. Immediately before her were the hairy tarsus and claws of a spider-like creature. The stealthy movements of its forelegs, questing about delicately, had been the scraping she had felt; its jaws, working in jerking spasms, had gradually drawn down her cloak until the cold night air had awakened her.

Tara jerked upright. The creature drew back, its grey-white anterior legs splayed wide in a threatening crouch. Tara's heart leapt to her mouth. A forest of bristled forelegs twitched in the bright moonlight all about their upturned rock. A pale, eyeless head glistened so close to Tara that she could have touched it, had she dared.

Quivering, Tara freed her hands and brought them up to touch thumb-to-thumb in front of her. "Spark shower!" she called in a low, quavering voice.

The ring glowed obediently and out streamed sizzling, multi-colored, blazing strings. The spiders hastily withdrew, bobbing, to beyond its furthest reach, but, as soon as the shower had died away in an extended hiss, began to jostle and creep forward. As they advanced, they whispered and chittered menacingly amongst themselves.

"What's going on?" demanded Ariel, awake from the sudden light and sound.

"Ariel, get up! Quick! Solifugae!"

Ariel sat up with a start. "Huh? 'Soli'—who? What's that?"

"Spiders! Lots!"

"Where?" she demanded, her eyes still adjusting.

"Just right out there. Here, watch," and Tara put her hands together again and called forth another spark shower. This drove the spiders back again but not as far as the first time. Evidently, the sparks weren't really hurting them. Or, not hurting them as much, as—Tara swallowed hard—as they were hungry.

"Spiders! Oh, I hate spiders!" wailed Ariel, now beginning to see how many and large they were. They had begun to crowd the entrance to their shelter, and the questing tips of innumerable forelegs probed further and further toward them. Ariel shrank in revulsion.

"Me too, but they're curious, and, well, I guess, hungry! My ring isn't working against them!" Ariel didn't answer. Tara looked over. Ariel was staring wide-eyed at the foremost spider, well underneath the rock, and its chelicera making short, chopping motions.

Tara nudged her. "Hey! What about that horn of yours? The Horn of the Winds. Could that help?"

"Huh?" answered Ariel, as if from a daze. "Oh! The horn!" She fumbled in her bag for a moment and then whipped out the horn. "Watch this!" Ariel put the horn to her lips and, turning sideways and pointing the wide mouth at the spiders, blew. A powerful wind commenced from the horn, kicking up sand and small pebbles, and the spiders ceased to move toward the princesses. Some squatted down in the face of the wind or latched onto the rocks surrounding their impromptu shelter. "Again! Harder!" urged Tara, and Ariel blew again. The wind became a gale and, one by one, the spiders' tenacious holds were overcome and they tumbled up and away far, far out into the desert.

Ariel set the horn down. Tara breathed again. The two looked at each other in relief. "I can't believe how awful that was," whispered Ariel shakily. "I can't believe how many there were."

Tara looked back to the entrance to their shelter. Thank goodness: no solifugae. She turned back to Ariel, still wide-eyed from exertion and shock and, in spite of herself, began to giggle. Ariel was surprised and even upset at Tara's apparent mockery but, seeing how mussed and dirty they were, and in a great exhale of relief, also began to laugh.

"All right," said Ariel at last. "Maybe that was funny. In retrospect. But let's not do it again, right?"

Tara nodded. It wasn't something she wanted to repeat either. "Come on," she answered instead. "Let's see if we can get a little more sleep before tomorrow."

They awoke early the next morning, anxious to resume searching before the hoar frost ran out. Just as they had recovered their rods, having eaten what food remained from the night before, and were stretching out their still cramped arms, a pool of water formed at Ariel's foot. It steadily widened and a small fountain bubbled up from the sand.

"Marina!" the two princesses shouted together and retreated to atop a rock to watch as the pool steadily enlarged. When it had become the size of a small pond, the sand at the bottom welled up in a cloud and out poked three coral prongs flecked with gold. A moment later Marina's head appeared. She looked around, blinking, then, catching sight of her friends, waved. "Hi! Oh! How perfect! I came right up where you were! I wasn't sure!

"Gosh," Marina remarked, taking a closer look at Ariel and Tara, "You are so dirty! Like you need a bath!"

Tara recounted their adventure with the solifugae and how Ariel had had to employ her Horn of the Winds to blow them out into the desert. Marina flipped her tail back and forth a few times in a rhythmic plash-plash and gazed placidly at them. "Just spiders? I bet they're a lot like crabs. Not dangerous at all. Did you try to talk to them?"

Tara confessed that, no, they had not tried to converse with them, omitting the fact that they couldn't speak to the solifugae, even had they desired.

"Well, next time, instead of panicking, you might just try talking with them. They might have even told you where the golden balls were. They might have seen them."

Ariel sighed and bent down to dip her fingers into the pool. Straightening, she ran her fingers through her unkempt hair. "Next time. Next time maybe you'll be with us and you can talk to them for us."

Marina nodded, signifying that this was a sensible suggestion. Then she bent down and, with a short grunt, heaved the trident up and deposited it at the water's edge. "Aren't you going to ask how my trip was?"

"How was your trip?" asked Ariel, obligingly, with a small smile at Marina's cavalier dismissal of the solifugae.

"It was tough. I had to go through a lot of rock. So I had to carry the trident pointing forward practically the whole way. It's so heavy! I had to rest every now and then. That's why it took me so long to get here. Carrying that thing," with a nod at the trident resting on the sand. "Sure is heavy. Anyway, I've probably changed the geology of this part of the world forever, mowing a path through bedrock like that. But I'm here and ready to find those balls, which are here somewhere." She looked up and around. "Unless you've already found them?"

The princesses shook their heads in unison.

"I figured not. All right, well, let's look for them. What do you think?"

"Sure," the other two agreed and turned wearily to a cluster of rocks they hadn't examined the day before. Marina watched from the pool, blinking in the bright sun. "You know I'd help if I could," she called. "But I don't have legs."

"We know," responded Tara.

"I'm just here in case there's trouble," called Marina back to Tara, who, behind a rock, was out of view.

Ariel's voice suddenly rose from beyond another outcropping. "Hey, Tara! Look at this!"

Tara immediately stood up from the small hollow into which she had been peering. It had looked like a likely spot for a ball to have rolled into, she had been thinking. "What is it? Did you find them?"

"No. Something else. Come over."

Tara found Ariel pointing beyond the rocks to a deep crease in the sand. Near the crease was a substantial, faceted, transparent crystal. "What do you suppose it is?" whispered Ariel. Tara shook her head to signify that she was mystified herself.

"What is it? What did you find?" demanded Marina behind them, from the pool. "I don't have legs! I can't see!"

Tara, walking alongside, began to trace the crease. "Look how straight it is. It can't be the wind. Some animal must have made this!"

"And what's the crystal? It's too big to be a diamond," said Ariel, pointing.

Tara turned back to look. "Hey, and there's another one. Two crystals, just alike!"

Ariel started forward in the direction of the crystals, as if to pick one up. Tara frowned and held her back. "Let's not touch anything until we know what this is. What if it's some kind of trap? What if something made the marks, and the crystal is a lure?"

Ariel stopped, a little abashed at how she had nearly taken what could be bait.

Tara continued to follow the crease. "Follow it in the opposite direction," she called to Ariel. "Let's see if they meet."

Tara followed her line out and then out into the desert. Shortly, she saw that Ariel was just opposite her by about six feet and moving parallel. "I think they meet up," she said, simply, and they stopped.

Ariel walked around to re-join Tara. "What do you think we ought to do?" she asked.

Not for the first time, Tara had no idea. "Let's just test it a little," she said and picked up a handful of sand and threw it to within the area bounded by the two creases. Nothing happened.

Ariel threw some too. Nothing. With her foot, Ariel pushed some sand into the crease and then walked across it. "Nothing's happening. I guess it isn't anything after all."

Tara took out her telescoping rod, extended it and drew in the sand beyond the crease an outline of a fluffy cloud and then, to Ariel's delight, a castle-like structure atop it. They waited a moment, listening into the absolute silence of the desert, but still nothing occurred.

Must be some freak of the desert winds, guessed Tara. "False alarm, sorry! Let's go check out the crystals."

They both began to walk toward them, Ariel shuffling her feet, kicking forward tiny clouds of sand before her with each step. Suddenly, the ground undulated beneath them, and Ariel staggered. "What was that?" she gasped.

Tara grabbed her hand and pulled her upright. "Get off! Now!" Another undulation sent them reeling, but the edge of the crease was still close by, and in another second they had scrambled across. They turned.

The sand across which they had been walking only moments before was coalescing and combining, the crease they had just leapt across deepening. The great expanse of sand contracted and solidified into a massive, vaguely human shape, the only sound the faint whisper of sand crumbling from the edges into the depression left behind. Shortly, one end of the mass, where the crystals had been, took on the rounded shape of a head, the crystals as its eyes, and hauled itself erect. A gaping mouth formed below, yawned like a cave mouth, and emitted a protracted and unearthly grinding, like that of rocks being crushed.

The growl wavered, subsided, and distinct words became intelligible. "Why do you disturb me?" the form grated, and it heaved its vast bulk to its knees, then to club-like feet to come fully upright to a height approximating that of a medium-sized tree in the forests of Brythrony.

"We're very sorry," offered Tara immediately, eyes wide at the sheer enormity of the giant that had arisen from the sand. "Please don't take offense!"

The great crystal eyes fastened on Tara. "You poke, and you prod, and you probe! Why?"

"We didn't mean to!"

"How can this be, when you moved purposefully?"

"What I mean to say is, we didn't know we'd disturb you. We didn't know that you were lying there!"

"It's a sand golem!" whispered Ariel to Tara. "It's solid sand! I've heard of them!"

"What is this whispering?" roared the golem. The faceted eyes switched to Ariel, then back to Tara, and the upper body with its massive head inclined toward them. Tara had the distinct feeling they were being evaluated, and she feared it was for their capacity to defend themselves.

"Please," she asked, if only to interrupt what she worried might be a hostile train of thought, "we're looking for something we lost. Maybe you might have seen it?"

The golem pulled back in surprise. A request?

"Yes! We're looking for three balls, gold in color. About this size." Tara formed a circle with her two hands to approximate their circumference.

The crystal eyes stared back vacantly.

"You wouldn't have seen them? Three balls? Golden?"

"I don't think it has!" whispered Ariel anxiously, tugging on Tara's arm.

"It doesn't seem like it," allowed Tara hurriedly. "We'll go. We promise not to disturb you further." Flexing the fingers of her right hand to ready her ring, she and Ariel began to back away.

"Golden? Gold?" demanded the golem, with umbrage.

"Gold only in color," corrected Tara, didactically. "Not solid gold."

"Gold!" bellowed the golem with certainty. "All gold here is mine! All! You come to steal!"

Why was everyone in the desert always trying to claim everything in the desert, wondered Tara. Hadn't the Desert Witch said the same thing!

"We didn't come to steal anything!" insisted Ariel hotly. "We came looking for three lost golden balls, that's all!"

"I will crush you with my great fist!" answered the golem truculently and took a ponderous step toward them.

"Oh, no, you won't!" responded Ariel, lifting the Horn of the Winds to her lips. She blew hard on it, and the fierce wind whipped up a billowing cloud of sand. But the golem was unphased. It was too heavy for the wind to budge, and the sand, if anything, only seemed to increase its bulk.

"Hold on, Ariel," shouted Tara over the wind's blast. "Let me try!" She put her two hands together in front of her and called forth the Spark Shower. But the sparks bounced harmlessly off the golem's legs. The golem laughed in an awful, scraping, grinding din and took another step closer.

Tara gritted her teeth. She didn't want to hurt the golem, but it had threatened to pulp them with its enormous fist. Pointing her right index finger, she invoked a meteor swarm.

The ring pulsed and three brightly burning balls soared up to impact the golem's midriff with a dull thud-thudding. When the flames cleared, Tara and Ariel could see three spots on the golem's trunk glowing a dull red but, other than that, no change.

The golem fixed the princesses with its two crystals and laughed again, more loudly and with the rattling and sliding noise of sand being violently shaken in a metal box. "Run!" shouted Tara. "Back to the rocks!"

"At least we can outrun it!" panted Ariel.

"Fly, Ariel! Fly! Don't stay for me!"

Ariel unfolded her wings and commenced to beat them. "I'll fly; it's easier than running. But I'll stay with you; I won't leave you!"

Tara didn't have the breath to protest. "Back to Marina! I hope she's still there!"

The two rounded the rocks to find Marina lounging in the pool she had created, sunning herself at the water's edge. "That hoar frost makes the desert quite comfortable. It's just like a beach!"

She sat up, a trace of alarm entering her voice. "Why are you running?"

"We're... running... from...!" gasped Tara.

"A golem!" finished Ariel, and flung an arm backwards by way of pointing.

Marina followed her gesture and gasped. The head of the pursuing golem, scowling fiercely, had appeared above the rocks surrounding the pool. It seized one of the larger outcroppings and began to wrestle with it.

"It's going to throw it at us!" cried Ariel.

"Quick, use your trident against it!" urged Tara.

Marina scrambled for the trident still lying at the pool's edge.

"Throw it, Marina!"

The golem, seeing one of them seize an object with the clear intent to attack it, bellowed again and, with a mighty wrench, yanked the rock from the sand. Though the weight was staggering, it hoisted the enormous rock to its shoulder to hurl it.

Summoning the desperate strength of those in mortal danger, Marina flung the trident. Tara was impressed: the trident was heavy, but up it lanced, straight and true, directly into the golem's right knee.

The three princesses held their breath. The trident hit the golem and the points of the trident rang with the impact. But the trident's prongs failed to hold and it tumbled to stick upright in the sand at the golem's feet.

Tara was dismayed. The trident had been no more effective than flinging a fork. Harsh laughter echoed to the sky. With a shudder of tremendous effort, the golem hoisted the rock high above its head.

Then it staggered. Where the trident had struck, a pool of water was rapidly forming and expanding. A fountain had commenced to bubble and gush, just at its right instep. The sand softened; the golem took another step, then lost balance from the boulder's weight above its head. With a terrible, rasping howl, one leg collapsed into the surging geyser, and the boulder overhead came crashing down to drive it deep into the pool as a hammer would a nail. There was a choked cry of rage, and the head was gone beneath the surging waters of the spreading pool.

Ariel and Tara cautiously approached the edge of the newly created pond. Far below, they could see the remnants of the sand golem dissolving in a settling cloud and the water clearing to a brilliant sapphire blue.

"Great throw, Marina," said an awed Tara, at last, turning back to her friend, still at the edge of the other pool.

Marina heaved a sigh and shook her head. "It was the trident, really. It brought up the water. That's its power."

Ariel turned to Tara. "Great idea to want that along with us," she whispered.

Tara knelt at the water's edge. Deep, deep down, she could clearly see the trident, undistorted by the depth, so clear was the water. "Guess we'd better retrieve that," she said, standing. "Marina, do you think these two pools communicate?"

She nodded. "Deep enough down, I'm sure they do. Let me see." Marina dove and a minute later reappeared in the pool where the golem had vanished.

"Hey," she called excitedly, brushing back her blonde ringlets with one hand, "you'll never believe it! There's all sorts of stuff down there! Like, jewels and things!"

Tara nodded. "The golem showed a lot of interest in gold and said it belonged to him. It must have been inside it?"

"There must be all sorts of things down there, collected over the years!" said Ariel.

"Dive and see what you find, Marina," encouraged Tara.

She blinked at them. "Why not come down too? The water's beautiful!" She smiled. "And you could both use a bath!"

They both were alongside Marina a moment later and enjoying the crisp, fresh water. They couldn't dive as deeply as Marina, but the sand golem had dispersed its treasure across all the pond. On repeated dives, a variety of gems, coins, and trinkets accumulated at the edge. Towards the bottom, Marina found the three golden balls that had been the object of their search.

"Wonderful, Marina!" exclaimed Tara. "Now we can return those to Atalanta!"

Deeper still, Marina discovered two enormous quartz crystals. She placed these at the edge of the pool and the three princesses regarded them solemnly. They had been the creature's eyes.

"What shall we do with them?" wondered Ariel.

"I don't think we should leave them out here," replied Tara.

"You mean, we should take them with us?" asked Marina.

Tara nodded. "Yes, I think so. Why not you, Marina? You take them. As a kind of trophy. Because you defeated the golem."

Marina smiled broadly. "Gosh, thanks awfully much! I don't really feel like I did all that much though. Not really!"

"You threw the trident. That did what needed to be done."

"All right, I did that. But, not much more, really."

Tara pushed the crystals toward her. "Put them in your princess purse. It'll carry them easily. Show them to your father. He'll have an idea of what to do with them."

Marina placed them in her princess purse. "What about the rest? There's quite a bit!"

The three princesses turned to the glittering hoard, wet and sparkling in the brilliant sunlight. "First some more hoar frost, then let's take a closer look," Tara said.

The three of them sifted through the pile—"And there's more down there," added Marina, with a glint in her eye.

"But there's really only so much we can take with us. How about we divide up what we have here and then leave the rest for another time? It should be safe."

Marina pointed and smiled shyly at the collection arranged on the sand. "Could I have the jewellery set with emeralds and sapphires, please? They remind me of the oceans and rivers."

Ariel asked for any diamonds set in platinum or silver, since they reminded her of clouds and raindrops.

Tara sifted through the remaining objects. That left for her those in gold and any other stone. It was all the same to her, she thought. Besides, weren't there other items down in the pool that they could come back to at some other time? "Fine with me," she said. "Here you go," she continued, passing two bracelets and some gemstones to Marina. "And for you," she said, giving Ariel a necklace, a bracelet, and an intricately woven circlet.

"This leaves me these gold coins," she concluded, holding up distastefully for inspection, one after another, various round and square coins stamped in an unknown writing, "what looks like a crystal rod, and this medallion and chain." Tara surveyed her items critically. Somewhat of a miscellany, actually. But probably valuable, even if not as valuable as that which her friends had received. Tara felt a pang of envy but reminded herself that her friends had joined her on her request, and that they surely deserved more of a reward than she for enabling Tara to restore to Atalanta that which had been sacrificed to save Tara's life.

Tara shook her head. No, it was fair that her friends receive more than she. Tara had had a debt to repay, and they had not. "Are you all right with this division?" she asked, resolutely. "I'm fine with it."

The others agreed. "Now what?" asked Marina, stuffing the last item into her princess purse which, though it carried objects without betraying weight or bulk, appeared full to near bursting.

Tara looked around. Nothing else here of interest. Moreover, they had the three golden balls. "Won't Atalanta be delighted to receive her balls back! I'd like to give them to her as soon as we can. Ariel, could I ask you to take us to Atalanta's castle in your sky chariot and we'll return them to her right away?"

"You won't need me for that," asserted Marina. "But after you see

Atalanta, why don't you meet me back at the Secret Island and we'll return the trident to my father? Hopefully he hasn't noticed it's missing yet."

Tara calculated that she still had a day or so left before she was due back at Stonedell. "Sure. That makes sense. We helped take it, so we can help return it. Right, Ariel?"

"Thanks, both of you," replied Marina, obviously relieved. "Tell Atalanta 'hello' for me too! I sure want to meet her someday!" And with that, she gave a quick goodbye wave, grasped the trident and vanished into the pool's depths.

It wasn't much later that Ariel and Tara were aloft in the sky chariot, the team of cygnet swans straining in their leads ahead of them. Ariel was examining her bracelet with delight. "Isn't it perfect!" she exclaimed. "It's a lovely silver, and set with diamonds. At least, I think they're diamonds. But it's so nice! Don't you think?"

Tara agreed readily.

"And see this necklace? Look at it, against my skin! Beautiful!"

Tara admired that as well. "Why not put it on? Even just for a moment."

"Would you help me with the clasp?"

"Of course! Here, turn around." Tara worked the clasp open and linked the two ends together at Ariel's nape. Ariel turned back. "Well? What do you think?"

"Fabulous!"

"How about that gold chain you have?" asked Ariel, generously, remembering herself.

Tara hauled it out of her princess purse. "Oh yes, this. Right here." The two examined it. Tara thought it looked rather heavy and old-fashioned. A bit big and bulky for her, she thought. "I'm thinking I might give it to my father," she said brightly. "He likes this sort of style." Maybe he did, she thought. Fortunately, he seemed to like most everything Tara gave him. Or at least he said he did.

Just then, the golden balls next to them stopped rolling with the motion of the chariot and lifted perceptibly from the seat. "Look," exclaimed Ariel. "They're coming to life!"

"We must be close to the castle," agreed Tara. "And to Atalanta." She knew that, if the balls had sensed Atalanta, she must have sensed their nearing presence as well.

A short time later, the sky chariot was circling Orlaith Palace and a small crowd of curious on-lookers had gathered below. Ariel set the chariot down in an adjacent field and they stepped out. Tara turned back for the golden balls, thinking to present them to Atalanta personally, but they were no longer where they had been but a moment before, just beside her on the seat. Her brow furrowed. How could they be gone, just like that?

"Ariel, have you seen Atalanta's three balls? They were here just a minute ago!"

Ariel laughed in delight and pointed. "Don't look for them here. Look there!"

Tara followed Ariel's finger to a distant figure racing toward them. In elliptical, ever-shifting orbits around the figure's head, flashing intermittently with reflected sunlight, were small, whirling, bright dots. Three, to Tara's eyes. She sighed happily. They were back where they belonged.

Atalanta was with them a moment later, breathless and flushed. "Ariel! Tara! You brought them! You found them!"

Tara nodded. The balls were zipping about Atalanta's head with dizzying speed. She had never seen them move so quickly. Elation, maybe, thought Tara. Perhaps even golden balls could feel rapture. Tara smiled broadly. Why should she want silver, sapphires, and circlets when she had the full joy of returning Atalanta's heart's desire to her?

Tara and Ariel left the next morning for the Secret Island. The two spent the journey discussing what Atalanta had told them at dinner the night before.

"It sounds like Atalanta is doing really well," Ariel said in summary.

Tara nodded. "There's rainfall now, and things are growing again. It's much better than before."

"Atalanta said her people have asked for her to be their leader. By acclaim."

"That's really nice. That shows their real confidence in her. She deserves it too, having restored the rainfall."

"By sacrificing her three balls. Which she has back again."

Tara thought for a moment. "Atalanta said that she had heard stories about sand golems and the giant quartz crystals that are their eyes.

"She didn't remember much about them, only that the crystals were important. I'm glad we took them. Even if we don't know much about them."

"She said she'd see if there was anything in her library on it."

"We can ask Marina's father too, when we get to the Coral Castle."

Ariel motioned to the uninterrupted blue tableau that had unfolded below the chariot. "Speaking of which, it looks like we're getting close to the Secret Island. I'd better take the reins. If we overshoot the beach when we land, we'll wind up in the water."

As Ariel busied herself directing the chariot's tightening spiral down to the island, Tara smiled to herself at their continued reference to it as 'secret'. It was hardly secret, being in the middle of the ocean, but they persisted in calling it 'secret' even so. Marina had christened it such long ago, when she had imagined it to be her own special hideaway. Now it was their regular rendezvous spot, being accessible both to her and to her above-water friends, though still far removed from the sight of others.

"Nice landing, Ariel," Tara complimented her friend when they had slid to a stop. The chariot still had the runners affixed to it for landing on the sand dunes; these had been the perfect skids for the Secret Island's beach. Tara alighted and helped Ariel tow the chariot to the nearest copse of palm trees beyond the edge of the sand and the highest tides. The swans were released from their trammels and Ariel provided them with food and water from inside the chariot. Now to wait for Marina to appear.

They didn't have to wait long, as they soon heard Marina's cheery voice calling them from the breakers. They found her waiting for them on the largest and flattest rock at the water's edge with two bags of the seaweed that allowed landlings to breathe underwater and withstand the pressure far, far below, where Marina and the other merfolk dwelt.

Tara hated the taste of it but swallowed it without complaint. After all, she had to have it and it worked. "Ready to go?" asked Marina, both hands full, holding her father's trident. Without waiting for their response, she flipped her tail fin to splash them with cold saltwater.

"Hey! Stop that!" protested Ariel, still chewing.

"Oh, you'll be wet soon enough anyway, won't you?" teased Marina, now in the water up to her neck, only her fair head visible, her blonde ringlets past her shoulders swirling and flowing around her with the flux of the waves. "Come on!" she called over her shoulder and vanished beneath a passing wave.

"I guess she's right; we might as well get on with it," said Tara, wading in slowly as she stuffed the remainder of the seaweed into her princess purse. The seaweed also seemed to inure her somewhat to the water's chill, though that took longer than the breathing ability.

The three swam deeper toward Coral Castle. All the water looked the same, Tara observed, and not for the first time. How could Marina know in which direction the castle lay without landmarks? Because she was a mermaid and just knew these things. Maybe she navigated not by landmarks but by watermarks. Tara imagined that for Marina to explain how she knew where Coral Castle was in relation to where they were was like her explaining to Marina how to gauge roughly the time of day from the shadows cast by the sun. It was just something you understood, innately, just like that, imagined Tara.

The three entered the castle through the same skylight, it seemed to Tara, from which they had exited at the start of their adventure. Staying to the shadows, Marina put her finger to her lips to signal that they remain quiet. "We just want to get this trident," which she shook for emphasis, "back into its case. Then everything should be fine."

Rounding a bend, Marina suddenly stopped, and there was a confused babble of voices. Marina turned and waved her two friends away. "Swim! Quick, as fast as you can!" Turning back again, she spoke haughtily down the passageway. "Who are you to address me, Princess Marina of Coral Castle, in such a manner?"

Ariel and Tara hesitated. Marina had told them to swim away, but how could they leave their friend if she were in danger?"

"Go!" she whispered fiercely, then, loudly back down the passageway, "How dare you! You will refer to me as 'Your Highness'!"

"Seize her! Take her to the King!" came an authoritative voice.

"Unhand me!" they could hear Marina saying, who could no longer be seen. There were the sounds of a struggle. "I have nothing to fear from my father, the King. I demand to see him at once!"

Tara pulled Ariel back. They should heed Marina's warning and swim away. Clearly Marina had been taken prisoner. While Tara imagined Marina had little to fear from her father, no matter what the reason, what might happen to them might be a different matter.

They heard the voice ring out again. "The Princess Marina was with others. Quickly: search the area!"

Though Tara and Ariel kicked furiously to get away, it was impossible to outswim mermen. Shortly, there came a chorus of sharp orders for them to stop and, moments later, nets came spinning down over them. Unceremoniously, they were towed back to Marina and allowed to settle like a net full of lobsters to the floor beside her.

Marina flushed angrily. "Free them this instant! I command it! They are princesses of other realms and merit the same treatment as me!"

The guard evidently in charge declined with an elaborate upper body inclination. "No, Your Highness. That may not be released. By orders of His Majesty." He turned to his complement. "Lock them in the lower levels." He scanned Ariel and Tara expertly and quickly. "If they are indeed royalty, there is no need to search them. Now, away with them!"

"Where are you taking them?" demanded Marina.

"Your Highness, you must come with me," was his only reply, and Ariel and Tara were dragged away.

They were pulled, still confined in the net, through a winding series of passageways and down shafts to what they imagined was the castle's base. A warden, who looked like a sort of platypus, eyed them critically and motioned wordlessly to a cell at the end of a passageway. Into this the both of them were rolled, and the door closed with a swirl of water.

"Let's get out of this net first," said Ariel at last, when they thought they were alone.

It took the better part of an hour to untangle themselves, during which a small slot opened near the door and through which a covered flat pan was slid. "Looks like dinner," determined Tara upon taking a closer look. "Hey, not bad for prison food! Seaweed, I'm thinking, but with something crunchy mixed in."

"Not exactly the reception I expected," observed Ariel, sardonically, in between bites.

"No, me neither."

Ariel looked forlornly at the empty pan when they had eaten all of it and sighed. "What do you think they did with Marina?"

Tara had been wondering about that herself. She shrugged. "Hard to say. But I can't believe the King would punish his own daughter harshly! King Aenon doesn't seem the type."

"But maybe it's not about the trident at all."

"What do you mean?"

"Maybe there was a coup and he's not the king any longer."

Tara didn't answer. It was too chilling a thought. If that were so, they might be kept locked up forever, as associates of the family of an *ancien régime*. She shrugged again. "Could be, I guess. But I don't think so." She considered briefly. "After all, didn't the guard call Marina 'Your Highness' after she protested? I don't think he would have if there had been a coup."

Ariel sat back against the wall. "So, maybe—I hope!—she's okay."

"I think so. But that doesn't mean we should wait here for that to be sorted out."

"What do you mean?"

Tara winked and sidled closer. "Well, what if she's in trouble, for example? We should try to help her."

"But we can't even help ourselves! What do you mean that we should help her?"

Tara glided still closer, keeping her back to the door through which they had entered. She slid her princess purse around to the front of her body and jiggled it significantly.

Ariel's face assumed a look of perplexity, then one of dawning realization, as Tara reached inside and extracted, just so it peeped out from the purse, her telescoping rod.

"You think?—" whispered Marina.

Tara nodded significantly. Then she floated over to the cell's barred window and looked to either side down the passageway outside. No one was in sight. She returned.

"They didn't search us. So we still have these," indicating the rods. "And did you notice? The cell door opens outwards—probably so prisoners can't meddle with the hinges." She winked at Ariel. "Let's wait a little longer then use these to force the door." Tara gestured to the wall behind Ariel. "I think the rods will seat very securely in these coral blocks. There're plenty of crevices in which to position them."

Ariel smiled. So typical of Tara to be thinking of escape even though they had been thrust into prison just an hour before! But was it advisable, she asked her friend, gently.

"Of course it is!" replied Tara confidently and with a sly smile. "Probably this is all a big mistake. So they'll let us out as soon as they realize the error. In which case, what harm will it have been to have already let ourselves out? On the other hand, if they don't mean to let us out, ever, we should try to escape as quickly as we can, in case they mean to do something fearful to us!"

Ariel thought the logic dubious, but Tara was set on it, and she could hardly stay behind if Tara were successful. They settled down to wait. Without the transit of the sun, it was impossible to know the hour, but they judged it had become "night" by a gradual but noticeable dimming of the light through the barred window. The lantern fish, which periodically toured the cell block, must have gone to rest.

"All right; let's do it!" whispered Tara, and they placed the butt ends of their rods firmly against the wall opposite the door, one above the other, and ordered the rods to extend until they were just touching the unhinged side of the cell's door.

Tara checked the cell's window one last time to make sure nothing was watching then re-joined Ariel. "Extend!" they commanded together, and the rods quivered as they pushed against the cell door. The door flexed but, though it was clearly very strong, the bolt was no match for the marvelous rods. It vibrated and strained, and there came a cracking sound from within the door.

"Retract!" whispered Tara. They didn't want to send the door flying, just to break the lock so the door could be pushed open, which Ariel accomplished simply by putting her shoulder to it.

"Quick," motioned Tara, after a moment's jubilation. "Let's go! And close the door behind you!"

In the uppermost chamber of the tower to which she had been confined, Princess Marina swam round and round, despairing. She had invited her friends to her Coral Castle home, and they had been locked up in some dark, desolate dungeon cell. This was merfolk hospitality? What would happen to them? What would happen to her?

Yes, it had been as she had feared. Her father was furious. She had left without telling him where she was going, without considering the dangers she was risking and, as serious, she had taken his trident without permission, risking its loss. He had been incensed, and it had been on his orders, she had been informed, that she had been virtually imprisoned in the tower in which she now found herself.

The only item of furniture in the room was an old and obviously unfashionable couch of carved rock and nacre. At length Marina reclined on it out of sheer fatigue. Shortly, though, there was a knock on the door and, a moment later, it swung open. Her mother, Queen Seafoam, drifted forward. Over her shoulder, she dismissed the guards. "I surely won't need an escort to meet my own daughter!"

"Marina!" Seafoam began, very sternly, upon closing the door. "Your father is especially angry with you!"

Marina assumed an expression of contrition.

"Marina! I am amazed—simply amazed—that you stole your father's trident!"

Marina remained silent. She couldn't resort to her traditional excuse, which was something along the lines of "she hadn't meant to." Since, of course she had meant to take it, and exerted considerable effort to do so.

Her mother interpreted her silence as an admission of guilt. "You know you've done wrong, don't you?"

Marina nodded, sorrowfully.

"I should hope so. You can't just take something like that; it's enormously powerful. You don't know how to use it. It's dangerous in the hands of someone who doesn't know how to use it."

Marina thought she had some idea how to use it but thought it best to stay silent.

"And what if it fell into the wrong hands? Well? What if something or someone took it from you? What would that mean to Coral Kingdom? All the ocean?"

Marina nodded gloomily. That was not something she had imagined. Her friends had been with her all the time, and they certainly weren't going to take it from her. But she supposed her mother was right that there *could* be things out there more powerful than the three of them together.

"And, lastly, it's the symbol of our reign over the Undersea World. We can't lose this symbol or allow it to be misused."

Marina stared at the floor.

"Well?"

"You're right," Marina admitted at last. "I shouldn't have taken it." She looked up hesitantly. "I should have asked if I could borrow it."

Her mother snorted. "I doubt he would have let you have it! But you are correct that it was wrong to have taken it." Her mother drifted a bit closer. "Are you sorry you took it? Very sorry?"

Marina nodded, vigorously.

"Very well. If you are well and truly sorry—and promise not to ever even think about doing that sort of thing again!—you need not stay in this tower any longer." Her mother looked around in distaste. It was a small, bare room, part of an addition from maybe decades before, and Seafoam could not even remember why it had been erected.

"Yes, you are free." She put a consolatory arm around her daughter. "I release you and I'll speak to your father on your behalf." Queen Seafoam looked away, down to the main part of the palace, where King Aenon must surely be. "He's quite upset, but I think if you say you are very sorry, he'll forgive you."

Seafoam put her hand beneath Marina's chin. "Come, look up. Let me see you." Marina turned sorrowful eyes up to meet her mother's gaze. Queen Seafoam appraised them, and evidently finding true penitence there, responded with a hug for her youngest daughter. "It was very wrong to take the trident! Why in all the seas did you want it? Where were you with it?"

Marina mumbled some words about being with her friends and wanting to show it to them. The rest was lost though, as she buried her face in her mother's arm.

Seafoam's voice shifted back to disapproval though softened by maternal understanding. "Marina! It is not a toy, something to show your friends. Well. Now you know better. Come with me," she said, arising and pulling Marina up with her. "Let's go down to see your father."

Soon they were in the Great Hall, where they found King Aenon at rest on his enormous clamshell throne. He eyed Marina with irritation but said nothing.

Seafoam dismissed with a wave the several courtiers who always seemed to be drifting around the King and propelled Marina forward. "Marina has something to say, don't you?"

"Yes, mother."

"That you're sorry, isn't that so? For having taken the trident."

"Yes."

"You recognize that it was wrong, don't you?"

"Yes—" began Marina, but was interrupted by her father.

"I'd like to know why you believe it was wrong. Because it *was* very wrong!"

Marina swallowed and summoned her resolve. "It was wrong because... because it could have fallen into the wrong hands." She flicked her tail very gently and the tiny eddies created spun away in all directions to dissipate in the dim, far corners of the room. Marina looked up into her father's face, which was still set with anger. "And it's very powerful, and in the hands of someone who doesn't know how to use it—and I don't know how to use it like you do—it could be dangerous."

"And also, it's the symbol of our reign over this world. We can't lose that or let it fall into the wrong hands." Marina thought she had recited the several reasons her mother had given. She glanced covertly at her mother. She was nodding, and Marina's confidence grew.

"I'm sorry. I shouldn't have taken it."

Her father frowned and looked over to his queen. "Do you think she really is?" he growled.

"Yes. She's sorry."

He turned back to Marina, now eyeing her thoughtfully. "Why did you take it? Did you use it, and if so, how did you use it?"

Marina thought hard, and her eyes roved around the floor as she did so. The floor was strewn with sand and mica to give it a glimmering, opalescent quality. Bioluminescence from the lanternfish that hovered ever-nearby reflected and refracted from the mica in tiny rainbows. "I... well..." Marina straightened. "I took it to the desert. The Lost Quarter."

Her father's brow contracted and he sat up on his throne.

Marina felt compelled to explain. "To the Lost Quarter. We—my two friends and I—thought we'd need it. We went to recover the three golden balls of Princess Atalanta. They were removed to the Lost Quarter in saving Princess Tara's life."

"Princess Tara? The same Princess Tara whom you rescued from a shipwreck?"

"Yes. And Princess Tara wanted to return them to Atalanta, because they are very, very, well, magical. So Ariel and I went with her to help her. I took the trident in case we needed water in the desert. Because I knew it could produce water."

Her father leaned forward in interest. "And did you?"

"Yes," replied Marina, now recollecting with satisfaction how they had concluded their adventure and even her role in its success. "We discovered that a sand golem had found the golden balls and wanted to keep them. When it attacked us—it tried to squash us!—I used the trident to create a spring. This dissolved the golem and saved all of us.

"We found the three golden balls at the bottom of the pool the trident created; they had been inside the golem."

Her mother gasped. Her daughter had ventured into a desert with just two other girls and confronted a sand golem. "Marina, that's so dangerous!" she sputtered.

Her father half-rose from his throne. "You used the trident to save your life and that of your friends?"

"Yes," proclaimed Marina, increasingly proud of herself, even if the spring's creation had been unexpected and even accidental. "The trident created the spring, which washed away the golem. Without the trident, we might have been killed. And we certainly wouldn't have found the golden balls!"

Her mother's face darkened at her daughter's foolhardiness. Marina had courted danger to a degree she hadn't imagined. But Aenon arose and approached her with arms outstretched. "Well done, my daughter! Well done! You saved your friends and yourself! That was noble of you, to accompany your friends and help them. And to find these balls you mention and which I gather are very important."

Marina nodded confidently. "Ariel and Tara returned the golden balls to Atalanta and then came with me back to Coral Castle to help me return your trident." She frowned. "They're locked up right now."

Aenon compressed his lips to a thin line. "Yes, I sent the two landlings to the dungeon. Of course, I didn't know then what I know now, that you were helping them in a noble cause." He summoned a courtier. "Have the two landlings released. Escort them here to us."

The king seized his daughter by both arms and gazed into her face. "I am proud. You were wrong to have taken the trident but it was to assist your friends. You saved their lives, and you returned to this other princess something important, which she could not have regained on her own."

Marina blushed.

Aenon, moved, took his daughter's left hand in his and then reached out to take with his right his wife's hand. In a sense, he wanted to speak to them both. "You are right, Marina, that the trident is an important symbol of our rule over this undersea kingdom. But it would be more accurate to say that we are this kingdom's first servants, and that this trident is a powerful instrument to be used in its service.

"We cannot let this trident fall into the hands of those who would merely rule this kingdom and not serve it. It was this I feared most when I found out that you had the trident. But, as I have learned, this was not the case. You used the trident in the service of others, not yourself, and service to others in a righteous cause is service to Coral Kingdom.

"And I am proud of you for this."

Tara and Ariel stepped forward from the shadows where they had been hiding. "Your Majesty," Tara began, attempting again the curtsy customary beneath the sea consisting of, for a mermaid, lifting the right flipper of the tail back with the right hand and inclining the upper body, but this time performing it with greater success than previously. "Your daughter performed heroically in the desert. And," she added, with a nudge to Ariel, "we are honored to call her our friend and to be hers."

Later, King Aenon asked about the sand golem. Marina pulled the crystals from her princess purse and all gathered around to admire them.

The king picked one up and inspected it with great interest. "The eyes of a sand golem!" he remarked. "Quite a trophy! Very well done, all of you!

"But you must be careful with these," he said. "We have more on the topic in the library, I'm sure, but don't idly place them in the sand. Placing crystals such as these is part of the process by which another sand golem is created."

Marina noted that all the floors of the Coral Castle had at least a fine layer of sand over them. "Yes," her father explained, "but golems require deep sand. That sand can be anywhere, and I have encountered some at the bottom of the sea. They are very dangerous."

He handed the crystals back to Marina, who replaced them in her princess purse. "Take care of them! I believe that their size has something to do with how intelligent they are, but I'm not sure. And that can be researched later."

He turned to Ariel and Tara. "I do, again, most sincerely apologize for having imprisoned you!

"And now I forget myself. You must be famished." Aenon called for refreshments to be laid at the banquet table off the Great Hall. Turning back to his guests, he invited them to the table. "Come; I want to hear the entire story now! It sounds exciting! Tell me everything, omitting no detail!"

With that, the five moved from the Great Hall to the banquet table, and Marina picked up the story of their adventure from Tara's first message bubble. Tara smiled. The three golden balls had been returned to Atalanta, the trident had been returned to King Aenon, and the three friends had been restored to the good graces of Coral Kingdom. All in time for Tara to make it back to Stonedell and demonstrate better manners. Why not try to practice those better manners here and now, at the Coral Castle? Wouldn't her parents be proud of her? Tara thought of them as she joined Ariel and Marina at the banquet table. Surely they would be. Of course they would be, as proud as King Aenon and Queen Seafoam were of Marina.

Silicana

As Princess Tara had been making her way back to Stonedell, far out in the Lost Quarter a cloud of sandflies began to swarm. Attracted first by the bright, fresh water King Aenon's trident had produced, they soon began to cluster about a small silvery tablet at the water's edge. This too had been within the sand golem, but the girls had discarded it as a piece of scrap metal, as it was neither bejeweled nor of any obvious value, and its composition was indeterminate.

Though not of interest to the three princesses, to the flies it was irresistible, and they settled on it and each other in an ever-accumulating mass. The mass grew into a squirming, seething heap, the tablet at its center, to gradually coalesce into something entirely different from its original constituents. After a time, having gathered enough mass, it tottered upright in a series of drunken lurches to cast its first shadow, that of an enormous and hideous insect-like creature. Its first act was to emit a lengthy series of shrill chirrups. There was no corresponding answer. With a great shiver, it shook itself, and errant flies settled into the mass to complete the shape. Enormous irregularly paned gossamer wings fanned briefly and shimmered in the intense heat. Higher and louder, the creature emitted its chitter: still no answer, nothing but the rustle of the sand against its many feet as it took its first, hesitant steps forward. And so, the creature, as its second act, chose a name for itself: it chose "Silicana."

The creature paused and drank greedily from the pool. Settling back, it regarded its immediate surroundings and, with a swirl of its wings, whipped up a column of sand and dust. The column rose higher and expanded, and Silicana became entirely obscured.

Princess of the Realm Tara lay on her bed and stared at the ceiling. She was thinking about her manners. Doubtless her mother, Queen Armorica, would have approved of this, as she was quite convinced that Tara did not think enough about her manners. But this was not exactly how Tara was thinking of her manners. Rather, Tara was recollecting how she had had to improve her manners because of her latest adventure. She had promised her parents that she would spend a week with Duchess Eunice to improve them but had done no such thing, having used the week instead to retrieve and return to Atalanta her three golden balls.

Now she was having to conduct herself as if she had learned a great deal, even though, on that topic, she had learned nothing. It had never mattered so much to Tara how she ate with a fork; that she was using one seemed to her to be something significant.

But now her parents were watching her closely. Tara had decided that the best way to prove that her manners had improved was by watching closely her parents, especially her mother, and imitating them. Easiest of all was to eat very little at meals with her mother and father, as it left less for them to evaluate. Yet it did leave her feeling very hungry the rest of the day.

Tara stared up at the ceiling. She wondered if Marina had to learn merfolk manners. The merfolk never used forks and spoons; why couldn't Brythrony be like that? Maybe, Tara started thinking, she should ask for her room to be repainted a sort of sea green, like Marina's undersea kingdom. But her parents would have all sorts of questions as to why she wanted that color, and Tara wasn't in the mood to provide answers.

Tara frowned, arose, and shuffled to the chest of drawers where she kept her most precious mementos. These were mainly from her adventures. In the top drawer, and toward the back in a small, plain, wooden box, was something especially dear to her. She placed the box on top of the chest and opened it. Inside was a handful of cowrie shells—money cowries, she had learned later. They had been woven into the bodice of the beautiful seagreen dress she had worn that day she and Marina had departed Coral Castle for the promontory on which had stood the remains of the ruined city of Syssalin. They were all she had left of what she had worn that day, the dress having long ago disintegrated from not being immersed in seawater, fabricated as it had been out of woven seagrasses.

It was there, at Syssalin, Tara recollected fondly, that the two of them, and then with the help of Ariel, had found the princess purses.

Tara ran her fingers through them, and they clinked and clicked against each other musically as they tumbled, one by one, back into the box. How happy she had been, riding in Aenon's chariot that day on their way to the city. The sun had been brilliantly bright, the ocean a shimmering, rippling expanse of blue-green broadcloth. What an adventure that had been, figuring out the map they had extracted from the scrimshaw cylinder!

Tara smiled nostalgically. Of course, she had more than the money cowries to remind her of that day. She had—they all had—the princess purses. Hadn't that been the main souvenir of that adventure, the purses? And each other's friendship? She was being silly, she reproved herself.

Or was she? Because the cowries, in and of themselves, were totally innocent. Their sole function was decorative, and they had nothing to do with any of the other memories so closely interwoven with the contents of the princess purses. They were only pretty shells, plain and simple, and of that day and moment. Nothing more. Not like the dazzle dust which was so frequently used in emergencies, like blinding bandits in the Great Forest. Or, the telescoping rod, which she had used to escape the Desert Witch.

She returned the box to the drawer and rummaged about in it for other items she knew to be there. Her hand closed finally on the crystal rod she had awarded herself at the oasis in the Lost Quarter. She picked it up and inspected it. It was of fine workmanship and appeared to be of solid rock crystal. She hefted it with one hand: it was heavy, like a crystal rod might be. She looked deep into it. It was nearly flawless, with only a few inclusions deep within. It was faceted all the way around its stem and flared at the top; a small ball at the other end would seem to denote its base.

Tara took it over to her bed to contemplate it. Was it more than a crystal rod? Or was it just a crystal rod, something the golem had picked up in its tireless shuffle across the trackless dunes? She looked up and out of the window, wrinkling her nose. How had it come into the desert anyway? Who knew. Maybe lost from some long-ago caravan.

Tara rolled it back and forth across the blankets atop her bed idly, musing. It didn't seem to have any particular power, but then, how would she know? Her only attempt at magic had provoked a drought and nearly brought down Ariel's Cloud Castle. She cupped her chin in her palm. While it was true she had her Ring of Shooting Stars, that didn't make her magical. It was still the ring working the magic. Tara was just commanding it.

Impossible to approach her parents, either, about magic. They hadn't the faintest idea of what magic was, and probably even feared it.

Tara sighed at last and returned her crystal rod to her chest after rolling it back up in a piece of clothing too worn to wear. She supposed she could ask Marina's father, King Aenon, but when would she see him next? She flung herself back on her bed, listless. Maybe she could consult Stonedell's small library. But she imagined it highly unlikely she would find anything there; its books all dealt with useless subjects, such as the plants and people of Brythrony.

Tara at last roused herself and went down to the castle's stables to see her horse Daystar. Geoffrey, the stablemaster, greeted her warmly.

"Hi, Geoffrey," she replied, somewhat distantly. She grabbed a curry comb and stepped into Daystar's stall. "Hey, boy," she cooed to him. Daystar tossed his mane and nickered softly in recognition. She began to comb him in long strokes, back and forth, gently but firmly. "How is that, hey? Yes?"

Geoffrey's head appeared over the stall door. "Your Highness, very sorry to disturb You, but I believe Your mother, the Queen, has requested your presence in the reception hall."

Tara let her head fall into her horse's mane in frustration. Couldn't she have even a little time alone with her horse? She lifted it back up then gave Daystar a last stroke. "Sorry, boy, I have to go. Promise I'll be back for some exercise!"

She handed the comb to Geoffrey, suppressing a grumble. It wasn't his fault, she knew; he was just the messenger. He bowed as she passed then retired to return the curry comb to its accustomed position next to the tack rack.

Tara trudged back to the castle's front door. The guard opened it with a salute, which Tara, uncharacteristically, ignored. Her face darkened as she entered the hall and spotted her parents at the other end, off to one side. Even from that distance, she could see her father gesticulating with his left hand, as if expostulating. Her footsteps echoing as she approached them, she saw her father suddenly stop, straighten, and turn to face her. Queen Armorica's face all too quickly set itself in a sunny expression of welcome.

Tara's misgivings deepened. On the several occasions before when she had seen the two of them in this sort of colloquy, the ensuing discussion had always become a confrontation. And today, of all days, she did not want a confrontation.

She forced a cheery note into her voice. "Hi! You were looking for me?"

Her mother's smile broadened. "Dear Tara! How are you?"

Oh no, thought Tara immediately. This was surely going to be bad. Probably worse than she had been expecting. Her sense of foreboding was only increased on seeing her father dismiss the sole servant occupying a distant corner so that they were completely alone. "Um, I'm fine, thanks. How are you?" she answered, warily.

"I'm so very well, thank you, dear!"

Tara eyed her father. Oddly, he had not spoken yet.

Her mother advanced several steps and took her right hand in both of hers. "Darling—but why do you start like that when I touch you? I'm not going to hurt you!

"But Tara, our princess, your father and I have been talking, and we agree that—"

Tara darted a quick glance at her father. He was staring off at the far wall, as if purposefully disengaged. Not, she thought, the picture of someone in full agreement with what his wife was even then saying.

"—it makes sense that you should be thinking of your dowry. Now, usually this is something that the mother and father—"

"What?" asked Tara, suddenly comprehending what her mother had said. "My what?"

"Dear, that's hardly a pleasant tone in which to ask me a question."

"Sorry about that. My what, though? Did you say 'dowry'?"

"Why, yes, I did. I did indeed. This is something that we need to think about."

"Mom, are you being serious? I mean, really? A dowry?"

Her mother drew herself up stiffly. "Princess Tara! I am always serious on these matters! You will not address me in that manner!"

Tara's head reeled. A dowry? How could her mother possibly be serious? She hadn't even met any boys—princes or otherwise—in whom she was even vaguely interested! The thought was impossible, absurd. Her eyes roved the room until they locked on her father. Now studying the flagstone-paved floor, he seemed to be studiously avoiding her eyes.

"Mom, look, I'm sorry, but, well, I just don't understand."

"Oh, is that it?" Her mother brightened and half-turned to her father, arching one eyebrow. "This is simple," she replied, turning back, some of the original cheerfulness returning to her voice. "A dowry is customarily given when—"

"Yes, I know what it is. But why? I mean, why now? Why at all? When I am no way near to getting married?"

Armorica's face creased in a frown, and she began to speak with exaggerated emphasis as she invariably did when her frustration began rising. "Dear. There is no way to know when you might meet your Mr. Right. And then you must be ready. This is a simple matter of preparation, that is all."

"But I don't know any Mr. Rights."

"True, maybe you haven't met any Mr. Rights yet. Yet. But a dowry is all about preparation. Just that: preparation."

Tara didn't like the sound of the word "yet" in her mother's response. Yes, it was true that she hadn't met anyone—yet. But that seemed to presuppose that she *was* "looking" for someone or that she wanted to "meet" someone. At least they were no longer encouraging her to get together with Prince Halliad, surely because the rumor was that he and the Lady Alina were engaged in some sort of dalliance. That was just as well to Tara. She wasn't interested in meeting or looking for anyone, except perhaps a friend to go riding Daystar with.

But could her mother have plans to move her in some other princeling's direction, wondered Tara. She compressed her lips and narrowed her eyes in dissatisfaction. Was this what was behind her mother's sudden interest in a dowry?

Her mother peered into her face uncertainly. "Just preparation," she repeated. There was a brief pause. "Because the Season will be starting again soon, and who knows…"

So it was as Tara had suspected. The "Season" again, the ball and reception season, which Tara always did her best inasmuch she could to avoid, or become sick during, or otherwise be absent from. Now her mother was saying that she might "meet" someone during the upcoming Season, which could only mean her mother had some definite plan which she had not yet unveiled.

"Mom, I don't need a dowry. The only male in my life who's not related to me is Daystar. I think this is all premature, and I, well, I just don't think I need one." Tara thought for another moment. "And, come to think of it, I don't even think we have the sort of things that go into a dowry anyway."

Armorica shook her head but was encouraged by her daughter's willingness to have any discussion about the concept. "Not so! On both accounts!" She hurried on, as she saw her daughter launching into further objections. "And with respect to what's in a dowry, of course we have those things!"

"Mom, such as what? What sort of things could be in my dowry?"

"All sorts of things. Many and various! Like land. Or buildings. Such as a castle. Or jewels and jewellery. And such."

Princess Tara looked askance at her mother. What could she mean by this talk when they were hardly the richest kingdom around, and all of them knew that? "We don't have any of those to spare for a dowry."

"We are not so destitute that we could not provide you with a handsome dowry! Especially with a bit of saving!"

Her father at last interrupted. "Tara, look, it's just something we—" he glanced significantly at Armorica "—have been thinking about, that's all. Nothing more than that."

"A bit of saving," her mother had said, and the expression rang in Tara's ears. Was that it? This conversation wasn't about a dowry but that her parents needed help with money. Could that be what her mother had been driving at, however confusingly? And her mother had simply cited the need for a dowry as the reason?

Tara caught her breath. Their finances must be really poor for her mother to have brought this topic up like this. Maybe they were even on the verge of financial ruin!

Tara nodded with dawning understanding. No wonder her mother had mentioned jewels. And jewellery. It made sense: the House of Hession must need items of value it could sell quickly to stabilize its financial situation. "Sure, Mom, I understand. Of course, we could use those—like, for a dowry. If it came to that." Jewels and jewellery. Like the heavy gold chain with the medallion on it from the pool into which the sand golem had fallen, and which she meant to present to her father on his next birthday. Hadn't Marina said that there were plenty more like that in that pool of water? That was what Hession needed. More of that.

"Why, that's wonderful. Thank you! Yes, thank you, Tara. How thoughtful of you. To agree like that."

"Sure, Mom. If that's what a dowry might require, I understand. And I could, uh, help save too. Help with that, like you said."

"Like I said?"

"Yes! Because you mentioned 'with a bit of saving'."

"Tara," interrupted her father, "don't worry about these things. Honestly! There's plenty of time for all this. The dowry and the savings—and it's not really 'savings' in that sense. More like identifying what you want and accumulating it. That's all! You shouldn't worry about it."

"Sure, Dad. I won't worry."

The three stood in silence for another long moment until Tara smiled innocently. "Is it all right if I get back to Daystar and exercise him?"

"Of course, dear! Of course!"

Tara left. Childeric turned ponderously to his wife. "I told you I didn't think it was a good idea to bring this up with her!"

"Why? She seemed to come around to it in the end."

Childeric shook his head. "I have no idea what she means by helping us. It's too ambiguous. Did you hear how she suddenly dropped all her objections? Something went through her head right then, that's what happened. And only she knows what it was."

Armorica laughed dismissively, but the laugh came off as hollow. "Starting her thinking about what she wants in a dowry won't hurt her a bit."

"You called it 'saving'. Like saving up for it."

"Oh, very well: 'accumulate'. Let her see what she wants to see in it. What's the difference?"

"A big difference, I think," retorted the king, and the two left the hall, still in dispute.

Outside, leading her horse from the stables to a nearby field, Tara was formulating a plan. Tara knew she didn't have any income. She had never given that any sort of thought before. Her parents had just provided for her, that was it. She guessed that was how it was with all the other princesses she knew too. She didn't think they had their own lands or property but rather they were completely dependent on their mothers and fathers just as she was.

Suddenly, Tara was acutely aware that she didn't contribute anything toward the palace's income but must account for some fraction of its expenses.

Her parents had revealed that they needed money and had, essentially, expressed the desire that Tara might help by being a bit more parsimonious. She was ready to help. In fact, she could do that one better by bringing in some funds. Not for a dowry, that thought being repugnant, but to the general credit of the kingdom's treasury.

And it would be easy to do too! Tara grinned. Marina had said there was a lot more treasure at the bottom of that pool in the Lost Quarter than had been brought up. All she had to do was return to the pool and pull up whatever else was down there. Why, what else would it do there anyway? Just lie there for all eternity. There was no sense in that.

Tara knew she wouldn't be able to do it alone, of course, but maybe Marina might come along? Marina liked jewellery, that was for sure, and Marina would have no trouble diving to whatever depth the pool went. Getting there could be a problem, but maybe she could ask Ariel if she might be interested in joining. Sure, she could go by Cloud Castle. Then the three of them could split the treasure three ways. There was so much at the bottom, there should be plenty for all. And they already knew where the oasis was so no problem finding it again.

How much simpler could it be? As simple as picking up coins out of the bottom of a fountain! She'd even take along the crystal rod she had in her top drawer; there'd surely be enough time for Marina and Ariel to take a look at it and maybe figure out what it was for.

Tara stopped and looked up through the dark mosaic of shadowed tree leaves interspersed amongst the brilliant blue tesserae of the sky. It really was that simple. All she needed was a pretext for getting away for a few days. That shouldn't be too hard either. She could say that she wanted to visit one of the daughters of the nobility that her parents were always trying to get her to see. How about Countess Abernathy of the Eastern Hills, who had offered many times to host Tara? She was sufficiently far away to give Tara enough time but close enough not to be improbable. Her parents would love it.

With a light heart, she dug into her princess purse and pulled out the vial for creating message bubbles. The first would be for Marina, the second for Ariel. Tara wet one palm with a splash of water from her canteen, dribbled a few drops from the vial to her other, then brought one to the other and, pulling them apart, created a bubble. Smiling, she whispered into it.

A day later, Tara received a response. She was riding again, out in the fields, and urging Daystar to jump over some obstacles she had dragged onto the paths. While a fast horse, Daystar was reluctant to jump, Tara had concluded. She felt obliged to give him some training in this, even though she knew little technique herself beyond, "Come on, boy, you can do it!" and other simple encouragements.

The bubble floated over her head and into her field of vision just as they had finished the third pass through the obstacles. Daystar's chest was heaving and flecked with foam; Tara had stopped to water him. She noted the bubble's presence with pleasure and stretched out her palm to receive it.

It was Marina. "Hey, Tara! That sounds interesting! Sure, I'm in for a third, like you say. Let's work out when we'll arrive and I'll start. My father—with his trident—will accompany me as far as the continental shelf, but then I'm on my own." Tara could almost picture her friend's eager smile turn momentarily into a frown. "And without the trident. He says I can't take it with me this time."

That was too bad, thought Tara. But not unexpected. Shouldn't be too much of a setback though, as they had already dealt with the sand golem. Now she just needed to hear from Ariel.

Ariel replied later that day in the same way, with the bubble arriving while Tara was brushing her hair and preparing for bed. She was game for a third too. When could they start? Tara smiled to herself. It was hard to know what was motivating her friends more: cupidity or adventure. Maybe both. Tara found herself starting to wonder about just how much there might be left at the bottom of the oasis pool. But she reassured herself: the sand golem must have roamed the desert for a long, long time. It had really liked gold too. It had to have picked up all sorts of treasures on its wanderings.

The next day, she brought up the idea of seeing the horrid Countess Abernathy with her parents. They were delighted, Armorica insisting she take two ball gowns with matching shoes. Tara assented readily. Why not? She intended to leave them at Cloud Castle anyway while in the Lost Quarter and pick them up again on the way back.

Tara, for her part, made sure to catch the name of the messenger to be sent to the Countess. She had to intercept him and prevent the message going out. Otherwise the Countess would wonder where she was. Daystar would still be in the stables, which would normally be a tipoff for sure that Tara had not gone to the Eastern Hills, but her parents never ventured there so would never know.

In short, all was arranged within a day and Tara promptly sent out reply bubbles to her friends. Let's get started, she told them. Ariel would be overhead in three days, she heard back. Be in the usual field by ten that morning for pick up. Tara considered: three days should be enough of a head start for Marina to show up at the rendezvous point more or less when they would.

Three days later, Tara and Ariel were standing on the Vista Terrace, each with a glass of a chilled liquid. Tara sighed in sheer delight. "This absolutely is my favorite spot on Cloud Castle! It's so beautiful!" Tara gazed down at the lands far below her, intermittently visible through the wispy cirrus clouds seemingly just below her, a tattered carpet almost at her feet and upon which, if she imagined it just so, she thought she might hopscotch across the sky if she could only stand upon them.

Ariel nodded, pleased. She always took Tara to this spot almost as soon as she arrived, because she knew Tara loved it so. Indeed, Tara always said how much she loved it, each and every time, as if it were her first time beholding it. On this occasion, she had requested one of her incorporeal servants, which she called Breezes, to bring them some refreshment.

"What is this drink?" asked Tara, holding up her crystal glass, shaped much like a flute, close to her eyes. It was filled with a pale blue liquid such that, when the sun shone through it, a blue-tinged spectrum of light spilt across the bodice of her dress.

"Oh, it's just melt from cloud ice—which is very pure—with a bit of flavoring from the west wind."

"From the wind? The west wind?"

"Yes. That's the wind that tends to blow over farmlands and gardens, so it picks up the most heavenly herb and fruit scents. When I'm able to catch and distil it, I can get the most wonderful dew! Just a little bit in each glass of ice melt creates this heavenly juice drink."

Tara studied the glass of powder-blue liquid another moment then took another sip. A drink flavored from the essence of the west wind! No wonder it tasted so light and refreshing. She looked around her, taking in the Vista Terrace and the tables and chairs and pavilions surrounding it. This was simply incredible, she thought. No way would Ariel ever have to wonder about a dowry when she found someone. Just look: the entire castle was the most beautiful that anyone could possibly imagine.

A dowry. Tara frowned. She might as well tell her friend everything. She didn't want to. It wasn't exactly wonderful, like Vista Terrace and a glass of pure, melted cloud ice. Then again, she realized with a rush, she did want to tell her everything.

"What's wrong? You look so unhappy all of a sudden!"

"Um, yeah. So, I should tell you…" Tara's voice trailed off.

Ariel prompted her at last. "What is it?"

"Well, so, well... I..."

Ariel watched with veiled amusement mixed with apprehension as her friend stumbled forward.

"Look, I sure appreciate you and Marina coming out to the Lost Quarter again with me. To look into the pool for whatever might be still there. But I guess I have some reasons of my own to go."

"What's that?" Ariel's amusement turned to real interest. What could Tara be hoping to find at the oasis pool? A set of golden balls for herself? Another sand golem to march back to Stonedell and put to gainful work in Brythrony?

"Yes." Tara looked miserable for a moment. "Look, it's because I need a dowry."

"A dowry? Are you getting married? And you didn't tell me?"

"No! No! That's not really what I mean. What I mean is that, well, I'm being told I need to save up for a dowry, which I don't really need, because I'm NOT getting married, but if my parents are telling me that I need to start saving—they really did tell me this—then it must mean they don't have a lot of money. For a dowry. Or anything else.

"So I think they need money. I suppose they're—we're—maybe... I guess we're broke."

"Tara, no! That's shocking!"

"I know." Tara looked around her, downcast. It was so gorgeous at Cloud Castle. So light and beautiful and with as much wind drink as you could want pulled directly out of the clouds. "Yeah. I guess we're about penniless. So I thought I'd try to help my parents out a little by trying to find some treasure for them. I mean, they've given me everything I've ever had all these years."

"Tara! Really? But, really?"

Tara nodded, sombrely.

"Why didn't you say something before? I mean, if you need some help, we could give it to you. Lots and lots! You just have to ask for it!"

Tara turned away, ashamed, unable to meet Ariel's earnest gaze. Everyone was so nice to her. Tara suddenly felt that all she ever did was think of herself.

"Really! I mean, Marina must have oodles of pearls at Coral Castle. She could give you boatloads! For her, it would mean, like, you giving her..." Living as she did not on the ground but in the clouds, Ariel struggled

473

for an apt simile for Tara. "Like you giving her… leaves from a tree! Right! Like leaves. From a tree!"

That could be true, thought Tara. She hadn't thought of that. "But I don't want to beg from my friends! I want to do this myself. I want to help my parents on my own. And I appreciate everything you want to do for me, but I want to share with you fairly and equally. I don't want charity, just a little help. So it needs to be one third for you, one third for Marina, and one third for me."

"Tara, no; you take—"

"No. We share. Equally. All of us."

"But you need—"

"No. Equally." Tara sighed. "I just wanted to tell you why I was doing this. I guess I didn't have to, but… well, I wanted to. To be honest."

Ariel put both her hands on Tara's shoulders. "You're a sweet girl," she said softly. "And I appreciate what you just told me. Hey, there's no need to tell anyone else if you don't want to. This can just be between you and me." An idea occurred to her. "So we'll share equally. But you choose first from whatever we find. How about that?" Tara began to object, but Ariel silenced her with an outstretched hand. "This whole expedition was your idea, so you get first choice. I insist!"

After a little more back and forth, Tara reluctant to accept even this concession, she consented, and the two princesses returned to the view.

"When will we arrive?" asked Tara at last, absorbed again by the panorama and starting to relax once more.

Ariel gazed up into the deepening blue of the sapphire sky. How alike it seemed to staring into the midnight-blue depths of the ocean when she had last swum with Marina and Tara to the Coral Castle! Far, far up she could discern tiny stars starting to peep forth, signaling the quickening onset of night. She smiled to herself then assessed some instrumentation nearby. "Tomorrow," she gauged expertly. "Around mid-morning, if these winds hold."

Tara finished the last of her glass then placed it on a nearby table for a Breeze to remove. She gazed dreamily out across the Vista Terrace. "Sounds wonderful. It sounds simply perfect."

As Ariel had predicted, they arrived the next day at mid-morning. Tara and Ariel were on the Vista Terrace again. Both were studying the landscape below. There was no sign of the oasis Marina had created the last time they were there.

Tara looked up at Ariel. "Seems hard to believe it's gone! But we're in the right place, yes?"

"I've double- and triple-checked."

Tara looked down again through the translucent flooring. There was no pinprick of blue like she would expect from the presence of water, such as from an oasis. Could the desert have reclaimed it already, it being created unnaturally by a trident? She looked up again. "You don't have any way to look more closely at what's below, do you?"

Ariel shook her head. "I could really use that too. I'll have to think about how to make that improvement. Sure would be useful now!"

Tara nodded thoughtfully. Maybe no oasis. Did this mean that all the treasures were buried under tons and tons of sand? But couldn't Marina bring water up again, and they could find them again? This was definitely an unwelcome twist.

Tara looked again. Instead of blue, there were various lines and contours in the sand. What could those be? "Those lines," she said aloud. "They must be where the sand golem arose?"

Ariel shrugged. "I don't know. I think we'll have to go and see. On the ground."

"Guess we might as well get going then. Marina should be arriving anyway." They stood up and Tara slung her quiver around her shoulder. Then they picked up two bags of provisions and walked to the waiting sky chariot.

"What in the world is this?" demanded Ariel, as they walked across the sand, having alighted from the chariot and sent it back up to the castle, where it was cooler.

Good question, thought Tara. Sprawled in front of them was what could only be described as an enormous sandcastle but of the most otherworldly and bizarre construction. Instead of tall and spindly towers challenging the sky, it consisted of rounded blocks and blobs, sometimes surmounting each other, sometimes jumbled together. They approached it cautiously, anxious footstep by anxious footstep, until they stood within the shadows of its exterior walls.

"Have you ever seen something like this before?"

"Never."

Tara touched the walls. They were composed of sand, as she had expected. She looked up. The wall wasn't too high; she could probably climb it if the sand held. "Say, could you, maybe, fly up and take a peek across the wall? Just to see if anything is there?"

Ariel grimaced. "Like, there and maybe lying in wait for us? What if it shoots me with something?"

Tara promptly lowered her voice to a whisper. "Of course we don't want that! But if something wanted to shoot at us, wouldn't it have started shooting already, when we were walking?"

"I guess you're right," admitted Ariel grudgingly. Didn't Tara always have an answer for every objection! Ariel unfurled her wings silently then gave a little jump. In another second she was airborne, hovering. Ever so carefully, she rose until her eyes just peeked over what looked to be the wall's parapet. She gentled descended until she stood next to Tara again. "Nothing there," she confided. "Plus, it doesn't seem like anything has ever been there. Unless they have wings. Because there aren't any footsteps anywhere."

Tara nodded. "Well, shall we go in and take a look?"

Ariel thought to object but then asked herself, what else were they there for? "Okay," she replied, unenthusiastically. "You don't have to climb, by the way. I can lift you, since it's only for a short distance."

A moment later, they set down on the other side of the wall. Truly, Tara had never seen anything like it before. The space between the wall and the next structure was of varying distance, sometimes enough for several to walk abreast, and sometimes no distance at all—the wall seemed to merge with the next "building." The wall also curved and twisted with no apparent logic to it. The top of it also seemed to be of varying widths, such that, at points, it was easy to walk along it, but at others, far too narrow. Tara turned to her friend. "Ariel, I don't think people built this!"

Ariel's face assumed a worried expression. "I think I agree with you. It doesn't look like it was made for people."

"Yes, it looks like some kind of fortress, but it doesn't have the characteristics of a fortress."

"Then, what made it? And why?"

"Funny, I was just wondering the same thing."

The two stood in silence for a moment.

"Hey," said Ariel at last. "Let's send Marina a message bubble and find out where she is." Tara assented at once and, with that, Ariel created a bubble, whispered a question into it and blew it into the air with a puff of breath.

The bubble hovered over them for a moment then darted, as if with purposeful intent, up over the sand structure next to them. The two princesses looked at each other. "It was moving as if Marina was—"

"—really close by!" finished Tara. Of course, that was impossible. The bubble moved with the same speed and purposefulness to find its recipient no matter how far away that person was, or where. But, for some reason, it seemed more decisive on this occasion. "Follow it, Ariel!" whispered Tara and Ariel, not needing further encouragement, unfurled her wings, leapt up and followed as quickly as she could.

Tara was left alone. "Guess I might as well try to keep up," she muttered and dug her toes into the structure next to her and began to climb.

The bubble floated up and over the structure and then down amongst the alleys and avenues of the sandcastle. Ariel caught sight of it again after a minute by hovering a little higher and catching a ray of sunlight reflecting from it. "There it is!" she whispered to herself and sped after it. But she lost it again amongst the corners and was forced to rise again to try to spot it. She thought she saw it a few "streets" away and flew as quickly as she could after it, but when she arrived, it was gone. What she did discover, though, was what looked like an entrance into the complex. Funny, she thought, this was the only entrance they had encountered. Otherwise, no doors, no windows, nothing. It really wasn't built by people for people. It was built by… something else for that something else.

There was nothing to be seen around the entrance, so Ariel flew to the top of the building into which it opened and marked it with a large "X" by dragging her heel across the sand. Then she hastened back to Tara.

She found her rounding one of the corners to a "street" with a confused expression on her face. "Wow, Ariel, am I glad to see you!" she exclaimed. "It's so confusing here!"

"I know," allowed her winged friend. "Less for me, because I can fly, but it must be super confusing for you!" She told Tara of what she had seen. "Follow me to the 'X' and, if you run into an obstacle, I'll try to carry you over it."

They were soon at the entrance. It was little more than a large hole in the sand, without door, lintel, or any other indication it was anything other than a simple aperture. Tara looked to Ariel. Ariel gave a wry smile. "I think this is where the bubble went in. So, somewhere in there must be Marina."

Tara heaved a sigh. "If she's in there, we can be in there too. Come on, let's go." And with that, Tara ducked and entered, Ariel following a moment later.

Very quickly they discovered that, if it was a labyrinth in the desert sunlight, it was doubly so inside, with the only light present from occasional chinks in the wall to the outside and the confusing twists and turns of the passageway. Worse still, it narrowed and widened in a way that, to the two princesses, made no sense whatsoever. Too late, Tara thought to start making marks on the wall to show they had passed by there already. A few minutes more, and they turned to each other with the same thought in mind: they were lost.

"Well, what do we do now?" asked Ariel in a low voice.

Tara considered. "Well, the bubble led us in here; maybe another could lead us on to Marina?"

Ariel agreed. "Follow the bubble. Good idea." She poured another two drops from her vial and whispered to the resultant bubble that they were looking for her, and then spoke "Princess Marina" and loosed the bubble. It hesitated next to them for a moment then floated down the passageway. The two princesses hastened to keep up with it, Tara running as fast as she could and Ariel even taking flight at points, though not always, as she had to remain mindful of the occasionally very low overhead.

"Around this corner!" shouted Ariel and disappeared, running, around a bend. Tara gasped to keep up. Marina must be nearby! She couldn't keep running forever!

Ariel suddenly gave a cry of surprise and Tara heard a great splash. Too late! Tara was unable to stop. After a short skid on wet sand, she fell, with a heart-stopping drop, into a deep pool of water. She came up, floundering and blowing, to hear her friend calling to her in the darkness from what sounded like right next to her.

"Ariel, is that you?"

"Yes, it's me! Is that you?"

"Well, it's Tara, if that's the 'you' you're looking for!"

Ariel snorted and splashed Tara with her hand. "Who else would I be calling for?" she demanded, slightly irritated.

"All right, all right, I'm sorry. That was obnoxious of me. I'm sorry." Tara paddled for a moment longer. "Let's get out of this water. We must be close to the edge."

"Right. It's got to be close by!"

"If only we could see!"

The darkness seemed wet, warm, and claustrophobic. Tara couldn't see anything. It made her feel panicky, not knowing where solid ground was. Then, to her utter terror, she felt a stirring in the water next to her, as of something rising from the depths and reaching for her. She gave a short shriek and jerked back, flailing wildly. "Ariel! Something—something's coming for us! Help!"

Ariel shrieked as well, and it echoed and re-echoed about them. "Get out! Get out! It wants to pull us down! To drown us!"

A dark round shape popped up above the surface nearby. Marina's voice spoke. "You two are so silly! Come on, it's only me! Marina!"

Tara's fright subsided. "Oh! How were we supposed to know?"

Marina laughed. "The bubble you followed took you here!"

"But look, come down with me underwater so we can talk. Take a bit of the seaweed I brought and we'll go underwater out of the heat."

Ariel and Tara were more than happy to do this, and soon they were lying or sitting on a bed of sand far beneath the surface where they had lately been treading water. Marina placed a handful of bioluminescent algae next to them to provide a feeble light and commenced to chat with them in her familiar and cheery way.

"Well, not really very much happened, except, well, I guess we met a giant blue crab along the way."

"A giant blue crab?"

"Yes, it threatened us with its claws and greedy feeders, until my father—he came with me part of the way—used his trident—he brought that along— and washed it far away with an undersea current so strong even the crab couldn't resist it. But then he said I had to go on alone when I reached the continental shelf.

"So, I asked again if he would lend me his trident, but he still said 'no'.

"So, where am I? Where are we?" continued Marina, looking up and around her. "I mean, where's the sunlight? The pool should be open to the sky; that's how we left it after we took care of that sand golem! But it feels enclosed now, there's no breeze, and the air smells!"

"Yes," answered Ariel. "It does smell, that's for sure. The pool's no longer open to the sky, but it's now inside some sort of chamber."

Tara described to Marina the strange nature of the structures around them and how neither she nor Tara could imagine their origin. Marina was baffled as well. "I have no idea what built this. But I'm a mermaid, and what do I know about the desert, or the land in general? So, if you don't know what built it, how could any of us?"

The three mulled this certain verity for a moment, but then Ariel brightened. "But what's the difference? We've found the pool, and we can look for whatever still might be here at the bottom. It's awfully dark, of course, that's the only problem. Then, when we're ready to go, we just follow Marina out underwater!"

Marina hesitated. "Yes, we can look for a little bit down here. But there's a problem. It's," and she hesitated again, "I didn't bring any more of the seaweed for you. Just that little bit I had left in my bag from when you came down to the Coral Castle."

Tara remembered that. It had been when they had—very briefly—been imprisoned.

"So, I don't have any more for you. And the little bit I gave to you won't be nearly enough to get you all the way back out."

"That means we'll have to go out the usual way: walking."

Marina nodded, wordlessly.

Tara dug her fingers into the sand and let it sift through her fingers. This was unfortunate. Because they had no idea of how to get back to the outside desert, having totally lost their way amongst all the twists and turns. She looked over to Ariel. "I'm glad we found Marina. But it looks like we'll have to find our own way out of here."

"Sorry, guys," mumbled Marina.

Tara shrugged. There was nothing to be done about it. They had walked in; they would have to walk out. "All right," she said at last, "let's see what we can do with Marina's help. As for getting out, Ariel and I will have to figure that out on our own."

The three at once started searching in the algae's dim light. Without stopping to assess what they were collecting, they piled up a trove of what appeared to be precious stones, necklaces, coins, and anything else that wasn't sand. Tara was sure that some of it was of very dubious value, but speed was essential. They could sort through it all later.

Before long, Tara could feel the effects of the seaweed starting to wear off. She was feeling the pressure a little more each time she dived. She motioned to Ariel that it was time to go up; Marina would stay with what they had found, so Ariel and Tara would not be burdened while they searched for a way out.

Tara and Ariel surfaced and hung to the edge of the pool. Still totally dark. Stirred by curiosity, Tara heaved herself out to determine where the nearest wall might be. She soon found one but, unnervingly, it seethed and shifted beneath her fingers. She pulled back her fingers, repelled, and returned to the pool. Marina brought up the bioluminescent algae and, in its wan glow, what they saw horrified them. The walls were covered with swarming, seething larvae.

"Horrible! Disgusting!" gasped Tara and shook the fingers of the hand that had touched the wall. "I simply have to get rid of them!" She turned to her friends and urged them to swim to the lower depths of the spring, explaining that she would use her ring to reduce the maggot swarm to ashes. "In this enclosed chamber, they'll be incinerated instantly!"

"Be careful," warned Marina. "We don't want you incinerated as well!" She and Ariel, who had eaten a slightly larger piece of seaweed, swam down as deep as they dared and seated themselves on the sand, back-to-back to await the fireball's sudden blaze of light.

At the water's surface, Tara crooked her finger so the ring was just above the surface and commanded it to emit a fireball, speaking into the water, but nothing happened. Had the water caused it to malfunction? Or was it, it occurred to her, that she had to speak the words of command such that the ring "heard" them? Meaning, she groaned inwardly, she couldn't be underwater!

Wincing, Tara surfaced. But as she did so, one of the darting, flying larvae landed on her lips and several others alighted in her hair. "Ugh! Horrid!" There must be thousands, maybe millions, all milling about this chamber! Choking and sputtering, Tara sank back below the surface until just her lips, barely, were above. The fireball would be intense. She'd have to speak the words and immediately dive as deep as she could, as the water's surface might well boil from the heat.

Crooking her finger again but keeping her lips just above the water, Tara spoke the command then spun and dove. The fireball roared and flames flashed overhead from one end of the chamber to the other. The surface of the pool smoked and intense tendrils of heat reached after her; Tara briefly felt one lash her leg. But the reach of the flames was limited and the duration of the fireball brief, and within a few seconds it had subsided. Superheated water mixed with cooler water, and shortly Tara felt it safe enough to return to the surface.

The other two came up behind her. Tara stepped from the pool and tentatively reached out. To her satisfaction, all that was left of the larvae was a fine film of soot. Maybe it had been excessive to use a fireball against larvae, but Tara had been nauseated. Besides, she asked herself, what could have spawned so many larvae? The thought made her gag. Whatever had was either big or numerous—or perhaps both.

The three princesses conferred at the edge of the pool, Tara dangling her legs in the water. "Well, that took care of that problem," announced Tara, not mentioning her misgivings about the origin of the larvae.

"But still, how do we get out?" asked Ariel.

Marina swished her tail thoughtfully. "I'm sorry I can't help you on that." Then she brightened. "But, on the other hand, it means I can search the pool thoroughly to find absolutely everything of value!"

Ariel and Tara agreed that would be helpful and there wasn't anything else she could do anyway. Tara picked herself up and offered a hand to Ariel. "Guess we might as well get going?" With that, and waving goodbye to Marina, they set off to find an exit.

It took only a few minutes of groping in the dark for Ariel to stop and state flatly that they had to have some light. "This is impossible, just feeling our way forward like this! What if we run into something… horrible?"

Tara admitted she was right: what if something lurked just ahead that preferred darkness over light? But they had nothing they could burn to create light, and they couldn't strike a spark anyway. All they had was… Tara's ring. She examined it closely. Could it be controlled finely enough so that it generated only a glow, rather than sparks or flame? She had never attempted it before, but then she had never faced the necessity. "Hold on a moment," she called. "I've got an idea." Concentrating mightily, she imagined the ring as a sort of aperture to a source of power and that she was painstakingly closing the opening to the narrowest slit so that it was only just wide enough to let through the tiniest amount of energy.

An entire minute went by in concentration, but gradually, waxing and waning, the ring at last achieved a steady, sullen red glow. A bit longer and it turned whiter and brighter, and another minute later and Tara had caused the light to shine in a narrow beam from the center of the ring, modulating it mentally such that it shone brighter in a narrow cone forward that fluctuated only slightly from minute to minute.

Tara turned to Ariel. "How about that?"

Ariel clapped her hands. "Nicely done; I like it! Let's go!"

The two set off to investigate the opening now plainly evident in the far wall. Princess Tara held the light at an angle, shielded, minimizing the beam, while Ariel peered within. Nothing. Ariel motioned for Tara to come forward and, together, they entered. Down another passageway, another, and still another, until, ahead, Ariel thought she heard sounds.

"Like what?" asked Tara.

"I don't know. Like, sand being shaken in a box. Something like that?"

"Maybe we're close to an exit!"

"Do you think? But why would the sand sound like it's being shaken?"

"Uh… the wind's blowing it?"

Tara now heard the noise too. It didn't sound like sand being shaken in a box, or anything else she had ever heard, come to think of it.

Maybe Ariel thought the same, because the closer they got to the sound, the more unsettled they felt. "Turn up the ring!" begged Ariel urgently, stopping. "Give us more light!"

Tara imagined opening the aperture through which light shone from the ring just a little wider. Little by little, the beam broadened and brightened, then she was almost knocked down by Ariel recoiling violently. Tens, if not hundreds, of enormous sand mites were swarming toward them out of the darkness. Ariel screamed. Tara lowered her hand to point at the floor just in front of the foremost mites and invoked a storm of shooting stars. They impacted and the flames sprayed down the passageway to engulf the approaching cloud.

Ariel and Tara gagged until Ariel's fanning wings cleared the thick smoke. "Yuck!" coughed Ariel. "That was incredibly disgusting!"

Tara nodded, but her mind was elsewhere. What on earth, she was wondering, was this sand structure with its larvae and sand mites? How did these insects come to be in this sand maze in such numbers? When they had regained their breath, Tara addressed her friend. "Look, we don't have the faintest idea of where we are. We're lost. Plus, I don't like these disgusting insects we keep running into. First, the larvae, then the mites, and—honestly—what's next? I think we need help."

"Marina can't help us."

"I'm not talking about Marina. I'm thinking of Atalanta."

Ariel thought this over. "Atalanta. Atalanta. She lives somewhere around here. Maybe she could help!"

"Right. Let me send her a message bubble right now." A moment later, just such a bubble was floating back down the passage from where they had lately come.

That must be the quickest way out, thought Tara. "Come on, let's follow as long as we can!" she called to Ariel. But this was not far, as it led them back to a point just twenty yards back, where the ceiling was very high, and up the bubble drifted until it vanished through what looked like a sort of crack or hole far, far up. The two princesses looked at each other.

"At least it's free," mumbled Ariel.

Tara tried to find some silver lining in what they had just witnessed. "Maybe, do you think, the wall could be a little thinner here? And we could break through and climb out?"

It was worth a try, they determined and, after gulp of water each, began knocking on the walls to determine if any section sounded weaker. Tara was thinking of the hole overhead through which the bubble had passed. Could their telescoping rods reach it, maybe, if both were bound together somehow?

Their renewed efforts to find a weak spot in the wall were interrupted by the chittering of hundreds of insects. They turned to put their backs up against the wall. "Ariel, I don't like the sound of this!"

Ariel's eyes widened as she peered into the dim light, the humming and buzzing growing ominously louder. "Me neither! Get your ring ready!"

Tara shrank back involuntarily. Out of the darkness, a nightmarish shape began to form. Now it was obvious why this sandy structure was the haven of so many insects. Shambling toward them was a great, seething, monstrous mass of them, swarming about some common core.

"I've never seen—we need to call for help! And we need to do it now!"

Ariel stared, fascinated by the grisly thing lurching unsteadily toward them. "We did that already, remember?"

"We need more!"

"It'll see the bubble go out through the hole! And maybe send one of those insects to try to pop it!"

"Turn and send a bubble back to Marina. I'll distract whatever that horrid thing is; you just send the bubble!"

Tara forced herself to take a step forward. The quivering, convulsing mass of insects drew closer. Tara felt herself grow faint; she thought she might retch, the thing was so hideous. Still, she steeled herself. Maybe it was friendly! They should give it the benefit of the doubt. "What are you? What do you want?" Tara called, trying to keep her voice even.

The thing said nothing and advanced another lurching step. Tara called again, hardening her resolve. "Please, get away from us! What are you?" Then, thinking to set an example, she added, "We are Princesses Tara and Ariel!"

Then the thing spoke, and its voice came in a strange susurrus of whispers, whistles, whirs, and buzzes, as if composed of a chorus of cicadas. The words growled around inside it for a moment, as if implementing the proper organs of speech to communicate. Then the words were articulated in a horrible, slurping sort of way. "Wonderful," the words came. "Wonderful!"

Tara caught herself. Was this thing, this creature, actually greeting them? Could it actually be friendly, as disgusting as it appeared?

"Wonderful," said the monster a third time, then clarified. "Such rich blood! So fresh! Two of them!"

This was more along the lines of what Tara had expected, unfortunately. In fact, in a weird, strange way, she felt better now that she had been so disgusted. It truly was as vile as she had thought it on first impression.

The creature slowed its advance, as if anticipating resistance, and spoke again, the voice softening to a chittering crackle that shook and stirred, moving up and down in volume like a sighing wind. "Of course, you would come for the light. I knew this. Now be still. Now I feed."

"Use the ring!" whispered Ariel, nudging her. "Fry it with the ring!"

It made sense, Tara readily admitted. The awful thing wanted to munch on them. Tara raised her hand and even paused, hoping the minatory gesture might give the thing pause, but it took no heed. You asked for it, thought Tara, and whispered for the fireball, bracing herself for the very slight kick the ring always delivered. But to her astonishment and horror, nothing happened. She stared down. How was this? She pointed the ring and again demanded, "Fireball!" but again, nothing. A sudden fear gripped her, and she saw that the ring's usual faint, reddish glow had faded to the dull, reddish-brown color of dried blood. The ring no longer functioned.

How could it, she raged, shaking her hand frantically. When they needed it most! It was like a lantern that had run out of oil, all its fuel used up! Could there still be enough fuel for another function, one less intense? She put her hands together and commanded the spark shower. The ring responded with only a sputter.

The insect thing chortled. "You have no power against me! I am Silicana, and I command the sands and all that is in it!"

Tara reached for Ariel's hand. This could be the end. That horrible thing wanted to eat them, or suck their blood, or something equally unimaginable. Ariel swallowed hard and squeezed her hand back.

But instead of advancing further, Silicana unfurled its wings until they nearly touched the walls to either side. Then, with a sudden jump and another vocalization of that horrible, gurgling laugh, it spun, and its outstretched wings whipped up the sand in a blinding cyclone. The princesses were driven to the wall behind them and pinned at the wrists and ankles by a band of sand so strong that it was as if their limbs had been cemented in place.

Silicana laughed and turned away. "Stay there," it called after them, with a final whistling, coughing snicker. "I will be back shortly!"

Across the sands at the edge of the Lost Quarter stood Orlaith Palace. In its throne room, on its throne, sat Atalanta, of the House of Orla, nearing the end of an audience for those petitioning for justice. Though she had become somewhat inured to their length, holding them several times a week, today the queue seemed exceptionally long. It was a tedious responsibility, but she conducted it fully and faithfully and without complaint. She remembered well the time not so long ago, before the rains had resumed, when no one had come to her for justice—for anything—as no one had cared even the slightest bit about her or the House of Orla.

Now, her subjects respected and loved her. "Queen," they called her. Atalanta was acutely aware of how precious that love was and knew instinctively that the prompt and fair administration of justice was critical to maintaining it. Thus, though she sometimes stirred restlessly, she knew that every case before her was an affirmation of her authority and her people's trust.

Next to her stood Chuffney, her chief adviser. She kept him beside her as she adjudicated to signal that, whenever he should preside, he was entirely trusted and fully authorized to act on her behalf.

A slight distance away, just off to the side, materialized a tiny golden shadow. It began to drift in an irregular diagonal across the flagstones toward her, growing ever bigger as Atalanta watched from the corner of her eye. She glanced up. High above her, through a lancet window at the very heights of the hall, had floated a bubble. It glowed in the sunlight, a growing golden orb streaked minutely with iridescence. Atalanta nodded very slightly in recognition, so slightly her supplicant could not see that she had. It was a message bubble.

In a single motion, Atalanta stretched out her left palm to receive it, while begging her subject for a moment's leave. The bubble alighted; Atalanta breathed on it softly to collapse it, and she heard, as if speaking at her very side, the voice of her friend Tara. What was this? Tara was saying that she was back in the Lost Quarter, where they had found the three golden balls, and that she feared she was in trouble. Ariel was with her, as was Marina. Could she please help in any way? The tone of urgency was unmistakable and troubling.

Atalanta turned back to her subject and heard him out. She thought gravely for a moment and proposed a solution which would seem at least to partially satisfy all parties to the conflict. They bowed, thanked her and were escorted out. Before the next party could approach, Atalanta clapped her hands twice and announced that the audience for justice must end and that the next audience would take place as scheduled under Chuffney.

Atalanta called for her courtiers to tell them she would be traveling. She stood, waited for all present to bow or curtsey ceremoniously, and then, with a swirl of her glittering emerald-and-gold gown, departed the throne room to ascend the stairs to her private suite. Her three golden balls, ever weaving about her head in their own unknowable pattern, silently trailed her.

Reaching her room, she pulled from the back of her wardrobe her unlovely, if sturdy, traveling clothes. Around the hanger on which they were hung was her princess purse with its precious contents. This, along with her golden balls, was all she needed.

But how to find her friends? She communed briefly with her golden balls to assess their knowledge of that part of the Lost Quarter where Tara had said she was. They replied that though that stretch of sand was distant and unremarkable, they could lead her to its approximate location. That would have to be good enough: Tara sounded like she was in danger and speed was essential.

And so Atalanta would fly. For just such an emergency, she had had fashioned a kind of sled that the three balls would hold aloft and keep stable. She had experimented with it some and been satisfied. But this would be its first real test.

Her preparations were interrupted by a respectful knock on the door. Atalanta was confident she knew who it was but asked nonetheless. It was Chuffney, as she had expected, and she granted him permission to enter.

He stepped across the threshold and doffed his soft cap of gold thread with its yellow-and-green badge of authority affixed to the left side. "Your Highness, a thousand pardons," he began in a low voice.

She dismissed these with a wave.

"Your Highness, will You be absent from Your realm for long?"

"You have all my authority, as always, in all matters, Chuffney," she replied by way of answer.

He half-twisted his cap in his hand then caught himself and straightened it. "Your Highness will be away."

"Yes. I will be away for a little bit, Chuffney. As I have been before, on occasion."

"Will Your Highness be away long?"

How persistent he was! "I hope not. I hope only a day or so."

"Your Highness knows best, as always."

Atalanta folded up a spare cloak for the inevitable chill of the desert night and straightened to look Chuffney in the eye. "Thank you, counsellor. But, as I say, I do not expect to be absent long."

Chuffney twisted the cap in the reverse direction from before. He did not wish to presume on the queen's patience, yet he still felt obliged to speak his mind. In fact, hadn't she told him it was his obligation, on more than one occasion?

"What is it, Chuffney? What troubles you?"

"Your Highness, I just… I just worry. A bit. About your absence."

"I have confidence in you, Chuffney. You should also."

"It is not that, Your Highness. It is this which troubles me. I fear that Maurienne may be unsettled while Her mistress shall be away from Her throne. If that should be for some space of time."

The golden balls circled Atalanta silently, unobtrusively passing just over the top of her forehead, above eye level, as if watching and listening. Atalanta gazed at her counsellor thoughtfully as she cinched around her waist the belt she had attached to her princess purse. It was obvious he meant well. It must be the case, as he said, that the realm was at its most secure and settled when she was present. But then her mind strayed back, as it oft did, to how her father had lost the kingdom by reneging on a sworn promise to help others; how she, Atalanta, had regained it and restored the rains by redeeming another promise; thence to the princess who had played such an instrumental role in bringing all of this to pass; and finally her pledge to come to that princess's assistance whenever and however she might require it. "You may be correct, Counsellor Chuffney," she replied in the soft tones she reserved for when she wished to be her most emphatic. "But I shall most certainly forfeit this throne if I do not go."

Chuffney bowed deeply. She was decided. There would be no further discussion.

Atalanta gave a quick nod of dismissal to Chuffney and grabbed the travel bag of some water and provisions she had had sent up. Turning, Atalanta exited through a door hidden behind a tapestry at the rear of the room. The austere ruler in the emerald gown of half an hour before would hardly have been recognizable as the weather-beaten traveler she appeared as now—save for the presence of the three continuously circling balls.

Atlanta ascended two flights of stairs just beyond the tapestry to the rooftop. It was there, secreted in a low, shed-like structure, that she kept her recently constructed sled. The sled was something she had conceived of one afternoon while wrestling with the frustration she felt at the fact that she could only travel by either horse or foot. Couldn't she go faster, she wondered, thinking of Princess Ariel's Cloud Castle. But, she didn't have the magic that Ariel had, nor did she have her wings. At length she had asked her golden balls for suggestions.

The sky sled had been their answer.

Atalanta opened the shed door and dragged out her sled. The sled was a sturdy platform sawn in the dimensions of a golden triangle, with a bowl affixed to the underside at each vertex such that they were open to the ground. Also on the underside of the platform, and next to the bowls, were nailed three rough blocks, large enough such that the bowls were open when the platform was resting on them. Upon these feet the platform stood. Two wheels had been attached to the rear of the sled at the base of the triangle.

By tilting the sled up high and pulling it by a handle affixed to the underside of the apex, Atalanta could tow the sled for short distances, the sled rolling on the wheels.

Atop the platform she had had a seat attached and, just in front of it, two stirrups into which she could slide her feet. Behind the seat was affixed a small, tightly covered storage bin. Otherwise, the sled was bare, as Atalanta considered it to be purely functional in purpose.

She took the seat, adjusting for comfort the belt and its attached princess purse, and slipped her feet into the stirrups. As a silent command, she let fall to either side her outstretched arms and the golden balls floated down and entered the overturned bowls underneath.

Up she raised her palms. Next moment, the three balls, working together to keep the platform level, silently lifted the sled from the rooftop. Another moment and the sled began to slide forward through the air, gaining momentum, each ball leaving a faint trail of golden sparkles in its wake. Another moment more and she was moving at speed toward Princess Tara, the rolling desert below her become a grey-brown blur.

Princess Atalanta skimmed over the desert floor toward the location her three golden balls had insisted they had lain. The sun was starting to set, far, far out on the distant, western horizon. The sky still blazed a brilliant yellow and orange, but toward the upper reaches of the hemisphere, toward its zenith, the blue was deepening to a flawless sapphire. Tiny points of light overhead, still more distinct behind her, were starting to show in the heavens. It was nearing twilight; soon it would be night. Atalanta glanced down at the sand below her. Her speed and height were blending its contours into a gentle rumple, like it had been yanked roughly from a bolt of khaki cloth. Here and there, lengthening shadows stained its expanse like spilt water.

Atalanta returned her gaze to the horizon. There was no time to contemplate such things. Princess Tara was out there, somewhere in the sand. She had asked for help, and she, Atalanta, would render that help. This must occupy all her thoughts, she told herself: how she might aid Tara best and most speedily.

The balls had stated that the place was an empty stretch of sand, marked only by a nearby outcropping of rocks. Yet, as she approached the spot they had identified, on the horizon loomed a mound-like structure much like a giant hive. Even from this distance it seemed vast and sprawling. She asked her golden balls if this was present when they were there last. "No," they answered, shortly.

"But you're sure this is the place?"

"Absolutely," they answered, in unison, as they always did.

Curious, observed Atalanta silently. How did it suddenly appear? In the uninhabited desert, no less, where generally all was one sinuous, endlessly undulating dune.

The vast hive bulked higher and higher on the horizon as she neared. Atalanta slowed as she approached and began to guide her balls to take her not directly down to it but at a more oblique angle. As she did, another bubble rose toward her. Stopping her raft to hover high up above the ground, another voice, which identified itself as that of Marina, spoke in urgent tones. Tara and Ariel had encountered some creature, she was saying and, not hearing further from them, feared the worst. "But come see me first before going after them! We'll need each other to find them!"

Atalanta resumed her descent. Marina had to be in the mound below somewhere. But where? Atalanta slowed the raft again and slipped her hand inside the princess purse. Marina's bubble had found her; why couldn't one from Atalanta find Marina and she, Atalanta, follow it?

Good, Atalanta told herself, pleased, and removed the vial, uncapped it and dripped out two drops onto her outstretched palm. Now to create the bubble. But her other palm was dry, and moisture was needed to create the bubble. Grimacing with displeasure, she licked her right palm, clapped it to her left and pulled it apart to form the bubble. Into it she whispered, "Go now to Princess Marina, and with this message: 'I'm on my way! Even now!'" Then, with a breath, she blew it into the softening light.

The bubble hovered for a moment and dove. Atalanta's sled followed in a great swooping arc, three glittering trails streaming from the underside of her sled. Yes, Marina was inside that sand hive somewhere.

Atalanta landed on the flattest space she could find and alighted to inspect the hole through which the bubble had vanished. It was small, not much more than the size of a fist; just enough to let in some light—and a message bubble. She ran her fingers around the edge of the hole. It was like a rough and crumbly cement: she could break off small bits of it with her fingers but nothing larger. Atalanta considered. She needed a way to enlarge the existing hole enough to fit through. Then she could extend the telescoping pole to the ground below and slide down.

Atalanta took another step back and summoned her three golden balls. They positioned themselves above the hole equidistant from each other and, in quick succession, commenced cycling up and down rapidly, punching the hole bit by bit wider with each pass.

Atalanta noted their progress with satisfaction and readied the telescoping rod. Then she paused. Could there be something below, perhaps waiting for her, just off to the side? She brought forth a half a fistful of dazzle dust. Best to drop some and let the fading sunlight off it briefly illuminate the space below to check. It fell, flashing and coruscating, sparkling and gleaming, to reveal only bare sandy walls and floor.

A few minutes later and Atalanta was standing within the mound, the hole through which she had slid just moments before a pool of light high overhead. Her options appeared limited, she determined with a frown. Either she went one way down the passageway or the other. She decided to send one ball in each direction as a scout. Look for water, she commanded them. Marina would be in the water. Surely there could be only one source within this structure.

Shortly, one notified her that it had discovered a wide pool in a large cavern-like structure. Marina must be there, determined Atalanta, and promptly set off in that direction, recalling the other ball.

She arrived in the cavern a short while later. The pool of water was as still as if glass, unruffled and undisturbed. Yet this must be where Marina was hiding. Atalanta tossed a few pebbles into the pool and shortly a shadowy figure surfaced in its middle.

"Are you Atalanta?" the figure asked hesitantly.

"Yes. I'm Atalanta. Marina?"

The mermaid sighed with relief. "I'm so glad you could come! It's been simply awful, waiting and wondering what has happened to Tara and Ariel!" She looked more closely at Atalanta. "Hey, you're a lot like Tara described you!"

Atalanta was unsure how to interpret that comment but decided it was complimentary and nodded as if in understanding. She crouched down at the water's edge. "We have a lot to catch up on, and quickly, if we are to find them. Tell me what you know."

Marina quickly recounted their adventure, from how they returned to the pool to look for more treasure, how they had discovered it enclosed instead of open to the sky, and then the discovery of the revolting larvae.

She concluded with the message bubble she had received from Ariel about the creature they had encountered while looking for a way out.

"Why didn't Tara's use her ring, if it threatened them?" wondered Atalanta aloud.

Marina shook her head. "Don't know. Maybe the creature was immune? Or something? But it sounded like they're in real trouble!"

Atalanta agreed. "I'll go look for them; they may be in grave danger. The balls will explore ahead for me. I'll let you know by bubble what I find." Saying this, two balls flitted away down the open passageway and she waved good-bye and followed after them. Marina watched for a moment, then dove back underwater.

Even though far down the passageway, Ariel and Tara could hear Silicana approaching, sizzling and swishing and whistling and chattering to itself as it intermittently hopped, swirled, or glided forward. Sometimes its wings fluttered out, causing little eddies of sand and wind to fly before it. Sometimes it was still, as if listening, or internally conferring, or simply waiting and testing the air. Then, satisfied, it would hop forward again and chitter anew.

Ariel and Tara had already discussed in hurried whispers what they thought they could do. As it was, not much, except to play for time. The longer they could stall Silicana's "feeding," the greater their chances, they figured, of rescue, escape, or of persuading Silicana to let them go.

Silicana appeared at the entrance to the chamber at last. Its bulk nearly filled the space from what they could make out by the moonlight filtering down from above.

Ariel mustered as much defiance as she could, though the quaver in her voice was still obvious. "Who are you, and what do you want? Let us go, now, or there won't be any mercy for you!"

Silicana gave its queer, hoarse, choking laugh. "Empty words! There is nothing you can do." The wings swirled briefly. "I am hungry. Which shall be first? The first will not have to watch the other suffer; that is to be prized!"

"You first," said Ariel, immediately, to Tara.

"No! No, you first. I do this for you!"

Tara had immediately understood what Ariel was thinking: feign a heated argument. Any delay would be valuable. Even if, she thought grimly, only one of them would realize its benefit.

"That's what you say. But you just want me to die first!"

"And wouldn't you be happy to see me die first?"

Silicana sputtered and chortled with a grotesque amusement.

"I'm offering you the chance to go first because I've always cared for you! More than for myself!"

Though the two continued like this, sometimes pretending to be at a loss for words, sometimes pretending to be overcome with anger, with a steadily sinking feeling, Tara realized that their pretended argumentation could never forestall the inevitable. Silicana still appeared to be entertained by the manufactured row they were staging, judging by the way it hopped back and forth between them and hissed and seethed with apparent enjoyment. But Atalanta would never be able to reach them in time to save them—how could she?—and Marina was confined to the water. Why not go out with dignity? Further, Tara knew, it was she who was to blame for this horrific mess. She had come looking for her dowry; Ariel had only come to help.

Quietly, Tara spoke during one of their pauses. "It's all right with me, Ariel. You choose which way you want to go: first or second. You decide."

Ariel stopped in mid-breadth. "Tara? Huh?" she managed at last. "Me? I choose?"

"You choose."

Silicana inched forward. "Very good, very good! At last. Well, which do you want, One-With-Wings?"

"Uh—I have to think about it. Tara, are you sure?"

"Enough! I will choose!" screeched Silicana, losing patience, with sustenance so close. "I choose the other! This one," it motioned to Tara. "This one. Because," it added superfluously, "it does not have wings and will taste better."

Tara closed her eyes tightly. This had to be the end. For sure. And how horrible. She only hoped it would be quick. Maybe she would even faint.

Silicana's chittering drew closer and the foul stench the creature exuded swept over Tara. Involuntarily, she began to retch. But then the whispering and muttering died away and the stench lessened. Tara opened her eyes just a crack, too curious to keep them shut. Silicana had backed away and was wavering, as if uncertain what to do next.

"What... what is it you have? On you?" it asked at last, still hesitant.

Tara thought hard. She had nothing but her clothes and her princess purse. The purse contained only the usual dazzle dust, message bubbles, and telescoping rod. But then she remembered something else. She had also taken the mysterious crystal rod from the top drawer of her chest in the hopes of finding out more about it in the Lost Quarter!

Just then, out of the corner of her eye, Tara spotted a golden ball loitering in the darkness high overhead. Her heart jumped as she recognized it as Atalanta's. She had to be close by! Tara had only to stall a little longer and there would be help.

Tara motioned with her head and called out, "Do you see the ball up there, at the ceiling? It guides powerful friends to our rescue! Escape while you can! Soon it will be too late for you!"

Silicana whirled to look in the direction in which Tara had motioned, just in time to see the spinning orb rise further into the darkness. Silicana hesitated again, weighing its hunger versus the probable necessity of dealing with new enemies. There was a long, sibilant buzz and, rather than turning back toward them, Silicana shifted its orientation by recomposing itself with a momentary blur. "My needs first. There may be confrontation. Drink now; attend to others when and if they come.

"One-With-Wings, now. The other, later."

Silicana chuckled in its horrible, gurgling, whispering way and lurched toward the princess it had called One-With-Wings. Ariel twisted frantically and she gagged as the foul, fetid stench of Silicana enveloped her. Tara heard herself screaming in horror. Silicana's wings were fanning out to embrace Ariel when, from high up in the darkness, the golden ball flashed down to strike a thudding blow to the top of Silicana's head. The creature screeched and staggered but held its balance. The golden ball took flight again to hover just beyond the reach of Silicana's wings.

"What is this?" Silicana hissed and extended one wing to bat at the ball. The ball withdrew further back and commenced to manoeuvre erratically, as if to taunt. "This object?"

The creature and the ball seemed to evaluate each other for a long minute when, in a single surprising bound, Silicana crossed the space between it. Both wings reached greedily for the ball, but a second came hurtling from the opposite direction to strike Silicana squarely from behind.

Silicana howled a terrible rasping note that rose from an angry buzz to beyond their hearing. One portion of Silicana's head was blacker than the rest, as if it had been bruised or punctured. Clearly, Tara could see, riveted with a fearful fascination, it had been hurt. Strangely and awfully, the wound seemed to crawl and seethe instead of ooze.

Silicana retreated from the princesses to the other side of the cavern, as if to size up its opponents. The two balls, hovering side by side, interposed themselves between Silicana and its prey. But Silicana was clever and had backed away only to gain the space to deploy its vast wings. Unfurling them, it swept them forward in an arc to enfold both balls.

Silicana's whispery laugh mocked them from out of the darkness. "This, that, was your rescue?"

"Not all of it, creature!" echoed Atalanta's voice down the passageway. "Hold there!" she called and stepped forward, the third ball hovering at her right temple. "Prepare to face your reckoning!"

The ball streaked forward and Silicana instinctively threw up its wings to shield itself, but the ball halted in mid-flight. A ruse! In deploying its wings, Silicana let go the two captured balls, and they returned straightaway to Atalanta.

Tara and Ariel cheered. Silicana tensed and a low, guttural crepitation developed somewhere deep within it. The sound emerged as a grim, rattling noise that trailed off ominously into the silence and the darkness.

Atalanta slipped off her traveling cloak and let it fall. Underneath, a shirt of chainmail gleamed in the dim light. At her belt, next to the princess purse, was a short sword, maybe several times longer than a dagger, which she drew with a sound like faintly ringing crystal. Tara sucked in her breath. Atalanta couldn't possibly fight Silicana alone; she and Ariel had to free themselves to help her.

"Free them," Atalanta commanded. "Now." In the moonlight flooding in from overhead, the three balls, whirling in and out of the soft silver beam of moonlight, circled, ready to strike again.

Silicana vented the same crepitating rattle as before but this time let it trail off slowly in a long, menacing hiss.

"A last time, creature: release them, and this instant," she added, gesturing with her sword in the direction of Ariel and Tara, "or it will go very harshly for you."

Silicana studied this third one. What weapon did it really wield? A grey stick of metal, nothing formidable. And the pesky floating balls, which were quick, and hard, but not deadly. Silicana could catch them again with its wings. Plus, Silicana had further powers, such as that to control and mold sand. Tentatively, Silicana unfurled its wings and advanced, whispering in its rustling intonation, like sand blown across the dunes, and questioning of itself what might happen next, how, and when.

Atalanta fell back, slow step upon slow step. It began to occur to her that, whatever this creature was, it was big. Bigger than her golden balls and much bigger than her sword. "I focused my efforts on getting here," she muttered to herself, "but might have thought a bit about what to do when I arrived."

To Tara's dismay, she saw Atalanta raise her hands, as if in surrender. With a tumble of jubilant clicks and clucks, Silicana hopped forward and Atalanta flicked the fingers of her upraised hands. The balls streaked forward to impact Silicana in its head and thorax, eliciting something between a shriek of rage and a roar of pain. Another hit, muttered Atalanta as Silicana recovered, but this is far from over.

Now was the time to wriggle free, Tara realized with a start. Now, while Silicana was thoroughly distracted. She began working furiously to free her right wrist, which did not feel as tightly bound as her left and her ankles. Seeing that Ariel's pent left hand was close enough to her own right so as to offer some assistance, she called to her softly. "Ariel!" she whispered fiercely. "Help me if you can!"

Shortly Tara slipped a hand free, the blood drawn from the abrasion to her raw wrist a grisly, if effective, lubricant and immediately pulled from her princess purse the quartz sceptre. Unlike at Castle Stonedell, it was glowing faintly from deep within its interior. One sharp knock on each of her bonds with it and she wrenched herself free.

"Enough!" sang Tara in a voice cracking with emotion. "Enough, Silicana! Away, or this is your end!"

The three glared at each other. It was a stand-off. Down the passageway stood Atalanta, her sword at the ready, her balls hovering above her head in formation; to the other side stirred Silicana, hissing and hesitating but, just perceptibly, starting to back away. In between, against the wall stood Tara brandishing her sceptre, rivulets of blood from her wrist streaking her arm.

"Be careful, it could mean to trick you!" warned Ariel from behind.

"Great point," replied Tara, keeping her eyes locked on Silicana. "Move further around the other side of the creature, Atalanta, so it can't take us both at the same time!"

Silicana heard Tara's warning but vacillated. What was to have been its next blood meal had become a threat. The sceptre hurt its sensory organs and weakened it. Perhaps retreat would be best.

But Silicana had never retreated and refused to now. Humans were weak and for feeding upon. Its dim mind enveloped by a blind, red rage, Silicana stretched its wings and lunged for Tara. Rend the one with the terrible sceptre first! Wings and claws, weight and speed, and then the other and its floating metal spheres!

Tara beat wildly back in self-defense. Distantly, she felt a long tearing scrape down the length of her left arm, thrown up to deflect the on-rushing creature. Croaking, Silicana stumbled back, but Atalanta's three balls crashing into it from behind shoved it forward again. Tara landed a body blow to the creature's side and Silicana collapsed, crippled and wailing. Yet, and as if in a last attempt at treachery, it extended a foreleg to ensnare Tara and pull her down. Tara jumped away and, with a furious fierceness that surprised even herself, pounded it mercilessly on its head and carapace.

The wings fluttered feebly and the legs kicked in jerks. Tara landed a final blow on its back, which gave with a sharp crack, and the sceptre splintered into a dozen pieces. Something within Silicana had shattered, and the creature imploded into a storm of, for all Tara could see, sand-flies.

Tara straightened in amazement as they rose in a cloud around her. "Ugh!" she cried in disgust, waving her arms to shoo them. "More flies!" The sandflies rose in a flurry and milled for a moment. Then, scattered by the gesticulations of Tara and Atalanta, they ascended to the ceiling and vanished into the night through the moonlit hole overhead.

The three stood and stared. Just like that, Silicana was gone. Whatever it had been, all that was left was a tumble of husks, broken bits of wings, and shards of quartz scattered about.

Tara and Atalanta kicked cautiously the remains. "What was it?" muttered Atalanta.

"Don't know," answered Tara. "But little's left. Just fragments. It looked like it was just sandflies, honestly."

Atalanta bent down for a closer look, still wary. "Maybe so. Now. But a minute ago, it was something a lot more."

"Come free me!" cried Ariel dolefully behind them.

The other two freed Ariel and they turned back to what remained of Silicana. Atlanta was right, thought Tara. How, just a few minutes before, had Silicana been such a threat? She bent down to pick up a piece of the quartz sceptre. When she had held it in the presence of Silicana, it had glowed. The fragment in her hand still retained some faint radiance. Tara shook her head, thoroughly puzzled.

"Hey," she called to the other two. "Let's gather up the pieces of Silicana. Into a pile, over here."

"Why? To give them last rites?" asked Atalanta.

"No. Just to see what's left. And maybe what was at its… core. Yes, the core. What made Silicana something more than—I guess—sandflies?"

The three scoured the floor for all that they could find, and they did find a deal but obviously not all. Some small pieces must have been flung off into the darkness when Silicana collapsed. Ariel suggested they use the remains of the sceptre to locate it, thinking it would glow again when in proximity, and Tara thought she had a great idea, but the sceptre had gone lifeless.

Atalanta was unenthusiastic, and even Ariel was ready to leave before long. "Come on," she urged them. "Aren't we all tired and hungry? I'm exhausted!"

"All right," agreed Tara. She could only keep them so long in an effort that, really, made little sense. They should get back to Marina. They left, Tara casting a look back at the fragmentary remains of Silicana on the cavern floor. For why she did not know, and perhaps only out of a morbid curiosity, Tara had stuffed into her princess purse a few shards of the sceptre that had destroyed Silicana, along with those few mysterious bits of the creature that were not obviously insect.

Two days later, Princess Tara was back in Castle Stonedell, lounging on her bed. She and her two friends had returned to the oasis pool and had found Marina waiting anxiously for them at the pool's edge.

"There you are!" Marina had shrieked in delight. "I've been absolutely beside myself with worry! What happened?" She had gasped. "And let me get you something for your wrist! And that terrible scratch down your arm!" Marina had reached into her princess purse for a bandage and the sea life-derived healing ointments she kept within to provide some first aid, but Tara would ever afterwards conceal the thin, puckered chalk mark of a scar down nearly the length of her left arm from, as she would ruefully recollect in later years, a gigantic, bloodthirsty sandfly.

The three had recounted the confrontation with Silicana and how Tara had used the sceptre to destroy it. Tara had added that, while the sceptre had been efficacious, "It's in pieces now."

"It is," Atalanta had dryly replied. "But good thing you brought it. Otherwise, we wouldn't be here now."

"But you did and you are," Marina had quickly answered. "Now take a look at what I recovered from the pool. Something for each of us. Then we'll leave this terrible place once and for all!" They had gathered around, their curiosity overcoming their fatigue, to inspect what Marina had dredged up. She had explained, "It's quite a lot, really, but not all of it is of any value. Some of it's just junk, stuff swept up from the desert over the years."

They agreed that they would take turns choosing, Marina insisting she be fourth since she had not risked the dangers the others had. The others chorused that that was very kind of her, which made her smile and, embarrassed, hide her face in smoothing her hair. Tara smiled too. How typically wonderful of Marina, she thought to herself

Atalanta had used her golden balls to punch several holes in the wall so as to let in the dawn. In the shade of the chamber, illuminated by several circles of steadily brightening light to either side, Tara had chosen first. She sifted amongst the piles of jewellery, gemstones, chunks of engraved tablet, figurines, and all sorts of miscellany and selected an enormous emerald.

Atalanta, who had come to their rescue, was next. She had chosen a long strand of pearls.

Ariel had decided on a ruby, which would remind her of the sun, she had explained.

Marina had picked up a wide golden collar worked in a delicate fretwork and of antique design—"I had my eye on this one all along," she revealed with a mischievous grin.

They had continued until nothing had been left of value. Then, those who could had stood, and with warm embraces, they had bid each other good-bye. "It's not tears," Marina had maintained, trying to avoid the sympathetic expressions of the others at her downcast face. "I'm just leaking a little saltwater, that's all."

Tara stepped forward and warmly embraced her friend (well, she'd dry out quickly in the desert anyway, she had chided herself). "Poor Marina! We'll miss you. I'll miss you. Hugely! Here," she was suddenly moved to say, and from where and by what she hadn't the faintest idea. "Here! Take this, for your beautiful blonde hair!" Tara reached down and pulled from her pile a bejeweled comb and pressed it on Marina. "For all your help. For being such a wonderful friend. To me and to all of us."

All Marina's resistance had collapsed, and she succumbed completely to tears. "You guys are so wonderful to me," she had sobbed. "You're such friends!"

The others had crowded around and hugged Marina then each other in turn. Even the undemonstrative Atalanta had been moved to heave a heartfelt sigh. At the last, Tara had asked Marina to take with her the remains of the sceptre and Silicana for her father, King Aenon, to examine. Maybe he might be able to unravel the riddle of Silicana's end and what to do with the fragments.

And then it had been time to return to their homes. With a final sorrowful wave, Marina had slipped back into the pool and vanished into its crystalline depths. Then Atalanta, after another handshake, had boarded her sled and, rising to a hover of just about head height, favored them with a quick nod and was gone, off over the sands, glittering sparks from the three spinning balls catching the morning sun as the sled lifted higher and higher into the sky.

Last, Ariel and Tara had ascended to the Cloud Castle in her sky chariot. A day later, she had been set down in the field near Stonedell—the usual field—and now, here she was. Lying on her bed.

Sure, it was good to be back. Maybe not as adventurous as confronting giant sandfly things, but then again, not as dangerous. Better than going to a ball at the country home of the Countess, that was for sure.

Tara lolled on her bed, and her thoughts drifted to her treasure, now safely and neatly organized in a box in her chest of drawers. It could be a dowry, she thought distastefully, but it would be of more immediate and greater use as a contribution to Brythrony. She sat up and walked thoughtfully to the chest to review its contents again.

Deep under the sea, Marina was speaking with her father, King Aenon. The sea king listened avidly to her story as they swam to his library with its extensive collection of mother-of-pearl books. He was particularly fascinated by the fragments of the crystal sceptre and examined them with great interest. "Very unusual," he commented when she had finished. "This creature, which called itself Silicana, arose from the sand, and this sceptre had great power against it."

Marina nodded.

Aenon placed the shards of the sceptre on a table and turned his inspection to the fragments of Silicana Marina had also produced. "These are very interesting also!" he enthused. "Very! I have never seen anything like them." He compared the shards of the sceptre with those from Silicana then sighed and put them both down. "It's unfortunate that we'll never know what the sceptre really was or all its potential. Did it have other, perhaps much greater capabilities?" He shrugged. "We'll never know.

"And these bits and pieces of Silicana," he said, tapping them thoughtfully. "I wonder what they represent. You say you don't think you found every bit of Silicana?"

Marina shook her head. It had been dark, and her friends had been very tired.

"That's also interesting, that. Because these pieces, here," tapping them again, "look inert. Something is missing. Yes, these are pieces of the vital part of this Silicana creature, but something else was at their center. And that, unfortunately, looks to be the part or parts we are missing.

"Nothing we can do about it now, but it's too bad," he concluded, "as it must have been incredibly powerful. Each piece contributed something, I would suppose, such that, when a whole, it prompted something akin to life and even a kind of intelligence. Even from an agglomeration of very small creatures! Simply fascinating."

Marina nodded again. "We looked, for sure, but couldn't find everything. Tara said she beat on Silicana pretty hard, and some must have just flown off into the darkness." Marina giggled privately at the thought of Tara hammering away at the insect-thing her three friends had so vividly described. "But I'll be sure to tell Tara what you said. I'm sure she'll be interested!"

Tara descended the stairs to the lower levels of Castle Stonedell carefully. She rarely went down to these depths, preferring instead to roam the fields and the forests with Daystar. She had waited until she was confident her parents were away, presiding over some local festivities. She wanted to be sure she would not be interrupted for at least a few hours.

In one hand she carried by a handle a small box. In the other, she carried a lantern. As it turned out, this level of the castle had been built into the hillside so that windows cut in the wall offered regular intervals of light. Tara had brought the lantern just in case the light was poor, but it wasn't, and now she felt somewhat silly carrying it.

Tara was looking for the kingdom's treasurer. "Silvers" was what he was called. That wasn't his actual name of course, just a sort of respectful nickname. He had been the treasurer for as long as anyone could remember. This was, in part, because he was expert at managing the kingdom's finances. It was, also in part, because he was known to be scrupulously honest. For the final part, it was because he was invariably impartial and never weighed in on what to do with the kingdom's resources, or on the relative wisdom of such a use, but confined himself to opining only on how much any enterprise would cost and how the funds might be raised.

Tara had been told where she might find Silvers, though she had had to find this out in somewhat of a circuitous manner to avoid arousing suspicion. He would most probably be in a room on the lower levels, the entrance to which was flanked by several of the king's private guard, who would only admit by express invitation.

The guards saluted her, and she asked to see Silvers. Upon gaining permission, she passed through the doorway to find Silvers at his desk, with several enormous ledgers to his left. The room was more dimly lit than she might have expected for the close examination of endless rows of finely transcribed numbers.

Silvers was an elderly man, somewhat hunched in his chair and with an unruly shock of greyish-white hair upon his head. Conceivably, the thought passed through Tara's mind, his nickname might have come from this aspect of his physical appearance as well. One hand held a pen, as if out of habit, or security, and the other—betraying just the slightest tremor when at rest—lay across a small notebook.

"Princess Tara," he observed, rising slightly, before Tara waved him to seat himself. "To what do I owe the honor of this unexpected visit?"

Tara smiled at his courtly words and formal tone.

"Eh? You rarely come here, Your Highness. Down to the subterranean corridors of the castle to visit me and—" he gestured sweepingly to his ledgers "—mine, my constant companions."

Tara's smile broadened incrementally. "I thank you, Silvers, for your willingness to receive me without notice. I know you are always very busy."

Silvers bowed his head slightly.

"Silvers, I come to see you on a matter which, well, I should say, requires your discretion."

Silvers bowed his head again, slightly more than the last time. He had heard this sort of prefatory phrase before. "Your Highness does not face troubles? I hope?" he allowed himself, in a low voice just above a whisper.

"No, not at all, I am glad to say. Rather…" Tara let her voice trail off. How to broach this? She considered for a moment, and her eyes roved the room. It was so dark, she could hardly make out the walls, but she could descry, just barely, on the wall opposite a portrait of her father and mother at their coronation many years ago. Her resolve strengthened and she straightened. "Rather, I should say, the opposite."

Silvers's eyebrows lifted in surprise and perplexity.

"Silvers, I've come to make a contribution. To the kingdom's finances."

Silvers dropped his pen in surprise and blinked. Many had come to him over the years asking for funds but few, if any, had ever come to provide them. "Your Highness?" was all he could manage for sheer astonishment.

"Yes," she continued and lifted from her lap to the desk the small box she had been holding. "Yes, I have. It is not a large contribution, but maybe it will mean something." She opened the box, turned it and slid it across the desk so that Silvers could see what was inside. He leaned in, and she could see his eyes flicker rapidly across its contents, appraising them with the practiced eye of someone who had done this before many times under a variety of circumstances. He looked up at her, his eyes now with a bright spark in them.

"Your Highness is exceedingly generous! These items. They are… items that have come into Your possession recently?"

"Yes, recently."

"And Your Highness wishes the treasury to safeguard them?"

"No. I wish the treasury to have them. To do with them as it likes, for the kingdom's wellbeing."

"To sell them?"

"Yes. Including to sell them. If you judge, in your discretion, that the kingdom would benefit best in that way."

Silver smiled, then frowned, then his face settled into one that betokened curiosity. "Forgive me, please, Your Highness, but I must ask. These items—they are Yours and Yours alone to decide their disposition?"

"Yes. Absolutely."

Silvers bowed. "Just as You say, Your Highness."

"I thought to help the kingdom, Silvers. That's all. I hope it will help?"

"Yes, Your Highness. Everything helps! The kingdom is always beset with costs. For this and that. Here and there. The harvest has not been the best this year, I regret to say. We have had to borrow in recent months to meet expenses. Which we have not had to do for some years." Silvers drummed his fingers on the nearest ledger for a moment, and his eyes looked for a space into the distance. "Not for a time."

Tara's mind returned to the conversation she had had with her mother and father before departing for the Lost Quarter. She had guessed what their actual meaning had been, and maybe she had been correct.

"I hope this will help some?" she enquired again, hoping to better gauge how much, if only out of curiosity.

"I will have to see, Your Highness," replied Silvers with a sigh. "To see. Yes, it helps. It will. We shall see how much."

"But everything helps! As I said."

Tara nodded in understanding. She would have to wait to find out more, so much was clear. One more thing before she left, though. "I'm sure I know the answer to this question, but..." she looked about. No one else was present.

Silvers leaned forward attentively.

"But I can count on your discretion on this, yes? No one can know of this."

Silvers straightened. "Your Highness. Absolutely. No one shall know."

"The Guards...?"

He smiled thinly. "They will say nothing. Nothing of Your visit. Nothing."

"Thank you. Because, because I wouldn't know how to bring it up to my parents. Or explain it. I don't think they would understand."

Silvers eyed her for a long instant then lowered his gaze. "I think I understand, Your Highness. I understand. Neither shall ever know from me. Ever."

"Thank you, Silvers."

"Your Highness," he replied, bowing his head again, more deeply than the last time.

Tara arose to take her leave.

"And if Your Highness might permit me..."

"Yes, please, Silvers," replied Tara, turning.

"Your Highness, there have been rumors that You have figured in some astonishing adventures and feats. Incredible feats!"

He paused, but Tara, rather than replying, only allowed a faint half-smile.

He continued, "These are only rumors. Only rumors. I do not repeat them, of course. To anyone."

Tara regarded the elderly man thoughtfully. He had half-risen from his chair in deference to her departure, one hand, slightly crabbed around the dropped pen, twitched, while the other leaned heavily on the ledger. But though his posture was bent and even unsteady from moment to moment, his eyes still burned bright with a quick and lively intelligence.

"That is good of you, Silvers, and I thank you. No, there is no reason to repeat rumors. After all, who knows how and whence they originate?"

The old man nodded significantly.

"And, Your Highness, if I may be so bold…"

"Yes, please."

"Your Highness's interest in the finances of the kingdom reflects very creditably upon You. Very. Your Highness is clearly preparing Herself for rulership. And most nobly."

"Thank you, Silvers. That is very kind of you to say so."

Tara exited the room to return to the upper reaches of the palace. There. It was done. It was in Silvers's hands now. He could be trusted. Those lovely jewels and gold and such would be put to good use. She could have tried to explain it to her parents, but it would never have worked. Her mother would have raised a scene.

Tara stopped for a moment on her way back to the stairs to gaze out one of the windows along the corridor. Outside, the grass was green and the sky was blue. The fields and forests, framed in the sunlit casing, unfolded before her, rolling gently away to the horizon. Brythrony was such a verdant and pleasant kingdom.

Tara turned to head back up the stairs. Silvers was a funny man. Very capable as a treasurer, to be sure, but odd. She stopped and thought again. But those last words he had said to her: she smiled. They had been sincere and genuine. They had, in fact, been one of the finest compliments she had received in a very long time.

The Homecoming Games

"Honestly," Princess Tara muttered to herself, slogging through the surf up to a stretch of empty beach, "this is the worst part of it!" Tara stumbled through the rolling breakers, up and over a sandbar, then across another, surprisingly deep length of water. Getting back to land always seemed such a drag. The fun part, aside from being able to swim underwater without worrying about holding one's breath and the pressure, was getting a ride from Princess Marina's dolphins. They would tow Tara as close as they dared to shore and wait just beyond the surf, watching attentively as she swam, coughed and staggered her way in. Tara gained solid footing, stood, turned and waved to them. She heard in the distance a series of chirping and clicking noises, and the pair vanished. So nice, she thought, those dolphins. She almost thought they knew her now.

Tara looked around the beach. This was roughly where she had set out much earlier that day. She called for her horse. "Daystar! Daystar!" There was a whinny from the trees where she had left him, untethered. Perfect, she thought, and made her way toward him. In the saddlebags was a change of clothes identical to the ones she had on but dry. She changed quickly, ordered her hair with a fillet and stuffed the wet clothes in the now empty saddlebag. "Time to go home, right, boy?" she asked softly. "Off we go, yes? Take us back along the river, right?"

Daystar neighed gently then set off at a brisk canter toward the River Vahaval and Castle Stonedell. Some royalty lived in palaces. Not they. Tara knew she shouldn't complain, because there were still other royalty and nobility who had it far worse. But living in a draughty old castle that passed as a palace was not her idea of the tippy top of life. It was not at all like Marina's amazingly alive Coral Castle or Ariel's beautiful floating Cloud Castle. It was just plain old Castle Stonedell, that was it.

Tara wondered idly if she would ever be able to show her friends Stonedell in the same way they had shown her where they lived. She sighed. Not to Marina, surely, at least not until Stonedell was underwater. Ariel, maybe sooner. Now that her parents knew about the both of them. She recollected well the day she had had to reveal their existence. That had been a bad day. A very bad few days. Her father had known about Ariel since Sundra and her bandits had attacked several villages on the edge of the Great Forest, but neither had known about Marina. They had cornered her one morning after returning from a ball at which they had spoken with the Duchess Eunice and had discovered, and been scandalized, that she had never shown up for her supposed week of training in proper manners. That was when Tara had had to confess that, instead of visiting the Duchess, she had been with her finned and winged friends the entire time, though she had omitted the details about spiders and sand golems and such that would surely have horrified them.

Her mother had taken the deception especially hard. She had been upset for days that Tara had—Tara preferred the word "misrepresented" over that which her mother had used—where she had been, what she had been doing, and with whom. Tara almost felt that her mother would have taken it better had Tara told her she had eloped with Prince Halliad. Her father had tried to help but had been implicated all too quickly in the cover-up of Ariel.

Tara reflected sorrowfully on the whole episode. Her mother didn't understand. As far as Tara could tell, her mother just wanted Tara to stay at Stonedell all day, every day and tend her hair. That, and be atwitter about the next ball in the Season. But Tara couldn't, simply couldn't. Her mother had come around before too long, thankfully. Tara was guessing, but hadn't asked, that her mother had partially persuaded herself that her daughter's friends just might be imaginary, or at least have imaginary characteristics like wings and fins, and that she would outgrow them. Her father, more cognizant of the role Ariel had played in saving Rohanic in the Great Forest, had simply decided to leave well enough alone.

Arriving at Castle Stonedell, Tara dismounted and led Daystar to his stall. She removed his saddle, bridle, and reins, and lugged them to the tack room. No one offered help. She grinned. They knew better than to ask; Tara always took care of Daystar herself. No one else was even allowed to come near him, save for Geoffrey, the stable master.

Tara entered the castle through a side entrance. The rooms were cool, sometimes cold, even in the heat of summer, because the walls were solid stone and feet thick at points. Tara stopped again to check her hair and dress before a mirror she had positioned in an out-of-the-way corner for just such a purpose. Both looked good. Well, at least reasonably good. She practiced her smile too, on and off, several times. Finding that passable as well, she continued to the royal family's private apartments, where she expected to find her parents.

They received her there with great joy, her mother throwing out her arms to her. Tara curtsied before them as she knew they liked and embraced first her mother and then her father.

Her mother, Queen Armorica, spoke first. "Tara! Where've you been? We've hardly seen you at all these last few days!"

Tara, immediately on guard on the question as to her whereabouts, cautiously granted that it seemed to have been that way.

"We've missed you!"

Tara responded that she had missed them too.

"Why, you've hardly been around at all!" exclaimed her mother. "You went to see that Countess Abernathy for a week, I believe—"

"Which we all thought was a good idea!"

"—Yes, yes, but you've been out most every day since!"

"I guess I've been out, yes… mostly riding Daystar. Things like that."

"Of course, dear; I know how much you like that. But we thought to inform you that we shall be receiving foreign dignitaries on Friday evening. What do you think of that?"

"Um, that sounds great, Mom." Tara knew from experience that she was to understand from this statement that her attendance would be mandatory.

"We thought you'd think so. How fun, right? And you can wear that lovely azure-blue dress I had made for you."

Tara nodded. It would make her look like the sky princess, but that was fine. She giggled: what would Ariel think of her?

"What's so funny, dear?"

"Nothing! No, I was just thinking of how beautiful I'll be in it, that's all."

"I'm so glad to know that! In fact, I chose the color myself, knowing how well it would suit you. After dinner, won't you please try it on, just in case it needs alterations?"

After dinner, Tara lay prone on her bed, deep in thought, her head propped in her hand. She was not thinking of the reception for foreign dignitaries though, or the azure-blue dress, or of what she had been doing these past few days that had kept her out of the castle so much. She was instead thinking about two things that had been on her mind for days: the missing piece of Silicana and her now lifeless ring. Inwardly, she groaned. After extensive internal debate, she was very seriously considering yet another journey back to the abominable Lost Quarter. The purpose would be to find the missing piece of Silicana to repower her Ring of Shooting Stars. She would have to go alone because she very much doubted any of her friends would want to join her.

The more she thought about it, the more certain she was becoming. The ring lacked power and it was certainly worth an effort to try to restore it. King Aenon had said that an important part of Silicana had been left behind in the Lost Quarter, maybe that which had functioned as its source of vitality. It must be a small bit because Tara and her friends had missed it in their efforts to gather up the remains of Silicana. Well, the ring was small, too. The fragment must possess a great deal of energy in order to have created Silicana. Wasn't that what the ring needed, something with a great deal of energy? If found, such a fragment might be joined to or inserted into the ring. Then, perhaps the ring would regain its abilities.

The chain of logic had seemed far-fetched at first, but Tara was gradually reconciling herself to it. After all, no other energy source Tara knew could possibly do the trick.

Marina had asked her what had been occupying her thoughts while she had been with her that day. She had, well, "misrepresented" and said that she was just thinking of home. She had dared not say she was thinking of returning to the Lost Quarter. She was certain that Marina would feel obliged to offer help or even insist on accompanying her. No, decided Tara resolutely, she had to take responsibility and either find the missing piece on her own, without endangering her friends, or some other equally capable energy source.

In her room following the reception, which had gone better than she had expected, as she had indeed looked fabulous, Tara toyed with various items from past adventures and even briefly entertained leafing through the magic book stowed way back in her top drawer for a spell she might try, before finally forcing herself to act. Out came the princess purse and, from inside, the bubble message vials. Wetting her hands at the basin in her room and with a drop from the vial, she created a lovely, round, clear bubble and whispered into it a request for some of the items that she had had on her first desert foray. "You know," she explained, "ice arrows, hoar frost, and a shard of ice to talk with you. Thanks ever so much, if you can!" Then she whispered, "Ice Princess Florence!" to it and puffed it away with a breath.

There, that was done. But, that had been the easy part, hadn't it? With a heavy heart, she now approached what she knew to be the very hardest aspect. Not crossing a desert, or battling gold-hoarding creatures, or anything like that. No, it was telling her mother and father that she needed to go away again. They would certainly not like that, particularly since she had only recently come back from "visiting" the Countess. Tara sighed. This time, she wanted to be honest and not "misrepresent" her intent.

A few mornings later, at breakfast, Tara summoned what she thought to be sufficient courage. "So, Mom, Dad, I don't know how to say this, but…"

"What is it, child?" answered her mother after a delicate pause.

"Well," continued Tara hesitantly, "I think I need to go somewhere. Before too long."

That statement was met with stunned silence. At last they responded, "But you just came back!"

The Princess of the Realm said nothing and stared miserably at the table.

After an interminable moment, her mother spoke. "Why on earth would you be leaving? Is it these friends of yours, who want to drag you off again on some errand?"

"No, Mom."

"It's not that weird fish friend of yours, is it?"

"Mom, she's a mermaid! Not a 'fish friend'!" She's not "weird" either, thought Tara sullenly.

"Or that other friend of yours, that fairy friend? Maybe it's her?"

"She's not a fairy. She just has wings. And her name is Ariel."

"Whatever! This Ariel thing, is it her?"

"She's a princess, a person, just like me! Princess Ariel!"

"Oh, all right! It's not that Princess Ariel person pulling you away again, is it?"

"No, Mom. And Dad. This time it's for me. For me."

Another long stretch of shocked silence. "What could you possibly mean, 'for me'? For why?"

Shortly, and to Tara's distant surprise that it was only now coming at this late juncture, "And where are you wanting to go?"

But inevitably, and as Tara had feared, "Is it that you don't want to be around us?"

Tara thought hard on what to say next. How could she explain to her parents how important it was to recover fully the capabilities of her ring so that she could defend herself at a moment of extreme need? That she be able to protect her friends should they need help? Or—possibly, and maybe even eventually—should it be necessary to save their kingdom in perhaps an hour of very great need? Her friends could swim through the seas or fly on the winds, but what did she, Tara, do? Only think on her feet. And wield this ring. Which was now useless.

Time for something dramatic, Tara decided and with characteristic impulsiveness. She removed the dull and lusterless Ring of Shooting Stars from its chain about her neck and laid it on the table, where it rolled back and forth in a short semi-circle a few times before stopping. All three stared at it. "I see it's a ring," stated her father at last, unimpressed.

"It's my ring. It's a Ring of Shooting Stars."

"What's that?"

"It's—well—it's very special."

"Honestly," replied her father, eying it sceptically, "it doesn't look that special to me."

"Well, it is special. It used to be even more special. And, well… it could be special again."

Her parents looked at each other, now thoroughly confused. "What do you mean, that it was 'special', but it could be 'special' again? Even though you're also saying that it's 'special' now?"

Tara sighed. This was going very poorly. She would have to give them a little more. "It's saved my life a number, well, a few times."

"What do you mean by that?"

Tara stopped. Dare she tell them about the spiders or the sand golem? Or the several times she had had to use it in Silicana's sand warren? But Tara didn't dare, fearing they might become hysterical.

"Let's just say it saved my life a few times. Through some pretty special things it can do, like send out sparks and balls of fire… and so on."

There was another longish pause while her parents regarded her steadily. Then her father leaned forward with a peculiar intensity and, in a low voice, enquired, "Just where did you find a ring like this with such capabilities? And what dangers are you running that require such powerful magic to defend yourself?"

Tara rushed ahead, deliberately ignoring her father's incisive questions. "But now, it won't. Because it's out of energy. So I need to re-power it. And yes, I have to do it and no, it's not about Marina or Ariel or anyone else. Just me."

Her parents settled back in their chairs and considered this pronouncement. Her mother sighed deeply; her husband reflexively offered her a handkerchief with which she daubed at her eyes, though Tara noticed no moisture there. Her father cleared his throat. "I think what we need to do," he said at last, "is think about this some more. It's not apparent that you have an immediate re-powering need, is it?"

"And you won't be going anywhere alone either!" Armorica burst out.

Childeric laid a soothing hand on his queen's arm but his voice remained firm. "This isn't something you need to do right away, is it, Tara?"

Tara, relieved at the placatory turn in the conversation's tone, agreed. "No, I don't need to do anything right away! Of course we can think about this some more." Though, she added silently, my mind is made up.

Her mother composed herself at last. "Well, that's good," she allowed, mollified. "That's good, because we've decided to hold some games in your honor."

"Games?" wondered Tara aloud.

"Yes, games. Celebratory games. Other kingdoms have done something similar for their children upon returning from a time away. There'll be jousting, swordplay, poetry, and even painting. And horse archery! We thought you'd like it!"

Tara nodded her head. Games would be popular. People would come from kingdoms away to participate. This could be the event of the Season. But at the same time, the games could run on for weeks. Tara gulped. It could be forever before she got started back for the Lost Quarter. Or see her friends again.

"Maybe," asked Tara, trying hard to adopt an agreeable tone, "maybe we could have a costume ball one night? In honor of those coming to the games?"

Her mother and father exchanged glances. "Why not?" exclaimed her mother. "Great idea! A masquerade! We'll have it on the seventh night, just after the finals, to give everyone ample opportunity to prepare. Superb idea!

"I do believe you're warming to this idea, dear!" said her mother, letting enthusiasm creep fractionally back into her voice. "And I'm so happy for this. Princes from all over will come to participate. There'll be many handsome ones for you to dance with!"

Tara nodded gamely. Sure. Plenty of princes. Yet her thought had been on inviting her friends. They could come as they were naturally, such as a winged human or a mermaid. At least she would see them sooner rather than later. "Lovely," replied Princess Tara to her mother, still smiling and clearly waiting for a reaction. "I'm sure many princes will come."

"Yes. Absolutely," replied the king, definitively. "And now, your mother and I must excuse ourselves, as we must tour the preparations already underway. Surprisingly complicated, I've discovered." The two left, arm-in-arm, flanked by the palace architect and seneschal.

Princess Tara watched them leave then stood to return to her room. What to do, she was thinking, about Marina? While she could get close to the castle by River Vahaval, how could she get to Stonedell from there? But just then, a small bubble floated through her open window. How wonderful: a message from one of her princess friends! She held out her hand, palm up, and the bubble settled into it softly. The voice that spoke was that of Florence, the Ice Princess.

"Oh, Tara, how wonderful to hear your voice! Gosh, it's been ages, hasn't it, since we've spoken. Of course, I remember how you brought back so much dazzle dust for us when we were nearly out! So, yes, I'd be happy to send you some more of what you need for the desert, like ice arrows and hoar frost. And sure, an ice shard, so we can talk!"

Tara smiled. Flo could be wordy at times.

"So, do let me know when you would want them. But are you sure that's all you'd need? The Lost Quarter (and the voice of the Ice Princess trembled): it's so horrible! Let me check with my sister Crystal to see what she thinks. Anyway, I'll speak with you again soon. Let me know when your plans firm up!"

Princess Tara relaxed at the chair at her vanity, happier and relieved. Flo was wonderful. Those items would be critical to success in the Lost Quarter. With those practically in hand, Tara felt as if she were already halfway to restoring her ring.

Tara descended the stairs to find her mother and father intently studying an enormous sheet of paper spread across the table. Something from the palace architect, she surmised, and politely stopped to inspect it with them.

"Hello, Princess," said her mother, who insisted on more formal address in the presence of the household staff. "Do you see this?" She motioned and indicated a circle within a square in the middle of the page, toward the top.

Tara let her eyes rove up the paper. "Yes, I see it."

"It's a dais. On which you shall be seated. To officiate over the games!"

Tara licked her lips. Would she really have to be on view in a chair, day upon day? But Tara was loathe to protest; her mother was still unhappy about her desire to venture out to re-power her ring. "Um, like every day? Every minute? That seems like a lot!"

Armorica and Childeric exchanged glances. One corner of Armorica's mouth turned down, and the other corner moved as if half-mouthing words. Childeric understood. She had complained about this before and not without reason. With dawning displeasure, he was beginning to conclude that maybe she was right. The increasing impression even he was being left with was that Tara was shirking her royal duties. Childeric sympathized with her spirit and inclination toward being in the outdoors, at the center of adventure, but her responsibilities as Princess of the Realm and heir to the throne were indisputable, and she had to accept them. Being present on the dais and presiding over the games was a reasonable royal duty. Tara would have to bend on this. "Tara," he finally answered with a frown, "not every minute. But most every minute. And definitely for the finals."

Tara's face brightened. For the finals, he had said. Just the finals.

"Of every competition! Each and every one!"

Tara's face fell a trifle, but she perked up right away. "Sure! The finals!" An idea smote her. Why not enter an event herself? Anonymously, of course, so that her parents would not die with worry. Her mind raced. Daystar had to be one of the finest horses in the land, and she considered herself a good horsewoman and archer. She'd enter the horse archery competition. In this event, contestants aimed at targets arranged along a course while riding at speeds from a fast trot to a full gallop. The winner was the one with the highest point score, consisting of best aim with the bow and arrow combined with the best time.

Further, the protective helmet all contestants wore would render her unrecognizable, perfectly completing the necessary disguise.

"Yes, yes," agreed Tara, preoccupied. "'Of every competition.'" Tara hung around a little longer to scrutinize more closely the plans for the arena in which all the equestrian sports, including the horse archery, were to be held. How fun and mysterious. She'd play the apathetic and indifferent officiant judging from the dais most of the time but, at others, actively participate on the field itself.

Yes, that could be quite fun, she decided. But first to invite her friends to the costume ball to be held on the seventh night. Tara raced up the steps to her room and whipped out the vial for creating message bubbles. With the first bubble she invited Marina and even though she didn't think there was a way for the mermaid to join them in the castle. "Seventh night!" she repeated then blew it gently so that it was whisked high into the air on the current of her breath, hovered for a moment, then drifted slowly and purposefully out of the window and tacked toward the ocean. She did the same for Princess Ariel, noticing the vial was only two-thirds full. She frowned. It had been an adventure to replenish the dazzle dust, and the quest for the energy source to re-power her ring had not yet begun. How would they get more bubble liquid? But that was for another day. Tara shrugged and sent messages to Ariel, Snow Princess and Ice Princess. After all, she could hardly send a bubble to one Princess and expect her to convey the details to all the others.

Tara spent her hours the next week honing her archery skills, fletching her arrows and attending personally to even the most minute details concerning Daystar, as she didn't fully trust the castle stables to look after him like she could. In between, she was fitted for a new ballgown for the official reception and, reluctantly, and upon the receipt of stern "recommendations," she accompanied her parents to inspect the facilities under construction.

She also had to choose a costume for the masquerade ball. This stumped her for a while, but then she decided to combine her plan to compete with the need for a costume by dressing as a huntress in the colors of her family's house. These colors were blue, white, and brown, with blue representing the kingdom's skies and waters, white its snow-capped mountains and the clouds overhead, and brown the trees of its forests and its tilled farmlands. In her house's colors and with the same bows and arrows used in the arena, she thought to rather dramatically reveal herself as having been a contestant.

Each day, she hoped to receive a bubble from her friends informing her that they would come, but was each day disappointed until just two days before the games were to begin when a message from Marina arrived, declining, as expected, citing her inability to make it to the castle from the river, though she appreciated the invitation.

On the other hand, Ice Princess announced by bubble the next morning that she would be able to join. Regrettably, her sister would not. Though she would like to come, some of her wildlife friends were ill, and she was too worried to leave them. Accentuating the positive, Flo added hurriedly that she would bring with her those items Tara had requested for her journey to the Lost Quarter.

Though Tara had decided to keep her entrance in the horse archery contest a secret from her parents, it would be impossible to keep the secret from Geoffrey, the stable master. Geoffrey knew everything that happened at the stables, and Tara would need somewhere to change into and out of her riding gear anyway. He was willing when she took him into her confidence though, and frankly told her that he thought she would do well. "I'll enter you in the lists tomorrow," he told her. Not the first to enter and not the last; somewhere in the middle, he winked. He also had an assumed name to recommend. "How about 'Fléchette'? It means 'Little Arrow'," he suggested. Tara liked it, rolling it around in her mind later that day as she cared for Daystar's tack. Not bad at all: Little Arrow. She liked the diminutive too as maybe that might throw the other contestants off a little.

The next day, she walked the arena with Geoffrey. "It's one of the largest spaces set up for the games," he told her as they stepped around tools and timber scattered on the ground.

Tara picked up for him. "Because contestants will have to ride at a gallop at points."

He nodded. "Still needs some work, but it'll be ready in time, I expect." He stopped to point to where the dais would stand, though at the moment it was just a frame visible over the barrier marking one side of the course. "That's where Their Majesties, Your parents will be watching." He smiled knowingly. "You, too, some of the time!"

They continued past some bushes that had been moved in large pots to create a barrier. "Aim, control, and skilled manoeuvring even while loosing an arrow will win top prize." He paused and turned to her. "Your Highness, it's a challenging event. But I think You'll do very well. You handle Daystar with great skill."

Tara thanked him but demurred at his confidence. "I suppose only a few have entered? I may place well but only because of that?"

"No, Your Highness. Twenty already. I counted." He considered, recollecting. "Most, I'm guessing by their names, are from the West. Good horsemanship out there—some even said that their ancestors were centaurs."

Tara smiled at that. That was silly, of course, but they were reputed to be very good.

"Don't you worry, Your Highness, You'll do just fine. You and Daystar!"

"Are there any names you recognize?"

He shook his head, no.

At last, the day dawned for the start of the games. During the preceding days, hundreds had arrived in baggage trains from around the kingdom, some from many miles away. The palace guards reported that tents filled the fields all around. Judging from turn-out, they told her father and mother at the final review before the official start, the games should be a success.

Tara joined her parents at that final review, an appearance which surprised her mother but earned her approbation. Tara listened intently to the order of events, paying particular attention to the announcement that the opening round of the horse archery contest was to be the very first day of the Games. It was then that, from behind, she felt a slip of paper thrust into her hand. She turned to read it covertly. It was from Geoffrey. Fléchette had been scheduled for that first round, and it was to commence in two hours. Tara gave a little start. That was sooner than she had been expecting! But why not jump right in right away? If she were eliminated, well, then she'd join her parents on the dais sooner rather than later, and they'd be happy.

After the briefing, her parents turned to Tara, who had already started to sidle toward the door to race toward the stables. "Darling, we know how much you like archery; won't you join us on the dais in the royal box?"

The color drained from Tara's face. She was supposed to be competing at the very same time. "Uh, Mom, sorry, I, uh, can't, because I'm not feeling well."

Her mother peered into Tara's face and took on a look of alarm. "Dear, your face is completely white! What's wrong? Shall I send up the doctor?"

"No, no, that won't be necessary! Just some rest. All I need. That's it. I think my legs hurt, that's all. Walking so much, getting ready for the

Games. You know."

Her mother turned to her father. "I've said this before. Her room at the top of the tower is a problem! Too many stairs. She should move to the main floor where she'll be closer to us."

"No, Mom, I don't think that's it! It's really just fatigue. That's all." She waved and began climbing the stairs to her room but stopped as soon as she was out of their sight and, when she guessed they were several rooms safely away, dashed back down to make for the stables. Minutes later, she was at Daystar's stall. "Hurry," she said excitedly to Geoffrey. "I need to get dressed!"

"No worries," reassured Geoffrey with his characteristic calm. "Daystar's ready, for sure. I combed some dye into his coat this morning to darken it. See: I painted out the star on his forehead so no one would recognize him. He's ready!" Tara fit the mask to her head and tossed her hair, that same mischievous light flashing in her eyes that her father had noted on more than one occasion with disquiet. "Now I am Fléchette!" she cried. The stable master bowed, peeked out of the door to see if any were watching and rolled the door of the stable open. Tara gave a last wild laugh of gaiety mixed with excitement and tore from the stable at a gallop.

Fléchette appeared at the arena gate, smoothing the mane of her now chestnut-brown horse. Through the mask, Tara could see the enormous crowd in the stands. They've come to see me, she realized with a shiver. Me. Tara gripped Daystar's reins tightly. She could not disappoint them—disappoint herself—and give anything less than her best. High in the stands, in the royal box, would be her mother and father, watching. Her mother would surely be seized by the romanticism of a masked contestant, never guessing it was her. With a crooked smile, she could imagine they would not have approved of her doing what she was; they would think it inappropriate. But no, she reminded herself fiercely, it *was* appropriate. For competing, and maybe winning, was *always* appropriate for her, her family, and her house. "Let's go, boy," she murmured to Daystar. "Let's show them how to do this!"

On signal, Tara advanced into the arena. With a flourish, she saluted the king and queen, as she had watched others do, then saluted the crowd. Tara laughed in pure delight and, as if in sympathy, a frisson of excitement seemed to pass through the spectators like a wave, rising and falling as it swept around the ring. Tara turned back to the king and queen to await their permission to begin and, receiving it, spurred Daystar forward.

A thrill surged through Tara. How fun this was! All the excitement of her past adventures but with none of the dangers. How easy it would be to hit targets when she had done it before on so many occasions, only without all the witches, golems, spiders and the like pursuing her! The tension she had felt when she had first stepped into the arena vanished, and she laughed for sheer joy. Reaching behind her, she nocked an arrow from her quiver to her bow. Aiming it quickly down the shaft, she let it fly at the first target as soon as it hove in sight.

It flew, unerringly, into dead center. There was scattered applause from the crowd up above, but Tara scarcely heard. She urged Daystar faster, and he, sensing her excitement, responded enthusiastically. His hooves flew across the course. Tara reached for another arrow, nocked it and, guiding Daystar with her knees, loosed the arrow just as the target showed. Bulls-eye again.

So it went, back and forth along the prescribed course. With each arrow, the applause built, until at the last Tara wheeled abruptly to ride away from the target and, heedless of any possible penalty, aimed over her shoulder Parthian-style to score the last bullseye. The crowd erupted in approval. Tara brought Daystar around again and to a halt in front of the royal box, where she bowed deeply. She made a last flourish to the crowd and cantered out.

As soon as she had exited the ring, she brought Daystar back to a gallop for the stables, certain that someone would give chase to learn her identity. But Geoffrey was waiting for her with the door already open and he rolled it shut as soon as she was inside. Tara was out of the saddle in an instant. "Shhh!" she whispered to Daystar, kissing him on the nose rapturously and offering him a carrot from her vest. "Well done, boy! Wonderful work!" She stopped and listened. As she had feared, outside, Geoffrey was confessing ignorance as to the whereabouts of a chestnut horse and its mysterious masked rider.

She met her mother and father back at the palace a short time later. "You should have seen him, Tara," her mother gushed. "Simply amazing, this Fléchette! He must be a natural horseman!"

Tara smiled at the impact of her skills on her mother. "Must be, Mom. I'm sorry I missed it!"

"Oh, dear, you simply must meet him! He must be royalty, to have such training! He simply must be advancing to the second round. We must meet him! We will!"

"Maybe you already have, Mom?"

"What? Met him already? How? How would you know this?" demanded Armorica sharply.

"Uh, because, well, he wears a mask! Meaning, we don't know who he might be. So, maybe we have already met him and we just don't know it."

Her mother considered. "Yes, I suppose. Possibly." But her imagination very soon re-asserted itself. "Still, how glamourous to wear a mask! Why? What could he be hiding?" Tara hadn't had a ready response to that question, but it had been intended rhetorically only, as her mother hadn't really paused for an answer anyway. "And what is just as amazing is that there were TWO masked riders!"

"Two?"

"Yes, two!" picked up her father. "The other called himself 'Shadow'. Riding a jet-black horse named 'Shade'. All in black and grey. Silver trim, with a short brown cape. Very dashing, I thought."

"How did he do?"

"Oh, very well also. As well as the one calling himself Fléchette, I believe."

Tara was silent. There had been another masked rider, who had also shot well. She had not expected that.

"Yes, I thought the masked riders were the best out there. Put the others in the shade, I should think!" Her father chuckled at his inadvertent joke.

Tara conversed a bit longer with her parents, but her thoughts were elsewhere. She expected to advance to the second round of the competition, consisting of the top eight riders, but what she was wondering about was the other masked rider, who would undoubtedly advance as well. It was intriguing and a little off-putting. Why would such a person ride masked? Quite apart from the fact that she was choosing to do the same! She resolved to investigate some before the second round took place in two days.

Between her duties as hostess and attending to other events, she had little opportunity to enquire about Shadow. All too soon, it was time to get ready for her turn on the course. All that she learnt was that Shadow was clearly an accomplished horseman. She consoled herself by imagining that Shadow must be wondering the very same about Fléchette—and, as frustratingly, learning nothing.

As before, when it was Tara's turn, Geoffrey manned the stable doors to roll them open and shut for a costumed Tara to make a just-in-time-from-nowhere appearance at the arena. Bowing to her parents, the king and queen, she grinned wryly to note the empty seat beside them for herself. This time she had told her parents that she had a headache. Not a great excuse, but it had sufficed.

The course was harder this time. As she knew it would be. Compared to the first round, her aim was not as good and her control of Daystar not as exact. Finishing, she whirled her prancing mount and bowed gallantly to the royal couple and the crowd but was disappointed with herself inwardly. The first round had been an absolute thrill; this round had been more like effort. She might well be one of those eliminated, as the final round consisted only of the best two.

It had only been a game, she told herself, as she walked back to the castle from the stables, her entry in the horse archery event, the costume, the dramatic appearances and disappearances. But quite against her expectations and even realization, she had become rather caught up in it. Now she expected to be eliminated. That meant that she could watch the finals from the box, as her father had insisted she must. Well, that was good. But the consolation was flat and empty. She wished to be out in the center of the ring, competing for the honor of Brythrony and even bearing back the prize for her house.

Her low mood was improved a little by a message bubble from Princess Ariel, confirming that she would attend the costume party. That was nice, she thought: two would make it. It would be nice to see Princesses Florence and Ariel again. This she received just before she entered the castle through a long-disused side door but which put her, by traversing a few dim hallways, near the reception hall. After a suitable effort to make sure she was presentable and that nothing from the stable might still be clinging to her clothes, she located her parents off the Hall, exclaiming to themselves how well the Games were going. They switched to the second round of horse archery when Tara joined them.

"Dear, you simply should not have missed it. It was such a marvelous display. Such skill! And the horses, so well-groomed and beautiful!"

"It must have been wonderful."

"Yes! Oh, and how is your headache?"

"Fine, Mom. Much better, thank you."

"Good. We're sorry you missed it, but you'll be there for the final, after all. And guess what! Guess!" Armorica let her voice trail off expectantly.

"Um, I'm not sure, Mom. What do you mean? Guess about what?"

"About the finals! For horse archery!"

"You mean you know who will be in the finals?"

"We received the results just before you arrived!"

Tara indicated that she could not possibly guess who would be the finalists.

"Well, wouldn't it be romantic if the two masked horsemen were the two finalists?"

"Sure, Mom. That would be really mysterious."

Armorica nudged Childeric, who smiled back. "Well! The two finalists are Shadow and Fléchette!"

Princess Tara was thunderstruck. She was advancing to the final round after all! Her spirits surged on the news. A moment later, she wavered. It would necessitate that she break her promise that she would be present at the finals to officiate.

"Isn't it exciting?" exclaimed Armorica. "But dear, what's wrong? It's improper to stand there as you are with your mouth open."

"I'm just really… surprised. That's it. Of all the contestants, that the two masked ones would be the ones to advance. That's all."

"It's perfect. As if we had arranged it. Though we didn't, of course!"

Tara excused herself very shortly thereafter. She was advancing to the finals, even though she thought she had done poorly. Could she really be one of the best horse archers in the land? It seemed like it—at least of those who had chosen to participate.

But behind that wonderful thought loomed the problem of how to explain her absence at the finals to her parents. It was impossible to observe the competition and participate at the same time. She had no choice, she knew. She simply had to participate. She couldn't possibly forfeit to this masked Shadow person. It would be unjust to herself and the interested spectators. It would also be unjust to Shadow, whoever he was, as he must also be looking forward to the finals. To forfeit would be to rob him too of the opportunity to win or lose by his own merits. She would have to explain to her parents that she was Fléchette and that was why she had not joined them for the previous two rounds and could not for the finals.

Tara mulled this thought of fairness over in her mind some more and liked it. "Fair." That was it. Fair to her, to the spectators, and fair to her competitor. Plus, it was time to stop deceiving her parents. She had done that for far too long with the existence of her princess friends. Now was the time to stop that practice. Tara laughed to herself at how surprised they would be. They would never have supposed she was Fléchette, the mysterious accomplished archer! How proud they would be of her!

She found an opportunity the evening of the next day. The three were taking their evening meal together, having come in from an afternoon of assessing poets vying for the prize of laureate of the Games. Tara had bridled her lack of interest in the competition, disinterested as she generally was in literature, poetry, and most of the arts. She knew it was an important part of the Games, and that her mother very much liked these less violent and physical competitions. So, doggedly, Tara had born up and tried to find something to like in each. Armorica had appreciated her daughter's efforts at culture but could not help but be disappointed in Tara's disinterest, no matter how mightily her daughter worked to hide it, and her mouth twitched intermittently in disapproval when she thought Tara wasn't attentive.

The conversation, such as it was that evening, had focused on the merits of the poetry they had heard that day. Tara had a hard time distinguishing between the many poems they had heard, as was evident from the way she stumbled in recollecting their verses.

Childeric tried to be kind, knowing his daughter's weaknesses. "No, Tara, that was a panegyric to Brythrony. Not an ode."

Tara had mumbled a half-hearted apology. Childeric had fixed Armorica with a brief frown, intending to convey to his wife that Tara was trying. Besides, he thought, it was not as if Armorica identified correctly all the forms of versification herself. Nor could he.

When the talk turned to the next day's events, which would include the final round of horse archery, Tara brightened. "Mom, Dad, I need to tell you something."

"What is it, princess?" replied Childeric kindly, placing his cutlery down on the table to listen to her.

Tara checked the faces of both parents to make sure they were paying attention then pressed forward. "I need to tell you that I will not be able to officiate at the final round of the horse archery competition tomorrow."

Armorica's dropped cutlery rattled loudly on her plate. "What do you mean?" she asked sharply, the blood mounting to her face.

"There's a good reason," protested Tara, suddenly aware of how painfully silent the room had become. The wait staff had fled at hearing Armorica's tone, probably to hover just beyond the doors, out of sight but not out of earshot.

"You said you would join us! You promised!"

"But wait! Listen!"

Armorica's accusatory finger stabbed repeatedly at Tara with each point she made. "You haven't shown up for a single round of that event! Even though we planned it especially for you! Because we thought you'd like it!"

"But Mom!—"

"Don't 'but Mom' me! I cannot believe how ungrateful you are! Spoiled child! If you don't want to attend, then don't! Go, then, and ride that horse of yours, or do whatever you want!" With that, Armorica rose from the table, upsetting a goblet of water in her anger, and stormed out.

"Dad!—"

"No, Tara," he replied sternly. "You have angered her. And me too. This is selfish behavior." Childeric pushed himself away from the table and stood to follow Armorica. But, after taking a few steps, he stopped and spoke, his voice soft and reflective, and rendered fainter still in addressing the doorway he had been about to pass through rather than Tara. "I am very disappointed. I am. One day you are to reign over this kingdom, but you have shown so very little interest in your responsibilities that I really worry what will become of Brythrony when you succeed us. If you ever do."

He left without another word and without turning around.

Tara was so upset that, for a time, she simply remained at the table, staring at the seats lately occupied by her mother and father. No one was here for her, she thought blankly, dully. She could climb the stairs to her room, but no one was there for her either. Her friends weren't due to arrive for another two days, for the costume ball. She didn't know where to turn and she felt utterly alone. At last, she stood and left for the stables. At least Daystar was there for her and would not reproach her.

"Hi, Daystar," she said on seeing her horse. He whinnied in recognition, and she entered the paddock and wrapped her arms around his neck to bury her face in his mane. He was warm and comforting, and suddenly hot tears at what she felt was unjust persecution started in her eyes. "You know the truth," she muttered into his glossy coat. "Do I really not care about Brythrony? Am I so spoiled and ungrateful? Am I?"

Daystar whinnied again, as if in response.

"I don't think so either. I tried to explain, but they wouldn't give me a chance." Tara was so discomposed that she began to think about withdrawing altogether from the competition and how best to do it gracefully. How could they be so unfair? They hadn't even let her speak! They thought she was mean and thankless for not joining them at the horse archery when, really, she was only trying to win them all honor. Why couldn't they make an effort to really hear her, instead of just accusing her?

Just then, she heard behind her the stablemaster entering the paddock.

"Your Highness?" he called into the dimness. "Is that You?"

Tara's muffled voice came from deep within Daystar's mane. "Yes, Geoffrey. It's me."

"Your Highness is distressed!"

Tara wasn't accustomed to showing her emotions to others, but she couldn't help it this time. She wiped her eyes dry as best she could on Daystar and turned her head to the side so Geoffrey could hear her better though still not see her face. "Yes. Yes, I am."

"I'm terribly sorry to hear that, Your Highness. Is there anything I can do for You to help?"

Tara sighed. There was nothing he could do. No one could intercede with her parents for her. Still, taking a deep breath, she recounted to him the events at dinner.

He listened sympathetically. "I'm very sorry for Your Highness." He paused, then continued quietly, backing up to lean against the stable wall. "What does Your Highness wish to do?"

Tara didn't answer and turned her face back into Daystar's mane.

"Your Highness doesn't need to make a decision just now if She doesn't wish. I mean, on the competition. She can wait until tomorrow."

Tara shook her head, rubbing her face back and forth in Daystar's coat. It was smooth, but turned rough with friction. Her skin stung ever so slightly from the mix of tears and horsehair. "I don't know. I don't know."

"Your Highness doesn't need to decide just now."

Daystar neighed softly and arched his head back to blow on her cheek. Tara considered. "Maybe you're right, boy. You're always right. No, I'll go ahead. I'll do it."

Geoffrey waited a space further in case the Princess of the Realm might change her mind. But she gave no sign of wanting to do so. "Very good, Your Highness. Having made up Her mind, Your Highness must focus to do well. Because there is no point in doing it if not to do it well." He lowered his voice to a soft undertone. "You'll have to clear Your mind of distractions. So that You may do Your best. Then, when You win—as I am very confident You will—then You can explain to Their Majesties. I say 'explain', because winning never needs an excuse."

Tara turned her head toward Geoffrey. It was nice to be believed in, not just by Daystar but by a real person. She thought to thank him, but the words wouldn't come to her.

Yet Geoffrey understood anyway. He nodded. "Go the full distance and win, Your Highness. For You and Your noble house. And," he concluded with a grin, "for Daystar and the stables!"

Tara straightened and smoothed Daystar's mussed mane. "What do you think?" she asked him, and it seemed almost as if Daystar nodded and pawed the ground. "You're ready to go, aren't you?" She turned back to the stable master. "I'll do it." There, she thought as she half-heartedly pulled down her costume as Fléchette to verify its readiness. There. She had said she would do it. But her heart wouldn't be in it like it had been in the first round. It had been so fun then. Now it had all sorts of other emotions mixed in. Now she was mainly finishing because she had started. And, maybe, somewhere way back there, to show her parents she could win.

The next afternoon, having diligently avoided her parents all morning, Tara pulled up sharply at the rear gates of the arena, just as on the two previous occasions. But, unlike previously, there was another rider present, dressed all in black and sporting a short, brown cape. Shadow, obviously. But why here at the same time? A herald stepped forward to explain the rules of the final round. As before, riders would be timed, and accuracy would win points, as would the faster time. Unlike in previous rounds though, they would ride simultaneously, only on different parts of the course to avoid injury. This way, the spectators would be able to watch both at the same time.

Tara listened and considered the new terms even as, covertly, she studied the figure next to her. She recalled what Geoffrey had said to her, about staying focused. Had this unexpected change been introduced to test their focus? She felt a little of the thrill of the first round mount within her as she savored the edge that she felt his words of the day before gave her.

This brought to mind a mischievous idea, an irresistible urge. If focus were key, why not unsettle her opponent just a little? He could never imagine he was competing against a woman; the sudden knowledge of this would have to disturb his focus. Tara chuckled slyly, turned and spoke, openly and plainly, to Shadow. "May the better of us win," she said, with a gesture to her helmet in salute.

Shadow turned toward her, saluted Tara similarly and then, in a voice of haughty disdain, spoke. "May the better of us win. But that will be me, Princess Tara. Oh, does it surprise you that I know who you are? But do you know who I am?"

Tara caught her breath sharply. Shadow wasn't a man but a woman! And she knew her identity! Who was Shadow? How did she know who Fléchette really was? When Tara had no idea who she was? Tara took a deep breath and concentrated. Instead of throwing her competitor, she, Tara, had been thrown.

The same herald stepped forward to assess their readiness, and Tara nodded absentmindedly in response to the formal question as to whether she was prepared. Focus! she reprimanded herself. She and this person calling herself Shadow would be competing at the same time, riding back and forth across the course, aiming perhaps at the same target at the same time.

"Good luck, Princess Tara," hissed she who called herself Shadow. "Watch out for my arrows!" She pulled a small bundle of sticks and fibers from a case at her side and, with a flick and a jerk of her arm, it opened with a snap and became a bow. From a case at her thigh, she withdrew a short arrow with a black shaft and silvery steel tip.

Tara straightened in her saddle. Shadow might try to hit her? But Shadow had proven herself to be an expert shot! Impossible, realized Tara. No one would dare injure her in front of the entire kingdom. This was a transparent attempt to throw her still further off!

Daystar neighed and shifted restlessly beneath Tara. "Steady on, there, boy," Tara whispered to him, leaning over to speak into his ear. "Steady on. Remember: we maintain focus." Daystar quieted, and Tara straightened and kept her eyes straight ahead. In previous rounds, she had been impatient to begin; this last round, she was grateful for the unexpected delay.

As she cleared her mind, she realized the identity of her opponent. Of course. That accent. That tone. She should have recognized it instantly. Even if it was a voice she had not heard for a long time.

Tara swallowed and without looking over to her opponent, stated calmly, "But I do know who you are. You are Maribess. Of the Underground Kingdom. Furthermore, I should think your aim is better than hitting me with an arrow by accident. Or," she couldn't resist adding, "could you be making excuses for missing the targets already, even before we've started?"

Tara sensed that Maribess might be preparing a retort, but she was interrupted by the re-appearance of the herald. "Riders! Places!" The gates to the arena swung open, and both she and Maribess entered to salute the king and queen. The officiant drew and raised his sword. "Ready," he called, letting his voice hang in the air for a second, eying both, then bringing his sword down in a sweeping arc. "Begin!"

Off they dashed in opposite directions, Tara intent on keeping her eyes on the ground ahead of her rather than on Maribess. No, she reminded herself sternly, stay focused. Focused on her aim and her horsemanship. On winning. A lot was at stake: her reputation before the entire kingdom and her parents. Her own self-confidence. She reached back to her quiver to retrieve the first of the ten arrows allowed her and nocked it to her bow. There it was, she murmured seeing the first target coming up fast, and her mind's focus contracted to a pinpoint. Only the target: now, aim and loose!

The arrow darted through the air to sink deeply into the bullseye. Tara was dimly aware of cheering, but her mind was already on the next target, which, unlike the first, would already have Maribess's arrow in it.

There it was, she saw with satisfaction, around the hedge, just visible through the leaves. She goaded Daystar forward to gain a few seconds then swung wide around the hedge for better aim. Grasp arrow, set to bow, draw bow, just like before—except that the black shaft fletched in vanes of grey and brown of Shadow was already present—and in the bullseye. Tara frowned in concentration: focus! Tara kept her eye trained on the target for a split second longer than necessary to see where it landed and was pleased to see it land next to Maribess's. Then she was spurring Daystar toward the next target. There could be no time for gloating.

Eight targets left. Look sharp for them, because she could neither afford the time to ride back for a missed target nor forfeit the points from missing it altogether.

Around the bend were targets five and seven, Underworld arrows in neither yet; Tara drew and shot, not wasting a moment to determine just how they hit. Around the next bend were targets six, eight, and two. Tara saw Maribess had ridden through since each target already had one of her short, dark arrows sunk to its shaft at its center. She is a great shot, whispered Tara then sternly reminded herself to remain focused. Targets three and four were about next to each other and went by as a blur, Tara riding at full speed, aiming and shooting in one fluid motion even as she spurred Daystar on at top speed toward the final target. She was feeling good about her aim. Her arrows were finding their marks. Not all were bullseyes, like the first two, but they had to have been about as good as those of Maribess. They must have nearly the same scores.

Up ahead lay the last target. Tara mentally reviewed the course's plan as she had ridden it. The nine targets had been arranged in a kind of symmetry with respect to the two halves of the course split, not around an axis perpendicular to the centrally located royal box, but parallel. That is, wherever there had been a target on the half of the course closest to the royal box, there had been another facing away. That half of the course closest to the royal box lacked one target to be equal with the other: the final target must lie there. Without a further thought, Tara spurred Daystar sharply in that direction, hoping to gain a few more seconds.

Tara gasped in relief. She had been right! But closer than she had expected; she reined Daystar in sharply, so much so that he reared up with a startled snort of surprise and discomfort. Tara strove to control his prancing; each second was valuable. Quick, get the arrow up and to the bow! Daystar shied and swerved, and Tara nearly dropped her arrow. For a wild second, Tara truly thought she might be thrown, but with a firm squeeze of her knees, she brought her mount back around through a full circle, aimed quickly and, not daring to let slip any more time, let the arrow fly. There, it was done! She wheeled Daystar about to the direction of the finish gate and gave him his head to gallop as fast as he liked. Just as she exited, she dared glance back to see where her arrow had struck. Next to outermost circle, she saw with deep disappointment.

She slowed Daystar to a trot and steered him in a wide circle back toward the arena. The last target, and she had done so poorly—but she had only seen one arrow in the target: her arrow. Could Maribess have been so far behind? Then, arriving in the arena, she saw with amazement that Maribess was already present. Could it be that, though Maribess had finished before her, Maribess had missed the last target altogether? Tara reined in Daystar to bring him snorting and panting alongside Shadow. Otherwise, the four waited in silence for the officiants to add up the scores and determine the winner.

The wait seemed interminable, but at last one of the officiants stepped up to the royal box and spoke with the king, who nodded in response and descended to the field. Both riders caused their horses to bow and dismounted.

The king stopped directly in front of them and eyed both of them, who were still masked. He lifted his voice, so that the spectators, dead silent now, could hear. "This King's Cup I award to the rider who completed the course with the fastest time and the best aim. I would have wished my daughter to be awarding this cup, but… but it shall be my pleasure instead." There was a pause, as if from disappointment. "And so, without further ado, and because this rider had the aggregate of best aim and best time, I award the King's Cup to… Fléchette!"

The king lifted high the trophy and advanced a step toward Tara. Tara bowed deeply and, pausing a moment, on impulse brought her right hand up to her helmet's chinstrap. As she straightened, and in one single sweeping gesture, she removed her helmet and the attached mask. Though her face was gritty and grimy and her chestnut hair matted and mussed, her eyes flashed forth in triumph. The king and crowd gasped in recognition. Fléchette was none other than the daughter he had known since birth, standing a bit taller than before but otherwise the same refractory and recalcitrant, and now victorious, Tara.

"Tara!" Childeric stuttered. "Why didn't you tell me?" He hesitated a fraction of a second. Was it fair to award his own daughter the trophy? But she had ridden incognito, and the course had been kept secret up until an hour before the final round. He shrugged: she had won fairly. He lifted the trophy high overhead for all to see, and in a booming voice so that all could hear, announced, "I award you, Fléchette, Princess Tara, this King's Cup! Congratulations!"

Later that day, in her room, Tara gazed at the trophy placed on her dressing table. How sweet to have won it and to have done so coming from behind! Maribess, she was told later, had been ahead through a better aim up to the last target but had lost because she had ridden so hard past it, she had overlooked it. Tara had been slower but had at least put an arrow in it.

Suddenly, there was a flutter of wings at the window and a rap at the casement. Tara turned to see her friend Ariel just outside, floating. Tara threw up her arms in greeting. "Hey there! How are you?"

"Hi, friend! How are you!"

"I'm great! I just won a tournament!"

"Hey, like, wow! Tell me about it!" Ariel settled herself gently on the sill of the window, her feet dangling fifty feet above the ground. Tara opened her mouth to caution her friend that it was a long drop and the seat seemed perilous, but she reminded herself that, for Ariel, sliding off the sill would be the same as standing up from a bench to Tara.

Tara recounted the story of the tournament.

"You are incredible! Of course you could do it!"

"Thanks," blushed Tara. "I didn't think I could, honestly."

Ariel waved her hand to dismiss that objection. "The rest of us have seen your aim. Many times. And in some pretty dangerous situations!"

"Thanks again. You're so sweet.

"But, hey," Tara interrupted herself. "There's a twist. My competitor—and I was saving this—is someone we know."

"Know? Know and love?"

"Not quite."

"Like, know and not love?"

Tara nodded.

"Who?"

"You'll remember her. We've had to deal with her before, though it's been a while. It's Maribess. Remember her? She came with that Underworld Sundra lady when she tried to take over Brythrony!"

Ariel nodded, suddenly serious. "Oh yes! She's the one who found me at the stockade trying to help Rohanic!"

"Right. I should have had her arrested, right there in the arena, but, well, I didn't want to cause a scene in front of everyone." Additionally, realized Tara, it would have required her to reveal just how deeply she had been involved in arresting the raids on the villages ringing the Great Forest.

"Probably so. At least all she wanted to do was compete in the games, right?"

"So far. But I'm a little worried that she's not done yet. Thankfully, you'll be here with me and—did you know?—so will Princess Florence."

"That's good. She's a big help."

"Because guess who else will be present?"

"Maribess."

"Right! Because every finalist is invited. So, I may need your help if Maribess tries anything."

Ariel agreed. "It'll be good to have Florence too. We may need all the help we can get."

Tara continued. "But here's something I've been thinking. While Maribess knows you and me, she doesn't know Florence. Maribess will recognize you soon enough, but she won't know we have a third ally. Florence will be a complete surprise to Maribess."

"That's true," allowed Ariel. "So, while Maribess is watching the two of us, she won't know that a third is watching her!"

Tara nodded her head in agreement, more vigorously this time.

"Okay, sounds like a plan," announced Ariel. "Listen, I'm going to head back up to Cloud Castle now—no thanks to the offer to stay with you since my place is just overhead—but I'll be back tomorrow for the ball. What time did you say it starts?"

"Around five o'clock."

"Right. So I'll be by early, say around four, just in case you need any last-minute help. I'll come through this window again, if you don't mind."

"Sure."

"Right. So what I'm saying is, please don't lock it!"

Tara giggled. "No, I won't lock it! Heaven forbid that you should have to come into the castle through the door like everyone else!"

They both laughed and, after a quick hug, Ariel flew out of the window with a quick flutter of wings. "See you tomorrow!" she called behind her as she ascended to the large, dark cloud directly overhead and upon which Cloud Castle rested.

Tara half-closed the window after Ariel departed. "Now I just have to wait for the Ice Princess to show! I hope she'll be in soon!"

But Tara grew tired and at last went to bed without any sign of her other friend. Tara wasn't worried: Florence always showed, even if sometimes a little late. Sure enough, in the middle of the night, Tara awoke to a distinct chill. Though Tara had left the window open, the cooler night air didn't account for the tumbling temperature. Tara sighed, gathering up the blankets around her. It could only be Florence. She didn't have to be preceded by dramatically lower temperatures, she just very much preferred that. Tara sat up to see a steady shower of ice crystals rain down through the open window and accumulate near the foot of her bed. Florence. Tara hoisted herself out of bed, wondering what time it was, and pulled on a robe. By the time she turned back around, there was Florence, coolly surveying her and her bedroom.

"Hey, darling, how are you? Great to see you again! How've you been?"

"I'm just fine, thank you, Florence. It's good to see you again. But could I ask you to let up on the chill. Just a little?"

"Sure! No problem!" Immediately the air began to warm.

"I appreciate that." Tara sat down at the edge of her bed. "Long trip, huh?"

"Yes. But I wouldn't miss it for the world! I love parties!" Princess Florence's mild, nearly colorless, eyes sparkled with laughter.

Tara had to smile. Florence was fun, and she would be good to have along if there were a confrontation with Maribess. Though she could be talkative, she was dependable and absolutely trustworthy.

"I also have everything I promised. In the bag here."

"Wonderful! Thank you!"

"But you're right. I'm exhausted! Coming such a distance is tough! Can I spend the night here?"

Tara smiled again. "Of course. I have a room set up for you next door. Let me also bring you up to date on something." Tara led Florence to the spare room while she summarized recent events.

"Maribess, huh? She sounds pretty bad, but there are three of us and just one of her. But hey, could she have others with her? Like, helpers we don't know?"

Tara hadn't considered that. "It's a great question," she admitted. "We'll watch for that. I'll also instruct the guards to admit only those who were in the competition."

With that, they went to bed.

The next morning, Princess Tara asked for her breakfast to be sent up to her room and for twice the usual amount than usual. "Because I'm very hungry this morning; I have a really big day ahead of me!" she explained. When the servants had departed, she called for Florence. "Breakfast is served!" Tara had thought it better not to bring Florence down until she and Ariel were "in costume," and Ariel's wings would not receive undue attention.

Ariel was soon knocking politely at the window. "No thanks," she replied to Tara's invitation to join them for breakfast. "I've had something already. But well, okay, I'll take a cup of tea." Of course, she was very happy to find Florence already there, and the three of them were quickly caught up with each on where they had each been and what they had been doing.

Flo was still puzzled by Maribess's motives. "Why is she here? Did she really come all the way to Brythrony just to compete in some games?"

Tara took another nibble from her pastry. "I've wondered about that too. She came all this distance to get a trophy? I think we'll find out tonight, but I don't know how or what it will mean."

Florence suddenly remembered. "Oh, here are the things I mentioned to you last night. For your journey," she said, handing Tara two bundles wrapped in a silvery sheen of frost but which were not cold to the touch. "They'll open only to your voice—which I got off your message bubble—so no one else can use them except you."

"Oh, how sweet," Tara murmured, adding her thanks.

"What's that?" demanded Ariel.

"Um, just that I'll have to get some more power for my ring." Tara held out her hand to show the dull, lusterless jewel atop the band on her right index finger. "I used it up in our last encounter with Silicana."

"Oh, yeah; I remember that."

"Florence very kindly offered me these items to help me along."

"But why not ride on the Cloud Castle? I'll take you there! It's no problem."

Tara considered. It was super thoughtful of Ariel to offer, but she was reluctant to involve her friends in yet another expedition out to the Lost Quarter. "That's so nice of you, Ariel, but honestly, it would be the third time going to that hateful desert! I couldn't ask you to do that again."

Ariel waved Tara's concerns away. "No worries, right? I can drop you off as I drift by! Why go by land when you can go by air?"

Tara hesitated, but the advantage was obvious. It would be far safer and quicker. "Wow, I'd love to accept! As long as you're sure it's no problem!"

They were interrupted by a polite knock on the door and a voice from the other side reminding Tara it was time for her to start getting ready for the ball. Tara made a face. "I gotta go, sorry. Florence, would you like to come along with me?"

Ariel inclined her head toward her wings. "I'll fly back home and get ready there. See you back here in a few hours!"

The three re-joined in Tara's room. Tara was dressed much as she had been as Fléchette, in her house colors of royal blue and arctic white with a brown semi-cape across her shoulders, but in finer fabrics. A blue-black mask had been fitted to her eyes, and her quiver, empty since arms would not be permitted in the hall, was slung across her back. Without cajoling, she had permitted Sullijee to arrange her tresses such that they were away from the mask and tumbled down her back in an elaborate cascade of curls and waves. Armorica, who had supervised intermittently, had been pleased and complimented the hairdresser. As for Tara, she had been admonished to keep her movements conservative so as not to disturb the delicate equilibrium atop her head.

Ariel took her dressing cues from her home above the clouds. Over her eyes she wore a white mask speckled with crystals to recollect the ice crystals in a cloud. Her collar, straight and tall behind her, was edged in gold as if from crepuscular rays of sunlight. Her dress was white at the bodice, to continue the theme of a cloud, but shading to the blue of the skies below as it edged to the hem, which floated above her feet. A golden coronet nestled delicately atop her honey-blonde hair, and Tara had brushed her wings with the thinnest layer of dazzle dust so they would shimmer and glisten in the chandelier light.

Like Ariel, Florence looked to her home for costume cues. Her dress was largely white but with the blue striations of sea ice, and studded with so many crystals and sequins such that it sparkled like a snowfield in a bright Arctic sun. Her gown was straight and dropped to the floor, unlike Ariel's, which puffed outwards; concentric rings of white and ever-deepening blues with matching sequins ringed the skirt down to the hem.

"You look dazzling!" they said, almost simultaneously, one to the other.

"Let's go downstairs!" said Tara excitedly. "So I can introduce you to my parents! I've been dying to do this for so long!"

They found her mother in the Hall, attending to finishing touches and making final adjustments to the decorations. "Oh, there you are, darling! And... who are these ladies with you?"

"These are my friends, Florence and Ariel," replied Tara as the other two curtsied deeply.

"And how beautifully costumed you are," exclaimed Armorica. "Why, you look just like a fairy, and even have wings!" She eyed the glimmering wings curiously for a brief moment, then shrugged. "And you," she resumed, turning to Florence, "why, well, I guess… you're an iceberg?"

Florence smiled gently at the inelegant assessment of what she wore. "I'm an ice maiden," she explained. "From the North!"

"Of course, dear! How silly of me! And you very much look it!"

Armorica peered closer. "And I've heard so much about you from my daughter. And you seem so reasonable and nice now that I've finally met you in person!"

"Thanks, Mom," muttered Tara, wryly.

Next, the queen turned to Ariel, her eyes at once drawn to her wings. Tara suddenly recollected her mother's term of "fairy friend" for Ariel and cringed. This was going to be totally embarrassing!

But Tara was to be surprised. "Ariel!" the queen said graciously. "Tara has spoken of you also! How lovely to meet you, too!" Armorica's eyes drifted down to check the feet of both Ariel and Florence. "But what about your other friend, the one with the? —"

Tara took each friend by an arm. "Mom, it's been great talking with you, but we should get going. There's still so much to do to prepare for the ball! We might meet a prince too!"

"Oh! Well, of course! And there will be princes too. Speaking of which, it's just as well that that Shadow person wasn't a man after all; he would have been far too short for you." Ariel and Flo suppressed smiles at Tara's discomfiture, who mouthed a reproachful syllable to her mother as she dragged her friends off. "Have a lovely time," called Armorica after them. "See you at the reception!"

Shortly, the winners of each competition were called to pair with their runners-up to form a line stretching from the doors to the reception hall into the antechamber outside. Tara was soon standing next to Maribess and saw that she had had the same idea as had Tara for her dress that evening, largely retaining her costume as Shadow, only in richer fabrics and deeper hues and consisting of a full black-and-grey velvet gown with a faint silvery wash of sparkles across much of it, the brown fur-trimmed cape falling dramatically down her back. A lovely costume, allowed Tara, possibly even more eye-catching than her own. But because the person within was merciless and mean, could she ever really be lovely?

Maribess greeted Tara with a hiss. "So! If it isn't Princess Tara!" She snickered. "More like Princess Tara-ble!"

Tara counterfeited an exaggerated smile, which went wasted, as her mask obscured it. Hadn't she heard that one before, many times, and even from her own mother? "Very nice to see you again, Maribess," replied Tara evenly, also in a whisper.

"We'll be even soon enough," Maribess asserted under her breath. "For the Sebastas!"

Tara wondered briefly what the Underworlder could mean but decided she couldn't attempt anything in the reception hall with so many watching and the palace guards within immediate call. "Oh? In the arena? Are you looking for a rematch?"

"You knew in advance where the targets had been placed. You knew where to look for the last target!"

Tara bridled at the insinuation that she had cheated. She had had no more advance knowledge of the course than anyone else. Maribess was trying to goad her to act un-princess-like in front of the guests. "That's untrue," she replied flatly, striving to confine herself to that response alone.

Maribess compressed her lips. She was the best aim in Pentenok. She had won tournament after tournament in many throwing weapons, including the very same folding bow she had used against Tara. Yet she had ridden right by the last target when this dilettante princess had seen and hit it. Only because, she had concluded, Tara had had some sort of inside advantage. But soon it wouldn't matter, she told herself. Deep down, she had known that, even during the tournament. "I could have won if I had wanted to!" Maribess continued at last, in a taunting tone.

"You didn't want to win? Or, do you mean you wanted me to win all along? Maribess, I didn't expect such generosity!"

Maribess sputtered something incomprehensible and Tara smiled a tiny smile behind her mask.

A soft fanfare sounded from the reception hall, and the line began to march into the hall, with the names of event, winner, and runner-up announced by a herald. As much as Tara disliked having to stand next to her, it did allow Tara to monitor Maribess for mischief.

Upon entering the hall, the contestants were proffered flagons of wine and guided into a series of concentric circles around the king and queen to offer them a toast. Afterwards, and to her surprise, Childeric called her up to join the royal couple. "Now, please, all contestants," he began, motioning with his hands for silence. "May I beg your indulgence in a second toast? This time, to my lovely daughter Princess Tara, who throughout the horse archery contest, we thought was in her room, or elsewhere, when, in fact, she was competing!" He turned to Tara, continuing in an affectionate tone, "I think it would have better had you been on the dais with us but, well, I suppose you couldn't help yourself."

He turned back to the crowd and lifted his voice and the flagon in his own hand. "Please! To Princess Tara, of our royal house, and the champion of horse archery!" There was a roar of approval from everyone except Maribess, whose face below the mask, if anything, turned a shade sourer. Tara also noticed that Maribess appeared to be discreetly working with something at her hip. What could she be up to now, Tara wondered. She caught the eye of Ariel and, with a few quick jerks of her head in the direction of her erstwhile competitor, motioned for her to investigate.

Maribess started in surprise to see the cloud-like Ariel appear beside her. "You! You also!"

"Yes, me! How very nice to see you again!" replied Ariel innocently and made a show of glancing down at Maribess's hand, which was just then secreting something like a small purse within the folds of her gown. "Tell me what you're doing there? Scratching at something? An itch?"

Maribess sneered. "The only itch I have is to settle scores with you and Tara. And those surrendering guardsmen of this pathetic little kingdom!"

Ariel adopted a tone of admonishment. "Dear me; do watch your temper. You are a guest here!" Maribess looked as if she might try to step away into the crowds, but Ariel pressed forward to stand very close. "It's been so long since we've seen each other, I think I'll want to stay very close and catch up on the so many things that have surely happened since our last encounter."

Tara joined them from the dais. "Why, Maribess, I see you've met my friend, Princess Ariel."

Deigning not to reply, Maribess turned to a passing attendee attired in the colors of a dragonfly and greeted her, her voice suddenly modulated pleasantly. The dragonfly stopped short, surprised and fascinated by Maribess's costume.

Ariel used the opportunity to lean in close to Tara and whisper, "She's got something there all right! At her waist; in a little purse!"

A bell began ringing to indicate that the banquet would be served imminently. Maribess spoke in lofty tones in the general direction of Tara and Ariel. "I hope you'll excuse me, friends," she said, deliberately emphasizing the final word, "but I would like to wash my hands. Surely you needn't accompany me to the washroom, yes?"

"She's quite a piece of work, huh?" muttered Ariel as Maribess walked away.

"A lot like that Sundra she reports to," agreed Tara but, glancing around the room, changed the subject. "But where's Florence? I still haven't spotted her."

Perhaps she was way in the back, speculated Ariel, as she hadn't either, even though her costume should make her stand out. They moved toward one of the columns further in, where they could take a step up from the floor, the better to search for Florence and see when Maribess returned.

"What's that she's holding?" demanded Ariel in alarm, pointing in the direction Maribess should be coming from. Tara strained her eyes but was unable to discern where her hands were, much less what they might be doing. But Ariel had always had the sharpest eyes of them all.

"It… it looks like a wand of some sort—no, like a reed. Or straw." Ariel squinted. "And now she's fiddling with that little purse of hers! What's she doing?"

Tara's mind raced. What on earth could Maribess be intending, standing in the entrance to the Banquet Hall with a reed in one hand and manipulating a small purse with the other? What could one do with a small, hollow cylinder? Then, in a flash, a thought occurred to her and she gasped. "It must be a kind of blowpipe! And she intends to fill it with something from the purse! We've got to stop her; she can't possibly mean any good!"

Ariel turned to Tara. "Dust? Like, magic dust?"

Tara was already moving forward. "Can't say. Maybe to make us sleep. Or control us!" Tara didn't dare mention what she feared, which was that the dust might be poisonous and intended to kill them all.

"We've got to stop her," agreed Ariel. But the crowd was still entering for the banquet, and it was difficult to force their way back against the press. "There's Florence!" exclaimed Ariel. "She's just about right behind Maribess! But Maribess is filling the reed from her purse!"

There was too little time to send a message bubble. "Fly, Ariel!" urged

Tara. "Do it! Shout to Florence to stop Maribess from blowing on that reed!"

Ariel's wings were already moving. With a short leap, she was airborne, her wings a brilliant blur behind her from the dazzle dust still on them. The crowd gaped and fell away as Ariel soared above them, her dress streaming behind her. "Stop her, Flo; don't let her put that straw to her lips!" Ariel cried, pointing and diving for Maribess.

Maribess hesitated, the pipe midway to her mouth. To whom was this awful Ariel calling? Maribess glanced wildly about, but everyone was watching in dumb amazement. A ruse, another desperate ruse, just like at the campfire in the Great Forest! But not again; she would eliminate this winged accomplice of the hated Tara. Maribess brought the pipe to her lips, aimed it into Ariel's path and blew a black jet. Ariel threw up her arms as if to ward off the dark cloud, then her wings faltered and she tumbled to earth, her fall broken only by some of the banquet's hapless attendees.

Pandemonium ensued. Costumed creatures ran this way and that, shrieking and bellowing. Tara fought her way as best she could through the crowd, but saw that Maribess had already reloaded her blowpipe. Tara would never reach her in time to stop another dust cloud!

Fools, thought Maribess, there is no escape. "For the Sebastas!" she cried triumphantly and lifted the blowpipe.

But she did not know Florence, behind her, finally had a clear line of sight to the dark huntress, the crowd having cleared. Florence's right arm flashed up and down, and a thin crystal rod appeared in her right hand from a slit in the long glove. The tip of the rod described a small circle in the air and stabbed toward Maribess, and a jet of ice streaked from it to encircle Maribess, mounting higher from her feet with each lap. Maribess had the pipe back to her lips, but the ice built so rapidly that, by the time Maribess blew, the ice was higher than her head. The dust billowed out but was contained within the dome by which she was completely covered. Through the translucent sheet, Tara saw Maribess's eyes widen in disbelief and horror, and then she collapsed to the floor, the dust settling silently over her still form in a thin, grey-black pall.

Silence fell. Not a person stirred. Childeric, in outrage mixed with concern, at last spoke from the front. "What is happening here? In my very own banqueting hall, before my very eyes?"

Tara knelt at her friend's side. "Ariel, are you all right? Ariel?"

Her friend did not stir.

Florence was beside Tara in an instant. "Is she okay? Was she hurt?"

Tara looked up to Florence. "I don't know! Is she... she couldn't be...?"

In answer to Tara's unspoken question, Florence snapped the fingers of her left hand and, instantly, an irregular shard of ice, as smooth as glass, appeared in it. Florence held it to Ariel's mouth. In a few moments, the shard fogged. Florence turned to Tara and held out the shard. "She's breathing, at least."

Just then the king shouldered his way through the circle of the curious and amazed onlookers around the two standing and two fallen girls. "Tara!" he demanded. "Just what is going on? People flying and falling and this dust—everywhere! What is the meaning of all this?"

Tara struggled to keep her voice calm. Gesturing, she spoke, her voice rising with each identification. "Father, Princess Florence, beside me, and Princess Ariel, on the floor, have surely saved our kingdom from some terrible plot of Maribess, who lies over there under ice!" Tara cast her eyes down upon her friend, lying insensate at her feet. "We must get Ariel some help; we don't know what this dust is!"

Childeric gazed down at the crumpled form sprawled across the flagstones of the hall. So, this was the Ariel who had helped to save Rohanic and his detachment in the Great Forest, this jumble of dress, limbs, and arms? And, over there, beneath a dome of ice, the Maribess who had attempted some plot against his guests and his kingdom? His features softened. "Very well then: bring me this instant my personal physician!"

"But don't touch the dust!" cautioned Tara. "We don't know how harmful it might be!"

The king immediately understood Tara's concerns. "Quite true! Everyone, away to the table! It's high time we started the banquet anyway!"

The guests grudgingly tore their eyes from the spectacle of Ariel being lifted and taken to the nearest bedroom to be examined. Tara briefly considering having Maribess removed to a prison cell but relented, reluctantly, as she was unconscious and, however errant, a guest. "But," muttered Tara, "there will be justice for what she did to Ariel when that opportunity comes." Florence broke Maribess's ice prison with a touch from her rod, and she too was carried away.

Tara too took her seat at the table, next to her father and mother, having let it be known that she would only provide the background to what all had seen if and when they took their seats. Now all eyes focused expectantly on Princesses Tara and Florence.

Florence elbowed Tara. "You go first!"

Tara mouthed a dry "Thanks ever so much" back but stood and surveyed her audience. A thousand eyes seemed to be upon her, of all hues and colors, but all bright with curiosity and wide with wonder. Tara took a draught of her wine, raised an arm to signal for silence, which was hardly necessary, and pondered how to begin. Let's see, she wondered silently. How far back do I take them to provide enough background but not make the story too long? How much do they really want to know?

The crowd waited in growing anticipation, but Tara simply stood at the table, silent, eyes unseeing, looking into the table, flagon of wine in one hand and her other arm in the air.

There was the inevitable muted cough. Princess Florence nudged Tara. "Hey! What's wrong? Start already!"

Tara started, then blurted, "They'll die! They'll die if we don't do something!"

Florence rocked back in astonishment. "What do you mean?"

"Don't you see? They'll both die from thirst and starvation if they stay unconscious long enough! We need to do something!"

It was true, thought Florence. While unconscious, they couldn't drink. They would die from dehydration. "What shall we do?"

"We've got to get them food and water. Water first!"

The guests at the banqueting table remained absolutely still, fascinated by what appeared to be yet another chapter in this story unfolding right before their eyes!

There was another interminable pause. Then Tara spoke again. "On the other hand, maybe they won't need food and water."

"But didn't you just say they had to have food and water or they'd die?"

"Well, yes, they have to have food and water. Or be such that they don't need food and water!"

Florence rolled her eyes in exasperation. "Tara! You're talking in riddles!"

Tara grabbed her friend by the shoulder. "Think about it: they have to have food and water or they die. But they can't eat or drink while they're unconscious. So we need to make it so that they DON'T need food or water."

Florence was absolutely baffled.

"Don't you see? We need two stasis bottles, quick! We'll put Ariel and Maribess in them so that they stay alive but don't need food or water!"

Florence jumped up immediately. "Stasis bottles! Of course! No one trapped inside ever gets hungry or thirsty, so they're perfect for indefinite imprisonment. But, used like this, the bottles would save their lives!"

Tara nodded in delight. Florence understood!

"So we need two stasis bottles right away! Do you have any here?"

Princess Tara darted a quick glance at her mother and father, whose faces were the very picture of bepuzzlement and confusion. "Here? No; we'll have to find them elsewhere."

"Marina?"

That "fish friend" of hers, as her mother had termed her. Surely the Coral Kingdom would have a bottle or two. "Probably. But it would take too long for a message bubble to reach her and then for her to get them to us. We don't have much time. Maybe two or three days!"

"But what then? What shall we do?"

Not a person breathed around the entire table, so mesmerized were they by the drama unfolding before them. Tara looked down at the table, off to the left, frowned, off to the right, and up to the ceiling. Suddenly, she brightened. "I know! From Ariel!"

"Tara! Stop talking like that! That's impossible when she's unconscious!"

"What I mean is we'll get the bottles from Cloud Castle. You'll have to go. I can't and I'm too heavy to carry."

True enough, agreed Florence. While she could ascend to Cloud Castle in the form of a sleet storm, she wasn't able to take Tara with her in that form. "Fine. But I've never been there and I don't know my way around."

"We'll use the ice shards. I still have the one you gave me earlier. And don't you always keep one with you? I'll guide you from down here."

Florence whistled. "Super quick thinking, Tara! We can do it! I know Ariel has several. All I have to do is grab them and come back. Done!"

Princess Tara turned to her parents. "Dad, Mom, I'm sorry, but it looks as though you won't get the story behind all this just yet. But I promise you'll have it after we've saved Ariel and Maribess. I hope that won't be long."

Her father was annoyed. "Princess! When will all this stop? Can you not even be present for the concluding banquet of your own games?" Surprisingly, though, Armorica squeezed his arm to calm him and gestured with her other to Tara and Florence. "You go ahead, dears. It sounds as though their lives depend on you."

"Well," her father added, his voice edged with irritation, "it would have been nice to have had some sort of explanation for all this, at least! But I guess we'll have to wait on that too!"

"Sorry!" Princess Tara called over her shoulder, and she and Florence leapt from the table, Florence grabbing a chicken leg from a passing platter as she ran after Tara.

Tara located amongst the items she had set aside for her journey to the Lost Quarter the ice shard Florence had given her earlier. But Ariel's Cloud Castle was no longer directly overhead. Florence pointed away into the sky. "There it is. Way over there; I recognize it. But it's still no problem for me to get up there."

"The winds must have carried it some," agreed Tara, though inwardly she wondered just how far the castle would drift without anyone controlling it. "No time for that," Tara muttered to herself. "First we get the bottles."

"Huh? Oh, right, the bottles. Get ready; I'm going up!" With that, Florence turned a flat white all over, and the top of her head began to gradually disappear diagonally, down her face and through her neck as she gradually dissolved into sleet, which vanished out through the open window. It was a little unnerving to witness Florence's dissolution, layer by layer, thought Tara as she watched, but it sure was a handy way to travel. A moment later, and the last of Florence's feet were gone.

Tara sat down on her bed to wait. Florence would be at the Cloud Castle in just a minute or two. It was just a question of when Florence would raise her on the ice shard. That moment came sooner than Tara expected, when the ice shard next to her suddenly glowed and Florence's face appeared. "Tara, I'm here! I'm on a large deck and across the way are several doors; one of them looks like a stable door!"

Tara knew where that was. She had alighted there several times. "That's the main landing area for arriving visitors. Good place to arrive! The middle door leads to the main reception. Once there, we'll look for the fireplace in the adjacent room; last time I was there I thought I saw a stasis bottle on the mantlepiece."

"Right. By the way, there are all sorts of birds watching me!"

Tara smiled. "Like hawks?"

"Very funny! But it feels strange. They're everywhere! Big ones, mostly."

"You'll see a lot of them. She keeps them, uses them as her messengers." Tara even remembered how she had first met Ariel. It had been a sharp-eyed albatross that had brought her plight to the attention of Ariel. "Only the strongest and largest of birds can fly so high as to land on Cloud Castle. Don't pay them any heed."

Flo's face faded but reappeared a minute later. "I've found the fireplace, but I don't see a stasis bottle on the mantlepiece. There's just a sort of glass sculpture that looks kind of like a bird. That can't be it."

No, that couldn't be it. Tara frowned. This might be more complicated than just going up, grabbing the bottles and coming back. "We'll have to check her room. Or her treasury. First, her rooms, because I know where those are. Not so much the treasury."

"Fine. Where do I go?"

"There should be an especially large chair against one wall. Look to its left, where there's a tapestry hanging. I believe it depicts a nesting eagle—something like that. But the tapestry conceals a door leading to a stairway to her chambers. Give it a try!"

The shard went silent again as Tara imagined Florence finding the tapestry, pushing it aside, fumbling for the door, and then climbing the hidden stairway. A minute later, Florence's voice returned. She was in Ariel's rooms. "Good," said Tara, slowing her voice so she spoke more carefully and slowly, as she was less familiar with this part of Ariel's castle. "Good. As I remember, there's a door off to the side. Still in the bedroom. Towards the back, I think. I believe it leads to a strongroom. It's where she keeps important things—and I think she'd keep a stasis bottle there, as I know they fascinate her."

Florence's voice floated back a moment later. "Found the door. It's locked, but there's a keyhole."

Tara groaned. Of course, it would be! She thought fast. "Wait, wait… She must have the key on her! How silly of us not to have searched her first! Wait there while I run and check to see if she has any keys." Tara raced down the stairs of the North Tower, past the Banquet Hall where dinner was still in progress, and to the bedroom in which Ariel had been laid. The guard outside saluted her and opened the door. Inside, with only a few candles burning, Tara found Ariel, stretched out on the bed. Feeling very odd rifling the person of her unconscious friend, but pressing ahead nonetheless, Tara checked for keys on a necklace or in any pocket. Nothing. Oh, but the princess purse! "Ha!" she exulted: one of the keys on the ring inside had to fit! She whipped out the shard right away. "Hey, I've found a key ring. Fly back to my room to get it. Then back up you go to Cloud Castle!"

Florence only nodded, and Tara rushed back to her room, arriving just in time to find Florence nearly completely arrived, with the very top of her head filling in. A moment later, she was whole and her normal color. Tara had just enough time to place the key ring into Florence's outstretched hand and say, "You'll have to try them all; I don't know which one works," before Florence dissolved again and was out through the window.

Tara sat back down on the bed to wait for Florence to re-establish contact. She certainly hoped that one of the keys would work. Her doubts were put to rest a few minutes later when the shard glowed again and she heard Florence say, "Good news: the fifth key worked. I opened the door."

Tara breathed a sigh of relief. "That's great! But I can't help you any further. I've never been beyond that door; I've only seen it from the other side."

"No worries; should be easy from here," came Florence's voice, though lacking some of its usual upbeat confidence. "Uh-oh," she said, a moment later. "Another door. Locked. Let me try all the keys over again…"

A sudden shout of enthusiasm told Tara that one of the keys had worked. "Found them! And there're three bottles!"

Tara jumped to her feet in elation. "That is the best news! Will it take two trips to bring two bottles back?"

"No, I think I can do it in one. So glad to find more than one though. Just think if we had had to stuff both of them in the same jar." Tara wrinkled her nose at the prospect. It would be a lot more problematic to revive Ariel if she were in the same bottle as Maribess.

Both patients placed in separate bottles and secure from hunger and thirst, Tara and Florence relaxed. "Guess we might as well sneak back to the banquet?" asked Florence.

"Yes, let's. We need a break. As for how to wake those two," gesturing back toward the two patients as they walked back to the banquet, "and what exactly to do with Maribess, I don't know. Also, what about Cloud Castle?

We wouldn't want it to drift into a mountainside."

"Maybe," said Flo hopefully, "maybe the sleep is temporary. Maybe they'll wake up naturally in a few hours or a day or so."

Tara agreed that that would solve all their problems. But if they didn't? A sudden thought occurred to her. "Say, do you have your princess purse on you?"

"Of course! Don't we carry them wherever we go?"

"Sure! But, could you whip up a quick message bubble for me? I need to ask a favor of Marina."

Florence created a bubble and held it out for Tara. Tara asked Marina to ask her father if he knew of the dust Maribess had blown from her pipe. Perhaps, concluded Tara, might he consult his library for any mention of an antidote for poor Ariel—and, yes, the less-deserving Maribess? With that, she whispered Marina's name to the bubble and blew it gently, whereupon it wafted gently toward an open window high up in the room to find Marina.

Tara winked to Flo. "Now let's get back to the banquet!"

By this time though, the meal was nearly over, and the guests were in the middle of dessert. "Where have you been?" demanded Tara's father upon catching sight of his daughter, his face dark with exasperation.

Tara was taken aback. He was normally so supportive! "Dad, we were saving Ariel and Maribess from certain death!"

Childeric dismissed her words with an angry wave, as if unconvinced of their veracity. Forgetting himself momentarily in his irritation, he addressed her by her given name, rather than her title. "Tara! Why can't you take your royal duties seriously? We organized these games and this banquet in YOUR honor! To follow the costume ball YOU proposed! But you hardly showed up! Except for the very beginning and very end!"

Her mother reached out to tug at Childeric's arm. "Dear, she's been busy on something important. I think, this time, it's been real."

"'This time'!" her father huffed. "I think I've been too generous in the past! No: when will she take her duties seriously and stop playing the teenage adventurer? When will she finally become Princess of the Realm?" He hesitated, on the verge of saying more, but didn't and instead turned and pointedly launched into a conversation with the poetry recitation laureate.

Tara fell silent. She had no enthusiasm for continuing the story she was to begin earlier. She looked around. No one seemed to care anyway. Her father had said she had only appeared at the beginning of the banquet and then at the very end. Well, this had been because she had been saving Ariel. She picked at the plate before her. Ariel had needed saving because of Tara. The only reason Maribess had been able to blow her dust was because Tara had let her get away in the Great Forest. Now Ariel was unconscious, the banquet ruined, and a strange and toxic dust lay scattered across the hall which no one dared touch. All because of her.

Suddenly, all her exploits with her friends, all she had seen, and all she had done with them and which she had treasured for so long, curdled. What had they brought, ultimately? They had been nothing more than the pointless risking of lives. They had brought nothing good to Brythrony and maybe even brought real danger. They had just been a self-indulgent distraction, more trouble than benefit, more harm than good.

Tara laid her fork down on her plate and at the next pause in her father's conversation asked in a voice barely audible if she might be excused. Hearing no response, and with a meaningful glance at Florence, she pushed her chair back and left.

Florence's appetite was gone too. She felt terribly for her friend. Not that there needed to be three cheers for them, but didn't they deserve better than this? Shortly after Tara left, Flo quietly begged permission to leave and slipped away to join her friend.

Flo caught up with Tara as she was trudging up the stairs to her bedroom. "I can't believe it!" Tara stopped to expostulate on the first landing. "We just saved this stupid kingdom, and all they can think about is that I missed dessert! No thanks, no nothing! Just 'Where were you when the vegetables were being served?' That's it!"

Florence took her friend's hand. "It's totally unfair. I'm sorry. I don't think your parents understand all you've done for them and everyone out there."

"'Understand'? They have no clue! Maybe it doesn't matter. Or, maybe it would have been better to let Maribess take this horrible kingdom and pass it to Sundra! Because it's no prize; honestly, it's a punishment. And— why not?—as soon as we revive her, I'll give her the keys to Stonedell. 'Take them!' I'll say. But, pretty quick, I know she'll be begging me to take them back!"

Florence reached out to enfold Tara in a close hug. "I'm sorry. I'm sorry they don't understand," she murmured.

Her friend's voice came back in that certain quaver that betrays one is on the brink of tears. "They don't even care! It's just as well that I've never told them all the things we've done and all the places we've been. They would have only cared that I wasn't at some ball or reception, that's all. And, 'How come you haven't met Prince So-And-So yet?' Because nothing I've done matters. Not a bit!"

"Come on, let's get back to your room," said Florence softly, tugging on her from a riser above.

In her bedroom, behind a locked door, Tara dejectedly threw herself onto her bed. "It's no use. I give up. I should just run away. I'll never be the princess they want for Brythrony. I know: I'll go out to re-power my ring and never come back. They won't miss me at all—at least, not until the dessert course!"

Though Tara was obviously upset, Florence couldn't suppress her laughter and, despite her best efforts, began to giggle uncontrollably. Tara, seeing her, burst out, "Right? Isn't that right? Am I right?" Florence tried to shake her head, no, but was overcome by laughter, to the extent that even Tara found herself smiling ruefully. "Right? Am I right?" she kept saying and shortly was laughing herself.

Florence flopped down beside Tara. "I'm so sorry; they really don't understand. But they mean well. I think they just want to see more of you and doing official things."

Tara shook her head. "Gosh, I guess I'd love that—I think—but there's so much going on. I mean, we've had Sundra try to invade Brythrony, Maribess try to put us to sleep for who knows how long, and the Desert Witch, and the Sea Witch, and all sorts of other things in the meantime... I don't know. It's not like, really, we can kick back on our thrones and hope things just work out for Brythrony."

Florence nodded in sympathy.

Tara vented a heartfelt sigh. "But, I guess, we need to start thinking ahead. And not about the past. Like, what are we going to do with Cloud Castle? We can't just let that drift randomly across the skies. And then how are we going to revive Ariel? And what do we do with Maribess?" Tara shook her head gently as she lay on her bed. She'd have to wait on re-powering her ring. First things first, after all: Cloud Castle couldn't be allowed to wander the sky, they had to bring back Ariel, and then they had to decide what to do with Maribess. Each one of those tasks was big, even life-and-death in nature.

Meanwhile, her parents were focused on whether she had been present for a silly banquet.

Tara closed her eyes. Okay, so maybe that was unfair and a little exaggerated, but still, it was sort of like that.

Florence spoke after a long moment. Funny, what she was about to say was the sort of thing that Tara was the one generally to say. Florence frowned. That Tara had not said it yet was proof of how upset she was. She began, slowly, feeling her way forward through a space they all generally left to Tara. "Well, I've been thinking about this. A little. And you can tell me if I'm on the wrong track. But I was thinking I might go up to Cloud Castle, take a look around it and see if I can keep it out of trouble."

Tara mumbled that this sounded like a good idea. "I guess you're right. Funny it should need attention, though, because Ariel has joined us for days before and I can't remember her ever worrying about Cloud Castle."

Florence shrugged. "I don't know. Maybe she tethered it to something on those occasions but didn't tonight because she thought she'd be gone such a short time? But you saw how far it had drifted in just a few hours."

Tara imagined Cloud Castle crashing into a mountainside and massive blocks of it raining down on the innocent and unsuspecting people below. She shook her head. "True. No telling where it would go."

"Right. So I should get back up there and see if I can get it under control."

"All right. I'll wait for anything Marina might find out about that black dust Maribess had."

Tara hauled herself upright to give her friend a hug. "You should get going. Who knows where the winds are taking Cloud Castle."

This thought made Florence pause. "You know," she replied cautiously, "I have no idea what to do up there. I've never even been there before. Not before earlier this evening."

"I know. But you'll be doing your best. Which is very, very good. I know." No, Flo had no idea of how to navigate the Cloud Castle. Still, she wasn't stuck there if something went wrong: she could get off in a matter of seconds. Flo would be fine.

Florence smiled. Tara was, just a little bit, starting to sound more like the confident, encouraging, and upbeat friend she had always known. She'd be fine.

With that, they hugged again, promised to stay in touch by ice shard and waved good-bye to each other.

Florence turned that strange grey-white all over and her features froze, then, starting from her head but moving stealthily slice by diagonal slice, particles of her flew out of the open window until the space was empty and Tara was alone.

Tara turned glumly back to her room. She was alone again, up in her high tower. What next, she asked herself, as she made ready to go to bed, totally worn out from the day's excitement. She removed her huntress costume, disheveled from the evening's adventures, and hung it on a peg at the back of a wardrobe.

Tara paused and regarded her reflection in the vanity. She was uneasy, and she didn't quite know why. Maybe it was the inaction. She disliked inaction. She wanted to be involved, doing something, bringing about success. Maybe she could do some research at Castle Stonedell. She was unlikely to find much on Ariel's condition, but she could give it a try.

But no, that was not what was bothering her, was it? Tara stared out of the window, frustrated. No, realized Tara slowly. The question bothering her was what she was to do with her parents. It was slow and painful coming around to it, but she was, gradually and crabwise. It was this: Tara was confronting something wholly and entirely different from all her previous escapades with her friends. Heretofore, Tara had sneaked out to the ocean or the desert or the forests to do something or get something that had not had much consequence. It might have been dazzle dust or Atalanta's golden balls or just to find a library. But it most always was important only to her or one or two other persons, and no worries if Tara came up short. As a result, Tara never felt the need to tell her parents anything.

But this was different. Two lives depended on what she and Florence were doing, and maybe more, depending on what happened with Cloud Castle. Her parents knew about Ariel, had seen her fly, and met Florence. It was no longer possible to minimize her friends and their abilities.

Even if Tara wanted to any more, she thought, with a twitch of her lips.

No, there was a lot more at stake now, and the difference between now and what had happened out in the Great Forest was that Tara was fully aware of the stakes from the very start.

Tara sat down on the bed and cupped her chin in her hands. What to do? When she had been young, she had looked to her mother as a model. Well, of course, she still loved her mother, but she wasn't really much help in situations like this. Her mother was mostly concerned about social events and Tara's dresses and her hair.

Tara thought about her father. His counsel was more useful and applicable but still only went so far. He would be more focused on protecting her as his only child and heir to the throne. He couldn't really understand either.

That left, Tara decided, just one person. Her grandmother. Whom she had never known. What would Ysolde do, she asked herself. Ysolde had been an adventuress herself, and bold, and strong, and had saved Brythrony. Ysolde would have to offer her guidance.

But Ysolde wasn't able to speak to her. So Tara would have to imagine her counsel. Tara thought hard. As near as Tara could guess, Ysolde would urge her to tell her parents about her friends and all she had done. At least, she guessed, most of what she had done. She'd urge honesty, full and complete.

Tara thought back to her complaints from earlier in the evening, the ones she had voiced to Florence. Her parents hadn't understood and appreciated all she had done for Brythrony. But this was because she, Tara, had never really told them all she had done. Tara sighed, and with the dawning understanding that she was, herself, at least partially to blame for her unhappiness earlier that evening. It wasn't fully her parent's fault that they weren't grateful. They couldn't be grateful when they didn't know all Tara had done. If she wanted their understanding, she would have to tell them more, and much more.

Tara got into bed and composed herself for sleep. Turning, she glanced out of the window, a window she kept open now, rain or shine, summer or winter. She didn't want to block incoming message bubbles or a possibly arriving Florence or Ariel. The stars were bright through the trees, she saw. Somewhere up there, though, was a cloud with a castle atop it, and Florence was up there with it. Out there, beyond the clouds and the trees and even the forests of Brythrony, were the ocean, other fields, other forests, and yes, even the Lost Quarter. Tomorrow, she would have to share them, share them with her parents. Tara was a little downhearted about this. It was nice to have one's own secret adventures. But the only way forward was to reveal them to her parents. Most of them, that is. Ysolde would have insisted.

Tara went down to breakfast the next morning in a mood of determination mixed with fatalism. "Hi, Mom and Dad," she greeted them on arriving at the far end of the family breakfast table.

"Aren't you going to say good morning?" asked Tara, in response to their silence.

"Why, of course, dear. Good morning."

It wasn't the most auspicious way to start, but then Tara wasn't in the best of moods either. They must still be mad from the night before.

Her mother set down her cup and fixed her with a studied gaze, which Tara soon found unnerving. Her father, instead of looking at Tara at all, stared determinedly into his plate. Uh-oh, thought Tara and took a tentative bite of her porridge, suddenly unsure how to begin.

At last her father looked up from his plate and spoke. "Look, Tara, I'm sorry about last night. I shouldn't have been angry with you. You were doing something important, which was saving your friend. You had a good reason to be away from the banquet."

Tara murmured something along the lines that she was grateful for the understanding.

"I didn't understand all that you were doing, what with this talk of bottles and so on, but it must have been important and it clearly helped her, so I'm glad about that."

Her mother picked up. "We just wanted you to enjoy yourself and have a good time. At your ball and your banquet. So that's why we were…a little upset that you weren't there for all of it. But saving Ariel is more important. We understand that."

Tara set down her spoon. If this wasn't the opening she needed, what was it? "Um, well, thanks Mom. And Dad. I'm sorry I couldn't really enjoy the ball and banquet either. But Ariel—"

"We understand, dear."

"Right, we—Florence and I—had to save Ariel. She's okay now." Tara swallowed hard and then plunged forward, explaining as best she could what a stasis bottle was and, as background on Maribess, a few more details of the confrontation in the Great Forest. Poor things, she would recall later, they were being confronted with all sorts of things and people that were totally beyond their experience. Her mother's cheeks went ashen at some of the details on what had happened in the Great Forest and the Lost Quarter, but her father bore up reasonably well. "I don't know what to do next," Tara concluded. "But I don't want to leave them in stasis bottles.

There must be a way to revive them. Maybe," and here Tara hesitated out of long habit over sensitivities to mermaids, "Marina might have some ideas."

Armorica didn't say anything. Childeric mused for a second then asked, "But why revive Maribess? Why not just leave her be?"

The thought had crossed Tara's mind. "I don't think that's a good idea. I don't know what the dust does to someone over a longer period. Does it just induce sleep? Or are there any other effects? Then Maribess deserves justice. We all do. We can't get that if she's asleep." And, well, Tara didn't want to say it, but what if there were other Underworlders on the way on the expectation that Maribess had been successful? Brythrony might need Maribess to deal with them.

Her father picked up the thread naturally though, being more accustomed to having to think strategically. "I guess," he added, "what if her friends come looking for her?"

Tara nodded.

"So then, what are you thinking of doing?" asked her mother at last.

"Great question, Mom. I think I just have to wait. To see if Marina has any ideas." As she had expected, her mother brightened measurably. "Also, I guess I could try to do some research around the castle to see if maybe we might have anything that might help."

Her mother and father exchanged another quick glance. "We have a library," began her mother, hopefully. Her father nodded solemnly.

"That's a great start. Maybe there's something for me there."

For the first time that morning, her mother smiled, happy that Tara wasn't proposing some extended absence as the means to revive Ariel. Tara smiled back, acutely conscious of why her mother was happy, even as she was happy for her, and even though she fully expected that some sort of absence would be necessary ultimately. But some other day. Not today.

"Of course, dear! What a wonderful idea! It's in the East Tower. Across a suite of rooms on the second and third floors. An older gentleman takes care of it for us; he's also our bard."

Tara knew what a bard was. He was a musician who played a small harp and could sing songs about the distant past for entertainment. Songs mostly about heroes, kings, and queens. And princesses.

"Thanks, Mom. What's his name?"

"Bardwell. Fitting, isn't it?"

The rest of the breakfast passed pleasantly enough and, at its conclusion, Tara jumped up and told her parents that she would be heading to the East Tower. Her parents bade her good luck and remained behind at the table. To talk about her, obviously. Tara shrugged. It was understandable. She had dropped an awful lot on them that morning.

On the second floor of the East Tower, Tara found a thick wooden door that, when she pushed on it with sufficient force, creaked open. Before her were shelves stacked high with books, except for a small oasis consisting of a desk and chair, though themselves strewn with an assortment of folios, compendiums, scrolls, and notebooks. "Hello? Anyone here?" called Tara, tentatively.

Tara approached the desk. She ran her finger across an exposed corner of the desk. The desk hadn't been dusted for years. Clearly Bardwell only managed the books, not the housekeeping.

She moved the chair from the drawers. Maybe there was something in here? But she stopped herself. She was there to find the books she needed, not to rifle through some old desk that hadn't been dusted in years. "Hello?" she called more loudly. "Is anyone here?"

"Hello!" came a voice immediately behind her. Tara whirled to find a thin, elderly man gazing at her in curiosity.

"Hi. Are you... Bardwell?"

"Yes! Yes, yes, yes indeed! I am!"

Tara and Bardwell stood in the dim light from the far windows filtering through the books and dust motes suspended in the thick air, eying each other speculatively.

"And who might you be?" he enquired at last.

"I'm Princess Tara. Of the Realm, Tara. Of Brythrony," she added automatically.

"Oh! Oh ho!"

What a very different man, thought Tara. Just a different generation, she guessed.

But he didn't bow elaborately, as she might have expected from such a prior generation. Instead, he simply asked, "Well, Your Highness... how can I help You?"

"I'd like to do some research. A friend's in trouble and I need to help her."

"Ah! Hm! Really! What sort of trouble?"

Tara explained, confining her story to the relevant bits.

"You say she used a sort of straw, a blowpipe, to puff out the dust, hm?"

"That's right. In fact, I have with me a sample of the dust."

Bardwell pulled back. "Careful! We could be put to sleep as well!"

The sudden alarm elicited a smile from Tara. "No worries! I scraped it from the floor into this bag so we'd be safe."

Reassured, Bardwell drew near again and cautiously examined the fine powder Tara gently shook onto a piece of paper on the desk. Shortly, he was studying the powder intently, his concerns apparently forgotten as his eyes were so close to it that Tara became apprehensive.

"Hm! Interesting! Hey! So, maybe we take a look at it through my magnifying glass?"

"What's that? What sort of magic is that?" Tara had never heard of magic in Brythrony. Could this glass be new and powerful?

He smiled into the distance as he pulled a thick piece of glass from the desk's belly drawer and began to scrutinize the dust through it. "It's not magic. It's optics. It's glass that's been shaped so as to make things beneath it look larger."

Tara leaned over to look. The dust underneath the glass did indeed look larger. But it wasn't actually larger, it just looked larger. To Tara, it did seem to be a kind of magic though. She had never seen such a thing, despite journeying across many more corners of her world than most others and having seen much in her travels.

"It looks purple. And black," she remarked, softly.

"Yes! Oh, yes! And see here: this speck here. Here, look at it closely. Do you see?"

Tara didn't see. It looked like the others, blackish-purplish in color and with irregular edges.

"Does it look like anything you've seen before?"

Not to Tara's recollection, and she said so.

"Does it look like sand?"

"No. Not like sand. As best as I can remember." Tara cast her mind back to all the different types of sand she had seen, when she had first met Marina on the Secret Island, in the Lost Quarter when dealing with the Sand Golem and Silicana, and on other occasions. "Not to me."

"I don't think so either. It doesn't look crystalline." He looked up at Tara. "Sand is from crystals, You know. Mostly quartz crystals." This was also new to Tara, though she had never given the origins of sand much thought.

Bardwell continued. "Take a closer look. What else does it look like? You may have seen it before, also as a fine dust."

Tara thought hard, thinking of all the fine dusts and powders that she could imagine that occurred naturally. "Pollen!" she said at last. "Like pollen."

Bardwell nodded vigorously. "Yes! Yes, yes! I think so too. See the jagged edges of each little particle: it looks like pollen."

They gazed a few moments longer at the fine dust, and then Bardwell replaced the magnifying glass in the desk. "Hm! Possibly pollen. Maybe not. But maybe so! So, let's look it up in a book on plants. I know its somewhere in this library."

Now they were really making progress in figuring out the nature of the dust Maribess had blown on Ariel, thought Tara. "Yes! The book!" she replied, unconsciously imitating Bardwell.

Bardwell wandered around several stacks then stopped in front of a shelf that, to Tara's eyes, looked like the others. "Here! Here, I believe!" he mumbled excitedly and began removing and replacing books after a glance at their titles. Tara watched intently as at last he pulled out a modest book bound in green cloth with black lettering on the cover. "Here it is!" he cried triumphantly and, pulling her by the sleeve, placed the book atop several other books on the desk and opened it to its table of contents.

"Now, this is a book on plants," he told Tara. "We think Your dust could be pollen, so I'm hoping this book may help. You say Your friend—and Your enemy—are unconscious, is that right?"

Tara nodded.

"Good—well, not good, but You know what I mean!—this book lists all the useful plants we know in this kingdom and then some. I seem to remember, in a section at the back, mention of a plant that has unusual sleep-inducing properties. Let me see…

"Here!" Bardwell turned to the back to a section entitled simply, "Other unusual plants." Scanning the sub-headings, he found an entry and read it to Tara of a plant whose spores, when breathed, cause the victim to fall into a deep sleep.

"That's it!" exclaimed Tara.

"Yes! Yes! Furthermore, and if the spores are properly treated, they cause death!"

Tara's blood ran cold, yet neither were dead. Had Maribess meant to kill them but had not treated the spores correctly? Or had she purposefully not treated them, for fear of falling herself a victim of them somehow? "Where is this plant found? And is there an antidote?"

"Hm! Hm! It says that this plant is only found underground—"

"That's it! Sundra and Maribess are from the Underground Kingdom. But what about an antidote?"

"I'm reading! I'm reading! Yes!"

The moments crept painfully by, so much so that Tara wanted to snatch the book from Bardwell to read it herself. But that would not revive her friend any sooner, so she quelled her impatience, though having to grit her teeth in doing so.

At last Bardwell spoke. "Hm! Yes, it does mention something that is useful. Shall I read it to you?"

Tara crossed her eyes and bit her lip but nodded silently.

"Here it is! Listen:

'We found that one of our party—'"

Bardwell broke off to turn to Tara, "This is from a diary entry, and the author was with a group that was exploring and happened upon the plant.

'... *after breathing in the spores, or pollen, of this plant, fell fast asleep and could not be awoken. We searched in haste for something that would revive him, but nothing, neither water, nor smelling salts, nor anything else, was successful. At last, in desperation, we concluded that the antidote might come from the very same plant that empoisoned him, much as antidotes to snake venom are frequently derived from the venom itself, and so we ground to a fine powder various parts of the plant for our unlucky comrade to inhale, as he could neither drink nor eat. At last, the plant's leaves had the desired effect and he awoke. Further inhalations brought him altogether round, and he was most thirsty.*'"

Bardwell pointed to a line drawing and some other sketches of the leaves and its spores accompanying the text. "There. The leaves. Ground to a powder." His hand traced an arrow running across the page. "Here, the author calls the plant 'mycolix'. He doesn't say why."

Tara nodded, her mind far away. It made so much sense that Sundra, who had to be behind this, would have chosen a substance with which she would be familiar but which she knew would be utterly mysterious to surface dwellers. Now Tara needed the plant's restorative leaves, which meant she would have to venture underground herself again.

Unless, it suddenly occurred to her, Maribess had thought to keep some on her own person.

"Bardwell, you've been a tremendous help." She smiled up at the elderly man, who beamed in response. "May I take notes from the book on the plant? I'll want them should I go searching for it."

"Absolutely! Yes!" agreed Bardwell. "May I copy all this for Your Highness and have it delivered to You in a day or so?"

Tara smiled sweetly. "That would be so nice of you! I'd appreciate it an awful lot!" Normally, Tara would have done this herself, as she hated to ask others to do what she thought she could do herself. But she had some things she wanted to get to right away, such as searching Maribess for the antidote and speaking with Florence to see how she was getting along. Plus, if she were to have to journey to the Grey Mountains back to the entrance to the Underworld, she might want to ask Florence if her sister, the Snow Princess, might join. "Yes, Bardwell, that would be awfully nice of you."

Bardwell bowed.

Tara glanced out of the window to check on where the sun might lie in the sky. "Oh, my goodness, look at the time! I should get back to meet my parents! So sorry to leave you like this but I have to go!" Tara seized and shook the astonished Bardwell's hand and dashed off without another word.

"Good-bye, Your Highness!" called Bardwell after her, waving at the vanishing figure leaping down the stairs of the East Tower two at a time.

Tara, now back in her room, was speaking to Florence via the ice shard. "So, I checked, but didn't find anything."

"No? Nothing? But what a great idea that was! To check Maribess herself for the antidote!"

Tara had been rather pleased herself. "Thanks! Yes, it's really too bad I didn't find anything. It's looking more and more like I'll have to go back to the Underground Kingdom. The book seemed to suggest the plant was not uncommon there; maybe I won't have to go very far down."

Florence only nodded on the other end.

"How are you getting along up there on Cloud Castle?"

"Okay, I guess. My news is that I've found what looks to be a control center. It's like a small cabin with windows all the way around, and it's forward and in the tallest tower, so it has a great view. There're a whole bunch of levers there too, but I don't know what they do. I've been too afraid of touching them and pitching everything to earth!"

That made sense, agreed Tara. "There are no instructions or labels or anything to help?"

Florence shook her head. "Not really. Some squiggles and signs and numbers at either end of the levers but not much. At least it doesn't look like I'm in danger of hitting a mountain, as the winds have blown us out to sea, and to the east, as far as I can tell."

That was a relief. At least Florence and the castle were safe for the moment. "That's great! Another thought is that you could just take Cloud Castle up high enough so that you could never possibly hit a mountain."

Flo frowned through the shard. "That was my thinking too, at first. But it's a lot colder the higher up you get. 'Course, I don't mind that—" and she smiled "—but I've come to learn that a lot of birds roost here. Long-time friends of Ariel, I guess. So, I'm afraid to take the castle too high, as it might be too cold for them."

"Oh," replied Tara, disappointed.

"Plus, I've come to find that other birds are accustomed to visiting at certain times of the day. So, Cloud Castle has to descend intermittently so it's at an altitude they can reach. It looks like only the stronger birds make that sort of trip, but still, I couldn't let them try and then fall back to earth from fatigue."

Wow, thought Princess Tara. She hadn't imagined it was so complicated managing Cloud Castle. "I still wonder how Ariel manages the castle's flight while she's away. It sounds complex."

"The same thought has occurred to me." Florence sighed. "Near as I can tell, a lot of it happens on its own, like when it ascends and descends over the course of the day." Flo sighed again and glanced away, to the side at something outside the shard's range. Then she turned back. "It'd sure be nice to have you here, Tara: you're really good at puzzles like these."

"That's awfully kind of you! Thanks so much!"

Flo nodded. She knew this. All the other princesses knew this as well.

Tara brought the shard closer to her so she could lower her voice. "So, like I said before, I'm going to have to go back to the Underground Kingdom. The entrance is in the Grey Mountains. Do you think there might be any chance that your sister, the Snow Princess, might be able to meet me to give me a little help, if only in the mountains?"

Ice Princess Florence considered the request thoughtfully. "I'm sure she could. She's not one for adventure, but I think she'd help out on this. She's awfully much a homebody but, once she gets going, she can really be useful!"

Sounds just like the sort of person I'll need, mused Tara silently. Aloud, she replied, "Great. How can I reach her? Because in the past, I only ever saw or spoke with her when I was with you."

"No, she doesn't have a princess purse, so she doesn't have message bubbles. I'll raise her on one of these ice shards and ask for you. If she's willing, she can find you on the ice shard you've got—they're all linked."

Good, thought Tara, that's settled. "Thanks for that. Speak with her as soon as you have the opportunity, because I need to get going. The sooner the better."

The ice shard went opaque and Florence's face vanished. The next step was one that Tara was not looking forward to, but she knew she would have to do it. She would have to tell her parents of her coming departure. She wondered what her parents would say. At least it was to revive Ariel, which they both knew was critical. But Tara would have to tell them about Snow Princess Crystal too. Yes, it was more effort, but she would have to keep her parents informed. It was almost like a "promise" she had made to her grandmother. Anyway, she wouldn't be leaving that very day; she still had to prepare. They should like that, she figured.

As it was, they did not. Not that they weren't glad that she wasn't leaving that very day, but rather, they weren't mollified by the fact that she was staying only as long as it took to prepare to depart on another trip.

"Why? Why?" complained her mother. "And who is this snow person you'll travel with?"

"Mom, she's not some random 'snow person'; she's Snow Princess Crystal."

"I don't know who that is."

Tara stifled the near-overwhelming impulse to roll her eyes. Wasn't this conversation so much like the one she had had with them when they had been talking about Ariel and Marina? No, she allowed, her mother couldn't know Crystal. But, on the other hand, why was that so important? "Mom, please, I have to revive Ariel. She helped save our kingdom, remember?"

Her father was much more understanding. "Tara is quite right. Ariel was trying to save us and everyone present at that banquet. It's our duty to do whatever we can to bring her back. We owe her that."

"Thanks, Dad."

"But I don't like you traveling alone to the Grey Mountains to look for this plant."

"But that's where the plant is!"

"So I'm going with you."

Tara was so shocked that she caught her breath. What an unbelievably bad idea. "Um, Dad, that's super kind of you. It's a great idea… and all. But I don't really think that it'd be such a good idea."

"What do you mean? How can it be 'a great idea' and yet not be?"

Tara concentrated hard on phrasing her objections. She dared not say it was too dangerous, because then they'd say it was too dangerous for her. "What I mean is that I think it's a great idea for you to come along but not such a great idea from the perspective of the kingdom. After all, you're the king, and you should stay in Brythrony in the palace. To rule. Like that."

Her father was pleasantly surprised. This was the first time Tara had taken into consideration the good order and proper functioning of Brythrony. "You make a good point, young princess, but we shouldn't be gone that long, I expect. Besides, your mother would be here, and she's just as capable as I am."

Armorica straightened to her fullest height and nodded confidently. "You know, I have done this sort of thing before."

"Well, all right, but—another thing—it's really not that comfortable, traveling like I do. On horseback. All the way to the Grey Mountains."

Her father chuckled and his eyes twinkled. "Can I seriously be hearing this? You know, I've been on many campaigns with no comforts whatsoever! No, I'm going too. It'll be a good father-daughter adventure."

Tara cringed. Yes, she would have to do it; Ysolde would insist. Plus, he seemed determined. Whatever would she tell Snow Princess Crystal? On the other hand, hadn't Marina's father once journeyed with them halfway to the Lost Quarter? Though it was also true that his trident could do all sorts of magic and Aenon was, well, how to put it, good to have along. While her father, she feared, was probably far less so.

"Well, okay. I guess. But I've warned you!"

Her father dismissed this with a wave. "Young lady, I know more about privation in the field than you can imagine."

Tara didn't say anything. No, she didn't know of his campaigns, since they had been undertaken before she had been born. But he couldn't possibly imagine all the incredibly scary stuff she had faced already with just Daystar and her friends.

"Okay, okay, you're coming. But I'll be leading, as I've researched this plant. Also, we're taking Maribess—in the bottle—as I'm thinking we'll leave her with her own kind under the mountains."

Her father looked puzzled for the first time, which inordinately satisfied Tara. "Under the Grey Mountains?"

"Right. And you'll have to trust me on this. That's where she's from, and they should take her back. Also, remember Crystal should be joining us. Don't worry, she should be able to take care of herself."

"Who is Crystal anyway? But fine; if she can take care of herself, I don't mind her joining."

Oh yes, thought Tara. If Crystal was anything like Florence, she could certainly take care of herself. "Super, Dad. Glad to have you along. We'll be leaving in a day or so, so you'll need to get your horse and pack ready. We'll want an early start too, to make real progress on our first day."

Her father snorted in disbelief and looked to his wife. "Listen to this! Me, a veteran campaigner, getting orders like this!"

The queen smiled back at him, her eyes twinkling with amusement. "You'd better do what she says! She's in charge, and you agreed to it!"

Tara left for the stables to find Geoffrey and oversee Daystar's preparations. As she walked, she felt again, keenly, how vulnerable she was without her Ring of Shooting Stars. She would be in the Underground Kingdom again, but now with her father, for whom she felt some measure of responsibility. Poor man: he was great and all and was probably ready—she had to admit—to undertake this journey as much as she was. But how would he handle the Underground Kingdom, and what if they encountered magic? Whatever sort of magic. It was not as if he had done so well in handling Maribess's black dust. They still didn't—really—accept Ariel.

But there was nothing she could do about that. She had to find the leaves of the mycolix plant, and she wanted to turn Maribess over to the Underground Kingdom, which she assumed the Sebastos Reynam still ruled. Tara didn't want to think much further ahead than that. Deep down, she was hoping she could count on Reynam for help in finding the plant if she had trouble. Maybe he would even provide her an escort back to Brythrony if there was any sort of trouble. In spite of these uncertainties, Tara was feeling better at last. She had never been much interested in detailed planning anyway; now she was back where she was most comfortable: acting and forcing events to go her way rather than strategizing and preparing endless and intricate contingencies.

Princess Crystal

Two days later, Princess Tara and her father bid Armorica good-bye and mounted their horses. A troop of the palace guard would accompany them to the foothills of the Grey Mountains, which were about two days' ride away. From there, Tara and her father would proceed alone, as the terrain became more rugged at that point, and Tara thought the guards would be more hindrance than help.

Despite Tara's insistence that she would make all the decisions surrounding the expedition, her father had balked at her initial intent to make the journey without any accompaniment whatsoever. It would not be wise for the two of them to go alone, he had maintained, as he was king and she was princess, even if he were skilled in arms and she had won the tournament in horse archery. She had protested that it would not be possible for a vast retinue to make their way at any decent pace into the upper reaches of the mountains. Eventually, in a compromise painstakingly brokered by Armorica, Tara had consented to being escorted by ten horsemen to the base of the first peak; Childeric had agreed that their escort would encamp there and hold the horses of Childeric and Tara. From there, father and daughter would continue alone to the entrance of the Underground Kingdom.

It was there, at the entrance or thereabouts, that Tara expected Princess Crystal would show to provide any assistance they might need.

Thus, the pair, so accompanied by ten horsemen, headed for the mountains. But hardly had they ridden for the morning when her father called a halt. Why on earth so early, asked Tara of her father, with a touch of irritation, pointing to the sun, which was still high over the treetops. He had replied grandly, "Because, dear daughter, we are king and princess, and come the night we must have a tent in which to sleep and a fire about which to warm ourselves. These take some time to prepare, as you will see." Tara vented a sigh of exasperation that she did not altogether try to hide.

What about the privations of the field, she had wondered. "But, at this rate, it will take us days to get to the Grey Mountains!"

"Why don't you," he countered, "hunt up some dinner? Put your archery skills to good use!"

Fine, thought Tara, reaching for her quiver. As long as she didn't have to dress the game, as that was icky, loathe though she was to admit it. Ariel had always done that for them, as that sort of gore didn't bother her, surrounded by birds of prey as she was at Cloud Castle.

About mid-morning the next day, and after breakfasting and furling their tents, they started again. It was nice to have the companionship of the Guard, she admitted, and without question they were safer, but she was unused to it, and it seemed to make the journey, in many senses, so much more complicated. Though they did not quite reach the foothills of the Grey Mountains by the end of the second day, they were close enough that she was comfortable in suggesting that the guard camp there and she and her father proceed by themselves the next morning.

Just then, Tara noted a small globe floating in the air approaching her. "Ah!" she exclaimed, recognizing it as a message bubble. She hesitated a moment, as this would be the first time anyone other than a princess had witnessed this means of communication. But, she shrugged, it was time to tell and show all, so she extended a hand to receive it.

Her father watched her curiously. "What is that? What are you doing?"

The small globe landed gently and soundlessly in Tara's right palm. "A message bubble," answered Tara airily. "You needn't be alarmed!" she added, though she instantly regretted her superior tone. After all, how could her father know what these were? "It's from one of my friends," she explained, contritely. "Listen!"

Tara blew gently on the bubble and, after a whispery "pop," she heard a familiar voice. "Oh, Tara, I got your message! We looked everywhere, my father and I—"

"It's Marina," Tara told her father.

"—and we couldn't find anything on what to do with Ariel! Absolutely no mention in the library of any sort of this dust or how to handle it! We're so sorry! Please let us know if we can be of any other assistance though!"

That was sweet of her, thought Tara. Even if she and her father couldn't help. Anyway, she felt they were on the right track as it was.

"Is Marina the mermaid?" asked her father when the voice had died away. "And how does she talk through a bubble?"

Tara considered first her hand, still outstretched, and then the sky. "Well, Dad, it's kind of a long story. But this is how we—my friends and I—send each other messages. We do it a lot. To help each other, mostly."

"Oh," was all he said, though he eyed her hand suspiciously.

By the afternoon of the next day, Tara and Childeric were above the tree line, and the ground beneath them had turned rocky, necessitating ever more care to pick their way forward. Childeric paused to rest after skirting a particularly difficult slope. He was carrying a heavy pack and finding the going hard. Still, he said not a word of complaint, conscious as he was that he had asked to come on this adventure.

"Let's stop for a rest, Dad," counselled Tara. Though also burdened with a pack, it was not as heavy as her father's. Then, also, she could see she was in better condition than her father who, perhaps, had enjoyed a few too many banquets since his campaigning days.

"No, we can't do that. We need to keep going and make as much progress as we can by nightfall."

"But I'm tired," lied Tara. "I'd like to rest a moment."

"Of course! Why didn't you say so?" answered her father, but he seemed more than happy to relax a moment. They both shed their packs and sat down against a particularly imposing boulder that looked big enough that it would not be moved by their weight.

Tara eyed her father covertly. He was red in the face and breathing heavily. Poor guy. She didn't dare ask how he was; he'd only deny what she could clearly see. Instead, she said, "It's been a climb so far, hasn't it? But I think we're making good progress."

Her father answered, after a short pause, "Yes, we're making good progress. You're doing well too."

"Thanks, Dad. That's really nice of you."

"But if you're getting tired, just let me know! I can take a little more from your pack, if it's getting heavy for you."

"Thanks again, Dad. No, it's not too heavy yet. But if it gets heavy, I'll definitely let you know. And thanks for the offer."

"No problem."

Tara mused over this offer. It was thoughtful. But the way it was looking, she would be taking some of his load sooner than she would be giving him hers. Tara looked up into the sky. It wasn't so clear and blue any more. "Say, Dad, I need to speak to my friend for a moment, so I'm just going to step away for a minute, okay?"

Her father jerked his head around. "Tara, are you going crazy? How are you going to speak with anyone up here?"

"Well, with this, Dad," replied Tara, and she flourished briefly the ice shard. "I'm going to speak to Flo. Just to check in with her." And to ask if the Snow Princess would be showing up, because it was starting to get cold.

Her father was awfully curious, she could tell, but he stayed where he was—maybe because he was tired—and Tara stepped around to the other side of the boulder. "Are you there, Flo?" she whispered.

Florence appeared after a few seconds' delay. "Hey! How're things?"

"Fine. We're making our way up the mountain to the cave. Probably more than halfway up, based on where I remember it was the last time we entered."

The Ice Princess's face brightened. "Great! You're making super progress!"

Tara nodded. "Did you speak with Crystal? Will she be able to come?"

"Oh! You know, I haven't checked in with Crissy for a while. Let me do that right away. Keep the shard on you; she'll find you by that." With that, Florence vanished, and Tara was left again with a flat piece of ice that, inexplicably, was never either cold or melted. Tara fingered it a moment, always fascinated by it, then turned to the horizon. It would be dark before long. Given the altitude, the night would be fiercely cold.

Just then, the wind down the slope whipped Tara's cloak, and she winced at its bite. The sky was darkening fast. Maybe a storm was coming. "Dad! I think we'd better start looking for shelter!"

His voice came from around the other side. "I agree, Tara. But with this wind, we won't keep our tent if we try to pitch it! I think we'd better dig in as best we can here, in the lee of the wind."

Tara had a terrible flashback of the last time she had sought refuge amongst boulders. It had been when she and Ariel had been in the Lost Quarter. How different that had been from where she was now: for Ariel, substitute her father, and for the desert heat, fierce gales and possibly an ice storm. At least, she consoled herself, there couldn't be spiders. She shook her head to clear the memory and raised her voice so that her father could hear above a wind that was rising steadily to a sustained howl. "I think you're right, but let's be sure first there's nothing already living there before we get too comfortable!"

The best they could find from a quick search in the falling light was protection on two sides, one side of which only half-shielded them. They stacked their packs as a further measure against the wind. The one good side was solid though, comprised as it was of an enormous boulder that looked immovable. The boulder's slant also provided a bit of an overhang, under which they could huddle from a light rain mixed with sleet that had begun to fall in swishing gusts. Night was drawing on fast, and the rain had already yielded to a driving sleet interspersed with snow flurries.

"Looks like it's getting worse," observed her father, stoically.

Tara nodded, her father's face barely visible in the fading light. She was beginning to regret the journey. She reproached herself. As usual, she had come much worse prepared than she should have, and this time she had insisted on being the leader. Now she and her father were—possibly—in danger of freezing. No, it was not the first time she had thought herself in deep trouble, and everything had always worked out in the end. But at what point would it come down to being the last?

Tara's teeth began to chatter. "N-n-nope! N-n-n-not g-g-get-t-ting any b-b-better!" she managed.

The snow flew wilder about them and washed into their makeshift shelter in scurrying eddies. The two crept closer together, and Tara's father tried to tuck in their cloaks still more tightly to keep the clawing wind and temperature at bay.

"No," her father said, firmly, and through nearly clenched teeth as an especially strong gust of wind pelted them with a shower of snow. Tara thought she would freeze solid, she was so thoroughly numbed.

"Anybody here?" came a voice suddenly, so mild and tentative that they would have never thought it was real had it not, seemingly, come from immediately beside them. "Princess Tara? You are here somewhere, right? Tara?"

"Here! H-h-here!" croaked Tara, so difficult was it to keep her vibrating teeth from stifling her words.

"Oh! There you are! I thought I'd find you through the ice shard. That's what Florence said. Gosh, you look cold!"

"Who's that?" demanded her father, momentarily forgetting how cold he was.

"Th-that's S-Sn-Snow P-p-p-princess C-c-c-Crystal!"

He father had evidently heard only the last word. "Crystal? Your friend? You can't be serious! Up here?"

"Someone with you, Tara?"

"C-c-c-Crystal, c-c-could you warm us up a l-l-little? P-p-please!"

"Sure! I'm forgetting how cold it is for you. Sorry!" Almost immediately, the wind died away and the snow gusts ceased, and a kind of warm glow slowly diffused about them. Before them stood a girl of Tara's age, with platinum blonde hair braided into plaits, mild light-blue eyes, and a handsome rectangular face distinguished by a strong chin and high cheekbones. She stood casually dressed in a dove-grey dress, fur-lined through the sleeves and with a hem that swept below her knees to skim the tops of her doeskin lace-up leather boots. "Hi! There you are!" she called, he right hand half up in a somewhat hesitant wave and smiling at them with a genuineness and warmth that belied their freezing conditions. On her head was a circlet of a silvery metal with irregularly shaped diamonds or crystals inlaid in them; Tara saw that it looked much like the one her sister sometimes wore.

Tara's father gaped. "Who... who are you? Have I died from the cold? And you're a vision?"

Crystal looked to Tara, puzzled. Tara elbowed her father. "Dad, it's Snow Princess Crystal! Come on, remember yourself!" That was very awkward, was all Princess Tara remembered of that moment afterwards, though she had to admit that, had she not known about Crystal—much less expected her to appear as she did and could—she might have feared she had lost her mind also. But her father, wincing from the sharp thrust of Tara's nudge, said nothing more than an uncertain, "How do you do?" Otherwise, he stared.

Crystal smiled again and inclined her head. "Hi! I'm Crystal!"

"And this is my father. He joined me to... help out."

"Oh. Right. Nice to meet you."

Tara spoke up quickly to take the conversation forward and before her father could cause any further awkwardness. "We're so glad you to see you, Crystal! You came just in time. It was getting awfully cold."

She appraised them both critically. "I can imagine. You're not so well dressed for this altitude. But no matter. I can take you wherever you need to go from here."

This was unexpected. Tara had imagined the three of them continuing up the mountain together, walking. "You can take us from here? But how? Flo couldn't take me up the Cloud Castle; I was too heavy."

Crystal thought for a moment, turning her head slightly sideways and gazing off into the frantically swirling snow just beyond their circle of warmth and calm. "Hm," she murmured. "You can't be that heavy. And my sister's pretty strong. Oh! I know! It's because your castle, from where you were starting, was too warm. The colder it is, the stronger we are. Both of us." She gestured to the mountainside where they stood, and the snowstorm that had gradually intensified into a blizzard, but by which they stood untouched within Crystal's protective globe. "Here, up on the mountain—and moving further up the mountain too, right?"

Tara nodded.

"Right, that's what I thought; well, it's cold enough that I can transport both of you. That's what I mean."

"What do you mean, 'transport you'?" interjected her father, still confused.

Crystal's eyebrows twitched, and her face became quizzical. "Well, I mean, just like that. Transport you. I'll take you up."

"Take us up?"

"Dad, why don't we just get going? Yes, now, I'm thinking. After all, no reason to stay here. Let's just gather up everything and get ready to go."

"No need to pack," said Crystal brightly. "Just grab it and hold on to it. You know roughly where we're going?"

"Roughly."

"That's good enough. I won't set us down anywhere unsafe."

Tara and her father hastily assembled their backpacks and blankets about their feet, her father still dazed but coming around to accepting that all this was truly happening.

"Now, whereabouts are we going?" enquired Crystal, and Tara pointed up the mountain's slope. "All right; hold on to your things!" With that, the globe shrank in around them and they were obliged to move closer to Crystal until they were standing next to her. A thick, soft carpet of snow speedily gathered underfoot, though neither Tara nor her father felt the slightest chill, enveloped as they were by the Snow Princess's protective bubble. There was an intensified swirl of snow around them, the ground fell away beneath them, and they moving up the mountain.

Childeric gazed down at the mountainside sliding below them in amazement.

"Wow," marveled Tara. This was so much easier than going on foot!

Crystal flashed a smiled at her. "Seems so natural to me! I don't get to do this much with others. It reminds me how much fun it is!"

Though the blowing snow and darkness made discerning details of the mountainside difficult, Tara remembered that the mouth of the cave leading to the Underground Kingdom had been large enough for pack animals to exit. She also remembered it as being uncommonly sheltered, as if an intelligent hand had played a role in its construction. Funny though, she thought: where she expected to see the mouth, none was present. Could it have collapsed, she wondered?

"Try over there," she suggested to Crystal. "That ledge looks familiar. Even though I don't see a cave. But maybe a landslide covered it."

Crystal set the bubble down on the ledge. "Here we are! Tara, you think it's here?"

Tara's father peered into the gloom. "I don't see how you can tell one way or the other; it's getting so dark!"

Crystal looked up into the sky. "Hm. There's nearly full-moon tonight. Let's see if we can use that to help us." She moved her hand in a small arc, leaving behind a glittering trail of snowy motes. Another manipulation of her hand and she brought forth from the motes a curved piece of ice. This she held up into the sky and, by twisting her hand one way or the other, reflected the moon's light such that it played quite brightly along the rocky face of the cliff before them.

"It's like a torch," exclaimed Tara.

"A little. But I need a source of light to gather and focus."

Tara eyed Crystal's curved piece of ice with interest and curiosity. What did it remind her of? Why, that was it! It reminded her of the curved piece of glass that Bardwell had produced to magnify the dust from Maribess's blowpipe. A "magnifying glass," he had called it. She wondered if Crystal's snow-ice used the same principles as did Bardwell's glass. "Optics," he had called them.

Crystal played the reflected moonlight along and about the rocky face in front of them. "I don't see anything," she murmured.

Tara stepped forward to take a closer look. She was confident this was where she had entered the Underground Kingdom, only this time there was no cave. "Over here," she requested. Crystal shined the light. Nothing. "What about... over here?" asked Tara again, and this time in the light the cliff face was oddly regular.

Childeric ran his hands over the surface Tara had identified. "Why, it feels like a wall of some sort," he said softly. "It's far too smooth."

Crystal gazed at Tara in admiration. "Great work, Tara. You found something! How about if we take a closer look into this?"

Crystal checked to make sure Tara and her father were safely beside her then stretched her arms out in front of her, palms to the rock face, all ten fingers spread wide. The snowstorm around them immediately intensified. Tara winced at the tumult's resemblance to a howling, wounded animal, rising ever in volume. Snowflakes whipped around the bubble such that the world beyond turned a roiling grey-white. Tara feared they might be swept away, but Crystal remained unperturbed, a beatific smile slowly spreading across her face. She closed her eyes, humming softly, and balled her hands into two fists. Bringing them together, she commenced churning them around each other.

A rush of ice and snow, driven by winds of unimaginable force, slammed into the rock face with enough force to scatter nearby boulders like pebbles. During brief pauses in the assault on the cliffside, Tara could occasionally make out large, regular cracks that had been opened in the rock face and which roughly resembled an enormous door. Crystal opened her eyes narrowly. "I see it," she murmured. "There is something there. Yes."

Crystal's hands churned faster and the wind strengthened. The cracks widened until, all at once, large chunks of the face collapsed inwards and the storm swept within. Crystal opened her eyes wide again and lowered her hands; the storm faded to the same intensity as before. She turned to Tara, a touch of appreciation in her pale blue eyes. "You were right. There is a cave; it was just blocked up. Shall we take a look?"

"Sure," replied Tara, recovering from the spectacle of the destructive potential of tightly controlled elemental furies. Her father just stood staring. Tara could only imagine what he was thinking. She was sure she'd have to circle back to him and reassure him all this was normal for her friends, but just now they had a cave to explore. This had been part of the reason why she had been reluctant to let him join, after all: not because of the hardships but because of the shock and surprise of her friends.

"C'mon, Dad," she whispered to him, tugging at his sleeve. "Let's go take a look."

Her father started and recollected himself as he walked alongside Tara to the mountain face. "Can, uh, your other friends do… things like that?" he asked in a low voice.

Tara answered carefully, keeping her voice similarly low. "They can all do things but, you know, they're all different."

The three of them, still within Crystal's protective bubble, gingerly stepped over the rubble. Crystal played the light from her curved piece of ice about. "Yes. The cave was blocked up. See over there," she said, pointing with her beam of light at what looked like mortar connecting the natural rock with the remains of the wall that had blocked the cave mouth.

Childeric ran his fingers over two joined blocks. "It's skilled work. See how smoothly the mortar is finished and the stones are chiseled. Also," he continued, stooping to inspect where the stones met the cave floor and summoning Crystal and her light, "see how closely set these stones are. And," picking up one of the stones that had faced the outside world, "this one is dressed so it appears to be natural rock face. It's very well done."

Tara turned to Crystal. "This is the entrance to the Underground Kingdom for sure. But why was it walled up?"

Crystal shook her head. "I don't know. But we might as well stay here for the night. At least it offers shelter." She glanced around. "I can erect a snow wall that will reach the ceiling to prevent anyone from approaching us from further down the cave. Then we can all get some sleep." She looked enquiringly at Tara and her father. "What do you think?"

"Won't it get cold? Even with the wall?" asked a sceptical Tara, even if there didn't seem an alternative.

"I'll keep the bubble up," replied Crystal. "We'll be okay." After directing Tara and her father to stand to the side, she summoned a great quantity of snow from outside and, lifting her hands to successively higher levels, massed the snow so that it touched the very roof. Then she turned back to the broken wall and engineered a snow drift to accumulate there, leaving only a small stretch across the top of the bank, which she closed with solid ice. "That's to let in some moonlight," Crystal explained.

"Now watch," she continued in a soft aside, and the surface of the bubble in which they stood expanded and glowed brightly such that it radiated heat and light, like brilliant summer sunshine. After a minute, she contracted the bubble and the melted exteriors of the drifts before and behind them fused to a sparkling crystalline hardness. "There. That'll hold. We should be fine like this for the night!"

Tara and her father agreed enthusiastically and prepared to bed down for the night. They both declined Crystal's offer of a snow "mattress," even though she assured them it was very soft. They couldn't see how it would be warmer than their blankets. "Suit yourself!" she replied and, without a further word, stretched herself across a slab of snow she had arranged atop what amounted to an ice platform. Tara shivered. It sure looked cold, even as Crystal's breathing became regular with sleep. Tara and her father helped each other arrange blankets and, with a last look around the cave, lit only by a sliver of pale silver moonlight slanting through the ice which capped the snow drift, settled down to sleep.

Tara was asleep almost instantly. It had been a long and exhausting day. Childeric lay awake longer. The day had been as exhausting for him as it had been for Tara. But Childeric's mind was still reeling from his encounter with Crystal, whereas Tara was used to the extraordinary powers of her princess friends. Childeric was having trouble coming to grips with the reality of all this. Floating up a mountainside in a bubble! Channeling gale force winds to blow down well-built masonry walls! Molding snow drifts into defensive barriers! All accomplished by, for all the world, an ordinary, if oddly dressed, girl his daughter's age! Childeric shook his head on his pile of blankets. At least, he was not freezing on the mountainside. He fell asleep, dwelling on that comforting thought.

Childeric was awakened the next morning by his daughter's movements. Sheepish at having slept later than they, he being the experienced campaigner, he stood to find Crystal and Tara sorting through some of the rations they had brought to assemble breakfast. "Sorry about that," he mumbled, burning at the thought of the two girls preparing a meal while he slept.

Tara hardly glanced around. "Dad, no problem! Don't worry; Crystal and I can find what we need!"

Very shortly, the three were seated on their packs munching on dried meat and fruit. Though not particularly hungry, having eaten something vaguely crystalline earlier, Crystal thought to give the rations a taste. "I'd like to try them. Because I don't get out so much," she explained. Childeric chewed them stoically, being all too familiar with them. Tara was indifferent; she had had far worse in her travels. Far better too, of course.

Tara set down her mug of snow melt after washing down the last of her dried fruit. "Crystal, thanks so much for rescuing us yesterday and keeping us safe last night." Crystal acknowledged this with a slightly abashed smile. "But we've only made it to the mouth of the cave. We still need to find the plant called 'mycolix' to revive Ariel."

She paused for a moment to let her audience apprehend these words. So far, so good: no questions, no quarrels. But this had only been the obvious and established. On what was to come next, Tara hadn't thought too deeply, so intent had she been on getting to this cave. Now that she was well and truly here… well, now it was time to think up the next steps.

So, and as usual, Tara pressed on, if only because she could not go back. "I've been here before, with Ariel and Flo, though it was a little bit ago. Anyway, as I remember, it's all rock—walls and floor—for about half a mile or so down. Only then does it start to change. Maybe that's where we might start encountering mycolix."

At this natural pause, her father gave her an enquiring look, which Tara knew to represent a question. "What about the people—or creatures—down here? How might they react to us?" he asked. Tara mused on this for a moment. Her father continued, "The one person I've met so far from this Underground Kingdom is Mary Bess—"

"Maribess."

"—Maribess, who tried to put us to sleep. What about the rest of them? I can see that they're good stoneworkers from the wall they put up. Clearly they didn't want anyone to come in. Maybe they don't want us here!"

"That's a good point, Dad," allowed Tara. It had also occurred to her that maybe the cave had been walled up so as to prevent anyone from the kingdom from getting out, but that was hardly reassuring either! "A great point! But when last we were here, we personally delivered Sundra and her two sidekicks to the person she had overthrown."

"How'd one get out then?" asked Crystal.

"I don't know. But however it happened, I've got her in a bottle. Right here," and Tara patted her pack, "and once we find the proper authorities, we'll turn her over for whatever justice they think appropriate."

"Do you think Sundra's brother still rules?" asked her father.

Another good question, thought Tara, because, what if Sundra had regained power somehow and had sent Maribess against them? "I don't know. I hope so."

There was another moment of silence. Then Crystal nodded her head. "But no matter what, I'm sure you'll do super. I'm glad I was able to help you too. But hey, I suppose I ought to be getting back home."

Tara wrinkled her nose. She had been afraid that Crystal might want to leave. Now was the hard part of what she needed to do. "Um, Crystal... actually, I was hoping you might stay with us. For the whole journey."

Crystal involuntarily jerked backwards fractionally. "What? Sorry? You want me to go with you?"

"Yes. In fact, we need you. You're really important."

"But... hadn't you been planning on going just yourselves?"

Tara bit her lip. There was that planning problem of hers again. "Not really. We thought—I thought—that, well, you'd come with us. I was even sort of counting on you. Coming along, I mean."

"Oh." It was not a happy sort of "oh"; it was more like the sort of "oh" from someone who was not at all glad at getting some news but was unwilling to say so just yet.

Tara thought to make another effort, using a different tack. "Honestly, I was counting on you because, otherwise, it's just the two of us. My dad and me. And I wasn't sure if that would be enough. But we had to get started, because we really need to help Ariel!"

Crystal mulled this over silently while the other two watched, affecting, as best they could, not to be preoccupied with Crystal's internal struggle. Crystal was not at all enthusiastic about the underground realm and would much rather get back to her glittering ice caves and chandeliers, where she was comfortable and content. But she did know from her sister that Ariel really needed help, and Tara was right that the two of them on their own wasn't enough.

Tara saw Crystal hesitate and continued gently, "We don't have nearly the sort of abilities you have."

"I'm not sure they'd work underground. I need cold temperatures."

Tara looked surprised.

"Yes, yes! Otherwise, I'm not sure what happens. Just, maybe wind, that's all." Crystal shook her head and frowned. "Maybe not even that. I don't think I'm of much use."

But there wasn't anyone else to turn to. "That could still be a big help. And we want you along for more than just your powers. We want you along for you! For everything else you can do, even if it isn't magical!"

"Really?"

"Yes," added Tara's father, to even Tara's surprise. "It's not just about magic. Not at all. It's for you. After all, take a look at us: we don't have any magic, but we're going down!"

Crystal considered this truth glumly for a moment. "Okay," she answered, hesitantly. "I guess I can go with you a little. Maybe not all the way, but some."

Tara smiled. "Some" was better than none, and maybe she could be persuaded later to stay still longer. "Thanks, Crystal! It's really important to us. I'm sure it won't take too long at all!" So she hoped.

"Right," continued Childeric, after a moment. "That's settled then! Crystal, it's great to have you along. We really appreciate it. So, I'm thinking we'd better break camp and get going?"

That was her dad, thought Tara. He couldn't resist trying to take charge of everything.

The three of them packed up what they had and readied to leave. Tara noted that Crystal had her princess purse snug at her hip, though it was a lighter grey in color than Tara's, so that it was near indistinguishable from the rest of her garb. Must have faded somehow, mused Tara. But by the snow and ice? But it didn't matter, decided Tara. As long as she had her message bubbles; the telescoping rod could also be a help.

When they were ready, Crystal turned back to the cave mouth. "I'll pull down some of this wall," she said to Tara. "So that we have a little more access to the elements down the cave." With that, Crystal spun her hands in reverse, and there was a muffled roar of wind outside and, gradually, the snow piled in the breach in the wall was sucked away into the void outside. "Now," she continued, "for the berm I put up last night." Tara and her father stepped aside and Crystal called in the winds again to disassemble that. "Okay! We can get going now!"

"Pretty nice," commented Childeric, admiring Crystal's handiwork. "Sure would be nice to have that along on a winter campaign."

"C'mon, Dad," replied Tara. "Let's get going. We've got to save Ariel." With that, the three of them stepped over the broken snow wall that had protected them overnight and started for the Underground Kingdom.

Just as Tara had remembered, all there was to see and feel for a time as they descended deeper was rock on all sides. But the further they got, the more noticeable a faint glow became. It was from the bioluminescent lichens Tara had seen before growing on the walls, ceiling, and even, at points, the floor and which provided enough light to obviate the need for another source. The eerie, greenish, shadowless light was unnerving at first but surely better than any smoky flame they could carry. Crystal stopped before a particularly large clump. "Wow," she muttered, with obvious disdain, crinkling her nose. "I've never seen anything like this. It's really… different." She picked up a rock and nudged the growth. It gave slightly but sprang back, spongey and elastic, its glow undimmed. She tried to pry some from the rock, but it sprang directly from the rock itself, without being rooted in soil or water. "Gee. I wonder how it lives," she questioned by way of conclusion and turned away, casting a distrustful eye over her shoulder as they resumed their trek deeper underground.

Tara had been curious about the lichens the first time she had been down but had come to accept them as simply another aspect of the extraordinary Underworld environment. Rather, other thoughts preoccupied Tara, namely the sketch she carried of the mycolix plant from Stonedell's library. Would it be difficult to find the plant, much less a specimen with sufficient leaves to pick to revive Ariel? How many leaves were needed? She reviewed yet again, mentally, the line drawing Bardwell had reproduced. Had he copied all the important details? Suppose there was a plant that closely resembled it but lacked any restorative power? It had seemed so obvious when the book had been in front of her at the library. But here, she couldn't wave away her doubts. What if she were walking by mycolix at that very moment without recognizing it?

Another consideration, if secondary, was Maribess. When would they meet someone from the Underground Kingdom to hand her off to? How long would Crystal stay with them? Just push forward, she told herself resolutely and banished those worries from her mind.

King Childeric was thinking himself as he picked his way forward, more or less following in the footsteps of his daughter. He wasn't claustrophobic or nyctophobic—afraid of the dark—but he wasn't especially glad about being in a cave who knew how deep underground. There was light, and it was limitless and unceasing, if greenish and dimmer than sunlight. Childeric smiled involuntarily: who would have thought that, deep underground, one would find continuous light? Anyway, here he was on a mission he had insisted on joining. While he wasn't exactly glad to be there, he knew he had to be, because he simply couldn't allow his daughter to take such risks by herself and for the entire kingdom.

He thought about Tara. She had clearly been getting around and doing things he had never dreamt of. She had never been one for "princessing," as she called it, but she was going in directions and into situations that mystified and even worried him. What else had Tara done over the previous months that he and his wife didn't know? Maybe, he thought, he should ask her, as seemingly silly as that was? "Hey, Tara!" he called to her, stepping carefully around a pile of broken rock.

Tara stopped, her head cocked, as if to perceive something in the darkness ahead. Hesitantly, and rather than turn around, she lifted her hand to signal him to stop.

"Tara!" he called again, but she jerked her hand up and down anxiously. "What's wrong?" asked Childeric quietly, drawing nearer.

"Shh! I thought I heard rustling. Up ahead, off to the side. Over there." She pointed into the darkness, which pressed on them as far as the luminescent lichens permitted.

Childeric tore off a ragged chunk of glowing fungi which, on the rocks next to which they stood, resembled a section of old tapestry. He wadded it distastefully into a loose ball. "Probably just a rat, something like that," he explained and heaved it heavily in the direction she had pointed.

At once, there came a sharp chittering sound that rose quickly into a kind of rasping snarl. Tara started back, almost stumbling into Childeric, whose hand had flown to the hilt of his sword. Crystal, behind them still a few steps, stopped abruptly in confusion. To Tara's horror, a ghastly white form reared up from the darkness, several grasping members clawing out to seize Tara and her father. Childeric yanked Tara with his left hand, his right already unsheathing his sword. Even as the appendage reached for Tara, his whirled the sword under and around his wrist until it was poised high above then brought it down in a whistling arc to cleave the groping extension in two.

The stump retracted abruptly back into the darkness, and the slithering, chittering noise rose briefly into a fierce chattering that, aurally, reminded Tara briefly of the pelting of hailstones on the window of the family castle, far up and away somewhere, out in the sunlight. Unbidden, her mind raced back: had she not heard that sound before? Yes: it was the sound that that Kobemy person had used to call for Underworld reinforcements but which had instead summoned the Sebastos Reynam.

Childeric grabbed Tara by the shoulder and pulled her back further. Just in time, as a monstrous shape, partly resembling an eyeless centipede but mostly composed of legs, mouth and antennae, lurched toward them from beyond the path. "Get back, everyone!" Childeric warned. "It wants us!"

Tara scrambled away, slipping and stumbling on the rocks. Crystal gave a small cry and shrank back. Childeric thrust Tara behind him, his sword upraised, as a member terminating in impatiently snapping and clicking pincers quested toward them.

"Dad, watch your left!"

It was a simple ruse but effective against the unwary or unalert. Childeric, though, was both wary and alert. His sword flashed out to lop off the pincers of the left then swung back to parry the darting arm to the right.

The centipede-like creature hoisted itself further on to the path to more readily bring to bear more appendages. Childeric retreated a step. He wouldn't be able to fend off all of them at once.

"Stand aside, Dad; I've got my bow!" called Tara, fitting an arrow to her string then bending the bow back almost double before letting the arrow fly. At near point-blank range, she could not have missed. But she was aiming for what she imagined to be a sensory organ, where she thought the arrow would sink deepest. The bow sang; the arrow flew and sank almost to the fletching just above what Tara figured to be its maw. The effect was immediate. The creature writhed violently in a great spasm and a dozen armored arms beat the path all around them. Rocks of all sizes rained down around them in a clattering hail.

"Stay back, Dad! I'll hit it again!" she shouted. But her second shot glanced away off the contorting creature's chitin. Tara grimaced; she didn't have unlimited arrows.

The thing pulled itself onto the path before them and began to lurch unsteadily toward them. The wound above the maw oozed a greyish ichor. The rattling of its antennae and arms quickened, as if signaling its determination and fury.

Tara found herself next Crystal, who stood wide-eyed at the monster's approach. Tara seized her by the arm. "C'mon, we can't stay here," she said tersely, and Crystal jerked to life.

"Any cover back there we can take?" Tara asked shortly, fitting another arrow to her bow. If only she could get another shot in, but the creature's arms and pincers were always snapping at them, and it was moving in such a lumbering, lurching way that it was a difficult mark, even though it was so close. Each time an arm got too close, Childeric would hack at it, but there were seemingly another five for each one lost.

"Nothing!" wailed Crystal. "Oh, what do we do?"

Great question, thought Tara fiercely. The unarmored area around its mouth was the target, but it was small and all those squirming, wriggling mandibles complicated her aim. Aloud, she asked again, more insistently, "Is there really no place for us to hide?"

"N-n-no. No," answered Crystal, glancing hastily around. "Just a bend in the path!"

The underbelly of the creature also looked vulnerable. Maybe she could get in a shot there?

Just then, the creature reared up, as if to confront something on its right. What, wondered Tara, but the distraction was welcome. As it repositioned to grapple with whatever was coming at it from that direction, it exposed its underbelly to Tara again and, in that brief moment, she fit another arrow to her bow and loosed it in one fluid move. Tara's arrow flitted into the darkness and sank deep into the space between two abdominal plates.

"Great shot!" called Childeric, jubilantly.

The creature twisted, chittered and beat again at the path. In the middle of the tumult, out of the darkness, came a scream, suddenly stifled. Childeric re-joined Tara. "I think someone's over there; maybe a few people," he breathed. "They must have distracted it; probably why you got in another shot."

Tara nodded, even as she reached back into her quiver for another arrow. She couldn't tell exactly how many there were, but there were at least two bipedal forms as best she could make out in the lichen light. "I guess they're with us if they're against this creature!"

With a final heave, the creature flopped the rest of itself onto the path from the ledge below where it had been hiding. In the gloom, Tara discerned that it was little more than an enormous, white, articulated tube, terminating at the far end in a fluke or stinging appendage, which the narrowness of the passageway, mercifully, prevented its use against Tara's party.

Silhouetted against the creature's pale bulk, Tara spied a figure lunge, as if flinging something. A quiver ran along the length of the horror, and it flexed its fluke upwards such that it hovered menacingly over the figures.

"Watch out!" Tara yelled. "The tail!"

Impossible to tell if they had understood, but the figures did pull back sharply and darted toward the three from above ground. Just in time, as the tail swatted empty space when it flicked around to sweep them away.

Tara and her companions made out the two figures as they drew close as being of medium height and, when closer still, wearing a fine mesh of matte-black chainmail. Round shields were slung over trim backpacks, and those over waist-length black capes. In their right hands they held short, sharp swords; at their hips were hand-held projectile throwing devices more for use against humans and too small to have an impact on the creature. A second sword, more like a longer and slenderer rapier, hung from the opposite hip. Their boots were of a dark-grey leather and atop their heads were crested matte-black helmets. They were people of the Underground Kingdom, Tara realized and, by their weaponry, some sort of patrol.

"They look like Maribess!" gasped Crystal, recoiling.

"Welcome!" cried Tara.

"We have not time for greetings! The mocurra is upon us!" answered one, whom Tara gauged to be the leader. Even so, they stared for a long second at Crystal, who was dressed all in white and dove grey, whereas their weaponry, armor, shields, and helmets—save for a red emblem embossed on the breastplate—were a near lusterless black.

Tara had a sudden idea. "Crystal, can you still churn up a snowstorm?"

She shook her head. "It's not cold enough for a Snow Blast."

"But you said you might be able to call up wind. Even without cold."

"Maybe. I haven't really tried before."

Time to try it now, thought Tara, eyeing the shifting mocurra, which had repositioned itself to recommence sliding and slithering toward them, its pincers and grasping members again snapping. The chittering came louder, and the mandibles at the mouth organ began fluttering, as if in anticipation of ingesting one of their number.

Tara stifled an impulse to vomit while, aloud, she maintained her composure. "Okay, here's the plan! The mocurra rears up when wounded. So, we wound it, as badly as we can. Crystal, you start summoning whatever wind you can. When it rears, you send the wind toward it with all the force you've got. We want to blow it off the ledge and back down to wherever it came from!"

She looked to the others to assess if there were any objections. No one said anything. That's because, she knew immediately, no one else had other ideas. "All right then! I want that thing hurt: aim for the area around its mouth and its underbelly. Use anything and everything!"

"When I shout 'Duck!' get out of the way fast! That's when the wind's coming!" cried Crystal.

Tara checked faces again, but there were no questions and no comments. "So, then, let's go!" she commanded and yanked from her quiver another arrow.

Her father stepped off to the side. "I'll hold this flank, but let's do this as quick as we can, as I can't hold off all these pincers for long."

The two Underworld soldiers conferred for a moment. The one with the taller crest spoke quickly. "I will take then the other flank." He indicated his companion. "Corporal Lotho will inflict the wound, taking both our spears. And now," he nodded to Princess Crystal, "summon this force, and may it be strong!" He reached around to his pack and pulled from it a short, stout pole which, with a single jerk, extended into a short, stout spear with a razor-sharp tip that snapped into place. This he passed to the soldier he had named "Lotho" and stepped to the side opposite Childeric. A second later, his shield had fended off a pincer, and the short, thick-bladed sword had hacked off another, for the towering mocurra was upon them.

"Crystal, get ready!" Tara shouted, scrambling to evade a claw that had stretched out of the mass of pincers and sinuous hooks, squirming for her. The frenziedly working mandibles lunged for her. In the dim light, she saw the mocurra's coloration to be the cream of soured milk, though mottled with grey-and-blue patches rather than uniform, and its glistening hide knobby rather than smooth. An overpowering stench poured from the maw; Tara thought she might faint. Dimly, to her right, she saw her father hewing frantically then, suddenly, the reek cleared, and the creature curled back upwards and to its side again. A single black spear protruded from above the mouth, not far from her first arrow.

Lotho! she exulted, and the beast writhed again, more violently than before, and Tara spotted the shaft of a second spear, just under the first. "Crystal!" she called over her shoulder. "Now!"

Crystal was already churning her hands as quickly as she could. "I'm trying, I'm trying!" she called back, breathlessly.

"Duck!" Tara cried. "Quick!"

A whistling had been building down the passageway, and Tara just had the opportunity to throw herself behind a largish rock before the whistle became a scream, and the creature reared high up into the darkness and swayed slightly, as if hesitating. The air was suddenly filled with dirt, pebbles, and loose luminous lichens. Tara raised her eyes into the howling wind to see the mocurra's appendages and stumps waving and clutching as its segmented trunk swayed violently. The mandibles chattered a last horrible chorus that climbed to a frenzied shriek, and it toppled backwards into the blackness. All of them listened intently for the sound of it striking the bottom of the abyss, but there was nothing but the dying breeze, or the depths were too deep for the impact to reach them.

Tara looked up to find her father standing next to her. "Close call." She grinned.

He nodded, making a fair effort at appearing sanguine. "Who are our new friends, who showed just when we needed them?"

Crystal joined them. "It worked, didn't it!" she exclaimed. "Are you okay?" she added.

Tara and Childeric thanked Crystal profusely. "It was easy," she replied, shyly. "I was glad to help. Good thing I came along!"

The three hastened to check on the Underworld soldiers, who had been so critical to defeating the mocurra. Tara raised her right hand in a salute when they found them just down the path. "Hello to you. Are you unhurt?"

Their leader nodded as he was joined by his corporal. "All well with us. You also?"

Childeric spoke. "Yes, thank you. We owe you a great debt of thanks. You came to our aid just in time against that creature, which I recall you called a mocurra."

The leader bowed slightly. "We are all allies against the mocurra. It is a terrible creature to confront and impossible to battle alone. We could not have let you face it, just the three of you."

Childeric bowed in return. "We owe you some introductions. Let us start. I am King Childeric, of the Kingdom of Brythrony, above your world. This is my daughter, Princess Tara, and the third member of our party is Princess Crystal."

"The Snow Princess," added Princess Tara quickly.

"Interesting, and thank you," replied the soldier. "With me is Corporal Lotho, who so accurately aimed the spears at the mocurra. I am Captain Farrell, this patrol's leader. I regret to say that we are missing our sergeant.

He was lost to the mocurra when we first encountered it."

Tara recollected the scream she had heard earlier. That must have been the sergeant. All three of them offered their condolences and thanked them again for having saved them and especially for the sacrifice of one of their patrol.

At length, Captain Farrell asked, "What brings you to our world, so distant, in so many ways, from your own?"

Both Crystal and Childeric looked to Tara. "Yes, what brings us to your world? Let me answer that for you!" She thought briefly and then, with a flourish, reached around to pull from her backpack a fat cylinder. She held it out with both hands to show to Farrell and Lotho, who stepped forward involuntarily to look more closely at it.

Farrell looked up to Tara. "My Princess, there is a person inside this cylinder?"

Tara nodded, noting the curious honorific Farrell used for her. "It's a stasis bottle. And inside, completely protected, is someone from your world. Someone you may know."

Both Underworlders gazed intently into the bottle. Farrell looked up after a moment and spoke in a lowered voice. "It is Maribess, a well-known, even notorious, confidante of the Sebasissa Sundra! Her whereabouts have been unknown for some time!"

Tara replied in an equally low and significant voice. "She came to our kingdom intending to cause much harm. Perhaps motivated by vengeance, perhaps to assume control over it. She blew dust from a plant that we know as mycolix at a number of my people to make them unconscious. Unfortunately for Maribess, but fortunately for us, she breathed some of the dust herself. We have kept her in this bottle so that she would not die of thirst or starvation."

Farrell nodded gravely. "The plant is indeed called 'mycolix', and it is an offense to employ the spores of the mycolix in this manner. This is because, as is clearly obvious to you, if the victim is not revived quickly, she can die."

Tara was gratified to know that what Maribess had done was wrongful below ground as well as above. "This is very sensible. But it is possible to revive those affected by the spores, isn't it? By powdering the leaves and inducing the victims to breathe them, is that so?"

"This is the only known antidote, My Princess."

Tara chose her next words carefully. Then, remembering something she had packed in her princess purse days before, she fumbled inside it until her fingers closed around what she sought. Now was the time, because she had to accomplish two objectives and quickly, both of which required the assistance of the Underworlders. "Yes, that is what we understand also. As I mentioned, in addition to affecting herself, Maribess affected another person in our kingdom, who is still unconscious. We would like sufficient leaves of the mycolix plant so we may revive her. Would you be willing to help us locate one with sufficient leaves?" As she spoke, Tara produced the seal that Reynam had given her when they had parted on the capture of Sundra, Maribess, and Kobemy at Starmers what seemed like ages ago.

The impact on Captain Farrell was immediate. He gazed down at the seal for many seconds, as if to evaluate its authenticity and as if to reconcile himself to the impossibility that an overlands princess was in possession of the royal seal of Pentenok, but after long seconds, he looked up to Tara and, in a voice lower and more respectful, replied that, if one knew where to look for the mycolix plant, it was not difficult to find, and that they would be honored to help.

This cheered the others from above ground, who had not seen what Tara had shown Farrell. Tara continued, returning the seal to her purse, "Though Maribess committed her wrongdoings in our world, after consultation amongst ourselves, we think it best to turn her over to you, the people of her own world, so that she may face justice she may better understand and accept, rather than our own."

Farrell nodded gravely as he received the stasis bottle from Tara. He examined it curiously for a moment then passed it to Lotho to keep, who stowed it carefully in his pack after a brief study himself. "This is fair and generous. You can be assured she will not go unpunished, as the evidence of her crime will be apparent just in seeing her in this bottle as she is!"

Farrell took a deep breath then turned to the subject of the mycolix. "This plant grows only in the deeper parts of the caverns. This means we must descend into—" he paused as he saw the faces of the three overlanders sink "—yes, down into those very realms where we just threw the mocurra."

Tara swallowed. "Down there? That's the only place where they grow?"

"The only place."

"Are there many of those... mocurra down there? I mean, I don't expect the one we just encountered to have survived the fall?"

"It is impossible it survived the fall as far down as the bottom is. But we need not journey all the way to the very lowest reaches, as the mycolix is also in parts above."

"And mocurras?" demanded Crystal. "Where are they? Will there be more?"

Farrell shook his head. "My Princess, they hunt alone, and it is unusual to find one in the upper realms, where we are now. They keep to the deep and to the larger ledges. Thus, we may not encounter one at all, if we find a plant toward the mid-regions, which is very likely and yet which would still be above where the mocurra frequent."

Tara turned to her companions. "None of you need to go on this part with me. You've come far enough already."

But Childeric shook his head emphatically. "Ariel risked her life for Brythrony, so I'll go too. Besides, you can't go alone!"

Crystal agreed too, reluctantly. Tara understood: it was not as if Crystal could reasonably remain alone on the path, waiting for Tara and Childeric's return! What if another mocurra or something equally horrible came along?

Tara turned back to Farrell. "We'll all go. We're ready!"

"Then we will take you," he answered. He waved to his corporal, who had stood beside him placidly, awaiting his orders. "We take the first path we find to the lower realms. I expect to find such a path close by, it being the route, surely, the mocurra used to ascend."

With that, Farrell and Lotho began to walk the edge of the path, scanning with what must be practiced eyes for a route downwards. Tara marveled at how sure-footed and noiseless they were despite the uneven path; the three stumbling Overlanders were hard pressed to keep up. Then Farrell and Lotho stopped and conferred. Farrell pointed to the others when they caught up. "This is the path that the mocurra probably used. Do you see how wide it is?"

Tara squinted into the darkness. She couldn't see much beyond a rocky incline sloping into the darkness. "Shall we take this path down then?"

As if in answer, Farrell and Lotho stepped off the path and into the darkness. They paused for a moment, motioned for the three others to join them then vanished into the murk.

The three scrambled hastily after them and re-joined Farrell and Lotho, around what very much looked like a rock lying to one side of the descending path. "The spoor of the mocurra," explained Farrell tersely, as if in confirmation of their hypothesis that this path had been its route.

They continued until Lotho stopped short and held up his hand. Farrell turned to them and explained. "Corporal Lotho believes the conditions are excellent here for finding the mycolix. He suggests we stop and search here."

The five decided that Lotho and Tara would conduct the search, since they knew what it should look like. While Farrell knew it too, Childeric and Crystal asked that one of the Underworlders remain with them and keep lookout for anything that might appear on the path.

While Childeric enquired, out of professional interest, of Farrell as to how the mocurra hunted, Lotho led Tara off the path and explained why he thought this location was promising. "The mycolix prefers to grow upon granite having striations of a certain kind of calcite, the name for which may be unpronounceable for you.

"This calcite, My Princess, we find here," pointing, "and here again," motioning to layers in the rocks that Tara dimly could see were slightly lighter in color than those between which they were sandwiched. He continued, "The mycolix also wants moisture, not so much as to be found at springs; wherever a small amount of moisture naturally collects is sufficient." Here again, Lotho pointed by way of example. "Finally, mycolix keeps to the shade, which is why it is not generally found on the pathways of the upper realms."

It struck Tara that all of the Underground Kingdom was "shady," but clearly the term was relative and must refer to those areas where there were fewer of the bioluminescent lichens. Yet again, Tara was glad to have encountered Lotho and Farrell. Their party might never have come across the mycolix if it didn't grow along the upper pathways.

Lotho stopped and Tara concluded that their search would commence here. Lotho had a last admonition for her. "We want to search thoroughly but quickly. There is no telling what might happen along the path upwards or downwards."

Tara needed no further prompting and began searching in earnest. Shortly, off to the side, she spotted a ledge that looked as if it might be worth checking. It looked awfully dark there, which was good for mycolix, but then again, it looked awfully dark there, which could be bad for someone like Tara, who was unfamiliar with the Underworld. What if something were lurking deep within? She stepped carefully along the scree and then stretched herself, fully supine, atop it so as to be able to drop her head down and peer under it. There, beneath the ledge, she beheld a deep darkness, spangled only intermittently by what she guessed must be dots of light lichen.

"It's almost like looking into the night sky in Brythrony," she breathed in wonder, fascinated. "Only I'm looking down, not up!" How strange, the inversion of the Underworld, she reflected, lifting her head. The shallow upper reaches of the Underworld were deep for those from the world above. What was shady to them was very dark to us. Tara pushed these thoughts from her mind; probably they had been stimulated by the blood rushing to her head from hanging upside down! She had to focus on the leaves and making sure she was not taking foolish risks investigating the ledge.

Tara ducked her head to look again, and her heart beat more quickly. Was that mycolix, and a sizable clump of it, thriving beneath the ledge, just before her? She gently tore off a leaf, sat up and called softly for Lotho.

He scrutinized the leaf closely. "Very well done! You listened carefully to me, because this location meets all three requirements of the mycolix. See, for example, the chalky rock, here and here, that provides it with the nutrients it requires," he added, tracing with one hand the striations. "Let us take enough and from several, so as not to impact any one, to provide for the revival of both your friend and Maribess. Even though I expect the royal dispensary has sufficient to hand for such emergencies."

Back with the others, Farrell was impressed that Tara had been the one to locate the mycolix plant. "My Princess, you have sharp eyes. But you should not have gone on the ledge without security. Ledges can crumble and you would have been lost to the abyss below, much like the mocurra!"

Crystal glanced around worriedly. "Let's get going. I don't think it's altogether safe here." The others agreed, and they immediately began heading back up the path, Lotho resuming his accustomed silence and acting as rear guard, alert for anything that might try to follow them. Before long, they regained the point from which they had originally departed the path, at which Captain Farrell asked if they might like an escort back to the cave mouth by which they had entered. "We cannot take you all the way though, because the full distance is outside our patrol area. Still, we can take you much of the way and along a quicker route than you doubtless originally took."

The three happily accepted, and shortly Farrell was leading the others, Tara just behind, with Lotho, who seemed most disposed to silence, again bringing up the rear. Farrell inclined his head to Tara once they were started and spoke to her in a low voice. "We of the Underground Kingdom know you already, My Princess?"

"Captain, sorry, I'm not sure I understand you? We have never met before, if that is what you ask."

"No, My Princess. Not me, but my people. You have visited us before, yes, to have with you the seal of the Sebastos Reynam?"

Tara hesitated, not certain how much of that episode was a state secret but declared that he was correct, and that was how she had come into possession of the seal.

"And, My Princess, may I ask if this visit was in connection with our Sebasissa Sundra, who you may also know as Princess Sundra?"

Tara affirmed that it was.

"Then, you are she who took such a role in completing the restoration of the Sebastos Reynam to the throne of Pentenok!"

"Yes, Captain, I was. But there were two others with me. The Princess Ariel, whom we seek to restore with these leaves, was one."

"The Sebastos, I wish for his continued health, will be very happy to learn that we have in part repaid his debt to you by rescuing you and your party from the mocurra. Though we lost a member of our patrol, his sacrifice is doubly honorable, as it was in your service and thus the service of the Sebastos."

These words moved Tara. "You are very kind, Captain. Of course, we—my companions and I—were happy to assist the Sebastos. We encountered him in pursuing Princess Sundra—like with Maribess, because of certain misdeeds she committed in my kingdom."

"The Sebasissa Sundra remains under close guard. As are her closest confederates. Inexplicably, Maribess escaped. This was still being investigated when my patrol departed. We are most glad to have her back; her capacity for mischief is very great, and she is known for being fanatically devoted to the Sebasissa. Once she is revived, she and the Sebasissa will be questioned, as the first would not do anything without the permission of and the knowledge and connivance of the second."

Princess Tara thanked the Captain for these reassurances. Then she enquired as to the health of the Sebastos.

Captain Farrell thanked her for her interest. "He is well, My Princess. Pentenok is fortunate to have him as Sebastos." He paused a moment in his conversation. "Of course, My Princess, upon our return to Pentenok, I must make a full report of meeting you and your party and of our adventures."

Tara encouraged him to do so and that he must not fail to mention the gallantry of their sergeant.

"Yes, My Princess. Would there be any message you might wish me to relay to the Sebastos in my report? I expect I would have that opportunity."

Tara understood the thrust of the Captain's meaning. "This is very intelligent of you, Captain. Yes, please. In addition to conveying to the Sebastos my greetings and very best wishes, and after delivering Maribess to him for justice, may I ask that you might beg of him how we might perhaps cooperate on frustrating any of Princess Sundra's further machinations? Perhaps, we might establish some means of communication between our two kingdoms, so as to better alert the other, should Princess Sundra cause any other difficulties?"

"Yes, My Princess. You suggest some enduring means by which our two kingdoms might communicate to forestall further problems from the Sebasissa Sundra in the Overlands."

"Just so, Captain. For the good of both realms."

"Yes, My Princess. As you say."

"I'm thinking also that such a means of communication could to lead to greater cooperation between our kingdoms and to a greater—if unknown as of yet—good?"

"Yes, My Princess, yes."

Surely Reynam would understand, added Princess Tara mentally. It was high time that the Underworld got a grasp of the true menace to both worlds that Sundra represented.

It wasn't long afterwards that Captain Farrell came to a halt and stated that this was the limit to which patrols from the Underworld were allowed to venture. He pointed up the path. "You are not far now from the entrance you know to the Underworld. You should be safe too: nothing from the Underworld ever comes this close to the surface. If you encounter any creature or person at all, it will be from the Overlands, not the Underworld."

The three travelers bid the captain and corporal good-bye. The Captain, ever gracious, saluted them, replying that it had been an honor to have been of service, and that he was certain that these actions would reflect well upon him in the eyes of his Sebastos. There was a last exchange of salutes, and the Underworld pair vanished back down the path.

Princess Crystal stared after them wistfully. "They were really nice," she murmured as the three resumed their ascent. "Not at all like Maribess!"

"I can't wait to take a proper bath!" exulted Childeric, upon at last spying the light from outside through the remains of the snow berm.

Tara was thinking of something else. "Before you leave, Crystal, could you take us back down the mountainside the same way you brought us up? It would be a really big help!"

Crystal, upbeat and reenergized by the colder air pouring in from the snowbound world outside, responded breezily, "Sure! But I can't all the way: it's not cold enough at the lower elevations to transport you safely."

"Take us as far as you can. Thank you so much!"

"Sure. Happy to help! Any time you're ready…?"

Tara glanced to her father, who nodded vigorously. "Let's go! The sooner, the better."

Tara looked around a last time. Too bad about the now-ruined wall that had blocked up the cave mouth. She had neglected to ask Captain Farrell why the Underworlders had walled themselves in. Who had they intended to keep out? Or keep in? But Ariel had to be the priority now. "I'm ready too. Let's go!"

The three of them stepped carefully around the ice that paved the cave floor to its very mouth and put down their packs. Crystal raised her arms slowly, dramatically, and a shimmering outline formed around her. The whistling wind at the mouth seemed to still, and the air became calm. Swirling snowflakes slowed in mid-flight to hang in the air. All traces of color drained from Crystal's face, but whereas that would have been cause for alarm with anyone else Tara knew, in Crystal it appeared healthy and fit. The flickering colors suffusing Crystal expanded into a globe that encompassed Tara and Childeric, and ice rapidly accreted below their feet.

Crystal looked expectantly into the faces of Tara, then her father, but seeing no reason not to continue, she motioned them forward another step. The cycling colors of the globe accelerated to a blur, and the ice platform beneath their feet grew thicker and harder. Humming softly and rocking her head from side to side, as if in time to some unheard, happy tune, Crystal raised her hands, and they arose from the ledge into the bright, pure, clear mountain air shot through with sunlight.

Tara remembered with a start that Florence was still wrestling with the controls of Cloud Castle. She whipped her ice shard from her princess purse and breathed on it to bring it to a shine. "Flo!" she called. "Flo, can you hear me?"

"Oh, good idea," observed Crystal. "Here, let me alert her you're trying to reach her." She concentrated for a moment then smiled at Tara. "She'll pick up in a second. She says she's in something like a 'wheel house'." Crystal's face became puzzled. "I don't know what that is."

Tara did but didn't know if Flo's presence there was good or bad. Just then, the shard glowed, and Flo appeared. "Hey, Tara! I sure am glad to see you! How have you been? Any luck?"

Tara detected a note of worry in Flo's voice, and her face seemed lined. Clearly not everything was going well. Tara kept her voice encouraging. "Hey, Flo! We're glad to see you too! Good news: we found the mycolix plant and we brought all the leaves we should need!"

Flo was visibly relieved. "Such great news! Great job, all of you!"

"We couldn't have done it without Crystal!"

Crystal smiled self-effacingly at her sister's face in the shard and waved.

"Crystal IS the greatest!"

"I know. But hey, how are things in Cloud Castle?"

Flo's face clouded. "Not so great, I'm afraid. I haven't had much success in learning steering. I thought I was, at first, but it was just favorable winds. Now, the winds have turned and it looks like I'm heading for some mountains. I'm really not sure if I'll be high enough to clear them. So it's really great you've got the leaves. You've got to revive Ariel so she can get up here and steer Cloud Castle to safety!"

Tara nodded. It was as she had feared. Flo had not been able to figure out the controls for Cloud Castle.

"If only Ariel had left some kind of instructions!" Flo was saying dispiritedly.

"Guess she never expected this. Look, stay with it and do your best! We're on our way back to Ariel. Shouldn't be too long now!" Tara dared not project anything but absolute confidence.

"Don't worry, Flo," chimed in her sister, leaning over to appear partially in the shard's field of view. "I'll set Tara and her father down as far down the mountain as I can. That should speed them on their way."

Florence agreed but encouraged them again, and superfluously, to move as fast as they could. Clearly she was worried.

"Just stick with it, Flo; we're coming with help!" repeated Tara.

"I sure hope those leaves work," replied Flo and signed off.

"'Work?'" questioned King Childeric. "What does she mean by that? Of course, they'll work, right?"

"Sure, Dad! Of course!" Of course they would, she repeated to herself. The book and Captain Farrell had said they would. But, she realized suddenly, she had forgotten to ask the Captain how to prepare the leaves for a victim. They were to be ground up, she thought. But how, if in any way, should they be prepared beforehand? Tara grimaced. She didn't dare think of that now. It was too awful to contemplate, having gone all the way to the Underground Kingdom and come back but not knowing the correct way to prepare the leaves. A terrible, rising panic clawed at her, enough to almost make her dizzy. Fortunately, she reassured herself, she had plenty of leaves. Even if she got the first effort wrong, there would be plenty for a second and even a third attempt.

Which she hoped would not be necessary. As there might not be enough time. For Cloud Castle.

Crystal was setting them down on the mountain side, in a clear spot in a boulder field. "This is as far as I can go safely," she apologized. "Sorry about that."

"No problem! We're grateful for the ride!"

King Childeric thanked her graciously. "You were very kind to accompany us underground. We could not have done what we did without you. You were very brave on our behalf."

Crystal smiled shyly. "Oh, hey, no big deal. Probably a good thing for me to get out more anyway. Besides, Ariel needed our help." Crystal considered for a moment and frowned slightly. "Come to think of it, maybe I'll go up and see if I can help my sister some at Cloud Castle. Before I go home." With that, and with a last muted wave of her hand, Crystal brought her arms up and over her head and clapped her hands. There was a sudden flash of white, and she vanished.

"Wow!" exclaimed Childeric, still blinking. "I didn't know she could do that!"

"Me neither. Must be something she can do when she doesn't have to carry extra weight, like us."

Sure was easier going down than up, remarked Tara to herself, and it was nice not to have to carry the stasis bottle, even if it hardly weighed anything. But aloud she said, "Dad, I know that when we came here we had a tent erected for us each night, but I think we ought to hurry back as quickly as we can. For Princess Ariel's sake.

"Or," she added quickly, "I could go ahead—maybe with a few of the horsemen—and you could follow along behind with the remainder?"

"Nonsense!" Childeric cried. "We'll go together. You'll see: we'll move quickly tomorrow. No use in starting tonight, as it's too late. No, don't complain!" he broke in quickly, seeing that Tara was ready to object and guessing what her objection might be. "You'll thank me tomorrow! We'll ride faster after a decent night's sleep!"

They arrived at the castle late the next night. Tara was exhausted. Staggering up to her room, too tired to even eat dinner, she had to admit that her father had been right. It had been an incredibly hard ride, even with the horses doing most of the work! While she wanted to start processing the mycolix leaves, she was simply too tired to concentrate on what should be a very deliberate process. She didn't dare make a mistake and ruin a goodly portion of the precious leaves.

"Go on," her father had told her gently. "Get to bed. You can start tomorrow when you're fresh and focused." For one of the few times in her recent memory, she had simply nodded and begun the ascent to her room which, on this occasion, had seemed to involve a stairway to the stars, it had seemed so long.

Tara awoke the next morning later than she felt she ought to have. Guiltily, on account of the late hour, and still saddle-sore from the day before, she staggered down the stairs. She flung herself into a chair at the table and immediately signaled to one of the servants to approach.

Her mother had already breakfasted but had stayed. She eyed her daughter sympathetically. "Tara, my child, what will you be having this morning?"

"Oh, hi, Mom. I'm kind of hungry, I think. Maybe something along the lines of what Dad often has for breakfast?"

Tara heard a sharp intake of breath from her mother. "Goodness! That? You know that's not good for you. Or him, for that matter! And what about your figure?"

Tara made as if rubbing her face in her hands to hide her expression of exasperation. "Mom! I'm just hungry, that's all! Could I have something to eat, please?"

Her mother acquiesced, though with further admonishments that she could be more mindful of such things than she was being at the moment, and motioned for the servant to fetch her what Tara had requested.

Be careful of what I eat, repeated Tara to herself. Not that I've had anything very tasty over the past few days, which had consisted mainly of dried fruits and meats with hard bread. "Where's Dad? Is he still asleep?"

Her mother nodded that he was. Tara smiled to herself. So the ride had been as hard on him as it had been on her!

After breakfast, she got to work. First, she visited the unconscious Ariel in her stasis bottle. Poor thing, she murmured. Don't worry though! I hope to have you out soon. With that, she pulled the mycolix leaves from her princess pouch and, studying them, wondered as to the best way to pulverize them so as to drop them into Ariel's bottle. Simply crumbling them and dropping them in didn't seem like it would be effective.

She frowned. She couldn't afford to be uncertain. Ariel couldn't afford for Tara to be uncertain. Tara looked to her tiny friend, lying helpless and motionless in the bottle. What to do? Back to the library, she decided, to consult that diary again. When she had first looked at it, she had been focused on how Ariel might be revived. Now that she had the leaves though, her interest was in what to do with them. Maybe there might be further clues in the entries missed the first time?

She found Bardwell where she expected to find him: in the second floor of the East Tower, still sorting through stacks of books, papers, and pamphlets.

"Ah, Princess Tara! Your Highness! How lovely to see You again!"

"Hi Bardwell! Good to see you, too."

"Yes! Your trip to the Underground Kingdom…?"

"Was a success," concluded Tara for him, and she withdrew a leaf from her purse as evidence. "I'm here again to find out what I should do next. I thought I might consult that book again to see if it had further details?"

"Great idea!" enthused Bardwell. "Let's see… Where did we find that book?" He jumped up and took a few hesitant steps toward the rear of the room, but Tara guided him toward the next aisle, remembering it being somewhere in the middle of that stack. Within a few minutes, they had found it and were back at the desk, turning pages to locate the section addressing how to handle the antidote.

"Hm! Hm! Ah! Here we are; here is where it was," and Bardwell read aloud for them both:

"*'...and so we ground to a fine powder various parts of the plant for our unlucky comrade to inhale, as he could neither drink nor eat. At last, the plant's leaves had the desired effect, and he awoke.'*"

Tara looked up at him. "It doesn't provide anything further. Just that the leaves were 'ground to a fine powder'. Nothing more."

"No. Nothing more. How did they do that when they were underground and had no equipment, I wonder? Just cutting the leaves with a knife would hardly do, I should think. But hey! Let's read a little further, nonetheless."

They skimmed further, and Tara was ready to give up, when Bardwell suddenly jerked upright and began to laugh in triumph. "Ha! Ha! Look! Read!" He spun the book so it faced her and pointed to a passage. "See? See!"

Tara read. The text mentioned the party breaking camp and in the process gathering their equipment, putting out the fire they had built and checking the perimeter of their makeshift encampment for misplaced items. She looked up at him, mystified.

"Do You see? A fire! They put out the fire!"

Tara wondered what the significance could be of putting out a fire. Why, they had built a fire most every evening to cook and to provide warmth. Then Tara's mind went back. Deep underground it had not been that cold, and a fire had not been needed, neither to cook, subsisting as they had on dried fruits, nuts and meats, nor for warmth, since the temperature had always been level and moderate. Of course, thought Tara, the light dawning on her. The fire had been lit to dry the leaves, to remove all the moisture from them so they could be crumbled to a fine powder and so introduced to the victim's airways!

"That's it, Bardwell! Wonderfully done! I need to roast the leaves to reduce them to a fine dust!" With that, Tara dashed out of the library, leaving behind an amused Bardwell, still in mid-bow to her.

"Good-bye, Your Highness!" called Bardwell after her. "Good luck!"

Here goes the first effort, thought Tara. In her hands, at the end of a stick, she held the small grid that was used to toast bread over a fire. Tara had repurposed it to hold the leaves and was flipping it back and forth quickly over the kitchen fire, to the amusement and confusion of the kitchen staff. Several of them stopped to watch but dared not ask what the Princess of the Realm was doing, much less why she was in the kitchen at all, where her family never went except to supervise preparations for important feast days. "There, nearly done," Tara whispered and pulled back the grid to examine the leaves closely. A little singed, but she could cut that part off. She didn't know if that was necessary or not, but why take the chance? Just a little more, she thought. Just to make sure. She returned the grid to the flames.

"Your Highness, I would be more than happy to bring you a slice of toast!" interrupted the head cook with a polite cough. Tara smiled, cognizant of their discomfort with her present in the middle of preparations for lunch.

"No, no thank you!" she answered quickly and with the most easy-going smile she could manage. "But I'll be out of your way in a moment!" She retrieved the grid from the fire one more time and examined its contents closely. They looked dry, that was for sure.

"Good! I think that will do!" announced Tara after eying the dried and curling leaves in the gridiron critically, and she emptied them into a bowl she had pulled from a dishrack by the vast porcelain sink where it had been drying. This scandalized the scullery maids, as the bowl had been the same that His Royal Highness King Childeric had used just that morning for the royal scrambled eggs. Tara further upset the good order of the kitchen by reaching again into the dishrack to grab the closest plate, which she clapped over the bowl. Yes, her mother liked to use that plate for her butter each morning, but how else was Tara to keep the leaves in the bowl from whirling out and away as she ran to the bedroom where Ariel still rested?

Tara could hear a susurrus of voices behind her as she exited the kitchen.

"What on earth was she toasting?"

"It looked like a pieces of paper!"

"Why? What's she going to do with them? Eat them?"

"And what's she doing with the royal breakfast flatware?"

"What will the king and queen say?"

"What about the head cook?"

"I'll be back with them, don't worry!" shouted Tara over her shoulder, but from their faces, she feared it only made them more firmly convinced that she had lost her mind. This struck Tara as hilariously funny and, laughing wildly, she dashed off to the bedroom where Ariel was.

"Yes, yes, yes!" muttered Tara to herself. "This has got to be it!" She seated herself on the bed, the stasis bottle on the bedside table, and uncovered the bowl. The leaves inside had already been reduced to fragments from the dash to the bedroom. Good. Tara took a pestle she had seized from the kitchen and commenced to powder the remainder while she considered the bottle in which Ariel lay supine. Best, she decided, to introduce the dust to the bottle with Ariel still in it, rather than first pull her out. Tara stared a moment longer then shrugged. Might as well give it a try.

Tara sprinkled the lighter particles into the mouth of the stasis bottle and blew ever so gently into the bottle to circulate the particles throughout the entire bottle.

Nothing.

Maybe she needed more dust. Tara pulled out the pestle again and fiercely ground the dust more finely then lightly shook it, bit by bit, into the bottle and blew again. Didn't the dust have to work? Hadn't Captain Farrell said the leaves would revive Ariel?

Still nothing. Nothing!

Wait! Was that Ariel, stirring? Tara got down on her knees next to the bottle and peered in closely, so that she must have looked to anyone within as an enormous, cyclopean eye. Yes, it must be! It was! Ariel was stirring, just very slowly. Tara jumped up and danced about the room in excitement. It was working!

When Tara looked again, it was clear that Ariel was coming around. She just needed a little bit of time, that was all. Tara thought hard. She'd be hungry, of course. And thirsty. Tara pulled hard on the bell to the kitchen to ring for a maid. Food and water should be ready for Ariel when she came around. Also, thought Tara, she should alert Crystal and Flo. Who knew what they were facing up in the Cloud Castle?

A maid knocked on the door and entered just as Tara was calling into the ice shard the names of Crystal and Florence. "Are you there? Either of you?" she was calling, shaking the shard as if to add to the urgency of her call. Tara looked up. The maid had a frightened, worried expression. "Don't worry, I'm just talking to my friends," Tara reassured her, waving the shard. "But, in the meantime, may I have some water and lunch, very quickly? Please? Thank you!"

The maid exited with the hastiest of curtsies. Just then, Florence's face swam into view. "Tara! There you are! Any luck? It's getting urgent!"

"Yes, yes! All sorts of luck! Ariel's coming around!"

Florence looked relieved. "Great! How soon can she fly up?"

Tara looked down at the bottle, where Ariel was struggling to sit up. "Um, I don't think she's in any condition to fly. Can you come down and help?"

"It's not cold enough!"

"Is Crystal still with you? What if both of you do it together?"

"Let me see." Florence disappeared for a moment, she and Crystal reappearing a moment later together. "Crystal thinks it's worth a try. Wait there!"

There was a flash beside Tara, and Crystal stood with her. On the other side, Flo began accumulating rapidly, greyish-white layer on top of greyish-white layer. The three exchanged hugs as soon as Flo was whole.

"How's Ariel?" demanded Florence, glancing at the bottle. "Oh, she's coming to! Hi, Ariel!"

Tara reached for the bottle. "Time to pull her out, I think," she said and, with an effort, reversed the procedure that had put Ariel inside. Crystal caught Ariel as she emerged and promptly collapsed. "She's not all the way revived yet, I'm afraid."

Ariel moaned and her head lolled.

"Let's get her back to Cloud Castle. Maybe the air there will clear her head."

The two sisters exchanged glances. "Ready?" they said simultaneously to each other, and Flo took Ariel's shoulders as Crystal held her legs. "Let's go!" With that, Flo began to vanish from the head down, and Crystal began to glow. The three seemed to merge and then were gone. Tara slumped on the bed in relief. Now it was up to Crystal and Florence.

There were voices outside the door. She crept closer to overhear them. It was her mother and father.

"—No, that's not true! I was never enthusiastic about her going!"

"What do you mean? You said you could easily rule in my stead. And that you'd done it before!"

"Well, what does it matter? The poor thing's lost her mind! That's what they told me! There she was, in the kitchen, cooking paper over a fire. Next she ran away to eat it, laughing crazily. Now, she rings for actual food while shouting names at a broken piece of glass!"

"I think I can explain the glass. It's not as bad as it looks."

"It sounds very bad. Probably calling for her imaginary fish friend. No, she should never have gone on that adventure; it's unhinged her!"

Tara threw open the door in a single, bold thrust and stepped through the portal. Her parents jumped back in alarm. "Mom, Dad: great news!"

The two glanced at each other. Let me handle this, Armorica mouthed and, turning to Tara, assumed a tone of exaggerated sympathy. "Dearest daughter, do you recognize us?"

"Mom! Don't be silly! Of course I do!"

"Good. That's very good. I hear you've been… well, doing things."

"I certainly have! I've been rescuing Ariel!"

"Huh?"

"Yes! I just ground up the leaves we brought back yesterday, let Ariel inhale them and awakened her. She's revived!"

Her father was surprised and pleased. "Really? Really?" He turned to his wife. "You see? Everything's fine. The leaves I was telling you about yesterday worked!"

Her mother looked sceptical, but there was her father vouching for her. "But where is she? Where did she go?"

"So, she had to leave. For her castle. Which, I think, even now, she's setting to rights!"

Her father eyed her suspiciously. He knew that tone well. It meant there was a lot more to this story than Tara was telling, but she wasn't going into it. Tara said no more and stood silently in front of them, smiling innocently.

"Come on," said Tara quickly, intuitively sensing her father's train of thought and moving to interrupt it. "Let's go to lunch! I'll meet you at the table after I wash my hands!" Tara ushered them out in the direction of the dining room then turned and proceeded down a hallway toward a water pump, where she could wash her hands of the residue of the mycolix leaves. Glancing over her shoulder to make sure no one was behind her, she whipped out the ice shard she had secreted in her blouse before she had opened the door to confront her parents. "Hey! Flo, Crystal, are you there?"

The shard clouded for a long moment, and then her friends appeared across the surface, whooping and shrieking. "We did it! We did it! We saved Cloud Castle!" Flo was jumping up and down, bobbing in and out of the field of view, intermittently blocking and revealing Crystal, smiling shyly but genuinely.

Ariel's face suddenly appeared off to the side and looking a little disheveled. "Hey, Tara! I'm okay; I made it. Thank you for saving me. It was kind of close," she continued, casting a worried look over her shoulder, "but we made it in time to swing the castle around and prevent it from crashing. Good thing we came when we did, that's for sure!"

Well, that was good, thought Tara. Those poor, innocent villagers she had imagined being crushed beneath raining debris had been saved!

"Thank you for waking me and helping me get here just in time."

"Thank you for saving us and Brythrony from Maribess," replied Tara, soberly. "It was the least I could do. I hope you're okay?"

"I'm fine, thanks. Hungry but fine." Ariel grinned at the realization.

This gave Tara an idea. "I can imagine! You'll all have to come back down to Stonedell Castle for a banquet when Cloud Castle is set to rights."

The three on the shard, their faces crowding together to be seen, laughed gaily. Ariel spoke up first. "Probably easier, I think, for you to come up and banquet with us!"

Tara smiled back happily. She had revived her friend and saved Cloud Castle and all that before lunch. This was going to be a good day! "Why not," she replied with an easy chuckle. "We can do both."

Later that evening, as Tara was preparing for bed, there was a knock on her bedroom door. Tara hastily stashed her hair brush in a drawer, fearful for a wild instant that she might be caught caring about the state of her hair, when she had so vehemently insisted so many times that she was not and could not be so concerned. Who could that be, she wondered, closing the drawer with the tiniest of slams. The knock came again, a firm rapping, more rapid than the usual from her mother. "Who is it? Dad? Is that you?"

"It's me," came her father's voice. "Can I come in?"

"Um, sure, Dad. Let me get the door." What could he want? So rarely did he come all the way up to her room in the North Tower.

Tara opened the door. Her father stepped through. She motioned him to the chair at her vanity she had vacated, as he was simply standing uneasily at the door, as if he were preparing to speak at some length. "What's going on, Dad?"

"Hi, Tara. I wanted to come up and see you."

Tara smiled. "And here you are! Welcome to my room, Dad!"

He smiled too. He was being silly, he knew it. Reaching into his pocket, he withdrew an object which he kept in his hand but tight within his fist. Tara eyed it for a moment but gathered she wasn't to know what it was yet. She returned her eyes to his.

"Tara, I came up to say something to you. Well—ahem!—to say that, in short, I can't tell you enough how impressed I was with you when we were in the Underworld."

"Gee, Dad, thanks!"

"I mean it! You were brave, you showed leadership, and you took risks to make sure that we were successful. Now, I thought some of the risks were unwise, like when you went out on that ledge on your own to get the leaves of that plant—don't frown at me like that when you know I'm right!—but, by and large, I thought you did really well."

"Thank you, Dad."

"Especially against that giant centipede thing."

Tara nodded in acknowledgement, suddenly feeling a little bashful.

"And so, because of all that, I wanted to give you something."

What was in his hand, she thought, unbidden. What was it?

"It's this." He opened his hand. Within it was a large, ornamental brooch in the shape of a sunburst, at its center a yellow sapphire, the rays of alternating lengths (as she was to find out later) of citrine and yellow opals, a corona of blue opals surrounding the whole.

"Dad! It's… it's beautiful. What it is it?"

"I thought you'd like it. It belonged to your grandmother. She used to wear it at state occasions. She called it the 'Sunburst of Brythrony', because Brythrony has so much sunshine and—she would say—looks so brilliant in the sunlight." He extended his hand to her.

Tara picked it out of his hand. Its stones seemed to blaze with a captivating, internal fire. She looked up. "Queen Ysolde used to wear it?"

"That's right. Not often. Only rarely. Mainly when she was going to some especially festive event. It's lovely, isn't it?"

Tara didn't have anything to say. It was gorgeous, she kept saying to herself. Her grandmother had worn it and only at particularly important state occasions. No wonder: it was simply incomparable.

"She told us that, if the kingdom were ever in financial trouble, we should sell it. It would fetch a lot, she said, and it was only stones. But I always kept it, because it had been very special to her. We almost had to sell it, maybe a little while ago…" Childeric paused, as if the memory were painful, "… because the crops hadn't been so good and, well, we were having some money troubles. But then, everything sorted itself out, and we didn't have to. Turns out I was right to hold on to it, right? I mean, I figured things would work out in the end."

"That's right, Dad. They worked out just fine in the end, didn't they."

"Yes. So I can give it to you now. It's yours. For your bravery in the Underworld. Which, in a sense, saved all of us in Brythrony. That's why I thought the sunburst especially appropriate."

Tara stared down at the brooch for a long moment. "I won't ever sell it, Dad. Never."

"I know you won't. I don't think you should, either."

Childeric watched in clear satisfaction at Tara's delight. "You know, one more thing, Tara. If I could."

"What's that, Dad?"

"They're really all real, aren't they? Not just the flying girl and the snow person, but the, uh, the mermaid and the ice lady too? All of them?"

Tara nodded wordlessly, her hand folded about the sunburst.

Childeric sighed. "I thought as much. Look, let's keep this quiet for just a little longer. It might be too much of a shock for your mother all at once. We'll tell her about them slowly and gently. So she won't get upset. What do you say?"

Tara smiled softly, her fingers gently tracing the contours of her grandmother's brooch. "Fine with me, Dad. That's fine with me."

The Ring of Shooting Stars

Tara listlessly stirred her porridge, wondering if she should add more butter. It would taste better but then, hadn't she already added a lot? She turned her eyes up to gaze idly out the window overhead. Another beautiful day. Brythrony was having a string of those. The weather had been perfect, the air as crisp as a newly picked apple, for showing Princesses Crystal and Florence some of the kingdom. Not so hot such that they were uncomfortable, being sensitive to warmer temperatures, but not so cool as to leave Tara and Ariel wanting heavier clothing themselves. They had left the day before though, for their wintry homes, leaving her alone at Stonedell and, just at that moment, sitting at the breakfast table.

Tara meditated on her current state. She felt anxious. It had been fun showing her friends around, and it had been nice to have some extra evenings with her mother and father, but now she was again confronted with her greater goal of restoring the powers of her ring. On more than one occasion she had missed its powers in the Underground Kingdom. Obviously, it would have been of tremendous use against the mocurra; she would have simply incinerated it. Without it, the Underworlders had lost their sergeant and all of them had very nearly been eaten.

No, she was confident that she needed something powerful of her own to safeguard herself. She couldn't just keep looking to others for help whenever she was in a dire situation.

Hadn't her father also told her something like that in other, or similar, contexts?

Tara tapped her plate absent-mindedly. She would have to get going again, and soon, to look for that bit of Silicana she expected would re-power her ring.

"Tara! What in the world are you thinking? You've hardly touched your breakfast!"

"Uh, Mom, not really, I guess. I think it's because I ate a lot last night. Still full from that." Here was something that would surely resonate with her mother. "Just watching my figure, after all!" she added buoyantly.

Her mother gazed sidelong at her, but Tara held her happy smile long enough to assuage suspicion. Her father held her gaze a moment longer. Tara looked back into her bowl. It might be the case, she cautioned herself, that her father didn't quite believe this explanation. What should she do about that, she wondered. Tara took a mouthful of her porridge, which she knew was filling and healthful but which she found bland and mealy. She would have to tell her father what she was planning. He would be more understanding of what she had to do. He had about said as much after Ariel had been revived, when he had been in her bedroom. Tara stirred the cooling porridge to better distribute the butter already in it. She'd talk with her father some time after breakfast. Before lunch.

Tara puttered around the castle and in and out of her room for the better part of the morning until she saw that it was getting on toward noon. Reminding herself that she had vowed to speak to her father that morning, she began a reluctant search for him.

He wasn't in the throne room.

He wasn't in the stables, though she knew it was unlikely he would be there. Rather, she knew that it was where she would want to be. She stopped long enough to give Daystar an apple, who whinnied his appreciation.

At last she found him in the kitchen gardens, one of the last places in which she would have expected to find him. "Hey, Dad," she greeted him.

"Hi, Princess," he replied warmly.

"What are you doing in the vegetable gardens?"

Her father smiled. "I like to be in a lot of different places by turns. Just to see what's going on around Stonedell. To check in on how things are running and so on. That sort of thing."

"But I wouldn't expect to find you here either! What brings you to the vegetable gardens?"

"I was looking for you."

His Majesty spread his hands. "Well, you've found me. Here I am!"

Her Highness followed for a moment an insect creeping along a wrinkled, plump spinach leaf before looking up again at her father. "I needed to talk to you for a moment."

Her father nodded and guessed the topic was one that couldn't be answered by a simple "yes" or "no." "Sure," he said and indicated a cluster of fruit trees nearby. "Why don't we step over there, into the shade."

Tara hesitated. "Dad, I know you and Mom may be upset about this, but I think I'm going to have to go out again."

Her father nodded again. "Go out again" he now understood as a euphemism for leaving on some other adventure. Armorica would definitely not be happy, but then Tara already knew this. Not that it was making much difference to his daughter anyway. "What's going on?"

Tara looked up to him, directly into his eyes.

That's better, Tara, he encouraged her silently. Maybe you're getting better at this. Best to look me straight in the eye than stare at the ground, into the tree trunk, up to the sky, or anywhere else.

"I mentioned it to you before. You and Mom. My ring. I guess I didn't describe it all that well then, but it's a special ring. It needs to be, well, re-powered." She paused to assess if her father understood.

"I seem to remember that conversation," replied her father, slowly. "You showed it to us. You said it was 'special'. A 'star ring'; something along those lines."

Tara resisted the impulse to sigh deeply. If he didn't remember exactly, he didn't remember. That was that. Just explain it to him calmly and patiently, she instructed herself. "Somewhat along those lines. It's a Ring of Shooting Stars." She unfolded her hand to show him the ring upon her index finger. "I know it lacks all luster now, but it shouldn't."

Her father eyed it critically. "What should it look like?"

"It should glow to varying degrees, depending on the angle. It should have flecks of, like, well, fire in it."

Tara looked up from the ring, which she had unconsciously bent her head to examine also, even though she knew full well it didn't have any fire. "It doesn't. But I think I know how to restore it."

"Does this ring have anything to do with your friends? Like Ariel? And Crystal?"

Tara thought for a brief second. "No. No, it doesn't. Not in the sense that it's theirs or anything like that." But her father looked confused, and Tara realized the true thrust of his question. "But if you mean that I've used it when I've been with them, and that it's been… important… to us on those occasions, yes, it does have to do with them.

"Yes," she affirmed, confidently.

Her father nodded knowingly. "I thought as much. I figured they were a part of this. These friends—I don't quite know how to describe them…"

"How about 'different'?"

Her father smiled faintly. "All right, 'different'. These 'different' friends of yours…" His voice trailed off as he groped for words. "They take you to strange places, and I'm not altogether sure I like—or would like—them. The places, that is.

"But it's also true that they saved us from that Merry Bess or whatever her name might be—"

"Maribess."

"Her, right. That awful Marry Best person. And, I suppose, possibly others? But her at least."

Tara waited for him to conclude. She thought she liked the way his reasoning was moving, albeit tortuously.

"And we should want to retain our friends and allies. Especially when they can be of such importance to the kingdom. That suggests, I guess…" Childeric grimaced and he leaned back against the fruit tree. "That we should support your effort to restore that ring."

Tara glowed in appreciation.

"What does that ring do that's so important?"

"Like I told you and Mom before, it can do a lot of things. I've used it to help myself and my friends when we needed some, well, frankly, firepower." Tara left it there, reluctant to furnish more details, as she feared her father might decide she was leading far too dangerous a lifestyle.

Her father mumbled something along the lines that he could guess as much as that. But, more loudly, he said, "Look, I understand. You need to go and fix that ring. Your mother will be upset. Let me try and manage that.

"But you may have to make promises about when you return."

Tara grinned. "You mean another round of Homecoming Games?"

Her father returned the smile. "That's not what I'm thinking. I'm imagining something far more ordinary and social. But of your mother's choice!"

His daughter wrinkled her nose in mock dismay. "Ugh! Well, if I have to!"

"You'll have to."

With that, father and daughter turned to walk back toward the kitchen garden and the castle. "When do you think you'll want to leave?"

"Pretty soon. Ariel has offered to take me most of the way to where I need to go. And I'd like to get maybe one or two other friends involved before they get caught up in something else. Just in case I should need them.

Which I don't expect," she added immediately.

Her father glanced sharply at her. "'Just in case' you should need them. I see. Let's tell your mother tonight and you can get started in a day or so."

Her mother had NOT been happy about Tara leaving. "What do you mean, you're leaving again? Already?"

"Mom, I've been here a while. Remember the Homecoming Games?" Gee, protested Tara silently, was it so long ago that you sent me to Sea Sprit, telling me I had to get out and about more? Now you're saying I'm away too much!

"You just went out to the mountains to get some plant leaves!" Tara hadn't told her about the Underground Kingdom and the mocurra; evidently her father hadn't either.

"Yes, Mom, that's right. Sorry; I forgot about that."

Her mother's face had momentarily assumed a triumphant expression.

"But Mom, that was only for a few days. Not even a week."

"So? You were gone!"

Tara groaned softly. "It was a short trip. I had to save Ariel."

"Which is why I didn't say anything about it. I understood. You had to do the right thing by your fairy friend, since she had very much done the right thing by us. Risked her life, even."

Tara ignored the reappearance of the "fairy friend" term.

"But what," continued her mother, "is this adventure about? Is it to save someone else?"

"Not really," Tara conceded. She turned to her father for support. Now would be a good time to say something, she communicated to him by a twist of her mouth and a veiled pleading look in her eyes.

King Childeric cleared his throat. "Armorica," he began, if hesitantly, "I think this is something Tara needs to do."

"Why? What is it?"

Childeric shifted uneasily. He was reluctant to be at odds with his wife, preferring as he did consensus. But he had been persuaded that this ring of was important and that she had to fix it. Further, and ultimately, it was becoming clear to him that this ring, and Tara's friends who relied upon it in whatever unexplained capacities they had, could be important to the kingdom. Childeric was coming around to the belief that Tara's request was, in a larger sense, really more for Brythrony, and not just for her.

"Armorica, I think we can trust Tara that, if she says she really needs to leave, then she really needs to go. No, no," he added, anticipating cross-examination, "I'm not really sure, not exactly sure, as to what it requires. But I believe her."

"And," he added, "she was here for the Homecoming Games. And for the ball afterwards."

"Hardly so, that," muttered Queen Armorica.

"Well, that was only because it was interrupted. As we both know and saw. I saw what she can do when we went to get those leaves, and I believe she can be trusted. I don't think we should stand in her way on this."

Armorica's face had twisted with the passage of various conflicting emotions as Childeric spoke until, after he had finished, she said, and with a faint note of resignation, "When will you be back?"

Tara considered. She should be specific enough to allay her mother's natural suspicion that Tara might be evading an answer, but not so much so that she could be confronted later, should she be delayed. And boy, how many times had that occurred! It was a fine line to walk in answering her mother, but maybe she could do it. "I don't know, Mom. But I'll really try to go and come back just as quickly as I can."

Clearly, she had not walked that line well enough. And so this proved to be yet another occasion in which Tarra concluded she could never be a diplomat. The queen's face clouded still further until she at last burst out, "I can't understand why you don't want to be around us any more! It didn't use to be that way! You used to like us!"

"Mom, I *still* like you. Of course I do! It's not that at all!"

Mercifully, Tara's father stepped in. "Now look, Armorica, I don't think it's that way at all. Just something Tara needs to do. Then she promises—promises, right?" with a sharp look over at Tara, who agreed instantly "—That she'll be back right away.

"Then we'll all have a wonderful time together."

"Don't patronize me!"

"No, of course not; I would never do that," Childeric assured her quickly.

"I don't want you running off every which place, into danger or whatnot, without any really good reason for doing so, just whenever it suits your fancy! You're a princess, and you're supposed to be in the kingdom, doing princess things!"

Tara didn't need to ask what "princess things" were, being already familiar with what her mother was thinking. "Mom, when I get back, I'll do some princess things. For sure. Tell you what: you and I can do some princess things—together. Yes. We'll do some princess things together. What do you think?"

"You're just saying that!"

"Together! And you can choose!"

Her mother was only slightly appeased by this concession. She heaved a heavy sigh. "I guess I'll have to be satisfied. All right: go. Come back quickly."

That was how it had ended. Tara had ruminated on it in her tower room later that evening. She didn't mean to make her mother unhappy; that wasn't her intent. It was that she had to go find that last bit of Silicana to re-power her ring. Her mother didn't understand the necessity of it, even though it was important. She was grateful for her father's support, but even he didn't really understand what it was about. What was it about? It wasn't about her friendship with Crystal, Flo, Marina, and Ariel, or about contributing to their collective defense in an emergency, although that was important; no, it was about being able to defend Brythrony and keep it safe from whatever unguessable malevolent forces were out there, Sundra being the perfect example.

At least it was done. She'd been given grudging permission to go, not at all the encouragement she thought she deserved for the service she was rendering Brythrony. The price for her selflessness was that, upon her return, she must submit, willingly, to "princessing." She wasn't sure what exactly those duties would entail, but it would surely involve carriage rides and a ball or two and other like events. Of course, enduring a ball would be far easier than, say, battling Silicana. Only, sadly, without any of the potential reward afterwards.

Earlier, Tara had released a bubble for Ariel into which she had whispered the question as to whether Ariel would still be willing to transport Tara to the Lost Quarter. "Sure!" had come back the prompt reply. "Wait there and I'll send the cygnet swan chariot to fetch you."

"Great," Tara had replied. "Come just before daybreak the day after next. I'll be waiting where I always do, in the field outside the castle walls, the one screened from the castle windows by a copse of trees."

And now she found herself far above the earth, the sun clearly visible even though it was early morning, walking with Ariel across the reception platform toward Cloud Castle's main receiving room.

"Great to have you back at Cloud Castle!" Ariel was saying. "Thanks again, also, for waking me up. And getting me back here in time to save my home!" Ariel frowned in remembering those moments. "It had been sort of close. I mean, an hour or two later and… well, I don't know. I might be still trying to build another castle rather than with you now!"

Tara waved off her friend's thanks. "Come on! You were the one who stopped Maribess from putting us all to sleep forever. It's the least I could do!"

"You left her in the Underground Kingdom?"

Tara nodded. "I turned her over to Captain Farrell and Corporal Lotho. They told me they would take her back to their authorities to face justice."

"Do you know if that happened?"

Tara shrugged. "No. I don't have any way, either, to find out if they actually did it or what happened to her."

Ariel opened the door that led off the landing platform and they stepped inside. "Now you're off to the Lost Quarter?"

"Yes. I'd like to find the tablet that animated Silicana and use it to re-power my ring. It's the only source of power I can imagine that's strong enough but small enough to fit into the ring to work."

Ariel opened another door, and they stepped into her main reception, which always resembled to Tara an enormous lounge. "I can't think of anything else either, but then, I haven't put the thought into it that you have. But I'm happy to help in any way I can."

"I appreciate that. My mom is really pressuring me to get back quickly. Just you taking me there will be a big help."

Ariel nodded wordlessly in agreement as she rang for one of her Breezes to bring them something to eat and drink. Folding her wings behind her in that complicated but entirely unconscious process that fascinated Tara, Ariel relaxed into a divan, waving Tara toward a couch opposite.

"So, yeah, as soon as I fix this ring—" Tara hoped, fervently "—I can get back to Castle Stonedell and resume princessing with her."

Ariel laughed as a plate appeared soundlessly next to her. "I'm sure it will be a nice change of pace! A lot less dangerous."

Ariel murmured a word of thanks to the Breeze as it offered a goblet identical to the one Tara had accepted, then dismissed it. "You know, if you really want to get this problem solved as quickly as you say you do, you should be asking for more help."

Tara fixed her friend with a quizzical look.

"I mean, you should be asking not just me for help but the other princesses too."

"I didn't want to cause a fuss. They're busy enough, I expect."

"That's nonsense, Tara! They'd be happy to help! This is important to you. Even to all of us. And, you shouldn't be alone in the Lost Quarter. I still remember that terrible night when we faced the spiders!"

Tara remembered it too. "And that's just my point: you were out there for me, to repay Atalanta. I feel like, most of the time, I'm just causing problems for my friends, more often than not!"

Ariel frowned deeply, sat up straight and assumed a stern expression. "Princess Tara, stop this immediately. You went out to the Lost Quarter originally to search for more dazzle dust, and that was for all of us. So, of course, we were happy to help you. Besides, all of us are happy to help each other, no matter when and where!"

"You sound like my mother!" Tara mumbled, though she knew Ariel was right.

"Then I think your mother is right. Who knows when any one of us will need help next? We all need it from time to time. Marina, Crystal, Flo, you, and me. Atalanta too. Which brings me to another thought: we should contact Atalanta. She's very dependable and solid. She'd be a great help."

"Marina too," added Ariel, as an afterthought. "And I wonder if she could bring that trident again?"

"I doubt it. Her father didn't let her on the last occasion we went to the Lost Quarter." Tara shook her head at the memory.

"That's true. All right, let's start sending message bubbles to get you some assistance. You send to Atalanta, and I'll send to Marina."

"Thanks, Ariel," admitted Tara after they had sent their bubbles. "You're right. I should be more willing to ask for help. It's just that I hate to be a bother all the time."

Ariel dismissed this concern with a sweep of her hand.

Tara continued, "I haven't contacted Flo or Crystal, because I don't see them doing well in the desert. Because of the heat."

"That makes sense. Marina can only handle it because she travels by underground springs."

"Right. But not so the two sisters. Although," ruminated Tara for a moment, thinking hard, "it does get awfully cold at night in the desert. They couldn't handle the daytime heat, but the night might be different."

"Good point! I hadn't thought of that! You are the smartest of us all!"

Tara smiled in gratitude at Ariel's kindness. "I also brought some presents from them. More hoar frost and ice arrows, like those they gave me before. And the communication shard. If we should really need their help, I'm guessing they could show up quickly."

"In which case, we should be fine. Good, then. I think we'll be ready for the Lost Quarter. Meantime, what about this ring of yours? Can I take a look?"

Tara pulled it from her finger and crossed the floor to hand it to her friend. Ariel turned it over in her hand and, holding it up to the light, spoke in a meditative voice. "We need this examined more closely. It would be nice if we had someone with experience in this sort of thing, but..." Her voice trailed off and she looked up at Tara. "I'd like to ring for another Breeze and ask it to investigate the ring. Would that be all right with you?"

"What could a Breeze find out?"

"Probably not much," admitted Ariel. "But one could investigate it more patiently and more completely than you or I. A Breeze wouldn't be able to draw conclusions, but it could tell us what it found."

"It couldn't do any harm?"

"No. Because it's only air. But it could examine the ring minutely. Every crevice and cranny."

"So a Breeze could more or less map the ring, in a sense, in tremendous detail. Is that right?"

"Right!" agreed Ariel triumphantly. "Map it! Then tell us exactly what every angle of the ring looks like—inside and out—and what it's found."

Why not? Tara asked herself. The more she thought about it, the more she liked the idea. Tara could recognize a good idea when she heard it, a recent example being that she should ask for help now, before it was necessary, and just in case. Tara nodded again. "Sounds good! And further, thank you so much for making me ask for help earlier. That was silly of me to be resistant."

Ariel glowed. "Gosh, Tara! That's so nice of you to say that to me!"

"I really appreciate your advice, and your willingness to give it to me."

Ariel's smile broadened. This was why it was fun to help Tara in her adventures. No, she didn't have any magic powers, but she didn't need any. She was so clever, and so easy to get along with, that everyone just *wanted* to help. But to get back to business… "Hey," she said, remembering something she had been wanting to show Tara. "When was the last time you were here?"

Tara cocked her head and tried to remember. "It's been a while, I guess."

"That's what I thought. Come with me; I want to show you what I've done with the Sun Room and the Vista Terrace. More of the floor is glass, so we can view what's below!"

Strolling the Vista Terrace later, and after a light supper, Ariel's hair fluttered for an instant, and she lifted her right hand as if to order it. "It's one of the Breezes," Ariel told Tara. "It would like to show us what it's found. I've said we'll meet it in the main reception and take a look there."

They sat together on the couch that, earlier, Tara had occupied alone. Ariel drew up a small occasional table to place before them. With the barest breath, the Breeze passed, leaving the ring in its wake. Ariel collected it, and her face assumed an expression as if listening intently. She nodded a few times, murmured something while holding up the ring to examine it minutely then listened again. Tara watched, fascinated. She had never seen Ariel converse with her Breezes, though she had witnessed their tireless service at meals on the occasions she had visited Cloud Castle.

She could hardly contain herself as she waited. Was there really so much to know? If there was, how could she have missed it, having had it on her finger for so long?

At last Ariel turned to speak. "Wow, interesting! So, as you know, the Breeze took the ring for investigation. It passed all around the ring at least a hundred times and explored every possible part of it. Really, really closely."

Tara imagined that it had, and uniquely so since the Breeze, technically, was incorporeal.

Ariel continued, "It didn't find all that much out of the ordinary about the ring, only this: that there is what looks like to be a tiny panel, hinged on the outside, just under the ring, in the basket of the setting. The Breeze thinks the panel can be sprung, and even showed me how I might, though it couldn't do this itself. The Breeze is confident there's a space behind this hinge and that something's within it." Ariel paused. "Does this make sense?"

"How does it know there's a space behind the panel?"

"From the dimensions of the ring, and because some space is otherwise unaccounted for."

That is impressive, thought Tara, that though the ring wasn't that big, the Breeze could still measure it so exactly!

"What do you think? Do you think the Breeze is right?"

Tara nodded excitedly. "I sure do! I figured some sort of tablet had to be inserted in the ring to power it; this has to be where! I would never have known for sure without the Breeze!"

Ariel nodded happily. "So now we know where to insert the tablet."

Tara agreed, but her smile was lopsided. "We still need to make sure we can open the panel. But maybe we wait on that until we're ready."

With that, they went to sleep in the hopes of receiving responses from Marina and Atalanta the next day. They woke to find that the topography far below had changed visibly from the rolling green of forested hills and fields mixed with the brilliant blue of lakes and streams to that of flat, featureless, brownish scrub and wind-etched stretches of tan grasses.

At last, a bubble floated in through the window as evening was drawing on. Both princesses stretched out a hand to receive it, not being sure to whom it was destined. Ariel crowed as it wavered between the two of them, then alighted on hers. "Marina!" they both exclaimed.

It was Marina. The bubble burst on a puff from Ariel, and they both heard, with Tara crowding close, the soft but excited tones of their mermaid friend. "Hey, you two! So glad to hear from you! I can't believe you're going back to the Lost Quarter a THIRD time! But sure, I'll join!" They heard her laughing. "I've been there so many times, I'll have no trouble finding it!

"I know you're on your way, so I'll start right away to meet you there. Don't have all the fun before I arrive!"

Tara clenched both fists and raised them exultantly. "Marina's coming! That's so great!"

Ariel agreed. "She'll be a big help. I want to hear from Atalanta too!"

But they hadn't heard from Atalanta, even as they approached the spot where Ariel maintained that, far below, they had vanquished their old foe Silicana. They returned to the Vista Terrace and to a particular section that was translucent rather than opaque as with the rest of the deck. "Here it is," she said proudly. "Now we can use it!" Ariel passed her hands over it and sprinkled something from what looked like a brazier nearby, and the section glowed briefly. When it cleared, Tara was looking down on the landscape below, only much more closely, as if she were hovering only a short distance above it rather than from a great distance. How amazing, thought Tara. The section—what was the word?—enlarged the landscape below so they could see it better. Wasn't this like the glass that Bardwell had used to look at the book on plants? This section of the Vista Terrace was the same as Bardwell's glass, except larger and more powerful.

Ariel gestured to one corner of the screen, which showed a jumble of shadows and lines. "See that? I think those are the ruins of Silicana's labyrinth, where we were trapped. You remember that?"

How could she forget, Tara replied. She would always have the scar on her left arm to remind her.

"I can imagine. Anyway, I believe those shapes are their ruins. Just another few hours, and I expect we'll be overhead them, if the winds hold."

Tara pointed to something close by the ruins of the labyrinth. "What's that?"

Ariel frowned. "I saw that too. I don't know. I've increased the magnification until it's at its limits but I still don't know what it is."

Tara put her eyes right up to the transparent screen. "It's weird. I can't tell what it is either. It's not the same as the ruins, so it's probably not more of that. In fact, it almost seems to move! Did you see?" she pointed excitedly. "I thought it moved!"

"It's hard to say," Ariel admitted reluctantly. "Honestly, I'm hoping it isn't moving. I don't want to deal with another Silicana!"

Tara nodded. "Me neither." But she knew better than to offer her friend the opportunity to back out, even if there were another Silicana. Ariel would have been insulted at the suggestion that she would shy away from facing another or several Silicana. "How about we go down tomorrow, really early, before it's too hot, to see what it is. I'll take the hoar frost and we'll see if we can locate the fragments quickly."

"Sounds good. But by the way," asked Ariel, in afterthought, "how are we going to find that tablet of yours? What was your plan on that?"

Tara grinned abashedly. "Um, I hadn't really thought of that. I guess I thought I'd figure that out when I got there!"

Ariel formed her mouth in an "o" but said nothing. Typical Tara, for sure! On the other hand, things with Tara always had a way of working out anyway. Surely they would this time too. "All right. I expect you're right. Now let's get to bed! We're up early tomorrow!"

The next morning, before dawn, the two of them stood on the desert sands, watching the swan chariot ascend back to Cloud Castle. Tara shivered. It was cold and dark, and the pre-dawn sky still spangled with a thousand pinpricks of starlight. A faint, wispy cloud was all that relieved the monotony of an otherwise pale blue sky where the sun would be rising soon. Ariel looked meaningfully to Tara and clasped her hands. This was when, Tara knew, she was supposed to be explaining her plan for finding the tablet. She glanced at the endless expanse of dunes that gently rolled into the horizon in all directions save one. "Over there," she said, pointing to the jumble of shapes and mounds of sand that they had seen from the Vista Terrace. "That's where we'll start."

The two made their way over to what they surmised were the ruins of Silicana's lair. It had tumbled down fairly quickly, they could see, what with the wind and without anyone to keep it up. Even so, as they neared it, they could see that the larger parts of it were still intact.

They stepped over a fallen wall to survey the interior of what had once been a passageway. "I wonder if we ever went through this one," muttered Tara, thinking back to when they had wandered the labyrinth together. But there was no way they would ever be able to tell. All of them had looked alike at the time: just packed sand and darkness.

Back and forth they criss-crossed Silicana's ruined "palace." At one point, they came across a section of wall, collapsed outward, that was blackened across a large section. "This is different," remarked Ariel. "What do you think could have caused this?"

Tara inspected the black substance on the sand closely. She drew her finger across it and then held it up. "It looks like soot," she said and thought back. Hadn't she flung a fireball from just below the surface of the pool in which the treasure had lain? That would have been into the large room where she had discovered all the larvae. Tara suggested this explanation to Ariel.

"That makes sense," Ariel agreed, kicking at the sand speculatively with her foot. "But where's the pool? I don't see any water."

"It must be back below the sand. Probably Marina will show here when she arrives. Assuming the spring still comes close to the surface here."

Dawn was spreading across the eastern sky and the two girls scrabbled up a broken wall to watch. "Lovely, isn't it?" remarked Ariel.

"Sure is," replied Tara but recollected how ferociously hot the sun would be soon. They had less than hour before it got unbearable and they would either have to seek shelter or use the hoar frost.

"Say, what's that over there?" asked Ariel, pointing into the sun. "Those shapes."

Tara peered, shading her eyes. "It's hard to see; they're right in the sun. Maybe whatever we saw but couldn't identify from Cloud Castle?"

"You mean the things you thought might be moving?"

The two looked at each other. Tara wordlessly swung her quiver around so that the ice arrows Flo had given her would be within easy reach. "Just in case," she reassured Ariel.

The two edged a little closer, darting in and amongst the sand banks but always being sure to be behind one for cover. By the time they had made their way so far forward the sand bank no longer afforded much concealment, the sun had risen enough into the sky that they were no longer looking directly into it.

Ariel gasped when next she peeked over a berm. "What are those things? They're moving all right!"

Tara peeped over the edge and promptly ducked back down. "Scorpions," she said, with a heave. "Enormous ones. I can't believe how big."

"There must be a hundred of them!"

Tara dared another peek. There were a lot. They seemed to be clustered around something too.

"What are 'scorpions'?" asked Ariel. "I mean, I guess I've heard of them. But I don't really know them."

"Well, they're insects. I mean, they're arachnids. Spiders. Like spiders. But they have big claws up front and a curving, stinging tail. The stinger is sometimes venomous." Is *probably* venomous, and very much so in this case, knowing their luck, added Tara silently.

Ariel considered this information wordlessly.

"They live in the desert. But they also shy from the heat and the sun. They prefer the night when it's cooler."

"I wonder why they're still out when the sun is rising?"

Ariel peeked around again. "But wait: I think they're moving!"

That made sense to Tara. It was starting to get hot. That reminded her to pick out a handful of hoar frost and sprinkle some over Ariel's and her own head. Ariel looked up with surprise, and then a broad smile spread across her face. "Wow! Thanks for that! That must be the hoar frost, right? It's so much cooler now!"

Tara smiled back. "Nice, huh? Works beautifully! Thank you, Flo!"

"Now," Tara continued, indicating with her hand the creatures just beyond them on the sand, "as soon as they go to bed, we'll check out that area."

"Tara! Why on earth should we go out to the scorpions? It's got to be dangerous!"

"Because," began Tara, fumbling at first for words, "because—well, do you remember what Silicana was? Just sandflies? And the tablet caused them to grow and combine? To make something far bigger?"

Ariel nodded.

"Well, I've got a terrible feeling that the scorpions have the tablet. That's why they are all gathered in one place. Because they don't do that naturally. Anyway, I'm thinking that maybe its power has caused them to grow as well. Maybe—I don't know—they've even combined in some way. Just like Silicana. It just seems to me there could be a connection."

Ariel glumly considered. She supposed Tara could be right; very often, after all, Tara *was* right. But it struck her as a little far-fetched to believe that, just because Silicana had arisen from a cluster of sandflies around a tablet, it meant that scorpions gathered together for whatever reason were necessarily around the same tablet.

The two sat in silence, waiting, until Ariel looked again and informed Tara that it appeared as though all the scorpions had departed. Exchanging wry smiles, they stood and walked slowly and resolutely forwards.

Out of the corner of her eye, Ariel saw Tara reach back into her quiver and pull out a blueish-silvery arrow. "An ice arrow," confided Tara. "Just to be on the safe side, in case something is still hiding there. An ice arrow might be more effective than a standard arrow against a desert creature."

Ariel unfurled her wings, something she did unconsciously whenever there was danger and in case she had to take to the air quickly. Tara noticed; she knew what it meant: she was getting ready for possible trouble too. Ariel, a little embarrassed, muttered an apology.

By that point, they had nearly arrived at the spot where they judged the scorpions had been. It looked to be just a stretch of hard-packed sand. Tara and Ariel circled it then threw some rocks into the center to see if there might be a reaction, but nothing occurred.

Ariel turned to Tara. "There's nothing here."

But Tara thought it didn't make sense and she said so. Why would scorpions be clustered here if there had been nothing to draw them? How could it be coincidence that this gathering point was in about the same place—in a vast desert—where Silicana had met its demise?

Then, also, what explained their tremendous size? Not that she was an expert on them, but they had seemed enormous, so large they had been visible even from the Vista Terrace. Weren't they generally about as large as her hand?

"No," Tara concluded, "I don't see anything either. But something has to be here." She looked up into the achingly bright blue sky and continued, slowly, "I think we should wait until nightfall, when the scorpions come out again. Then we'll investigate further."

Ariel was dismayed. "Really? You really want to do that?"

"Yes. I think the scorpions are gathering around something. Something important, and something we want. For some reason though, I'm thinking, it's only visible at night."

Ariel considered this distressing recommendation for a moment then surveyed the sky. "Could we have another sprinkle of hoar frost, please?"

Tara quickly produced it, as she could clearly see that her friend was having a harder time with the sun than she.

Ariel visibly relaxed in the renewed comfort of the frost, and the two began walking back to the sand berms they had come from. "All right! All right! I have an idea!" exclaimed Ariel, suddenly.

"What's that?"

"If you really think those scorpions have something, maybe we can distract them once they gather around it. Then we can grab it!"

"Go on. What are you thinking?"

"Well, something like this: you'll distract them, like, by running in front of them and getting their attention. That's when I'll swoop down and grab whatever it is they're looking at, or worshipping, or whatever." Ariel nodded, pleased with the idea.

Tara gasped. "Hang on: alone? Alone I'm going to distract and face them? All of them?"

"Well," Ariel objected, "you'd have your bow and arrows! And I wouldn't be long. I'd just dart in and then back out again!"

"But what would I do after that? I'd be all alone against, like, a hundred giant scorpions!"

"C'mon, Tara, there aren't *that* many!"

Tara glanced dubiously back at the patch of sand they had lately inspected. "Look, I appreciate your confidence in me, that I can face that many giant scorpions with just a bow and arrows, but, well, I'm less sure myself. I'm thinking that maybe we might need some help for that. Along the lines of what you suggested in Cloud Castle."

Ariel brightened. She had suggested that, after all.

"I'm also wondering where Marina might be. And Atalanta. They'd be a big help. Then also, come dusk, as it starts to get colder, why couldn't we ask after Flo and Crystal?"

"Good idea! Then it wouldn't be just you against so many. Why, you'd have loads of help distracting them. I'd have plenty of time to swoop in. Maybe Atalanta too; pretty nifty how she can turn those golden balls into a flying carpet!"

Tara reflected for a moment that they had not heard back from Atalanta. Odd, she thought, and wondered why. But she agreed with Ariel. "Good. Let's do that! I'll contact Flo and Crystal. Maybe we won't need them, but why not, just in case? We'll gather everyone here at dusk and then deal with these scorpions!"

Just then, in floated a bubble on the breeze. Both princesses spotted it with a cry of excitement. From whom was it? Who would be the recipient? The bubble landed on Tara's outstretched hand. She blew gently on it, and it burst. A voice spoke. "Sorry it's taken me so long to get back to you, but I'm on my way now. I won't be able to stay long, but I'm happy to help in any way. See you at Silicana's old place!"

"Atalanta!" rejoiced Ariel. "She's on her way!" Tara's spirits lifted also. Atalanta was a recent addition to their band, but she was so capable and so calm and collected under pressure that Tara instantly felt like their chances had improved a hundred-fold. She smiled. Some time ago, Atalanta had sent them all message bubbles informing them that she had become queen of Maurienne and so was no longer a princess; should she return her princess purse? After a quick conference, Tara and the others had decided unanimously that Atalanta would forever be an "honorary" princess and that on no condition should she return her purse.

"Meantime," murmured Tara, reaching for her ice shard, "I'll contact Crystal and Flo and enquire about their availability for this evening."

Tara and Ariel spent the rest of the day wandering around the ruined walls and chambers of Silicana's sand palace, staying to the shadows as best they could. Midway through the afternoon, Atalanta appeared, first as a dot on the horizon, then as a dot atop a platform supported by brilliant golden specks. The two girls waved to Atalanta as she circled and soon she had landed and joined them, the three balls, as ever circling her overhead. After fond greetings, Tara explained to her their plan. Atalanta listened carefully. "Sounds good to me. Where do you want me? Distracting the scorpions with you, Tara, or swooping in with Ariel to see what's got them so enthralled over there?"

Tara thought hard. "Good question. I'm thinking you join Ariel, because I'm expecting help on the ground from Marina and hoping for it from the Ice and Snow Sisters. So there should be two of you in the air to see what the scorpions have."

Atalanta nodded. That was good enough for her.

It wasn't long afterwards that a message bubble floated in. All three of them stretched out their hands and looked at each other, wondering for whom it was. It was for Ariel. They gathered about her and she breathed on it. It popped with a tiny sigh and they heard Marina's breathless voice. "Hey, where are you guys? I'm here and don't see you!"

The girls looked at each other. "Guess we better find the place where that pool was," said Ariel.

They returned to the place where Tara and Ariel had found the charred sand. "Got to be here," the three said, with Ariel looking to Tara, who looked to Atalanta, who looked at Ariel. "Well, let's call for her!" prompted Atalanta and, feeling sheepish, they began yelling for their friend. "Marina! Marina!" they called.

Suddenly, a plume of sand erupted from one side of the area ringed by the charred sand, followed by a small fountain of water. The jet rose higher and a pool formed, and they saw Marina's blonde head appear. "Hey, guys!" she called. "It's me! I made it! I'm here!"

A greeting from Marina was always wet because of her submarine nature and because her hugs were always extended. But hey, reasoned Tara, even as she was just about to embrace her, wouldn't this heat dry her clothes quickly anyway?

After another round of their customary rejoicing at seeing each other again, they conferred on how to approach the evening's work. Tara told them she had contacted Princesses Crystal and Florence and both said they could show as soon as the temperature was meaningfully lower, probably a few hours before midnight. Tara suggested that as soon as the two sisters were with them, they should approach the scorpions.

"My father wouldn't let me bring his trident," said Marina. "But I did remember to bring along the two quartz crystals we found the first time we were here. Do you remember? From the sand golem? Also—listen to this!—I've researched how to create a golem with them!"

Tara hastily provided the background on that encounter to Atalanta. She shrugged. "Sure hope we don't have to call on that sort of thing for help. I mean, only if we really, really need it! 'Cause I don't know how we'd handle it, and this time we don't have a trident."

This caused all of them to fall silent for a moment until Tara brought them around again. "Look, we'll just keep that in reserve. With all of us working together, we should have no problem discovering what's pulling those scorpions together; if I'm right, it's the tablet. All we have to do is grab it and then we're done."

"But what about the scorpions? They won't like that!" asked Marina, with concern.

The rest of them laughed. Atalanta commented, "The scorpions can go back to being just plain scorpions. They don't need to be gigantic, super-sized scorpions."

"But that's not what I mean," Marina protested. "I mean, what are they going to do when we take their tablet away, or whatever it is?"

Indeed, what would they do, asked each princess of herself privately. All eyes slowly swiveled to Tara. "Look," she said, "I can't say what will happen. But do you remember Silicana? Once the tablet was out of her, she dissolved into her component sandflies. Buzz! Off they flew! I'm thinking the same might happen with these scorpions: they'll shrink down to regular-sized scorpions and cease to be super-sized."

These reassurances mostly satisfied the others, as that was what had truly happened to Silicana. "I'm thinking," Tara continued, seeing the others had accepted her prognostication, "we could have a longish night tonight. Why not try to get some rest and be ready?" With that, Tara sprinkled hoar frost over all of them and they lay down and made themselves as comfortable as possible in the shade of the sand berm.

Tara awoke in the early evening to find Marina already awake and lounging serenely in the pool she had created. Tara walked over and seated herself beside her friend. "Thanks so much for joining us. It's great to see you again."

Marina smiled one of her characteristic radiant smiles and said she would not have missed it for all the fish in the sea. "Why, we're all here! It's great to be together!"

Sure was, acknowledged Tara. "But too bad that it isn't for something more celebratory than facing down scorpions. Wouldn't it be nicer if it were for something like a party?"

Marina shrugged. "That's what brings us together, isn't it? Seems like it, at least… Not so much the fun times but the difficult ones. When we need each other the most. That isn't so bad, is it?"

Tara opened her mouth to try to say something clever in response then shut it again, realizing just how truly her friend had spoken without even affecting great wisdom. "You know, Marina, that's got to be the truest thing I've heard in a long time."

Marina smiled shyly. "Aw, thanks! I mean it too! We've always come together when one of us really needs the others. Isn't that why we're here tonight? We'll always be there for each other. Like we are now for you."

Marina flipped her tail back and forth once or twice, in and out of the pool, and looked over Tara's head into the star-strewn desert sky. "And do you remember? I was the first one of us—" gesturing to the others sprawled about in the near distance "—you met? And you've helped us all along the way. So, of course I have to be here for you when it's your turn!"

Tara gave her friend another hug, longer than any before and absolutely oblivious to how wet it would leave her. "That's so sweet of you, Marina," was all she could manage, and found herself glad, even, for her friend's dampness, as it masked completely the tears of gratitude that had commenced to course down her own cheeks.

Marina smiled again then her face lit up as she remembered. "Hey, let me show you the quartz crystals I mentioned earlier. The ones from the sand golem!" Marina rummaged around inside her princess purse and hauled out, one after the other, two exceptionally large stones, and handed them to Tara.

Tara eyed them warily. They were identical crystals faceted in a round, brilliant cut. At first glance, they appeared to be clear and even flawless. As Tara looked more deeply into one though, she thought she saw inclusions and cavities deep within it, but they began to swim before her eyes the harder she focused on them. She handed the crystal back to Marina after a few moments, a little dizzy and her mind whirling.

"Yeah," whispered Marina. "You can't look too long into them. There's something about them that makes your head spin! They both have inclusions and fracture lines deep inside them, but the shapes and patterns they form are different. Still, the effect is pretty much the same."

"Are you sure they're safe?" asked Tara, handing the other over.

Marina assumed a look of confidence, though it was clear misgivings lingered. "I think so. I mean, I read up on how to use them. I found a text on it in our library. You have to have both crystals, and you have to say the right words!"

"Really? Then what?"

Marina's voice became excited. "It works like this. First, you put one crystal down in the sand where you want the first eye to be. Next, you recite the incantation, which I have here," and she patted her princess purse. "Then, you place the other down where you want the second eye. Because the crystals are the eyes. The distance you put between the two eyes determines how tall the golem is and how big overall it gets. Because the height and size is proportionate to the distance between the two eyes. Does that make sense?"

"Yes. It makes a lot of sense."

"So that's how you decide how big you want your golem to be. By how far apart you space the eyes. So, if we needed one, we could just make a small one. Not a big one, like how we found originally. And, as it turns out, the intelligence of the golem depends on the size you make it. But in the sense that, the bigger you make the golem, the less intelligent it is. The smaller it is, the more intelligent."

Tara thought about this for a moment. Maybe that could be useful after all. "All right, then we have our golem. Then what? How do you tell it what you want it to do?"

Marina beamed at her friend triumphantly. "I knew you'd ask that! You always ask such good questions! As it turns out!—"

The two girls were suddenly pelted by particles of ice borne by a sudden blast of cold air. A small pile of snow was accumulating several feet away, though instead of drifting, it was piling straight up. "It's Flo!" exclaimed Tara and, indeed the Ice Princess stood before them shortly. She shook herself and smoothed her hair back. "Hey, how are you? Gosh, it's warm here!"

Marina and Tara glanced at each other. The temperature must have halved over the past several hours, but it was still warm by Florence's standards.

"Hey," she said, after greeting everyone and turning to Tara. "Guess what I brought you?" Without waiting for an answer, she produced a bundle of silvery sticks. Tara recognized them as the shafts of another fifteen ice arrows.

"Wow, thanks!"

Flo smiled. "No problem! I thought you might need them. WE might need them, that is!"

Tara asked her about her sister.

"Oh, Crissy's right behind me," she replied and pointed. Her sister had just stepped out onto the sand, her plaited hair pulled back and her light blue eyes crinkled in delight.

"Hey, everyone!" she called. "Hi, Marina! It's been so long since I've seen you in person!"

Now that all were present, it would be best to get going, because some couldn't stay for long, decided Tara. Tara checked over the sand berm to ensure the scorpions had returned to where she and Ariel had seen them that morning and, finding that they had, began to marshal her troops. The first three calls for attention were ineffective; only after several further requests to "listen up!" did they finally stop chattering and gathered around in a ragged semi-circle.

Tara explained her plan which as usual—but unbeknownst to the others—she was hastily improvising even as she was speaking. Tara, Crystal and Flo would strive to get the scorpions' attention by whatever means they could to draw them away from whatever it was that they were gathered around. Ariel and Atalanta would be in the air, high up and back. As soon as the scorpions were distracted and sufficiently far away, the two princesses would swoop in to grab whatever was there that might look like the tablet they sought. Marina, whose mobility was impaired by lack of water, would remain back. For her, though, Tara had a special role: could Marina cause a spring to appear, even a very small one such that it formed a stream? Tara was thinking that, if it ran for enough distance, it might function as a sort of barrier to the scorpions. As at home in the desert sand as the scorpions were, maybe water might deter them from giving chase to the three grounded princesses if it should come to that.

Just in case things started to get out of control, Marina would have ready to hand the quartz golem crystals. They would be used only in emergency, in case, for example, the scorpions didn't shrink in size when they had the tablet.

"How will the three of you distract the scorpions?" asked Atalanta.

Tara hefted her bow and quiver of ice arrows. "I think a few of these will be all that'll be necessary to get their attention."

"We can help also," affirmed Crystal and Florence eagerly.

Tara thought for a moment. "Marina, it might take some effort to bring up that spring where we need it to be. Maybe you should start now?" Marina agreed and, wishing them all luck, and adding confidently that she would see them all again shortly, vanished beneath the surface of her pool.

They waited a few minutes in silence, the five remaining shifting expectantly from foot to foot while they imagined Marina was making her way beyond the sand berm, then Atalanta spoke up soberly. "We might as well get going. We'll see you out there." Ariel waved, and the two flew off into the brisk desert night.

That left only Tara, Crystal, and Flo. Were they really going to take on all those scorpions alone, wondered Tara, a sickening feeling of panic starting to creep into her confidence. Yes, there were three others out there, but still, it was just the three of them facing the scorpions. And two of them could vanish almost on command. All of a sudden, the ice arrows she had in her quiver were looking very puny, while the scorpions were growing bigger and more numerous.

Crystal and Flo must have sensed her worries. "Don't worry," said Crystal. "We're with you! We won't let those nasty creatures get you!"

"Thanks, guys," replied Tara nervously, bracing herself. That was of some assurance, though she still wasn't sure how they were going to stop so many scorpions any more than she could. But it was kind of them, at least. "Well, what do you think? Should we get going?"

The other two nodded. Tara pulled an ice arrow from her quiver and put it to her bow. At least getting their attention would be easy. The three stepped through a gap in the berm and commenced to stride forward toward the scorpions.

As they drew closer, Tara remembered her conversation earlier with Ariel, in which the latter had suggested Tara distract the scorpions and Tara had guessed there to be "a hundred" scorpions present. As they approached the knot, Tara revised her estimate downwards to more like twenty or thirty, though still the biggest group she had ever seen in one place. Not that this was the time for this to cross her mind, it occurred to her, but she sure hoped the tablet was what had drawn the scorpions! But she brushed the thought away. What else could it be, if not that?

Crystal must have been thinking the same question. "What is up with those scorpions that they want to gather here? I guess you're right, Tara: something's attracting them."

"Maybe they'd like to move it. But they don't have hands!" Flo giggled, in spite of the tension.

Tara strung her bow with the ice arrow. "Let's keep walking until either they see us and come toward us, or until we're just within bowshot," she whispered to the others. "Then I'll shoot right into their midst. It won't matter if it hits one of them or not."

"Yeah, they'll come after us no matter what," breathed Flo.

Tara motioned them to stop. None of the scorpions had made a move. They just stood in place, their forward pincers—pedipalps, Tara thought they were called—twitching, and their tails gently swaying, as if to some offbeat rhythm. "Here we go. After the arrow lands, let's shout at them too, to make sure they come after us."

Tara bent the bow back as far as she dared and aimed into the sky at a steep angle. She let go, and with a long thrumming, the arrow soared skyward in a high, arcing, parabolic flight. "Lovely shot, Tara," whispered Crystal.

Tara had never shot an ice arrow at night before, and what she saw amazed and delighted her. As the arrow flew, it trailed faint, glittering blue-and-white sparks, which the girls could follow through the apex of its flight and as it plummeted earthwards. Its faint trace was soon lost in the distance, but they knew it had hit ground from the instant effect on the scorpions. There was a sudden, surprised flurry of movement, and one pedipalp lifted above the rest and gesticulated stiffly; Tara grimly surmised the arrow had found a mark. The others began to mill about wildly in a sandy scrum.

"Hey! Over here! Scorpions!" sang out Flo. "You told us to start shouting, right?"

Crystal joined in, hesitantly at first but soon lustily. "Hey, over here! Here, scorpy-scorpy, are you looking for us? Over here!"

For good measure, Tara pulled out another ice arrow, strung it and fired it in the same high arc into their midst. There was another sudden movement, then at last it looked as though the scorpions had put together that these three figures some distance away were the source of the harassment. Several, waving their pincers intimidatingly, began advancing toward them in a kind of scuttling, scurrying movement that was alarmingly quick.

"Gosh, they look pretty big," observed Flo. "Like, about ten feet tall or so at the top of their tails!"

"Wow, like, how'd they get that big?" wondered Crystal aloud.

Tara resolutely strung her bow again with a third ice arrow. "Closest scorpion wins the next arrow!" She waited a long moment then loosed it at the nearest scorpion. The bow sang; the arrow sped; the scorpion stumbled as one of its front legs collapsed beneath it.

"Nice shot; you got him in the leg!" called Crystal. Tara waved back with her bow.

All of them were heading toward them, each in that curious scuttling movement that arachnids use. There sure were a lot of them, whispered Tara, and scanned the skies quickly for Atalanta and Ariel, but she didn't see them. Tara gauged there was just enough time for one more ice arrow before they would have to flee and, on sudden impulse, lowered her aim to shoot at the desert floor in front of the most advanced scorpion, the crippled one having been well overtaken but advancing, haltingly, nonetheless.

"C'mon! Let's go!" Tara shouted. To her immense satisfaction, her instinct had been correct: the arrow had created a sheet of ice and the leading scorpion had gone skittering across it, a mass of clawing legs and pedipalps, to pile into the sand dune just beyond.

Flo barked with laughter. "Nice one! But time to retreat, huh?" Tara got off one more arrow, Parthian-style, over her shoulder, but her aim was poor and it did little.

Just then, a spout of water erupted off to the side of them. "Hey, guys!" Marina called cheerily, her head just above the still rippling water. "Look at what I made!" Then she looked back in the direction from which her three friends were running. "Oh, wow, there really are a lot!"

Crystal, Flo, and Tara splashed through the stream that Marina had made and turned at the other side to face the scorpions, which were gaining on them fast. Crystal and Flo were winded; Tara guessed that, flying all the time as they did, they weren't much used to running. Tara whirled and began firing as fast as her hands would move. "Tell me how you like these," she muttered.

The arrows flew, and most connected, but the onrush only slowed when the arrow hit a creature around the head. Most often, Tara would hit a wildly brandished pedipalp, turning it a curious white color; the owner would stop and club the ground in confusion, perhaps at the loss of sensation, but quickly resumed its advance.

"Do you think we've distracted them enough?" asked Crystal, nervously licking her lips. Unasked, she began to compose herself in that way that Tara recalled was preparatory to creating a windstorm.

"The water should stop them," stated Tara, forcing confidence into her voice. Where were Ariel and Atalanta? She wished she had time to send a message bubble, but there simply wasn't. "Let's keep their attention just a little longer. I'm sure it'll be enough!

"Marina!" Tara called anxiously. "Can you make this stream any wider? Just to make sure they won't try to cross?" The scorpions weren't showing the wariness of the water Tara had been expecting. They were awfully big, those stingers, jabbing the air atop the weaving and darting tails.

Marina looked doubtfully down at the sluggish brook she had created. "I don't know. There's not a lot of water to work with. But I'll try!"

Tara, eyeing the oncoming rush of scorpions, was just about to encourage her, and strongly so when, *en masse*, they skidded to a stop and turned to face where they had just come. The four friends stopped likewise, even Tara, midway in the process of stringing another ice arrow. Far off, from where the scorpions had originated, the sand had erupted in an enormous fountain of dust and grit. Out of the vast, billowing cloud clambered a terrifyingly large scorpion with not one tail but two and with gigantic pedipalps that looked like they could slice a warship in two. It hoisted itself up to stand silhouetted against the stars while, on the opposite side of the stream, the assembled scorpions bobbed up and down in a kind of grotesque obeisance.

"Good golly," exclaimed Tara, softly. "It's the grand-daddy of all scorpions. Right here!" With a start, Tara suddenly grasped where Ariel and Atalanta had been. They must have accidentally awoken this monster in their searching.

The four girls looked at each other simultaneously. "Give us a windstorm," Tara urged Crystal. "The best you have! Before they turn around!"

Crystal nodded wordlessly and promptly shut her eyes in concentration. "Get down!" shouted Tara. "Now!"

A breeze swirled around them. It wasn't cold enough for frost or ice, but it was wind and it was building. The scorpions instinctively faced into the wind and hunkered down to squat close to the desert floor. The sand whipped and the wind began to scream, but not an inch did they give.

"More, Crystal! More!" pleaded Tara. "Please! Every little you've got!"

But Crystal shook her head, her face anguished. "I can't! It's not cold enough! I can't summon any more!" Even as she said this, Tara felt the wind lessen. So did the scorpions, which began to relax and straighten. Behind them, ominously, the giant scorpion shook itself free of the last of the sand and, flexing an enormous claw high overhead, commenced to lumber menacingly toward them.

It'll be here any moment, thought Tara. *It must be twenty feet tall!* A sudden thought occurred to her. "Marina!"

The mermaid, mesmerized by the giant scorpion and its two stingers, each as large and curving as a scythe, didn't answer.

"Marina!" screamed Tara.

The mermaid jumped and, abashed, spun to face Tara.

"The two crystals! The sand golem! Quick as you can!"

Marina reached into her princess purse and pulled out the first quartz crystal, which she tossed into the sand a short distance away. "Here," she said, turning to Flo and handing her the second, "put this down over there, a couple of feet from the other one, as soon as I point to you."

Flo nodded tightly and gripped the crystal.

Marina reached back into her purse to retrieve a sheet of mother-of-pearl, hinged in several places. Unfolding it, she hastily began mumbling what sounded to Tara like an incantation. Hurry, Marina, she urged her silently, one eye on Marina and the other on the approaching scorpion, for whom the others seemed to wait in deference.

Marina closed her eyes, waved her free hand in a semi-circle and, snapping her fingers, pointed to Flo. "Do you… do you want me to place it now?" Flo asked, hesitantly.

"Yes, Flo! Place it!" cried Tara.

"Right!" shouted Flo and hastened to where Marina had pointed. But, whether because Flo had been looking at Marina, or because she had been distracted by the steady approach of the giant scorpion and its clicking and clacking claws, Flo took but three steps before tripping and sprawling headlong. The crystal bounced and rolled away to come to rest far beyond where Marina had indicated.

Crystal gasped in stunned amazement. "Oh no!" she breathed. "Oh no!"

"Run!" Tara shouted frantically. "The sand golem! It's going to be really, really big!"

It was going to be really, really big, much taller than anything the princesses had ever seen in their lives. The two crystals were to be the golem's two eyes; the distance between them to determine how tall it would be. With the distance between the two crystals as great as it was, the head would be mammoth and the rest of the body sized to match. The ground rumbled and the dunes stirred and sloshed. Crystal pulled her sister erect and they scrambled to take flight with Tara. Marina took one look at the forming golem and dove into her stream to hide underground.

Tara glanced back, unable to resist. A vague human-like shape was becoming discernible from the deepening cavities in the dunes. The sand surged beneath them like a wave, tossing the princesses as if they were insects on a carpet, and Tara feared for a wild moment that they might be sucked in as the spell seized sufficient material to form the golem's gargantuan proportions. Behind them, an indistinct shape was rising from the desert floor.

The figure stirred again and heaved itself to newly formed knees then upright with a rasping, snarling moan. It reared up high, higher than the tallest treetops, and its colossal head, visible only as a blot against a sky swarming with stars, swung ponderously as it dully sought its creator.

"Over there," panted Tara. "Hide! On the other side of those dunes!" It was all she could think of, even though it could hardly be called a refuge. The princesses peeked over the top of their meagre cover as soon as they had scuttled to the other side to see that the giant, two-tailed scorpion had easily forded the small stream Marina had created as a barrier. The rest of the scorpions were following hard behind.

Just then, there was a whir of wings and a swirl of dust eddies next to them, and Ariel alighted with a thump and a small cloud of dust. "Finally!" she said, and in a slightly frustrated tone, "We've finally found you!"

"And where's Marina?"

No one replied. They were intently focused on something on the other side of the dune, so much so that she looked herself. She started at the giant scorpion and sized up the stretch of sand between it and them. "You can't stay here, you know. That thing is coming this way fast."

Atalanta landed a moment later. "Great job distracting them, guys! I've got the tablet!" Atalanta held out what looked like a jar in which, rattling around within, Tara could make out a tiny pebble.

"Say," Atalanta continued, motioning beyond them, "don't know if you've seen it, but you'd better do something about that really big scorpion coming. You know what I'm talking about?"

The princesses nodded wordlessly.

"Well, Tara, do you have any more of those ice arrows on you?"

Tara frowned. As if she were unaware of the scorpions' relentless advance! Sometimes her friends were too much. "Unfortunately, the ice arrows aren't stopping even the smaller ones. I can't imagine they'd have any impact on the big one. Their carapaces are just too thick!"

Florence and Crystal looked at each other in alarm. "So, what are we going to do?"

The air reverberated with a single, thundering boom, and the ground trembled.

"What on earth was that?" demanded Atalanta.

"The sand golem," replied Tara casually. What else could happen next, she wondered? She was beginning to think that maybe it would have been better if she had stayed at Stonedell. This had turned into a disaster. And all for the ring she wore, she thought, glancing down at it broodingly. Even princessing would have been better than this.

"Uh, Tara, that really big scorpion with the two tails is getting closer!" warned Ariel.

Tara sighed. It wouldn't do any good, but she might as well go down fighting. She unslung her bow and reached around for an ice arrow. Popping her head up over the dune, she took aim at the giant set of gesticulating claws and the greedily wriggling chelicerae advancing on them. Above, and weaving about as if of independent minds, were its two tails, each armed with its own venomous extended stinger.

Tara took aim and pulled back hard on the bowstring. But just then, out of the sky descended the gigantic right foot of the golem to land directly on top of the two-tailed arachnid. The twin palpi jerked vertical and flailed; a portion of one tail sticking out from under the foot twitched spasmodically.

"Just in time!" breathed Flo. "You must have planned it, Tara! Great thinking to use that golem!"

The remaining scorpions, enraged, commenced a frenzied assault on the golem's leg with a flurry of snapping claws and repeated stinger jabs. The golem hesitated, momentarily confused. Then, with a single, sudden swipe of its foot, it flung the mass of them far, far out into the chill desert night. One more yet clung; another massive shake and this one too sailed away into the darkness.

Tara watched dispassionately a moment longer then ducked back down behind the crest of the sand dune. "We don't have to worry about the scorpions any more," she declared matter-of-factly. "They're gone."

"That's great!" exclaimed Crystal, delighted. "What a relief!"

"But what about the golem?" added Flo worriedly, picking up seamlessly from her sister.

Well, what about that golem, wondered Tara. She peeked back again above the dune. The golem hadn't moved further either toward them or away. Was it looking for them? Or awaiting instructions?

She ducked back down again. "Where's Marina?" she whispered sharply.

They looked at each other. The last they had seen of her she had been diving into the stream she had created. "Underground, I guess," muttered Crystal. "She can't run, after all."

"I'll send her a bubble," volunteered Flo. "It's her golem. Maybe she knows how to deal with it."

"Yes," echoed Tara. "Now that we're done with it, we'd like it to go away." Tara shuddered at the thought of being flattened like the two-tailed scorpion. "Yes, please send her a message bubble. Oh! And, I know, can you and Crystal blow up some sand to help hide us from the golem? Just in case it's looking for us?"

The two sisters nodded eagerly and joined hands to gather strength.

Tara returned her gaze to the golem looming above them. Think, Tara, think! she urged herself. In the past, she had always come up with a plan for every situation they had faced. This couldn't be the one time she'd fail; it simply couldn't. She looked down at the ring, which had been their reason for coming, and a sudden thought occurred to her. Long ago, Tara had watched in fascination a farrier shoe Daystar. While the white-hot horseshoe to one side had hissed furiously in a barrel of water, Tara had noted that the sand lining the center of the furnace had taken on a crystalline glaze. The farrier had explained that sand, if heated hot enough, would change to glass. But this, he had added, required a very high temperature, much higher than that his furnace could produce.

Maybe one day, she would fail to come up with a plan when she was in a tight corner, but it might not be tonight! "Atalanta, you found the tablet?"

Atalanta held up the jar proudly. "Sure did! As soon as those awful buggers moved away, Ariel and I located it; it kind of—"

Tara turned to Ariel. "Ariel, can you open the ring's basket, where the Breeze said there was a panel? Really quickly?"

"Why? Oh! You want to put the tablet in? Now?"

Tara nodded energetically. "Yes, please." No time like the present. Especially with a towering, uncontrollable golem hunting for them. "Yes, exactly!"

"But why?"

Tara gestured frantically with the ring. "I need to make the biggest, hottest fireball ever!"

"But, putting that tablet in? It could be dangerous! We don't know if it will work!"

A sudden boom and a bone-jarring tremor signaled that the golem had taken another step. "It's already dangerous. It's got to work!"

As if to underscore Tara's urgency, the princesses then heard the most unearthly noise they had ever heard and would surely remember for the rest of their days. It rose from a low, rasping growl to crescendo in an ear-splitting, ululating howl of bewilderment and fury. But it didn't come as a voice from anything living; rather, it roared into the night like the gnashing and grinding of a sandstorm forced through a trumpet. The bellow rose and fell and then, even as it trailed off, the thud of the golem's foot sounded again, rattling the princesses' teeth.

The roar came again, closer. Crystal and Flo crouched lower; Tara shrank down herself. Ariel, without further prompting, began intently fiddling with the ring to open the panel the Breeze had identified.

Atalanta looked around quickly. "I think I'd better take a look and see what's going on. We can't just wait for this thing to find us."

Tara answered in a voice bordering on panic. "But we can't give our location away!"

"No worries. I'll skim out a little way before turning back. Maybe I can even buy you some time." While she had been speaking, her raft had levitated obligingly. With a curt wave resembling more a salute, Atalanta boarded and was gone.

"Doesn't waste time, does she?" murmured Ariel. "Didn't even say good-bye."

"I'm hoping this isn't good-bye. More like, 'see you soon,'" said Flo.

A moment later, Ariel exclaimed, "Opened it! The panel is SO tiny! But I still had a nail or two with which to spring it!"

Tara handed Ariel the jar containing the tablet. "Careful," she cautioned. "We'd never be able to find it in the sand if you drop it!"

Ariel looked up with a faint smile. "Sure we would! Because it glows a little. That's how we first found it!"

"Just got a bubble from Marina!" called Flo from the short distance away to which she and her sister had removed themselves. "She says she's having trouble coming up, because the golem's steps have smashed the water table into bits!"

Tara groaned. No wonder Marina hadn't reappeared!

Overhead, Atalanta was banking steeply in a sweeping arc, returning from the safe distance she had flown out to in leaving the others. The golem towered above the dune where the others had sheltered. It sure was oversize, she muttered to herself. One bad step and the dune and all four princesses would be mushed. Atalanta caused the three balls underneath to brighten and she took the raft higher. She had to distract it yet stay out of reach of its arms. How, she wondered, as she jammed her feet deeper into the stirrups affixed to the wooden raft. It wouldn't hear her shout, and she couldn't try to ram it. The best she could come up with to attract its attention was to cause the three golden balls to blink and for her to buzz its head, as close as she dared. Setting her jaw, Atalanta banked again, directly toward the golem, the three balls commencing to wink brightly in unison.

Far below, Tara's attention was caught by three blinking dots traversing the night sky. Their formation, like that of birds, seemed far too consistent, their path too purposeful, to be natural phenomena. Brave Atalanta! There she was, high above them, flying straight at the colossus! Tara whirled back to her winged friend. She couldn't rush her; the operation was too delicate. But she sure wished she'd hurry!

Ariel wailed in frustration. "It's no use! I can't seem to get it!"

Tara closed her so eyes tightly she thought she might have seen the world cross-eyed had they been open. With a mighty effort, she forced calm into her voice. "Please. Please, Ariel. Try again, really, really hard!"

Ariel shook her head in vexation and bent again in focus but almost dropped the ring on another stupendous roar. The golem again, Tara knew; if only she had had the forethought to learn from Marina how to control it!

Atalanta manoeuvred as close in as she dared. Forcing her feet as deeply into the stirrups as they would fit, she took the raft up steeply in a climb that had it zipping past the crystals that were its eyes then cutting hard to starboard and letting the raft drop down its back in a plummet that seemed to leave her stomach high above. A terrific peal buffeted her, and she was lashed by a wash of stinging sand grains. Ugh, she scowled. The thing was shouting at her!

"Got it!" exulted Ariel, down below. "I think I got it!"

"Oh, Ariel! That's great!"

"I think! But are you sure you want to use it right away? I mean, what if it explodes or something?"

"I'm sure it won't," Tara reassured her but not convincingly. The same thought had crossed her mind already, but she reasoned that at least she would take the golem with her. After all, all of this had been on Tara's account, and no one should pay the ultimate price except her. "Don't worry about that!"

Ariel's face was pained but she said nothing and handed Tara the ring.

Tara put it on instantly. It felt different. It pulsed and throbbed and was warm, even hot, against her skin. Tara looked intently into the ring's center stone. When she had first found it, it had been a sullen amber, then a dull black when it had lost power. Now, with the tablet inserted into its gallery, the stone had reddened to a brilliant vermillion and flames appeared to leap wildly inside it. Surely that was some kind of trick of the light? What exactly was this tablet that had she asked Ariel to put into her ring? Tara stared at the ring, transfixed.

The thunder of another footfall jarred her back. The golem stood almost directly over them. It was too late for second guessing. Tara smiled bravely at Ariel though with a fixedness more suggestive of fatalism than humor.

Ariel peered intently at her through the gloom. "Tara, are you okay? Tara?"

"Yes, I'm fine. All right, here I go!"

"Go, Tara!" called Ariel after her then, appositely, "Stay safe!"

Tara clambered over the dune and through the cloud of dust the sisters were still raising. The golem soared hundreds of feet high above her. It was not looking down but wrathfully and vainly clutching at Atalanta and her sky raft and its three blinking lights.

Tara shook her hand in pain; the ring had begun to burn and ache. It's too hot, she thought, it has too much power. Without a further thought, Tara pointed into the dark at the giant's waist and called for a fireball, if only to ease the burning sensation. A gout of fire billowed forth and Tara was flung back into the dune behind her.

There was another grinding, shrieking moan, and the head swung ponderously down to search the sands.

It's all or nothing now, determined Tara. She lifted herself from the dune by her left hand and pointed her right with the ring at the golem's knees. Meteor swam, she uttered softly to the ring. Give me meteors.

The ring quivered and, with a kick that forced Tara deeper into the sand, vomited an enormous tongue of flame that licked across the golem's knees and up to its waist. The thing howled and bent down toward her, stretching out its arms to grope for the source of the fire. Tara rolled away, keeping the ring trained on the golem. Up she raised her aim to its head and called for all the power the ring could deliver.

A column of white fire gushed from the ring. The golem staggered backwards but, unpityingly, Tara played the stream across the head and neck, then down again through the waist and legs. In a moment, the entire body of the creature was glowing red and had ceased to move.

Tara cut the flames but kept the ring trained on it. She stumbled to her feet and scrambled back over the dune to re-join her friends. If the heat had vitrified the golem, it might topple any second.

"Well? What was all that light?" demanded Ariel.

"Run!" answered Tara breathlessly, dashing past her. "Crystal, Flo: run! This way!" she shouted over her shoulder, not pausing a moment.

Why was Tara running so frantically, Ariel wondered, unfurling her wings. What's the urgency?

Crystal and Flo sped by. "Come on, Ariel!" they urged and raced away.

Good enough, Ariel concluded and, with wings beating and a running leap, was airborne. As she rose above the dunes, she comprehended Tara's urgency. Behind her was the titanic outline of the golem, still upright against the thousand pinpricks in the night sky that were the desert stars. Only now, it was glowing a dozen shades from orange to crimson from its lower legs through its head and neck.

Before her very eyes it swayed but, so great was its height, it tottered at a stately, even majestic rate. The arms fell away in their component granules to shower the desert floor below. The head and neck, still a radiant red, tumbled in slow motion from the disintegrating shoulders to land in an enormous spray of sand atop the dune behind which they had so lately hid. The trunk, down to the waist, was now pouring itself out in a dark, almost liquid cataract, covering the fallen neck and head. For a moment longer, the feet and knees stood, swaying, still faintly glowing, then the right one buckled and toppled like a felled tree into the mound left by the trunk.

Only the left foot and leg up to the calf remained upright, a broken glass column raggedly silhouetted against the deep black of the desert night.

Ariel caught her breath, circled the smoking ruins of the golem once and then hovered over where the head and neck lay three quarters buried. Atalanta pulled up beside her. "Guess that's the end of it," she observed, laconically, eying the still-smoldering wreck over the side of her raft.

Ariel stared, still fascinated, until she shook her head and looked over to Atalanta. "I think so. The scorpions. And the golem."

She scanned the sandy wastes of the Lost Quarter where—somewhere—Tara, Flo, and Crystal had to be. "Wonder where they are out there? Shall we go find them? Marina too?"

Atalanta turned her gaze to join that of Ariel. "We should. Then, what do you think? Can we get some breakfast at your place?"

Ariel laughed for what seemed like the first time in hours. "Sure! And a bath! I must be covered in sand!"

"What about the quartz eyes of that thing?" asked Atalanta quietly, as the two descended toward the ground to search for their friends. "You know, the crystals Marina brought?"

Ariel tossed her head carelessly. "Look for them? No way! They're somewhere way down in the sand, probably encased in solid glass. I say let them stay that way for a long, long time!"

Epilogue: Princessing

Princess of the Realm Tara waved with studied politeness to the crowds lining the parade route. They had gathered for her and her mother, who were attending a ribbon-cutting ceremony for the opening of a reconstructed bridge over one of Brythrony's many rivers. This particular river tended to overflow more frequently than others, and the old bridge had at last been extended and strengthened so as keep the road open during all but the most severe floods.

"Yes, Mom, it is important," acknowledged Tara dutifully and in response to Queen Armorica's observation that this was an important event.

"Oooh!" gasped her mother as they rounded the last bend and the multitudes assembled began to clap and shout with renewed vigor. "Look! Look how rapturous they are to see us!"

"Yes, Mom, they are," repeated her daughter. Tara let her hand droop, though she maintained the smile in which she had set her face. Yes, she owed her mother. Meaning this, the parade. And the smile. She had promised that, were she ever to get beyond that golem and back from that terrible desert, she would gladly open a bridge, or school, or any other public project, without complaint. Now, it was time to make good. Tara widened fractionally her practiced smile and lifted her hand to wave again. How good it was to be riding in the royal landau with her mother and greeting their loyal subjects.

Well, it was better than facing a sand golem or a sand fly creature.

Tara sighed. Her eyes fell upon the lap dog her mother had brought with her that day. It was of an indeterminate breed; some sort of mix. It panted contentedly in her mother's lap and its moist eyes regarded Tara languidly. A slip of a pink tongue darted in and out arrhythmically with each of Armorica's idle caresses of its carefully combed coat, ears and collar finished with a selection of parti-colored ribbons. Tara sighed again, mentally, and glanced out of the carriage.

For a moment, Tara wondered what her loyal subjects would really think of her if they were more fully informed of her many recent adventures.

What would be their opinion if they knew of the many risks she had run, some certainly for them, but some for her family, and still others just for herself. Some of the problems had come looking for her rather than she for them, but still, she was the kingdom's only heir apparent and she had placed her life in jeopardy on more than one occasion.

Tara sighed aloud and her mother looked over. "What's wrong, dear? Look, what a lovely day it is! And how fun it will be to cut the ribbon! It is important. They need this bridge; they've waited a long time for it."

Tara adjusted by a fraction the tiara atop her meticulously arranged hair, mindful of the hour of preparation Sullijee had lavished on it. Tara spread the white tulle—seemingly all spangles and sparkles—that underlay her sapphire gown of taffeta such that it fanned across the seat in a perfect semi-circle. The White Wave of Sea Sprit pinned her white sash of royalty to her left waist; the Sunburst of Brythrony held the sash at her right shoulder.

Her mother inspected her approvingly. "The dress looks good. Sullijee did so well with your hair too! You look beautiful!"

Tara thanked her mother and turned her gaze back out of the carriage. Her mother was right. The bridge was important. The day was lovely. Her gown was beautiful. Yes, and she owed her mother this appearance. She waved again to the spectators and searched for the bridge they were to open. In doing so, she caught sight of the red ring on her right index finger. The center crystal had been an angry, even livid, red when it had first been re-powered. Flames had seemed to leap in its interior. Tara considered it now. It no longer seemed to harbor the violent, furious energy it had before, and the color had receded to a sparkling bronze overcast occasionally by sullen reddish tinctures.

Tara waved to the crowd. She knew opening the bridge was her penance for the adventures she had had and the ring she wore. Her grandmother had had to do penance too; her father had told her so when he had given her the Sunburst of Brythrony. Tara reflected. Ysolde had princessed; was it so very wrong that Tara had to princess also? Wasn't it even Tara's job, just as it had been Ysolde's? Tara's life couldn't all be adventure. Ysolde had boarded Captain Jarvis's *Gyrfalcon* but in the end never set sail. This had to mean that though Ysolde had walked the ramparts of Stonedell in its defense, she had also had to play the diplomat and even attend the Season. And even princess rather than sail on some exotic oard *Gyrfalcon*.

 stopped abruptly with a jerk, interrupting her thoughts.
 go!" called her mother excitedly, and she stood to exit the
 ...er door held open by a footman.

Tara steeled herself for hours of badinage. "Yes, Mom, I'm right beside you!" She gathered up her skirts and balanced herself to alight from the carriage. A footman at the last of the retractable steps proffered his hand to steady her. Smiling innocuously, Tara accepted and carefully stepped to the ground, distantly amused at the care she was taking not to soil her ecru satin shoes on the rocky path. She found her footing and gazed around mildly then, blinkingly, up into the flawless blue dome of the sky arching overhead. She looked across into the eyes of her mother, who had come around the carriage to join her. Donning the "court" accent, she observed lightly, "What a lovely day it is, Mother! Shall we cut the ribbon and open the bridge?"